Reign of Vengeance

No one messes with the Queen's family and lives to tell about it.

De Luca Mafia Series
Book One

Annalynn Nicole

Copyright © 2021 by Annalynn Nicole
All rights reserved.
No part of this publication may be reproduced, distributed, or transmitted in any form or by any means, including photocopying, recording, or other electronic or mechanical methods, without the prior written permission of the publisher, except as permitted by U.S. copyright law. For permission requests, contact author.annalynn.nicole@gmail.com .
The story, all names, characters, and incidents portrayed in this production are fictitious. No identification with actual persons (living or deceased), places, buildings, and products is intended or should be inferred.
Book Cover by Crazy Knight Book Creations
1st edition 2023

Dedication

To all my dark romance readers,

who ignore all the red flags and

question their sanity after reading a dark book.

And who like their men dark and dirty

with a filthy mouth that makes your run for your

B.O.B.

This is for you.

Single mom, Emilia Lombardi, escapes from the clutches of her daughters abusive father and is staying with her childhood friend until she can get back on her feet. They feel like they are safe, but she catches the attention of the Italian Mafia Boss, Mateo De Luca. He is known as a ruthless beast.

Mateo had everything he could want. He is the Boss of the Italian Mafia; he has his family, and women are at his disposal. Until his father comes to him and tells him he has one year to pick a bride, of his choosing, or one will be picked for him. Emilia catches Mateo's attention, and he decides she can be the solution to his bride problem. He figures this single mother will be an easy arranged marriage.

But Mateo has no idea that this mother daughter duo are about to flip his world upside down.

Read At Your Own Risk

This is NOT a clean romance; this is a dark mafia romance filled with graphic and explicit content. For content warnings scan the QR Code below or go to my website at

www.annalynnnicolebooks.com

Table of Contents

[DEDICATION](#) 3

[READ AT YOUR OWN RISK](#) 5

[DE LUCA FAMILY](#) 11

[DE LUCA MAFIA MEMBERS](#) 12

[PROLOGUE](#) 13

[ONE](#) 15

[TWO](#) 17

[THREE](#) 19

[FOUR](#) 27

[FIVE](#) 35

[SIX](#) 45

[SEVEN](#) 54

[EIGHT](#) 64

NINE	72
TEN	83
ELEVEN	93
TWELVE	102
THIRTEEN	112
FOURTEEN	124
FIFTEEN	131
SIXTEEN	138
SEVENTEEN	144
EIGHTEEN	155
NINETEEN	164
TWENTY	172
TWENTY-ONE	179
TWENTY-TWO	186
TWENTY-THREE	196

TWENTY-FOUR	**203**
TWENTY-FIVE	**212**
TWENTY-SIX	**219**
TWENTY-SEVEN	**227**
TWENTY-EIGHT	**235**
TWENTY-NINE	**245**
THIRTY	**250**
THIRTY-ONE	**256**
THIRTY-TW0	**265**
THIRTY-THREE	**272**
THIRTY-FOUR	**278**
THIRTY-FIVE	**286**
THIRTY-SIX	**292**
THIRTY-SEVEN	**297**
THIRTY-EIGHT	**303**

THIRTY-NINE	**307**
FORTY	**312**
FORTY-ONE	**315**
FORTY-TWO	**322**
FORTY-THREE	**330**
FORTY-FOUR	**337**
FORTY-FIVE	**346**
FORTY-SIX	**355**
FORTY-SEVEN	**361**
FORTY-EIGHT	**364**
FORTY-NINE	**374**
FIFTY	**380**
FIFTY-ONE	**383**
FIFTY-TWO	**391**
FIFTY-THREE	**398**

FIFTY-FOUR	407
FIFTY-FIVE	420
FIFTY-SIX	426
FIFTY-SEVEN	431
ONE	441
TWO	444
THREE	447
FOUR	450
FIVE	453
AFTERWORD	457
ACKNOWLEDGEMENTS	458
ABOUT ANNALYNN NICOLE	459
FOLLOW ME	460
REVIEWS	461

De Luca Family

Giorgio De Luca & Francesca De Luca-Grandparents

Abramo De Luca-Son of Giorgio and Francesca

Adriano De Luca-Son of Giorgio and Francesca

Abramo De Luca & Asimina De Luca(deceased)

Eleanora De Luca-Second Wife

Mateo De Luca-Son of Abramo & Asimina

Emilia (Lombardi)De Luca-Wife of Mateo

Alessia (Lombardi)De Luca-Daughter of Mateo and Emilia

Julietta De Luca-Daughter of Abramo & Asimina

Adriano De Luca & Anna De Luca(deceased)

Salvatore De Luca- Son of Adriano & Anna

Vincenzo De Luca-Son of Adriano and Anna

De Luca Mafia Members

Mateo De Luca-Don

Salvatore De Luca-cousin, guns

Vincenzo De Luca- cousin, shipments

Marcello Giordano - Capo, security

Vittorio Giuseppe- Capo, Girl's personal bodyguard

Raffaele Esposito -Capo, Night Club

Eduardo D'Angelo-Capo, Casino's

Fabio Sorrentino -Capo, P.I./Hacker

Damiano Morelli -Capo, Gentleman's Lounge

Roman Bianchi- Capo, Doctor/Drugs

PROLOGUE
EMILIA

Have you ever felt like you were seeing your whole world fall apart in front of your eyes and there is nothing you can do to stop it? Well, that is me right now.

"No, no, no. Let me go in there, my family is in there." I say against the firefighter who is holding me back from entering my family's house, which is engulfed in flames. Mama, Papa, my older brother, Franco, and my baby kid brother, Giovanni, are inside that house. I got off work from working at the diner when I saw my family home on fire. I feel like a rock was dropped into my stomach.

Mama loved that, Franco and I still lived at home even though we were both old enough to have our own place. It helped us save up for our future, and Mama soaked in every second of us still living there.

"Why aren't you all doing anything? They are dying there!"

"I am sorry ma'am, it's too dangerous for us to enter."

I feel so much rage, I turn my body and slap him. "Too dangerous for you all to enter? What about my family? You are trained for this, they are not. If you are not going to help them, I will." And I try again to get out of his arms, but he refuses to budge.

"I am sorry, ma'am, but I can't allow anyone else to get hurt."

I continue fighting to get out of his hold and hear wood splitting as the house collapses.

"NO! MAMA, PAPA, FRANCO, GIOVANNI!!! NO, NO, NO, PLEASE." I yell out sobbing hysterically. My family, my perfectly crazy family is most likely dead inside of our house. "No please..." my breathing starts to become uneven.

"Ma'am? Ma'am, are you okay?" I don't answer him because I can hardly breathe. It feels like someone is squeezing all the air out of my lungs. I feel myself being carried in someone's arms and I am laid on something. I hear mumbling voices around me and then I feel my whole body being driven somewhere. I pay them no mind; I just feel so empty and numb. What am I going to do without my family?

No more Mama and her wanting me to find a man so I can get married and give her grand babies to spoil. Papa would tell her no boy would be good for his *principessa selvaggia (wild princess)*. Franco would tell Mama that they would have to pay someone to marry me, no one would willingly want to be with me which would turn into us wrestling. Sweet Giovanni would jump on Franco to help me out since Franco is bigger than me, despite him being a hacker, he was also a gym rat. He loved going to the gym and you could tell. Frankie was built, and he looked intimidating.

No more playing soccer with Gio in the yard to help him practice. For a ten-year-old he was so dedicated. No more watching Mama and Papa be sickly sweet with each other while also one day wanting what they have with my own someone. My last thoughts before I pass out are of my family.

When I wake up to hear a constant beeping in my ear, I reach over, thinking it is my alarm clock. It's not there. Wait! This bed is too hard and doesn't feel like my bed. It has a disinfectant scent, not my vanilla smell. I open my eyes and the harsh light hits them. I quickly groan and try to cover my eyes with my hand, but I feel something attached to the top of it, I squint to look at my hand and I see an IV in it. "What in the actual fuck?"

"Even after passing out, the first thing you do is cuss?" I look over and see Mama Mimi; she looks like a mess. Her usually perfect brown ponytail is in a messy bun, her blue eyes are red and swollen, she has dried tear marks down her cheeks. She isn't just the owner of the diner I work at, she's also Mama and Papa's friend. I am then hit with what I hope is a terrible dream.

"Mama Mimi, tell me it isn't true?"

She shakes her head as she squeezes my hand, "I wish it wasn't true my sweet angel. They found three adults and one child dead in the house, but they are going to use dental records to identify them because the bodies were burned beyond recognition."

I don't say anything but pull my knees up to my chest and rest my face on them as I sob. I rock myself back and forth, Mimi sits next to me and just holds me. We don't have to say it. We know the chances of my family being the ones who died inside of my house is very high. I just sit there and just weep; I feel like someone just cut my heart out of my chest. "What am I going to do?"

She runs her hand through my hair, "You are going to stay with me for as long as you want. You are the daughter I never had, and I will always take care of you. I love you, Lia."

"I love you too Mimi, beyond my last breath." I say the last part out of habit because that is what my family would say to each other. And thinking of my family again sends another series of sobs through my body.

"Shh, I know it hurts, angel. Let it out, it's going to take a while for the pain to lessen, but I am here. You are not alone." I nod at her; I stop rocking back and forth but I keep sniffling as tears continue to make their way down my face.

How do I live without my family?

ONE
EMILIA

Seven Years Later

    As I drive down in this old truck that I bought off the side of the road, I wipe the tears going down my face. I quickly look up in the rearview mirror and see my dark brown hair is matted with blood and my lip is busted. Before all of this I had beautiful tan skin, but now I am covered in cuts and bruises. My once vibrant green eyes now look dull and lifeless. My six-year-old daughter, Alessia, looks almost exactly like me, except her hair is curly instead of straight and her eyes are a deeper green.

    I hope Alessia's father, Seth, and that sick son of a bitch Boris don't look for us, but I know that is highly unlikely because who else will be Seth's cum dumpster and maid?

    Seth was your typical bad boy, with deep green eyes and short brown hair that was slightly spiked on the top. I used to run my fingers through his hair or run over soft stubble of his facial hair. He never grew it for more than a few weeks before he would shave it off and let it grow out again. He had this rugged, bad boy attitude that I found attractive when we met, and because I was being stupid and grieving my family through drinking, partying, and wild sex with Seth, I became pregnant with Alessia.

    When I told him that I was pregnant, he didn't believe me but made me live with him. I didn't know he lived with Boris and some employees.

    The thought of Boris creeps me out. He is a pig; I don't think he understood the concept of proper personal hygiene. His face and hair were always oily, he constantly smelled like old cigars and whiskey. He had wrinkles all over his face, more than a man in his forties should have, he kept his oily brown hair to his ears. He would make me uncomfortable when his beady eyes would never leave my body regardless of what I was doing. You could see he was high most of the time because of how huge his pupils were; you could barely see the brown in his eyes. I always felt uneasy around him because I was worried he would do something to Alessia. I can be sure their work is illegal, but I never asked. I probably should have asked, but I didn't want to find out the consequences of doing so.

    I am still very afraid of them, and my mind keeps replaying our past. I keep wondering how I could have let things go so far. I was being a coward and put my daughter's life in jeopardy. I am a terrible mom. "I am so sorry *Principessa della mamma (Mama's princess)* I promise from now on I will do whatever it takes to make sure you are never in harm's way again."

TWO
EMILIA

Two *Days Ago*

  I'd just finished cleaning the house when I heard Seth yell my name. I walked downstairs to see Boris here and that is never good. He is a nasty and sadist mother fucker. If I could, I would have killed him years ago, but everyone here acts like he is some kind of royalty.

  "Yes, Seth," I say while bowing my head as he likes. I absolutely hate it, but I do it, so they won't hurt Alessia, which is pathetic since she is his daughter.

  "I want you to cook steak for dinner. We will be having two guests and I don't want to see or hear you or the brat. If I do, you know what will happen. I will enjoy taking you up to my playroom for the night." Seth says with an evil smirk on his disgusting face.

  He loves to use my body for his pleasure, but he can't even keep an erection the whole time. The only way he can stay hard is if he beats me and when I say beats me, I mean to the point that I am bruised and bloody and barely conscious.

  I keep my face blank, knowing he loves when I give him a reaction. I nod my head and make my way into the kitchen and start to cook. I look and see, once again, we don't have much food. He must have just gone out and bought the steak for tonight's dinner. I decided to make mixed vegetables with mashed potatoes as sides.

  While I am cooking, I feel someone wrap a hand around my waist and pull me flush to their chest. Just by the smell, I know it is Boris. He starts to use the hand he has in my hair to turn my head to the side, kissing up my neck and biting hard on my ear lobe to the point I am sure it is bleeding. I bite my tongue to hold in my whimper from the pain.

  "You better make sure this is perfect because this is a very important client, and we can't afford to have any mistakes. And maybe if you are good, we could make the girl a big sister. Wouldn't you like that?" I shake my head no. I don't regret having my baby, but I wish we were living in a safer place. This is no life for her staying cooped up in our small bedroom all day and night, but I know she is safe and out of harm's way if she is in there.

  "Well too bad, you might have been Seth's booty call before you got pregnant, but I have my eye on you. In time you will be all mine, and we can leave that abomination here so you can just focus on being on your knees for me all day long. My slave." He says angrily after he slaps me hard enough to make me fall to the floor.

He bends down and grabs my throat tight so I can barely breathe. "Look at me." I do, knowing he could hurt me more than he is now. "Never tell me no, do you understand?" I just nod my head. "Good girl. Now get cleaned up and finish dinner." He kicks me in the ribs once then stomps out of the kitchen, slamming the door behind him.

I slowly limp to the bathroom that is next to the kitchen to clean up my bleeding ear lobe and wash my face, then lift my shirt to look at the bruises all over my ribs. I sigh, knowing my body will constantly be covered in bruises. I return to the kitchen to finish cooking and wait for the doorbell to ring and for everyone to walk into the living room. I rush to put everyone's plate and glass of wine on the table before grabbing mine and Alessia's dinner of a sandwich and a piece of fruit with water, running downstairs before anyone can see me.

When I open the door, Alessia is snuggled up in our small twin-size bed looking out of the window. I sigh sadly, knowing she wants to play outside; I wish she could.

I call her name. She looks over at me and smiles. She sits up in the bed, I sit next to her and hand her today's dinner. Alessia whispers a thank you, and I give her a kiss on the cheek.

We eat dinner quietly, and I put the plates aside and pull Alessia into my arms once we're both finished. She wraps her body around me like a monkey and we sit in silence, enjoying the rare peaceful moment.

A little while later I am called. I tell Alessia to stay in our room, so she grabs her book and settles back into bed. I walk upstairs and Seth tells me to sit on the couch. Seth and Boris are sitting across from me, both with a drink in their hand.

Seth looks at me. "Emilia, you need to start grooming Alessia to be Boris' wife. She will be married to him by the age of 16 and will fulfill every duty a wife should," he says, his eyes never leaving mine.

Screw the consequences. I jump off the couch, filled with rage. "No. Absolutely not. I will not have my daughter marry that disgusting monster!"

Boris pushes off the couch towards me and punches my cheek, the same one he slapped earlier. "Since you are no longer a virgin, she will be my wife in ten years. I am giving you plenty of time to come to terms with it. She will be my wife regardless of what you say."

I look up at Seth from my position on the floor in absolute disgust. "How can you be okay with this? She's your daughter."

He smirks with an evil looking smile and crouches down in front of me, roughly grabbing my chin. "That is not my daughter, only a bastard child that I wish would die. At least I get money from her at the end of this." He harshly lets go of my face, causing me to fall back.

I hear a small whimper and turn to see Alessia standing in the doorway with tears running down her cheeks. Before I can tell her to go back to her room, Seth marches over to her, picking her up by her throat and slapping her across the face.

"Seth, don't!" I scream. "Please leave her. Hurt me but please don't hurt her." He goes to hit her again, but I already have a lamp in my hands. I smash it against his head, and he loses consciousness, dropping Alessia. "Go, Alessia," I yell to her. She wastes no time and bolts for the stairs.

I am so distracted by making sure Alessia is out of their reach that I don't expect to be grabbed by my hair and thrown across the room. I see black dots in my vision, but I shake it away. I need to be strong to get us out of here safely.

I use the wall to brace myself for Boris' next attack, trying to trick him into thinking that I am weaker than I am. Sure, my body hurts but adrenaline is pulsing through me, and the strong will to protect Alessia is overpowering my pain. He rushes at me, but I move out of the way just in time and he runs into the wall headfirst.

"You fucking bitch! I should kill you and fuck Alessia now."

That sends a new wave of blinding anger through my veins, and I see red. I gather my strength and punch Boris in the temple, causing him to stumble back a couple steps, then I kick him as hard as I can in the nuts. He groans, bending over to grab his pathetic cock. I grab his face and knee him in the nose. He falls over and I take the opportunity to straddle him and punch his face repeatedly. When he stops fighting back, I check his pulse. He is still alive, so I run downstairs, change my clothes, and pack all our things into a bag. I also grab cash that I have been stealing off both of them, from a coffee can I have under the kitchen sink. I am not proud that I am stealing but I need to get us out of here. I pick up Alessia, who has cried herself sleep, grab the bag, and run to the bus stop.

We barely make it in time before the doors on the bus close. The bus driver does a double take when she sees me. "Are you okay, hun?"

I shake my head and say quietly, "Can you please get us as far away from here as possible?" and go to hand her money for the tickets.

She waves me off, "Don't worry about it, I can tell you are running from someone, and I can tell they aren't the friendliest. I can get you to Brooklyn, New York, but that's the furthest I can go. Go sit down. If you need anything, please ask, okay?"

I thank her and take a seat by the window, keeping my head down to avoid attention. I just want to leave Virginia and get away from Seth and Boris so I can keep Alessia safe. I need to put as many miles as I can between us.

THREE
EMILIA

I find a quiet parking lot to rest for a while so we can continue to Maine, where I can buy us plane tickets to Florence, Italy, where my friend Theo lives. Seth knows nothing of Theo, so I will hopefully be safe there until I can get on my feet. Tomorrow, I will go to a library so I can get Theo's information and contact him, let him know I am coming. I finally get a look at my face in the mirror. I have a swollen black eye and a busted lip, I am sure my wrist is sprained, and I know some of my ribs are broken or at least fractured. I am in agony, but I will worry about myself once I know we are safe. With a plan formed, I let myself shut my eyes and relax for a moment.

I wake to small fingers running over my busted lip and I open my eyes to see Alessia with tears in her eyes as she signs, "I am sorry, Mama. You are hurt because of me."

"No baby girl, don't you be sorry. It should be me that is sorry that I didn't get us out of there sooner" I tell her as I hug her close to me and kiss her head.

"Mama, you took all of those beatings to keep me safe. Why Mama?" she signs while looking up at me.

I push her hair behind her ears, gently rubbing my fingers over her bruised cheek. "I want you to listen to me, Alessia, and I want you to listen to me well. It is my job as your Mama to protect you and I will do so until the day I die. You are my world, and I am sorry we had to live there so long, but after we eat, we are going to go to a library so Mama can contact her old friend and we will live with him for a while."

"OK Mama," she signs for me, and I kiss her forehead. I am lucky to have her as my daughter. We get out of the truck and, after locking it; we walk into this cute diner. We are greeted warmly by a beautiful woman. I smile shyly at her as I take in her features. She has a heart shaped face with soft features and gorgeous hazel eyes. She has her brown hair in a messy bun on top of her hair with a pen sticking out of it.

When she sees mine and Alessia's appearance, she leads us to a booth in the back of the diner and grabs my hand with an encouraging smile on her face.

"What do you need, hun?" I start to order pancakes and she shakes her head no. "I will take your order in a minute, but what can I do to help get you both somewhere safe?"

"Can I use a phone and computer to look up my friend's number so I can get his address in Italy, please?"

She nods to me, "Of course sweetie. My name is Aurora. What is your name?"

"My name is Emilia, and this is my daughter Alessia."

"Welcome, this is my café. I will place your order on the house, and you will eat, then I will take you to the office. My husband will be done on the computer by then." She takes our order and then leaves.

I look over at Alessia who is enjoying coloring in the coloring book Aurora gave her. "The nice lady, Aurora, is going to let us use her phone and computer, instead of going to the library, but you still need to be on your best behavior."

"I like her Mama. She is really nice," she smiles as she signs to me.

"Yeah, she is," I agree as Aurora comes back to our table with our food. I thank her and we dig in, enjoying the taste of something besides sandwiches. Once we finish, I go to pay the bill, and she insists that it is on the house, which I am so appreciative of.

She leads us back to her office and we are met with a man with huge muscles and broad shoulders who is covered with tattoos. His brown hair is styled in a comb over. Even though he seems rugged when he looks over at us with his green eyes, his rough exterior seems to melt at the sight of his wife.

"*Mi amor (My love)*, is this who you were talking about?" he asks Aurora.

"Yes, Ace, this is Emilia and Alessia," she says. He bends down to talk to Alessia, but she tenses up and hides behind me.

"Alessia, you are safe here sweetie," he says gently to her.

"You won't hurt Mama like the other men?" she signs, and it breaks my heart. Aurora and Ace look at me, confused. I tell them she is mute and repeat what she signed, taking a deep breath to swallow my tears.

Ace sucks in a breath and tells her. "No, princess. Would you like to color while your Mama uses the computer?"

She looks up at me. "Mama, can I?" she signs, bouncing on her feet as she gets excited. I nod my head as Ace stands up and holds his hand out for her to grab. She looks at it and slowly wraps her small hand around his big one. They walk over to the coffee table, and Ace pulls out a box of crayons and a princess coloring book.

Aurora looks at me, "Do you need any medical help?"

I shake my head, "No, I have had a lot worse than this. I just want to get us to my friend's house." She nods but I can see she wants me to get medical help.

Once I know Alessia is settled, Aurora ushers me over to the laptop. I sign into my Facebook account that I have not used since Seth took over my life. I find the old message from Theo and write down the address and phone number he sent me. Even without me asking, Aurora hands me her phone. I thank her and dial the number.

After two rings someone picks up the phone with a groggy, "Hello." I feel bad, I probably woke him up.

"Theo, it's me Emilia."

"Emilia...? Wait Lia is that you? Are you okay? What happened?"

I start to tear up. I missed my best friend.

"Yes, it's me Theo. We are alive. I hate to ask this Theo, but I need somewhere to hide outside of the states until I can get back on my feet."

"You don't even have to ask. And who is 'we'?"

"My six-year-old daughter and me. We had to run away before they hurt us more than broken bones."

"I won't ask details now but when you get here, I want to know."

"I know thank you."

" Where are you now?"

"In New York. Brooklyn in a café."

"I have a friend who can sneak you two into the country. I will call them and give you a call back."

He hangs up and I clutch the phone tight in my hand as I wait. When Theo calls back a few minutes later, he tells us that his friend Roman will come get us in an hour and put us on a plane. He promises he will pick us up when we land, and I thank him again before hanging up.

I turn to Ace and Aurora and tell them that Roman will be here soon, then sit next to Alessia and lean over to kiss her forehead. I am so lucky I have her. She is my world, and I will do anything to protect her. Ace leaves the room, coming back with another man.

If this is Roman, he is early. He has dark brown eyes, and his hair looks to be the same color. It is spiked slightly in the front. He is wearing faded jeans with a leather jacket and boots. I stand in front of Alessia to protect her and he gives me a gentle smile.

"You must be Emilia. I am Dr. Roman Bianchi. Theo called me to get you to Italy." he says as he offers me his hand to shake.

I slowly reach for his hand and shake it. I don't trust men after everything that has happened in our past. I turn to face Aurora and Ace.

"Thank you both. You have no idea how much I appreciate it," I tell them with tears in my eyes.

"I was in the same position as you are once. Here are our numbers and email address. Call if you ever need anything and I want you to call when you land." Aurora moves to hug me.

I hug her back as tight as I can with my injured ribs and thank her and Ace yet again. I grab Alessia's hand, and we follow Roman out of the diner. I tell him we need our bags from the car. He nods his head at me. I grab our stuff and slide in the backseat of his expensive SUV with Alessia.

Roman keeps his eyes on the road as we drive. After a short drive, we pull into a deserted field where a plane waits.

Roman grabs two hats and two sweatshirts from the seat beside him and turns to hand them to us. "Put these on before we get out of the car, keep your head down and quickly get to the plane. I will get your stuff."

We do what he says, choosing seats at the back of the plane to keep all attention off us. Alessia grabs my hand and squeezes it, I squeeze back. I know she is scared, I am too. I just hope our lives will make a turn for the better. Once we are at cruising altitude, Roman stands and walks over to us.

"Now that we are all settled, let's check out your injuries."

"Oh, you don't have to worry, we don't want to be an inconvenience to you."

"It isn't an inconvenience for me. Let's go back to the bedroom so we can have more privacy." We follow him back to the bedroom and sit on the bed as Roman squats in front of us and takes a good look at us. "Now, I see you are pretty roughed up," he says to me before turning to face Alessia. "What about this little angel, did she get hurt?"

I nod my head with tears in my eyes. "She was grabbed by her throat and slapped on her cheek by her father," I say, looking down. Roman looks at her cheek, where there is a clear bruise in the shape of a handprint. "What's your name, little angel?" He asks Alessia.

"This is Alessia, she is selectively mute from witnessing me get abused for years," I tell Roman.

"Wow, such a beautiful name for a beautiful girl. Now, I heard your father hurt you. I am sorry about that, no man should ever hurt a woman. I am going to see if I can make it better, ok?"

Alessia looks at me and I nod at her. Roman smiles back at us. "Good, now can you turn your head and look at your Mama and make a silly face?" Alessia looks at me and sticks her tongue out. I chuckle and stick out my tongue back at her which makes her smile. Roman then gets her to turn and look out the window next to her.

"Good job, Alessia. I am going to move your head, so you are looking at the ceiling." He moves her head up and Alessia whimpers, so I scoot closer to her, wrap my arm around her shoulder, and kiss the side of her head.

"I am sorry little angel, that part is done. Now, I want you to do one last thing for me. Can you do one last thing for me?" Alessia nods her head. "Can you open your mouth really big?" Alessia complies and Roman shines a light down her throat, then applies ointment to her cheek and throat where the bruises are.

"Ok brave girl, you are all done. There is a very nice lady out there with brown hair who will get you a drink of water and sit with you so I can check your Mama out, ok?" Alessia looks at me.

"If you need me, just come get me, ok?" I am nervous to leave her with a bunch of strangers, but I am a door away and I can get to her fast.

"Ok, Emilia. It looks like you took most of the beatings." I nod my head, still hating the fact that Seth was able to put his hands on Alessia at all.

"By the looks of it, you protected that little girl and got her out of there. You are her hero. Be proud of yourself for that. She only has a sore throat and a bruised cheek. She could have been hurt a lot worse."

I shake my head. "I should have gotten her out of there the first time they hit me. They should never have the chance to lay their hands on her."

"You can't change the past. But you push forward and make your future better than your past." I nod miserably, he is right, even though I still regret not getting her away from them years ago. "Good, let's see what injuries you have. Tell me what hurts."

"My ear was bitten, my cheek got slapped and punched. He also grabbed my throat and threw me across the room, and I landed on my right ankle in the wrong position. Then, my ribs were kicked multiple times." I tell him, and he gives a low whistle.

"Damn, you are truly a warrior. Let's get you all cleaned up." We are quiet, so I take time to think about how disappointed my family would be wirg me if they were still alive. Roman's voice brings me back to the present.

"Alright, you either have three bruised or broken ribs on your right side. I can't tell which without doing an x-ray but treat them as if they are broken until I can get you an x-ray. Your ankle is most likely sprained. I will put your leg in an elastic bandage try to stay off your ankle if possible. If you have to be on your feet, use crutches for the time being. I have cream I can give you for you and Alessia's bruises," he instructs.

"Um, I don't want to go to a doctor, they could find us."

"Where are you going to be staying?" He asks.

"With Theo until I can get back on my feet." I stand up and put the crutches under my arms, making my way back to Alessia.

"I will come visit tomorrow with my portable x-ray machine unless I get an emergency call. And don't worry, I won't say anything to anyone about you or Alessia. I know Dr. Walker, doesn't have an x-ray machine at his house." I stop walking and give him a puzzled look.

"I met Theo at college, and we have stayed friends since. He knew I was in the states at a conference, he was supposed to come with me but one of his patients had an emergency. He knows I have the connections to get you both out of the country undetected."

"Oh. Thank you again for helping us," I say. He nods in acknowledgment and walks out of the room to give me some privacy. I take a breath to pull myself together and I push the negative thoughts in my head away. I don't have time to deal with the what ifs or self-doubt that are buzzing around in my head, so I leave the bedroom and settle in my seat next to Alessia before we both drift off to sleep.

Hours Later

I wake with a start to someone shaking my shoulder. Was that a dream? Are we still stuck in hell? My vision clears and I realize we are still on the plane. I relax back in my seat as everything comes back to me and see Roman looking at me.

"We are here," he tells me with a small smile while grabbing our bags. I wake Alessia and lead her out of the plane, hobbling down the steps on the crutches Roman gave me.

The first thing I see is the familiar shaggy light brown hair in the same hairstyle it's been since high school. Those deep, piercing blue eyes have relief when he sees me but once his eyes scan my body and see all my injuries, his face shows how angry he is. Theo has always acted like my brother more than my best friend and has always been protective over me. Theo finally sees the crutches and he clenches his fist at his side, but he still comes over and wraps me in a tight hug. I smell the familiar smell of the Old Spice he's always worn. It makes the walls around my heart fall. Everything comes crashing down on me and I sob into Theo's chest. He tightens his hold on me.

"You're okay, Lia. I've got you now." He pulls away slightly to wipe the tears off my cheeks. "You were always an ugly crier."

I chuckle and lightly smack him in the chest, and he lifts me into the truck. Alessia climbs in the truck after me, giving me a worried look after seeing me cry. "It's okay. Theo is Mama's friend and I just missed him a lot."

"Thanks, Roman," Theo says to Roman, and they continue to talk for a couple more minutes. Alessia snuggles into my chest, and as I run my fingers through her hair, I feel like I can finally breathe.

Theo gets into the car and turns back to look at Alessia. "Now, let me introduce myself to the beautiful princess. Hopefully she isn't as difficult as her Mama."

I scowl and mumble "asshole" under my breath, and he returns at my glare playfully before facing Alessia again.

"Hello, Princess, my name is Theo. I am your Mama's friend. I know you both were hurt before, but I want you to know that you both are safe with me. Can you tell me your name?"

She looks at me for approval and give her a nod and I smile at her. "Alessia," she signs to Theo.

He looks at me confused but says, "She's deaf?" I shake my head no. "Mute?"

I say "Yeah, from witnessing the abuse."

"But you named her Alessia after my Mama?" He asks quietly, probably thinking about his sweet Mama, who was too sweet to have given birth to this overgrown brat. Unfortunately, she died from a heart attack when we were in high school.

"Yeah, Theo. I wanted her to be named after your sweet Mama. She was a saint to deal with us as kids." We both chuckle, remembering the hard time we gave our parents growing up.

He shakes himself out of his memories. "Well, it's wonderful to meet you Alessia. Let's get out of here and head to my farm."

Her eyes shine in excitement recognizing that Theo understood her. "Theo's *Nonno (Grandfather)* was deaf baby girl."

"Farm?" she signs with a sparkle in her eye. Alessia is an animal lover.

"Yep. We have lots of horses. Once you are settled, I will show you and your Mama around." Theo smiles at Alessia, and she gives him a smile back.

It takes a few hours to get to his house because of traffic, so we decided to get up in the morning and he will introduce us to the animals while he is doing chores. His farm is beautiful; it has a rustic feeling to it, but it is warm and welcoming. He shows us to our rooms, but Alessia decides she still wants to share with me, which I have no problem with. We've shared the same small twin size bed since the day she was born.

We lay cuddled together as Alessia falls asleep and I pray we will be safe. I just want my baby girl to be happy and safe.

FOUR
EMILIA

      I lay awake next to Alessia for hours and I still can't fall asleep, so I decide to go downstairs and get something to drink, hoping that will help me get some rest. I hobble down the stairs on my crutches, trying to be as quiet as possible as I limp into the kitchen, where I find Theo nursing a beer.

      "Hey, you want a drink?" he asks looking over at me. I give him a short nod, and he hands me a bottle of water. "Couldn't sleep?"

      I shake my head as I lower myself onto a stool at the kitchen counter.

      "No. A lot has happened in the past couple days; I haven't been able to process it." I say, taking a swig of my water.

      "I can imagine so. Now that Alessia is asleep, why don't you tell me everything that happened."

      "Okay, but don't interrupt me. Let me get it all out first." He nods and gestures for us to go sit in the other room. He holds his hand out to help me off the stool and I follow him, taking a seat on the couch. He grabs a pillow and props my leg up on it, then goes back into the kitchen and comes back with an ice pack.

      "Figured you could ice your ankle while you talk."

      I thank him and take a deep breath, closing my eyes for a moment, getting myself ready to finally expose myself and be vulnerable to Theo. I open my eyes and I look down at my lap, refusing to meet his eyes as I tell my story.

      "About eight years ago, while I was at work, my house caught fire. Mama, Papa, Giovanni, and Franco were all inside, and they died in the fire. All barricaded in so no one could get out. After that, I went on a wild careless streak. I started partying and drinking a lot, and I met Seth. We hooked up a lot, and I don't know if we ever used protection. I was always too drunk, until I found out I was pregnant. I went to Seth and told him that I was pregnant. I didn't want his help, but I wanted him to know. He wasn't happy, and we got into a fight about it being my fault.

      "He forced me to move into his house, and at the time, I thought he lived alone. I found out pretty quickly he didn't. He lived with his partner, Boris, who is a sick, sadistic, perverted old man. As soon as he saw me, he became obsessed with me. There were also maybe about ten other men, Seth and Boris' employees, who came in and out of the house regularly.

      "I knew something wasn't right from the start. I tried to leave, and I was caught. My punishment was given by Boris, and I will never forget that day. I had to spend a week in his room, naked and chained to his bed, and I wasn't allowed to tell him no. He raped me, over and over. In the beginning, I fought back but by the end of the first day, I just did what he told me to do."

I'm crying now, big, ugly tears and snot running down my face, Theo pulls me closer to him and I feel safe enough to continue.

"Luckily, Alessia was never hurt during that week. I was in so much pain, that I couldn't walk, so they ended up throwing me in the basement until I could gather my strength enough to serve the men. Once I recovered enough to move, it was decided that the only way I would be allowed to eat is if I cleaned the house every day and pleasured the men when they ordered it. Seth even joined in on the punishment and would whisper evil comments in my ear while he was raping me." I sob, and Theo tightens his arms around me. "I dealt with it because I was trying to keep Alessia alive.

"When I went into labor, they threw me in the bathtub and told me to shut my mouth and hurry up. I was so scared; I was petrified that one of us was going to die. I was in labor for over twenty hours, and I was so weak from the labor they called a doctor to come help deliver her. The doctor told Seth that I was lucky to survive, and I that shouldn't have sex of any kind for at least eight weeks because of the tearing. Seth played the doting boyfriend and new father part well. As soon as that doctor was gone, they put Alessia in another room, then dragged me to the kitchen and tied me to the table, facedown with my ass in the air, so they could take turns on my ass. Then, I was beaten with a spiked whip thirty times. I had to make a new deal with them to make sure Alessia could have what she needed. I was their guest's entertainment, anything they wanted, I had to give it to them. I was to obey them, bow when speaking to them, never tell them no, and be their good little slut.

"That went on for years. Alessia learned to stay quiet and never leave the bedroom, which isn't a life for a kid. I felt terrible, but I wanted her safe and away from them." I take a deep breath, knowing that I am almost finished, I've made it through this disgusting story that I have lived. "I finally lost it when Boris came to me on the night we left and declared I would groom Alessia to be his bride. I yelled at them, and Seth told me that he wished Alessia was dead. He told me that I was going to do was I am told because Boris bought Alessia from him. Seth tossed me around and Alessia came out of our room and whimpered. Seth went for her and that is when I attacked Seth with a lamp and knocked him out. After that, Boris told me he was going to kill me and fuck Alessia now. She is only six, still a child. I saw red and punched him until he was unconscious. I packed our bags, grabbed Alessia, and got on a bus that took us to New York, which is where I met Ace and Aurora. They helped me get in contact with you, and here we are." I am still a crying mess, shaking like a leaf in Theo's arms. "I've failed as a mother."

Theo pulls himself away from me to hold me by my shoulders and look me in my eye. "That is the worst bullshit I have ever heard coming from your mouth."

"It is my fault all of this happened to her. She is petrified to talk after seeing how Seth and Boris would beat me if I spoke out of line or didn't agree to what they wanted me to. She is afraid of men because of them. No little girl should be afraid like she is."

"Emilia, whether you want to admit it or not, you saved her. Yes, she has some trauma, but with time and therapy, she will get better. YOU took the beatings and all the other torture for her. That makes you an amazing mama. You knew her life was in major trouble, and you got both of you out of there. And the condition your body is in? How you went two days travelling like that, I will never know. Stop being so hard on yourself. Let go of the guilt and start looking toward a better future for you and Alessia."

I am sure he knows I don't believe him, but he doesn't say anything. I give him the tightest hug I can while being injured, and when he moves away, he starts telling me all about his life: owning a farm, being an oncologist, and his many boytoys.

"You are an oncologist and you run your family farm," I process out loud.

"Yes, you know I have to keep myself busy. Plus, I have staff on the farm," he tells me with a cheeky smile.

"You better be letting them help you." I give him a warning look, I know he likes to overdo it.

"They are," he puts his hands up and shakes his head. "Geez, don't give me the mom look," he says, shaking his head.

I shrug. "Well, after you have kids, you develop the mom look. It comes in handy when people do stupid things." I give him a meaningful look.

"Ouch. Emilia, I am hurt." He puts his hand on his heart dramatically, as usual.

"Oh hush, drama queen. You will be fine. But thank you for listening, and for talking to me, Theo. I really missed you." I give him a hug, and we end up watching reruns of The Nanny. I don't remember falling asleep, but I wake when I feel myself being carried.

"Theo! What the hell, put me down! I can walk." I protest and try to squirm my way out of his arms. He just chuckles at my attempt. Bastard.

"Emilia, you are on crutches. I am just saving you time getting to your room." I shake my head, knowing his stubborn ass won't put me down.

When we get to my room, giving me a kiss on my forehead, he tucks me in, and we wish each other goodnight.

The next morning, I wake up to small hands on my face, and it takes me a moment to remember that we are safe and at Theo's. I pretend I am still asleep but before Alessia can do anything, I grab her in a big hug and give her kisses all over her face. I get a big smile in return, one that I would do anything in this world to keep on her adorable face. I see Theo out of the corner of my eye leaning against the door frame with a small smile on his face.

"Good morning sleeping beauties." He comes over sits on the edge of the bed and starts to speak, but he is also signing as well. When we were kids, we never thought we would use sign language except to sign with his grandfather. "How about you two get up and get ready? I already have breakfast in the kitchen, after we eat, we can get in the truck and tour the farm."

Alessia's excitement is contagious as she starts jumping on the bed. I laugh "Go in your backpack, get dressed, and then I will brush your hair before we eat." She jumps off the bed and runs into the closet. As I am slowly making my way out of bed, she comes back and hands me clothes to wear. I kiss her head and thank her.

"I will be outside the door if you need any help," Theo tells me from the doorway.

"Thanks Theo."

Alessia and I take our time getting ready and open the door to Theo still waiting outside. He picks me up and tells Alessia to grab my crutches as we make our way into the kitchen where a great feast is set out. Waffles, eggs, bacon, sausage, mixed fruit, and juice are all waiting for us.

"Wow. Theo, thank you, but you really didn't need to go through all this trouble," I whisper to him.

"Of course, I did. Now eat up." We all ate silently, too hungry to speak. When we finished, Alessia and I helped Theo clean up, then we headed out to Theo's truck.

The drive to Theo's farm is scenic, with rolling green hills and clear blue skies as far as the eye can see. We pull up next to a beautiful white barn, get out of the truck, and are immediately welcomed by six horses running up to the fence, nickering at us. Theo chuckles towards them, "I know Alfred fed you this morning."

Alessia grabs Theo's hand to get his attention and signs, "Can I pet them?"

"Sure. Would you like to feed them some apples?" She bounces on the spot excitedly and Theo tells us to stay put as he goes get some. He goes into the barn and comes out a minute later with a handful of apple slices, then gives some to Alessia and shows her how to keep her hand flat as she feeds the apple slices to the horses. The smile doesn't leave Alessia's face the entire time She even lets out a few giggles, and I love seeing how much happier she is here. When they run out of apple slices, we go inside the barn and meet a sweet and polite young farmhand, Alfred, as he cleans out the stalls. Alessia scrunches up her face and waves a hand in front of her nose, causing all of us to laugh.

When we climb back in the truck, Theo drives us to the edge of an empty, muddy field, where he gives me a sly smirk.

"What are you planning?"

He doesn't answer, just hits the accelerator, and we go speeding into the mud. It flies all around us as Theo twists and turns with Alessia and I shrieking and laughing.

We slow to a stop a while later and Theo turns to us with a big smile on his face. "Did you have fun?" Matching smiles cover mine and Alessia's faces. "Good. Let's head back to the house before Dr. Bianchi arrives to check up on Mama."

We arrive back at the house as a range rover is pulling up. When we get out of the truck, Roman just laughs "Really, Theo? You better not have injured my patient any more than she already is."

Theo, dramatically as always, puts his hands on his hips. "What kind of doctor do you take me for? I would never hurt either of them!"

"A crazy doctor, but we already knew that," Roman taunts as he starts taking things out of his car.

"Ouch, Roman. And here I thought you loved me." I roll my eyes as Theo places a hand on his heart. "I will help you carry this stuff in as soon as I get the girls in the house. We can set up in the bedroom on the bottom floor."

Theo picks me up out of the truck and carries me inside to sit on the bed. Alessia joins me, and we sign about what she wants for lunch. Once Roman and Theo have everything set up in the bedroom downstairs, they start checking out my ribs.

"Yep, as I thought. You have three broken ribs, but it looks like this isn't the first time this has happened," Roman tells me after a few minutes of inspecting.

"Yeah, I am not surprised. The only time I saw any kind of medical help was after twenty hours struggling in labor."

Roman's eyes look like they're about to pop out of his head. "You mean to tell me even when you were pregnant with his child, he never took you to make sure everything was, okay?"

I shake my head. "He wanted me to have an abortion and told me that if I didn't, he wasn't going to help me with anything."

"Wow. What a bastard." He mutters, "Ok, let's check your ankle. It's not broken, but it is definitely a nasty sprain. Stay off it as much as possible for the next couple weeks and use the crutches if you need to go somewhere. And rest your ribs as much as possible. I will come back out in four weeks to do another round of x-rays and then we can reevaluate. Unfortunately, with those areas having been severely injured in the past you need to be extra careful when healing." He starts to pack up his equipment. That didn't take long.

"Ok. Thank you, Roman." I stand and crutch my way out to the kitchen. As I finish making lunch, Theo walks Roman to the door and says goodbye.

"Emilia, this is not taking it easy." Theo states glaring at me. I glare back.

"Theo, I can't stay completely off my feet. I am a mother, I have to take care of Alessia, I promise you I will rest when I can," I tell him with a shrug.

He throws his hands in the air, exasperated. "Fine!" He mumbles something under his breath about me being stubborn and the worst patient he has ever dealt with. I smile in victory.

After lunch, Alessia and I have a Disney movie marathon while Theo goes to work. As night falls, we eat dinner and get ready for bed, where Alessia signs to me, "Mama, I had so much fun today. You are the best Mama in the whole world." She snuggles into me. I kiss her forehead and whisper good night to her, and it isn't long until I fall asleep after her with a smile on my face.

MATEO

I stalk into my office, slamming the door behind me. I have just finished torturing a man for answers about where the money that he stole is. Stupid man was gullible enough to believe a greedy man, especially one who took off afterwards, leaving the idiot for me to find. No one steals from the Don of the Italian Mafia without being punished. They call me a beast for a reason.

There is a knock on the door. Pa told me he was coming by my office to speak with me. I can guarantee I know what he wants to talk about. He wants me to find a wife, but I have no interest in getting married to someone who wants me only for my money.

"Enter," I order. Pa walks in and sits down in front of my desk.

"*Figlio (son)*, how are you?" I am immediately suspicious and give him a blank stare. Obviously, he wants something. He is never nice to anyone.

"Pa, I am well. I know you are not here on a social call, so why don't you just tell me what you came here for."

He shakes his head. "You are so much like your mother, right to the point. This is not a social call. You need a wife. You have until your next birthday before I pick one for you and you already know who my choice is. I really don't see why you are against Zaira being your wife."

I take a deep breath to control my temper. I will never marry that woman. "I don't want a whore for a wife. She needs to be loyal, fierce, and protective of this family. Not someone who will spread her legs to gain status. Zaira would let the power go to her head and abuse it. I will not put the family at risk like that."

"Few women stay pure till marriage anymore. If you don't find a wife by your birthday, you will have no choice."

"It isn't about being pure. I want loyalty to the family and someone who is strong, who won't break when my enemy gets their hands on her. If that's all, you can leave. I have a meeting soon."

He nods and stands. When he reaches the door, he looks over his shoulder and says, "Don't forget about dinner on Sunday at Nonna's mansion." Then he slams my office door, pissed I didn't do what he wanted. I don't care. He can throw a temper tantrum for all I care.

I lean my head back in my seat, take a deep breath and my phone starts ringing. "One fucking minute of peace, is that too much to ask for?" I reach for my phone and see that Fabio is calling me back. He is one of my Capos and specializes in hacking. He is probably calling back with information about that mother and daughter that flew over here in my jet with Roman. I answer with a barked, "Hello."

"I have the information you asked for Don."

"Ok what did you find out?"

"The mother and daughter Roman flew over here, I found out from Roman that Emilia and Alessia Lombardi are on the run from her daughter's father and his business partner. He physically abused them, mostly Emilia, the mother. She has stitches in her ear, broken ribs, sprained ankle, and many bruises all over her body. Whereas the daughter, Alessia, only has bruises around her throat and on her cheek. His buddy from college, Theo Walker, grew up with Emilia before he moved out here for college and stayed after he got a job as an oncologist. When she escaped, she called him and asked if she could stay with him. Theo knew Roman was on his way home from the conference he went to in the states and hoped he would bring them to Italy safely. I also found out Alessia's father is none other than Seth Volkov."

"Interesting. Seth Volkov. Is he the Seth that is Boris's partner? Who gets him girls from their trafficking ring?"

"Yes, that Seth. And Boris is the business partner they are running from."

"Send me everything you have on Emilia and Alessia."

"Already in your email. Call me if you want me to look further into this."

We hang up and I open my email. This is why I asked Fabio to investigate for me. He is thorough in his work. I click on the email, which opens a couple photos. My first thought when I see the picture of Emilia is, "Wow, she is beautiful." She has shoulder length brown hair with vibrant green eyes. She looks like she is graduating in the first photo, she has her robes and cap on. The other photo is of both mother and daughter, both injured, but I can see Emilia's beauty underneath. I look at

Alessia next. She looks almost identical to her mother, except her hair is more of a reddish brown.

I continue to stare at the pictures and analyze their injuries. It sickens me. Yes, we are in the mafia, and we are evil but abusing women and children is disgusting, it is a death sentence. I have killed many men and women over this. I have been trying to shut down all human trafficking around the world with the Spanish Mafia, but it seems as soon as we shut one down, another five pop up. I might be in luck though, maybe Emilia will be my golden ticket to finally catching these two sick men who keep slipping through my fingers.

I decide I will have Fabio monitor Emilia and Alessia to see what they are like. Maybe Emilia will be the answer to me finding a wife problem as well. I call him back and have him put them under surveillance until further notice and tell him I want daily reports.

I call one of my whores to meet me at my penthouse to come suck me off. She is eager to please me, it's not like I must try hard to have a woman pleasure me. Women drop to my feet. My short dark brown hair is buzzed on the side and the front is barely spiked. Woman always want to touch me, but they're forbidden to.

When I arrive, she is already waiting for me by the door. I walk past her and towards the living room couch. "Don't talk. Get on your knees in front of me." She obeys, and I unzip my pants to pull my cock out. She opens her mouth and starts to bob her head up and down my length.

She isn't going down far enough, so I grab her hair and start to fuck her mouth. She has tears running down her face and puts her hands on my thighs and tries to push me away. I just tighten my grip on her hair. "Get your hands off me." I command.

She does so immediately, and I go back to roughly fucking her mouth. I close my eyes and imagine that it is Emilia with her mouth wrapped around my cock, causing me to go faster as I feel myself close to cuming. A few thrusts later, I cum down her throat. I open my eyes and look down, seeing the mess that is this blonde, made-up slut. I push her away and tell her to get out as I walk towards the bathroom. She obeys quickly scrambling, away and running out the door. As soon as I shut the door, I strip and step into the shower. Why did I think of Emilia sucking me off? I never do anything like that. I will admit she is absolutely beautiful, and I would love to enjoy her body, but no woman has taken over my thoughts while I was with another woman. I shake my head, trying to forget about the sexy brunette as I finish my shower and climb into bed wearing my boxers

FIVE
MATEO

"Did you really think you could steal from me without me knowing? Where is my money?" I demand Donald answer me. The stupid idiot thought he could steal two million dollars from me. He was the greedy man who tried to run, and for a bit we let him think he got away with it. We knew someone had been stealing money, so my Consigliere and I set a trap to catch them. We have a tracker on the money, so I know it is in the hands of the fucking Russians. Now it is time to make this rat start to spill. His hands and legs are tied to the chair and the chair is bolted to the ground.

"I don't know what you are talking about." He refuses to look at me. I let loose a menacing chuckle and punch him in the nose. His head flies back and blood starts flowing.

He groans. "Motherfucker."

"L'ultima volta te lo chiederò. Dove sono i miei soldi?" (*Last time I am gonna ask. Where is my money?)*

"Vaffanculo" (*Fuck you.)* I give him a dangerous smirk. That's okay, he will be singing like a canary soon enough.

"Strap him to the table." I order one of my soldiers. Once he strapped to the table nice and tight so he can't go anywhere, I walk over to my tools and spend a minute deciding, before picking up coal, gasoline, and a blow torch.

I turn to my underboss Vincenzo, who is also my cousin. "Vincenzo, go get our guests." Roman looks over at me and smirks as Vincenzo walks back into the room with a metal cage. The rat inside is already squeaking and squealing, making Donald even more nervous. "Donald, did you know that when a rat is in an enclosed area that is too hot, it will burrow its way out?" He shakes his head as the sweat gathers on his bald head.

Vincenzo sets the rat on Donald's stomach and slams a metal bowl over it roughly, pulling a strap over the bowl to keep it in place. I lay the coals on top of the bowl and pour gasoline on top of the coals, then turn on the blow torch. I heat up the coals, quickly setting them on fire. The squeals of the rat as it scrambled to get away from the heat filled the room, then the sound of ripping flesh. Not even ten seconds go by when Donald starts begging for me to stop. I let him suffer more, he doesn't deserve my mercy. He stole from me then refused to answer when I asked nicely. He disrespected me, and I value respect.

"Fuck!" he screams. "Stop, I will talk. Just stop!" I turn off the blow torch and I give him a minute to catch his breath since he is crying.

"Alexei contacted me offering me more money to steal from you. He said he would protect me from you if I got caught." I give him a blank look. He really is a dumbass.

"Well, you are dumber than I thought. The only thing Alexei cares about is himself." His eyes look like they are about to pop out of his head as he realizes his fate. I am going to kill him.

"Don. I am so sorry. Please, I will do anything. Please don't kill me."

"Why should I keep you alive? Hmm?" I turn the blow torch on low and have it graze the side of his face. "I can be a spy for you."

"Why would I trust you? You broke Omerta' when you accepted the enemy's offer of more money. I should probably thank Alexei for showing me where your loyalties lie." I turn up the heat and the rat continues to burrow through his stomach. He cries and begs for me to stop, but he broke Omerta, so he will die painfully. I turn off the blow torch and hand it to Vincenzo.

"Finish him however you want, then dispose of the body." Vincenzo rubs his hands together; he loves to torture people. I get myself cleaned up and head to my meeting with Fabio about my future wife.

I arrive at one of my legal companies, an energy provider company, De Luca Corp. I also own bars, strip clubs, malls, real estate, and a hotel chain called Jasmine, named after Mama, Asimina. Her name means Jasmine in Italian.

Fabio is already in my office waiting for me. He nods his head in acknowledgment as I sit behind my desk. "What do you have for me, Fabio?"

"We have had men watching Emilia and her daughter Alessia for six weeks now. She is living with a Dr. Theodore Walker. They were childhood friends until he left for college, and they fell out of touch. Their friendship seems to be platonic, and we have yet to see any kind of relationship that is more than sibling like.

"The girls are on the run from Seth Volkov, Alessia's father. He never wanted Alessia. Emilia got raped and beaten, not just by Seth but by any man who walked through the doors. She didn't fight back in fear of what they would do to Alessia. This happened from the time Emilia moved in at three months pregnant until they escaped a month and half ago, which was roughly seven years. When Roman assessed their injuries, Alessia had a bruise on her cheek and on her throat. Emilia got stitches on her ear lobe and had bruises on her face and throat, three broken ribs, and a nasty sprained ankle. Alessia is a selective mute from watching her mother being abused for years."

"Fabio, are you telling me that little girl witnessed her mother being abused?" I ground out, my fists clenched.

He nods, "Yes, Emilia did everything she could to keep Alessia out of danger, but Alessia still saw and heard things no little girl should have," Fabio tells me.

"Fabio, where are they right now?" He gets on his phone, turning to me with their location not even a minute later.

"They are at Theo's home. Theo is working a twelve-hour shift at the hospital."

"Good. Call Vittorio, Salvatore, and Vincenzo. Tell them we will meet with them out front in fifteen minutes with a couple guards and two SUVs." I smirk. "We are going to pay my future wife a visit."

Fabio nods and puts his phone to his ear as he walks out of my office. I head over to the private mini bar and pour myself some whiskey, then sit back at my desk to get another look at her photo. I run my finger over her face. She is beautiful, and she will look great on my arm.

"You look like a stalker, running your finger over that picture, cousin." Vincenzo smirks at me as I shoot him a glare. "So, what is this about visiting the future Mrs. Mateo De Luca?" he asks as he plops himself in the chair across from my desk as Salvatore takes the chair next to him.

"Well, you know how my father told me I had until my next birthday to be married?" They both nod. "Roman escorted a mother and daughter using my private jet about two months ago. They were on the run from the abusive father and his business partner. I have had Fabio and his team keep them under surveillance and what he reported back to me has me very intrigued. She is beautiful, loyal, fierce, and protective, which will be perfect for my queen. But this will only be a marriage on paper unless we need to put on an act in front of people."

Salvatore looks at me, "Are you really going to drag an abused mother and daughter into this world when we all know you won't treat them right? Mateo, you are a selfish bastard, you won't stay loyal in this marriage and your stepmother is an evil and cunning bitch. Also, you have Zaira you are obsessed with, and I can guarantee that will make their lives hell. Are you willing to protect them from that as long as your enemies are their enemies?"

"Of course, I will protect them. I am the Mafia Don. I will keep them safe." I say, giving him a knowing look. I am the Don, I can and will keep them safe. I know I sound cocky, but I am the king for a reason.

"When this bites you in the ass, don't come to me asking for my help. You are taking on more than you know. Abused victims need more than money. I feel bad for them, and just so you know, I will be treating them like family regardless of what the "bitch crew" says about it," he tells me.

"I know what I am doing. *Andiamo*." *(Let's go.)* I say, and we walk out to the front of the office where everyone is waiting.

At Theo's House A Couple Hours Later

When we pull up into the street they are staying on, I tell Fabio to kill the cell service so she can't call for help. We park the SUV's in the driveway as I have my men surround the house and I walk up to the door. I knock on the door, and I hear some murmurs and shuffling around. I am about to knock again when the door opens, just enough that Emilia can block my view of inside of the house with her body.

"May I help you?" She has the most angelic voice. I take her in from head to toe. Holy fuck. The pictures don't do her justice. I leisurely lead my gaze back to her face and find her glaring at me. *Shit focus.* I chastise myself. It feels like those piercing green eyes can see into my soul, and I can imagine myself wrapping my hand in her beautifully shiny brown shoulder length hair as I fuck her mouth.

"Yes, sweetheart I am looking for you, *La Mia Tigre," (My Tigress)* I put my hands in my pockets, taking a casual stance.

She glares at me as if she can bury me six feet with a look. "And why would you be looking for me?" I chuckle at how adorable she is.

This marriage is gonna be fun. I think to myself. "Well, I heard you rode on my plane over here from New York. Tell me, why were you so desperate to leave New York?"

She puts her hands on her hips, "I thought Dr. Roman did it as a favor for Theo. What do you want as payment? For me to drop to my knees and suck you off?" She raises an eyebrow at me. Well, I wouldn't say no to that.

I am taken out of my lustful fantasies when I hear the safety of a shotgun being clicked off and realize that the barrel of the gun is at my lips. Where the hell did that come from? I hear my men turn the safety off their own guns. *"Metti giù le pistole" (Put your guns down)* I tell my men and they do. I put my hand on her gun, using my strength to lower it. She tries to fight it, but I easily overpower her.

"Tigre," (Tigress) that isn't a very nice thing to do to a guest." I step closer to her. She takes the gun from my hand and swings it to try and hit me, but I catch it. That's enough of her feisty attitude. I pull the gun from her hands and toss it to the side. I turn her body so her back is facing my chest. I have both of her wrists pinned to her sides and my arms are wrapped around her. She tries to pull her hands from my hold on her, but I won't let go of her.

Emilia is fighting me. "Let go of me, you fucking bastard." I lift her off the ground and carry her into the house. "Fucking stop, you mother fucker." I chuckle at how much anger is in a small body.

"We are gonna need to work on that foul language coming from those pretty lips."

"Yeah, good luck with that, asshole." Oh, once she is married to me, I am gonna be spanking that sweet ass every time she decides to curse.

I push her into a chair, "Okay, Tesoro, *(darling)* are you going to sit and behave so we can talk, or do I have to tie you to the chair?"

She glares at me and says, "Go to hell."

"Okay being tied to the chair it is. Vincenzo, bring me the rope." He comes in a minute later, meanwhile I am fighting to keep her sitting in the chair.

He hands me the rope and chuckles, "Good luck with this one."

Emilia's sassy mouth responds back with, "Great, another egotistical, small prick asshole."

Vincenzo chuckles, "Darling, if my cousin didn't want you. I would show you how I am far from small."

I tie the rope around her from her chest to stomach so she can't wiggle her way out of it.

I take a deep breath, so I don't lose my patience. "Now that we have that settled, we can talk, my name is Mateo."

"I never said I wanted to talk to you."

I tower over her and whisper in her ear, "Oh I think you do since you don't want Alessia to go back to living with Seth." The color from her face drains when I mention Alessia being with Seth again. The fear is all over her face.

She sighs and looks down at her feet and says, defeated, "What do you want?"

"I have a proposition for you." I lift her chin so I can look into her green eyes, she doesn't say anything but nods, so I continue. "You will not be able to keep her safe here. Seth's brother-in-law Alexei, he is the boss of the Russian Mafia. And Seth has already asked for his help in finding you and Alessia. I am a very powerful man myself and I can keep you both safe, but I won't be doing this for free." I back away from her to give her a bit of space. You can see the worry and fear all over her face.

"I don't have the money to pay you. So, I can't accept your offer."

I raise my eyebrow. "Who said anything about you paying me with money?"

She mumbles, "Great another man who wants to use my body."

I put my hand over her mouth "Did I say anything about using your body as payment?"

She shakes her head no, and I move my hand. "Well then how else am I supposed to pay you for keeping Alessia safe?"

I shake my head. "Not just Alessia, you as well."

"I don't care about my safety as long as she is happy and safe, that is more important to me."

She will make a wonderful Queen to stand at my side, I think to myself. "You have done a wonderful job at that so far but let me help keep you both safe. All you have to do is marry me."

Her green eyes lock onto my blue ones, then she starts laughing. "Good joke but seriously, what do you want me to pay you with for her protection?" Emilia stops laughing when she sees I am not joking, and she looks shocked. "Wait, oh fuck. You are serious?"

I take a step closer to her and kneel in front of her, so we are eye-to-eye. I do put my hands on her calves to prevent her from kicking at me, since my Tigress seems to be very feisty and vicious. "Yes, I am serious. I need a wife so I can have ownership of my late mothers' estate, and my father will only do that if I have a wife."

"Wow, either you are a man whore, or your father is a piece of work."

I chuckle at her comment, "Oh he is a bastard, but I am no virgin." I was hoping to get reaction out of her, but her face was blank.

"I am sure a man like you can get any girl to be your wife. Why choose me?"

I take a step closer and tuck a piece of hair behind her ear, but as soon as my hand gets near her face, she slightly flinches. It pisses me off that someone laid a hand my Queen. I might be the boss of the Italian Mafia, but I do not tolerate abuse of women and children. I will personally have them meet their maker for doing this to her and Alessia.

"Don't give me that look of pity. I did what I had to do so we could survive."

"That is why I want to marry you. You are strong and I need someone like that as my wife."

"And why do you need someone strong to be by your side as your wife? Will I have jealous mistresses to worry about? Cause honestly, I don't care what you do in your free time as long as they leave Alessia alone."

I chuckle again at her feisty attitude. "No darling, I need someone who won't crumble if my enemies get their hands on them. And the other ladies who throw themselves at me usually cry over breaking a nail."

"Why would your enemies want to get their hands on me? I am nobody."

"But you will be my wife and you will be my biggest weakness."

She rolls her eyes, "Well, they will be in for a rude awakening when they learn I am not."

I grab her chin in my fingers and make her look at me "This may be an arranged marriage, but you will be treated with respect and be safe."

She tries to pull her face out of my grasp but when I don't budge, she just rolls her eyes. "Why are you so important that your enemies will want to get their hands on me?"

I smirk at her, "Well *Tesoro*, soon you will be married to the Boss of the Italian Mafia." Her eyes look like they are gonna pop out of her head.

She shakes her head and says, "Yeah I am not gonna marry you."

I give her a hard stare, "And what makes you think you have a choice?"

"I am not putting Alessia in danger of being tied to one mafia when another one is after us."

I lean up and whisper in her ear, "It's cute that you think you have a choice. Emilia, you will be my *moglie(wife)* because you know Alessia will be safer with our protection rather than without it."

"CHI CAZZO PENSI DI DIRMI COSA FARE CON MIA FIGLIA?" *(WHO THE FUCK DO YOU THINK YOU ARE TO TELL ME WHAT TO DO WITH MY DAUGHTER?)* She yells at me; she doesn't back down when I glare at her.

"She will also be my daughter and will have my last name like you will."

Her nose starts to flare, "Who the fuck said she was going to be your daughter? You only talked about marrying me, not adopting Alessia."

I knew she was protective of Alessia, but I had no idea it was this extreme. "I will adopt her so she will be protected under our family. This is not for discussion." Emilia head butts me in my nose, and I lean back, I use my sleeve and wipe the bit of blood from my nose. "What the fuck was that for?"

She glares at me. "Never tell me anything to do with my daughter. It isn't up for discussion; you may have a lot more money than me, but I will always have final say when it comes to Alessia."

I stand back up and look down at her. I grab her hair firmly so she can look me in the eye but not enough to hurt her. "I will be adopting her so she will be safe and under my protection. She will be my daughter in every way but I will go at her pace so we can form a bond. She will learn to trust me and the other men in this family like you will."

She is grinding her teeth together. "If anyone, and I mean anyone in your family hurts her in any way I don't care who they are, they will be at my mercy, and I will not hold back. Remember that, and I would advise you to tell everyone my warning."

I nod at her. "She will be happy and safe."

"I will believe it when I see it."

"Now, can I untie you so we can go discuss with our daughter about you both moving into my mansion?"

"Cut that daughter shit out. You will not say anything until I get to discuss it with her. She is already petrified of men; you pushing her into being your daughter when her own father made her scared isn't gonna help anyone. AND you will stay out of the room so I can talk to her alone first. But are you absolutely sure you want to be married to an abused woman and have a mute stepdaughter?"

"I already made my decision and I stick to my decisions. I will give you an hour to gather all of your and Alessia's things." I say to her as I untie the rope from around her and then I stand back up.

"An hour?" she huffs at me.

"Yes. We need to make it somewhat believable that we are in a relationship. And then we will get married in three months. You now have fifty-nine minutes, and we will be leaving with or without your stuff so move it," I say to her, helping her up off the chair. She glares at me and storms her way upstairs. As her foot touches the second step, I say, "Oh Emilia, don't think about trying to escape. I have men outside and if you run, they will catch you." She flips me off and continues up the stairs. I chuckle and say to myself again. *This will be an interesting marriage.*

I give her about twenty minutes before going to check on her. I make my way upstairs, the door is cracked open, and I see Alessia, who Emilia's is mini me, sitting on the bed in front of Emilia, who is bent on her knees talking to her while holding her hands. I don't pay attention to what Emilia is saying anything, when Alessia looks up at me.

She curls in on herself with her legs to her chest and her head on her knees. Her hands are covering her face. She starts to shake like a leaf. She catches me off guard at how scared she is of me and that breaks my heart. My heart drops to my stomach. No little girl should be that afraid, she is supposed to be a ray of sunshine with a huge smile across her face. I will make sure from now on she is nothing but smiles.

She looks so much like Emilia the only difference is the shade of green in her eyes and her hair is a brighter brown than Emilia's. She truly is an angel. I already feel so protective of this little angel, my princess. Holy shit, if this girl is still my stepdaughter when she gets older, I am going to be threatening a lot of horny boys to stay away. I start thinking about private tutors, extra protection and more guns to keep the boys away. I shake my head and decide to worry about that later.

I slowly walk in to show them both I am not going to hurt them. You can see Alessia is petrified. I get next to Emilia and mock how she is kneeling on the ground. "Hi Alessia, my name is Mateo. Did your Mama tell you how you are gonna come live with me so you and your Mama can be safe?" She barely nods her head that is still on her knees. She hasn't looked up yet. "I am a friend of Dr. Roman and I want to help keep you both safe so no one else hurts you or your Mama." I stop so I don't overwhelm her. I look at Emilia. "Can you translate between us since I don't know sign language?" Emilia nods at me. "I promise that you and your Mama will be safe from all those mean people."

Alessia looks at Emilia and signs to her. Emilia says, "Yes, Mama said you have extra people to help keep us safe. But we must leave soon. What about Teddy, will we see him again?"

I look at Emilia and ask, "Who is Teddy?"

"Teddy is Theo's nickname. Alessia calls him that because he gives great hugs like a teddy bear," she says with a chuckle. She is so precious and adorable.

I smile at Alessia and tell her. "Of course, *Principessa, (Princess)* Teddy can visit. Let's finish packing all of your stuff so you both can get settled and I will introduce you to the family at dinner."

She finally looks at me, I get a small very timid smile from Alessia, she signs to Emilia. "She says thank you." Emilia tells me.

"Of course, do you need any help with anything?" I ask.

"No, we are about done, Alessia just needs to change her clothes." I stand up and leave the room, waiting for them outside their door. When they both exit the bedroom, I see they each only have a backpack of stuff. "Is that all you want to bring?" I grab both of their backpacks; Emilia goes to protest, and I give her a look to shut her mouth, and we keep walking to the car.

"This is all of our stuff," Emilia says with a small smile.

"We will fix that. I will give you my credit card and you both can go shopping."

"Mateo, I don't want you for your money, the only reason I am doing it is because I want Alessia to be safe."

"I know that Emilia, but you both are De Luca's, and, in my family, we take care of each other."

She puts a note on the table for Theo and she locks up the house. We continue to walk to the SUV, and I pull out my phone to let them know we are leaving. As soon as we approach the men, Emilia stops and bends down to pick up Alessia. Alessia's body starts to shake as though she is sobbing. She hides her face in Emilia's neck. Emilia quietly whispers to Alessia while rubbing her hand up and down her back. I have all the men except for Salvatore, Vincenzo, and Vittorio get into the SUV's, to hopefully help Alessia calm down.

I stand slightly behind Alessia, and I quietly start talking to her, "*Principessa,* it's okay these men won't hurt you. Those two are my cousins, Vincenzo, and Salvatore." (I point to them) "Vittorio will be you and your Mama's head bodyguard. It is his job to keep you both safe at all times, if you ever feel scared and can't find your Mama or someone you trust, you find Vittorio, okay?" She looks up at my men quickly but then nods into her Mama's neck. "Good, let's get you both into the SUV. I hand the backpacks to one of the guards to put in the back of the SUV.

"Alessia, I am going to hold you while your Mama gets inside the SUV and then I will hand you back to her. Okay?" She nods, she reluctantly lets Emilia get in the SUV, though she grips onto me tight, still shaken in fear. Watching her shake in Emilia's arms has been heartbreaking. But now I have her in my arms, it makes me want to hold her in my arms forever and never let anyone hurt her. Once Emilia was settled, I handed Alessia back over to Emilia. She basically wraps herself around her. But she looks at me, I smile at her.

      I climb in next to them, it's silent except for Alessia's sniffles and Emilia quietly talking to her to calm down until she falls asleep. Before she falls asleep, she reaches for my hand and holds it. She looks at me, I smile at her and tell her, "It's okay princess." I gently squeeze her hand. I run my thumb over the top of her hand, Emilia looks at my hand holding Alessia's and smiles.

SIX
EMILIA

I sit in this expensive SUV with Alessia in my arms, with Mateo and his men. Am I nervous? Scared? Pissed at myself for even having both of us in a situation like this? Absolutely. These men are strangers, and I am putting my daughters' safety in their hands. I just felt like I could trust them. Not like I had much of a choice anyway. I would do anything to keep Alessia safe from those sick motherfuckers. I turn to face Mateo, and he is on his phone, while he holds Alessia's hand. I was shocked she wanted to hold his hand but watching how gentle he was and how he reassured her made me feel a lot more confident I am doing the right thing. I don't say anything to him because let's be honest, I have nothing to say to him. I am still pissed about him pushing his way into Theo's home, manhandling me, tying me to a chair, and forcing me to marry his spoiled ass. I can't help to think why in the world he would want to marry an abused mom where he could have any beautiful model or celebrity. I am so deep in thought while rubbing Alessia's back, I don't realize Mateo is looking at me until he starts talking.

"*Tesoro, (Sweetheart)* what are you thinking about so hard?" Mateo asks.

I glared at him, "I am not your *Tesoro.*"

"So, if you don't like *Tesoro* how about *Amore (love)*?" I glare at him and don't say anything, he isn't gonna give me any cute pet names. The last pet name I had was kitten, and that was from Seth. I get shivers from that name and not the good kind. "That must be a no…. I know, how about *Angelo (Angel)*?"

I snorted. "Do I look like an angel especially earlier when I held the gun to your face?"

He chuckles, "No, but I was very much impressed. That confirmed that you were made to be at my side." I roll my eyes. "I will think about it and find the perfect nickname for you," he says with a smirk.

"That won't be happening."

He smiles at me but doesn't respond to my snarky comment. "After you both get settled, Vittorio will watch Alessia while we discuss a couple things in my office." I look at him with wide eyes. I worry about leaving her with strangers.

"Can he give you updates while we are talking? This is all so new to both of us, and I need to make sure she is safe." I ask because I really don't know any of these men and I don't trust them.

"Of course."

I nod my head at him and say, "Thank you."

He gives me a small smile. Then his phone rings, he gives me an apologetic look and picks up the phone. I tune back into my thoughts, ignoring his phone call.

Next thing I know Mateo has rounded the car and opens my door and says, *"Benvenuti nella tua nuova casa."* (Welcome to your new home.) He helps me get out of the SUV with Alessia in my arms.

I follow Mateo to the mansion, the guards open the door for us and nod to Mateo saying, "Boss or Don."

I walk in, and it takes my breath away. Mateo doesn't slow down at all so I can look around. I will have to do that later. His mansion is just too beautiful not to admire. He finally stops in front of a door and opens it for me to walk in. I go to lay Alessia down on the bed and she clings tighter to me. I know it's gonna be a challenge to unhook my little spider monkey from me. I lay down next to her on the bed and slowly replace myself with a pillow, but she still wakes up. Her eyes pop open and look around scared, until she looks at me.

"Shh, Alessia you are okay. Remember Mateo moved us to his house, so we are safer away from Seth and Boris?" I ask her, and she nods at me and sits up. Mateo walks over and sits on the edge of the bed next to Alessia and lightly touches her hand, she tenses for a second but then relaxes.

"Alessia, I am going to talk to your Mama in my office. Vittorio will be staying with you until we come back. If you need anything, he will get it for you, okay?" Mateo asks as he motions for Vittorio to come over. Vittorio is a huge man, nothing but all muscle, his head is bald, and his brown eyes soften as he bends down on his knees next to the bed.

"Hi Alessia, my name is Vittorio, but you can call me V if you want," he says and signs at the same time.

"You can sign?" she asks.

"Yes, little one I can. My Mama was deaf, so I know how to sign," he tells her chuckling.

"Mama he can sign like us," she signs excitedly.

"I see that baby girl. Now you behave, and I will be back soon, okay."

"Ok, Mama," she sighs, looking at Vittorio like he is God. I kiss her head and follow Mateo to his office.

"Ok have a seat, Emilia." I sit on the couch in his office. He goes over and grabs a file and sits across from me on the chair. "Ok, I know I told you we would be married on paper only and act like a happy couple around other people. We both will always wear our wedding rings, but I will keep you and Alessia out of the spotlight as much as possible for your safety. If you go out, you will have a minimum of four guards and Vittorio with you. I am a very powerful man and with that I have enemies, you both are my weakness and people will use that against me."

"That's fine."

"Do you have any questions about anything so far?"

I nod. "Yeah, I know you are the boss of the mafia, and I don't have to know any information you don't want to tell me, but please say you do not participate in human trafficking?"

"God no! I am working with the Spanish Mafia to take down trafficking rings around the world but unfortunately, when we take one down, it seems like five more pop up. I will not lie and say we don't do illegal things because yes, we do, but human trafficking is forbidden, along with abuse on woman and children. We sell guns, drugs, we do have strip clubs, night clubs, casinos, restaurants, and other legal companies. You and Alessia are safe here; you will have your own security team, including guard dogs in a couple months after their training is complete. I want you both to be comfortable here, and if you need anything just ask and I will make sure you both have it."

"Good. I am pretty sure Boris ran human trafficking. Unfortunately, he had an eye on me and Alessia, which is why he never sold us. But Mateo, I mean it when I say I am not marrying you for your money but for our safety. And I know we are not in love, but I would like to be at least friendly with each other. I also am not expecting you to be loyal to me. It is not easy being with an abused woman and you have needs. But please don't have them around Alessia. She doesn't need the woman you bring home to hurt her."

"I promise you that I will deal with each person that had a hand in hurting you and Alessia. I know you are not marrying me for my money. I could tell when I met you that you are not after my money. Just because you went through all that abuse does not make you damaged to where you can never be in a healthy relationship again. I am not going to lie. I am not innocent, and I meant what I said, we will only be married on paper, but I respect both of you enough not to bring the woman where you two live."

"Thank you. Mateo, can you tell me about your family? I would like to at least know a bit about everyone before I meet them."

"Sure. Well, my *Nonno (grandfather)* is named Giorgio De Luca and my *Nonna (grandmother)* is Francesca De Luca. *Nonno* can be a hard ass, but once you are a part of the family, he loves you fiercely. *Nonna* is bluntly honest and doesn't sugar coat anything. She will spoil Alessia rotten. She loves kids, don't be surprised if her closet is full of clothes and she has a lot of toys. Next, we have my *zio, (uncle)* Adriano, and his wife, my *Zia, (aunt)* Anna, she almost died from a car bomb, but after barely being alive she was shot by the Russian Mafia over ten years ago. He is closed off emotionally because they were childhood sweethearts, and he could never love someone else like he loves her."

I put my hand to my mouth. "Oh my god. They are fucking terrible."

He nods at me and says, "Yes, they are. Adriano has two sons. My cugino *(cousin)* Salvatore is the older one by two years; he also lost his sweetheart to the Russians a little before his Ma got killed. He is more closed off than Adriano; he is very observant and only talks when he thinks it is necessary but is very protective of the women in the family.

"Vincenzo is a clown; he makes it his job to make his loved ones happy. He is more of a player than I am. Usually, you will find him at the strip club. I personally think one stripper has his attention, but he refuses to admit it. He helps me run all the shipments for all the merchandise. My *padre, (father)* Abramo, is an evil bastard. He is the one who is forcing me to get married before my next birthday or he will not give me the house my late *madre (mother)* Asimina, owned; he will sell it. Usually, I wouldn't care but that house has a lot of memories and one day I want to move into that house. And he wants to try and take back the mafia from me, which I have worked hard for.

"My sweet *madre (mother)* died from cancer when I was sixteen and my *sorella (sister)* was ten. He was having an affair with the woman who we call our *matrigna, (stepmother)* Eleanor, who acts like an entitled bitch and never came to see *Madre* while she was sick. After *Madre* died in less than a month, he was remarried to her, and they left us with *Nonna* and *Nonno* to raise us while they explored the world. I took over as the Boss at sixteen, after my Nonna paid him to step down and helped raise my *sorella*. My *sorella* is Julietta. She is six years younger than me and because of our *nonni (grandparents)* she turned out to be an angel. I sometimes worry people will take advantage of her because of how sweet she is. That is the De Luca's, now my capo regimes or capos will be there, but I will introduce you to them at lunch." Wow that's a lot to take in.

"Has Vittorio checked in?" I ask.

"Yep, I was about to tell you that they are watching Moana together," he says, showing me a picture of Alessia snuggled up to Vittorio on his chest. I smile seeing how she is comfortable with him. She is happy but also makes me sad she has never gotten to experience anything like this in her six years of life. I am glad she trusts him after her breakdown earlier today.

Mateo must have noticed my look. "You okay *Tesoro*?" he asks.

I say, "I am not your *Tesoro!* But it is just a bittersweet moment. I love seeing her so happy and carefree but also feel guilty she has never gotten to experience what most six-year-olds get to because of the situation I put her in. I wish I never told Seth about her. Yes, I probably would have struggled, but at least she would have had a somewhat normal life."

"But she will now. You both were deprived of a happy life for years but now you both can be happy." He ignores my nickname comment, I refuse to have some sickly cute nickname.

"Anyway, what will we say to your family about who we are to you and how we met?"

"That I met you after Roman brought you over here to escape Alessia's abusive father as a favor for a friend of his. As my girlfriend, you both are living with me. Only a few members know that I plan on making you my wife soon, but they will not say anything in fear of my punishment." He looks at his watch. "Let's go get Alessia, lunch will be ready soon."

He stands up and grabs my hand to help me up. I follow him out of the office to the room Alessia is in. I expected him to drop my hand, but he doesn't. We open the door, and the sight we are greeted with has me giggling. Vittorio is dancing to Moana with Alessia on his feet. Seeing a huge, buff man dancing with a small little girl who is smiling ear to ear is simply adorable. Mateo clears his throat and both jump. I look over at him and glare at him for ruining a sweet moment. He just shrugs his shoulders.

"Uhm, Boss, you're back?" Vittorio says, rubbing the back of his neck nervously.

"I am." He turns his focus to Alessia, "*Principessa*, did you have fun with Vittorio?" he asks as he bends down to her level.

She nods her head. "I loved the princess movie," she signs, and I translate for him.

"I am glad, and we can get you more movies if you want," he says, and she nods her head.

She looks at me and signs, "Can I hug him, Mama?"

"Do you want me to ask him?" I ask her. She nods her head. Mateo is looking at me.

"Mateo, Alessia wants to know if it is okay to hug you."

He looks at her and smiles. "You never have to ask to hug me." She smiles and hugs him tightly; he hugs her firmly against his chest. I must look up at the ceiling to stop the tears from falling. It really is so emotional to watch her finally be happy and not scared. At least these two men will cherish her like she should have been.

"I know things are scary, but we always protect our family. Alessia told me about what you both have been through. Don't blame yourself, you did everything you could for her, and you kept her safe. You are the definition of a queen. It's okay now to rely on others to help protect the both of you." Vittorio says next to me.

"Thanks, it's just bittersweet seeing her like this," I say.

He nods his head, "I am sure it is."

"Ready, *Tesoro*?" Mateo asks me while holding his hand out to me. I smile and walk over, grabbing his hand. He is holding my hand

and his other arm is holding Alessia, who has a huge smile on her face. We walk out together, looking like a family. I look over my shoulder and Vittorio is taking a picture and he winks at me. I give him a small smile in return. When we enter the dining room, everyone stops talking. Mateo hands Alessia over to me. He then wraps his arm around my waist, and whispers, "Relax" into my ear. I have to force myself not to cringe and flinch away from his touch.

      He looks at everyone in the room and tells them, "I would like everyone to meet Emilia, my girlfriend, and her daughter Alessia. I will introduce everyone to you *mio caro (my dear)*. We have my Nonno Giorgio, Nonna Francesca, Padre Abramo, Matrigna Eleanor, Sorella Julietta, Zio Adriano, cugino Salvatore and cugino Vincenzo," he says as he sweeps his hand across the table, pointing to each person. "And these are my Capo regimes or Capos, Damiano, he runs the Gentleman's Lounges, Eduardo, runs the casinos. This is his wife Luciana, you know Roman, he is our doctor and also runs the drug labs, this is his sister Zaira. Fabio is my P.I. and hacker, that's his wife, Lucilla. Raffaele oversees the night clubs, Marcello is the head of security, and you know Vittorio, who is in charge of your and Alessia's security."

      "*Ciao è molto bello incontrare tutti,*" *(Hello, it is very nice to meet everyone.)* I respond.

      "*Parli italiano?*" *(You speak Italian?)* Nonno asks me. Nonno has dark brown hair with grey streaks in it. He has laugh lines and sharp features on his face. His brown eyes look to be the same color as his hair.

      "*Sì, parlo fluentemente italiano, spagnolo, russo, posso firmare, inglese. I miei genitori erano italiani e credevano che avremmo dovuto conoscere più lingue.*" *(Yes, I can speak fluent Italian, Spanish, Russian, can sign, English. My parents were Italian and believed we should know multiple languages.)* I tell him.

      "*Wow, Mateo è stato fortunato. Lei è intelligente e bella.*"*(Wow, Mateo got lucky. She is smart and beautiful.)* Nonna says, then she turns to Mateo. "*Mateo si affretta e la sposa. Ho bisogno di più nipoti per rovinarmi.*"*(Mateo, hurry up and marry her. I need more grandbabies to spoil.)* Nonna is absolutely beautiful. She has these deep blue eyes that are as blue as the ocean. Her dirty blond hair is in a wavy bob hairstyle that stops around mid-neck. She has a heart shaped face and soft features. You can see she wears her emotions on her face and is a sweetheart.

      "*Nonna stiamo insieme solo da un po'.*" *(Grandma we have only been together for a bit.)* He pauses to look at me for permission to tell everyone our story, and I nod at him.

      "I will go at Emilia's pace because I will not treat her like Alessia's father did," he says, looking at me. I give him a small smile.

      "What? Let me guess, she said she is some damsel in distress and wants you to save her." Zaira says. I eye Zaira down. She has bottled bleach blond hair with green eyes. She is skinny and small framed, almost on the unhealthy side, but I am not here to judge. She is dressed like she is desperate for someone's attention; her face is caked with makeup and her dress is tight and very short.

"Zaira, right?" I ask.

"Yeah, that's my name."

"Let me guess, because of Roman you live a pretty comfortable life. Have you had to be raped so someone you love could eat a meal? Or how about you got beat because you were a minute late bringing a meal to a table? We ran after I was beaten to an inch of my life because I refused to have Alessia be married to a man that is forty years older than her who is a monster and one of my abusers. He is a sadistic perverted fucker; I wouldn't wish my enemy to be at his mercy. And for your information, I did not seek out Mateo, he pursued me. We were staying at my friend's house while I was recovering from my injuries until I could get back on my feet and provide for Alessia."

Everyone's mouths were wide open from shock except Roman, Vittorio, Salvatore, Vincenzo, and Mateo. As I was looking around the table, I didn't realize that Zaira walked around the table and was next to Alessia.

"Is that true girl?" she says to her and when Alessia didn't answer. Zaira slaps Alessia across her cheek hard enough that she falls into my leg. I quickly handed her to Vittorio. I grabbed Zaira by the top of her dress, so she is standing in front of me. I drill my hand back and punch her in the nose.

She screams, grabbing her nose. "You broke my nose."

I then grab her by her throat and throw her against the wall. She looks at me in fear as I slowly approach her. She is still on the ground when, just to instill fear, I put my cowboy boot over her throat, not enough to stop her breathing but enough to get my point across. She grabs at my boot to get me off of her.

"Let me make myself clear, no one will damage one hair on my daughter's head. There's nothing in this world that I will not do to keep her safe. This is a warning to everyone; next time, I promise your brother will be putting stitches in you. You don't fuck with my daughter. You have no idea the length a mother will go to protect her children. Don't play with a real woman, little girl," I say, finally, lifting my boot from her.

I look at everyone else and say, "Sorry for ruining lunch. Have a nice meal." I grab Alessia from Vittorio's arms and walk into the kitchen. I grab Alessia an ice pack and we go to the room we were in before. I sit her in my lap. I look at her cheek and it is already starting to bruise. She is silently crying. "I am so sorry baby girl," I say, kissing the top of her head and humming a lullaby to her as I rock her in my arms. I should never have brought her here. We haven't been here for more than a few hours, and she is already getting assaulted. She fell asleep a couple minutes later. I kick off my boots and lay down with her in the bed. I hear a knock at the door, and carefully lay her down. When I open the door, Vittorio and Roman are on the other side. I open the door to let them in.

"Hey, Emilia, how is she?" Roman asks.

"She fell asleep from crying so hard," I state, not trying to let my anger seep out. It wasn't his fault his sister is a bitch.

"I am so sorry, Emilia. Zaira should never have put her hands on Alessia. She has been obsessed with Mateo and wants to marry him. Having Mateo claim you as his girlfriend and you two here made her react badly. I know she is a spoiled brat and after I treat Alessia's wounds I will be dealing with her," he says.

"Thank you Roman, I don't blame you. Zaira did this, not you. I did put ice on her cheek before she fell asleep, unfortunately it has already started to bruise." I tell him and he frowns. He walks over and kneels next to her bed and lightly touches her cheek; she winches but doesn't wake up. He opens his medical bag and grabs a tube of cream and lightly puts it on her.

After he is done, he hands it to me "Put this on twice a day until the bruise is gone like last time." He gets up to leave the room. "Again, I am sorry. Tell Alessia that too." I nod at him. He leaves and Vittorio puts his hand on my shoulder. I turn and look at him.

"You okay, *Regina*?" he asks.

"Honestly, no. I thought she would be safe here but not even twenty minutes into meeting everyone, she gets hurt. I feel like this is all a mistake," I reply.

"Zaira is a bitch. And she will be bitter from Roman dealing with her and you beating her ass which was completely badass like the Queen you are," he says chuckling.

"Why do you keep calling me Queen anyway?"

"The way you protected Alessia is the way a Queen would act. And if Mateo is smart, he will make you our Queen and we would be lucky to have you," he answers. I chuckle at him.

"The bond between me and Alessia is very tight. As I said, I have gone through so much for her, to protect her. Vittorio can you promise me something?" I ask.

"What's that?"

"Promise me regardless of what happens, if it ever comes to a choice between mine and Alessia's safety, you always chose hers. I can handle anything thrown at me and if not, I will at least be at peace knowing you will protect her."

"Emilia, what are you saying?" he asks me, sitting on the edge of the bed.

"I don't trust anyone with Alessia's safety besides you. I saw how you jumped up after Zaira attacked Alessia. Mateo nor anyone else reacted in that way. And by the look of some of the people at the table what I did will not go unpunished. And I am fine with whatever happens to me but please keep her safe even if you must bring her back to Theo's," I say, basically begging him with my eyes.

"Okay," he says.

"Thank you." I take a huge breath of relief and give him a hug. We sit on the couches in the room and make small talk for a while. He really is a sweet man; he tells me his mom died when he was twenty and he joined the mafia not long after that and has worked his way up since then. That this became his family because it was only him and his mom and when she died, he was lost.

When the door barges open, Vittorio and I stand in front of Alessia to protect her. I feel her grab the back of my jeans. I see Eleanor march in the room, her hazel eyes swarming with anger and evil intentions. Her shoulder length hair bounces as she turns to the two men that came in with her as she tells them to grab me. I turn to Alessia, "You stay with Vittorio, he will protect you. I love you." I look at Vittorio "Don't forget your promise." He nods at me. He goes to protest but I shake my head and point to Alessia. He nods knowing he has his hands are tied. The men grab me and pull me out of the room. I am roughly pulled through the house, shoved down multiple sets of stairs. We are down in a basement, and I am thrown to the floor. I look up at the people in the room.

Eleanor comes over and steps on my hand, breaking my fingers. I bite the inside of my cheek to prevent me from screaming or crying. "You are a guest in my house, and you dare to disrespect the future Queen like that." They lock my wrists with chains and have me hanging from the ceiling. My clothes are cut from my body. I see one of the men grab a whip and walk behind me.

"Would you look at that she already has scars from being whipped," he says, and Eleanor skips over.

"Oh, let me see. She does. Get the whip with blades on it. Make it hurt; she must know where her place is." I don't say anything, I need to figure out if my silence will make them angrier or will settle their anger down. The guard comes over and starts whipping me. I look down, refusing to make eye contact with them. After thirty minutes being whipped, I start feeling lightheaded and I know soon I will pass out. And I welcome the feeling, at least I know Alessia will be safe with Vittorio.

SEVEN
EMILIA

Ugh not again, I think. They did a number on my body. Wait, no, I am not at Seth's anymore. Then it all comes back to me. Zaira slapping Alessia, me attacking Zaira, then Eleanor and the guard whipping me and probably broke my hand. I quickly open my eyes and I see that I am not in the chains anymore. They unhooked me and dropped me on the ground. I sit up, wincing at the pain. I am still in my bra and underwear. They didn't give me any type of medical attention, not like I ever got any in the past.

I look at the small window and it's dark outside, which means it's been hours and my so-called boyfriend has yet to come find me, or he let me get treated this way. Regardless, if this is his way of protecting us, we are better on our own. I turned my head to the door, and they left it open. What a bunch of idiots, or it's a trap. Well, I am not going to waste a chance of escaping. I stand up, my back and legs hurt like a bitch, but I need to get going. I push myself on shaky legs, open the door the rest of the way, peek my head out, and one of the guards is sleeping in a chair. I walk behind the chair and put him in a choke hold. He wakes up and tries to fight me. I just squeeze harder and within seconds, he stops fighting and his arms drop. I slowly release him and bring him to lay on the ground. I am glad Papa taught me to defend myself. I steal his shirt, so I am covered while running around the mansion. Last thing I need to do is attract more attention when I am trying to get me and Alessia out of here.

I quietly keep walking up the stairs, a couple times I must stop and hide when guards pass by me. I finally get to Alessia's room and quietly open the door. The T.V. is on and I see Alessia asleep on the bed and Vittorio is asleep, sitting up on the couch in an uncomfortable position. I feel bad for doing the same thing to him as I do the guard, but he is loyal to Mateo. I need to cut all ties with anyone associated with him or his mafia. I put him in a choke hold, but I put more pressure on his neck than I did the guard. He wakes up but I squeeze my arms with everything I've got, and he quickly puts up a fight but passes out. I lay him down on the couch. I change into my clothes and boots. I write a note to Vittorio.

I stick the note on the bed.

I am glad we never unpacked our stuff and that Theo barely let me use the money I have. I see Alessia is in her PJ's. I wake her up. "Shh Alessia, we need to leave, but you need to be very quiet." She nods at me when I hand her clothes she does as I asked and quickly changes. I grab her PJ's and pack them in the bag. I give her a small smile. I grab her hand and we quietly walk out of the room. We had to hide in the bathroom during the guard shift change.

Once the hallway was cleared again, we snuck out the back door. We were crouched down behind a bush; I was looking for a way to either distract the guards or to sneak past them so we could get over the gate without being spotted. I heard two guards talking to each other and they were talking about how one was leaving for the day. I watched as a guard was loading stuff into the back of an old pickup truck and walked back into the mansion. I tell Alessia to wait by the bush. I go and look, and he has a bunch of gardening tools and tarps already in the bed of his truck. I quickly throw the bags in the back and grab Alessia. I put her in the back of the truck, and I got in behind her. We climb underneath the tarp.

"Lay as flat as possible. Hold my hand the whole time and once we are somewhere safe, I will explain everything to you," I whisper to her, and she nods her head. I can't believe how easy it has been to escape. I just hope I am not leading us to another trap. We hear the truck door open and close, and a minute later the engine turns on. He starts driving off, and I rub my thumbs over the back of Alessia's hands to reassure her everything is okay. I feel her squeeze my hand back.

The truck finally stops, and we wait for a couple minutes. I tell her to wait, and I pull back the tarp so I can look over the edge of the truck without sticking my head out. I see we are in a grocery store parking lot. I pull the tarp back and put both of our hoods over our heads, grab our bags, and we quickly get out of the truck.

"Hold my hand and keep your head down." I get us out of the parking lot and look for a train station. It doesn't take us long to find one, unfortunately it doesn't leave for another hour. The clerk told me that they have a small diner and motel not far from the train station. I decided we will go get something to eat. Once we are seated, I have Alessia sit next to me, and we are facing the front of the restaurant.

"Ok, Alessia, I will explain. After I left the room earlier, Eleanor and one of the guards decided to hurt me because I hurt Zaira when I was defending you. No, it was not your fault, but when I woke up, I decided that we are not safe there. So that is why we left Mateo's mansion and we are not going back to Theo's because they will look for us there and I don't want us to go back there."

She looks at me and signs, "Are you okay Mama?"

I smile at my sweet girl. "Yes baby, as long as you are safe, I am okay." She hugs my arm and I soak in this moment with her. The waiter comes and we order our food. While we wait, I hum to Alessia while running my hand through her. The food arrives; we separate so we can eat, and I keep my eyes going between cars outside and the door. I don't know how long it will take for Mateo or someone else to notice that we are gone. I am hoping that it will not be until after we leave on the train. I am glad they didn't ask for I.D. for our tickets. Either she didn't care, or she could tell we needed to leave quickly. We finish, we head back to the train station, and we board the train.

"Keep your hood up and head down until I tell you otherwise." I whisper in Alessia's ear. She nods her head, and we find a seat. I put her next to the window, we sit down, I put our stuff at our feet, and tuck her head into my chest. And I look around but make no eye contact with anyone. I watch everyone board the train to see if anyone is suspicious or looking for us. So far, we seem safe but won't know until we get to Spain. Once we get there, I am going to get a hold of my godmother, Esmeralda. That has been the plan since I escaped Seth and Boris, but I knew I couldn't go straight to her, just in case they knew where I was.

Finally the train starts to move. "Go ahead and go to sleep baby girl. We have a long ride ahead of us. Once we stop, we are going to call someone who will help us," I tell her, and she nods her head. I hum and run my fingers through her hair until I hear her breathing slow down. I look around to watch the people on the train with us. Everyone seems to be doing something to pass the time.

I still don't trust that anyone on here isn't part of the Italian Mafia. It's gonna take basically two days on the train to get to Spain. The train will stop at Pamplona. We will find a motel and I will call Esmeralda. I am glad that when I looked up Theo's number back in New York I wrote down Esmeralda's.

A little while later, I decide to take a short nap while we are in a long stretch without any stops. I need to rest now because I must be on the lookout when we get off the train until we get to Esmeralda. I feel like I just shut my eyes when I feel Alessia shake me. I open my eyes and realize one of the workers is asking what we want to eat from the restaurant car. I ordered food for both of us. When she comes back, she has extra snacks and drinks for us. I smile at her and thank her.

I tell Alessia she can sit up but do not look anyone in the eyes. She does and we start to dig into our food. After we finish, I put the extra drinks and snacks in my bag and put all the trash together at the end of our table. Alessia signs to me, "How long will it take Mama?"

"Almost two days, sweet girl," I tell her, and I kiss her forehead.

"Okay, Mama, I am going back to sleep; the train is making me sleepy," she signs to me, and yawns.

I lightly chuckle, "Go ahead baby girl."

It takes her no time at all to fall asleep. The girl comes back and collects our trash.

"Here I brought you some magazines. Let me know if you need anything."

"Thank you," I say to her. She walks away and I pick up some random fashion magazines, and as I am skimming through them, I see Zaira is a model. Not that I am surprised, but she is a terrible role model if she reacts that way to anyone who gets in the way of what she wants. Oh well Mateo and her can be happy together for all I care. I am no longer associated with the Italian Mafia. I sit back and try to relax as I look at the magazine to kill time.

MATEO

I am trying to get caught up on paperwork after wasting my time talking to Zaira. Let's say she was pissed that I kicked her out of my mansion and chose Emilia over her. Obviously, I would because Emilia is my soon to be wife and Zaira had no reason for slapping Alessia. She is damn lucky I don't believe in laying a hand on a woman, but Emilia took care of that. Zaira had to have security drag her out of the mansion, she kept begging me and trying to hold onto me. When that didn't work, she was throwing anything she could get her hands on.

I hear a knock on my door, and I tell them to enter. My office door is open and Vittorio walks in. I continue to work on my paperwork.

"Yes Vittorio," I say.

He takes a deep breath and says, "Boss we have a problem."

"What is the problem?" I ask.

"They are gone, Emilia left a note."

I shot my head up to look at him, hoping this is some sick joke. By the look on his face, he isn't joking. Did she really think she could escape out of my life? I told her she would be my wife and I will make sure she would be. Is she really that careless of their safety that she would run like that? And how could she get past all my security? He hands me a shirt with blood on it, a note, and a broken phone.

Vittorio,
Sorry about me putting you in a choke hold but I can't have anyone stop me. Eleanor and the guard tortured me, and no one came to find me after being there for hours. I don't feel like we will be safe here. Oh, and give the guard from the basement his shirt back and apologize to him for knocking him out too.
Thank you for all you have done while we were here. You will always hold a special place in our hearts. Tell Mateo the deal is off and don't bother looking for us. Our safety is no longer his concern since he failed to protect us on the first day.
Love,
Emilia and Alessia

"What the hell does she mean about Eleanor and a guard torturing her?" I ask.

"A little while after Emilia and Zaria's altercation, Eleanor came and dragged Emilia out of the room. I wanted to go after her but beforehand she made me promise to protect Alessia to keep her safe. She had a feeling that something would happen because of her attack on Zaira, and I am assuming from her note that she was right. One of Eleanor's guards broke my phone, and I had no other way to contact you and I was not going to put Alessia's life at risk. She already got hurt by Zaira and to be honest, I don't know where anyone else stands with them being here, and I knew I had to do whatever I could to keep her safe. I must have dozed off after Alessia fell asleep because I woke up feeling like I was being choked and the next thing I knew I was passed out again. When I finally woke up again, I couldn't find Alessia and all their stuff was gone, and I found the note when I was tearing the room apart hoping that Alessia was just hiding. But, Boss, I am worried because there is a good amount of blood on her shirt and there is a trail around the room and in the hallway. I was going to follow it after we talked."

I nod at him and call Fabio. "You have thirty minutes to be in my office with your surveillance equipment and to bring a new phone for Vittorio," I tell him, and hang up before he can respond. I look up to Vittorio. "I will get you a new phone and let's go check the blood trail."

We walk back to Alessia's room. I walk in and you can see there is a light blood trail all over the carpet from the couch to the closet, to the bed, and back out the door. "Fuck this isn't good." I say, and Vittorio nods at me.

We continue walking and see one path leads us to the back door which is how she escaped. It leads to the employee parking lot, which means she either had help or used one of their cars to escape, but they wouldn't have had let her through while she was driving, and I none of them better have been scared by her to follow her commands. If she could scare them, granted she is a force to be reckoned with, but they don't reserve to be in my mafia.

"Well, we know how she escaped, now let's see where the blood trail began." I say, and Vittorio doesn't say anything. We keep walking in silence, and we find the second trail of blood. It leads right to the basement door. I walk down and we hear yelling. I see my stepmother and two guards yelling at each other inside of a cell. Well, if this isn't too easy. I walk in the cell and slam the door behind me. They all jump as I look at them. I see Eleanor with her eyes wide, fear written across her face. She even has small sweat beads on her forehead. One guard is slowly moving himself away from me towards the wall and the other one is missing a shirt and has a bruise around his neck.

"What seems to be the problem here?" I ask, and no one answers. I look down at my watch and realize Fabio should already be in my office. "Well, since no one wants to answer, you all can enjoy sitting in here while I have Fabio look at the surveillance and see if the note Emilia left me is true. And let me tell you, if I find out any of you have anything to do with her disappearing, I will personally punish you. Eleanor, my father won't be able to save you from my wrath this time."

I look over to Vittorio "Give them each their own cell. I am going to call Marcello to come down here." He nods at me and grabs Eleanor first. She is causing a scene as usual, but he just grabs both arms behind her back and pushes her forward.

"Don't manhandle me."

"Shut up bitch. I am giving you the same treatment your guards gave Emilia earlier." She starts to respond again but catches the look of pure anger on my face and decides to stop fighting and talking. I pick up my phone and call Marcello.

"Hello," he says groggily.

"Sorry to wake you Marcello but I need you and two of your men in the basement now."

"Yes Don." and he hangs up.

Vittorio is already grabbing the guard without a shirt and walking him to his cell. After he walks out, I look at the guard who is hiding in the corner like a scared little girl. He is dead regardless. I can't have a weakling like him in my mafia. Pathetic.

I walk out as Vittorio is locking the cell he just walked out of. "Don, it doesn't look good," he says to me.

"No, it doesn't." I respond.

We stand there waiting for Marcello to come down. When he and the other two guards arrive, they all nod their heads at me saying. "Don."

"I need you to keep these three in their cells until I come back. Marcello, I want you personally to guard this one that has Eleanor in it." He nods his head without a word. "If anyone comes down asking questions, tell them it is my order that they stay locked up until I say otherwise, and they can come discuss it with me. I will be back once I have my answers. Marcello, I expect hourly updates."

"Yes, Don," he responds, and all three of them go stand in front of the doors with their hands folded across their chests. I motion for Vittorio to follow me, and we walk back to my office. When we walk in, Fabio is already there with his laptop set up on the coffee table in my office waiting on my order. Vittorio sits down in one of the chairs and I make my way over to the mini bar and pour myself a drink.

"Vittorio, what time was Emilia taken out of her room?" I ask.

"About 5:30 this evening." He replies.

"Ok, Fabio, I want you to follow her from the moment she leaves dinner," I say, and he nods, I turn my back to both and look out the window. Are they safe? How bad is Emilia hurt? Thoughts keep running through my head.

"Boss, you're gonna want to see this." Fabio says. I walk back over and take a seat next to him and he starts the surveillance video. We watch Emilia attack Zaira and damn, does she not look like a Queen? We see her get ice for Alessia; I cringe at Alessia crying on her mother's shoulder. That should have never happened. They walk into her room, and you see Emilia applying ice to Alessia's cheek and they lay down in the bed.

A little while later she gets out of bed. Roman and Vittorio come in and Roman checks on Alessia and he hands her a cream then leaves the room. Emilia and Vittorio talk to each other for a while before suddenly, the door swings open and both jump in front of Alessia to guard her. Emilia turns and tells Alessia something and then looks at Vittorio, basically begging him, and he nods but you see the hesitation in his eyes. Then she is manhandled out of the room and Vittorio goes to pull out his phone, but the other guard grabs it, throws it against the wall, and breaks it. During all this, Eleanor has an overly happy smile on her face that is psychotic. Fabio then keeps switching to different cameras and follows them through the mansion. You see the guard physically dragging her down the hallway and roughly shoving her down multiple sets of stairs. Once they get to the basement, they throw her to the ground.

Eleanor comes over and steps on her hand. She never screams or cries. "You are a guest in my house, and you dare to disrespect the future Queen like that." They lock her wrists with chains and have her hanging from the ceiling. Her clothes are cut from her body. One of the men grabbed a whip and walked behind her. I throw my glass at the wall. Who the fuck does she think she is to treat Emilia this way? I am almost tempted to break my rules and torture her for hurting Emilia.

"Would you look at that, she already has scars from being whipped," he says, and Eleanor skips over.

"Oh, let me see. She does, get the whip with blades on it. Make it hurt, she must know where her place is." Emilia doesn't say anything. Fabio changes to another camera and I feel my heart drop to my stomach. All the scars on her body from the abuse that she went through with Seth are absolutely terrible.

"I don't think there is a part of her back and legs that isn't covered in scars," I say out loud.

Fabio says, "Holy shit. When she said what she went through during dinner I didn't think it was that bad, but fuck, this is horrifying." I nod at him, not knowing how else to respond.

The guard comes over and starts whipping her. She is looking down, refusing to look at them. He keeps whipping her for at least thirty minutes. Eleanor tells him to unhook her, and he does it and she literally falls into a heap on the floor. You see blood draining from her back and puddles around her legs on the floor. After a couple hours you see her get up and make her way out of the room. She puts the guard in a choke hold, lowers him to the ground, takes his shirt off, and puts it on herself. Then she sneaks past maids and guards and goes into her room.

She knocks Vittorio out, changes into her clothes, then writes a note and sticks on the bed. She gets Alessia ready, and you see the two of them sneak out of the mansion through the guard door. Eventually, they get into a pickup truck that drives out of the mansion gates. I sit there trying to control my anger. "Fabio, I want a copy of all of the surveillance. And look to see who's truck they got into and where they could be."

"Of course, Don. I will be in my office. It will take time to get you the surveillance after she leaves the mansion, but I will get you this as soon as possible." He stays for another couple minutes. "Don, the surveillance from the mansion is in your email."

"Thank you, Fabio." He nods and leaves. I motion for Vittorio to stop as he approaches the door. "Vittorio, I don't blame you, you protected Alessia. Thank you."

"Of course, when you assigned me to be their security, I would lay my life down if it meant protecting them. I am sorry Emilia got hurt," he says.

"Take the day off and rest. And go see Roman about the bruise around your neck," I tell him. He nods at me and leaves.

I sit down at my desk with my head in my hands. I knew Eleanor could be a bitch, but this time she took it too far. I wonder how they were able to coordinate this. I text Fabio "Look into Zaira and Eleanor's phone calls and text messages and see how they were able to pull this thing off within hours." I feel terrible that their first day here, both girls were hurt when I promised them that I would protect them. I don't blame Emilia for bolting out of here the first chance she got but I hope wherever she is that she is safe and out of Seth and Boris's reach.

But I don't go back on my word, she will be my wife. Even if I must drag her back here kicking and screaming. Which I can see her doing.

A couple hours later, I get a phone call from Fabio saying he has information about how Eleanor pulled this off, but he is still trying to track where Emilia and Alessia are. I thank him and I call all the De Luca's into the living room since it has more space for everyone while I show them what the lovely Eleanor did. I show them all the surveillance from start to finish, when they get to Emilia's time in the basement. Nonna and Julietta cry. The men except my father, look pissed. My father just watches the screen with a blank look on his face. Once it is finished, I look directly at my father and say, "Anything you want to say padre?"

"And why do you think I would have anything to say *ragazzo (boy)*?" he says with a snarl. How typical of him.

"Maybe because that is your wife, and you should watch who you're speaking to. He may be your son, but he is the Boss here. Your wife's life is laying in his hands. I told you not to marry that *cagna (bitch)* and now you get to pay for the consequences," Nonna stands, yelling at him. Nonno grabs her hand, sits her back down in her chair and calms her down.

My father pulls his gun out on Nonna. Nonno, Zio Adriano, Salvatore, Vincenzo, and I pull our guns out and point them at him.

"Wow, you all point your guns at me after the bitch disrespects me," he says, shaking his head.

I click the safety off my gun and shoot him in the hand which is holding the gun and he puts pressure on the bullet wound trying to slow down the bleeding.

"You are a worthless son of a bitch," he sneers at me.

I roll my eyes. "Just shut the fuck up, motherfucker."

I walk away from him and over to Nonna and kiss her cheek. "Thank you, Mateo." She smiles at me. "Bring my babies home, Mateo."

"Fabio is working on where they are right now, Nonna," I tell her.

"Good. Please keep me updated."

"Of course, Nonna."

"Padre, tell me why your phone has text messages to Sean and Angelo to help Eleanor to take Emilia down to the basement and do as she says," I demand.

"Because they needed to go, so you could marry Zaira. And the plan almost worked, they left but she wasn't supposed to be able to escape. We were going to bring them to France and make sure they never met the Italian Mafia again."

I motion to the guards outside the room. "Take him and put him in his own cell down in the basement." He fights them and is yelling about respecting him.

I walk back in the room and say, "If you hear anything about this, please let me know." They all agree and leave the room. I obviously need to do some house cleaning, since people are not being loyal to me, their Don. I walk back to my office and pour myself another drink. I sit back down, swivel my chair around, facing the big window in my office and I slowly take a sip. Looking out at the stars are twinkling in the dark sky and it is beautiful.

But I can't appreciate the view right now. I am really worried about the girls. I hope they are safe. Fabio is also getting information on Seth and Boris. I will enjoy taking down their trafficking ring little by little and watching them crumble. The way I am going to torture them they will beg for death, but I will not grant it. They will feel all the pain Emilia felt, but ten times worse. I smirk at all the different ways I am going to torture them. My inner beast craves to hear their screams and watch as the blood drains from their bodies.

As I am deep in thought, my cousins walk in. "What can we help with Mateo?" Vincenzo asks.

"I need all the information on Seth Volkov and Boris Smirnoff; they are associates of the Russian Mafia. After everything they have done to us and now, we know what they did to my girl, I am going to take down their trafficking ring and slowly and painfully torture them."

"Okay, I will see how much we can get but we might need Fabio for that." Salvatore says.

I nod at him, "He is already working on that as well, but it can't hurt to have more people looking for information."

I run my hand through my hair. "I already failed them, and they were with me for less than twenty-four hours. I should have checked on them and maybe I could have stopped it. I figured Emilia was too mad at me for what happened and needed her space to calm down, so I decided to busy myself with paperwork. What if I bring them back and I can't keep them safe?"

"Mateo, you could 'what if' until you're blue in the face. The only thing you can do when we find her is apologize to her. Hell, get on your knees and beg if you must. That's if you want Emilia and Alessia that badly. In the meantime, we will find those fuckers and have some fun," Salvatore says smirking. Ever since his Ma and Lilyana died, he is one evil fucker, especially about anything that has to do with the Russians. After they died, he went on a killing spree of anyone who was in the Russian Mafia for a year. I know he is holding that anger in and is waiting to release it.

"You're right. Alright, get to work and let me know once you find anything. I am going to call Fabio; I better buy him his favorite brandy for all this work he is about to put in," I say, and they laugh at me as they walk out of the room.

EIGHT

EMILIA

It has been six months since I have been in Barcelona with Esmeralda and Jose. Both Alessia and I have been working on recovering from our past. Alessia needed therapy to help with her mutism, but I refused to admit I needed help from all the abuse I went through. As I always have, I push my demons away and just focused on her, until Esmeralda tricked me into a session here at her mansion.

She literally locked me and my therapist, Maya, in for two hours. Maya knows Jose, who is Esmeralda's husband. He is the Boss of the Spanish Mafia. Esmeralda and my Mama Angelica were best friends growing up, which is how she became my godmother. Yes, I groaned that we were hiding from two mafia's inside of another mafia's protection, but Esmeralda and Jose are family, and I fully trust them.

Anyway, back to my forced therapy session. After I paced around the room refusing to talk, I finally calmed down. If Esmeralda and Jose trusted Maya then I could, and I started to spill everything that has happened since my family passed away. She diagnosed me with PTSD, which isn't a surprise, my past is far from pretty. Maya comes twice a week now for my sessions, and it helps.

For a while, I was depressed because I never really had a chance to grieve my family's deaths. That was a rough phase I went through. I felt lonely missing my family, unwanted by Seth, and with all the abuse, I started thinking all I was good for was to please men. I was longing for someone to love me, but I knew it might not happen because who wants an abused single mom who struggles with PTSD? I am fortunate to have the Garcia family that has been supportive.

As Esmeralda told me, "You are a gem and one day someone will be worthy of your heart. All those boys in the past didn't deserve a second of your attention. It is okay to let someone inside your heart because the right man will cherish it with everything they have."

That is the day I slowly started to come out of my depression.

Esmeralda wanted to fly to Italy and "beat some sense into those Italian cocksuckers for messing with her babies." Jose reminded her that if she did that then he would know where I am, and I don't want us to be found. Which is why we were given a small farmhouse on the back of their property to use when any other mafia families come and visit, so no one will see us. But Esmeralda loves fiercely and anyone who messes with her family is going to get it.

Jose has heard from other mafia families that Mateo is looking for me. Why? I have no idea; I clearly said our deal is off and he can be happy with Zaira or anyone else for that matter. I am trying to move forward in my life. He should as well, it's not like we had any kind of relationship. We must continue to lay low until Mateo gives up looking for us. Then we can move into our own place. I know Esmeralda loves having us here, but I feel like we are taking advantage of her kindness.

I am so thankful for everything that the Garcia family has done for us. I recall the day we got to the filthy motel, and I cried once I heard Esmeralda's voice on the phone.

Six Months Ago

We finally exit the train with the bags on my shoulder and our hoodies up. We walk for half a block to a motel; even though it looks run down and gross, we need to get off the street so we can hide. They never check for I.D. and just take my money, throw me a key, and tell me room 21. As we walk down the hall to our room, I pull Alessia closer to my body to protect her because it is very sketchy. We get in the room and I turn on the T.V. and play some cartoons for her. "Alessia, I am gonna call Esmeralda, okay?" She nods at me, I grab the phone, take a deep breath, and dial her number, praying she didn't change it. It starts to ring, and a woman picks up.

Esmeralda: "Hola, (Hello) who is this?"
Emilia: "Hello is Esmeralda García there?"
Esmeralda: "Yes, this is Esmeralda."
Emilia: "Esmeralda it's me Emilia. Emilia Lombardi, Angelica, and Alessandro Lombardi's daughter."
Esmeralda: "Lia, my little Lia bug. Oh, my baby. Where are you? I have been looking for you for years. Tell godmother where you are, and I will come get you."

And at that point I start bawling my eyes out, knowing that we will finally be safe and loved for the first time in years. And feeling the love of a parent which Esmeralda and Jose may have spoiled us, but they love us just as much as Mama and Papa did. She tells me to take a deep breath and after a minute, I start to calm down.

Emilia: "We need help. My daughter's father was abusive towards us, and we left there only to fall into another evil family's hands. Please help us. I just want my baby to be safe."
Esmeralda: "Oh my God, a daughter? My baby had a baby. Where are you?"
Emilia: "We are in some motel near the Pamplona train station."

Then I hear her shouting at someone, which makes me giggle. Her crazy personality always puts a smile on my face. Esmeralda is a force to be reckoned with.

Jose: "Emilia it's Jose. I heard you are coming home with your daughter. When you get here, we'll talk about everything. You are family and will always be family. We will be there soon. We love you both."

Then he hangs up.

I continue to let the tears fall and I feel little hands wrap around my waist. I look down at Alessia and say to her, "Everything will be okay now baby girl. Esmeralda will be here soon, and we will be safe." She gives me a big smile; I pull out some of the snacks that I had in my bag from the train, and we munch on them while watching cartoons.

A couple hours go by, and we hear several fast knocks and Esmeralda says, "Emilia baby. Open the door, it's Esmeralda."

I get up but the knocking continues. I start giggling and I hear a manly voice. "Woman, would you calm down and give her a chance to open the door?"

"Tell me to calm down again and see what happens to you," Esmeralda responds back.

I open the door and Esmeralda is pointing her finger at Jose. I chuckle at her; she is still the insane and crazy Esmeralda I remember. Before I process anything, Esmeralda gives me a tight hug and I wince from my injuries on my back, and she notices. "I have some injuries from when I was in Italy," I tell them.

"Are you okay?" she asks, worrying, holding me at arm's length.

"Yes, I will be fine. Come in and meet Alessia," I say, and open the door wider so they can come in.

Esmeralda looks basically the same except brown hair is now at her mid back instead of shoulders; but her piercing hazel eyes are scanning my body, looking for injuries. Jose has not aged much but can tell it is from stress by looking at the dark circles under his eyes. His shoulder length black hair is in a ponytail and his brown eyes have softened looking at me and Alessia. Alessia looks over at me.

"Alessia, please come over here baby girl. I want you to meet Esmeralda and Jose," I tell her, and she slowly walks up to us. While she is walking over to us, I whisper to Esmeralda and Jose that she is a selective mute from watching me be abused her whole life. They grimace but quickly cover it up with smiles.

They both kneel to her level. "Wow, Emilia, she is truly beautiful! She looks just like you when you were her age," Esmeralda says, and gently tucks a piece of hair behind her ear. "You look so much like your grandmother. So beautiful. I will have to tell you all kinds of stories about how naughty your Mama was as a child," Esmeralda says, laughing, and Alessia smiles while nodding her head.

"You, Alessia, are an angel. My name is Jose, and this is Esmeralda. We were good friends with your grandparents before they passed away and have been looking for your Mama," Jose tells her.

Alessia looks at me and I can tell she is nervous. Esmeralda catches on. "Alessia, I know you are scared and that is okay. I know people have told you to trust them and they broke that trust. You are family and we will keep you and your Mama safe. How would you like to get out of here and come back to our place?" she asks, putting her hand out for Alessia to grab.

Alessia nods and puts her hand in Esmeralda's hand. Jose grabs our bags before I can pick them up. Esmeralda and Alessia are already walking out when Jose turns to me. "Daughter, what happened?"

"After Alessia falls asleep, I will explain everything to you and Esmeralda."

He nods at me and says, "We missed you sweet girl." He hugs and kisses me on the top of my head. I smile up at him and follow him to the receptionist. I hand her the key and walked out with Jose and see a beautiful Range Rover. I climb in the back with Alessia and see her hugging a stuffed grey wolf toy with a huge smile on her face. Jose starts the Range Rover and starts driving.

I look at Esmeralda. "Really, Esmeralda, you already started spoiling her? I figured you would at least wait until we got back to your house first."

"Nope, I spoil my babies, which includes you. I have no one to spoil besides Mr. Grumpy over here. I did it when you were little and will continue till the day I die," she says smirking at me. Jose looks at her and grunts.

"You don't need to spoil me. I am an adult. And if I remember correctly, Mama and Papa would fuss at you every time you would spoil us," I say to her, and she rolls her eyes at me.

"They did but I didn't listen to them, and I won't listen to you now. You will be spoiled, especially since you are my god baby and I have years of spoiling to make up for." I give her a glare, but I know I won't win with her. Esmeralda turns her attention to Alessia and starts asking her questions about things she likes.

"Alessia, how would you like your room decorated?" Alessia looks at me, excited that she can pick how to decorate her room. She tells me she wants to decorate it with farm animals like at Theo's farm.

"Farm animals, especially horses," I tell Esmeralda.

"You like farm animals, Angel?" Jose asks her and she nods her head with a smile.

"Yeah, when we first came to Italy, we stayed at Theo Walker's farm. You remember Theo, Esmeralda?" I ask.

"Oh yes, the cute white boy. Me and your Mama thought you two would get married," she says.

"That would have been wonderful, except I don't have the right parts," I tell her, and her mouth drops open.

"He's gay?"

"Yep," I say.

"Damn, you two would have made beautiful babies."

I chuckle at her. We pull up to a private airport and board their jet. I see some men come on with our bags and nod to Jose. We all buckle up, and as soon as we are in the air, I tell them that I am going to make Alessia nap. She has been through so much and her little body is exhausted.

"Mama, I like them. They are nice and make me happy," she signs for me.

"Yeah, they are baby girl. They are family." I sit with her, hum to her a lullaby until she falls asleep. I lean down, kiss her forehead, and quietly leave the room.

I tried to quietly sit down in my chair while Jose and Esmeralda were in a deep conversation, but I should have known Esmeralda would know what I was doing. It's not that I am embarrassed about my past. But I am not proud of my past. I had no idea telling Seth about Alessia would turn into seven years of hell, but I survived and that is what matters.

"Not so fast. She is asleep. Now it's time to talk," Esmeralda says to me.

I told them everything and let me say, both were pissed. Mateo is one of Jose's allies. Jose was so pissed, he was about to cut ties with the Italian Mafia, but I didn't want him to do that. He couldn't risk the lives of his men and Mateo would know where we are. I want us safe and obviously being with Mateo we would not be safe.

"I know you want to treat my wounds and I will let you. But it will be painful, and I know I will scream, and I prefer not to do that near Alessia. My screams will scare her, and she also doesn't know how bad I am hurt. It isn't the first time I went without medical attention after being abused. I will be okay for a bit longer."

She goes to argue but after thinking about it, she agrees. "Ok fine, but you will go to the medical wing as soon as we land." I give her hand a squeeze and smile at her. She leans forward and kisses my forehead. I keep a smile on my face knowing everything will be okay and we are with family.

Oh shit, Theo. He probably has already had Mateo down his throat, asking about where we are. "Hey Jose, could you give Theo a message that we are safe, without the Italian Mafia knowing where we are?" I ask.

"Consider it done."

"Thank you," I say. After that, we talk until it is time to land. I go and get Alessia, and she is still asleep. Jose carries her out and tells me he will put her in a guest room and will stay with her until she wakes up. I thank him and follow Esmeralda to the medical wing. When we arrive, a doctor and a couple nurses are waiting for me.

"They already have been told about the situation. No need to worry about anything. I will be here the whole time."

I squeeze her hand and follow the doctor into the room. After the door is closed, I slowly undress to just my bra and panties. I hear Esmeralda gasp. "Oh, my poor baby. I am gonna skin those Italians. I am going to take some pictures to show Jose, he needs to know how bad you are hurt." I hear her take a couple pictures. I try to push the body shaming thoughts about my ugly scars out of my head.

Once I know she is done, the doctor has me lay down. The doctor and nurses quickly get to work cleaning and dressing my wounds all over my back and the back of my legs. Esmeralda stayed true to her word and stayed with me. She held my hand even when I squeezed it hard. And wiped my tears and tried to calm me down when I would scream out in pain. After that they gave me something to sleep in, and Esmeralda said she was going to take Alessia shopping to buy both of us clothes and other things we need. I knew she was more than safe with Esmeralda, plus it would distract Alessia from wondering where I was. I could relax knowing she was completely safe and having fun with Esmeralda.

Present Day

I am walking out of Jose's gym after a three-hour session with Nina. She is Jose's younger cousin who has been helping me learn how to fight, shoot guns, and throw knives. The little Spanish bombshell has black, straight hair that goes down her back, but she always has it in a ponytail. Her brown eyes usually can see through my bullshit, and she always calls me out on it.

This has helped me not feel so weak and defenseless, and I love how confident it makes me feel. I know I have a hard, bitchy exterior, but it is to protect myself, I will no longer be taken advantage of. I sent Esmeralda a text saying I would come get Alessia after my shower and I got a response saying they were already on their way back to our house. We have a small cottage on the Garcia's property so we can have some privacy and keep us hidden when Jose' has other mafia's here. I quickly shower and when I get out, I am welcomed with the smell of something sweet and chocolatey. I get dressed in a tank top and booty shorts and I am met by Isabella (Esmeralda's mama), Esmeralda and Alessia. I go over and kiss each of them on the cheek.

"Hello, honey, did you have a good workout with Nina? She didn't work you too hard?" Isabella starts asking. She has the same hazel eyes as Esmeralda, with short snow-white hair. This sweet old lady has called us her grandbabies and demands we call her Nana.

"Nana, I am okay. I feel better after I worked some of my anger out." I say smiling at her. I sit next to her and start to eat the chocolate churros they brought over.

She grabs my hand and pulls my head to face her. "I hate that you have so much anger in your small body my dear."

"But it has made me stronger." I tell her, and she smiles pushing a strand of hair behind my ear.

"That it has my dear. And I am so proud of the woman you are and how far you have come, especially since you moved here. You are so strong physically and mentally. You are a force to be reckoned with."

"I still say you should have let me skin those Italian fuckers." Esmeralda says, and I shake my head. When she starts talking like this, I am glad Alessia doesn't fully understand Spanish yet but just like me, Alessia enjoys learning different languages. She is learning Italian and Spanish right now and I told her after she learns those languages, I will let her pick what language she learns next.

"We all have told you, to keep me and Alessia hidden from them, you can't skin any of them. Regardless of how much they deserve it."

"Quit being hot headed. They are safe and away from them, that is all that matters." Esmeralda goes to argue but Isabella shoots her a look. "Nope keep it shut. Anyway, a little angel has dance lessons to get to. Plus, you need to talk to Emilia. We will see you two later. Come on Alessia." She holds her hand out for Alessia. She grabs it but she comes over and gives us each hugs and kisses on the cheek. She walks out of the house with Isabella.

I turned to Esmeralda. "What did he do now?" I ask her. The only time Esmeralda and Jose want to talk to me alone is about Mateo.

She takes a deep breath and says "He still is persistent in looking for you. Jose has tried everything he can to keep him out of Spain but unfortunately, he had to travel here for business. And will be here tomorrow."

"Are we safe here?" I ask.

"Jose says you both will have to stay in your house while he and his men are here and stay away from the windows so no one can spot you. I know it seems unfair, but we are afraid that if they see the jet not here, they will question, and all of our safe houses have been blown up by the Russians after we shut down the human trafficking in Mexico," she says with a sad look in her eyes.

"It's fine, Esmeralda, just ask Jose to have someone stock up the house so I can cook for us, and we can have mother daughter bonding time during that time. Just please keep me updated," I say with a smile. We sit there for a moment in silence, I worry that Mateo has finally found out that we are here, and he wants us back.

"What if he has found us?" I ask, looking down and picking at a loose string on my tank top.

Esmeralda grabs my hand. "We won't let them take you back."

"I know you will protect us but if it comes down to me staying here and anyone getting hurt or me leaving with them and everyone staying safe, let me go. I know you don't want to, but I can't stand by and watch as my family gets hurt if I can prevent it. All I ask is if you keep Alessia safe, I can take care of myself. She is a child, and she deserves to have the rest of her childhood with nothing but happiness."

"That won't happen," she says.

"I hope you're right." I have a bad feeling that my happiness will be coming to an end soon.

NINE
MATEO

A Week Earlier

I get in my car and drive off to the warehouse where all my visitors are being kept. My father has been a good way to relieve some of my stress from worrying about where Emilia and Alessia are and if they are safe. I hope they are. I don't think Alexei has them because it looks like his people are still looking for them as well. I just hope that I am right.

As for my father and stepmother, well, they look like shit. There is no other way of saying it, they are still in the same clothes they were wearing six months ago, although I am generous and make sure they get hosed off once a day. But that is more so me and my guards can tolerate even be in the same area as them.

"Well father. Are you ready to tell me about where Maxim's safehouses are?"

He glares at me, "Fuck you, boy."

I shake my head and cut off another finger, he only has two left on his hands. "I can cut more off than your fingers, you know that, right? You were the one who taught that to me." I snap my fingers, maybe threatening his whore will get those lips moving. I untie Eleanor from the chair and stand her in front of him. I will give it to him he either doesn't care about her or he is good at keeping his emotions behind his blank mask.

"Talk and I won't shoot her."

He chuckles, "Go ahead. She is no good to me down here if she can't suck my dick."

She starts to cry, "Abramo, please. He will kill me."

Father looks at her, raises his eyebrow, and asks her, "How is that my problem?"

Now her response is hysterical. "I AM YOUR WIFE! DOESN'T THAT MEAN ANYTHING TO YOU?"

He shakes his head, "All you are is a money hungry whore. All you had to do was look pretty on my arm and satisfy me. Since you can't do anything to get me out of here all you are dead weight."

I snicker at them. I let go of her and she takes a few steps back. "I will make you a deal Eleanor, if you can make it to the door before I get to five, you can walk out of this room alive." She nods and I start counting, "1… 2…" and she is tripping on her feet trying to get to the door. She is having problems using her legs since she has either been hung by her wrists or tied to a chair for six months. "3…4"

"Hurry Eleanor," I tease her. She isn't gonna make it, she barely made it ten steps. "5," I say.

She turns around to beg me, but I shoot her in the head. I will kill a woman if they have wronged my family, but I will not physically torture them. I tell my men to leave her body in here with him for two days.

I go into my office and use my personal bathroom and clean myself up. I shower quickly, so I can get back to looking for my girls. I walk out in a new suit and Fabio is sitting in my office. "Boss, I found them." I walk over to him and stick my hand out so I can read the file in his hands. What I see pisses me off.

"Are you telling me that Jose lied to me when he said he had not seen her?" I ask Fabio, gritting my teeth in anger.

"Yes, Boss it looks that way."

"Well, it's about time I went and checked on my businesses in Spain. It seems our friend Jose needs a reminder of what happens to people who cross me. Let Vittorio and Marcello gather a team of guards, we are leaving tonight. I will notify the pilot. I expect you to stay here and keep an eye on our guests in the basement. I do not want them trying to escape with me not here," I say to him, and he dismisses himself.

I called my pilot and let him know we are leaving tonight for Barcelona. I sit back in my chair; I am glad they are alive and safe. I have been so worried about them for the past six months. Not knowing if they were safe or if they were in Seth's clutches again. We will not go on to Garcia's estate the first day, I will make it look like it is a social call since I will be there to check on my business, but really, I will be going and dealing with Jose for going against me. He has no idea the danger he has put his Mafia and my girls in by letting them stay there. The Spanish Mafia is not as strong as mine, which is one of the reasons, we are allies with them in exchange for discreet weapons they make.

With the information we found out about Seth and Boris, it's even more important that the girls are with me. Alexei is the Boss or Pakhan of the Russian Mafia, and his wife is Irina, Seth is Irina's brother. They are heavily involved in the human trafficking business. We have been trying to find them for the past six months, but it seems as soon as we get close, we lose track of them. I suspect we have a rat, so it might seem careless to bring the girls back. But I can always keep them safer with me, especially when I plan on keeping them in my sight or one of their guard's sights at all times. Especially since my fiancée is sly and loves to escape, not that I blame her this time. But we need to keep a close eye on her.

I hope Emilia will not make coming home as painful as I think she will. I don't want to use force and seem like the bad guy. Well, okay I am a bad guy, but I don't want to be with my girls. Yes, I consider Alessia to be my daughter. She doesn't have my blood running through her body or my last name yet... but that little girl has captured my heart and soul in less than one day. I am a selfish bastard, but I want this marriage to eventually work. I am sure she will be beyond pissed at me, and anyone associated with the Italian Mafia, but we will move past that. I run my finger over the picture I have of the girls Fabio got from when they were running surveillance before we met in person. They look so happy they are riding a horse together. Alessia is sitting in front of Emilia, and both have the biggest smiles on their faces. *"A presto mia Regina e mia Principessa."* (See you soon my Queen and my Princess)

    I get up from my desk and walk to the dining room where my family will be eating lunch. We tend to have at least three meals together a week. That is just our family. We have reconnected on a deeper level since then, and I can now say it is enjoyable to sit with my family and just talk. My father and stepmother only added tension in the room. Since they have been in the cells, meals are now more relaxed, and we laugh and enjoy each other's company.

    I sit there listening to them talk, not talking to anyone. I am nervous about going to see Emilia and Alessia. Yes, the Mafia boss who is the beast of the underworld is anxious about meeting a fierce, petite woman and her angelic daughter.

    Julietta looks at me and asks, *"You okay big brother?"*

    I nod at her. "Actually, Julietta I have something to say."

    My grandfather looks at me "Well what is it son?" he asks me, putting his fork down.

    I take a deep breath because I know in a minute Nonna is gonna be in my face. "We know where Emilia and Alessia are. I have a team coming with me to get them and bring them home. We will be gone for about a week. Salvatore and Vincenzo, I need you both to run things here while I am gone."

    Before I finished talking Nonna was out of her chair and in front of me spouting questions at me. "Where are they? Are you taking a week to go get them? Are they in danger? Please tell me those sick fuckers don't have my babies!" She grabs my shirt in her hands, starts to shake me. I can feel the worry oozing out of her.

    "Nonna, one question at a time. They are not in danger but an ally of mine betrayed me by not telling me they were with him. We found out when they were out shopping with Esmeralda Garcia, Jose Garcia's wife. I plan on visiting my other companies in Spain first, to have them believe I don't know they have the girls. Then I will confront Jose about why he didn't inform me of their whereabouts. I am sure it will be messy and knowing Emilia, I will probably have my hands full with her," I say, chuckling to myself.

    I think back to how she took down Zaira for slapping Alessia. And how she was able to knockout one capo and one guard. And she escaped with her daughter, and no one knew until hours later. Not to mention the first time we met she had a gun pointed at me.

"Oh, you will. Can you have one of your men record it? It will be some good entertainment for us," Julietta says laughing.

I scowl at her while everyone else is laughing. "Well, aren't you a comedian?" I say to this little brat.

"It's one of my many talents," she says, while pushing her hair over her shoulder and winking at me.

"Sure, you definitely have the talent for driving me insane."

She puts her hand on her chest like I hurt her. "I would never. I just love my big brother."

"Oh really?" I say, and I look at Salvatore and Vincenzo and they smirk at me. We all look over to Julietta and stand up, slowly stalking towards her.

"No, no, don't you three dare. Uncle Adriano don't let them get me," she says running over to stand behind Zio Adriano hoping he will save her from us. Vincenzo swoops her up and has her over his shoulder.

"Pool?" he asks us, and we tell him yes. She starts yelling and hitting Vincenzo's back.

"Vincenzo, if you throw me in the pool, I will go to the strip club and tell all the women that you have an STD!"

He stops walking to the pool; that is a huge threat for him since that is his usual spot to pick up a woman. "You wouldn't dare."

"Try me," she says, smirking. He thinks about it and keeps walking. We think he is going to throw her in the pool but instead he throws her on the lounge chair by the pool and shuts the door and walks away. The three of us burst out.

Nonno glares at us and says, "Vincenzo did you really have to throw her in the pool?"

We start laughing again, taking a seat at the table. When Julietta comes bursting through the door, she marches right over to Vincenzo and smacks the back of his head and says, "You asshole. Really? You threw me on the lounge chair. Can't you act like a gentleman?" I see him give her a devilish smirk.

And Uncle steps in and says, "Don't you even think about making that kind of comment in front of ladies. Especially your Nonna and your innocent cousin."

I look at Julietta and my cousins, knowing very damn well my sister is no longer a virgin and has not been for a very long time. Julietta looks at him and says, "Uh Uncle Adriano, I hate to say but that ship has sailed a long time ago."

He shakes his head. "Nope. I didn't hear that. You are still as pure as the day you were born. Even after you have kids you will still be a virgin because I refuse to admit some boy will violate my niece like that."

We all laugh at how overprotective he is over Julietta. Since Aunt Anna, Lilyana, and Mama passed away, he had no biological daughter, he is very protective over all women in the family. I feel like poor Alessia and Emilia will be a bit overwhelmed when it comes to him. He can be a bit much, but he is coming from the right place. About a week after they escaped, he sat me down to talk to me about whether or not this is really what I want. I explained to him in more detail about what Emilia went through since her parents died. He explained what it was like for him to be a single father to Salvatore and Vincenzo though they were adults.

Emilia's situation is different but similar in some ways. Adriano felt heartbroken and angry from Anna's death. Emilia felt heartbroken and angry from the treatment she and Alessia felt from the hands of Seth. He was supposed to love and cherish Alessia and at least respect Emilia but no, he abused her and tried to sell his daughter for money. Now she is petrified that someone is going to hurt Alessia and will do anything to protect her. We all saw that firsthand with Zaira and how she willingly went with Eleanor and the guards for Alessia. She has issues trusting people and I know her coming back here is not going to have her trusting me, but she will be safe.

We also talked about if I understood what it meant to be a parent. He explained how your heart will walk outside of your body and all you want is to see them happy and will do everything in your power to keep them from being sad. He said this decision will be one of the most important decisions I will ever make and do not take it lightly. Alessia has been denied a father and I should not show up if I am not willing to give it my all. She deserves to have a father who is present. I agreed with him, and I told him I would take time and think about my choices. I want to be the father she deserves; she deserves to have a father who will love and cherish her. Unlike Seth did to her and my father did to me.

"I love you Uncle Adriano," she says walking over and kissing his cheek.

"I love you too, Princess." She goes back and sits in her chair.

"This is what family is about. Loving each other even if it's through silly banter. And soon we will have our Queen and youngest Princess with us. But we all know how Mateo will act like a gentleman when he is bringing them home especially with all the trauma they have gone through." Nonna says to me giving me a hard look.

I gulped and nodded at her, not wanting to be at the receiving end of her wrath again. The day after the girls escaped and Nonna found out how I never checked on them after what happened, well let's say my ass was sore from her smacking me with the spoon. That woman has never put up with our bullshit and has expected the men in our family to act like gentlemen and when we don't, her handy wooden spoon comes out. I swear she used to carry that thing around for me, Salvatore, and Vincenzo all the time as kids."

"Nonna, of course, but I am sure Emilia will not come along happily. Remember who is searching for her and she is safer with me than with the Garcia's. I know you already love Emilia and Alessia, so I have to do what is necessary to keep them both safe."

She nods at me. "I know you will my boy. Bring my babies back to us safely."

I smile at her. After we finish eating, I head back to my office to finish paperwork I must complete before I leave.

When it's time to leave, I have Marcello, Vittorio, and the security team with me. As soon as everyone is settled on the jet, I start to explain the plan with Marcello and Vittorio. "I will be doing routine checks on my businesses in Spain, which will take three days, then the last two days we will be in Barcelona, either at or near Garcia's estate. I will be informing him that I know about his betrayal of not informing me about our Queen and Princess's whereabouts. I am sure it will get hostile, so we will have the whole team with us just to be on the safe side. What he says will determine if we continue to be allies with them or not. I can guarantee that Emilia will be a handful, so we need to be prepared to subdue her without hurting her. We need her back in Italy as soon as possible so they can be safe. Seth has already reached out to Alexei for help looking for his girlfriend and daughter," I explain.

They nod at me, and Marcello has a smirk on his face. "Julietta has asked me to record you and Emilia," he says, laughing.

"Fuck off asshole." Marcello might be one of my capos, but he also is one of my oldest friends. We grew up together as kids, so it was a no brainer to make him a capo.

After that, we all go do our own things during the flight. I go and review all the photos and videos Fabio has of the girls. Since he found out where they were this whole time, he was able to hack into their surveillance and see what my girls have been up to.

"*Oh fuck!*" I say to myself. If what I just heard is true, we could have more problems. I already knew Esmeralda was gonna be on my back about what happened, but if she truly is Emilia's godmother then she is gonna be a whole new level of crazy, and that says a lot for her. That is not going to change my mind about bringing them home. I see the video of when Emilia was treated and how much pain she was in. She went basically three days without any medical attention for herself. This woman keeps shocking me how truly selfless she is.

I continue to watch, and I see how Emilia has been training, which is probably not going to be a good thing for me, but I am happy she will be able to protect herself and our family. Alessia is in all sorts of activities, and she looks so happy. She will be able to do whatever she wants when we get home. Then I see where a woman has Alessia crying while Emilia comforts her. I email Fabio asking who this woman is so I can decide if I need to kill her or not. I get a quick response saying her name is Maya Lopez and she is a therapist for both girls. That is another thing I will demand they both have when we get home. It will be mandatory until the therapist says otherwise. Maybe I can pay for Maya to move to Italy.

I continue to watch the surveillance for the past six months until we land. I pack my stuff up and walk out of the jet to the Range Rover. We all head to one of my hotels to get some sleep before we start visiting some of my hotels in Spain. I have a chain of hotels named Jasmine. When I lay down on the bed I crashed. I have been so worried about their safety and now I know they are safe and will be safer soon in my care. I feel like a huge weight has been lifted off my shoulders.

The next day I woke up and got ready. I just finished putting my pants on when I heard a knock at my door. I pull my gun from the back of my pants when I see a maid has brought my breakfast. I tell her to place it on the table. She is miserably trying to seduce me; I ignore her attempts, but she does not take the hint. She keeps trying to touch me or sticks her chest out. I finally had enough and asked her, "Is this what you do with all men or just the rich ones?"

She bats her eyes at me "What are you talking about Mr. De Luca?"

"Do I look stupid to you?" I ask with irritation in my voice.

"Of course, not sir." She tries to purr the sir part.

"I am aware of your miserable attempt to seduce me. You know I am the owner of Jasmine's, and I am also engaged."

She looks at me and laughs. "If you are engaged then why haven't you been seen with her in public?" she asks me, smirking.

I tell her, "What I do with my fiancée is none of the public's business. And by the way pack your stuff, you're fired." I say, then walk to the door and open it for her. She starts with the tears, begging me not to fire her. I ignore her, grab her by her arm, move her out of my room, and shut the door in her face. I called the manager and let her know she was fired.

I finally start to enjoy my breakfast when I see my Nonna calling me. I talk to her for a bit, she asks me about how the ride over to Spain was. We chat for a little more, then she hangs up. She always does this when I travel because she worries about me. I am truly lucky to have such a caring grandmother. Luckily the rest of my visit to the hotel was much better than I expected, especially after breakfast with the maid. The next three days went by well. We had some minor issues that were quick to solve but time also dragged on since I was so anxious to see the girls again.

On the fourth day in Spain, we park in front of Garcia's estate in two Range Rovers. Marcello and Vittorio follow me in, and we get escorted up to Jose's office where Jose, Esmeralda, and his underboss are waiting for us. We sit down and Jose greets us, "Welcome, Mateo. I hope your trip has been pleasant so far."

"Cut the pleasantries Jose. We all know why I am here. Why did you betray my trust and not tell me my Queen and Princess have been here for six months?" I yell with anger, clenching my jaw.

"When you first called, I had not heard anything from them. Later that day, Emilia called Esmeralda from a rundown motel, and we picked her up. After seeing the condition she was in and the fact she went three days without medical treatment, of course, I didn't tell you. Here, take a good look at what your people did to your supposedly future wife," he said while throwing some photos at me.

I look at them and my heart jumps to my throat and it is hard to swallow. My poor *Bella Regina (beautiful queen)* even with her back and legs all cut up you can also see the scars from her old injuries. "My queen is so strong. How is she? And how is Alessia?" I quickly ask.

"They are both happy and safe. But she is not your queen because you do not let your queen get treated like that." He basically yells at me; I raise my eyebrow at him. I know he isn't that stupid to raise his voice at me knowing how much power I have. We both hold hateful glares at each other and eventually he hears his phone ping and looks at it. When he looks back at me, I start to speak again.

"I will explain my side and then we will get into her past. After the incident where Alessia got slapped by my doctor's sister who has some fantasy that I will marry her, Emilia grabbed Alessia and went into her room. I had Vittorio, the girls' personal guard with them. I had no idea that the guards who came into her room broke his phone. Emilia gave him strict orders to keep Alessia safe and he had no idea who else was listening to Eleanor 's orders. He knew Emilia had been through worse and would be okay. He stayed with Alessia to keep her safe. When Emilia was able to escape, she knocked out a guard and Vittorio. Then she escaped. I had no idea what was happening at all. I had purposely given them both space to calm down. When Vittorio came into my office and informed me what happened, within an hour we caught how she escaped on surveillance and had been trying to track her ever since. We had no clue where she was until we spotted Alessia shopping with Esmeralda."

He looks at me chuckling. "Well, have fun with her when she hears the reason you had no idea what happened to her."

I groan knowing she is going to give me hell. "Any advice to help me live with a woman who wants my head on a platter?"

"There is a fire within her...If loved correctly, she will warm your home. If abused, she will burn it down. It is a quote her father used to describe her mother. Unfortunately for your poor soul, she is just like her mama in so many ways." He chuckles.

I smile thinking about her feisty attitude but before we get into lighthearted conversation, we need to discuss Seth and Boris. "Thanks for that. Later we will have to get back to the fact that Esmeralda is Emilia's godmother. But you need to hear how serious the situation is with her past. Did Emilia tell you about her past before she met me?"

Jose and Esmeralda nod their heads and Esmeralda speaks up, which to be honest I am surprised she has stayed quiet this whole time. "Yes, I was ready to skin them alive for what they did to my babies. Especially Boris, that sick motherfucker wants to marry my baby when he is forty years older than her. And don't worry I wanted to skin you too, but Emilia told me I couldn't do anything to you, so we wouldn't start a war. You're lucky she is my goddaughter, otherwise I would have not listened."

"I don't doubt that, Esmeralda. And both of those girls are angels. But Seth is Alexei Ivanov's brother-in-law. Seth has already reached out to Alexei to help him find his girlfriend and daughter. We both know you don't have the manpower to deal with the Russian's and I do, especially if I pull manpower over from the states. I am going to tell Emilia that we will be married in a month, and I will formally adopt Alessia. I know it isn't what she wants but if they are bonded to me, it offers them more protection." I tell them both my plan and hope they will see that it is the best way.

Esmeralda sighs and looks me in the eye. "No, she is not going to be happy at all, but you are right about them being safer, especially if they have your last name. But mark my words, if either of them comes to me hurt in any way because of you, I will do more than skin you."

I nod at in agreement with her. "I promise to protect them until I take my final breath. Let's go tell her preferably without Alessia around. I don't think our reunion is going to be a happy one." They laugh and Jose calls someone to stay with Alessia while Emilia comes and talks to us.

A couple minutes go by before his phone rings, and he laughs when he sees Emilia calling him to question why someone is watching Alessia. Eventually, she agrees to come to the office. Marcello goes and stands at the corner of Jose's desk, and I look at him. "Are you really going to record this for Julietta?" He just smirks and nods his head.

Esmeralda was about to question it when the door opened, and Emilia came in. Wow she took my breath away. She was always beautiful, but she is in a tight tank top and booty shorts that hugs her figure, which she has more muscle than it did before. Holy fuck. She is staring at me with so much anger. She runs at me and goes to punch me in the face. I grab her wrist, but she sends a kick to my ribs. I grab them and she goes to punch me again. This time I grab both her hands and spin her around, so we are facing each other. Her hands are being restricted by me behind her back. Then she stomps on my foot, it hurts like a bitch, but I won't react. She throws her head forward and her head connects with my nose, which starts to slowly bleed.

"I know you're pissed at me, and I understand that, but you need to calm down and let me explain some things to you."

She glares at me. I sigh and I just move her to the couch, so she is sitting. I gave her a look when I let go of her. "I will tie you to a chair if I have to. Behave."

"Not like it is the first time that has happened. What the fuck are you doing here?" she seethes.

I chuckle at her. "Now is that anyway to greet your fiancé who has been worried about you for six months?"

She scoffs at me and venomously tells me, "If I remember correctly, I left you a note with Vittorio that said the deal was off," she says, crossing her arms over her chest. "Yes, I did get your note, but the thing *Tesoro* is that I never go back on my word, which is a good thing for you."

She rolls her eyes, that habit will have to go, or she will spend a lot of time across my lap getting her attitude spanked out of her. I have no problem watching that juicy ass jiggle when I spank it.

"And why is that Mr. De Luca?" she says with more sass.

"Well, my darling fiancée, I found out that Alexei has sent more men out around Europe and North America looking for you and Alessia."

"I am going to kill them, even if it kills me. If they get their hands on Alessia, the things they will do to my baby." she says, starting to shake in anger.

"No one is going to hurt you or our daughter. You both will have my last name. You are my Queen, and she is my Princess." I go to pull her into my arms. She just punches me in the gut, and I am bent over holding my stomach. It takes me a few moments until I catch my breath.

"I know you don't trust me. I can keep you both safe after everything that happened. I have everyone who was a part of hurting you or Alessia being dealt with. Zaira has been banned from anything related to the De Luca's and if she doesn't follow my instructions, she will be in my basement. Now the two guards, and Abramo are being held in the basement and are slowly being tortured until you arrive home. If you want, you can decide their death." Unfortunately, I had to shoot Eleanor in the head already. She looks at me with a happy smile on her face.

Jose laughs "Good luck. She spent time with Esmeralda torturing people."

I groan, "Hopefully you are not as crazy as Esmeralda."

Esmeralda laughs and says, "Nope, she has a whole new level of creativity, and I never knew."

I just smiled knowing I would let her do basically anything she wanted. And let's be honest, I am very excited to watch her torture someone and be covered in their blood. That makes my inner beast very excited. We are all searching for someone whose demons play well with ours.

TEN
EMILIA

      Yesterday when Esmeralda told me about Mateo visiting, I knew he was up to something. I was called to Jose's office to speak to Mateo earlier today. Why were me and Alessia so important that Alexei had called in more men to look for us?

      I am livid, I know Seth didn't want her, but to put my little girl in the middle of a human trafficking ring just for money makes my blood boil. "No one is going to hurt you or our daughter. You both will have my last name. You are my Queen, and she is my Princess." Mateo says this to me and promises, "They will not get their hands on either one of you." He looks at me with such sincerity that he will protect us. I nod at him, and he starts telling me how he dealt with everyone's punishment. Not gonna lie and say I am not irritated that Zaira is basically off the hook but banned from being near us. She is too obsessed with Mateo to stay away. I am brought out of my thoughts when I hear Esmeralda laugh at Mateo's face over learning how creative I am during *interrogations* with Esmeralda.

      "Hey Esmeralda, remember Jose and Juan's (Jose's underboss and younger brother) faces during my first interrogation?" I say laughing.

      We both chuckled. "Mateo I will give you a piece of advice: don't piss her off enough that she wants to cut your dick off and make you eat it." His face pales.

      "Don't look so nervous, that was one of my calmer techniques."

      A buff, bald guy with deep brown eyes whom I remember as Marcello says, "If that is one of her calmer techniques. I hate to see what a severe technique is. Mateo you better not piss her off."

      I chuckle at him, and I look over and see Vittorio. "V sorry I knocked you out before. I hope I didn't hurt you too bad." I say with a smirk.

      "No *Regina Emilia, (Queen Emilia)* but you definitely will keep us on our toes," he says laughing, and I just shrug my shoulders.

      "Got to keep things entertaining," I say.

      Mateo was on his phone texting someone. I see him smile at his phone. Must be one of his whores. I try to rein my anger in, he isn't anything to me I must remind myself.

      Mateo grabs my hand and starts walking out the door. "Where are you taking me Mateo?" I ask, trying to pull my hand out of his.

      "To see our princess of course."

"And how do you know where she is?" I ask with a bit of anger in my tone.

He looks over his shoulder at me "Fabio is more than a pretty face *Tesoro*."

I just glare at him, "I am not your Tesoro, fuck face," and march past him. I know he will follow me regardless. Fucking Italian prick thinks he can do whatever he wants.

"Why are you angry, my Queen?" He asks, oh the nerve of this man, I think to myself.

"Look I appreciate you offering to protect us, but we will be fine on our own," I say to him.

He looks irritated. "You will not be fine on your own to protect Alessia from thousands of Russian men and women who would try and kidnap both of you."

I put my hands on my hips and glared at him. "We are not your problem, so if you need a wife that bad go finds one of your desperate whores to marry you. Shouldn't be that hard to convince them."

He takes a step closer to me, but I don't move from where I am standing. "I don't remember calling off our engagement."

"I am pretty sure the note I left for you, called off the engagement."

He shakes his head, "No that was you running away which won't be happening again." He is standing so we are face to face.

"Oh no, it will happen every time I feel my daughter's safety is at risk. I will run. And there is not a damn thing you can do about it," I tell him as I push him away from me, but he doesn't even budge. Well, what do you do accept when you are trying to move a rock wall?

"Since I know my fiancée is very sly and skilled in the art of escaping, I have increased your security. I need to keep extra eyes on you now," he says with a smirk.

"Don't you fucking patronize me, Mateo! Alessia is not safe in your so-called family. So why don't you and your mafia stay the hell out of our lives."

The smirk falls from his face. "It is your choice, Emilia. We can do this the easy way with you walking onto my plane, or the hard way where I throw you over my shoulder kicking and screaming. Regardless, you and Alessia will be on my plane in two hours, and we will be flying back home to Italy."

"I will not bring her back there knowing she could be hurt," I scream at him.

His glare hardens on me. "Every person that had a hand in hurting you or Alessia has been dealt with."

I roll my eyes. "Yes, because what you did to Zaira was dealing with it. Mark my words, she will be back. And if she hurts Alessia again, what I did before will seem like child's play compared to what I will do to her. I am not playing around Mateo."

He has a big grin on his face, and I arch my eyebrow at him. "I think your beat down on Zaira was a warning enough to everyone. Plus, it was very sexy to watch, and I can't wait to see you covered in blood after you have tortured someone."

I roll my eyes at him, "You're such a pig."

"What? I know it will be very sexy to watch my fiancée torture someone. We are the mafia baby; we are fucked up in the head."

I start to walk away but I stop and look back at him. "You and your whores stay away from Alessia. I have seen the kind of women you attract, and I don't want them around us."

I turn and continue to walk away but I am stopped by him hugging me from behind. "Is someone jealous?"

"What in the world are you talking about?"

"You seem to be upset when you talk about other women around me," he huskily whispers in my ear, and I shiver as his breath hits my ear.

"I saw the way you were smiling at your phone earlier. And I am not too stupid to know it must be one of your whores to put that smile on your face."

He starts laughing "Sounds like my sweet little fiancée is jealous."

"Why would I be jealous? I know getting someone to fuck me won't be a problem if I need to." Before I can react, he has spun me around to face him with one hand wrapped around my waist and the other has my chin between his thumb and pointer finger.

"The only cock that will ever be allowed inside of you is my cock. I am your fiancé, and I am a very possessive asshole. You need to be fucked, you come to me, and I will fuck you until you can't walk the next day. If you let another man or woman pleasure you, I will have you watch as I kill them. Understand sweetheart?"

I smile at him and say, "Sounds like a good time." He drops his hands as his mouth opens wide. I close his mouth and walk away, swaying my hips a bit more than usual.

He says to himself, "Yep, she is gonna be the death of me. Not the dangerous mafia I run; my little diabolical fiancée will be the one to kill me." He shakes his head and tells me, "Oh, and I was smiling at the surveillance of Alessia playing in your house that Fabio sent me."

"Whatever Mateo." He is next to me as we approach the house.

I unlock the door but before I open it, I turn to Mateo and his guards. "You will stay here and let me talk to her first. She is already scared of you all because of what we went through. Once I have her calmed and she understands, then I will allow you to talk to her." Mateo goes to open his mouth but I shoot him a glare while lifting the bottom of my tank top so he can see my holster around my waist with knives and my gun. He opens and closes his mouth; I think he is more shocked that I am carrying weapons on me. When he nods, I laugh to myself. For a mafia boss he really is a push over. Wait, he is just letting me do these things to get me to open to him. I am no weak bitch, he thinks a couple sweet gestures will have me forgive him for what happened. Yeah, good luck with that buddy.

I ignore those thoughts, open the door, and lock it behind me. I walk in and see Santiago and Lola playing with Alessia. They are probably the cutest older couple I have ever seen. Santiago with his brown hair in his military style haircut and green eyes. And Lola with blonde hair which is in a braid and her sky-blue eyes. After being married for over twenty years they still act like they are in the honeymoon phase and they raised such a sweet but badass daughter, Jade, who has become one of my good friends here. Jade has her Papa's brown hair and her Mama's blue eyes. The girl doesn't lack the attention from both the guys and girls which I can't blame Jade for. Jade is as sexy as hell, but her personality is just as fiery as her looks.

Santiago runs their weapons here and Lola and Jade run the strip clubs. When I met Lola and Jade, I was impressed at their confidence and Lola must have noticed my lack of confidence in myself. So she decided that me and Alessia would be around her because "my awesomeness rubs off on people" and she was right. Both of us are more confident in ourselves.

"Hey, thanks for watching her." I say, going next to Alessia and kissing her head.

"Of course, we love watching her. Well, I need to go get ready to head to the office. See you later," Lola says.

"Actually Alessia, please stay here. I need to talk to Lola and Santiago really quick, okay?" She smiles and nods at me. We walk to the front room and tell them how Mateo and his guards are outside. I explain how dangerous Seth is and how he has reached out to Alexei for help. And they don't like it, but they agree with me that going back to Italy is the safest thing for the both of us. Lola tells me to give him hell, and I tell her I plan too. They give me a big hug and tell me to call if we need anything. I walk them out and Mateo looks at me. I shake my head saying, "Not yet, give me a couple minutes."

I walk in and Alessia is sitting at the table drawing a picture. "What are you drawing, baby girl?"

She looks up at me and signs "You Mama. You are my hero."

I smile at her. "I love you Alessia."

She signs back to me, "I love you, Mama." I let her finish her picture and then I turn her body to face me. "Alessia, we need to talk about something serious." She nods her head at me. "Alessia, Mateo is here." Her eyes get wide, and she looks around. "Calm down, he is not going to hurt us. Remember how he said he was going to protect us from Seth and Boris?" She looks at me and slowly nods. "Well, Seth has a sister, and this sister is married to a powerful man whose name is Alexei. Seth told Alexei we were missing and asked for his help, but Alessia, Alexei is a bad man. Mateo has been looking for us since we left. He had no idea what had happened to us until hours later. And when he found out that Alexei was searching for us. Mateo got scared and started searching harder so he could keep us safe. Jose can't keep us as safe as Mateo can. I know you are scared because of everything that happened, but he has punished Zaira since she hurt you. He also has dealt with the people who hurt me."

She sits there for a minute and then signs "So he really isn't a bad guy, just he is surrounded by idiots?"

"You cheeky little monkey. Esmeralda is a bad influence on you," I say and tickle her. I hear her quietly giggle which is my new favorite sound.

After a minute, I hear the door open and I push Alessia behind me as I see Mateo, Marcello, and Vittorio enter. "I thought I told you to wait until she was ready?" I say giving him a glare.

He just smiles innocently at me. "I couldn't wait any longer to see my princess," he says, walking over to Alessia and bending down to her level. "Wow, *Principessa* you have gotten so tall since last time I saw you. Have you enjoyed spending time here with Jose and Esmeralda?" he asks, and without a beat she starts signing. "Slow down for me, *Principessa. I* am still learning to sign."

I gasp, "Wait, you've been learning how to sign?"

He turns his head and looks at me. "Of course. I want to be able to communicate with Alessia without a translator. It's not just me, all the De Luca's have been learning to. Vittorio has been teaching us."

We hear a smile giggle "Did she just giggle?" He asks.

"Yes, her therapist has been working with her and she started finally feeling comfortable enough to giggle again."

Alessia is looking at her feet, embarrassed that someone besides me and Maya heard her giggle. Mateo raises her chin, so he is looking into her eyes. "Alessia, that is such a beautiful sound, don't be embarrassed."

She smiles and hugs him. She really was sad to leave Mateo and Vittorio; she already felt safe with them when we were with them six months ago. "Okay now start again Alessia so I can know what you did here."

She starts to sign again and tells him about how she takes horseback riding lessons, her therapy sessions, her dance classes and how she helps me walk around the estate taking pictures. Then she starts telling him about everyone here.

"Wow you did a lot here and don't worry you can do all those things and anything else when we get back to Italy," he says.

"Really?" she signs.

"Of course, whatever my princess wants she gets," he says standing up.

She grabs his leg once he is at full height. He looks down at her and she signs for him to pick her up. He smiles at her and picks her up. She is super clingy for her age, but she is seeking out the adult comfort that she only got from me until recently. She hugs his neck tight and snuggles into his chest. He whispers something in her ear, and she looks at me and smiles.

I have to hold back the tears to see how happy he makes her. Even though I am still pissed at him, I am grateful for how sweet he is with her. I smile at them and kiss her forehead, walk into her room, and start to pack up her room. I start packing her carry-on bag with her stuffed wolf, coloring books and some extra clothes. Then I see Marcello walk in with boxes.

"Go ahead and start your room. I will pack Alessia's stuff for you. I left boxes outside your bedroom door. Alessia is giving him a tour of everything in the house," he says, chuckling.

"I am sure she is, and thank you, but leave her wolf and this bag out. It has stuff to keep her busy on the plane," I say.

"Of course, *Regina*," he says, I shake my head at everyone calling me a queen. It feels weird, an abused and used whore being called a Queen.

I walked into my room and start packing all my clothes. Esmeralda really went overboard with shopping for us. I have just finished packing the last of my clothes in a box when I hear a knock on the door and Mateo walks in, coming in stand next to me. "Need any help?" he asks.

"If you could take down the photographs of me and Alessia from the living room and hallway that would be great."

"No problem. And I have told Jose we will leave in about an hour. He told me he will let everyone know so they can come say goodbye."

I smile at him. "Thank you." He kisses my forehead and walks out of the room while chuckling at my blushing face. What the hell? Why did I blush? I have to tighten up the walls around my heart. I will not be taken advantage of by another man.

"No. Do not be affected by his kind gestures," I mutter to myself. I will not be fooled by his sweet gestures or words until he proves it, if he does prove me wrong. Seth was never sweet, but some of the men that Boris sold me out to would be sweet in the beginning then would turn violent.

Once we finish packing and our luggage is loaded into the SUV, it is time to say our goodbyes. I hug everyone goodbye and as I get to Esmeralda, she gives me a bear hug and whispers in my ear "If that dumb fuck does anything to either of you, call me. I will skin him and take you both away from there."

I shake my head at Esmeralda. "Of course, Godmother. We love you." I walk away from her with tears in my eyes, and Mateo helps me into the SUV. I climb in next to Alessia and we wave bye to everyone. I continue to look out the window, thinking about everything that happened in the past six months. Being with Esmeralda and Jose made me feel like I was with my family again. They were always like my second set of parents as a child. I felt safe and secure and to be honest, I haven't felt like that in years. I was able to let down my walls and be myself, not the cold-hearted bitch I pretend to be.

I am snapped out of my thoughts when I hear Marcello say, "Boss, we got company."

Mateo looks in the rear window and cusses. "Fuck."

I see four blacked out trucks following us. Then the SUV is being shot at Alessia starts to cry, and she is shaking. I grab Alessia and shove her down to the floor of the SUV and cover her with my body.

Mateo looks at me. "Emilia there is a gun under your seat, use it," he says.

I grab the gun and sit back up in my seat. I am sitting on my knees, facing the back of the SUV, and I shoot at one of the tires of the SUV next to me. It starts to spin, hits a tree, and then I shoot the driver in his head.

"Nice shot," Mateo says to me. I just give him a wink.

Marcello is trying to keep control of the SUV, but he is still jostling everyone around. Vittorio and Mateo continue to shoot at the trucks. After a couple minutes Mateo tells Marcello to stop, which he does. I look up and Mateo tells me, "Stay in the car with Marcello." Then he turns to Marcello and says, "Marcello make sure they get to the airport safely." Then Mateo and Vittorio climb out of the SUV.

"Yes Boss," Marcello drives off.

"Marcello, what about Mateo and Vittorio?" I yell over the sound of gunshots.

"They will be fine; they already took out three of the four trucks and injured two men in the last truck. No worries, they will be on the jet home with us," he assures me.

I get in my seat and pull Alessia off the ground to have her sit in my lap. "You okay Alessia?"

She nods her head and signs "Just scared. Where are Mateo and V?"

I quickly told her, "They went to check on the other vehicle and they will meet us at the airport." She looks at me skeptically but doesn't question me anymore. When we get to the airport, Marcello pulls up right next to the jet's stairs.

He turns and looks at us and tells me to go ahead and get in the jet, he will get our stuff loaded. I pick up Alessia and quickly run on the jet. I sit her down by the window and hug her next to me. She opens her bag and sees that her wolf stuffed animal was in there and gives it a big hug. We settle in, waiting for everyone else until about twenty minutes later, they finally board the plane. Mateo has his jacket and tie off and his sleeves rolled up with a few of his top buttons undone.

Fuck, he is one good looking man; he catches me checking him out. He is smirking at me as he walks over to me. "See something you like darling?" he asks me huskily.

I have had a lot of men around me, but this man has my body reacting to him like never before. I take a deep breath, look over at him and glare. He just chuckles. I am so tempted to choke him, the thought sounds very tempting. "Just looking to see if you are hurt," I say instead of wrapping my hands around his throat.

"I am perfectly okay," he says kissing the side of my head.

He goes and talks to the pilot and his men for a couple minutes then he comes back with Vittorio who has a bag in his hand. Vittorio crouches down to her level and asks Alessia, "Hey, *Principessa*, I got you an iPad with a ton of Disney movies. Would you like to come sit with me so we can watch them? Only if it is okay with your Mama?" Although he asks her, he looks at me questioningly.

Alessia looks at me and folds her hands together with puppy eyes silently begging me. I laugh at her. "Of course, go with V." She giggles, jumps up, grabs his hand, and basically drags him to a seat. Mateo is sitting in front of me smiling at me, "What?" I ask.

"Nothing, just admiring my fiancée's beauty." I rolled my eyes at him being corny and was about to respond with a sassy answer, but the pilot announced to buckle up because we were going to take off. Once we are clear to take off our seat belts Mateo has his off, stands up, unbuckles me, and throws me over his shoulder.

I start hitting his back. "Mateo! What the fuck? Put me down, fuckface." And he smacks my ass, twice! "Asshole, quit that shit." And he smacks my ass again, twice. Oh, this fucker is gonna get it.

He finally responds, "Every time you cuss, I am gonna spank you. Such dirty words shouldn't come out of your mouth."

I smirk "Good luck with that."

When we get to the bedroom on the jet, he tosses me on the bed. I open my mouth to protest but he cuts me off. "No, we are not doing anything sexual. We need to talk, and I don't want Alessia to overhear." I sit up against the headboard and he sits next to me. "The men in the trucks were sent from Alexei. They sent a message that Seth wanted what was his. We will be calling Alexei and Seth when we get back and offer them one chance to leave you and Alessia alone, or we will destroy his entire empire. He will also have to hand over Seth, Boris, and any men that had a part in your and Alessia's abuse." I go to stop him. "No Emilia, they are the reason my Aunt Anna and Lilyana are dead. They run a human trafficking ring and sell many kids to pedophiles, and they need to be taken care of once and for all. People like that don't deserve to live. I may be a monster but even that is sickening to me.

"Also, with that being said we need to announce our engagement. It is your choice if we make a spectacle out of it or keep it private."

I take a breath and tell him, "Let's keep the whole thing private, even the wedding. Since this is a business marriage, let's not waste your money on all the extra unnecessary stuff," I say looking down, playing with the bottom of my shirt. I know I will never get my happily ever after, and that is upsetting, but I know one day it won't bother me.

He gently grabs my chin and has me turn my head and look at him. "When I first proposed the idea to you, yes, it was just a business marriage, but I want us to at least be friendly with each other. And I don't want you to hate marrying me. I am doing this to keep both of you safe. I have thought a lot about this in the past six months and I want to give this marriage a real try. You are an amazing fierce woman. I would be the luckiest bastard to have you by my side." I give him a smile.

"Mateo, you need to know I am not ready for any kind of romantic relationship. The mental trauma I have gone through is bad. The psychiatrist I was seeing diagnosed me with PTSD. I don't know when or how long it will take me to be ready. It's not fair to you to keep you waiting."

He just smiles at me. "Emilia, I have not touched a woman since the day you entered my house. My cock only gets hard for you now. I have my hand and cold showers. Plus, it gives me time to think of the different ways I can explore that delicious body once you are ready. You will be ready one day; I will help you and I have already found both of you therapists to come to the mansion. If either of you don't like your therapist or don't feel comfortable, then we will find someone else. But you should know, I crave to be dominant, but I will never do anything to hurt you. If I do anything you are not comfortable with, I need you to tell me. I never want you to be uncomfortable with me," he tells me and tucks my hair behind my ear. I look down blushing, I am sure I am as red as a tomato. I don't want to cave but he is making it hard.

"Okay." I pause but then I say, "Thank you, but can I make a request that Alessia always has someone she trusts with her during her sessions? I just don't trust too many people with her."

"That was going to happen regardless, she is too young to be left alone with any strangers and especially with this Seth bullshit. I don't trust them not to threaten the therapist to do something to her if she were alone with them."

"Now that it is settled, lay down and rest. We have a long flight, and knowing my family, they will be bombarding you when we get home. Especially Nonna and Julietta," he says chuckling, as he pulls me into his arms and has us lay down. I try to wiggle out of his arms, not used to feeling a man hug me. "Relax my queen. We are just going to sleep." I try to calm down on my own by taking a deep breath, but it doesn't help. I start hyperventilating and I feel like I am back with Seth, being abused. He realizes this and he pulls me closer to him, so my head is on his chest. He is whispering sweet words to me while he rubs my back until I have calmed down. "That's it, good girl. You are okay." After a while I finally relaxed into him and snuggled closer. Mainly from the exhaustion caused by my episode and that was a small one. They always make me feel exhausted afterwards. He just holds me tighter and kisses the top of my head, and I fall asleep laying on his chest.

ELEVEN
EMILIA

      I start to stir when I feel a little body squeeze around my waist. I smile, knowing it's Alessia. I pulled myself out of Mateo's tight grip, which was difficult. Every time I would loosen his grip, he would pull me tighter against him. After I finally pried his hands off me, I pulled Alessia to my chest. She usually isn't a snuggler and if she does, something is bothering her. I move the hair away from her face, she looks up at me with a small smile on her face.

      "What's wrong?" I whisper to her, so we don't wake Mateo; he looks like he hasn't slept well in a while.

      "Are you happy Mama?" she signs.

      I look at my sweet girl. Despite what she has witnessed, she still has such a big heart. "Now why would you ask a silly question like that?"

      "You always make sure I am happy and safe but what about you?" she signs back.

      I slightly jump when I hear Mateo's hoarse voice next to me. "Alessia I will make sure you and your Mama are happy and safe."

      I looked over at him. "Sorry if we woke you up."

      "No, you didn't. I have been awake for a while but enjoyed laying down with you," he says, smiling at me. This cheeky fucker kept pulling me closer when I was trying to get out of his arms. Before I can respond he says, "How about we lay back down and watch a princess movie on the TV? We have another hour before we land." Alessia nods and asks for Aladdin. He puts it on, and she moves, laying between us, and snuggles into Mateo's chest. He looks down at her and has this sweet, genuine smile on his face while kissing the top of her head.

      After the movie is over, Mateo asks Alessia who her favorite princess is, and she tells him Jasmine because she loves her outfit. I had to hold back my laugh at his expression. His eyes looked like they were gonna pop out of his head. I can imagine him watching her run around in a Jasmine outfit with her stomach showing and totally losing his cool. He is already so protective of her.

      "Alessia, I feel bad for you when you want to date, Mateo is gonna give you such a hard time," I say laughing.

      He turns to me and says "If she finds someone, they will have to get mine, and all the De Luca's men approval. Plus, we will be watching them, and I will have no problem dealing with them if they make her cry."

      I look at him. "Really? You know she will be heartbroken at some point in her life."

"Not if I can help it. Anyone who makes my princess cry will meet my gun." I shake my head at him. We go and sit back and get ready for the jet to land.

I expected to see us land in the airport not at the back of an estate. "Mateo, where are we?" I ask as we climb in the Range Rover. "On the backside of the estate. I figured we would have unwanted company if we landed at an airport, even a private one, so I decided to land us on the estate itself to make sure you both get home safe." I nod at him.

After our luggage is loaded, we take off to the house which is only a couple minutes' drive. Our driver introduces himself to us, "Hello Queen and Little Princess, my name is Sergio I am going to be your driver when you need to go anywhere." He shakes both of our hands. Sergio is an older man with black hair cut in the military style and brown eyes.

"Hello, Sergio, my name is Emilia, and this is my daughter, Alessia. It is nice to meet you." He nods his head at us. Mateo grabs my hand, he already has Alessia on his hip and we are walking towards the door. We are greeted by a bald man with a grey goatee wearing a butler suit. "Hello, my name is Valente," he tells me as he opens the door. Before I can respond, I am grabbed into a hug which completely catches me off guard, and I tense up.

Julietta, Mateo's sister, has gotten more beautiful than last time. Her long brown hair shines in the light and her brown eyes shimmer with happiness. She puts me at arm's length and does a look over. "He didn't do anything to either of you right?"

Before I can respond, Mateo replies, "Wow, I feel the love, Julietta. And why would I do anything to my Queen and Princess?"

"Well, I do love them more than you cause you're annoying, along with these two idiots." She points to Salvatore and Vincenzo.

The three of them respond with, ouch, hey and brat at the same time, and not sure which response came from which.

She raises her eyebrow. "And that is my point," she says, and I shake my head laughing at them.

I do still respond to her question though. "No he didn't do anything too bad for him."

"There is hope for him after all!" He glares at her, but she ignores him and goes to Alessia and takes her out of his arms. She starts walking and we follow her to a room which looks like an informal family room. It has a huge sectional couch with a big TV mounted on the wall. Julietta whispers something in Alessia's ear to make her smile. Julietta has this happy demeanor that is contagious and it's hard not to smile around her.

"I heard someone likes princesses?"

Alessia nods her head and signs, "Jasmine is my favorite and I love her outfit."

Julietta smirks at Mateo. "Don't worry, Alessia, we will get you lots of Jasmine outfits to wear."

Mateo goes to responds but Nonna smacks him on the back of his head. "Keep that trap shut. She is a little girl and can do whatever she wants. Especially if she has all these overprotective men watching her every move." I give her a grateful smile.

He again tries to respond but this time Nonna tells him, "Zip it before I get the spoon out. You're not too old for the wooden spoon, I proved that six months ago." I see him gulp.

"Nonna, this sounds like a story I need to hear," I say with a smirk on my face.

She walks over and hugs me and says, "Oh I had to smack some sense into him after that bitch hurt the princess and this idiot didn't go check on you two until it was too late." I chuckle. He just shakes his head. It's clear he respects his grandparents, which is sweet.

Nonno comes over to me and gives me a big bear hug and says, "Well dear, since our last introduction was disastrous, welcome to the family and I want to apologize for my son and that woman who he married. What they did to you was horrifyingly awful. You are a fierce woman, and we are honored to have you as part of this family."

I smiled at him. "No need for you to apologize, you didn't do it to me and honestly, I have been through a lot worse than that."

Uncle Adriano, who has been quiet this whole time, speaks up. "You truly are an amazing woman and mother. If Mateo has any cells in his brain, he will do everything he can to not lose you," he says, giving Mateo a knowing look.

He has these piercing blue eyes that seem like they can stare right through your soul, and short, jet-black hair. I will think about why he seems so familiar later. Nonna says, "Alright, quit picking on Mateo. We will save it for next time he makes a mistake."

She laughs and hugs Mateo, and he hugs her back and kisses her cheek. "Thanks for the confidence, Nonna."

Vincenzo and Salvatore come back into the room and each of them carrying a huge gift bag. Vincenzo calls Alessia, "Hey, Princess Alessia, we have some stuff for you." She looks over at them and sees the huge gift bags and her eyes get wide in shock.

She slowly walks over to them. She pulls out a huge stuffed horse that is almost as big as her. She squeals and hugs it then hugs both of them. Salvatore tells her, "There is more in there, princess." She continues to look through the bags, and she finds clothes and princess outfits.

She signs to them, "Thank you."

They sign back to her, "You're welcome".

I can tell Salvatore and Vincenzo are brothers; they look almost identical except Salvatore has his Papa's bright blue eyes and Vincenzo has green eyes. Vincenzo's nose is crooked and has he higher cheekbones than Salvatore.

Nonno says, chuckling, "Seeing how happy and appreciative she is makes me want to buy her more stuff."

"At this rate you all will have her spoiled," I say to him, and he smirks, at me.

He says, "So? She is my *pronipote (great granddaughter)* and the baby in the house, so we are going to spoil her." Nonno and Nonna look at me and I sigh knowing I won't win but that isn't the worst thing in the world.

"As long as she doesn't become an entitled brat, I am okay with spoiling. She deserves it anyway."

"Speaking of spoiling. Since we don't want to risk being seen in public until those bastards are caught, I have arranged for a friend of mine who is a stylist to come tomorrow for you and Alessia so we can fill your closets. Plus, as a fashion designer you both get to be my personal models," Julietta tells me.

"Oh no, you don't need to worry about that. We have a lot of clothes from Spain, we are okay. I feel bad spending anyone's money," I say.

She rolls her eyes. "You are too humble to be with this blockhead brother of mine, but there is no such thing as too many clothes. Especially when you both have walk-in closets to fill." My mouth drops at the thought of having a closet that big. She smiles at me. "We will get your sizes later so she can bring over what we need." Then she walks over and sits on the couch.

"Okay, quit smothering my girls. You are going to overwhelm them," Mateo says, grabbing me and hugging me from the side.

Adriano rolls his eyes. "No, you just want to hog them. Alessia doesn't look too smothered watching Aladdin with her uncles and aunt," he says pointing towards the couch in front of the TV, where Alessia is sitting on Julietta's lap and has one uncle on each side of her. He just shakes his head, walks over to Salvatore, whispers something in his ear, and Salvatore nods his head at Mateo.

He walks back over to me. "We will be in the garden," he says to Adriano, grabbing my hand and walking me out of the room. I turn back, and all of the De Luca's are sitting watching Aladdin with Alessia. I see a couple maids walk in with drinks and snacks. Looks like she will be content for a while, I wouldn't be surprised if she had them watching a couple of movies.

Once we get into the garden there's a beautiful gazebo. He opens the door for me so I can go inside. He grabs my hand and has me sit next to him on the bench. For a while we sit together in silence, which I truly appreciate, so I can soak everything in. Not that his family's love and support is unappreciated but with my PTSD, sometimes being in situations like that can easily overwhelm me. I am used to having to use my body to have Alessia's basic needs met. Have them just throwing money and gifts at us is hard for me to grasp.

I have to force myself to remember that they are doing it out of love and don't want anything from us. I finally sort through my thoughts and turn to him and say, "Thank you, I needed this." I genuinely mean it.

"I could tell you were getting overwhelmed, but you don't have to say thank you, Emilia. You can always tell them to back off when it gets too much," he tells me.

"I know, it's just one of my triggers because for Alessia to get basic essentials to live before, I had to give my body to any of the men," I say.

Mateo clenches his fists, gets up, and starts to pace. "I really can't wait to get my hands on them," he says angrily. I don't say anything at first and let him calm down, but he doesn't after a minute.

I stupidly say to him, "Sorry, I won't talk about our past since it upsets you."

He stops pacing and kneels in front of me. He looks at me dead in the eyes. "Emilia I am not mad at you *il mio amore*. I am mad that Seth would do that to both of you. As a man, he is responsible for you and Alessia since she is his daughter, but he failed, and you suffered so much. I wish I would've found you both sooner, so you never suffered. Especially you, God, Emilia, you are strong, so incredibly strong," he says, kissing each of my knuckles and making me blush. *"È bellissimo,"* *(so beautiful)* he says as he brushes his knuckles against my cheek. He chuckles at my face getting redder and sits back down next to me.

"I know you don't like to spend people's money, but I want you both to be happy here. When Fabio originally investigated your background, it showed you were going to college to get your business degree. You were basically a straight A student. I want you to finish that and open your own business."

I am flabbergasted by his offer, as much as I would love to, I don't want to waste his money. "But the money," I say.

He laughs at me "Emilia, I can pay your whole tuition at once, stop working, and Alessia's kids would still have enough money not to work." I just open my mouth gapping at him. "You will have to do it online or I can hire a private tutor for you."

"No, I can do it online," I say quickly, knowing a tutor will cost him more money.

"I have to ask though, you were eighteen when you were pregnant, how do you already have two years' worth of college credits?"

I smile shyly at him. "I took AP classes through high school. And I was just shy of nineteen when I got pregnant with Alessia and dropped out. When I was in college, I worked the night shift and weekends and took my classes through the day. I was determined to finish college as soon as possible so I could start my photography business right away." I remember how excited I was to open my own studio.

"Good thing you are going back to college so you can have that photography studio. If that's what you still want to do." I smile at him and nod my head. "Alessia told me what she enjoyed doing while she was in Spain. Is there anything else you want her to do? I want her to be able to do anything she wants."

"She loved the different styles of dance lessons she had while we were: she was taking ballet, tap, latin, hip-hop and jazz. Plus, she had horseback riding lessons. I know she loves art, but I am not sure if she wants to do it as a weekly activity or just for fun," I told him.

"Well, she will have art and music included with her private tutor who will start next week with her. And if she wants to add dance and horseback riding lessons, we can look into it. I didn't realize she was taking so many dance classes," he says laughing.

"Yeah, Esmeralda kind of went overboard on her dance classes, but it is also an emotional release for her."

He nods, but he says, "As long as she tries hard in school and keeps her grades up. I don't mind her being in so many classes."

"Does the tutor know that she is behind academically? I tried my best with her, and she did learn a lot in Spain, but she definitely isn't on the level of a six-year-old."

"Yes, she knows, and she also knows that she is a selective mute, the tutor is specialized in speech therapy. And I want you both to learn self-defense. I know you have been learning and already can defend yourself, but I want Alessia to have a chance at defending herself. God forbid she is in a situation and doesn't have any of us around. I want her to have a chance to escape," he says nervously.

"I agree with you, plus, as everyone says, she is the princess and that puts a target on her back. It wouldn't hurt her to know," I tell him, and he nodded his head, agreeing with me.

"Now that all of that is discussed, let's go for a walk," he says grabbing my hand, and we walk through the garden just making small talk to get to know each other He is gonna be my husband and I hope one day we can be friends or at least cordial with each other. I know he wants more but at the moment, but friendship is all I can offer.

Mateo looks down at his watch and he sees it's been over two hours, so we decide to head back to check on Alessia. Alessia has her hair braided and is wearing a Princess Jasmine dress. Luckily, the belly part has a big band covering it. I bend down to her. "Well look at you. You are such a beautiful Princess Jasmine. Did you say thank you?" I ask her, and she nods her head.

"Nonna braided my hair and Aunt Julietta helped me into my dress."

I kiss her cheek and tell her, "Good. Just remember to always use your manners. Okay?" She nods at me and goes over and hugs Mateo, he smiles at her, and she motions for him to come closer. He bends down to her level and she kisses his cheek. Then he kisses her forehead.

Maybe I did shelter her enough from the abuse that she feels safe enough to be happy and carefree with the De Luca's. I smile to myself knowing it was all worth it.

"She is such a sweet little girl." Adriano tells me.

"Thank you. I am so lucky to have her. I am glad she feels safe enough to be so carefree around your family."

He gently grabs my shoulders and turns me so I am facing him. "No Emilia not my family. It's our family, I know this isn't a marriage of love but the moment you accepted Mateo's proposal is the moment you became family. We protect our family. It might take you a while to trust us, and that's okay, but know you can come to us." He hugs me and this time I willingly hug someone back.

Seth

That whore thinks she can escape from me. She has another thing coming. Her running away has cost me money. She didn't know but Boris owned many brothels, and the men would request her, and she always did what they wanted without complaining. She took all the abuse knowing I would take it out on Alessia if she didn't cooperate or follow directions.

I never wanted the abomination, but it was a good way to keep Emilia in line. Boris loved to beat Emilia anyway. He said it "kept her from getting any ideas of leaving." That's why when he told me he wanted to tell Emilia to start grooming Alessia to be his wife I didn't agree with him. I know how protective she is of Alessia. We saw how well that turned out, since she knocked us both unconscious and escaped with Alessia without a trace. I called my brother-in-law Alexei, who is the Boss of the Russian Mafia, to help me find his niece and the whore. He should be calling me soon to inform me of how the rescue mission went. Ah, speak of the devil and he appears. I pick up the phone.

Seth: *"Well how did it go?"*

Alexei: *"Why didn't you tell me she had ties to the Spanish and Italian Mafia?"* he asks, yelling at me.

Seth: *"What the hell are you talking about? After I caught her house on fire, she had no one. I made her cut off all communication with everyone."*

Alexei: *"Are you seriously telling me you had no idea that Esmeralda Garcia, the wife of Jose Garcia, who is the boss of the Spanish Mafia, is her godmother? And why were she and your daughter boarding a private jet with Mateo De Luca, the boss of the Italian Mafia? I* fucking told you when you first became obsessed with her, you need to know everything about her or it would bite you in the ass. If they get wind of how you and Boris treated them, you both will have a target on your backs. Plus, I already have bad blood with them anyway. You just added fuel to the fire.

Seth: "Well, I didn't care before and still don't care. I saw what I wanted and went after it. She has a good pussy and is good at sucking cock, nothing else matters," I say, getting hard thinking about Emilia on her knees in front of me. I unzip my pants and start to stroke myself.

Alexei: "Yeah and look how far that got you. A kid you didn't want and possibly two mafia's coming for you. The only reason I am helping you is because you are my wife's brother. Tell Boris to watch his back, I will be in contact soon." And he hangs up.

Fucking bastard thinks he can treat everyone under him like dirt just because he is the boss of the Russian Mafia. If that asshole hadn't saved my ass so many times, I would have killed him. I honestly would be a better boss. But soon I will kill him, my sister, and that little brat nephew of mine. I just have to bide my time a little longer and I will have the Russian Mafia.

I call in one of my whores to satisfy me. I tell her to get on her knees and, "Suck or I will kill you." She starts to suck my cock, but her mouth isn't as good as Emilia's. I pull my cock out of her mouth. She goes to say something but I stop her. "Don't fucking talk. Turn around." She does as she is told. I take my belt and tie it around her hands behind her back. I bend her over the couch and try to shove my whole length inside of her. I struggle to get my whole shaft inside of her, since she isn't wet. Oh well. She is crying and begging me to stop but that just makes me harder.

I kick her legs further apart. I grab her hips with both of my hands and hold her in place. I pull my hips back a bit. Then as hard as I can, I forcefully shove my cock inside of her. She screams out in pain. "Please. Stop. You're fucking hurting me."

This whore just cussed at me. I wrap my hand around her throat and squeeze it. I move my other hand from her hip and push down on her lower back. I lean down and bite her neck, hard. "You don't tell me what to do, whore." I push her head further into the couch. I imagine that it is Emilia that is bent over the couch in front of me and I cum.

When I am done, I put the whore on her knees in front of me. "Clean me up." She goes to stand up. "Where do you think you are going?"

She is scared, with tears still pouring down her face and her naked body is shaking. "To get a towel to clean you up."

I shake my head, "No, use your tongue."

Her eyes go wide. "But your dick has blood on it."

I raise my eyebrow. "So, get to it, unless you want me to fuck your ass?" She quickly starts to clean me up.

I got hard again, and I ended up fucking her for two hours. I fucked every hole at least once. She eventually passed out; she was okay, but I will have to do it until I get my hands on Emilia. I can't wait to punish Emilia for running away and taking Boris's wife with her

TWELVE
EMILIA

Last night my traitor daughter of mine and Mateo ganged up on me. How you ask. Well, I was expecting Alessia to want to sleep with me, but no, Mateo bribed her with a new stuffed animal earlier in the day. By the time we put her to bed, a tiger stuffed animal was sitting on her bed. Mateo was helping her get ready; once she changed into her pajamas and brushed her teeth, she suckered Mateo into reading three books when I usually only let her read two. When he was reading the third book, she looked up at me and gave me a cheeky smile. This little girl figured out that she has Mateo wrapped around her finger.

When he finished reading, she told me she was sleeping by herself like a big girl. After we kissed her goodnight, I tried to open the door to my room, but it was locked. I turned around to Mateo, leaning against the wall opposite my door with a cocky smirk on his face and his arms crossed over his chest, which makes his muscles bigger. Not that they need it. Focus, Emilia, you're pissed at this cocky asshole.

"Ok fuck face, why is my door locked? I need my stuff to go to bed," I ask him with a glare on my face and my hands on my hips.

"Fuck face? That isn't a very nice thing to call your fiancé, darling. Your stuff is in our room."

I looked at him, baffled. "And why would my stuff be in your room?" I emphasize the word your, trying to get through his thick skull that we do not, and will not, share a room.

"Because you are sleeping in our room with me, and all the other guest rooms in my wing are locked except Alessia's, so let's go get ready for bed." He reaches for my hand, and I shake my head at him. I refused to move another step.

"I'd rather sleep in the hallway," I say, crossing my arms over my chest. And I sit down with my back against the wall.

He shakes his head, laughing at me. "That's fine, we can do this the hard way," he says, bending down and picking me up, so I hang over his shoulder.

"Mateo, put me down asshole!" I demand as I smack his ass. I try to kick him, but he holds my legs still.

"You, my darling, are *la mia esuberante tigre.*" I shake my head at him as he opens his bedroom door, gently tosses me on his bed, and sits on the edge, looking at me.

I look around. He has a California King-size bed, a TV mounted on the wall, and two bedside tables. His curtains are closed, but the color scheme is dark with black, gray, and white. I glare at him with a look that should make him cower in fear, but no, he has the biggest smile on his face. What is wrong with this man? He sobers up a minute later, sits beside me on the bed, and holds my hand.

"Emilia, I know you haven't told me much of what you went through, and I won't pressure you until you are ready. But did you ever sleep through a night with a man that was not sexual?" he asks me while rubbing his thumb on my knuckles.

I shake my head. "No, once they were done with me, they would drop me in my room to get cleaned up." I start fidgeting with my shirt.

He covers my hand with his, gently pulling it off the end of my shirt. "We will share a bed and all we will do is sleep like we did on the plane. We will go at your pace. If you want me to hold you, I will, but if you're not comfortable, I will not. If I end up holding you in my sleep and you feel uncomfortable, wake me up. Okay?" I nod, still looking down, and he pulls my chin up gently, so I look him in the eyes. "I know this is new and scary, but we will slowly push your boundaries; right now, we will work on having you be comfortable sleeping in the same bed."

I shake my head. He is not telling me what to do. I walk over to the couch and grab the blanket hanging off the back. I go to cover myself with it and lay down for bed, but Mateo has other ideas.

"Good try, but walk your ass back to that bed," he tells me as he tosses the blanket across the room.

I stand up and ask him, "The fuck is your problem?"

"I don't have a problem, but you will have a very sore ass if you don't get your ass in that bed in five seconds."

I plop myself down on the couch. "That's okay. I am good right here."

He stares at me, then looks up at the ceiling as he runs his hands through his hair. He says, "I wasn't asking. You either walk yourself back to bed, or I carry you, but you are gonna sleep in the bed beside me."

I turn away from him and snuggle into the couch to get more comfortable; maybe if I ignore him, he will give up and leave me alone.

That was just wishful thinking, because he picked me up and tossed me on the bed. I go to get up, and he says, "If you even try to move, I will handcuff you to the bed."

I scowl at him. "What is with you and tying me to shit?"

He put a hand over my mouth and said, "You need to stop all the vulgar words that come out of your mouth." I lick his hand, and he quickly removes it from my mouth. I laugh at the bewildered look on his face. "Did you really lick me?"

"Yep," I say as I lay down on the far side of the bed, since I am in no mood to be tied or handcuffed to anything else.

He walks around to the other side of the bed and lays down next to me. "You looked very sexy when I tied you to that chair; the anger in your eyes as you fought me was extremely hot."

"Fucking pig." He smacked my ass again. I grumble but don't acknowledge him as he chuckles at me.

He doesn't hold me, which I appreciate because a man holding me just sends me back into my nightmares, and I do not want to be weak. Even though I am so far from put together, it isn't even funny, I refuse to have any man help me. Men will only help you if they can get something from you, and I will not owe a man another thing.

I feel myself being shaken and someone calling my name, but it's foggy, and they seem so far away. I know it's just a nightmare, but I keep replaying Seth telling me he sold Alessia to Boris. Then she is slapped, and he is choking my baby. "Emilia! Emilia, wake-up, it's only a dream." The voice sounds familiar, but who is it? I feel myself being held in someone's arms, they are more muscular, and the body wash smells like Irish Spring, which soothes me. Papa always washed with Irish Spring. I opened my eyes and saw Mateo looking at me.

He brings me back to his chest and just holds me while his hand goes up and down my back. I realize he is holding me after a nightmare and he must realize how messed up I am. I go to pull away, but he holds onto me, refusing to let me move away from him. "Shh, stop fighting me. Relax."

I shake my head. "No, I don't want to bother you. Let me go sleep on the couch or in another room." He pulls me back a bit so he can look into my eyes. I am surprised he isn't looking at me with pity, but he looks concerned and worried.

"No, you are right where you are supposed to be. Here, in my arms. I know you don't trust me, and that is fine. I wouldn't expect you to yet but let me hold you. I promise I will be here for you." He lays us down in the bed with me snuggled up to his chest. We don't talk anymore, but he holds me and runs his fingers through my hair. It doesn't take me long to fall back asleep.

This morning I was woken by whispers.

"Aww, look at them."

"Look at him being a teddy bear."

There were other comments, and I heard a camera click. I start stirring, and I hear Mateo hoarsely grumble, "You three better get out of here before I start shooting you for waking us up." He holds me tighter while I snuggle closer into him, and he kisses my head.

"Well brother, too bad Emilia needs to get up. Annabella will be here soon, and Alessia is already downstairs eating breakfast with Zio Adriano. And these two followed me up to make sure you share Emilia since you hog the girls," Julietta says to him.

He groans and tells them, "Go fuck off."

Nonna yells from somewhere, "Don't you be cussing in front of those girls." I chuckle at his groaning, and Nonna has no idea how much I cuss in an hour, let alone a day. Mateo finally surrenders and decides to get up, but I am perfectly content lying in bed all day. I hear the door close, and I close my eyes.

I feel him get out of bed, and I snuggle further into the bed. This bed is heaven, so comfortable I never want to get up. I heard Mateo chuckle, and I looked up to see him smiling at me. "Come on, beautiful, go get ready." He sticks his hand out to help me out of bed.

Once I am out of the warm and extremely comfortable bed, I face Mateo and say, "Sorry I woke you up twice last night."

He shakes his head while he hugs me again. He has been doing a lot of that recently "I told you I would help you through your nightmares, and I meant it. I honestly expected them to be worse. All you did was shake and whimper in your sleep."

"They used to be a lot worse, especially when I first started therapy. According to Maya, all the emotions I had been burying for years were finally coming out. It will take me a while to feel in control without being triggered."

"That's okay and you will get the help you need from your therapist and your family here," he says to me, kissing my cheek and getting up to walk to the closet. I blush but quickly walk to my closet so he doesn't see my pink cheeks. I put on a summer dress with a pair of sandals. It feels weird not wearing my boots but being engaged to the boss, I really can't go around wearing jeans and cowboy boots all the time. I quickly put a bit of mascara and lip gloss on, I was never a fan of heavy makeup.

Mateo is standing with his back to me, adjusting his cufflinks. Fuck, this man is a wet dream in a suit. Hell, I am sure he is in anything, or nothing. I am broken out of my lustful thoughts when Mateo clearing his throat. "You okay there? You seem a little distracted," he says with a glimmer in his eye.

I am not going to feed into his already huge ego. "Yep, just thinking how painful your sister is going to make trying on clothes, but Mateo, we really don't need anything. You are already doing more than enough by helping keep us safe from Seth and Boris."

"Yes, you and Alessia buy all the clothes you want, and this is the last I will hear about your complaining of you spending money," he tells me with a no-argument tone. I sigh and give up arguing with him.

He puts his hand on my lower back, and we quietly walk to the dining room. We greet everyone with a good morning and start eating. Nonno asked me if after Alessia tries on her clothes, they could have a grandparent and granddaughter date. I obviously say yes because I want her to experience the love of a family like I did as a kid. Plus, she was giving me puppy dog eyes. She was too excited for me to say no. It was adorable seeing how excited she was to spend time with Mateo's grandparents.

During breakfast, the doorbell rings, and a few minutes later, a beautiful woman with long blonde-haired and green eyes enters. I feel hideous being in the same room as her. Mateo kisses my hand and whispers to me, "You're beautiful." I give him a small smile; I don't believe it.

"Julietta! You liar, they are both so much more beautiful than you described," she says gushing over Alessia and me. "Oh, I am so excited to see you both try on what I have brought. Alessia, I heard you like princesses, especially Jasmine, or did Julietta tell me a lie?" She asks, chuckling and Alessia smiles at Annabella and nods.

"She is selectively mute," I tell Annabella.

Annabella, without missing a beat, smiles and says, "No biggie, we will still have fun."

After we all finish, we walk into a room literally filled with racks of clothes. Annabella turns to me and asks, "Do you want to have Alessia go first? Kids usually don't have much patience."

I chuckle and say, "Yes please. Little missy here has a date with her grandparents after this."

"That's exciting; let's put on some Disney music so we can make this a party." She goes over to her phone and starts playing "Let It Go" from Frozen, and Alessia is already smiling and dancing.

Alessia starts trying on all different kinds of outfits, everything from jeans to dresses. And let's not even get me started on all the shoes she has now, thanks to Julietta. Both of them love shoes, and Julietta is already planning shopping trips with her once everything is safe. One outfit was ripped white jeans with a black and white spaghetti strap shirt with a big bow on the front. It showed a bit of her stomach. Julietta knew Mateo would flip, so she decided to send him a picture of her in that outfit. Not even a minute later, her phone goes off. She reads the message, and she bends over, laughing. I read the text.

"No way in fucking hell will my innocent princess wear anything like that. Get rid of that pathetic excuse of a shirt, it needs to be burned. She is too precious for anyone to see her like that. She is no longer going to private school; I will find a tutor to homeschool her. No one is gonna see my baby girl. She is too pretty for any sleaze ball boy to even look at. I need more guns and guards for her."

I look over at Julietta and smirk. "We should let her wear this outfit for her date with the grandparents, knowing Mateo will see it later."

"Yes! I am so happy to finally I have another girl to help me deal with those three idiots."

"No worries, I have your back," I tell her with a smirk. I can see both of us enjoying giving the boys hell. After about an hour, Alessia is done trying on clothes, so Julietta and I walk her to the kitchen for their date. Alessia wants to learn how to cook, and I found out at breakfast that Nonno and Nonna cook the family dinners. They enjoy cooking together now that Giorgio is retired. I think that is so sweet.

Nonno raises an eyebrow at Alessia's outfit, and we show him the text. He laughs and says, "let me guess you both are just torturing him a bit?"

I shake my head no. "Just giving him a preview of what her teenage years will look like. I was a royal pain in my Papa's butt, fighting him with clothes and boys," I say, laughing at the memories. I say goodbye to Alessia with a kiss on her hair, but she doesn't acknowledge me. She and Nonna are looking through a cookbook. I grab my phone and take a picture of them; they look so adorable together.

When we walk back into the room, Annabella has all the clothes for Alessia in a couple piles, and the maids are already bringing them to her room. Annabella has "Sexy Bitch" by Akon playing and has a variety of alcohol out. I laugh at her, grab the wine, pour us all a glass, and take a drink.

"Ok, let's start," Julietta says. As I try on clothes, I have to admit Annabella truly has a gift. The clothes and shoes she brought me were absolutely beautiful. None of them are over the top with the bling or too gaudy. I have a simpler taste in fashion. I fell in love with all the different boots she had brought me. I hope Mateo realizes I will be wearing outfits that go with the boots instead of heels. I am not the type of girl who will get dressed up in heels, dresses, jewelry, and makeup every day. I don't mind if we have guests or leave the house, but I won't do it at home unless we have plans.

By the time we got to the lingerie, which they had insisted on me trying on too, I was not drunk but relaxed and carefree for the moment. In between outfits, I would drink a bit and start dancing around, and as time went on, I started to dance more seductively. I am currently in the last piece of lingerie to try on, which is a lace bra and thong with garters. We are blasting *"Tonight (I am fucking you)"* by Enrique Iglesias and singing along with the song. We don't hear a knock on the door, and the door opens.

I was teaching the two of them some of the seduction dances I learned when I was in dance class in college. They begged me to show them "my inner sexiness," as Julietta said. I see a new side to Julietta when she is tipsy, and she is hilarious. She is a little vixen, and I found out she has been secretly kissing a certain capo and her brother doesn't know.

I feel myself being spun around and I am faced with a Mateo whose eyes have darkened with anger and lust *"Che diavolo stai facendo?" (What the hell are you doing?)*

"Danzante" (Dancing) I say with a shrug.

"Oh, stavi ballando bene, ma quel tipo di danza è per i miei occhi solo a porte chiuse. Soprattutto quando indossi a malapena qualcosa." *(Oh, you were dancing all right, but that kind of dancing is for my eyes only, behind closed doors. Especially when you are barely wearing anything.)* He slowly looks over my body which makes me shiver in excitement.

Once he looks back in my eyes, I give him a smirk and say, "Beh, eravamo solo noi ragazze qui dentro prima di essere bruscamente interrotte." *(Well, it was just us girls in here before we were rudely interrupted.)*

He arches his eyebrow at me. "Are you giving me attitude, my tigress?" I roll my eyes at him. He looks over my shoulder to the girls behind me. "Do you still need her?" he asks them.

Annabella laughs, shaking her head. "Nope, Mateo, she is all yours." He unbuttons his shirt and puts it on me, including buttoning it up, I am laughing at his caveman act.

"What? Do you want to give me a show now?" I ask him, purposely eyeing his naked torso. Especially his washboard abs and the V-Line.

"Ti darò uno spettacolo bene," *(I will give you a show alright.)* he whispers huskily in my ear then the brute picks me up and carries me out of the room over his shoulder.

"Stupid brute," I mumble.

He tells me, "Tigress, you're gonna get yourself into more trouble with that mouth of yours." Then he smacks my ass. And the idea turns me on, but I stop myself. I don't need to go down that road with him.

Once we are in the room, he stands me on my feet. He locks the door, grabs my hand, and pulls me against his chest. "Is this too much?" he asks me and I shake my head no.

I decide to give him a bit of payback for smacking my ass. I push him against the wall and start grinding on him. I lean forward and whisper in his ear. "Did you know, Mr. De Luca, your fiancée used to take dance lessons and loves to dance... sexually?"

I hear him take a shaky breath. I run my hand down his chest. I get near his cock and purposely do not touch it, but lightly graze my finger around it. I went past his cock to tease him and started running my hand over every dip of his abs. He grabbed my waist tighter. He gulps, looking down at me in lingerie and I feel his not-so-little friend pushed against my thigh. I looked at his face, and he had his eyes trained on my face but had his jaw locked. You can see his restraint. He was so bad trying to hold onto it. I decide to see how far I can push him. So, I push him and grind harder against him, not that I am complaining, because it felt good for me too.

He finally had enough of me teasing him, and he spins us so he has me against the wall. He grabs my hands and pins them above my head, and he gives me slow, tormenting kisses along my neck. I moan when he kisses right below my ear, and I feel him smirk against my neck. He starts to give that spot extra attention as he nibbles and sucks on it. I start grinding on him to feel any kind of friction against my aching pussy, but he pins me harder to the wall with the other hand.

I whimper in protest. He chuckles at me, *"Non tanto divertente quando vieni preso in giro. Mmm mia piccola tentatrice."* (*Not so much fun when you are being teased. Hmm, my little temptress.*) He leans away from my neck and looks back at my face. He takes his hands off my wrists and runs them through my hair until he reaches the back of my head. We make eye contact, but his eyes keep going back and forth between my eyes and lips. You see he is deciding if he wants to kiss me or not.

"Fanculo," (*Fuck it*) he says and kisses me. Damn, he knows how to kiss. He has blown me away; he has made me feel amazing, and it's only our first kiss. If his kisses make me feel like this, how will I feel when we have sex? I can't wait to have his mouth all over my body.

He is gently kissing me, nibbling on my lips asking for entrance and without even thinking about it, I opened my mouth, the way he is holding the back of my head to angle my mouth so he can devour my mouth. Holy fuck I have always had aggressive and sloppy kisses but never had I had someone kiss me that makes me feel like I am on cloud nine. I would have thought he would be rougher with me seeing the fire in his eyes before he started kissing me, that's when I realized he was holding back. I barely pull back and I whisper against his lips "Don't hold back Mateo." He pulls back even more and looks into my eyes asking me without saying anything and I nod at him.

He wastes no more time and smashes his lips against me. I moan into his mouth, which earns a grunt from him. He grabs my thighs and lifts me up, I wrap my legs around his waist. He pushes me further into the wall if that is possible, and grinds on me hard. He moves his lips off mine and goes back to kissing my neck. I moan out loud, throwing my head back. He continues to assault my neck while grinding on me hard. I feel myself getting closer to an orgasm. He stops kissing me, takes a deep breath, and drops my legs back to the ground. With wide eyes, I look at him, looking for an explanation.

"That's what happens when you display your body off to anyone that is not me, *La mia cara fidanzata di Fiancée*" (*my darling fiancée*) he says with a dark and hungry look in his eye. "I am a very possessive man; you are my fiancée, and no man or woman gets to see what only my eyes get to see. I have never shared well, and I am not about to start sharing your body with anyone else," he says while twirling my hair between his thumb and pointer finger. "If you even think of it, you will be punished, and this is nothing compared to the kind of punishments I can give you."

I look at him, shocked that this motherfucker just denied me an orgasm. "Probably want to go shower and get yourself cleaned up." He pushes me toward the shower and pats my ass. I turn around and look for something to throw at him but come up empty-handed, so I just decide to flick him off and call him a cock block. He laughs at me, which angers me more. I go to close the door but a thought pops in my head. I give him an evil smile; he looks at me. "What are you about to do?"

I then turn my evil smile into an innocent one. "Me, I am not up to anything I am just gonna do what you want and shower." I shut and lock the door and say loud enough for him to hear. "And I will take care of myself since you don't want to."

I can hear him mutter "Fuck. She is gonna kill me." I laugh and walk over to the tub and turn it on. I can hear movement on the other side of the door, but I ignore it. I get in the massive tub and turn on the jets which only help intensify my need to relax.

Once I am settled, I start rubbing my clit because of how wound-up Mateo made me. It doesn't take long for me to reach my climax, and I shout out. "OH FUCKKKKKK!" I moan out with my head tossed back against the edge of the tub as I finish. I lay in the tub and try to catch my breath. I quickly finish cleaning myself up, climb out of the tub, and wrap myself in a towel as I walk out of the bathroom.

I see a note on the bed.

"You are so damn sexy. You are gonna get it you little minx. You wait until the day I have you. We will not be leaving the room all day and I will make sure you won't be able to walk for a week."

Mateo

I burst out laughing while also getting turned on by the thought of being stuck in a room with Mateo and being at his mercy to do whatever he wants with my body. Yes, I hate men, but I can't deny that Mateo is carved by the gods, and he knows how to turn a woman with by his sultry looks and his filthy mouth. The man also looks like he knows how to work his anaconda in his pants. So, he can help me when I have an itch that needs to be scratched.

As I am getting dressed, I pause and think about how he easily could have taken me, but he also respects me. Which makes the wall around my heart crack a bit. I wonder how it will be when he figures out when I need to "perform." I go to my safe place in my head. It was the only way I survived all those years. I never told anyone, but the first time I was with Seth, I don't remember anything I was also a virgin. And every time we would meet up, it would start off as drinks and would end up with me blacked out and naked in a motel room with a note from Seth saying to call him. Being drunk all the time because I was grieving, I was stupid to call him, but realistically I was just lonely. And then I got imprisoned when I told Seth I was pregnant. I never had an orgasm that I enjoyed mentally. Sure, I had them because my body would react to the constant physical contact, but mentally, I hated that I was having an orgasm against my will. If Mateo can make my body react that way by just kissing and grinding himself on me, I can't wait to see what he can do when we go further.

THIRTEEN
EMILIA

        I had just walked into the kitchen and stopped to watch Alessia interacting with her "new" grandparents with adoration. Nonno is teaching her how to make homemade lasagna. He helped her run the pasta dough through the pasta maker. She has her own pink apron with blue trim that says, "I am the official cookie tester." Alessia has flour on her face and her apron. I took a picture of the two of them. I already plan on some cute gift ideas with these pictures I have been taking of Alessia with the De Luca's.

        Nonna must have heard me and gave me a glare. "What?" I act innocently.

        "You know what, missy. She is safe. Now out you go. Shoo," she says to me, waving her hands at me.

        "I was just checking on her," I say. Next thing I know, she is grabbing her wooden spoon off the counter and about to smack me on the ass. I quickly dart out of the kitchen, but I am not fast enough. The crazy old woman smacks me right under my butt cheek, and fuck, that shit hurts. "Ouch, Nonna, that hurts."

        I turn around to see her with her arms crossed, and she says, "That's what you get for interrupting our date with Alessia. Now shoo," and I hear Alessia and Nonno laughing at me.

        Nonna shouts at me, "Go bond with Mateo or something. No bothering us."

        I shake my head, turn around, and say "Well what if I want to spend time with Alessia?"

        Nonna picked up her spoon that she laid on the counter and smirked as she walked toward me. "You want to ask me that again?" I shake my head and turn around to run away from this crazy old lady and her spoon when I feel her smack the same spot as before with that spoon.

        I jump up and yell "Nonna!"

        She just laughs and goes back to whatever she was doing in the kitchen. I turn and walk away while rubbing my sore butt. I wasn't paying attention and ran right into my fiancé.

        "Miss me that much?" Mateo asks with a smirk but stops smirking when he sees my face scrunched up in pain. He immediately starts to worry. "What happened, are you okay?"

        I nod my head and say "Yeah, I dared to peek at Alessia during her date with her grandparents, and I was met with Nonna's spoon." I pouted at him.

He winces slightly. He looks over my shoulder into the kitchen. "Nonna be nice to my fiancée," he says to her, but she waves him off, not even looking up from stirring her pot.

"Hush, boy. Get out of here before I give you a matching sore ass." He grabs my hand and pulls me away from the kitchen. I hear Nonno say something to Alessia, and giggles. I don't say anything as Mateo leads us through the mansion, and we eventually end up in Mateo's bedroom. Sorry "our" room, he has been trying to drill that into my thick skull. He opens the door and lets me walk in. I open the curtains, and the view of the garden is breathtaking. I turn when I hear a knock on the door, and see Mateo thank a maid as she hands him a bag of ice.

"That really isn't necessary, Mateo."

"Yes, it is. Can't have my fiancée in pain," he says with a smile on his face.

I shake my head. "You know a little bruise on my ass is nothing for me, right?"

He gets an angry look across his face and stalks towards me, and before I can react, he has my face cupped in his hands. "I absolutely hate that. But as long as I am breathing, I will do everything I can to keep you both safe," he tells me while looking in my eyes and I see how serious he is. I nod at him; he leaves a lingering kiss on my forehead. He needs to stop these sweet gestures, or the walls around my heart will start break, and I can't let that happen.

"Go in the bathroom, and if you need to, use this ointment on your delectable ass. Then come back here and lay down on your stomach so I can put ice on it," he says with a smirk. Oh he wants to tease me? Okay.

I nod, making him think I am going to do what he says. I take off my boots and then start walking to the bathroom, making him think I am going into there. Instead, I unbuckle my belt and wiggle my jeans down. Before my jeans hit the floor, I hear Mateo says, "Emilia, what are you... Holy fuck. Red is my new favorite color."

I look over my shoulder and see him licking his lips and staring at my red lacy thong. "Do you see any bruises?" I ask, and my voice must have snapped him out of his haze.

"No, no, but why don't you put your jeans back on and we will still put ice on it," he says, trying not to stutter, which is funny. Mateo the man whore, getting all nervous about seeing my thong-covered ass. I quickly pull up my jeans and buckle my belt and lay on the bed.

He comes and gently lays the ice on my ass; I shiver at how cold it is. He asks me if I am okay, and I nod at him. He kicks off his shoes and unbuttons his dress shirt and lays on his side facing me with his head propped up in his hand. He releases a big sigh. "I talked to Alexei while you girls were with Annabella." I nod and stay quiet to let him continue. "He refused to back off, saying you are Seth's property, and Alessia is Boris's property. He said he would be coming to get what belonged to his family. And his wife will be taking over Alessia's grooming, and you will move to their brothel."

I try to jump up in anger, no way is Alessia going to be groomed to be that abusive, sick, demented fuckers' wife. Mateo gently pushes on my lower back to make me lie down. "Lay down. Neither one of you is their property. And neither one of you will be in their hands. I can't imagine what grooming will be like for her. She is just a little girl; she shouldn't be worried about being a wife but enjoying being a happy little girl. The dominant and possessive man in me hates the idea of another man seeing what only my eyes will be seeing." He is already pissed off, so I decide not to remind him of my past.

I give him a small smile instead. "Thanks."

He pushes the hair that has fallen by the side of my head behind my ear and caresses my cheek. "We do need to talk about us getting married and me adopting Alessia. I might have to reach out to some allies, and the Irish tend to be very old school and won't help if you are not my family. He believes it is wasting his time if he helps, and you both don't have my last name. He is a mean bastard, but he is a great ally to have."

I look at him. "Okay, plus that was part of the deal anyway when you originally offered to protect us, and I will not go against my word."

He kisses my forehead, and I swoon at the sweet gesture. I finally have had enough of laying on my back and turn on my side to face him. He grabs me by the waist and brings me closer so our chests are touching, and I have to look up to look at him. "You can decide how big you want it." he says to me.

"Is that safe with the Seth drama?" I ask.

He smirks at me "We can have more security that day."

I think about it and make my decision. "How about we just sign it with your lawyers in private and have a small party. After all this drama is over, then we can have a bigger party if you want."

"Sure, I can have our family lawyer, Benjamin, here tomorrow, and we can have a party with our family. Do you want to invite anyone?"

I nod my head fast. "Theo please." I give him my puppy dog eyes with my lip poked out, knowing he is super jealous of Theo even though he is gay.

"Ugh, fine. I see where Alessia learned that look from." I shrug my shoulders, pretending to be innocent.

"Good, that's settled. I want to ask you about Alessia and Seth's relationship. I want her to feel comfortable around me, but I need to know what damage he did to her."

I look past him at the wall and take a deep breath, then look back at his face. "Honestly, they didn't have a relationship. He made her watch him abuse me. I will say he never laid a hand on her until the day we left. He would yell at her often, and the one time she called him Dada as a toddler, in front of his fling at the time, he got in her face and screamed at her. So, after that she was afraid of him. He noticed she was afraid of him; he kept doing stuff on purpose to make her more afraid of him. He would constantly yell when she was around or throw things in her direction. When she was old enough to understand, I told her that he was her father because she deserved to know, even if he was a sperm donor. I made her promise to never call him that because he doesn't deserve to be called a father. As she got older and barely talked, that is when I knew she was selectively mute because she would only talk to me when we were alone. I started to teach her sign language, so we had a way to communicate with each other."

I look at him, and he is clenching his jaw. "I am going to enjoy torturing him when I get my hands on him."

He looks over at me and sees me eyeing him suspiciously. "Sorry, sweetheart, the mention of what they put my girls through consumes me with anger."

I shrug my shoulders and say, "He deserves all the pain you want to inflict on him and more."

"I have a feeling many people will want a turn after what he did to you girls," he says, chuckling. After that, we lay in bed and just made small talk until, we got called for dinner.

We all enjoyed the lasagna that Alessia made with her grandparents. She was so excited to tell us about it that I had to remind her that everyone else is not as fast as I am at following her when she signs. After dinner, we all retired to our own living quarters. After I shower, I walk out to see Mateo and Alessia watching Aladdin on the T.V. into his room. She is so engrossed in the movie she doesn't notice me, but Mateo does and motions me over. I climb in the bed on the other side of Alessia. I kiss the top of her head and enjoy the peace of the three of us watching a movie together as a family.

EMILIA

Three Months Later

It has been a little over four months since we came back with Mateo to his mansion. Things have been pretty good. Nonna has helped me with my "hovering parenting," as she calls it. Even though we both know has to do with my lack of trust in people, which I am getting better at. I do trust the De Luca's, but I constantly worry about her safety. But having Marcello, who is now her personal guard, helps.

Those two are thick as thieves when it comes to sneaking sweets out of the kitchen. I swear he always has some kind of sweet in his pocket for her, or they are raiding the kitchen for something sweet. Nonna must keep moving where she hides them. She pretends to be mad, but we know she loves that Alessia brightens the place up with her smile and giggles. That's another thing, it seems like Alessia always has a smile on her face.

Alessia really enjoys her new therapist, Rachel, and has started to talk in small sentences around me. She is still not comfortable enough to talk around anyone else yet, but as Rachel has discussed with Mateo and me it can be a really long process, or she can bounce back; kids are very resilient. I am following Alessia to Mateo's office after her speech therapy session because she says she has a surprise for him. Alessia won't tell me what it is, but she is really excited.

She is about to open his door, and I say, "Knock on the door first, so we don't interrupt him if he is busy."

She nods at me, and she says quietly. "Okay." She knocks on the door, and we hear him say enter.

We walk in, and he looks up and smiles at us. He turns away from his desk and walks over to us. Alessia decides to launch herself at him and says, "Papa." My breath hitches, and I put my hand on my mouth. Mateo makes eye contact with me, and I see the tears in his eyes.

"Yeah, princess, I am your Papa." They hug each other tighter, and I start to cry. She finally has a man who will love and protect her as much, if not more, than I do. You can see love in his eyes for her.

These past couple of months, they have been spending a lot of time together, and she loves spending time with him. Her favorite is when they practice self-defense in the gym. That is their "bonding time," and no one is allowed to bother them. She didn't want to learn how to defend herself unless Mateo taught her. When Vittorio took her down to the basement, she refused to step into the gym and shook her head.

"I want Mateo to teach me." We tried to coax her, saying he was busy, but my stubborn daughter refused. Vincenzo was working out and called Mateo. He was there two minutes later and told Vittorio he would train Alessia. I made her tell us why she didn't want Vittorio to train her, and she told us she only felt safe with Mateo and me. That is what sealed the deal to for their one-on-one bonding time while they train.

He pulls away from the hug and asks her, "Are you excited to wear the dress Annabella brought over for you to wear tonight?" She nods her head. He tickles her belly, and her laugh echoes through his office. After a minute, he stops and puts Alessia down on her feet. "Princess, go with Marcello and have him bring you to *Zia* Julietta to start getting ready. I need to talk to Mama about something, then she will help you finish getting ready."

He opens the door, and Marcello is waiting outside the door for Alessia, and she walks up to him. "Hi, Celly," he chuckles and bows.

"Hello, Princess."

Mateo tells Marcello, "Take Alessia to Julietta to get ready. Emilia will join them soon."

He nods and then turns to Alessia, sticking his arm out for her to grab on like a princess. "Are you ready to go, Princess Alessia?" She nods yes. I clear my throat at her, waiting for her to respond but she rolls her eyes at me.

"Alessia Rose De Luca, you roll your eyes again I'm gonna tan that hide of yours, understand?" I say while arching my eyebrow at her.

She signs, "Yes Mama."

"Good. Now shoo, go see Aunt Julietta," I tell her while she quickly runs out the door with Marcello.

As soon as I shut the door, I am encased in a hug from Mateo while he is chuckling at me. "Julietta is rubbing off on her," I say while shaking my head.

He kisses my head. "Yeah, but I doubt we can separate them. Alessia is Julietta's shadow." I agree with him. He leads us to the couch for us to sit down. I go to sit next to him, but he pulls me into his lap. I roll my eyes, ever since that day after I tried on clothes and he caught me dancing in lingerie, he has been very touchy-feely, but never going further than I am comfortable with. We have gotten closer; I would not call us lovers. We have not had sex; we definitely have had a lot of heated moments, but he loves to leave me on edge before walking away. Those are the days I consider strangling him, but that is okay. It is fun to tease him back.

Mateo gets my attention when he asks me, "How are you feeling about announcing you and Alessia tonight as my wife and daughter?" he sticks my hair behind my ear.

"Honestly, nervous I know Zaira acted like she was the Queen, and I really don't want to deal with petty fights because of it. I won't deal with it, so if they start, I am probably gonna hurt some feelings."

"They need to accept that you are my Queen and Alessia is my Princess. It doesn't matter what they say, what we decide is the final word. We are the King and Queen of the Italian Mafia. And I trust you to deal with the ladies being catty bitches," he tells me with a smirk on his lips. I throw my head back and laugh, knowing he is referring to when I beat Zaira's ass for slapping Alessia.

I pull his hands away from my waist and stand up. "I am going to go get ready."

As I start walking away, he grabs my hand and pulls me back into his chest. I look up at him. "You forgot something?" he says.

I play dumb, pretending I don't know what he wants. "Nope, I didn't," I say with a cheeky grin. He just puts one hand in the back of my hair and the other one on my cheek and kisses me. He dominates the kiss holding me exactly the way he wants, and his tongue tastes every part of my mouth. I try to keep up with him but as soon as it starts, it is over.

He pulls away, smirking at my flushed face, and says, "Now you can leave." And he gently pushes me to the door and taps my ass as I walk out the door.

I turn around, glare at him, and mumble, "Ass man." He is always looking for a way to have his hand on or near my ass.

He laughs at my comment and says, "You know it, baby." I roll my eyes but sway my hips to give him something to look at. I hear him groan. "Damn, the woman is an evil vixen. I need another cold shower." I laugh as I walk out of the door.

When I walk into Julietta's room, I see Alessia coming out of the bathroom and walking over to sit in front of Julietta's vanity. I smile and kiss her cheek. "How do you want your hair, baby girl?"

She signs to me, "I want it to have princess curls."

I nod at her, and Julietta tells me, "Go shower. I will start working on her hair. I was thinking of putting it in a high bun with some curls to frame her face."

I nod, smiling at her. "That sounds perfect. Thanks, Julietta."

"Of course. Now shoo." I shake my head, laughing as I walk out and head to my room. As I was in the shower, I hoped that the party would be successful without any drama, but I know I am holding my breath. I get out of the shower and change into a pair of booty shorts and a tank top to get ready. I grab my dress and heels, then go to Alessia's room to get her dress and shoes. She is so excited that she is wearing "fancy" shoes, which are a pair of baby sparkly heels.

I walk in, and Alessia has her hair all done with lip gloss on. I look at Julietta. "You know Mateo is gonna be pissed about the lip gloss" I say chuckling.

She shrugs her shoulders. "Oh well. She is a little girl who can wear lip gloss. Now, what are we doing with your hair?"

I smirk, knowing how Mateo loves my hair down. "I want it down with soft curls. With simple make-up." I say the last part while shooting her a look because this girl loves to go overboard.

"Perfect, and yes, I know, Miss Simple," she says, rolling her eyes. She has been trying to break me out of my comfort zone with my clothes and make up, but I have yet to budge. I give Alessia her tablet so she sits still while I finish getting ready then I can get us both dressed. About an hour later, Julietta is finished, and I swear she needs to open her own salon. I can't believe this is me as I gawk at myself in the mirror. I look beautiful.

"Wow, I can't believe I look this beautiful."

Julietta stands next to me and says, "But you are beautiful, on the inside and outside. I am so glad you are my sister-in-law and not some stuck-up bitch. You are gonna make every girl jealous tonight." Then she starts getting herself ready. I continue to look at myself and tell myself that I can do this. I turn my focus back to finishing getting ready.

"Ready to put your dress and shoes on?" I ask Alessia. She looks up and nods at me. I kiss her cheek and grab her dress out of the closet. I help her step into her royal blue dress and slide it up her body. I have her put her arm through the strap since she is wearing a one-strap tulle princess dress. The top half has jewels and a royal blue belt with a brooch in the middle. After I zip up her dress, I help her step into her baby heels. She is smiling at herself in the mirror, admiring herself as she twirls around. My dress is an elegant, off the shoulder, lace mermaid with lace sleeves. I kept running my hands over my dress. It still seems unreal that this is our life now. I sit down and put on my black open-toe strappy stilettos.

We hear a knock at the door, and Julietta opens it to see Mateo looking very sexy in a black suit with a royal blue tie. He kisses Julietta on the cheek. "You look beautiful Julietta."

She smiles at him and says, "Thank you Mateo. You look very handsome as well."

Mateo turns and looks at me; he is just staring at me, speechless. Until Alessia walks up to him, which seems to snap him back to reality. "Wow, Princess, you are absolutely beautiful." He grabs her hand and twirls her around; she giggles at him.

When she faces Mateo again, he kneels in front of her and opens a box, and inside is a tiara. He takes it out of the box and puts it in her hair. He kisses her forehead saying, "A diamond tiara for my princess's first ball." I was going to protest giving her a diamond tiara, but if having the tiara helps her feel more confident tonight, then so be it.

He stands up, and his eyes slowly survey me from head to toe. I have to bite the inside of my cheek from nervousness, hoping that I look okay. "*Mio Dio. Sei il più assolutamente stupendo. Sono così fortunato che tu sia mia moglie,*"*(My God. You are the most absolutely gorgeous. I am so lucky that you are my wife.)* he says to me as he gives me a quick kiss on my lips.

He reaches into his pocket. "I picked up our rings today." He slides my engagement and wedding band on my finger, and I see he is already wearing his on his hand.

I look at him. "You know you really didn't have to spend a lot of money on my rings."

He pulls me in for a hug while chuckling, "Another reason I am lucky to have you, my darling. You don't want me for my money, and you are so humble. You are just happy with simple things." I just shrug my shoulders, but he knows the reason why I enjoy the simple things.

I start to walk towards the door, but he grabs my wrist and pulls me to his chest. I look up at him. "That's not all I got you." I start to tell him he didn't need to, but he stops me. "I know I didn't have to, but I wanted to. Now turn around." I do, and we are facing the mirror. Mateo puts a beautiful diamond necklace around my neck. I run my finger over the huge diamond.
   "It's beautiful," I whispered.
   Mateo kisses the behind my ear and whispers, "Not as beautiful as you." I blush but try to not look at him, he kisses my blushed cheek and chuckles. Alessia is watching us from the door with a smile on her face.
   I grab Alessia's hand and start walking to the limo together, with Mateo holding my other hand. It takes us a little longer because Alessia is being careful on the steps. When we get outside and into the limo, the rest of the De Luca family members are there, and they gush over Alessia and me. I compliment them back.
   It doesn't take us long to arrive at the one of Mateo's hotels that is hosting the ball. When we arrive, the paparazzi are already going crazy. Mateo signals Nonno and Nonna to go first then Julietta, Adriano, Salvatore, and Vincenzo will go after them. We will go after they all have exited the car. Mateo set up this ball with other Mafia families and other legal business partners. He did this hoping to get the Russian's to come out of hiding. He told me when he originally brought up the ball to me that he refused to play this cat and mouse game anymore. We have extra security; some we can see and some we cannot see, which makes me feel more comfortable.
   When Mateo gets out of limo and walks around to my side of the limo and opens the door, I am blinded by the lights from their cameras. He sticks out his hand as he smiles at me, I put my hand in his as he gently pulls me out of the car. And the questions start. "Who is this? Mr. De Luca, is this your latest conquest? What about Zaira Bianchi?" Then one of them sees our wedding rings and starts shooting questions about us being married and if we are only married because I am pregnant.
   Mateo smiles at me, kissing my cheek, and turns to the paparazzi. "I will answer all questions later."
   Mateo then sticks out his other hand back inside the limo for Alessia. She looks up at both of us, and we nod at her. When she gets out, the paparazzi absolutely lose it, wondering who Alessia is to Mateo. I look at her, and she comes over to me and hides behind my dress, I keep her face hidden and rub her back. At this moment, I am very grateful Mateo has security to keep the paparazzi back. We continue to ignore the questions and walk in.
   As soon as we are inside the ballroom, Alessia goes off with Nonno and Nonna. Once I see she is settled, Mateo takes me around and

introduces me to different Mafia families and their high-ranking members, along with other business partners. When I see Jose and Esmeralda, I hug them both. We catch up, and they are happy that we both are doing well and are happy. I swear Mateo was holding his breath when I was telling Esmeralda everything. Maybe he is afraid of her, she is a bit crazy. Okay she is really crazy, but I love her regardless of her having a few screws loose.

We meet back up with the De Luca family members and chat with them for a while. I notice that Marcello has been keeping a close eye on Julietta a lot more. I will have to ask her about that later, he might be the capo she is sneaking kisses from. Right now is not the time to ask her, especially since her overprotective brother has his hand around my waist.

Mateo leans over and whispers to me, "Go get Alessia and meet me by the stage where the band is playing."

I nod at him and walk over to Alessia, bending down to her level and looking her in the eye. "Baby girl, it is time to come stand with Papa and me on the stage. Remember what we talked to you about. You just smile and wave, you don't have to say anything, let us do the talking. If you get scared, you look at Julietta, Nonno, Nonna, Zio Adriano, Zio Salvatore, or Zio Vincenzo, okay?" She nods at me, and I stand up, we walk over to the side of the stage. Mateo is on the stage with the microphone in his hand and smiles at us.

The doors bust open, and I see Zaira walk in. I groan, knowing she is going to start drama. I swear, entitled brat is her middle name. I look at her dress. What the hell is she wearing? We are at a ball, and she is dressed like she is going to a club. Zaira is wearing a neon green, short strappy dress. It is one-sleeved with a thick strap across her lower boobs, a thinner strap above her belly button, and two thicker straps, one on her lower hip, and a bottom strap on her mid-thigh, with gladiator heels. She is barely covering anything. I turn Alessia to my side so she doesn't see her or that pathetic excuse of a dress.

"What are you doing here, Zaira?" Mateo asks with a bit of an edge to his voice.

She smiles sweetly at him, "I came here for our announcement, of course, baby."

He glares at her. "I have no announcement that involves you, and if I remember correctly, I told you almost a year ago, after you slapped my daughter in my house, you were kicked out of my house, and I never wanted you around my family."

She tries to walk up to the other side of the stage, but security blocks her. "We all know that was a misunderstanding, darling. It is me you want, not some whore and her bastard child."

Mateo responds, "I would be careful of what you are saying, Miss Bianchi."

I have had enough and decide to make my appearance. I hand Alessia over to Marcello and walk up to the stage with my head held high. Mateo hears me walk up the stage, he walks over to me, and I give him a small nod that I am okay. He holds his hand out for me, and I grab his hand. We walked back to the center of the stage.

"Honestly, Zaira, if he wanted to marry you, he would have. You were around years before Mateo knew me, but obviously, he didn't want you. I won't stand here and ridicule you or your character because I refuse to do that unless absolutely necessary." Mateo squeezes my hand and security escorts Zaira out.

"You are making a mistake; she is just a whore. She will tarnish your reputation." She is trying to fight them off her, she is calling me all kinds of names. I keep a blank face until we can no longer see her after she is through the doors. But she is loud as she is throwing her tantrum.

Mateo starts to speak now that we no longer hear her. "Now, before I was rudely interrupted," he turns to where Alessia is standing with Marcello. "Princess, please come here." Alessia runs up to Mateo, and he picks her up and sits her on his hip as he stands next to me. "I would like to introduce to you, my wife and daughter. Emilia and Alessia De Luca." He says as he kisses both of our cheeks. "Now, if anyone has any questions, I will only answer a few." We stand there as Mateo explains how we were seeing each other for a couple of months before we had a very small and intimate ceremony. And that we have stayed out of the press this long because of Alessia and how I didn't feel comfortable with her in the spotlight. Then he goes into explaining his new business project with his casinos.

Once that is done, people start dancing. Adriano is dancing with Alessia; she is standing on his shoes which is so adorable. I feel Mateo grab my hand and kiss it softly, "May I have this dance, Mrs. De Luca?"

"Of course, Mr. De Luca." He leads me to the dance floor, and we are slow dancing. I look at him and say, "Well, the evening went a bit differently than we expected."

He chuckles. "Yeah, you could say that. I was hoping she would take my warning and stay away, but now I have to deal with her," he says bitterly.

"How about I deal with her? Plus, if I do it, her anger will come out and when her anger gets too much, she will spill. I want to make sure she hasn't done anything to betray our family." He agrees and kisses me lightly on the lips. We enjoy the rest of the song dancing together, and for the next song, Alessia asks Mateo to dance with her. He agrees and they start dancing with her on his feet. I laugh and walk back to my seat with Adriano. I can tell, about halfway through the dance she is getting tired since it is way past her bedtime, but she refuses to stop. Mateo, being the doting father he is, picks her up so her head is resting on his shoulder and continues to sway with her as they dance together. He walks back to us; she is finally asleep at the end of the next song.

A couple of people smile at the sight of them. We say goodbye to Joe and Esmeralda. I can't wait to visit them again, but that will have to wait until after this Russian Mafia War is over. We decide to head back to the mansion to put her to bed. We climbed back in the limo with her fast asleep on Mateo the whole time. We don't talk but enjoy the moment of peace.

Once we are back at the mansion, we both put her to bed after changing her out of her dress and wish her a good night. We got ready for bed and laid down in with me wrapped in Mateo's arms. Hopefully tonight I don't get any nightmares.

FOURTEEN

ZAIRA

I can't believe Mateo would throw me out of the ball. Me! I am a perfect model, someone with status. I will make him look good. Unlike that whore. He has a special announcement, and as his future wife, I should be by his side. After the guards roughly escort me out of the building, of course, the paparazzi are there. I ignore them and try to flirt my way back in. "Boys, now we all know I belong inside, so step aside and let me back in."

"No, Miss Bianchi. Boss said that you are not welcome back inside the hotel tonight." One of the security guards grabbed my arm and turned me around, away from the hotel. "Oh, and all of the security guards are aware you are not welcomed back in, so don't even bother."

I glare at him and storm off. In the next moment, paparazzi swarm me and starts bombarding me with questions, and I smirk, thinking I either have Mateo play into my hands or give his publicists a mess to clean up from.

"Why were you kicked out?"

"Are you his mistress?"

"Why are you wearing such a scandalous dress to a formal event?"

Ok, that one was rude, I will have Mateo deal with them later, but I started to answer questions.

"To answer your questions, Mateo needs to clear up a misunderstanding between him and that other woman. She is trying to blackmail him into being with her but doesn't want me near that awful woman. He was trying to protect my image. As you can see, we are engaged, and we will soon release details of our marriage. Have a great night." I show them my ring, and I turn to enter my car. I smirk to myself, yes, the engagement ring he didn't buy, but that is okay. He obviously needs a bit of encouragement to have me become his wife. Abramo promised me after I helped him kidnap Lilyana. She confronted me that I was sleeping with Abramo and she is all about being honest and loyal in a relationship. Lilyana should have kept her nose out of my business, and she wouldn't be in so much pain. I have never done that because you can get what you want from any man when you sleep with them. I have been sleeping with Abramo since I was in high school. He said I was lucky to have his cock in me at all. Granted, he was never gentle to me but the money and knowing I will be Mrs. Mateo De Luca is worth it in the end, so my plan can work.

I will have so much power and money once we get married, and then Alexei will be able to take down the Italian Mafia. I honestly don't want anything to do with the De Luca's, but I was chosen at sixteen to become close. Kidnapping Lilyana was worth biting my tongue, being her friend. I could barely stand her; she was a bitch, but the look of hatred I saw on her face when I saw her in the cell with a big pregnant belly was worth it. I had to wait months to see her in Russia, and I had to play the grieving friend. It would have been better if I could have gotten a video of Salvatore sleeping with me, but the fucker was still hung up on his "one and only true love." Gag me, please, there is no such thing as love.

I climb into my Mercedes Benz and drive home to my condo to relax and wait for Mateo to do the right thing and get rid of the trash. I get home and change into cotton booty shorts with a crop top tank top. I go pour myself a glass of wine and sit down to watch the news and see what Mateo's "big news is." Of course, the paparazzi makes me look like I am some crazy obsessed psycho. I will have Mateo fix that.

I take another sip of my wine when I hear Mateo say, **"Now before I was rudely interrupted, I would like to introduce to you, my wife and daughter. Emilia and Alessia De Luca."**

I spit out my wine. I yell out in the room, "What the fuck is this bullshit? Fuck, Alexei is gonna be pissed at me. Fuck." Not even a minute later, my phone rings, and I see Alexei's name.

Alexei: Why the hell am I seeing Mateo is married, and it is not to you?

Zaira: I don't know, Alexei. It has been basically a year since I have been around the De Luca's for slapping that freak.

Alexei: And whose fault is that?

Zaira: Yes, I know, but I figured by now he would have gotten over his temporary lust over the whore.

Alexei: Obviously, you were wrong AGAIN. Twice you have made yourself look like a fool. It seems like I picked the wrong slut to do the job. How hard can it be for you to seduce him and open your legs or mouth for him?

Zaira: You think I haven't tried? I have told you he only sees me as a sister because of Roman. I would send him nudes, and he would just block my number.

Alexei: Mateo will call you in to meet and discuss the stunt you pulled tonight. You will threaten him to marry you, or there will be consequences. You better get the job done. I will release one of the many recordings of Emilia being raped.

Zaira: I won't disappoint you.

Alexei: Contact me when you hear from the De Luca's.

Then he hangs up the phone.

I chuck my empty glass of wine against the wall and storm into my bedroom. I call the maid and tell her to clean up the mess. If Mateo embarrassing me in front of everyone tonight wasn't bad enough, I then got a text from my modeling manager.

"What the hell was that stunt your supposed fiancé' did tonight? He just trashed your image. His publisher just informed me that you are not engaged to him. You look like you are obsessed with him, and this will destroy your career. I will have to do some major damage control. You shouldn't have commented back to the paparazzi. I may not be able to get you out of this one."

I text him back, "Do the job you are paid to do. I will call you tomorrow."

I want to go to a club and find someone to hook up with, but I need to play the loyal fiancée card, so the public believes my story. I pull out my dildo and pretend it is Mateo's big cock inside of me.

After I take care of myself, I get in bed and get some sleep so I can deal with getting rid of Emilia and Alessia, even if I have to kill them myself.

I wake up to multiple messages on my phone from Lucilla and other friends of mine. They can't believe Mateo married Emilia and adopted Alessia. They agree with me that they do not belong next to Mateo. I responded back to them that I would have to make him realize his mistake soon. I look and see an angry text from Roman, saying how I have embarrassed our family name again. I roll my eyes at his text and ignore it because it will turn into a fight. He doesn't care about what I want, just about the family name. Our name is already ruined with Papa in jail and Mama, who is a whore.

I need to save my energy for dealing with the De Luca's. I saw an email from Gary Stultz, Mateo's publicist, telling me to meet him at Mateo's office at one o'clock this afternoon. I decided to email him back and tell him I would not meet with him unless Mateo was there. Not even five minutes later, I get a response back that Mateo would be there. I emailed him back and let him know I would be there. I text Alexei.

Zaira: I am meeting Mateo at one o'clock this afternoon.
Alexei: Don't fuck this up, slut. This is your last chance.
Zaira: Of course. Talk to you after the meeting.

I lounge around for a bit and start getting ready to go meet Mateo. I decided to dress in an off-the-shoulder black lace dress that stops mid-thigh and has a small slit on the right side with black stilettos. I must look good for my fiancé. I leave my condo, and as expected, the paparazzi are outside. I just smile at them and tell them I will respond to all questions later. I drove myself to De Luca Corp. Soon, I will have my own personal driver when I marry Mateo.

I don't bother to check in at the front entrance. I just get in the elevator and hit the 75th floor button. I check my makeup and hair with my mirror as I wait for the elevator to get to the floor. I pay no mind to other people getting on the elevator, until I can feel eyes on me. I put my mirror back in my purse, and I look to see who has their eyes on me. I gag. He is an old man with a huge belly and greasy hair.

He smiles at me. "Hello, beautiful. You must be new here. I would remember an angel like you."

I roll my eyes at him and lift my hand up to show him my engagement ring. "Keep your disgusting eyes and hands off me. I am engaged to your boss."

He chuckles and says, while he is stepping off the elevator, "Well then I wonder why we had a meeting this morning when he introduced his wife and daughter to us."

I shake my head, thinking how much work he is giving our poor publicists to do. The elevator finally gets to the 75th floor, and I see his personal assistant Heather roll her eyes at me. I could never stand the old bitch; she always gets in my way when I have come to see Mateo.

"You can sit and wait for Mr. De Luca, " she tells me before I can say anything.

I lean over her desk and point my finger at her and say, "No. I will be walking into his office. I got an email from Mr. Stultz stating. I have a meeting with Mateo."

She grabs my wrist "First, don't point your fingers at me; god only knows where they have been. And second, Mr. De Luca was the one who told me to have you wait until he calls for you. Now sit down before I call security."

I walk away, but halfway to my seat I turn and tell her, "When I become Mrs. De Luca the first thing I will do is have you fired." She raises her eyebrow at me and then goes back to work.

I sat down and watched all the news coverage of the ball last night on my phone. Finally, after ten minutes of waiting, I hear Heather's phone ring. She answers, "Of course, Mateo, I will send her in," and hangs up the phone.

I smirk at her and walk into his office. As I open the door, I say loud enough so Heather can hear, "Mateo, darling. Your assistant needs to be fired. She is very rude to your fiancée." Before I can sit down, I look at who is sitting behind his desk, and in his chair is none other than Emilia. Mateo is standing behind her with his hands on her shoulders. "What is this bitch doing here?"

Mateo starts to rub her shoulders and kisses her head. She smiles up at him, I am about to go rip her away from him when he looks up at me. "Zaira, I was nice a year ago when you slapped my daughter, and I told you to not contact me or my family. Which you broke when you kept sending me nudes from different numbers. I overlooked that because of Roman, but after last night, I will not be lenient anymore."

"Mateo, you are making a mistake marrying her and adopting that freak," I tell him while leaning forward in my chair. I look to see

Emilia throwing a glare in my direction while she is grabbing the sides of the chair so tightly that her knuckles are turning white.

"*Rilassa la mia Regina. La gestirò.*"(Relax my Queen. I will handle her.)

I just smirk at her. She wishes she had a sexy body like mine. Then I hear him call her his Queen; what the fuck? She is not a Queen. A peasant, yes, but not a Queen. I then frowned at them.

Mateo glares at me. "Insult my daughter or wife one more time, and I will have you join Abramo and Eleanor."

I just gave a small smile to Mateo; this must all be an act. "How do we even know if you got married? No one in our close circle was at a wedding for you two," I say with a smirk.

Mateo grabs a folder and hands it to me. It was a copy of their marriage certificate and Alessia's adoption papers. "Again, no one was there. This could be fake."

Mateo rolls his eyes at me and grabs his iPad off his desk. He turns it on and hands it to me. It shows the De Luca family all in their backyard with the family pastor doing an Italian wedding. When the ceremony was over, they called Alessia up to the temporary altar, which was ugly. Mateo asks her ,"Alessia would you like to be my daughter and have the same last name as Mama and me?" She nods at him, and quietly you hear her say, "Yes, Papa," so the freak can talk.

"So, you had an official ceremony? Why didn't you invite any of the capos or any of your business partners?"

Emilia responds back, "Our reasons for having a private ceremony are really not your business but that is the way we wanted it." It must have been for show and not real.

With that thought, I stand up; I walk up to the front of his desk and look down at Emilia. "I have no idea what you blackmailed him with, but you need to end this now. He is mine! You are just a used whore, and your daughter is nothing more than an unwanted bastard child."

She stands up, gently pushing the chair away from her, and stands right in front of me, so we are eye to eye. "You are right. I was used for other men's pleasure against my will to protect my daughter. You are just bitter because the man you have been obsessing over for years continuously turned you down. You cannot get it through your head that he doesn't have any interest in you."

That just sends my temper over the edge, and I go to slap her, but she grabs my wrist with one hand, stopping me, and punches me in my nose with the other. "Ow. You are fucking psycho," I say, grabbing my bleeding nose.

"Emilia, I told you not to touch her," he says in a stern tone.

"Well, it was self-defense. She tried to slap me first."

I look up at her, smirking at him and him shaking his head. "You are too feisty for your own good my tigress." She just shrugs her shoulders; he kisses her cheek.

"Quit being cute with her; she doesn't deserve it. It is me who you need to be sweet with. I am your fiancée; I was promised by your father years ago, and I will be damned if I let some whores take that away from me," I yell at him while showing my ring to them.

"Wow, your desperation went to a new level. Buying your own engagement ring, is honestly sad, Zaira," Emilia says to me while making a sad face. I finally have enough. I take my gun out of my purse and aim it at Emilia.

"Zaira, you just signed your death certificate by pointing your gun at Emilia," Mateo says.

"No. I am getting rid of the problem." I go to pull the trigger, but the gun is removed from my hands by security. I feel my hands being restrained behind my back. I try to fight out of the hold they have on me. "Mateo, please tell them they need to let me go." I am being dragged away. I look up at them one more time when I say, "Mateo you are making a big mistake, she will only bring your reputation down."

He shakes his head. "No, Zaira, she will not. She is a true Queen. Yes, she has scars on her body, but that doesn't make her less beautiful. It shows how strong she is and how she will sacrifice herself for her family, and that is a true Queen. Unlike you, who is so vain about looks, you would put anyone and everyone else in front of you to save yourself. That is not someone who I want to stand beside me. Her heart is pure gold, yours is nothing but a black hole." He looks to his security and tells them, "Take her in my private elevator, and she can join Abramo and Eleanor."

My heart feels like it falls to my stomach. I keep my face blank, but I yell at them, "You both will regret this," as I am dragged into the elevator. They don't respond to me and the door closes. I finally look and see it is Dante and Nicolo, along with Raffaele. I put on my best seduction eyes and say, "Please let me go. I promise I will disappear. I will do anything you want."

Raffaele just glares down at me with the most hated look possible, which has me shivering in fear. "You must think we are stupid. We will not go against the Don or Donna, and we heard all the shit you were spewing in there."

I then realize I am going to die and start to cry. "Quit crying, or I will gag you. I don't want to hear your whiny voice." I keep crying, and he finally has enough and gags my mouth. I tried to fight against the gag, but with Dante and Nicolo holding me still, it didn't work. When the elevator opened, they placed me in the back of the van between Nicolo and Dante.

At this point, I am sobbing regardless of what happens. I either die by Mateo or die by Alexei for failing him again. I honestly don't know which is worse. They are both known to be ruthless with their victims. Alexei would probably make me a prostitute in one of his brothels or be a punching bag, but Mateo is still torturing Eleanor, Abramo, and the guard who beat Emilia over a year ago. Since I slapped Alessia and pulled a gun out on Emilia, I feel like his torture will be long.

  I just hope Alexei has her rape tape on the news soon. It will be worth all the pain and torture I will go through. The world will finally see her for the whore she is.

FIFTEEN
MATEO

After Zaira was escorted out of my office, it was just Emilia and me. I walked past her and locked my office door, so we would not be disturbed. Every time this woman stands up for herself or our family, she turns me on. It takes all my control not to devour my wife right where she stands. I turned around, and she was glaring at me, challenging me to do something. Especially with our conversation, we had earlier about how she wouldn't be caught doing something intimate in my office, I am going to prove her wrong on that. I have many ideas on how to have her in not just my home office but in all my offices, especially my clubs.

I walk past her and call Heather on the intercom and tell her I am not to be disturbed for the next hour unless it is an emergency, she nods.

I turn to see Emilia glaring at me. "I already told you, Mr. De Luca, I will not be caught in any intimate position in your office," she tells me with her arms folded across her chest and her hip cocked to the side a bit.

"Well, Mrs. De Luca, my office is soundproof, and the door is locked." I start stalking her like she is my prey. She starts backing up and brings her closer to the wall. Perfect. Just where I want my wife.

When her back hits the wall, she mumbles. "Fuck," to herself. I smack her ass for cussing. She raises an eyebrow at me. "Can you stop smacking my ass?" I smack it again just a bit harder this time.

"Then stop cursing. I told you dirty words like that should not be leaving such a pretty mouth." She is about to respond when I put my hand firmly around her throat and put my leg between her legs. I look her in the eyes like I am going to devour her soul which I show her when I kiss her. I don't go in for the soft, gentle kiss. I go in and push my tongue between her lips and taste every part of her mouth. I move my hand from her throat to the back of her head, so I can angle it to get better access to her whole mouth. She wraps her arms around my neck, and one of her hands grabs onto my hair. I groan in her mouth, and I slowly grind myself onto her. She grips my hair tighter; I leave her mouth and start kissing her jaw, and as I get next to her ear, I whisper to her, "Jump."

She does, and I catch her thighs and have her wrap them around my waist. I don't hold back and grind harder onto her; she throws her head back against the wall, moaning my name. Every noise she makes sends a jolt to my cock. I keep kissing my way down to her collarbone. She turns her head slightly to give me better access to her neck. I kiss harder on the spot between her shoulder and neck, and she starts to grind back onto me. Oh, fuck does it feels wonderful to have her willing to want me as bad as I want her. I decide I am going to taste my wife on my desk; since she isn't ready for me to sink my hard cock in her doesn't mean I can't enjoy tasting her. I hungrily place my lips back on hers as I walk us over to my desk. I toss my papers to the ground as I lay her on my desk.

"Mateo, you better not make Heather organize those for you," she tells me with a glare.

"Of course not, *mia Regina*." I kiss down her chest as I undo each button on her shirt. Once they are all open, I go and suck on her nipple through her bra as I keep grinding on her.

She moans out, "Yes, Mateo." I unclasp her bra and start sucking on her nipple like I was a starving man, and I play and tease her other nipple between my thumb and pointer finger. "Don't stop," she moans out as she throws her head further back into my desk, if that is possible.

I switch so both tits get the same amount of attention because that wouldn't be fair. Once I feel like I have given both nipples the proper attention. I continue kissing the way down to her pussy. I grab her by her thighs, so her juicy ass is on the edge of my desk. I pull her skirt up so it is bunched around her waist. I pull my chair, so I can sit down to be at eye level with her pussy. Her breath intakes as I grab her thong and rip it off her body.

"Mateo," Emilia shrieks but starts to groan. She shutters in pleasure. I continue to devour her clit. I go back and forth between licking and sucking on her clit. While I am doing that, my finger grazes over her hole and she shivers against me, and that is when I enter her with two fingers. I move my fingers in and out of her. She moans out, "Oh God, please don't stop."

Pulling my mouth from her clit, I respond back, "No darling, I am not God. I am the devil."

I go back down, but I don't go to her clit. I start leaving my mark on her upper thighs right by her pussy. She starts wiggling against me for some kind of friction to ease the ache between her perfect long legs, and I decide to relieve a bit of her torture and add a third finger and switch from plunging my fingers in and out of her pussy to moving my fingers in a curling motion hitting her G-spot.

"Oh, Mateo. Yes, right there." I can tell she is close with her legs shaking next to my head, so I decide to not torture her this time and drag out her orgasm, and I gently bite down on her clit. That sends her over the edge, and she screams out, "Mateoooo," as she is still coming down from her high. I gently lick and kiss her clit to soothe where I bit it, then I remove my fingers and lick them clean. I am not about to waste a drop of her nectar. I watch her as she lies there catching her breath. She looks up at me with a content smile.

I can't help but lean down and gently kiss her lips. She responds to me and wraps her hands around my neck. I sit us both up so she is sitting on my desk. She starts to unbutton my shirt, and after she has my shirt, my bare chest is exposed. She slowly runs her hands down my chest exploring every grove and divot of my muscles. She plays with the waistband of my pants, and I must control myself from throwing her down on my desk and tasting her all over again. She completely catches me by surprise by taking both of her hands and unbuckling my belt.

I pull away from the kiss and grab her hands while looking her in the eyes. "I am not expecting anything in return."

She just smirks at me and says, "I know you're not, but I am ready to start exploring my *marito diavolo (devil husband)*."

She takes her hands out of my hands and quickly unbuttons and unzips my pants. And she drops to her knees in front of me. I suck in a breath as she runs one of her nails from the head of my cock all the way to the base. She barely hasn't done anything, and I already feel like I could cum as fast as a teenager, granted it has been almost a year since I have been with a woman. I look down at her at her, at me with those deep green eyes, and fuck, she is the most beautiful woman in the world. I run my hand down from her cheek to her lips and slowly trace her lips with my thumb. She opens her mouth and starts sucking on my thumb.

"Fuck, Emilia," I groan at her, and at that moment is when she pulls my boxers down and is slowly moving her hand up and down my shaft. She lets go of my thumb with a pop and starts licking all around the head of my cock, licking off all my pre cum. She started taking more of me in her mouth, I couldn't hold back anymore and tossed my head back against the back of my chair.

"Fucking hell, Emilia. You have barely gone down on me, and I already feel like I could cum." She just chuckles, which sends a vibration through my body, I grab the sides of the chair to hold myself from fucking her mouth. I will not be rough on her when she is choosing to do this for me. She let's go of my shaft and grabs my hands and moves them to the side of her head. Her mouth is so damn soft, but she is literally attacking my cock with her mouth. She is going so fast on me; I look down at her, and she takes my cock out of my mouth.

"Don't hold back *il mio re,*" *(my king)* she tells me.

I ask her, "Are you sure?"

She nods her head and looks me in the eyes. "Yes, my king, unleash the devil on my mouth."

I look down at her. "Stop me if you start going back to your safe place, I never want you to go there when we are together." She nods at me and goes further down on me. "Fuck, my wife loves my cock, huh?" She looks up at me and nods her head while sucking on me. I grab the side of her head and start to fuck her mouth as she sucks on me.

I groan, and she looks down at us, but I tell her, *"Tieni gli occhi su di me. Voglio che tu guardi cosa mi fai."* (Keep your eyes on me. I want you to watch what you do to me.)

She does exactly as she is told and keeps her eyes locked on mine. I increase my speed; I am trying not to embarrass myself for cuming too fast, but once she has all of me down, her throat sucks hard and grabs my balls. I am done for. *"Fanculo alla mia regina, hai la bocca di una dea"* (Fuck my Queen you have a mouth of a goddess,) I tell her as I cum down her throat, I keep my eyes on her as she swallows it. She slowly releases me from her mouth but cleans me up with her mouth. I pulled her head away from me. "If you don't want me to take you again, you better stop that, regardless of how enjoyable that was." She giggles at me; I pull her up to her feet and pull my pants back up to my hips.

I grab her and throw her over my shoulder. "MATEO! Put me down, you caveman." I slap her ass and laugh when she tries to kick me, I just hold her legs down, and she gives up a huff at me. I sit her down on the bathroom sink, grab a washcloth from under the sink and start to wipe her clean. She should know after each time we are intimate, I will take care of her.

"Don't give me that look. You are my Queen, and I will take care of you in every way possible." She gives me a small smile while shaking my head.

"I know I am still getting used to it. I just got used to being used and pushed away after."

I lean down and kiss her head. "Never again. You are Emilia De Luca, my Queen, and will be treated like one. Anyone who doesn't will have to answer to me." I kiss her cheek. "But I am proud of you for how far you have come in under a year."

"Yes, but you have been so patient with me with each step I take. I also feel safe with you."

I smile at her "And I will continue to be with you each step of the way."

After we were both cleaned up and redressed, she sits on my lap and snuggles into my chest while I sit at my desk, finishing the never-ending pile of paperwork. While I was doing my paperwork, she was running her fingers through my hair when I felt her stop. I look down and see her asleep on my chest with her arms wrapped around my neck. Her head is tucked into my shoulder. I smile down at how adorable she is kissing the top of her head. I very quietly call Heather; I tell her to try and keep everyone out of my office so Emilia can get some sleep. She still struggles with her nightmares but refuses to sleep after Alessia is awake. Unless I force her to. And she refuses to take any kind of sleep medication. She is too stubborn, but hopefully, she will sleep for a bit until I send her home with Sergio. I pull her closer to me as I continue to work on my paperwork; she nuzzles her head into my shoulder when I move her. After another hour, I see my door open, and my cousins walk in. Salvatore gives me a sad smile saying without words he is happy for us, but he misses Lilyana. Hell, we all miss her. She was like another little sister, Julietta looked up to her, but Lilyana never complained about her hanging with us regardless that she was younger than us. Lilyana would want to spend time alone with Julietta. She truly was an angel.

Vincenzo sees us and starts taking pictures. I glare at him, but he just starts cooing at us.

"If you wake her up, I will shoot you." I threaten him, but I didn't realize my Queen had already woken up.

"Then you will have to explain to your princess why her uncle got hurt," she says, and I grumble at her knowing I can't do anything to upset Alessia.

"Now, why are you idiots in my office bothering us?" I was annoyed with them for disturbing my peace with my wife.

"Well, *cugino*, it is almost time for the meeting," Vincenzo says. I sigh, knowing I have to send Emilia home.

"Okay, let me walk Emilia down to Sergio, then I will meet you there." Salvatore nods, but Vincenzo wants to come to bother Sergio. Poor Sergio was our driver as kids, and let's say we made that old man earn every dollar he made.

Sergio sees Vincenzo, and before he can say anything. "Sir, please tell me that you are not torturing me by making me give this fool a ride along with our Queen." I shake my head, chuckling along with Emilia, while Vincenzo has a hand on his chest, acting like he is wounded.

"Sergio, I am hurt you think that low of me."

"I don't think I know how much of a fool you are. I was your driver as you were growing up, remember."

Vincenzo looks at me, and we just smirk. "We kept things interesting."

Sergio glared at him, "Not the three of you caused me stress and scared off every assistant your grandfather hired to help me."

"Unfortunately, you won't be enjoying my company today. I just decided to accompany the love birds down here to see you."

I push Vincenzo back towards the elevator. "Go help your brother so I can say goodbye to my wife."

He pouts at me, says goodbye to Emilia, and tells her to inform Alessia that their movie date is still on tonight. I roll my eyes at him, not sure if the movie is for him or Alessia. I hear Emilia giggle at him, but she gets in the SUV when Sergio opens the door for her.

I bend down, buckle her seatbelt, and give her a kiss. "Let me know when you get home safe."

"Of course, Mr. Overprotective." I chuckle and kiss her one more time before shutting her door.

Vincenzo snickers at me when I catch up to him in the elevator, I look over at him. "What?" He shakes his head.

"I thought this was only going to be a business marriage."

I chuckle, knowing that is what I had originally said.

"Yeah, that was my original plan, but those two girls have wrapped me around their fingers."

"Yeah, they are something special. The mansion is livelier and feels like home. It hasn't felt like that since our mama's and Lilyana have been gone."

"Yeah, you're right. Even Nonno and Nonna seem happier." I chuckle at the memories they are making with Alessia.

When we walk off the elevator Salvatore chuckles at us. "Did Sergio enjoy your visit, *fratello*?"

We laugh at Vincenzo's face when he tells Salvatore, "No, he says I was a fool and thought Mateo was torturing him by making me ride with them. I am a perfect gentleman."

That is when Zio snickers behind us, "You three were not gentlemen when you were younger, that man deserves a damn award for dealing with you and your shenanigans. And to be retired, but for some reason, he still wants to work."

We all shrug our shoulders, knowing we can't deny that we were little assholes as kids.

We enter the conference room with the board of directors for De Luca Corp. We're here to discuss our numbers for the past quarter and how they have gone up six percent. Time to go through each department and analyze each team member to decide if we should keep them where they are, move them, or fire them. We do this four times a year, and that is why our company is so successful because a company can only be successful with hardworking employees and a determined boss.

All the board of directors had left, and it was just my uncle and me talking when Heather comes running in, panting. "Mateo, Julietta just called and said you need to get home now. There is an emergency with Emilia."

I run to my office, grab my stuff, and get into the elevator. I get in my car and floor it to my house knowing I am about forty-five minutes away, but I can make it in about twenty. I called Julietta to see what had happened.

Mateo: What happened?

Julietta: We were watching TV together when a piece of breaking news came through, and it was a video of Emilia being raped.

Mateo: CHE CAZZO? Qualcuno morirà (WHAT THE FUCK? Someone is gonna die.) Fuck, how is she?

Julietta: Not good. She has backed herself into a corner, rocking back and forth. She keeps repeating, "Please don't hurt her. I will do anything; just don't hurt her." She won't let anyone near her. I tried to talk to her, but as soon as it happened. She just backed herself into a corner and refused to move.

  Mateo: Figlio di puttana (Mother Fucker!) Where is Alessia?

  Julietta: With Marcello. I told him to keep her away. She doesn't need to see her Mama like this.

  Mateo: No, she doesn't. I am on my way. I will be there as soon as I can.

  I hang up the phone and punch my steering wheel. My poor sweet *moglie* doesn't deserve to have her past all over the news and social media. Whoever did this will pay, they will beg for death, but I will drag it out. No one messes with my Queen without punishment. I call Fabio next so he can work on tracking down the mother fucker who decided to hurt my wife.

  Mateo: Have you seen the breaking news from tonight?

  Fabio: Yes, I saw, and I am already on it. I will call you as soon as I find something.

  Mateo: Thanks, Fabio

  Fabio: Of course, Boss.

  After I get off the phone with him, I call my publicist and tell him to work with Fabio to get this down and taken care of as soon as possible.

  I pull up to the mansion, I don't bother parking my car in the garage. I park it jump out and throw my keys to the butler Valente and tell him to park my car.

  I run into the mansion. When I get to Emilia, the before me feels like someone just put a dagger in my heart. My strong Queen is backed in the corner behind the couch, looking absolutely frightened.

SIXTEEN
MATEO

I see my wife against the wall, curled into a ball, crying, "Please don't hurt her. I will do anything, just don't hurt her." I signal for Julietta to leave, and I have one of my guards watch the door and keep everyone out. Julietta asks me to update her about Emilia later, I nod at her but keep my attention on Emilia. They leave the room, and I immediately walk over to her and sit in front of her gently grabbing her hands with mine. She goes to pull away. I don't let her; I continue to hold her hand and rub my thumbs over the top of her hand. I calmly told her, *"Shh Amore mio. Stai bene, sei qui con Alessia. Lei è al sicuro"(Shh, my love. You're okay, you are here with Alessia. She is safe.) "Non ci sei più" (You are not there anymore.)* For a couple more minutes, I keep repeating comforting words while she continues to rock back and forth while trying to pull my hands away from hers. I continue to sit here with her rubbing my thumbs on top of her hands and gently reassure her that she and Alessia are safe.

After about ten minutes, I feel her grip my hands back and slowly stop rocking. She looks up at me for a moment. She looks confused as she looks around the room tensely. After she has looked around, she sees it is just us in the room alone. You see the tension slowly leave her body uncoils.

She croaks out, "Mateo?"

"Yes, *il mio amore.*" She climbs into my lap, and her body shakes with sobs. I just sit there on the floor with her and just hold her against me as I run my hand up and down her back. *"Shh ti ho preso." (Shh, I got you.)*

After a couple minutes, she mumbles into my shoulder, "Can we go to our room?"

"Of course." I stand up with her arms, she is holding onto my neck tight with her head in my neck and her legs wrapped tightly around my waist. I hold her against me.

I open the door, and the guard nods at us. With her closer to me, I can feel how much she got herself worked up during her flashback; my poor wife was sweating from the fear and anxiety. I see my family in the kitchen as I pass. Nonna goes to ask. I just shake my head at her. I will explain everything to them later. They all look at Emilia with sadness, anger, or tenderness. It really shows how much they have accepted her as family.

I continue walking up to our room as soon as we are in there. I ask her if she wants to take a shower or a bath to wash the sweat off her and help her relax. She barely whispers, "Shower." I kiss her temple, walk into the bathroom, and sit her on the sink. I go and adjust the temperature for her. Once it is at a temperature she will like, I walk back over to her, and she is picking at the end of her shirt, looking at the floor.

I lift her face, so we are making eye contact. "You don't have to say anything right now. Take a shower and collect yourself, then we'll talk after, okay?" She nods at me. "Do you want me to help you get undressed?" She nods again. I smile at her and start by taking off her shirt and unhook her bra but keeping eye contact with her the whole time. I then stand her up and grab her shorts and her panties and bring them down her legs. I lift one leg at a time to have her step out of them. I grab her hand and lead her to the shower.

"Thank you, Mateo."

I shake my head. "You don't have to thank me. I told you I would be here for the good and the bad days. I will go get you some comfortable clothes and sit them on the sink. I will be in our room; just call if you need anything." She nods at me and finally gives me a small smile. I am glad when she is this upset that she can feel comfort with me. I grab her favorite shorts and one of my hoodies that she usually grabs when she is just having a "lazy day." I look at her through the foggy glass bathroom door, and she is just staring at the wall with a blank face. I will give her some time then I will come back and check on her.

I changed out of my suit and into sweatpants and a shirt. I sent my family a text about how Emilia saw a rape tape from when she was being held with Seth, and it set her to have a flashback. And for them to take care of Alessia for tonight and maybe tomorrow, depending on Emilia. I don't bother waiting for a response.

I decide to watch the video myself, even if it angers me. I am hoping for a face I can put a name to. I haven't been able to get my hands on anyone, but maybe this will be the lead we need. The more I watch this, the more my blood starts to boil; he literally bends her arm behind her back to at least dislocate it if not break it. To make matters worse, they have Alessia in the corner of the room blindfolded, listening to Emilia cry out in pain with a fucking knife to her throat. After they finish, they throw Alessia to the ground by her hair. My daughter is crying and shaking from fear. I have to pause it and look up at the ceiling, count back from twenty to calm down because counting to ten isn't enough. I have to do this a couple times; I have enough control to finish watching the video, and you see the bastard throw Emilia down on her bad arm and start beating her. After that, the video ends.

I text Fabio and ask him if he has any updates. He tells me he hasn't found anything on him, and he asks me to ask Emilia if she remembers. I am about to respond when I hear Emilia scream. It is the kind of scream of pure agony. It hits me in the heart. I drop my phone and run into the bathroom. I see Emilia crouching down on the ground, pulling at her hair, and screaming at the top of her lungs. Her knuckles are bloody.

I jump in, fully clothed, and bend down on my knees, pulling her hands away from her head. I make her look at me, and seeing my strong wife this destroyed is absolutely torture. She continues to cry. I stand her up. I hold her in my arms and say, "You are okay. Just let it out." And she sobs into my chest for a good ten minutes, probably a lot longer. I don't say anything. I just hold her, rubbing my hand up and down her back.

When she stops, she tells me, "I can't stand myself. All I am is a whore."

I turned her head to look at me. "Now I know damn well that I must have been hearing things when I heard you call yourself a whore."

She looks at me. "But I am. That video just proved to the world that my body has been used."

I grab her face with both of my hands. "No, you're wrong. Anyone who has half a brain who watched that video will see a strong woman. You were willing to do anything possible to save Alessia. Alessia and our future kids are the luckiest kids in the world to have you as a Mama who has and will do anything to save them. Now let's see what damage you did to your hand, *la mia tigre*" I just held her to me. She mumbles sorry to me. "Why are you saying sorry?"

"You jumped in here and got your clothes soaked."

I chuckled at her "Darling, the clothes can be washed; you are more important than clothes, silly woman."

She gives me a small smile.

"Are you okay if I take my clothes off? They are getting a bit heavy."

"Yeah, I trust you, Mateo. You would never do anything to hurt me."

"Never, *mia Regina*."

After I have stripped myself of my soaking wet clothes. I turn her around so I can start washing her hair. She relaxes into my hands as I rinse her, and I do the same when putting conditioner in her hair. I wash her body as well; even though she has such an amazing body, I don't focus on that.

I go to turn off the water, but her hand grabs mine. "What about you?" I arch my eyebrow, giving her a questioning look. "You need to shower as well, and you are already here." I go to grab my shampoo, but she stops me. "Let me do this, please."

"Sure, darling." I stand looking down, knowing I am too tall but want to get a bit of my sassy wife's attitude to come back.

"Bend down, giant," She huffs out. I chuckle and bend down so she can wash my hair; this woman has magic fingers. The way she runs them through my hair is completely tranquilizing. After she rinses my hair, I stand up, and she washes my body. I try to keep my cock from getting hard but as soon as she washes it, I lose the battle. She shots me a look and I shrug my shoulders.

"What? My sexy wife is naked in the shower in front of me, and her hand is on my cock. I am a man." She rolls her eyes at me with a small smile on her face.

I help her out of the shower and quickly wrap a towel around my waist. Then I turn my attention to Emilia and help her dry her off, and we both get dressed. I walk her to her vanity and start drying her hair with her hair dryer. I am so glad my Ma, not Eleanor, taught me how to treat a lady. She and my Zia drilled into mine, Salvatore, and Vincenzo's heads how our future wife should be treated. I look down at her, and she looks up at me with those big doe eyes, and you can see her emotions all over her face. Hurt, anger, but also comfort, and I would almost say love. I care for my wife; I realize I have fallen in love with her.

Obviously, now is not the time to say anything. Tonight is all about her and helping her come over this bump. I will stand by her side every step. We continue not to say anything while I finish drying her hair. After I finish, I put everything away, bend down and lightly kiss her lips.

I pick her up, and we walk over to the bed; I lay her down. At first, we were lying facing each other. But we both need each other closer, so I shift so she is laying across my chest. She wraps her arms around my chest, holding onto me like an anchor as she lays her head on my heart, listening to it beat. After a couple minutes of peace, I feel tears on my chest, and I feel her body shake lightly from crying. I tilt her head up to look at me.

"Alright, beautiful, what is going on inside that head of yours?" I ask, running my hand through her hair.

"I am worried about how bad I have brought down your reputation from that video being released?"

"Did you volunteer to be put in that situation?" She shakes her head at me. "Words, Emilia,"

"No, I didn't."

"Did you want to be used by many men without your consent?"

"No"

"Okay then. If anything, it will show how strong you are and if anything, I should be bowing and kissing your feet for being allowed in your presence."

"That would be a sight to see," she tells me, and I shake my head and kiss her head. I pull her closer and ask, "Do you know who that was in the video with you?"

"Yeah, the one who was raping me was Alec, and the one holding a knife to Alessia was Ivan. I don't know anything except they would come couple of times a week to Seth's house to rape and beat me."

"That will help Fabio, so hopefully we can catch these two assholes and hopefully they will have loose lips so we can find Seth and Boris. I have to admit that Alexei is doing a good job of hiding those two." I nod.

"Maybe now that you announced that we are married, and you adopted Alessia will anger them, and they will do something rash to leave some kind of hint for us."

"That would be wonderful, but let's talk about your flashback because I know you are trying to avoid it." She looked at me sheepishly, knowing that was exactly what she was doing. She sits up with her legs up to her chest and her arms wrapped around her legs. It is her defense mechanism she uses when she is about to say something that doesn't make her comfortable, or she will clench and unclench her fist.

"After I had Alessia, Ivan and Alec decided they were ready to have fun with me. At first, they would take turns raping me or raping me at the same time. I could block that out, and when I did that, it would piss them off, so that's when they would get creative and find different ways to get reactions out of me. It was severe beatings or they would viciously rape me, which seemed to work for a couple years. They got bored, and the video you saw was the first time they brought Alessia into the room already blindfolded, and I tried everything I could think of to save her from being a part of that but seeing me so upset got them really excited. It was sickening they took turns beating, stabbing me, then raping me so roughly to the point I was bleeding. This went on for hours because they fucked me until they were dry, they said, and Alessia had to be in the room the whole time blindfolded. When they finished, they tossed Alessia and me to the ground. I could barely open my eyes, but I crawled over to untie her blindfold and got the both of us cleaned up and up into the closet that they called our room."

I look up at the ceiling to control my anger after I have counted back from twenty a couple times.

"I am really going to enjoy torturing them. I think they will get to meet Lucifer and Lilith, my tigers. They haven't had any prey in a while," I say with a smirk.

"Do you really have Tigers?"

"Yes, they are on the back of the property. I do want to have them meet both of you." Her eyes look like they are going to pop out of her head. "Relax, they are protective, and I want them to know they have to protect my girls." She nods at me and goes back to talking.

"Why? Why me? I hate feeling so vulnerable. I am tired of acting like I am okay, but I am not."

"Then don't be okay; let it out. Be angry, be sad; it's okay. Emilia, you literally went through hell and have raised an amazing daughter. You don't have to keep it bottled in." I tell her.

"I am afraid to trust people again. If I didn't go back and tell him I was pregnant, we would never suffer the way we did for so long."

"I promise you I will never betray your trust. Don't blame yourself. You had no idea Seth was the way he is. You thought you were doing the right thing. You had no idea how sadistic and evil Seth and Boris are. Stop blaming yourself." She doesn't respond, but that is okay because she puts her head back on my chest. I don't push the conversation anymore, knowing she is mentally exhausted, so I continue to rub her back and hope she will fall asleep.

And she does.

I turn my phone on to vibrate and text back to Fabio the names of the two sick fucks who were in the video, and hopefully, with the name and how they are close to Seth and Boris, it will help us get our hands on them sooner. Fabio says he is still working to track the video, but it looks like it is coming from Russia. Gary says he wants to hold a press conference with Emilia and me about the video. I tell him I will have to talk to her because the press can be brutal, and her past is not pretty.

After I had answered and texted everyone, including updating my family, I sat my phone back on my end table.

As I lay there thinking about the past couple of days, I keep thinking back to Zaria's threat. Did she know about the video? If she did, and it is coming from Russia, she is involved with Alexei. I wouldn't be surprised because she has always chased whoever has more money. She thought everyone was oblivious to the fact that she was sleeping with my father before my mother died. We all knew. I just chose not to comment on it because I couldn't care less what my father did in his free time. It now makes sense what Zaira would gain from sleeping with my father if he promised her to be my wife. I am so glad I dodged the bullet on that one with her.

I wanted a wife who was loyal, and I got that with Emilia. I don't think there is a loyal bone in Zaria's body. I still have to deal with her on top of everything else. Maybe I will let Emilia deal with her. It would be a good way to get her anger out, and it's not like she doesn't deserve it. I will ask her that when she wakes up. I am excited to see the creative torture side of Emilia that Esmeralda told me about. I decided to take advantage of the opportunity and fall asleep with Emilia.

I also must keep a closer eye on Roman and make sure he stays loyal after knowing we are holding his sister in a cell and will be tortured too.

With that thought, I lean down, kiss her head, and whisper, "*Sogni d'oro mia Regina. Ti amo.*" *(Sweet dreams, my Queen. I love you.)*

SEVENTEEN
EMILIA

I woke up with a pounding headache and groaned as I tried to open my eyes. The pain shoots through my head. I decide to keep my eyes closed longer and take the blankets over my head to try and block out more of the sun shining through the windows. I hear people trying to talk quietly; it sounds like they are outside the bedroom door. I don't bother to try and eavesdrop because I can guarantee it is about the video that leaked yesterday. I start to fall back asleep when I hear the door open and footsteps. I assume it is Mateo walking back into the room. I feel the bed dip, and I smell Mateo's cologne. He tries to pull the blanket off my head. I mumble to him, "You pull the blanket off me; I will put a bullet in your hand." He climbs back in the bed next to me and gets completely under the blankets with me. He sees me rubbing my temple. I am pulled into his arms; he takes over, rubbing my head.

He quietly whispers to me, "Do you have a headache?"

I shake my head and whisper, "Migraine."

"I thought you would. I have some paracetamol for you. Come on, sit up and take it then we can lay down for a bit until you feel better."

I really don't want to because of the sunlight in the room, but I hear the curtains closing. I see he has the remote in his hands for the curtains. I thought it was laziness when he originally showed me that the curtains could close with a remote was crazy but now, I am very grateful for them. I slowly sat up; Mateo handed me the pills and a glass of water. I take the pills and finish the glass of water; he puts the glass back on the nightstand.

"Let's lay down for a bit longer, Julietta is going to be with Alessia."

My eyes pop open, "Oh my God. Alessia. I am such a terrible mother I completely forgot about her."

Mateo grabs me by my waist and makes me lie down on his chest.

"Relax. Julietta had Marcello keep her away during your flashback because we thought it would be best if she didn't see you like that. Alessia had her movie date with Vincenzo and somehow convinced Julietta, Vincenzo, and Salvatore to sleep in the movie room with her last night." He tells me.

I whisper, "She has everyone here wrapped around her finger."

He shrugs, "She is the young princess, and she can have whatever she wants."

I know no matter how hard I try to reign in the De Luca's from spoiling her, they won't listen, but she appreciates everything she has received from them. I lay back down on his chest and snuggle into him. Mateo chuckles at me, and I smack his chest. "Hush, you are my personal pillow." He pretends to be offended, he says. "I feel used." I shrug.

"You will get over it." He playfully growls at me, "You're lucky you have a migraine, Miss Smart mouth." He tells me and kisses my forehead. He gently rubs my head with his fingers.

A little while later, I wake when I hear his phone go off, and he gently moves me off his chest and onto the pillow. He answers the phone and walks outside to the balcony to answer it. After a couple minutes, he comes back in and kneels in front of me, moving the hair away from my face. I look him in the eyes, and he asks me, "How is your headache?"

I give him a small smile. "Better. I just don't want to see our family's disgusted looks after they saw that video yesterday."

He grabs my hands and kisses each of my knuckles. "They are not disgusted with you, *mia Regina*. They are pissed off at those fuckers who have hurt you and Alessia. I don't think they understood the extent of the abuse you went through until they saw the video, but they are also proud to have you as their Queen because of the strength you showed in that video."

"But…" He stops me from protesting, "Nope, you are incredibly strong, Emilia. We only saw one clip of your abuse. I am sure they did worse things to you while they were there." I nod at him.

I take a deep breath and decide to tell him about what I went through because I trust him. He was here all night and this morning with me at my lowest. He never strayed from my side and took care of me when I couldn't take care of myself.

"Mateo, I want to tell you everything that happened." I scoot over to make room for him, and he lays next to me. I wrap my arms around his chest. He has one hand on my waist and the other running through my hair. "About eight years ago, my house caught fire while I was at work. My Mama, Papa, and brothers, Giovanni, and Franco, died in that fire because all the doors were barricaded so no one could get out. After that, I went on a wild careless streak. I started partying and drinking a lot and that is where I met Seth. We met up a lot to hookup, and we never used protection because I was really drunk until I found out I was pregnant with Alessia. I went to him and let him know I was pregnant. He wasn't happy we got into a fight about it being my fault.

"He forced me to move into his house, and at the time, I thought he lived alone. But he didn't. He lived with his boss Boris, his business partner, who is a sadistic old man. As soon as he saw me, Boris became obsessed with me. There were also had about ten other men who were Boris's employees. They would come in and out of his house a lot. I knew something wasn't right. I tried to leave, but I was caught. My punishment was given by Boris. I will never forget that day. I had to spend a week in his room naked and chained to his bed, and I couldn't tell him no. He raped me over and over that week. In the beginning, I fought back, but after the end of the first day, I just did what he told me to do. Luckily Alessia was never hurt during that time. After that week, I was in so much pain I couldn't walk, so I ended up throwing myself in the basement until I could gather my strength to serve the men. It was decided that I would only eat if I cleaned the house and pleasured the men daily. Seth even joined in on the punishment and whispered evil comments in my ear while raping me. I dealt with it because I was trying to keep Alessia alive.

"When I went into labor, they literally threw me in a tub and told me to shut up and hurry up. I was so scared I was petrified I was going to die, and my child would be left in their hands. I was in labor for over twenty hours when they came back up, and I was weak, and on the verge of passing out from the labor, they called a doctor to come help deliver her. He told Seth that I was lucky to survive, and I shouldn't have any kind of sex for at least eight weeks because of the tearing.

"He played the carrying boyfriend and new father part well. As soon as that doctor was gone. They put Alessia in another room, dragged me to the kitchen, laid me on the table face down, and tied me to the table so I was bent over with my ass in the air, and they all took turns having many rounds on my ass. Then I was beaten with a spiked whip thirty times. A new additional deal came in place that I would be their guest's entertainment if I was asked so that Alessia could have what she needed. I was to obey them, bow when speaking to them, never tell them no, and be their good little slut.

"That went on for years. Alessia learned to stay quiet and never leave the bedroom, which isn't a life for a kid. I felt terrible, but I wanted her safe and away from them.

"I finally lost it when Boris came to me on the night we left and declared I would groom Alessia to be his bride. I yelled at them, and that is when Seth informed me that he wished she was dead. And that I would do what I was told because Boris was going to buy Alessia from him. Seth tossed me around, and Alessia came out of our room and whimpered. Seth went for her, and that is when I attacked. I attacked Seth and we fought, and I knocked him out with a lamp. After that, Boris told me he was going to kill me and fuck Alessia now. She was only six, still a child. I saw red and punched him until he was unconscious. I grabbed Alessia, packed our bags, and got on a bus that took us to New York, which is where I met with a couple who owned a café and helped me get in contact with Theo and, you know, the rest."

Mateo sat up and pulled me closer to him and took a deep breath. "He is going to beg for mercy for everything he has done to both of you." I don't say anything and continue to let him talk his anger out. "I am so sorry you went through that. I thought you were strong before, but you are you are stronger than I can put into words." He kisses my head, and we both lay there in silence.

"What has Gary said about this video for your image?" I ask him to break the silence.

"Well, he wants us to either have a press conference or we can meet with a reporter to clear it up, but the choice is yours, but we don't have to do anything at all," he tells me as he runs his hand through my hair.

"If it will help clear up your reputation, I will do it."

Mateo shakes his head. "No, you are not doing this for me. We will do this for you. I could care less what they think of me. I am a billionaire; I don't need anyone's approval. You decide if you want to make a statement, or I can take care of it for you."

I close my eyes and enjoy feeling his fingers through my hair while I think about if I am brave enough to confront the world about my abuse. Mateo said I am strong; I have nothing to be embarrassed about. I did what I did to protect Alessia, and I would do it again if I had to. I can do this. I will have my family by my side. I open my eyes back up and look at him. "I will have an interview with a reporter you trust."

"Are you sure?"

"Yeah, it's time to stop wallowing about what happened. I have nothing to be ashamed of; I was doing what I had to do so we would survive, and if I was in the same situation, I would do it again."

He stands up, leans over me, and whispers against my lips, "I am the luckiest bastard alive to be married to you. You are a Goddess, Emilia." Then he smashes his lips against mine. I reach up and grab him by his shirt and bring him down against me. He stands up but gets his legs tangled in the blanket, and he ends up faceplanting the pillow. I cover my mouth to stop myself from laughing at him. He pulls his head from the pillow, looks at my face, and starts laughing along with me. He rolls over next to me, and for a couple minutes, we just laugh at each other. Mateo smirks at me and is about to make a comment when the door flies open. Alessia comes running into the room and climbs on the bed. Julietta follows her in trying to stop her. "It's okay; we got her now. Thanks"

"Of course, *Sorella*." She smiles at us and walks out, shutting the door behind us.

"Mama, Papa!" She climbs up next to us and cuddles with us. I see Mateo look down at her in adoration and kiss her forehead.

"Alessia, I think we talked about knocking on people's doors before you enter their room, correct?" I give her the mom look.

She signs, "Sorry."

I look at her and say, "Words, little missy."

"S-Sorry," she tells me with a stutter; I kiss her forehead.

"That's okay; try to remember next time."

Mateo smiles down at Alessia. "I took the day off work today; how about we go out for a ride?"

Alessia perks up and signs, "On horses?"

Mateo looks at me, winking, but looks at Alessia to say, "Hmm, I don't know."

She interrupts him, "Pleaseeee, papa," with big puppy dog eyes and pouting her lip.

I burst out laughing. "Just say yes. You know you will give into her without her giving you the puppy eye pout."

He looks between us and says, "Of course, I will because my princess gets whatever she wants. Yes, Alessia, we will go for a ride. Go get dressed and meet us in the kitchen."

She jumps off the bed and runs out of the room, and I hear her yell for Marcello, or as she calls him Celly. She is close to him, and if we are not around her, she wants Marcello around. I smile at her carefree spirit.

I pull the covers off my body and get out of bed. I decided on a pair of jeans that hug my body with a tight tank top and my cowboy boots. I walk out and see Mateo in white riding pants and a black polo with tall black boots. I arch an eyebrow at him. "Are we going for a ride or are we going to a show?"

He looks at me. "What? This is what I always wear when I ride."

I shake my head. "Well, I can promise you, our daughter will be wearing jeans with a t-shirt and her pink boots. You *il mio re*, need to learn you don't always have to dress to impress. Sometimes simple is better." Knowing he loves his designer clothes, whereas I prefer bargain clothes, he gives me a hard glare. I pop my hip out at him with my arms on my hips and my eyebrow raised. I am not budging on this.

After a couple seconds, he throws his hands up. "Fine *mia Regina*, pick me out something to wear then."

I clap my hands, "Oh, goodie."

He groans, "I feel like I am going to regret this." I decide not to torture him too bad. I give him a pair of faded jeans with a tight gray t-shirt and a pair of his black boots. I walk out of the closet and hand him the clothes. I push him into the closet to change before he can complain.

I flop myself on the bed with my feet hanging off the edge of the bed and wait for Mr. Designer to get his ass out here. He walks out a couple minutes later, and I sit up. The only thing he changed was he added a belt, but fuck, I didn't realize how tight his clothes fit him. I gulped looking at him.

He smirks at me, "If I didn't promise Alessia we would take her out for a trail ride, I would be stripping us out of these clothes and enjoying every little noise that I would come out of that mouth." He whispers in my ear. He pulls me up on my feet, and we leave the bedroom and head towards the kitchen.

I laugh when we get there, Alessia is in a pink shirt and her jeans with her sparkly pink boots along with her pink cowboy hat. She is standing by the kitchen door with a pout on her lips and her hands crossed against her chest. When she sees me laughing, she goes from pouting to glaring at me. "Sorry, baby girl, I had to pick out Papa's outfit. He was trying to wear expensive clothes to the barn."

She gasps, and he looks at me. "Don't you dare have my princess side with you on your bargain clothes, woman!" I put Alessia on my back, smirk at Mateo while sticking my tongue out at him and run out the back door. Alessia is laughing at me. I hear Mateo's heavy feet running to catch up to us. I barely make it a minute before I feel arms wrapped around my waist, and we are lifted off the ground. "Gotcha," he says to us; Alessia giggles, and I just chuckle at him.

He grabs Alessia off my back and puts her on the ground. He leans over and gives me a small peck on the lips, and she says, "Eww."

I laugh at her, "One day, you will be kissing boys."

Mateo glares at me. "No, she won't, not until she's thirty; wait, no, sixty."

I laugh at him, "Whatever you say *Miele*." *(Honey)*

He shakes his head. "No, my princess, will not be kissing no boys. Boys are bad, right princess?"

She looks up at him and signs, "But Papa but then how will I live happily ever after with my prince?"

"You don't need a prince, baby. Boys will make you cry. And Papa doesn't want to see his princess cry."

"That's okay, Papa. Mama and Zia Julietta said they would help me go on dates when I want to have a boyfriend," she signs.

"Alessia, you weren't supposed to tell Papa. That was a secret."

She gives me a sheepish smile.

Mateo glares at me. "Your Mama and Zia Julietta won't be supervising any of your dates. Papa will if I think they are worthy enough of dating my daughter."

I roll my eyes, "No boy will be worthy enough in your eyes." He smirks at me.

"Exactly, plus she won't be able to meet any boys when she is homeschooled."

I roll my eyes again. He is being ridiculous; he smacks my ass. I glare at him; he has this dark hungry look in his eyes. Mateo whispers in my ear, "You are racking up your punishments." I gulp thinking about how he will punish me which usually leads to at least one of us naked. I ignore the ache between my legs.

We walk up to the barn, and we see Cash, Sundance, and Alpha, our horses.

We walk into the field to catch our horses. Alpha is an all-black gelding except for the end of his nose is a dark brown that fades from the black. Alpha automatically walks up to Mateo, and he can put Alpha's halter on with ease. Cash takes off running. "Go get the treats for your naughty horse Alessia." She nods at me; Mateo puts his hand out to her, and she walks up and grabs his hand. Mateo is leading Alpha in the barn with the lead rope in one hand, and the other is holding Alessia.

I turn and go to catch Sundance. He has brown fur on his body, and his mane and tail are black. He has a white star marking on his forehead, and his left hind leg has a white pastern which is a white mark from the top of his hoof to about his ankle; it looks like an ankle sock. He sees me and doesn't run away, but he also doesn't come up to me. I unbuckle the throat latch, the strap under the throat of the halter. I slide the crown piece up his face and over his ears. I tuck the crown piece behind his ears and then buckle the throat latch.

Once I have the halter securely in place, I give him a pat on his neck "Good boy, come on, let's go in the barn and get a treat." We walk to the barn, and he is nuzzling my hands and pockets, looking for a treat. I laugh, "Soon, boy. I promise I will give you one as soon as we get to the barn."

Once we approach the door of the barn, Mateo and Alessia are walking out with her halter and lead rope with some treats for Cash. Sundance sees her treats and starts moving toward her. Alessia smiles and opens her hand flat for him so he can eat a treat out of her hand. I tell her, "Go get that rotten horse of yours missy."

She nods and walks with Mateo out to the field. Let's see if they will catch him; Mateo has never had to catch a horse who loves to run away. I grab another treat for Sundance and put him in the stall to go walk outside to see if they will need help.

Cash is a dapple gray which is a dark gray all over his body with some white spots sprinkled all over him with a dark gray mane and tail gelding. Mateo is trying to catch Cash, and every time Mateo gets close Cash runs off. I look and see Alessia sitting on the ground with a metal bucket with the peppermint treats in it, and she gently starts to shake the bucket. Cash stops to look for where the noise is coming from and slowly trots over to Alessia. He stops right in front of her, and he sticks his face in the bucket to start eating the treats. She swings the lead rope around his neck, and he sticks his head up, confused about what happened. At that moment she quickly slides the halter over his head and behind his ears. When he hears the buckle click, he snorts at her but decides to finish his treats.

"Really?" I hear Mateo say irritated at Cash.

I just chuckle at him. "Don't worry, he has done the same to every other adult who has tried to catch him, but all Alessia has to do is shake a bucket of treats, and he is putty in her hand." Alessia smiles at both of us, and we all walk back into the barn. "I will grab the tack boxes."

"If you get them in the cross ties."

"Sure," he tells me.

I grab tack boxes. I see Mateo and Alessia have put all three horses in the cross ties. I put the tack box out, and we all started grooming our horses, from combing the mane and tail to brushing their body and picking their feet. I help Alessia with picking the feet because you have to be careful to not touch the frog in the middle of their foot because that can hurt and is very sensitive. After we are done, we put the tack box back, and we all grab our helmets, bridles, and saddles. We all tack up our horses, and we all walk out of the barn. Mateo gives Alessia a leg up onto Cash since she is a bit too short.

We start heading off for the trail, and Alessia gives me a smirk, and I tell her, "Warm up first." Knowing she wants to gallop through the fields, I chuckle to myself she is so much like me when I was her age, but she also amazes me with how fast she has picked up on riding and basic care of horses in the past year.

Being out here with just us as a family is so peaceful. We don't talk about the sex tape. We just make small talk, and Alessia talks to us without signing. She did get frustrated with her stutter, but we encouraged her through it. After about twenty minutes, we get to a big field and Alessia turns to me and smirks. I just laugh and shake my head.

She clicks her tongue as she nudges Cash with her legs, and she yells out, "Race ya, Papa." His eyes bug out that she is galloping away from us, through this open field.

"Alessia, slow down; you are going to get hurt."

He is already pushing Alpha into a gallop, and I am right behind him with Sundance. I yell over to him "She is fine. Relax and enjoy the ride."

He shakes his head, and it doesn't take us long to get caught up to her. I close my eyes for a moment and enjoy the sound of Sundance's feet galloping under me and the wind in my hair. I feel so relaxed out here with my family. Alessia has the biggest smile on her face. Mateo looks like he is about to have a heart attack from watching Alessia gallop on her horse. After a couple minutes, I tell Alessia to slow down so we can have the horses get a drink at the river. She slows Cash to a walk, and we all head over to the river. As soon as we get to the river, we loosen our reins so the horses can bend their necks down to reach the river.

"You are crazy just like your mother, young lady." Mateo attempts to be stern with Alessia.

"B-but I am b-beautiful like her too," she says with a smirk. I have to bite my tongue from laughing because she is finally engaging in her inner smart mouth.

Mateo looks at her. "Yes, you are." Then Mateo turns to me. "She is just as sassy as you."

I shrug and say, "I am not the only smart mouth person in our house."

He just shakes his head at me and mumbles, "I am screwed when she is a teenager."

I chuckle at him. "You have no idea."

On the way back, Alessia decides to not give Mateo any more heart attacks, and we have a leisurely walk back. At one point, she walks right next to Mateo and grabs his hand while they are riding. She looks at him and tells him, "I love you, Papa."

"And I love you, *Principessa*."

He looks at me, "This is perfect, just me and my family."

I smile at him. I am shocked his phone hasn't gone off since we have been out together. I am not complaining. We continue to enjoy the tranquility of this time together because we know it won't last forever. As soon as we get back to the barn, we untack the horses and put it away. Then we hosed off the horses and brought them back out in the field together. We laugh as they all run and roll around in the dirt. They buck at each other, squealing. After hanging up their halters, we walk to the house with Alessia holding our hands.

Nonna runs out with her phone and starts taking pictures of us together and decides we need to take more pictures of us looking "normal" for some family pictures, not pictures in stuffy outfits.

Nonna is the reason why they have the barn and horses, to begin with. Nonno built the barn for her as a wedding gift. We both are so similar in the fact we prefer to be out at the barn, and we both hate dressing up, especially in designer brands. Which is one of the many reasons we get along so well.

We sit there and listen to her tell us how to pose for a couple more pictures because she has her wooden spoon in her apron pocket, and we all know that she has no problem bringing that out. After we get done, I look at my watch and see it is almost time for Alessia's speech therapy appointment. I usher her into the bath, so she doesn't smell like the barn for her session.

"Alessia, I laid your clothes on the sink. Take a quick bath and then wait for Marcello or me to bring you to speech therapy."

She tells me, "Yes, Mama."

I turn and quickly make it to my bedroom and walk into the bathroom to take a quick shower. I am in the middle of washing my hair when I feel two arms wrap around my stomach and a chin resting on my shoulder. I look down and see Mateo's arms around me. "Mateo, I don't have time; I have to quickly shower because Alessia has speech therapy."

He nods and says, "Ok, I will behave. Do you think she would want me there?" he asks.

I turn around and tell him, "Yes. She asks every time if you are working because she wants you to watch how well she does."

He smiles and says, "She really looks up to me, huh?"

I grab his chin and make him look me in the eyes and tell him. "Yes, she absolutely loves you. She has told me she wishes that we never met Seth and always knew you because she thinks you are her personal superman."

He laughs at her comment.

"I wish I met you before Seth got his claws into you, but I am also thankful for him because if it wasn't for him, Alessia wouldn't be here. I also can't wait to get my hands on him."

I smirk evilly at him while rubbing my hands together. "Me too. You better include me in that. I have some special plans for all of them."

He grabs my loofah and body wash and starts to wash me. "Ok, my little *moglie diabolica*, you can think more about your evil plans later," he says and kisses my lips. We quickly finish showering.

Alessia gets all excited when she finds out that Mateo will watch her during her therapy session. As we watch Alessia work with her therapist, you can see she gets frustrated but works through it. At one point, I thought she was going to cry and give up, but her therapist had her stop and collect herself before trying again. I can only imagine having thoughts in her head that she wants to say but struggles to say them because of being behind in speech from being mute for over five years.

Mateo leans over and whispers in my ear, "Her therapist is really good with her and Alessia is so persistent learning."

I smile and whisper, "Yeah, they work really well together."

She has been trying to saying more than a couple words without stuttering. She has really been working hard. I am very proud of her.

After that, we continue to watch.

At the end of the session, she turns to Mateo and tells him slowly, "Did you see me, Papa?" It took her a minute to say, but she didn't stutter.

He opens his arms and picks her up. "Yes, princess, I saw, you did so well. I am so proud of you."

He kisses her hair. "How about some lunch? Then we will go watch a movie together." She nods happily and starts heading for the kitchen.

I clear my throat and tell her, "You are forgetting something, young lady." She looks confused. "What do you say after your session?"

She opens her mouth in an "O" shape and says, "Thank you," to her therapist. And barely waits for a response before making her way out of the room.

Serafina is one of the maids here who is absolutely breathtaking. Her dark caramel skin flows against her chocolate brown eyes. Her shiny black hair is pulled back into a ponytail. But I love Serafina. She is just a sweetheart. She already has lunch waiting for us.

We thank her, and once we finish eating, Alessia drags us to the movie room. On our way, we see Nonna, and she asks Alessia, "Where are you dragging your parents to, missy?"

"To watch a movie." Nonna smiles at Alessia and gives her a kiss on the cheek. "Well, don't let me stop you. Go have fun." Alessia gives her a hug and continues to drag us to the movie room.

We start by sitting together on the sectional couch but as soon as the music starts in Little Mermaid, Alessia is up dancing and humming. Mateo moves me, so my back is against his chest. "I can't tell you how much I appreciate everything you have done for us, especially Alessia. Seeing her this carefree and happy. I just never thought I would see her like this," I tell him softly.

"Don't thank me. I will always do anything for *mia Regina* and *la mia principessa*." He puts his kisses on the side of my head and I relax more into his touch. And we enjoy the rest of the day, just the three of us.

EIGHTEEN
SALVATORE

   I sit under Lilyana's favorite tree and silently cry to myself, missing her. Everyone says with time, the pain will lessen, and I will be able to move on with my life, but they are wrong. Today marks seven years since she was killed. She was my high school sweetheart, and it hurts every day that she isn't here with me. I can only imagine if she was still here, that we would be married with at least one kid. If I was lucky, we would have more. I hold onto my Irish Blessing necklace that I gave her for our last Christmas together. She loved Irish jewelry and loved visiting Ireland. Every morning I tell myself that we are one day closer to seeing each other again. And that gives me the power to live.

   The next thing I know, I feel someone rub their hand up and down my back. I know it is not any of the De Luca men because they all suck at emotional stuff and know to leave me alone. I tend to get angry when anyone interrupts my time alone grieving Lilyana. I look over, and through my blurry vision from my tears, I see Emilia sitting next to me.

   "What are you doing here?" I ask, my voice gravely from crying.

   "You have been acting off this past week. I looked outside and saw you crying out here. I'd figured I see what I can do to help?" she says with a sad smile.

   "There is nothing you can do unless you can bring people back from the dead," I told her.

   "Who is it that you miss?" she asks.

   "My high school sweetheart, Lilyana. She was kidnapped by the Russians, who tortured her before they Skyped me so I could watch them shoot her in the chest. And we found out right before she was kidnapped that she was pregnant. We were on our way to the mansion to tell the family when we were hit by another driver. I blacked out, and they took her from the car." I start crying again, I try to slow down my tears, but the pain of losing her never seems to ease. It feels like there's a permanent hole in my heart.

   Emilia just hugs me and whispers, "Don't hold it in, Salvatore. Trust me, it hurts more than letting it out."

   I turn my head, giving her a puzzled look. "Don't worry about it, we are talking about you, not me."

   "Nope I shared, now it's your turn," I say.

   "One day, while I was at work my family was killed in a fire. My family home set on fire, all the exits of the house were blocked, and they were all tied to chairs, except Mama, who was on the floor. The police never even bothered to look into who murdered my family, even though my Papa was a cop and my Mama was a nurse. When my family died, I had no one because my uncle turned his back on me after he got the inheritance. I slept on my boss's couch and spent every night partying, getting drunk off my ass. I did that until I found out I was pregnant. I told Seth because he was the constant guy I was sleeping with at the time, and then he took me to his house, and that is when my new nightmare began. So, because I was an idiot and never let myself grieve, I bottled it all up until the therapist from Spain made me talk about it, and the waterworks began that day, and I honestly cried for hours. Until I passed out from mental exhaustion."

"Wow. Emilia, I am so sorry you went through that." Holy shit, she is stronger than we believed. She went through grieving her family, plus the abuse from those bastards while raising Alessia. Damn.

She nods at me, and we both just sit there together, enjoying the peace and tranquility of Lilyana's memorial garden Nonna had built for me.

"Today is the day that Lilyana died. I usually come out here crying for a couple hours alone, then I go drink myself into oblivion," I told her.

"Not this year, you're not. I know drinking is good at numbing the pain but what I have heard about Lilyana is she would kick your ass for doing something so stupid," she tells me with a smirk.

"Yeah, she was feisty as hell and took no shit. I remember when we were still in high school, Mateo was being a pig and making some sexual comments about a girl. She told him to knock it off, but he wouldn't, so she took a book and threw it at his head hard enough that he had to get stitches." I say chuckling.

"Well, he deserved it. It sounds like we would have gotten along," she says, throwing her head back, laughing.

"I remember the first time I laid eyes on her. She was new to our high school and rumors were spreading about a hot redhead that started. I paid no mind, and I was walking past her locker, and when she closed it and turned in my direction, we made eye contact. I stopped walking, Mateo ran into my back, and I fell face forward into the ground. I was so embarrassed, and she made a smart-ass comment about didn't know the new girl was worth doing a faceplant on the ground. Of course, I tried using some cheesy pick-up line, and she dismissed me. But I was a young, hormonal teenage boy who saw a beautiful girl, and I knew she was my light in my dark world. I refused to let her slip between my fingers. I would talk to her every day and after a couple months, she either got tired of me bugging her or she started to like me, but she eventually said yes to a date with me. And from there, we would go on dates and spend time together, but she also enjoyed spending time with Mateo and Vincenzo as well. She even called out Mateo for his big ego and Vincenzo for being a moron. And she would glare at me when I would call her *"Giglio tigrato" (Tiger Lily)* because she was feisty like a tiger and lily for Lilyana. The look I would get when I called her that," I say, smiling at the memory of her putting her hands on her hips and giving me her mean glare, which I thought was so damn adorable.

"She was studying to be a pediatrician, and she wanted to specialize in treating kids with cancer. She wanted to help if she could and, if not, at least make them comfortable. She loved helping people. She had the biggest heart and would do anything for anyone. Don't get me wrong, she might have a big heart, but she wouldn't let anyone take advantage of it. She also was loyal and protective; I can't tell you how many times she beat Zaria's ass for trying to get with Mateo when he didn't want her. And since Mateo won't lay a hand on a woman, Lilyana had no problem stepping in." I stop to take another sip of my bourbon.

"One time, Zaria was all over Mateo in front of our family, like basically humping him and kissing all over his neck. This was as we were trying to have lunch, and he was being respectful, picking her up and setting her in a chair across the table, but she'd get up and start it all over again. Lilyana had grabbed her by hair and literally dragged her out of the restaurant as she was kicking and screaming. She comes back in a couple minutes later and apologizes to the family for what she did with so much class, like she didn't drag that bitch out by her hair. She loved to cook Irish food in Nonna's kitchen just to get Nonna all riled up, but Nonna loved her food at the same time."

"Let me guess, she would get the wooden spoon threat?" she asks with a snicker.

"Yes, and Lilyana would stick her ass out and say make it a good hit Nonna." I laugh but also remember what my rubbing lotion on her sore ass would turn into. I wasn't complaining about getting in between her legs.

"Oh my god! That is priceless. I may have to do that next time Nonna threatens to smack me with the spoon when I start cooking my 'disgraceful American comfort food' but yet that woman sneaks to eat the food later."

"Nonna is something else." I love Nonna, but she is crazy.

"She sounds like such a wonderful girl. Salvatore, it sounds like you were lucky to know her and love her."

"Yeah, I truly was, she loved all of her loved ones so fiercely, even that annoying mutt I got her."

"Wait. You have a dog?"

"Chance is an Irish Terrier. I got him for her as a housewarming gift when she moved into my penthouse with me."

"And why have you not brought him by so I could meet him?"

"He is a grumpy asshole, and plus, have you met your husband? Mr. Overprotective?"

"Ugh, don't remind me. That man drives me up the wall. Bring him by, it sounds like he needs some love and snuggles. Knowing you, you probably don't give him that because you two probably have a love-hate relationship," she says, looking at me. Shit! This woman is too smart for her own good.

"Guilty. Fine, I will bring him over tomorrow, but you have to deal with Mr. Cranky Boss," I say with my hands up in mock surrender.

"I will just tell him to behave, or he can keep the couch company," she says with an evil smirk on her face.

"You are an evil wife." I laugh with her.

"I know it's my job." She winks at me; Mateo is going to have his hands full with her. He will have gray hair in no time.

I take another deep breath, knowing what I say next is always hard for me to talk about. "Every time I close my eyes at night, I see her bleeding and bruised up while crying, telling me how much she loved me before being shot in her chest on camera. And the worst part was, we never received her body. I can't wait to get my hands on each person who hurt her. They will be begging for death after I get my hands on them."

"Oh, Salvatore. I am so sorry. I can't even imagine your pain watching that, but know we are here for you anytime you need us. And make sure they feel all the pain in the world and make their death slow and painful. I will help if you want. I am good at cutting off pathetic cocks and making them choke on it. No one gets to hurt our family and gets away with it."

I was not expecting that she would include Lilyana in our family even though she had never met her. She truly is a blessing for this family, but fuck, she is evil. But her being evil makes her a good match for Mateo.

"Thanks, Emilia, believe it or not, being around Alessia helps make life a little better. I have always wondered if my child would be a boy or a girl? Who would it look like? You know all of those things."

She nods at me. "Yeah, when I was pregnant with Alessia, I would pray she would be more like me than Seth since he is so evil," she said with anger in her tone, but her face was blank.

"I had bought an engagement ring and was planning to propose to her. I was going to take her back to Ireland and set up a fancy dinner at the National Botanic Garden and propose to her there. I was even going to fly both of our families out there to surprise her. I always wonder, would we be married by now? How many kids would we have? A girl that would be as beautiful as her or a stubborn boy like me? I just wish she was still here with me and how happy we could be together." Emilia doesn't say anything, she just gives me a tight hug. Knowing there isn't anything she can say that would make the pain go away. She just holds me for a few minutes.

"Mateo is a lucky son of a bitch to have you. He has an amazing woman as his wife, and I would have done anything to have Lilyana back in my arms." I start stuttering my words, I close my eyes feeling the heartache of her not being here.

EMILIA

We continue to talk until I see Zio Adriano coming towards us. "Hey *Figlio,* how are you holding up?" he asks and sits next to Salvatore.

"Better than usual," Salvatore answers.

Then Adriano smiled at me and said, "Ah, let me guess, our Queen worked her magic on you, so you're not drinking today to numb the pain."

I shrug my shoulders and say, "We just talked, and it seemed to help."

The next thing we hear is, "Emilia Rose De Luca!" Mateo is yelling my name as he stalks over towards me.

"Fuck," I say and go hide behind Adriano and Salvatore in hopes they will save me from the beast I poked earlier.

Adriano laughs, "What did you do to him this time?"

"Well, he should stop being a cock tease and leaving me all hot and bothered, thinking I won't get him back. I thought of sending him a video of me in the tub while he was having a meeting. Now save me from the beast."

Salvatore throws his head back, laughing, "Hey *cugino (cousin)* did you open the video during your meeting with the board of directors?"

"Yes, but as soon as I saw it was my wife naked in the tub, I stopped it, but her ass is gonna get it for sending me something like that during a meeting," he says, staring me down, and takes a step around Salvatore. That fucker didn't try and stop him. I take off running through the garden with Mateo on my heels. I am about to run into the mansion when he catches me and throws me over his shoulder like a caveman and starts walking into the mansion.

He smacks my ass when I keep trying to get out of his hold. "Behave, you're already in trouble, *mia cara moglie.*"

I mumble "fucker" under my breath, and he smacks my ass again. We pass Nonna and I look at her with a pleading look and my hands together, begging for help, and she just laughs and tells us to have fun.

I grumble to myself, and soon, I am tossed into bed. I glare at him as his back is turned to me. I hear him lock the door, and when he turns around, I see lust and hunger in his eyes. "Now, what should I do with you after that little stunt you pulled earlier?" he says and slowly walks closer to me.

"You are lucky that no one else saw that video. Your body is only for me to see, and only I can enjoy, see, and touch your body." He grabs my hands and puts them above my head. "It seems like my Queen needs some more attention from me. Hmm."

He stops, looking into my eyes for a moment, and says, "You always have control, my Queen." As soon as he finished talking, his mouth was on mine, and I responded immediately to him. He bites my lip, and I gasp. He plunges his tongue into my mouth, and I wrap my hand around his neck to bring us closer to each other. He grabs my hands and moves them above my head. "Keep them here, or I will tie your hands to the bed."

Fuck, when he gets all dominant on my ass, it turns me on so bad. I am ready to take it further with him since all we have been doing is intense make-out sessions and touching my clothes, I want to feel more of him, skin-to-skin. He stops kissing me and starts to take my boots off, then works on my belt. Once he has my belt off, he slowly peels my jeans off as he leaves kisses down my leg, and once they are off, he trails kisses up my other leg. He kisses right next to my pussy but never touches it, making me wiggle in need of him.

He then pulls my shirt over my head and lays me back down, still with my hands above my head. He sits up and looks down at me only in my lacey black bra and thong. He licks his lips and says, *"Bella, cosi fottutamente bella." (Beautiful, so fucking beautiful)* He stops and stares at me before asking, "Do you trust me?"

I look at him confused, why he would ask that, but I nod my head. "Yeah. Why are you asking me that?" He starts to untie his tie and leans forward, tying it around my head. The tie is now over my eyes, and I can't see anything.

"When you take away one sense, your other senses are heightened. I want you to feel everything I do to you. If it gets too much, just let me know."

"Okay" I say. I am excited to see what he is going to do to me. I lay there trying to hear what he is doing, but he is quiet until I hear him chuckle and goes back to kissing my mouth with dominance, and I let him. I rub my thighs together to ease some of the ache I have for him. Sneaking using my toys isn't the same, and I am aware of how big he is because I feel it against my ass every morning when he wakes up.

He lays his body on me so I can feel how big his bulge is right on my pussy. The pressure makes me moan out, and I start to grind against him. He started to grind back on me and started sucking on my earlobe. I threw my head back as he started lightly grazing his teeth on my skin. He worked his way down my neck toward my chest and started sucking on me over my bra. I kept grinding on him and moved my hands from his neck to his shoulders and held on tight to help keep myself grounded.

"Move them again, and I am tying you to the bed. I will make you cum and cum until you can't take it anymore." Fuck I feel completely soaked. He has barely done anything to me, and I am already feeling breathless. He unhooked my bra and lightly kissed my nipple, but he grew more aggressive, sucking on my nipple like it was his last meal while his hand was twisting my other nipple between his thumb and pointer finger.

"Oh, Fuck Mateo," I moaned out as he let go of my nipple with a pop and went to my other nipple just as aggressively as the first. At this point, I am grinding on him as hard as I can to help get any kind of pressure to ease the ache between my legs. He stops playing with my boobs and he puts his hand on my stomach to stop me from grinding on him, and he slowly grinds on me.

"Faster, Mateo," I beg but he doesn't. If anything, he goes agonizing slower.

He whispers to me, "I will make you remember who this body belongs to."

I feel him at the edge of my thong. He grabs it in his teeth and slowly drags it down my body. He tosses my thong somewhere in the room, grabs both of my thighs and puts them over his shoulder, and dives in between my legs. I throw my head back when he starts to suck on my clit, and his other hand is circling around my hole, just teasing me. I was so busy writhing in pleasure when he plunged one finger into me, and I yelled out his name. I can feel him smirk against my clit when he adds another finger and gently bites down on my bundle of nerves. I tighten my legs around his head.

I am about to come when he pulls his fingers out of me, and I whimper in protest. He leans up next to my ear and says, "Oh, not too fast. We are going to drag this out."

He goes back down on me and thrusts his tongue in me, and pinches my clit with his fingers, and again, I am writhing under him. He does this about three more times, bringing me to the brink of an orgasm and then denying me my release. Finally, he grabs my thighs and opens my legs as wide as they can go, so I am completely exposed to him. He cuffs my legs to the legs of the bed. "To keep you still," he says and as soon as he finishes, he is back on me. Three fingers curl inside of me, and he is sucking my clit. I arch my back off the bed, and my eyes roll into the back of my head as I cum hard.

I yell out, "MATEO." He continues while I ride out my orgasm. I slump back on the bed; he pecks my lips. He uncuffs me and unties the tie from around my head. I barely noticed he got up and started a bath until he picked me up.

I look at him and give him a questioning look. "Shh, just let me take care of you." I nod because I am so exhausted. He gently sits me down in the tub and strips out of his dress pants and boxers. Mateo climbs in the tub and places me on his lap. I rest my head against his chest, and he is running his other hand through my hair, which isn't helping me stay awake. After he washes me, we sit there enjoying each other's company. I realize he pleasured me, extremely well but I never did anything for him in return.

"I am so sorry," I tell him.

He pulls back from me and asks, "Why are you apologizing, my *tigre*?"

I look at him like he has lost his mind. "You went down on me, but I didn't do anything for you."

He shakes his head. "Darling, I was not expecting anything. I am just happy you felt safe enough to trust me to do that to you. It is okay at times for me just to pleasure you. I want you to feel completely safe when we are together." He kisses my head.

I chose not to respond and snuggled back into his chest. When the water starts getting cold, we get out. We lay down in the fresh bed and we just talked and caught up with each other. I love when we have time to just talk with no distractions. I run my hand over his chest, admiring his muscles, and he is running his hand up and down my back. I guess you could say we enjoy the quiet moments with each other but still have some physical contact.

He has been working really hard to get Seth and Boris in his hands. I know it hasn't been easy, plus he is so supportive of Alessia and me with us recovering from our past. I truly appreciate him. Yes, it was just a business marriage, but now, after everything he has done for us, it is hard not to fall for him. I am just petrified if I do. I am afraid that not only will my heart be broken but he will also break Alessia's heart as well.

"What are you thinking about in that pretty little mind?" he asked me.

I didn't realize that I had zoned out. I blush and say, "I was thinking about how much I appreciate everything you have done for Alessia and me."

"Of course, I want to do all of this for both of you, but really, I could give you both more, but you don't want to spend any money on yourself," he says, giving me a look, knowing our biggest issue is that I hate spending money on myself.

I shrug my shoulders. "I am working on it."

"I know you are my *Regina*," he says and kisses my forehead.

"Mateo, is there anything you need me to help you with, being as you are the boss of the Mafia? I don't know if the wife has any responsibilities, but if you need me to do something, just let me know."

"No, mostly the wives just organize balls and other social events that we have but otherwise, no, unless you want to help torture people. I remember Esmeralda saying you have a unique and creative mind for torture."

I smirk up at him and say, "I'd rather torture someone than host some snotty nose social event."

He chuckles at me, "I figured you would say that."

We lay in the quiet together until Mateo says, "One day, I want to have a loving relationship like Nonno and Nonna do. How they love each other so much and how they are each other's best friends."

"I do too, Mateo, but I am worried that my PTSD one day will be too much for you or that I won't be enough for you," I tell him. If I want this marriage to actually work, I need to be honest with him. As much as I hated him in the beginning, now I can see one day us being happy.

"Emilia, you are more than enough for me. If we are being honest, I should be on my knees, bowing at your feet for being allowed in your presence. And your PTSD will never be too much for me. Look at the progress you have made. When I first saw you almost a year ago, did you ever expect to consent to do what we just did together?" I shake my head. "See, you are making progress. Is it slower than you want? Yes, but that is okay because this goes at your pace. Even if you fall back, I will always be here to help you. Remember that."

NINETEEN
EMILIA

It has been a couple weeks since the video was released on the news. The following day the news station released an apology statement to my family and me. They said that they were hacked and released that video. Poor Fabio worked relentlessly for basically a week straight to find out the video was released by none other than Alexei.

Today is the day of the interview, and to say I wasn't nervous would be a lie. My hands kept shaking and are sweaty so I kept wiping them on my dress. I had Annabella get me a beautiful navy-blue dress that stopped at my knees, but I was still nervous that my appearance would reflect on Mateo. I kept looking over at myself. Was my make up good enough? Is my hair okay? Does my dress make me look like a whore? I feel two hands wrap around my stomach and pull me into a hard chest. I smelled his cologne and looked at him through the mirror. I gave him a small smile.

"You look absolutely gorgeous. Stop overthinking and nit picking at your appearance," he whispers into my ear.

I look at his eyes through the mirror for a second but then look down. "Sorry, my insecurities were buzzing around in my head."

He spins me around, lifts my head, and makes me look him in the eyes. "You don't need to feel insecure about anything. You are perfect and if anything, everyone else should feel insecure around you. *La mia Regina perfetta.*" He kisses my forehead. "Now come on, let's get this shit show over with." I nod at him, I grab my bag, and we walk out holding hands.

We say goodbye to Alessia. She is staying with Serafina, who has become her nanny now, instead of a maid. Marcello will be staying with her as well. Last week when we scheduled the interview, the whole De Luca family decided they would come with us to be there to support me. I was so floored that they would rearrange their schedules to support me today. When they told me they were coming to the interview, I was speechless. I scared them, thinking I didn't want them there, but after a moment, I told them how shocked I was to have their support during this painful emotional interview. Zio Adriano brought me into a bear hug and told me we are family, and, in this family, we support each other. "You are a De Luca, and we always have each other's back."

We all walk out to our cars. One of the security guards takes my bag and places it in the trunk of Mateo's car. Mateo opens the passenger door for me. I give him a kiss on the cheek and sit down in my seat. He smiles at me as he closes the door. He gives orders to the security team coming with us and then climbs into the driver's seat of the car. He grabs my hand and kisses my palm. *Starai bene. Prometto che sarò con te tutto il tempo."(You will be okay. I promise I will be with you the whole time.)*

"*Grazie lo apprezzo molto*" *(thank you, I really appreciate it.)* Then he starts the car, and we head out to the news station. We don't talk; both lost in our own thoughts. We exchange hand squeezes and smiles during the ride.

At the news station, the paparazzi are already swarming our cars. "Stay in the car; I will come and open your door. We will walk in together." He kisses my forehead.

I nod at him, "Okay." He puts his sunglasses on, then opens the door and gets out. The security team is pushing the paparazzi back, but you can hear them shouting questions at Mateo, and the flashes from the camera are going off like crazy.

He opens my door. "Put on your sunglasses on, *Tesoro.*" I do as he says. He has his hand sticking out. I grab it, and Mateo gently pulls me out of the car.

As soon as the paparazzi saw me, they completely lost their minds. They were yelling questions at me and pushed harder to get to me, but I didn't realize all the De Luca men had the women surrounded by them. So, the paparazzi must get through the security team and the De Luca men before they can get to us. Of course, this doesn't stop them. I can see them. Mateo had his arm wrapped around me and Zio Adriano was on the other side of me. Nonno was holding Nonno's hand. And Julietta was in between Vincenzo and Salvatore. Plus, our security team was between the men and the paparazzi. Vittorio mumbled while pushing the paparazzi back "fucking vultures" which made me chuckle. They are still pushing to get to me, but Mateo squeezes my shoulder and smiles at me. I ignore all the questions and hurtful comments being said which is hard, but I know it won't do any good. I don't give them any of my attention.

The look of everyone in the news station when they see the security team and all the De Luca's with me is comical. You could see the woman had an arrogant smile but as soon as she saw all of us her face paled quickly. She masked it and tried to be sexy while eyeing Mateo up and down.

"Hello, Mr. De Luca. My name is Ashlee. I am honored to be able to interview you so we can hear your opinion on this scandalous video. I am so sorry your image has been tarnished by someone else's shameless decisions in her life." Is this woman serious? Mateo has his arm wrapped around my hip, pulling me into him. She completely ignores my presence and downgrades my character.

"Ashlee, do you treat all spouses of good-looking and wealthy men with this much disrespect, or is it just me?" I ask in a sickly-sweet tone. I raised my eyebrow at her.

She looks baffled then she has a smirk on her face. "Well, if it wasn't for you being such a whore, poor Mateo wouldn't have to be defending his image." Before I can respond, Salvatore responds.

"How about you stop attempting to flirt with my cousin, who is obviously married, and get the interview started. We rather not waste our day listening to your whiny voice." Salvatore says with so much distaste on his tongue. Ashlee's face turns red in embarrassment, but she tells Mateo.

"Mateo, you and Emilia can follow me, and I will have Dave here escort your family to where they can watch the interview."

Before we separate each family member comes over, hugs me, and wishes me well wishes.

Nonna holds me the longest and whispers in my ear, "Remember you were protecting Alessia, so ignore that floozy's comments. And if she tries any shit in the interview, show her why you are Mrs. Mateo De Luca, the Queen of the Italian Mafia." She pulls back from the hug.

I nod at her and tell her, "I promise."

She smiles at me, "Good," pats my cheek lovingly and grabs Nonno's hand, following the rest of the family.

I turned to Mateo. "Nonna give you some extra advice and encouragement?"

"Yep," I tell him. He grabs my hand, so I move closer to him, he gives me a quick kiss on my lips, and we follow Ashlee, the anger on her face when she sees how loving we are with each other. Geez, she looks like she has steam coming out of her ears.

We sit and have people come and prep us to start. We sit in the back while Ashlee does her other segments while we wait. Mateo turns to me and leans down to whisper in my ear, "Now that we are finally alone. You looked very sexy putting Ashlee in her place earlier."

I quietly laugh. "Well, I am here to fix our image from the video, and I don't need a thirsty hussy trying to do more damage. I have a feeling that is what she will do during the interview."

He wraps his arms around my shoulder, "I think that too. Just defend yourself, and I will be there the whole time." I nod at him, and that is when we are told it is time for us to go on air.

"A couple weeks ago, a very scandalous and sinful video was released of Mateo De Luca's wife, Emilia De Luca. Today they are here to give us her side of the story." We walk out when we hear Ashlee introduce us. Once we sit down, Ashlee starts, "Welcome, Mateo and Emilia. Thank you for being here."

Mateo is quick to respond, "Of course. I want to clear up *La mia Regina's* image." Kissing my hand, I smile at him.

Ashlee responds, "Isn't that sweet. Emilia's video is very bothersome to watch. Why did you do something like that? And why would you let them record you? Have you no shame?"

"First of all, Ashlee, I did not want to be in that kind of situation. Do you know what it is like to have your heart outside of your body?" I ask her, and she looks at me confused.

"What kind of question is that?"

"Obviously, you are not a mother," I said to her.

"No, I am not."

"I can tell, because when you become a parent, the moment you lay your eyes on your child, you realize your heart now beats outside of your body. And a true parent would do anything in the world to protect their child. Do you know why Alessia was in the room while I was being raped?" I ask, my hands start shaking from the memories. Mateo holds my hands, rubbing his thumb along my knuckles.

She shakes her head. "Obviously not. I wouldn't put myself in that situation."

"They decided that raping and abusing me wasn't enough to torture me; they had to have my daughter there too. If you listened in the video, I begged them not to have her be there or hurt her."

"Well, why didn't you escape?" She asks with a snarky tone. Mateo squeezes my hand; I give him a squeeze back.

"You think I didn't try? I tried once, and they beat me until I was on the verge of death, and then I was still raped after the beating as part of my punishment. They had the house guard heavily, and I was afraid if I acted out, they would hurt Alessia. Fortunately for us, one day, we were lucky enough that we could escape. They thought they had scared me into not trying to escape, but one day they had loosened their security, and I took advantage of it. I got my daughter out of there and never looked back."

She rolls her eyes and then looks over at Mateo. "Mateo, I have to say, why would you put your and your family's reputation on the line for some bottom class whore?"

Mateo's hand tightens around mine. "A bottom-class whore, you say? I see a Queen who we all should be bowing at her feet just to be in her presence. You only saw a glimpse of the abuse she went through to keep our daughter alive. This woman has so many scars on her body from that pathetic excuse of a man and his friends. When our daughter's sperm donor said that she was to 'groom' Alessia, and I call him a sperm donor, not a father, because he doesn't get to be called that after all the abuse he put my girls through, for a man that was forty years older than my daughter to be his bride, Emilia did what any decent mother would do and protect her child."

"Well, how do you know it isn't an act just to try and get your money?"

At that, Mateo burst out laughing. "Have you seen Emilia out shopping?"

"No, we have only seen her out at the charity ball a couple weeks ago."

Mateo nods, "That's right. My wife is a very honest and humble woman. She rather enjoys the simple things like taking a walk or watching Aladdin for the hundredth time with our daughter. Our biggest argument is her spending money on herself." He says, chuckling, and I give him a sheepish smile. He just smiles bigger and puts his arms around my shoulder, pulling me closer. He kisses my temple, and I look up at him with a big smile.

Ashlee then turns to me. "Why wouldn't you spend his money? Any woman in your position would have designer clothes and jewelry."

"That's right most people would, but when you are abused for years and have to use your body so your daughter can have clothes on her back, materialistic stuff doesn't matter. What is most important to me is making memories with my family and having people around my daughter who love her just as much as me. Even if certain people are spoiling her too much." I say, giving a fake glare to Mateo, who just shrugs his shoulders.

"I am not gonna apologize for spoiling my princess, and I am not the only one," I chuckle.

"I know our whole family spoils her in different ways, but that is why she has flourished so much in the past year. I am so thankful for everyone loving her as if she is their own blood."

Ashlee gives us a fake smile. "You're such a great man, Mateo. Emilia, you sure are a lucky woman to have him. Too bad you didn't bring your daughter Alexis; I would love to meet her."

Mateo responds, "It's Alessia, and why would we bring her to see you? It is very clear you have a distaste for my wife. Why would I put my daughter in a situation where she is uncomfortable? My daughter deserves to only have people around her who will love and cherish her, not someone who will degrade her and her mother." Ashlee's mouth opens like she has no idea how to respond. I just chuckle at her. She can dish out the pettiness but can't deal when someone gives it back to her.

Finally, she snaps out of it. "Well, let's talk about your relationship; where did you meet?"

I look at Mateo and nod at him to tell her cause my self-control is getting thinner by the minute.

"Well, after my girls escaped the clutches of their abusers, they came to Italy. Emilia called her high school friend and he called my family doctor, who was at a conference in the states to have my girls fly back with him for safety reasons. When he landed, he told me how he escorted a mother and daughter back to Italy, and the mother had some pretty severe injuries. I wanted to meet this mother-and-daughter duo and make sure they were okay and if I could help them in any way. About a week later, he went to do a follow-up of Emilia's injuries at her friend's house, and I decided to tag along. When I got there and saw how bad her injuries were but how she still hobbled around on her crutches, still taking care of her daughter, grimacing through her pain. I remember thinking this beautiful, resilient woman in front of me was an angel. Of course, both were very hesitant to talk to me. Once I found out what happened, which took a lot of coaxing, I placed security around her friend's place. She was afraid she would owe me something, but I would never do that to her. After I left, I couldn't help but keep checking in with my team about their well-being, and after a week, I couldn't help it. I started to come around so I could spend time with them, and each time I would fall more for both girls. And a couple months ago, we got married and I officially adopted Alessia. Which was the best day of my life."

"Aw, you are like a modern-day knight in shining armor."

I have to bite the inside of my lip from laughing from the story he just spun and her thinking Mateo is some kind of knight in shining armor.

"It's so sad that you are off the market right now."

That's it, I have had enough of this nonsense. "Ashlee, I wonder if your viewers are as disgusted with your behavior during this interview as we are." Ashlee gives me a glare, and I give her a passive look back.

"Well, maybe if you weren't such a whore in your past and didn't put Mateo and the De Luca's reputation at risk. I wouldn't be so hostile, but someone needs to tell you, you are an embarrassment. I bet your parents are so proud that you open your legs for any man."

I jump up and glare down at her and say with venom in my voice, "My whole family was murdered when I was at work when I was nineteen." I can feel myself start to lose control; I want to beat her to a bloody pulp, but I also want to scream about losing my family because it still hurts. I feel Mateo turn me away from her, and he wraps me in a hug. I bury myself in his chest.

He whispers in my ear, "I got you." I nod and take a deep breath inhaling his cologne.

Mateo tells Ashlee, "We are done. Oh, I would pack your stuff. I will make sure you won't have a job by the end of the day." I look at her, and she is about to say something, but her boss tells her to go to his office. She shoots me a glare and walks off.

"Mr. and Mrs. De Luca, I am so sorry for Ashlee's performance during the interview."

Mateo cuts him off. "I know you are not. If you were, you or one of her supervisors would have intervened, but you didn't. Now, if you excuse me, we are leaving."

We met with the rest of the family, and the first thing was Nonno came up to me and gave me a huge hug. "You, my darling, are such a strong and beautiful woman, my granddaughter. Don't you pay her no mind." I pulled away from the hug.

"I know she was just being desperate for Mateo's attention and was getting nastier the more he gave me attention." He hugs me again.

"Good. I am so proud of you," he tells me as he kisses my hair.

"Thank you, Nonno." Everyone comes over and hugs me.

After that, Julietta looks over at her brother. "So, are you gonna get her fired?" she asks. I roll my eyes at her protectiveness.

"Of course, she is already in her boss's office, and I just made sure she can never find another job in Italy for that pathetic excuse of an interview, all she did was attack Emilia. If we have to do more damage control, we will hold a press conference because, obviously, reporters are incompetent doing their job. Now let's get out of here."

Mateo grabs my hand and walks me out of the news station and to our car. Paparazzi swarm us, but we pay them no mind. Before he opens my door for me, hold me close to him. I look up at him, and without any notice, he kisses the soul right out of my body. When we separate, he leans his forehead on mine. "What was that for?" I ask him, and he smiles.

"Because I am the luckiest bastard alive to be able to call you my wife. You held yourself during that interview with such class when she was acting like a petty bitch. You are so amazing, a true Queen."

Before I can respond I hear Vincenzo. "Okay, lovebirds quit putting on a show and get in the damn car." I roll my eyes at him.

Mateo chuckles and mumbles, "fucker" under his breath as he opens the car door for me. I get in the car and buckle up. After Mateo gets in and buckles his seat belt, I turn to him.

"What are you doing the rest of the day?"

Mateo sighs "Paperwork, why?"

"Oh, if you weren't busy, I was hoping we could finally go visit Zaira, but that's okay. I will go work out this anger at the gym."

"Emilia, I have no problem pushing my paperwork off until later. You need me, and I will always put my family first. Let's go home and change." I smirk at him; he narrows his eyes at me.

"The bag in the trunk has a change of clothes, doesn't it?" I smile at him.

"Yep. I had a feeling I would need to work out some emotional shit after the interview and I thought what better way than to deal with Miss Entitled Brat." He just laughs.

"Okay, let me tell everyone our plans." He picks up his phone and texts everyone then we head over toward the warehouse.

Mateo attempts to sing along with a song on the radio, but singing isn't one of his talents. I am pretty sure he is doing it to make me laugh but not even halfway through the first song we are both laughing our asses off at him being so off-key. But he continues to sing until we get to the warehouse.

When we get to the warehouse, I go to the trunk of the car and pull out my bag. I walk with Mateo into the warehouse. He opens the door to the bathroom and tells me I can change in here. I change into tight black skinny jeans with my black ankle boots. I topped it off with a very tight black fitted shirt and my leather jacket. I chuckle to myself, thinking about how Mateo will react when he sees me. I opened the door, and his mouth was wide open. I peeked down at his cock, and it was definitely being restricted by his pants. He looked sexy himself. He changed into black dress pants and a black button-up shirt with the first few buttons undone, and his sleeves rolled up. After he got over the shock of my outfit, he said, *"Così fottutamente sexy" (so fucking sexy)*.

I laughed at him as I walked up to him, and kissed his cheek, ignoring his protests about me going to change. As I attempted to open the door, he was standing right behind me with one arm around my waist and the other against the door, he spins me around so our chest is touching. "Were you ignoring me, *piccola moglie*?" he asked huskily in my ear, which caused a shiver to run through my body.

I looked up at him. "I would never do that, *mio caro.*" I said with my sassy mouth.

He lightly grabs me by my throat as he grazes his teeth along the shell of my ear until he gets to the lobe then he harshly sucks it in his mouth. I lean my head back into him and moan out. He stops, pushes my back against the door, and smashes his lips on mine. I sink into his embrace, but as soon as it starts, he pulls away, smirking at my face of disappointment when he doesn't continue.

He whispers in my ear, "That is your punishment for not changing into something not as sexy. Now I must control myself not to have a damn boner, watching you in that sexy outfit torturing Zaira. So, you will have to walk around with wet panties, but no worries, I will take really good care of you later." Fuck, this mother fucker knows how to get me riled up more than I already am.

He smirks at me and starts walking towards the stairs of the warehouse. I follow him, and we walk down the stairs to the basement. I see Zaira hanging from her wrists. She looks dirty. I chuckle to myself, "Well, well, well, looks like the almighty Zaira has fallen," I smile at her, as she gives me the most hateful glare. "I think it is time we had a chat, don't you, Zaira?" I say with an evil look.

TWENTY
EMILIA

I look from the De Luca's to Zaira. Oh, the satisfaction I am getting from watching a woman who hurt my daughter hanging by her wrists. "What, you have nothing to say? I thought you would since you were so talkative a couple weeks ago. And being down here all alone, I figured you would have found something… anything to tell me," I say as I slowly circle her.

"Well, it looks like you need some encouragement to talk. That's fine with me." I turn to my dear husband. His face is stoic, but you can see the glimmer in his eye as he watches me. *"Il mio re,* what do you want to know *il mio amore*?"

He stands there for a moment and thinks. "Well, *mia bella regina,* I want to know who she is working for since the video of you was sent from her laptop, but she was in our custody when it was released."

I walk over to him and kiss him knowing that because of her obsession with Mateo, this would get a rise out of her.

"Get off him, you whore."

I slowly pull away from him, smirking and grab a knife from the table of tools. "Me? A whore? I think you must be referring to yourself." I tell her as I stand in front of her. "Now, Zaira, this is your last chance to help yourself. Tell me who you are working for, or keep quiet, and you will suffer. I am feeling generous. I will give you 5 seconds to make a choice." She rolls her eyes.

"5," No response.

"4, I would open my mouth if I were you," I say to her.

"3," Still nothing.

"2," I roll my eyes.

"1, Last chance." She just gives me a nastier glare. "Ok then, you will be singing like a canary in no time." Then I stab her stomach, and she cries out in pain.

"Oh, sweetheart, if you are crying now. I hate to see what happens when we are really having fun," I say sweetly. "Mateo, I need salt and lemon juice."

He walks out of the room for a minute and comes back with the salt and lemon juice. I wiggle the knife around, and she is thrashing, trying to get away from me. I pull the knife out at a different angle. She is screaming; I ignore her and grab some of the salt and rub it right into the stab wound.

"Fuck. Fuck you."

I pour some lemon juice and have it drip down from under her chest and into the stab wound. She just screams and screams with tears pouring down her face. I stand there, waiting for her to settle down.

"Are you done being dramatic?" I ask with my hands on my hips.

"You have no idea how bad this hurts," she rasps out to me.

I start laughing. "You think this is painful? This is nothing compared to what I went through when I was with Alessia's father." I roll my eyes. "I have had my limbs stretched to their limits and still was expected to clean and cook. If I wasn't fast enough, they would cut me and pour acid directly into a cut," I tell her and lift the bottom of my shirt to show scars from my acid burns. She gasps because, honestly, they are very ugly, and it has been over three years since that happened. The only reason they stopped doing that was that I almost died, and then they would have a small little girl to deal with. I also was a favorite among the men to use so they would have lost money.

"Yet you think you are strong enough to be Mateo's wife."

I scoff at the thought, and I hear his family chuckle behind me. "You are not strong enough to be his Queen. Enemies will get their hands on me, no matter how hard he tries to protect me. We also know if they do, I can tolerate a lot of pain, physically and emotionally, because I have already gone through hell and survived. Unlike you, Zaira. When I broke your nose, you acted like it was the end of the world." I shake my head at her delusional fantasy.

"Now we have established all of that. Start talking about who you work for." I say, smirking. I put down the knife and switch it for the scissors, knowing Zaira is all about her beauty and appearance. Maybe threatening to cut her hair will get those lips moving. I turn around and face Zaira with an evil grin on my face. I swing the scissors around with my fingers. "Zaira, I think it is time for a makeover." She starts thrashing around, and I have her moved to the chair, that is bolted to the floor. She is strapped to the chair and a neck brace holds her neck still.

"No, please, no. I don't want to be ugly."

I run the edge of the scissors along her hair by her ears. "Well, get talking then."

"It was Alexei. He wanted me to get close to you so he could take over your empire," she says looking at Mateo.

Mateo walks up behind me. "How long have you been working for him?" She doesn't say anything, so I make the first cut right above her ear.

"Since I was a teenager. They kidnapped me and told me to do as I was told, or they would kill Roman," she sobs.

"Let me guess, you were fucking my father to try and gain the spot as Donna," Mateo asks.

She nods.

"Yes, he was also working with Alexei and Alexei's father, Maxim, before he was killed."

He laughs and says, "Figures. Go ahead and have some fun, my darling." He smacks my ass as he turns to go stand by the wall. I jump a bit from the shock and dig the end of the scissors into the side of her head a bit.

"Oops, sorry about that," I say, but I am laughing. I decided to finish the job and give her a unique haircut. It takes me about ten minutes to complete my look. I step back and shake my head. "I guess cutting hair isn't my talent. Oh well." I say her hair is hideous. Her body is shaking as she continues to sob.

"Mateo, is my box of tools that Jose and Esmeralda sent me here? I also need the portable battery charger," I ask him.

"Yes, darling. I will have someone get it." Then he has one of the soldiers get it.

I turn back to Zaira. "Now I know you are hiding more information from us, so I would advise you to talk before they come back."

"What else can you do to me? I am already ugly."

"Oh, I can waterboard you, beat you until you have many broken bones, burn you with acid, cut off parts of your body, burn you, skin you. I have lots of ways to hurt you and make you ugly, even though the inside of you is already ugly." The men walk in with my box of toys and the car battery charger. "Last chance Zaira and this one will make the stab wound feel like a paper cut." She just glares at me.

"Do you worst. I won't say anything else."

"Okey dokey," I say and grab the scissors I used to cut her hair. I hand them to a soldier.

"Cut her clothes off," I order and walk into my box of goodies, looking for what I need. I hear her thrashing around.

"No, don't do this!"

I look over my shoulder and laugh, "Zaira, why are you acting shy? It isn't like you have ever been embarrassed to show off your body before." I hear multiple men chuckle at me. Yes, I was a victim of sexual abuse, and I should be against this, but when you come after any member of my family, especially Alessia, my values go out the window.

"How can you be this evil?" she asks me.

I simply responded back, "You hurt my daughter and tried to hurt my family. We even gave you the chance to leave and never come back, but you didn't listen. Now you must pay for what you did." I grab the metal gag that is actually a horse bit and tighten the leather strap behind her head. I grab a pair of gloves because I don't know if she has any diseases from her sleeping with anything with a dick, and I don't want that shit touching me. Then I attach the clit clamp, which is also metal.

I attach the clit clamp, which looks like a spider. I grab the portable charger and car battery; I attach one side of each jumper cable to the battery and the other to the edges of the clit clamp.

I hear Vincenzo whisper loudly to Mateo, "*Cugino,* you better never piss her off. She is an evil genius for torture ideas."

I laugh loudly at Vincenzo, and I wink at Mateo. He looks at me, chuckling and tells Vincenzo, "My Queen is perfect. We are all searching for someone whose demons play well with ours and I found mine."

Salvatore shakes his head, "She is just as fucked up as you, if not more, Mateo."

"Aww, thanks, guys, for the compliment," I say, blowing them a kiss.

Mateo says, "Yep, she is my perfect *moglie demoniaca.*"

I turn on the portable charger, and it starts to electrocute her. Her body starts to spasm. The clit is one of the most sensitive parts of the body. I am going to use that to encourage her to start talking. She is already screaming louder than she has before, with fat tears rolling down her face. I turned it off for a minute. "Do you want to tell me what you are hiding from us?"

She nods her head, that was faster than I expected. I walk over and remove the horse bit from her mouth. Her teeth are all cracked, and her mouth is bloody from biting down so hard on the bit. I grab a bottle of water and pour it in her mouth, "Spit the blood out," I tell her. I move to the side so she can't spit it on me.

"I was the reason Lilyana was kidnapped. I had to pretend we were friends so I could get myself into the inner circle. She knew about me sleeping with Abramo and was gonna tell the family. I knew Lilyana and Salvatore were headed to the weekly family dinner. I told Maxim so we could take care of her because we couldn't have her ruin our plans."

I don't even hesitate and swing my arm back and punch her as hard as I can in her nose. I hear something hitting the wall, and I see Mateo and Vincenzo trying to hold Salvatore back from attacking the concrete wall anymore. There is a broken chair not far from where he is standing. I go over to him and just wrap my hand around his wrist. "Salvatore, stop. Let's go to the office." I don't wait for a response, and I walk him into Mateo's office. Once we were in the office, I let go of his wrist. He falls to the ground, and I go with him. He just completely falls apart. He cries harder than I have ever seen a man cry. I don't say anything and just hug him tighter. He finally looks up at me.

"My sweet Lilyana was betrayed by someone who was part of the inner circle," he says through tears.

"I know, Salvatore. It is not your fault; it is Zaira's fault. I will make sure they pay for what they did to her and your baby. I don't care how long it takes; I promise I will help you get revenge for her."

He smiles at me and hugs me again. "Thank you, Emilia."

"Don't thank me. As you all told me this morning, we are family, and, in this family, we support each other." I stand up and give him my hand to help him up, even though he could easily pull me back down to the ground.

"You okay now?" I ask.

He shakes his head. "Not really, but I will be with time."

I nod at him, knowing this probably makes him feel like he just lost Lilyana all over again. "Just remember you have family, and we are all here if you need us."

"I know. I need time to digest all this new information." We walk back out of his office. Mateo and Vincenzo are outside the door, showing their support without being overbearing. They both take turns hugging Salvatore. After they have their moment to console Salvatore, we walk back down to the basement.

"Well, Zaira, I was gonna let you die today but now, knowing what you did to Lilyana and Salvatore, you get to stay alive longer and suffer." I turn to Salvatore. "I know you guys won't physically have a hand in the torture of a woman, but Salvatore is there anything you would like me to do to her." He scratches his chin, thinking then he gives me an evil smirk. He grabs a metal bat wrapped in barbed wire.

"Use this and break as many bones as you want then we can pour acid on her."

I nod at him; I walk up and grab the bat out of his hands. I slowly walk up to her and start with the left leg and smash the bat into her shin and knee. You can hear her bones breaking. I go to the other leg and do the same thing. She is about to pass out. I toss the bat to the other side of the room against the wall, and she jumps from the noise. Her eyes are wide with fear. I go and get the heavy-duty gloves and the container of acid and slowly pour them all over her legs and watch as the tissue gets eaten up by the acid.

She soils herself in the chair. I turn to the soldiers. "Hose her off and have someone who isn't her brother patch her up. She is in for a nice and slow painful death." I turn to the De Luca men. "Are you all ready to get out of here?"

They all nod their heads at me, but Mateo responds, "First, you need to get cleaned up."

I smirk at him. "I wonder why?"

He shakes his head. "Oh, I don't know. You just spent over two hours torturing someone, darling."

I smiled at him. "I did, didn't I?"

Vincenzo shakes his head. "Seriously, you two are fucked up in the head."

"Oh, Vincenzo, don't be jealous of the special bond I have with your cousin."

He looks at me and says, "Nope, you two can share that. Yes, we are all evil, but the clit clamp is a new level of sadistic shit."

I throw my head back, laughing. "Oh, that is nothing for what I have planned for Seth and Boris."

Salvatore chimes in, "Jesus fucking Christ. I am honestly afraid for them, but then again, they deserve it."

"That they do."

I walk into the bathroom in Mateo's office and quickly shower. I watch as the water turns from red to clear. I step out in the same outfit I wore to the interview and just throw my hair up into a messy wet bun. When I walk out, I only see Mateo with his back facing me, looking out the window. I quietly put my bag down and walked over to him. I wrap my arms around his back. We don't talk for a minute; I wonder if I scared him too much. I kiss his back and quietly ask, "Did I go too far?" He slowly turns around and puts both hands on the sides of my face.

"Absolutely not. I am just afraid I have corrupted you." I laugh and shake my head; his hands fall to my waist. He pulls me right against him, and I keep looking at his face.

"No, that was all Esmeralda's doing. Jose threw the biggest fit when he found out what she was teaching me during our whiskey-tasting sessions." Mateo laughs.

"She is a woman not to cross."

"Yeah, but I am lucky she is my godmother and always there for me when I need her."

"Yeah, she is a special kind of woman. I hope one day she will not think of different ways to kill me." We both laugh at how crazy she is and how Jose deals with her, I will never know. I think about how much Jose and Esmeralda love each other. I want someone who adores me and understands me like that, like Mateo does.

Wait! Then it hits me how much I love Mateo. Shit, I love Mateo. This overprotective, possessive, pain in my ass man, who has been carved from the Gods but has a seat next to Satan. I love him with all my heart and soul. Sure, he drives me absolutely insane, and there are times I consider choking him, but I wouldn't want anyone else as my husband.

I lean up and kiss his lips, pushing how much I love him into the kiss. He is quick to react to me; he walks us towards his desk and lifts me onto it. We stayed like that for a few minutes kissing each other not with busy hands but me holding onto his face and his on my hips. We finally separate, and he pecks my lips softly. He leans his head on my shoulder and whispers huskily, "Not that I am complaining, but what was that for?"

I lean back and look him in the eyes and ask him, "I was just wondering how important is that paperwork that is waiting for you at work?"

He squints his eyes at me. "Nothing is urgent. Why?"

I jump off his desk and walk towards the door. I stop and look at him over my shoulder. I bite my lip and say, "Because I can think of some things, we can do together…." He is still eyeing me down, trying to comprehend what I am telling him.

I slowly lick my lips, then bite them again. *"Come consumare il nostro matrimonio. Questo è se vuoi anche tu?" (Like consummate our marriage. That is, if you want to?)* Not even three seconds after those words leave my lips, he grabs his stuff, and I am thrown over his shoulder. I burst out laughing at his eagerness.

He says to me, "I hope you're not planning on walking tomorrow because you have woken up my beast. And I am going to destroy your pussy."

TWENTY-ONE
MATEO

When Emilia said she was ready to consummate our marriage, I got harder than I've ever been. I was not going to have our first time on my desk in the warehouse. That is why I have thrown her over my shoulder and me racing to my car. I am taking her to my penthouse, so we won't be interrupted. I told her I would wait as long as it took until she was ready. Now that she is, I am going to enjoy ravishing her without interruptions. I am going to pull every moan and whimper out of that sweet mouth of hers.

I get to my car, gently put her in it, and buckle her up. I look at my beautiful wife in the face and kiss her. She immediately responds back; I plunge my tongue between those soft lips and begin to taste every corner of her mouth. She lifts her hands and glides it across my chest, going further down. I stop her before we can go further. I look her in the eyes. "Not here, don't worry, we will soon." I lean down to her ear, "And I will fuck you so hard that you will feel me inside of you tomorrow."

She shivers in delight. I stand up, smirking, and make my way around to the driver's side of the door. I get in the car and call my sister to watch Alessia.

Julietta: Hey, Mateo.

Mateo: Hey, can you do me a favor?

Julietta: Maybe…. But it will cost you.

Mateo: Fine, I owe you one but Julietta, please watch your niece for tonight and maybe tomorrow.

Julietta: Okay, that's not a favor, but why do you need me to watch her?

Mateo: Emilia and I are going to be spending time alone.

Julietta: Wait, is she okay? Is she upset from today? Tell her I will go deal with that bitch myself.

Mateo: No, she is fine from today. Sure, she was pissed earlier, but she is not now after torturing Zaira. We are going to spend time alone, uninterrupted.

Julietta: Wait… eww Mateo, I don't need to know about you having sex. That is not something I want to picture in my head.

Mateo: Well, how do you expect to have more nieces and nephews in the future?

Julietta: Miracle conception.

Mateo: Okay, crazy. Love you, and thanks. Call if there's an emergency.

I hang up the phone and text my cousins, telling them I will be at the penthouse, and only bother me if it is an emergency or something that relates to Alessia. After I hung up the phone, I saw Emilia's face red from embarrassment. I chose not to say anything, but she looks so adorable when she blushes, I want to kiss her to make her blush brighter. Luckily, we were almost there. I slowly glide my hand from her knee up towards her pussy. I won't touch it until we are inside, but I definitely will tease her. She tries to close her legs and shuffle away from me. I just chuckle at her. I do this a couple times, and each time I purposely get closer to her pussy.

She turns to look at me "Are you trying to get me all worked up?" she says.

I smirk, "Yes. Trust me, you are going to experience so much pleasure." I pull up to the front of my penthouse, park my car, and toss my keys to the valet. I open Emilia's door and pull her out of the car. I grab her hand and walk her right past the receptionist and walk to my private elevator that takes us right to my penthouse.

We get inside the elevator, and I push her against the wall. I kiss all over her neck, and she has her hands on my neck, gripping my hair tighter. She has moved her head to the side so I have better access to her neck. "Mateo, someone might see us," she barely says between moans. I chuckle against her skin.

"No one will see us, darling. This is my hotel, and we are in my private elevator that will lead us to our penthouse so we cannot be interrupted because I have many plans for my wife's sinful body." She moans out to that. "I know what angels sound like when I hear you moan my name." I whisper huskily in her ear, and I go back to my assault on her neck. The elevator doors open, and I scoop Emilia in my arms, bridal style.

She shrieks out in surprise, "Mateo!"

I look down at her.

"What? I couldn't carry you over the threshold after we got married, but I can do it before we consummate our marriage."

She snuggles into my chest. "You are something else, Mr. De Luca," and kisses my collarbone through my shirt.

I shudder at the contact. "Only for you, my darling."

I get her into the bedroom and place her on her feet. I take her hair out of the bun and let those beautiful brown locks fall. I kiss those luscious and already swollen lips; she kisses me back and pulls herself closer to me. I weave my hand into the back of her head and angle her head the way I want so I can get better access to her mouth. I put my other hand on her ass and squeeze it; she moans into my mouth. Fuck I am already hard as steel but hearing those sweet little noises makes me even harder, if possible. I can't wait to hear all the sounds she will make and her screaming my name. I keep kissing her as we walk toward the bed. Once her knees are at the edge of the bed. I slowly remove my mouth from hers. I kiss over her cheeks, down to her ear and suck her lobe in my mouth while I keep squeezing her ass. She grinds on me and moans again. I don't spend too much time on her ear lobe because I have more important parts of her body to worship. I pull away from her and look her dead in the eyes. "Are you sure you want this, Emilia?" She nods her head.

"Yes, Mateo. I want you inside of me." I take a deep breath, trying to keep myself from ripping off her dress and fucking her right now.

"Fuck. Woman, you are killing me. If you need to stop, just tell me." She nods her head, and I lower the straps of her dress. I grab the zipper on the side of her dress and watch as her dress falls off her body and pools around her feet.

I slowly raise my eyes from her feet all over her body. "*Cazzo diavolo. Sei così dannatamente bella. Mi godrò ogni momento mentre ti rapisco.*"(Fucking hell. You are so damn beautiful. I am going to enjoy every moment while I ravish you.)

I don't give her a chance to respond and go back to kissing her deeply with one hand on her hip and the other side of her face. I slowly lowered her to the bed. I push my cock against her pussy and slowly grind on it. Even with her thong and my pants still on. I can feel how wet she is for me. Emilia grinds back on me as she grips my hair in her hands. I groan in the back of my throat, and my hand that was on her ass travels up to her boobs. I pull down the cups of her bra and pull out her boobs. I take my free hand and slowly start grabbing and massaging it. But I am very hungry for my wife's body, and I start to twist her nipple in between my fingers. With my other hand, I finally unhook her bra and toss it somewhere across the room. I latch my mouth onto her other nipple, and I go from licking it to sucking on it until it is pebbled in my mouth.

She arches her back into me. "Yes, Mateo. Don't stop."

I take my mouth off her nipple with a pop, and she whimpers at the loss of contact. I chuckle "Don't worry, I have to give the other some attention." I immediately go into sucking her other nipple while I twist the nipple I was sucking on between my thumb and pointer finger. She is moaning a mess and squirming under me.

After a couple more minutes, I decided I have starved myself long enough of that sweet nectar that is sitting between my wife's legs. I slowly kiss down her stomach until I am at the edge of her thong, and I lick from one hip to the other. She is wriggling under me. "Please, Mateo," she begs and makes eye contact with those green eyes that make me melt. I put my hands on each side of her thong and rip it off her. "Mateo!" she moans.

"I will buy you more." I grabbed her by her butt and pulled her to the edge of the bed. I sink down to the floor on my knees and spread her legs as far as they can. I am at eye level with her pussy, and I lick my lips. I start licking slowly all around her clit purposely avoiding her clit; she whimpers in protest. I chuckle against her.

"Mateo, stop teasing me. Please." I dive my tongue deep inside of her. She grips the sheets. "Oh fuck," she moans out as she starts to ride my face. I thrust my tongue in and out of her; she has her back arched and is riding my face. I have to hold her legs apart, so they stay open. "Oh, please don't stop, Mateo."

Hearing her call my name out in ecstasy just feeds my ego. I do this for another minute, and she is whimpering and writhing underneath me. I have been drawing out this orgasm long enough. I move my mouth to her clit and start sucking on it gently but get a little bit rougher each time. I move one of my hands from her leg to one of her nipples and start to twist it. If possible, she arches her back even higher off the bed but finally, I insert two fingers into her. I move my fingers back and forth across her G-Spot, and I feel her walls tighten around my fingers.

"That's it, Emilia. Let it go; I want to taste all of you."

She yells out at the top of her lungs, "MATEO!"

I continue what I am doing until she rides out her orgasm. I make sure I lick up every drop of her nectar. I lick my lips; I am not about to waste one drop.

I stand back up to my full height, and she watches me through hooded eyes. Keeping my eyes locked with hers, I slowly unbutton my shirt and drop it to the floor. She gulps at my chest as her eyes lower to the very noticeable bulge in my pants. I unbuckle my belt and quickly pull it from my pants. I dropped it on the ground. With a snap of my wrist, I have the button on my pants undone, and I very quickly pull my zipper down.

I pull my pants off and step out of them. I stop at the edge of my boxers to ask her again if she wants this, but my feisty wife only sasses me. "Don't you dare ask me if I want this. I want you. If you don't, I will find someone else. I am sure I can find a man to come please me. Maybe one of your soldiers?"

Oh, she is gonna get it now.

I quickly pull down my boxers, I go to reach for a condom from the nightstand, but she stops me. "I have an IUD, but it is your choice," I smirk, and I nod at her. I climb into the bed and grab her by the back of her neck and give her a hard, punishing kiss. I purposely give her long slow strokes as I grind my hard cock along the lips of her pussy, making sure I hit her already sensitive clit.

I break the kiss and whisper down into her ear, "What was that about finding someone else to pleasure you?"

She barely gets out without moaning. "Well, you were taking too long. I was wondering if you still wanted it."

"You are asking for it, *moglie esuberante*."

She smirks at me. "Then give it to me." And I grab my cock; I run the head up and down her pussy a couple times. She is about to open that smart mouth again, and I push myself inside of her, I ignore my needs. She moans out and closes her eyes.

"Keep your eyes on me *il mio amore*." She does. I keep my eyes on her the whole time as I slide myself further inside of her. I decided I would not ram my cock inside her, and once I was fully inside of her. I stop so she could adjust. I lean down and kiss her; she responds back with just as much passion. I continue to slide the rest of me until our hips meet. "Fuck, Emilia, you are so damn tight," I groan out, and she gives me a smile.

"And you are so big; I don't think I have ever felt so full."

I start to thrust in and out of her. I grab her legs and wrap them around my waist. She reaches down and starts to play with her own nipples. "You look sexy as hell playing with yourself right now." I grab onto her hips and give her harder and longer strokes. Her eyes roll in the back of her head, and my dominant side comes out. I reach down and gently wrap my hand around her throat; her eyes pop open, looking at me.

"I told you to keep your eyes on me," I say between thrusts. She nods her head at me, "Tsk, Tsk. Words, Mrs. De Luca."

She barely whispers out in ecstasy, "Yes, Mateo." I lift one of her legs over my shoulder and pound into her hard and deeper. "Oh, don't stop; I am so close."

"I won't stop until you are shaking and begging me to stop. When I get done, you won't be able to stand on your legs."

Her hands that had been lightly scratching my back, now are scratching me harder as she reaches her peak of pleasure. At the top of her lungs, she yells my name, and her pussy squeezes my cock so hard that I cum. I keep thrusting into her until we both have come down from our orgasmic high. I lean down and kiss her sweaty forehead. She barely gives me a content but exhausted smile. I chuckle at her. I go into the bathroom, quickly clean myself up and start the water so we both can take a relaxing bath together. I grab a wet washcloth and bring it into the bedroom to clean Emilia up.

I gently clean her up and she quietly moans when the washcloth contacts her clit. "Let a woman rest. The anaconda in between your legs tried to murder my pussy."

I laugh at her "Crazy woman, I am just cleaning you up." I toss the washcloth into the laundry basket then I pick Emilia up in my arms, bridal style.

"Didn't I say let a woman rest?"

I just kiss her lips in silence. I step into the tub with her in my arms. I sit her between my legs, and she sighs out. "Thank you," she says as she lays her head back against my shoulder.

I look down, "Why are you thanking me?"

She gives me one of those sweet smiles. "That is the first time I've had sex that was completely consensual that I was conscious for the whole time." I go to open my mouth, but she stops me. "No, let me finish. The whole time you took care of me, not expecting anything in return. It has always been me who has to please them and never worry about myself. You also made sure I was okay and never drifted back to my safe space in my head. You took care of me physically and mentally while we were having sex."

I cup her jaw. "You always have the right to tell anyone no. What you do with your body is your choice unless you let anyone else touch your body. Then you get to watch me kill them in front of you. I don't share what is mine. Especially the ones I love." Her eyes bug out.

"You love me?" she asks, bewildered.

"How could I not? You are beautiful on both the inside and outside, you are an amazing mother, you love my family fiercely, you are loyal, fierce, and you look sexy as hell when you torture people even if you do frighten my men." I chuckle at the end, and she laughs along with me.

"Are you sure you're not saying that because of the sex?"

I turn her around, so she is straddling my lap. "No, beautiful. I have felt like this for a couple weeks, but I figured with everything going on, that it wasn't the best time to tell you. I actually was going to take you on a romantic date and tell you that way, but I couldn't wait any longer. I don't expect you to say it back." I tell her to wrap my hands around her waist and bring her closer, so we are cuddling in the tub.

She lifts her head and looks me in the eyes, "But I do. Yes, in the beginning, we didn't really have a good start, but that wasn't all your fault. Since we have come back from Spain, you have done nothing but be the best husband to me even if I was being extremely difficult, and you've been an amazing father to Alessia. You are a man, a father, who loves her unconditionally even if he spoils her rotten, but you also gave her a family. I never thought she would have anyone else but me who would love and protect her. You have dealt with me and helped me work through my past. It took us a year to have sex and you never once complained. I am the luckiest woman in the world to be your wife and be loved by you." She leans forward and gives me a soft kiss.

She bites her lip and starts to grind on me; I am hard as a rock as soon as she starts. "Why wash up when we are going to get dirty again?" she whispers in my ear.

I close my eyes. She grabs my cock lifts herself up, and then slides my cock inside of her wet hot channel. She lowers herself all the way down, we both moan about being intimate again. I barely get a moment before she is grinding on my cock, hard. She goes back and forth between grinding on me and bouncing up and down on my cock. After sucking on her nipples and rubbing her clit, it doesn't take long for both of us to cum again.

We wash ourselves, get out of the tub, and she wiggles her hips at me as she leaves the bathroom. I quickly dry off faster than I think I ever have in my life and chase after my sexy little vixen. We spent the whole night christening my penthouse. I had her bent over the couch and against the floor to ceiling windows. I pounded into her while she sat on the counter. She had the idea of eating cool whip off each other, so we had to take a shower, and I fucked her against the shower wall with her legs wrapped around my hips. Hours later, we are finally lying in bed, and she is fast asleep on my chest. I swear if I die tomorrow, I will die a happy man. All I know is that Emilia is going to be extra busy because now that I have had a taste of what sex with Emilia is like, I am going to crave more of it. She is the whole package.

I think Emilia might be joining me for lunch when I go into my office. I smirk to myself about bending her over my desk at work. Knowing Emilia's kinky side, which I found out today, I can see her enjoying some midday sex at my office as well. Especially the office at the clubs, where I have mirrors so she can watch herself as she cums all over my cock.

I fell asleep with a smile on my face with my beautiful naked wife on my chest and my arms wrapped around he

TWENTY-TWO
EMILIA

      I feel someone giving me feather light kisses down my neck, and I smell the familiar and soothing smell of Mateo's cologne. I sigh with content, and I turn my head to give him more access to my neck. He moves so his head is nuzzled between my legs and wastes no time before feasting on me. I grab his hair and use my hold on him as leverage as I ride his face. His tongue starts thrusting as deep as he can in and out of me. My head is thrown back, and I keep riding his face; his nose keeps lightly rubbing against my clit every time I thrust his face back and forth against my pussy. He can feel me tighten up around his tongue because his fingers move up to my clit and start rubbing it vigorously, and I moan when my orgasm hits me. "That was a good appetizer before my meal." He wastes no time and lies in the middle of the bed, "Sit on my face and put your hands on the wall."

      "But I will suffocate you."

      "Emilia, get your ass over my face, and don't worry about me I can move you if I want to, but I doubt I will. I want your pussy to be flooding like a waterfall before I will consider giving you a break."

      When I don't move fast enough. He sits up, grabs my hips, and drags me over his face. "Hands on the wall."

      After seeing the look in his eye, I do as he says. My legs are on either side of his face. Mateo grabs my hips and lowers me all the way down, so I am flushed with his mouth. He holds onto my hips and rocks me back and forth across his mouth. This is so fucking good that I end up grinding harder on his face. Mateo moves his lips to my clit and starts to alternate between sucking hard and sucking so softly I can barely feel it. When he adds two fingers inside of me and curls them in and out of me, my orgasm hits me so hard and fast.

      "How are you feeling this morning?"

      "Sore but very happy." He flips us over. so I am on my back, and he is leaning above me.

      "Is that so?" he asks me, and I nod at him. "Good, that means I am doing my duties as your husband." He leans down, kissing me nice and slow. The kiss isn't sexual at all but shows each other how much we mean to each other.

      We break apart from the kiss and I tell him, *"Ti amo."*

      He smiles at me like he just won the jackpot and responds, *"E ti amo."* Before I can kiss him again, he is swoops me into his arms.

      "MATEO!" I shriek out, and he just laughs at me. He carries me into the bathroom and sits me on the sink; he starts the water in the tub. Once he finds it warm enough, he adds my favorite bath oils to it. I go to get off the counter, but, shocker, Mateo already has picked me up and sets me in the tub.

"I am going to order us breakfast and get us clothes. I will be right back." He gives me a quick peck and walks away; I stare at his ass. He turns around sending me a wink, and I laugh at him.

I sink further into the tub. Last night was absolutely amazing. For years I had been afraid of men because I feared all they wanted from me was to use my body. Last night Mateo proved me wrong; he was so unselfish. He always made sure I had orgasmed before he did, and oh man, could he make me orgasm. I have never felt like that, and my body is no stranger to sex. My husband seems to keep surprising me every day with the way he dotes on our daughter, how much he loves and protects our family, how absolutely wonderful he is to me. Not to mention all the little things he does for me. Like random flowers he will give me, giving me time to take an uninterrupted bath when the demons inside my head are getting too much and I need time alone. Or just spending time talking to the two of us.

I am so deep in thought I don't even realize Mateo is sitting in front of me until he grabs one of my legs and starts to massage it. I moved my eyes to him and he asks, "What are you thinking about, *bello?*"

"Just how lucky I am to have you as my husband."

He shakes his head. "I am glad you and Alessia rode on my plane that day with Roman to Italy."

"Me too." He switches to the other leg, and I close my eyes and enjoy the moment of complete bliss, no Seth bullshit or Russian mafia drama. Just us in this peaceful moment, I know it won't stay like this, but I am enjoying it.

We help each other wash. I am not surprised he paid extra attention to my boobs, pussy, and ass. I kept trying to swat his hands away, but he would kiss me senselessly. As the kisses became more passionate, he started to knead at my breast. I threw my head back. He moved me, so I was facing him, straddling his lap. He was kissing all over my neck and face. One of his hands traveled to my clit, and I started grinding back on his cock. I finally had enough of teasing each other, so I lifted my hips up and sank down on his length until I had all of him inside of me. I moaned out once he completely filled me. I start to grind on him as he grips my waist tighter and groans.

And holy hell, this man keeps getting better each time. "Ride me…. Harder," he moans out with his head thrown back. I grab the edges of the tub on each side of his head. I do as he asks and grind on him harder. He opens his eyes and sees how close my boobs are to his face. He grabs one, puts it in his mouth, and starts sucking and licking my nipple while he twists and pinches the other one. This time it is me who throws my head back in ecstasy.

"Mateo, don't... stop." I say breathlessly. He takes it upon himself to thrust up into me. I can feel myself getting closer to my orgasm; my walls clamp around his shaft. I cum, and he holds my hips, and he thrusts up into me. I am still panting from my first orgasm, and he is pushing me into my second. I am moaning his name when my second one slams through my body.

Mateo yells out, "Fuck. Emilia." Both reach our highs. I collapsed on him, leaning my forehead against his forehead. After we have caught our breath, he gives me a peck on my lips.

"Fucking hell, Mateo. My pussy is going to die by your anaconda cock." I tell him, and he laughs.

"You have such a smart mouth, Mrs. De Luca. And I love it." He pecks my lips again. He stands up with me in his arms and brings us to the shower, and he washes me again. This time he was sweet and loving, leaving gentle kisses on my body as he washed me. I returned the favor, and after, we were done.

Breakfast was already waiting for us when we got out. I realize I have nothing to wear, and I go to ask Mateo for one of his shirts, but I turn around, and he is in sweatpants and has clothes in his hand for me. I grab them from him and see that they are clothes my size. I quickly get dressed in sweatpants and a baggy t-shirt like I love to wear on my lazy days at home. "How did you pull off having clothes for me?" He smirks at me and opens his closet, I walk in, and half of the closet has clothes for me. I am flabbergasted "Wait...when... how?"

He laughs, "All of my properties have clothes for both you and Alessia."

Once again, this man surprises me. I hug him, "You are too much, Mateo."

"This is not too much, Emilia."

"Yes, yes, it is. Let's eat on the balcony." I walk over to get our plates, but he beats me to it, so I grab our drinks and open the door for him.

We set everything down at the table and sit down. The food is amazing. The pancakes, French toast, eggs, and sausage are all delicious. "So, what time do you have to go back to the office today?" I ask him.

"I don't have to go at all today. Salvatore and Vincenzo are handling the mafia side of things today. Today is our day to spend together alone. We haven't been able to do that with everything going on between you finishing your degree and helping Alessia with her studies and me dealing with Seth plus my legal businesses. The few moments we catch each other during the day are nice but today I am being greedy and want my wife all to myself."

I just laugh to myself. "Okay, but I do want to call and talk to Alessia."

"Of course. We will check in on her, but let's finish our breakfast first."

We continue to have small talk while we eat; the view over the city is absolutely beautiful. Don't get me wrong, I love the mansion and the scenery, but I also appreciate the city views. We FaceTime Julietta to check on Alessia; it rings for a couple seconds.

Julietta: Hello, fratello. Why are you calling me? Aren't you supposed to have alone time with Emilia?

Emilia: *(chuckling)* Hello to you, sorella. I was calling to check in on Alessia.

Julietta: Sorry, sorella. I thought you were that pain in the ass I am unfortunately related to.

Mateo: Hey! You are lucky enough to be related to me.

Emilia: *(smacking Mateo on the back of his head)* Hush, your ego is already big enough.

Mateo: *(pretending to glare at me)* You will pay for that later. *(He smirks)*

Julietta: No, nope. As much as I want more nieces and nephews, I don't need to witness your PDA. Here is Alessia.

Alessia: Mama, Papa!!

Emilia: Hi, baby. Are you having fun?

Alessia: *(nods her head and signs)* Yep. I helped Nonna and Nonno cook dinner. Zia Julietta painted my nails pink with hearts on them. *(She shows her fingers to us)* and I played on the new playground Zii got me.

Mateo: Wow, it sounds like you are having a lot of fun.

Alessia*(signs)*: I did, Papa. Zio Vincenzo played with me on the playground because he is silly, but I had to give Zio Salvatore puppy eyes so he would help me across the monkey bars. Zio Vincenzo says Zio Salvatore has a stick up his ass.

Emilia: Don't say that again, it isn't very nice.

Alessia*(signs)*: Okay, Mama. I won't say it; I will be a good girl.

Emilia: We know you are a good girl. Zio Vincenzo just says naughty things, but we will teach him not to say those things. You be a good girl for everyone, okay? We will be back tomorrow morning.

Alessia*(signs)*: Okay, Mama. I love you, Mama and Papa.

Emilia and Mateo: I love you, Alessia.

Then we hung up. I turn to Mateo "Can I beat Vincenzo's ass when we get back home?"

He laughs "Of course *Tesoro*."

I smirk. "Good"

"Don't do too much damage. I still need my cousin." I pretend to think about it. "Emilia," he warns, and I still pretend to think about it, but he starts to tickle me. I try to wiggle away from him.

"Okay, okay, I will make sure he can walk after. Stop," I say, laughing. He stops and gives me a cocky smile. I mutter under my breath, "Cocky bastard," and take off into the other room. I know he heard me because I hear him running after me. We end up in the living room. I am on the far side of the couch, and he is on the other. We keep trying to juke each other out. I run to the other side of the room that leads to the door to the elevator, but I hear a big thud. I look over my shoulder and see Mateo jump over the couch and run over to me. With me stopping to look at him, he gains on me, and before I know it, he has his arms wrapped around my waist. He lifts me up off my feet, and we both are laughing hysterically.

He sits us on the couch. I am in his lap with his hands around my waist with my legs across his lap. We both are still laughing hard, but we finally stop. Mateo gives me a gentle kiss on my lips "What would you like to do today?" he asks.

I shrug my shoulders, "I honestly don't care."

He smiles. "Good, I have a plan, let us freshen up a bit and we can leave."

We both freshen up. I am wearing jeans with knee-high boots and a teal blue flowy short-sleeve shirt. Mateo is wearing jeans and his boots with a black, very tight-fitted short sleeve shirt. I love when he dresses casually, he looks hot. He sees me checking him out.

"Take a picture it will last longer."

I shake my head, "Nope, I am good; I can just ask to see my husband if I want to see something sexy." I wink at him.

He shakes his head "That smart mouth is gonna land you across my lap. That ass is going to be pink."

"Sounds like a good time." I walk past him to the door while shaking my ass at him.

He groans and mumbles "She is trying to kill me."

We walked into the elevator, and I ask him, "Any hint on this surprise?"

"Nope." I look at him and try to give him puppy dog eyes. Instead, he just kisses me to distract me.

"Did you just kiss me to distract me?"

"Yep," he says, dragging out the p.

"That's cheating!" I tell him with my hands on my hips, giving him a glare. He chuckles at me and pushes my hair behind my ear.

"No *mia Regina*, it is playing smart."

I mumble 'asshole' under my breath; of course, he hears and smacks my ass.

"Quit swearing, and I will not have a reason to smack that juicy ass. Actually, no, keep cursing; I don't mind smacking your ass. It is actually quite enjoyable," he says with a cocky smirk on his sexy face.

I keep my mouth shut and just glare at him. The elevator opens, and he guides me out to his car. Mateo being the gentleman he is, opens my door for me; I thank him and climb into his Range Rover. As I buckle the seatbelt, he climbs into the driver's seat. He turns the engine over and pulls out of the penthouse parking lot, and heads into the city. We sing along with the radio, Mateo being very off-key. I have to try not to laugh at him, while I sing along with him but after two songs, I lose it.

He lowers his sunglasses, so his eyes peer over the top of his sunglasses. "Mrs. De Luca, are you laughing at my wonderful singing voice?"

"*Miele*, you sound like a dying cat."

He pushes his sunglasses back up his nose and then puts a hand on his heart. "You wound me."

"Here, I thought Vincenzo was the dramatic one."

"Your sassy mouth is gonna get you in trouble."

"So, I have heard," I smirk at him knowing his punishments would end in both of us naked. At a red light, he leans over slowly and licks the shell of my ear while his hand travels further up my thigh to pop the button on my jeans. He pulls the zipper down, and his fingers lightly run over my folds through my thong. My breath hitches, and he pulls away from my ear, but he keeps playing with me. I arch my back into the seat of the car while thrusting my hips forward, hoping to get some kind of friction. Instead of him relieving me, he snaps the band of my thong against my skin. I whine in protest.

"Don't you move unless I tell you to."

Fuck, I just got wetter than I already was. He tortures me for a couple more minutes, moving his fingers all around my pussy but never actually going under my thong and giving it the attention, I desperately wanted.

Finally, he moved my thong to the side and thrusted two fingers inside of me. I squeak out, surprised at him thrusting his fingers inside of me so quickly. You would think he would start fingering me fast, but no, he is barely moving his fingers in and out of me. "Mateo," I whimper out, wanting more.

"Hmm, does my wife want more?" I nod at him. "Words, *moglie*."

"Yes, Mateo, please faster." He smirks and starts to finger me a lot faster. I am a moaning mess with my head thrown back against the seat and my eyes closed. I am on the brink of my orgasm when he stops the car and pulls his fingers out of me. I quickly open my eyes to see Mateo sucking my juices off his fingers. I am still panting and on edge. He zips up my zipper and buttons the button on my jeans. He gets out of the car and comes over to my side of the car. I glare at him for stopping me from cumming; he just smirks and quietly chuckles at me. He takes my hand and leads me into an empty building.

I look around and see it is basically empty, except for a small table with a folder on it and two chairs. He lets go of my hand and walks to the table to grab the folder. He picks up the folder and walks back over to me. "Go ahead and open it." I looked stunned at him for a moment but opened the folder. When I read what it was, my mouth opened.

It takes me a couple seconds to form words to respond to him, "Mateo, are you serious?" I ask.

"Yes, *Mia Regina*, you have finally got your business degree, and I know this was a dream of yours. I want you to have whatever you want, and we both know you would not have asked me to help you with this." Instead of responding back, I just give him a tight hug, and he hugs me back just as tight.

I whisper, "Thank you," into his chest.

"You don't have to thank me. I want you to be happy and to have everything you have ever wanted. But you are too selfless and always insist on not spending the money I give you for yourself. You chose, instead, to spend it on everyone else." He shakes his head, reaches into his wallet, and pulls out a black, unlimited credit card. "This is for you to buy whatever you want or need for the business. Since you can see, it is very bare." He looks at me giving me a look knowing that I am about to turn down his help. I decide to agree with him, knowing he doesn't want anything in return from me.

"Okay."

He cups my face and gives me a sweet kiss. After we break away from the kiss, he grabs my hand and gives me a tour. It has four rooms; one will be my office, another I will turn into my dark room, the third will be a boudoir studio, and the last will be my studio for all my other shoots. I grab the paper and pen Mateo had on the table and start planning everything I will need to get. After spending about two hours at the studio, which we ended up naming Mama E's Photography, we ended up going back to the penthouse. Enjoying spending more time exploring each other's bodies.

The next morning, we headed back to the mansion. As soon as Alessia spotted us, she ran up to us. "MAMA! PAPA!" she yelled and launched herself into Mateo's arms. We chuckled at her enthusiasm.

"Whoa, there speed racer. Where are you going so fast?" Mateo asked her while kissing her cheek.

"I want to show you my new p-playground."

Mateo kisses her head and puts her down. Alessia grabs both of our hands and drags us outside. As we pass, Nonna and Nonno laugh at their sweet great-granddaughter dragging her parents outside.

When we get outside, we both are shocked to see a huge princess-themed playground and a trampoline. Alessia takes off running to the playground, and Marcello follows her.

"Geez, when she said playground, I never imagined something so big." I said to Mateo; he nodded his head at me.

"And this summer we are putting a pool in for her as well." Mateo and I turn our heads to Adraino as he walks up next to me.

"You all are going to have her spoiled."

Adriano just shrugged his shoulders. "We might spend a lot of money on her, but she has yet to act like a spoiled brat. You raised her right Emilia; she is so appreciative of everything people do for her."

I blush, "Thank you."

"I should be thanking you and Alessia."

I turn and give him a questioning look. "Why would you be thanking us?"

"Yesterday was the first time since Lilyana died that I saw Salvatore have a truly genuine smile on his face when he was playing with Alessia on the playground. It kills me every day to see my son not living his life to its fullest because he misses his other half. And I know that pain as well. I miss Anna every day and probably will never move on, but I already had a lifetime of wonderful memories with her. Salvatore and Lilyana had barely begun their life together when it was snatched away from them. We all regret both Anna and Lilyana's deaths, wishing we could do more, but watching Lilyana be shot in her chest by Maxim live on the TV was torture for him. Salvatore lost it. If it wasn't for Mateo and Vincenzo holding him back, he would've destroyed his penthouse. I can't tell you how many times in the first couple of years one of us would find Salvatore completely drunk. Luckily, he never touched drugs, maybe due to the fact that Lilyana's mother used to get high and beat her. So, thank you both for coming into his life and making everyone in this family happier."

I smiled at him with tears in my eyes, thinking about losing my family, Salvatore had already told me about Lilyana's death, but my heart still ached for him. I gave Adriano a big hug and kissed him on the cheek, trying to not cry.

The rest of the evening we spent together as a family outside. The men were acting like children daring each other to do stupid things on the trampoline. At one point, they were getting stupidly careless, especially for Mafia bosses. I yelled over to them, "If any of you get hurt, you better hope between the three of you, you can help each other to the infirmary because no one will be helping your dumbasses." Nonno was laughing in his seat at the looks of hurt and betrayal on their faces. They started to protest, and I stuck my hand up and shook my head at them. They all huffed and chose not to say anything else, but did that stop them? Of course not.

I decided to sit down with Nonna and Nonno. I haven't talked to them much recently. Nonna asked me how I liked my gift from Mateo.

I was shocked at first that she knew, but, then again, this is Nonna we are talking about. She knows about everything that goes on in this mansion.

"I absolutely love it, and we have already started planning what I need to get it up and running." She looks over at me with a knowing look, and I know she is about to ask me about last night, and I prefer not to discuss my sex life with my husband's grandmother.

"So… Did you both have a nice night together…alone, without anyone or anything in the way?" Geez could this woman be any less discrete.

Thankfully Nonno comes to my rescue. "Woman! Don't pry into their personal business."

She smacks him on the arm. "Hush old man! I want to know how soon I will get more grandbabies."

I start laughing. "Nonna, I would love to have more children, and hopefully, one day, we will. We discussed that we would wait until after Seth and Boris are dealt with, because if I should get kidnapped again, I do not want to put another child through what Alessia went through. I also feel like if I was kidnapped by them and I was pregnant with Mateo's child, they would treat the child worse than they did Alessia."

Nonna huffs, "I understand, but I still want more grandbabies."

I smile at her and pat her hand. "Of course Nonna, and I should expect you to spoil that child just as bad as Alessia."

"Yes, and you will be too. Your last pregnancy you were treated like less than dirt. I will be surprised if Mateo lets you pick up a pen." I groan out because I can see it. "I don't want to imagine it."

They both laugh, but Nonna says, "Darling, if I remember correctly, you used to swear at me because of how overprotective you got after I was pregnant."

Mateo sits down next to me, all sweaty. He gives me a kiss and asks, "Nonno, what did you do to have Nonna glaring at you?"

Nonna smirks and says, "We were talking about, when Emilia gets pregnant, how overprotective you will be. And then your sweet Nonna reminded me how I was when she was pregnant with Abramo and Adriano."

Mateo smiles, looking at me, "When you get pregnant, you will be spoiled and be a pampered Queen. You won't have to lift a finger to do anything. I can't wait to see you round with our child. I will be there for everything; I missed almost all of Alessia's firsts. I will not miss any of our future children's firsts."

"Children? How many do you want?"

"Four kids sound good."

I chuckle at him. I wouldn't mind a big family with him and look over at Nonno and Nonna, who are holding hands and smiling at each other. I lean over and whisper to Mateo, "I want us to be like that when we are older."

"Me too," he says and pecks my lips softly. I lay my head on his shoulder as we watch Adriano, Salvatore, Vincenzo, Marcello, Julietta and Alessia all play together in the yard.

Alexei

I call my idiot brother-in-law because what I found out really has my blood boiling.

Alexei: "Are you fucking telling me you never got your daughter a birth certificate?"

Seth: "Well, hello to you too, brother-in-law. Yes, I never did; she was supposed to never leave the house until Boris married that brat."

Alexei: "Are you stupid or a complete moron? I honestly should expect you to be so fucked up. You are that pathetic woman's brother."

Seth: "So when can I get my hands on that whore?"

Alexei: "Well, because you are an incompetent idiot, it is going to take longer to kidnap both. Especially since Emilia is married to Mateo, and he also adopted Alessia."

Seth: "NO! They are mine."

Alexei: "Maybe you should have done something about it when you had her kidnapped and held her hostage for over five years. I have to go and figure out what to do next."

I then hang up my phone. I reach out to a spy within the De Luca staff at the mansion because we will burn the mansion down, and if they do end up escaping, I will just kill them.

I grab my phone and text, "Get everything ready and wait on my mark."

TWENTY-THREE
UNKNOWN

I hate working for these Italian fuckers. I had everything set in place last week after I got Mr. Ivanov's text. "Get everything ready and wait for my mark." Once we get that used-up whore and bastard child out of the way, we can take down their empire. I can't wait to set everything off and watch everything go up in smoke from a distance.

Today was the day, but I had to act normal and wait. My phone vibrates with a text.

"Go."

I smile and start our plan.

EMILIA
A Few Hours Earlier

I laugh along with Alessia as we swing our hands together walking towards the barn. Today all the De Luca's are out of the mansion, so we are having a full day of fun. Some overdue mother-daughter time together. Mateo went to Ireland with Salvatore to talk to Peter O'Sullivan, the boss of the Irish Mafia, about being an ally with us. Mateo has been trying to get as many people as possible to be allied with us. We have strength, but the Russian's have numbers.

Vincenzo went to the States to handle a casino that was having issues with people paying back their debt. I honestly was surprised when Mateo said, out of the three of them, Vincenzo is the most psychotic when dealing with torturing people. Mateo shuddered when I suggested that Vincenzo and I should pair up together. He said he would almost feel bad for whoever the poor soul was but then we don't torture innocent people.

Nonno and Nonna are on vacation in Canada. After he retired from being the Don, they kept Julietta. Now they take two vacations a year, each about a month long. They left a week ago, and Alessia was so sad. She thought they were leaving and never coming back. They both promised to come home, and they call every day.

But oh boy, the tears when Mateo went to leave was tough. She grabbed onto his leg and wrapped her little body around him. She bawled and promised to be a good girl and that she never needed any more gifts as long as, "Papa never leaves me."

It took Mateo, me, Julietta, Adriano, and Salvatore an hour to convince her that he would come home. He calls multiple times a day, and she calls him. If he can't answer her call, he has Salvatore talk to her.

Salvatore also promised if Mateo didn't call, he would force him to call her.

Julietta and Adriano are still around. Adriano has his own house but has been staying here while the three men are out of the country. I am pretty sure Mateo asked him, but he is also helping Mateo run things while he isn't here. Today he had to go to a meeting at De Luca Corp on behalf of Mateo.

Julietta is at her fashion company right now. She has a runway show coming up in a couple months and today is the final pick of the outfits that will be shown that day. She promised when she got back, we would have a girls' sleepover in the cinema room and do facials and our nails. Alessia was so excited, and already decided she wanted her nails painted teal and hot pink. Miss Thing loves pink; everything must be pink, and of course everyone is too eager to fill her in her love for pink.

My phone dings notifying me of a text from my darling husband.

Mateo: Hey don't have long to talk, but I wanted to check in on my girls.

Emilia: Aww, how sweet. We are headed to the barn so Alessia can have her jumping lesson.

Mateo: Is Marcello with you?

Emilia: Yes, he is. Try not to worry.

Mateo: I know. I am just worried that anything can happen since I am out of the country. But have Marcello record her riding and send it to me. I feel like I am gonna need something to put me in a better mood after this meeting.

Emilia: Sure, I can do that. Maybe tonight I can send you something before I go to bed.

Mateo: Really, are you trying to make my cock hard before I go into the meeting?

Emilia: I don't know what you are talking about.

Mateo: Sure you don't. Keep it up. and I will punish you when I get home. I have to go now. Give my princess a kiss. I love you both.

Emilia: Promises, Promises. We love you too.

I put away my phone before he could respond back to me. I quietly chuckle to myself, thinking back to the day he showed me my studio. I thought my punishment was done, nope. Put it this way, I was walking funny the next morning even after soaking in the bath, and of course, Vincenzo had to make some comments. And the other two snickered, but it was worth all the comments.

"MAMA!" Alessia yells to get my attention.

"Sorry, baby. What's up?"

"Can we give Alpha some treats since Papa isn't here, and he might be missing Papa?"

I smile at my daughter; she has such a big heart. "That sounds like a wonderful idea."

She starts to walk faster toward the barn, Marcello and I laughing at her excitement. Having her around the horses has really helped her.

Marcello turns to me, "Boss check in yet?"

I nod at him. "Yep, that was him. He asked if you could record Alessia riding today."

"Of course, Donna."

I roll my eyes at him. It still feels weird being called Mrs. De Luca, Donna, or Queen by the other members of the family, even though it has been months since I married Mateo. "Ugh, I am still getting used to being called anything but Emilia."

Marcello chuckles, "Well, you better."

"I know, Mr. Grumpy Boss hates when any of you refer to me as Emilia." I'm just adjusting from going from a "whore" to the wife of the Boss of the Italian Mafia.

We continue to follow Alessia to the barn, and she is calling back to Marcello. "Celly I... get to jum-mp Cash today." she tells him. Of course, he is already fully engaged with her. I love how he is more than a bodyguard for her. I need to find out when his birthday is and get him something.

"Your Mama told me *Principessa*, and I am gonna record it so we can send it to your Papa." She smiles at Marcello and goes to grab the treats out of the barn.

"I got them, Mama," she tells me as she is holding a handful of sugar cubes.

"I see, baby."

She unlocks the gate and sets her eyes on Alpha first. He walks over to her, and she opens her palm completely flat as he eats a couple sugar cubes out of her palm. She giggles as his lip tickles her hand. After he ate all the treats, she started to pet his neck. He nuzzles his big head into her chest, which is funny since his head is almost the size of her torso. I take a picture of them and send it to Mateo.

She gently talks to him, "I miss Papa too. He will be home soon, and we can go for another ride together when he gets home." After a couple minutes of them spending time together while I took some pictures, she moved on to catch Cash.

He sees her and starts to run away until she shakes the bucket of treats. He stops, and his ears perk up, she shakes it again, and he trots over to her. She can put on his halter without him running off. "Cash, you are so naughty," she tells him as she leads him into the barn.

Sundance finally sees me but doesn't walk over; he is content grazing. I chuckle at my lazy boy. Alessia diligently grooms and tacks up Cash almost on her own. She still struggles to put the saddle on his back because he is a bit taller than her. She puts on her helmet and leads Cash out to the arena.

I give her a leg up onto his back and I tell her to start warming up with a working walk while doing circles and figure eights using more of her legs and less of her reins for steering. She nods her head and starts following my directions. I lean back against the fence. I am proud of how far she has come in the past year.

I can't believe she will be eight in a week; I remember how last year Esmeralda and Jose spoiled her for her birthday. I can only imagine what the De Luca's have planned. I tune back in and see Alessia trotting doing the same warmups but now in a trot. I chuckle at her and call out, "Cheeky Monkey." She smiles at me but stays focused on what she is doing. After she has gone both directions, I call her over to me.

I pet Cash on his neck and walk over to her "Good job, now I want you to pick up a slow canter" I say the word slow because my dare devil daughter loves to go fast, and Cash is a willing participant.

"Ok Mama."

"Remember shoulders back, hands steady, and sit deep in your seat."

"Gotcha, come on, Cash. We have to go slow cause Mama might have a heart attack." She nudges Cash into a trot moving to the edge of the arena. I hear Marcello give a deep belly laugh. I look over at him and glare.

"She is your mini-me, including her sass."

I shrug my shoulders. "Yeah, she is, but her being sassy and confident, she will be able to stand up for herself."

He nods at me. "That is true, especially how far she has come since we met her last year."

"Yeah, I was thinking about that. I can't believe my baby is gonna be eight soon."

Marcello looks at me. "You know everyone is going to spoil her absolutely rotten."

"I know, and usually I would stop them or at least slow them down but honestly, it's only the second birthday she has celebrated. The first one with her family, and she deserves to celebrate it to the fullest, including the De Luca's over spoiling her." I see Alessia's feet are flat in her stirrups. "Heels down, Alessia," I call out to her and a moment later, I see her push her heels further down.

She does another two laps. I tell her to change directions, and she crosses the ring, breaking down into a trot. She is back on the edge of the ring, going in the opposite direction, then picks up the canter again. I set up a single jump that is only eighteen inches. I also set up poles before the jump since Cash tends to get excited before the jump and tends to take off early. The poles slow him down so he doesn't take off too early.

Once I have the jump set up, I see her slouching a bit. "Shoulders back." And she does it. "Good job, do one more lap, then you can let him have a break for a minute." Alessia nods her head at me. Once that lap is finished, she brings Cash down to a walk. She loosens her reins and let's Cash casually walk over to me. I grab the bucket of water for him to get a drink. "Ok, tell me three things to do while you are jumping," I ask her.

She is quick to respond, "Get in a two-point position, heels down, look ahead and hands down."

I chuckle "That's four, but yes, that's correct. But also to remember to lean forward but not to lay on his neck in a two-point position."

"Got it, Mama."

"Go ahead and jump the cross rail at a steady trot."

She nodded to me. "Aye, aye, captain." I shake my head as she is back on the edge of the arena trotting around towards the fence.

"Why do I let Vincenzo around her?"

"I am sure Mateo asks that question every day," Marcello says with a chuckle.

I watch her as her eyes look past the jump, and she is in the correct position. They jump over the fence with ease, granted it isn't that high for him. After they land, she rewards him with pats on his neck and tells him he is a good boy. That smile on her face makes me happy. "Good job, Alessia; go do it again." She goes around and does it again.

She ends up doing a small course, which she did well at. She takes her time to give Cash a proper cool down. We even decided to give him a bath. Somehow, we both ended up soaking wet, so I figured why not, and I took the hose and sprayed Alessia. I could see Marcello either recording or taking pictures. I was gonna give him some kind of snarky remark but honestly, it was a fun moment with my daughter, so I really didn't mind. Once we finished bathing Cash, we turned him out with a handful of treats as a reward for doing a good job. Not even thirty seconds later he gets down and rolls in the dirt.

Alessia pouts at him and says, "Bad Cash."

I laugh at her. "Most horses do that after they are given a bath, baby."

She looks at me. "Well, it's not very nice Mama."

I swoop her up and place her on my shoulders; she starts laughing. "MAMA," she squeals as I start running back to the house. Once we get to the mansion, we both take off our boots, fearing a whooping from Nonna. Even when the woman isn't here, she still puts the fear of her bringing out the wooden spoon and smacking your ass.

"Go shower and then we can have lunch. What do you want?" I ask her, and she starts bouncing on her feet.

"Can we have mac n' cheese with hot dogs in them like we used to have?"

I kiss her head. "Sure thing, go and shower and meet me in the kitchen." I go and see if we have everything we need. I see we don't have hot dogs, so I ask Alexandra if she would go grab some. I sit on the stool at the island while I wait for Alessia. I went through the pictures and videos of Alessia riding today that Marcello sent me. The smiles on both of our faces while we were bathing Cash and spraying each other with the hose, were priceless.

She comes and climbs on the stool next to me, and she leans over my shoulder to see what I am looking at. "I had fun today, Mama."

I kiss her hair, "Me too, baby. Alexandra went to get the hot dogs. She should be back in a few minutes." She nods at me. "Did you decide what movie you want to watch?" I asked her.

"Yep, *Frozen*, and then *Frozen 2*. Can we make brownies?"

"Sure thing, let's start that while we wait for Alexandra." We both hop off the stools and she help me pour and stir the ingredients together. I am about to put the pan in the oven when she tells me to wait. I turn to look at her, and she has the bag of chocolate chips in her hand. I let her add a big serving of chocolate chips on top of the brownie mix. While we were cooking, Alexandra came back from the store and put the hot dogs away for us.

I tell Alessia to go hop back on the stool, and I start to boil water for the pasta. She was talking to me about how excited she was for girl's night. How she wanted teal with pink hearts on her nails and if I thought Julietta could do that. Alessia was behind me as I faced the boiling pot of water stirring the pasta. When I looked up, I saw someone in the distance running far away from the mansion. I tried to look closer to see who it was but could not, but I did see them reach into their pocket and grab something. The next thing I know, I heard the glass window in front of me explode. I feel the pain of the boiling water and glass hitting my chest and face. I scream, and I am also launched into the island. My back makes contact before I slam into the ground. My head is fuzzy. I shake my head for a moment. I remember Alessia was in the room with me. I am groggy and I can barely see because of the fire and smoke. I hear heavy footsteps running in our direction.

I remember Mateo telling me a gun was hidden under the sink, and I limp towards it. I quickly snatch the gun from the cabinet, and I see Alessia slumped on the floor by the table. I grab her in my arms and make my way to the garage so we can get out of here. I hear footsteps approaching us, I move us into the formal dining room. I shoot the window out and jump out of the second-story window with Alessia tucked into me. I groan as I hit the ground. I take all the impact. I look down, and Alessia is still unconscious. I worry but I need to get us out of here first. I hear my name being shouted, and I see three men running toward men. I take off towards the garage.

"Emilia, stop. It's Marcello." I look over my shoulder, and I see Marcello with Raffaele and Damiano.

I run in their direction; they all look extremely worried but before they can say anything, I tell them, "We need to get out of here." Marcello grabs Alessia out of my hands and Raffaele grabs me and carries me bridal style. We run to the garage, and we all pile in the SUV. Damiano drives through the gate. Just as we make it through another explosion goes off, and we end up smacking the side of the car into a tree. I don't remember anything after I hit my head on the window.

TWENTY-FOUR
EMILIA

    I feel myself being shaken and my name being called. My eyes feel heavy, I groan out in pain, and my whole-body hurts. I think the list of what doesn't hurt is shorter. My eyes feel like they are taped shut. I can barely hear around me. I squeeze my hand, and I feel leather under my fingers. I hear yelling, "Fucking hell, Roman, answer your damn phone. Mateo doesn't pay you not to be available when people need medical attention, especially his wife and daughter. *Stupido motherfucker.*" Whoever is yelling needs to shut up, they are not helping.

    I groan out, "Whoever is yelling, if you don't quit I am gonna cut out your damn tongue with a rusted knife, slowly." I hear a chuckle, and I slowly turn my head to see Raffaele peering down at me. I look around and see we are inside the SUV. Then everything comes back to me; I quickly sit up, looking for Alessia, but before I can he is pushing me back down.

    "Lay down, Donna. Alessia is still unconscious, Marcello is with her." I nod with tears in my eyes worried something seriously is wrong with my baby.

    Raffaele looks worried. "Are you okay?"

    I shake my head. "How bad is she hurt?"

    He gives me a small smile. "I am no doctor but besides her still being unconscious you look a lot worse than she does."

    I nod. "Good. I would rather be hurt than her."

    He shakes his head, "You truly are something else."

    I hear Damiano start cussing. "Damiano, what's wrong?" I ask him.

    He looks at me in the rear-view mirror and sighs. "Donna, Roman isn't answering his phone and we are trying to avoid taking you to a public hospital."

    "Call Theo Walker. He is my childhood best friend and is a doctor." I give him Theo's number, "Put it on Bluetooth." I feel lightheaded. Theo picks up on the second ring.

    Emilia: Theo, it's Emilia. We need help. Someone set bombs to go off at the mansion. Alessia and I were inside and had some serious injuries. Roman isn't answering our calls, and we can't risk going to the hospital. Can you or someone you trust help us?

    Theo: I swear I am putting you in a bubble. I have a friend. We can use his practice it's private. What are your injuries?

    Emilia: Alessia is still unconscious but is bleeding from a head wound, and her arm is bent at a weird angle, but I don't know anything else. As for me, it would be easier to list what doesn't hurt. Text this number the address, we are already in the car.

Theo: Ok, be safe. I love you both.

Emilia: Love you too.

Then the phone is hung up. Raffaele and Damiano give me a look, and I roll my eyes. "It's a brotherly kind of love, plus he would prefer the company of you two to me."

Damiano's eyes pop open "Wait he's gay?"

"Yes, very gay. To the point that, when we were younger, we would compare guys assess."

Marcello laughs. "Why am I not surprised?"

I give him a small smile and start to close my eyes and feel exhausted again. Raffaele notices and tries to keep my eyes open. "Donna, Donna, you got to stay awake. Damiano, how much longer?"

"With me speeding twenty minutes."

"Well, go faster. We need to get these two-medical attention."

"No shit, dumb fuck."

I hear Marcello yell out to me, "Emilia, open your damn eyes right now." But I have no energy to keep them open, and my world is black again.

MARCELLO

"Emilia, open your damn eyes right now." Her eyes are closed. Raffaele mumbles "fuck" under his breath. I am just glad the girls were both unconscious when we had a shootout with the damn Russians. Boss will be happy we have one survivor so he can do as he pleases, and I will feel bad if Emilia gets her claws into them. That woman is worse than Vincenzo torturing someone and that says something. I hear my phone ring. "Fuck we forgot to call the boss," I answered the phone and before I could say anything, he was already yelling through the phone. Not that I blame him.

Mateo: *VUOI SPIEGARMI PERCHÉ STO SCOPRENDO CHE LA VILLA È IN FIAMME E HO SCOPERTO ANCHE SE LA NOTIZIA NON NESSUNO DEI MIEI UOMINI?"(DO YOU WANT TO EXPLAIN TO ME WHY I AM FINDING OUT THE MANSION IS ON FIRE AND I FOUND OUT THOUGH THE NEWS NOT ANY OF MY MEN?)*

Marcello: *Sorry boss. I am with Raffaele and Damiano. They were at the shooting range while I followed up on the lead you asked me to take care of, since the girls were cooking lunch. And I figured that they would be safe with security around. The girls were inside when the bomb went off. We got to the girls after we saw Emilia jump through a window on the second floor with Alessia in her arms. Roman hasn't picked up our calls, so we called Emilia's friend Theo. We are on our way* to his friend's practice. We ran into other trouble with Russians on the way. We killed all but one; he is unconscious in the back.

Mateo: *(He takes a deep breath)* Sorry, Marcello. I am just worried about them. How bad are they injured?

Marcello: Honestly, Boss, it's bad. Alessia has been unconscious the entire time, and her one arm is bent at a weird angle. Emilia kept coming in and out of unconsciousness, and when she talked to Theo, she said it would be shorter to make a list of parts of her body that didn't hurt.

Mateo: Fuck. Salvatore and I are pulling up to the jet now. We should be landing in three hours. Send me the address and contact Adriano and give him details he will contact everyone else. Keep me updated on their progress.

Marcello: Of course, Don.

As Mateo hangs up, we pull up to a small building and see a man with shaggy brown hair and blue eyes in a doctor's coat rush over to the back door.

"Are you Theo?" I ask.

"Yeah, that's me." He barely acknowledges me and barks out orders to the nurses. They first get Alessia on a gurney. He whispers, "My poor little angel. We will get you fixed up."

Nurses and one doctor take her inside, and I follow them. I look over my shoulder, they are loading Emilia on a gurney, and Raffaele is with her, Theo, and the nurses. Damiano goes to park the SUV, and I also know he is going to make sure our visitor stays unconscious. They rush them each into their own room, with nurses running in and out of the rooms.

I sit with my head in my hands; both of those girls have me wrapped around their fingers. I am in no way a holy man, but I pray for them to be okay. Once again, Emilia proves she deserves the title of Queen. We have no idea what she went through inside the mansion before she jumped out of the window. I sent Adriano a text letting him know the girls were injured from the bomb going off at the mansion and where we are. He responds that he and Julietta are on their way. Damiano and Raffaele come and sit next to me. We don't say anything. We just sit there watching the door, waiting for any kind of news.

It seems like the whole day has passed when Adriano and Julietta come running in. I stand up and hug Julietta, and she clings to me. I hear a throat clear, and I look at Adriano. "I won't deal with this now, but we will talk later." I rub the back of my neck, knowing I am probably gonna get my ass kicked by the De Luca men for loving their princess. Yes, I might have been friends with Mateo since we were children, but that doesn't mean I don't have to get the approval of the De Luca men. I don't regret it; I would do anything for my *fiore*.

She pulls away from me and asks, "Any news?"

I give her a sad smile and say, "Not yet *fiore*."

"How badly are they injured?" Adriano questions us.

Damiano responds, "Bad."

Julietta cries in my chest, and I just hold her close, rubbing my hand up and down her back. Adriano mumbles a "fuck" under his breath. I tell them all that happened that we know about, and I get a message from Mateo saying to drop our visitor off at the warehouse and to have someone ready to pick him up. Damiano volunteers to drop off the bastard and go pick up Salvatore and Mateo. He wishes us goodbye and tells us to keep him updated on the girls.

Julietta ends up crying herself to sleep in my arms. While we wait, Adriano decides he is going to ask me about our relationship. I told him we were not official and that I was going to ask Mateo's permission when he got back, but I didn't deny that we had grown closer. Adriano wishes me luck, laughing. I nod my head, giving him a knowing smile. Mateo will beat my ass; at the very least, he will probably shoot me. He is very protective over the women in the family, and no one will ever be good enough for Julietta.

"As long as you treat her right, I will have no problem with you. Hurt her, and you will be filled with bullet holes."

"I could never hurt my *fiore*." We don't talk much after that.

MATEO

I walk into the clinic and the door slams against the wall. I honestly don't give a fuck. All I am worried about is my wife and daughter. When Salvatore busted into the meeting with Peter O'Sullivan, the Boss of the Irish Mafia, and said the bombs went off at the mansion, I felt like someone had just punched me in the gut. My heart felt like it was being ripped out when Marcello told me how badly my girls were injured. We were on our jet within the hour, taking the longest three-hour flight of my life back to Italy. I am glad Salvatore was with me and not Vincenzo because he understands what it means to have your loved ones on the line. Unfortunately, Lilyana didn't make it, but he didn't make dumb jokes like Vincenzo would have. He let me pace the plane and understood how hard it was to feel this helpless. When we get into the waiting room, I snarl at Marcello seeing Julietta asleep in his arms, which will be discussed later.

I marched up to the nurse at the desk.

"How can I help you, sir?" She tries to be sexy.

"I want updates about my wife and daughter, NOW!"

She just smirks at me. "I don't know what you are talking about."

I lean forward and in my most deadly voice, I say, "You see those people in the waiting room?" I ask, pointing to my family and Capos. She nods. "They have been here since they were brought in. I just flew from Ireland in the middle of a business trip because my wife and daughter are severely injured, and I demand to know what is going on. NOW!" She goes to make a smart comment back, when my name is yelled out. I look over, and Theo is wearing protective gear from head to toe.

My stomach drops seeing blood on the protective gear.

"Follow me," he says, and I walk with him. I try to look in the room he walked out of, but the blinds are pulled closed. We walk into an office. "Have a seat, Mateo." I do, but my leg is bouncing from my nerves. Usually, being Mafia Boss, I hide my emotions, but this is Emilia's best friend and honestly, I don't care if he sees me like this.

"Ok, both girls are in recovery now. Alessia has a concussion from the swelling in her brain. We put her in a coma to hopefully help reduce the swelling. Her left wrist is broken. It was bad; luckily, she didn't need pins, she had three bruised ribs, and she fractured her left tibia."

I nod at him. "Do you think she will have any brain damage?" I am almost afraid of the answer.

He shakes his head. "I can't know for sure, but she is young, and they bounce back better than adults from injuries."

I nod my head and swallow the nerves before asking about Emilia.

"Emilia?" I ask.

He takes a deep breath. "Her injuries are a lot more severe. She only has a minor concussion; we had to heavily sedate her because of the pain she was in while we were treating her. Her forearms had third-degree burns, and she had glass in her arms as well. Her chest had only second-degree burns. It would have been worse, but her shirt protect her somewhat. Her right collarbone is broken, along with a sprained elbow and broken wrist. She has bruised ribs as well, and her right kneecap is shattered. We had to put pins in her kneecap."

He stops and lets me absorb the information for a moment. "Mateo, I won't sugarcoat it for you. It looks like the reason her injuries are worse than Alessia's is that once again, she protected her. Emilia is going to be in a lot of pain. I recommend her being heavily medicated for a week, at least. I have no idea what happened or why it happened, but you will need a doctor to be with her for a while."

I sit there with my head in my hands, thinking about what he said. Usually that wouldn't be a problem with Roman, but he is missing.

I look up at Theo, "How much could I pay you to be that doctor?"

He shakes his head. "I would do it for free. Emilia is like a sister and Alessia is like a niece to me."

"Seriously, I won't allow that, nor do I want Emilia on my ass if she found out I didn't pay you."

"Whatever you paid Roman will be fine, if you can have some security. Keep an eye on my farm to make sure I get no backlash from whatever happened today. It's no secret who you are and what you do. I don't want to be involved in that part, but I will help the girls recover."

"Nope, double what I paid Roman, plus security. You can argue with Emilia about this."

He slumps in his seat. "Hell no, I prefer one less migraine from her. I already know she is going to give me plenty because she is a terrible patient."

I chuckle at his statement knowing this is very true. "Theo, I can't tell you much, but I will say I believe it has to do with Seth."

"Fucking worthless bastard. Hasn't he already done enough?" he says, standing up glaring at his desk.

"Trust me, Theo, I am just as angry as you, but we are much closer to catching that son of a bitch."

He turns to me. "Good. Mateo," he says, and I raise my eyebrow at him. "Make sure he and Boris experience nothing but pain and drag it out."

"I will."

"Let's go see your girls."

We walk in silence until we get to two rooms. Theo turns to me to speak. "This is Alessia's room," we walked in, and the sight of my baby girl just about killed me as I cried quiet tears. I wiped my tears. I couldn't believe hours ago, she was full of smiles and giggles with her Mama having a water fight. Theo places a hand on my shoulder, and I look up at him. "I will go inform your family, and then, if you are ready, we can go see Emilia." I nod at him; he quietly walks out the door.

I lean forward and kiss her forehead and whisper into her hair, *"Il mio povero bambino. Non preoccuparti Principessa, papà è qui ora. Mi prenderò cura di chiunque abbia fatto questo a te e a tua madre. Ti amo principessa."* (My poor baby. Don't worry, Princess, Papa's here now. I will take care of whoever did this to you and your Mama. I love you, Princess.)

I sit back down in my chair, rubbing my thumb over the back of her hand. My poor baby has a cast on her wrist and leg, with her chest wrapped. I can't stop my silent tears; I hear the door open. I quickly wiped my tears. I look and see it is my zio, Julietta, and Salvatore. Julietta falls into my uncle's arms and sobs. Salvatore comes over and sits in the chair next to me.

He looks at Alessia and squeezes my shoulder. "How are you holding up?" he asks.

I turn to him "I am not. My whole world is lying in two hospital beds. When you told me about the mansion, I couldn't have cared less about the mansion itself, but I had so much fear run through my body at the thought of losing them. I am honestly afraid to see how bad Emilia is if it breaks my heart seeing Alessia like this."

He nods understandingly. "Emilia is truly a force to be reckoned with and she will do anything for Alessia."

I give him a small smile. "Yeah, I am truly the luckiest man in the world."

Uncle Adriano comes over to me and hugs me first, then Julietta comes and hugs me. She is still sniffling through her tears. She goes and sits in the chair I was in.

I look at Salvatore. "Can you stay with Alessia and coordinate security until we are able to leave along with who is picking up Nonna, Nonno, and Vincenzo?"

He nods at me, "Consider it done."

"Thanks."

Theo meets me by the door. I pause, my hand right above the doorknob and take a deep breath, knowing what lies behind this door is going to be hard to handle but I must be strong for her. When I open the door, she lies in bed looking so lifeless. Most of her body is covered in either a cast, sling, or bandages. It literally brings me to my knees, and I bawl my eyes out and cry. I am not holding it back; seeing both of my girls in this condition makes my stone heart crack. Theo says nothing but sits next to me until I can pull myself together. After a couple minutes, I look at him. "She isn't in pain, right?"

He shakes his head. "No, she is on some pretty strong pain medicine." I nod my head and slowly get off the floor. I take shaky steps up to the side of her bed. I sat in the chair next to her just to look over my wife. Theo clears his throat. "The next couple of months are going to be a rough recovery for her."

I nod, and then tell him, "With the threat, I want to leave here to a safe house as soon as possible. Let me know what you need, and I will make sure you have it at your disposal."

"I will have that done as soon as I am done checking on both girls; Emilia should be waking up in the next hour. Here is my phone number; call my cell if you need anything." I thank him as he is leaving.

"You have no idea how thankful I am that you saved our daughter today. I am sure you did more than what I was told, but, Emilia, you truly are a goddess" I say as I gently rub her cheek. "I have said it before, and I will say it until the day I die. I am the luckiest bastard alive to be your husband. You are so beautiful, Emilia, on the inside and outside. I know when you wake up you are gonna be scared and hurt but know that I will be with you every step of the way." I sit, stroking her cheek gently and talking to her. At one point, all the adrenaline I had pumping through my body wears out, and I feel exhausted. I lay my head on the bed next to her hips.

I have no idea how long I have been asleep, but I wake up to a groan and then a hiss. I quickly shoot up and see those beautiful green eyes that are identical to our daughter's, with tears flowing down them. *"Il mio amore,* you are awake! Why are you crying? Are you in pain?"

She shakes her head no and opens her arms for me to hug her. I wrap my arms around her shoulder and let her lean her head on my shoulder as I give her a firm hug without putting any pressure on any of her injuries. She just bawls her eyes out; I gently whisper sweet words in her ear as I rock her in my arms. She ended up crying herself to sleep. My poor Queen held it together, but she finally hit her breaking point. I am afraid of what happened today and what it has done to her mental health. She has been making so much progress with her PTSD. I hope this won't set her back, but I doubt it won't, since most of her nightmares and flashbacks are around them trying to hurt Alessia. Alessia was put in direct danger today so I am sure this will reverse all the progress we were making, but that is okay. I will still be here every step of the way.

She wakes up a little while later. I go to move out of the bed, so she has more room. Emilia shakes her head. "Please stay," she whispers. I stay in the bed and carefully hold her against me.

"Do you want to talk about it?"

"Not yet. I just need you to hold me." That is exactly what I do.

I assured her that Alessia would be okay and that she could see her later, even if it was through the phone. Her shoulders slumped back, and she relaxed.

Theo came in, "Hey. How are you feeling?"

"Okay, pain is tolerable. How is Alessia?"

Theo chuckles. "A lot better than you. We put her in a medical induced coma because of the swelling in her brain, which has gone down since the five hours you both have been here. She has a broken wrist, a couple bruised ribs, and a fractured tibia. We will try and wake her up tomorrow morning."

"Thank God she wasn't hurt worse."

Theo gives her a look. "Now, you on the other hand, are a different story. Your forearms have third-degree burns that have a lot of glass in them. You also broke your collarbone, sprained your elbow, and broke your wrist. Along with bruised ribs and a minor concussion." He gives her a pointed look, "And you won't be giving me any trouble and be the perfect patient?"

She has that look in her eye "Nope, got to keep you on your toes."

He throws his head back and groans but then gets a mischievous glint in his eye. "Misbehave, and I get to tell the De Luca's some stories of you. Maybe like ones of third grade?"

I look at Emilia and she is glaring daggers at him. "You wouldn't dare."

"Oh, but I would."

"Fine. Asshole."

He does a small victory dance. "But that is only the tip of the iceberg of good stories I have of you, Emilia...How about when you snuck into your grandparents' barn?" and before he could finish, she was throwing an empty cup at him. It hit him in the stomach.

"Rude," I shake my head; the family is going to be very entertained while he stays with us.

"Let me check over you and see how your injuries are looking," he goes and checks her. "You still have a concussion, but everything else looks good."

She gives him a small smile. "Thanks, Theo, for taking care of us; makes me feel safe knowing it's you."

"I will always be there for both of you." He gently pats her good shoulder and turns to walk away but before he walks out the door, "Keep your ass in the bed. There is no reason for you to get out of it." I can tell she is overwhelmed or just exhausted because she doesn't fight him or give him any sass. She nods at him.

After he leaves, I focus my attention back on Emilia; she looks at me and gives me a small smile. I run my hand through her hair, hoping this will relax us a bit. "Now, my fierce *Regina*, do you want to tell me what happened?"

She nods and goes on, telling me she was standing at the stove when she saw someone outside running from the mansion and pulling something out of their pocket. And when she woke up on the floor, she heard heavy footsteps coming toward them. She grabbed Alessia, made it to the formal dining room, shot out the window, and landed on the right side of her body. Caught up with Marcello, Raffaele, and Damiano, and after they passed through the gate, there was a second explosion. She woke up later to Damiano cussing because he couldn't get a hold of Roman.

"Yeah, Roman is MIA. So, he better be seriously hurt somewhere, or he will be a guest at the warehouse." She chuckles at me. "Rest, darling. I will be here, and Salvatore, Julietta, and Adriano will be with Alessia. Nonno and Nonna will be here in a couple hours and Vincenzo will be here tomorrow. You will need your rest for tomorrow."

She doesn't argue with me. She whispers, "I love you, Mateo, beyond my last breath."

I smile at her, lean forward, and kiss her forehead. "I love you, Emilia." I keep running my hand through her hair until she has fallen asleep.

I lean back in the chair and run my hands over my face. I need to talk to Theo about when we can safely move them because the sooner we get them moved and out of danger, the better.

Alexei you have made the biggest mistake of your life hurting my girls and especially with our new allies. You are going to watch your empire burn to the ground.

TWENTY-FIVE
MATEO

Once I know Emilia is going to be out for a while. I put my forehead on her forehead and whisper, "I love you, my Queen. I will be back soon, my love. I love you." Before I leave the room, I take one last look at my Queen.

I step out of the room and take off the scrubs I have to wear in the room with Emilia. I see Vittorio standing guard with two soldiers outside of Emilia's door, and I look at Alessia's door, and Marcello is doing the same. "Thank you for getting here, Vittorio," I tell him. He has been away for the past couple of months training the new security guard dogs, which now it looks like we will desperately need. Marcello took over as head of security. I was gonna put Vittorio back as the girl's main bodyguard, but I think I might leave it the way it is and just have Vittorio be head of security instead. Alessia is so attached to her "Celly" that I don't have the heart to remove him from her.

"Of course, Don. How are the Queen and Princess?"

"Emilia is severely injured, but due to heavy pain meds she is in and out of consciousness. Alessia overall only has a couple broken bones except for her coma, she was put in a coma, but soon we will start to wake her up."

"I am sorry, Boss. I hope they both have a speedy recovery."

I nod at him. "Emilia should be out for a while; I am going to talk to the doctor. No one enters that room but hospital staff, and if they enter, you enter with them and notify me."

"Of course, Don." I walk over to Marcello, "Why don't you switch off with someone else and get some rest" he goes to argue. I look at him with a hard glare. "That is an order."

He sighs, "Yes, Boss." He pulls his phone out. I am assuming to call someone to relieve his shift.

I continue my path to Theo's office. I knock on the door, and he mutters, "Come in." I walk in and sit in a chair in front of his desk. Theo has his back turned to me for a moment, and I see him making coffee. He turns around, giving me a small smile. "How do you like your coffee?" he asks me.

"Black," I reply back.

While waiting for the coffee to finish brewing, he sits in his chair and asks me, "What can I help you with, Mr. De Luca?"

I shake my head. "Theo, lose the formalities. You are my wife's friend and like an uncle to my daughter."

"Technically, you are my boss."

"You go ahead and argue with Emilia about that. Anyway, I want to know how soon you think we can fly them out of here?"

"I would prefer if Alessia was awake from her coma, and we got to do an MRI of her head before. Which, hopefully, will be soon because I have already taken her off the medicine to keep her in her coma."

"Ok, did you make a list of all the medical supplies you will need for the girls?"

He nods at me, "Yes," as he opens the drawer in his desk and hands me a file, then he turns around. Pouring two cups of coffee, he pours the flavored creamer like Emilia does. I mentally gag because of the sweetness of the coffee. I personally think coffee should be strong and black with nothing else to it.

I skim through the file. "Perfect, I will have all of this at the safe house before we arrive." He hands me my coffee; I close my eyes, enjoying the coffee. I needed this. I have been pushing myself to stay awake. I need to be there for both of my girls. But I am so exhausted.

After a moment of quiet, I start talking to Theo about Emilia's past. Like about how she was a troublemaker in school, which doesn't surprise me with her witty side. Suddenly one of my soldiers barges into the room, "Boss, it's the princess. She is awake, and she is panicking, and no one can get her to calm down."

I am on my feet; I shove my soldier out of the doorway, and I run to Alessia's room. As I approach the room, I can hear her screams and crying. The sound of her screaming for Emilia and me, feels like someone put a dagger through my heart. "I W-WANT MAMA AND PAPA!" she yells out.

I swing the door open, and I see Salvatore trying to hold her injured limbs steady. Nonna and Nonno are behind me as they have just arrived. I walk up next to her; I push everyone away from her. I gently pick her up in my arms. She is fighting me; I softly hum the lullaby Emilia will sing to her. She slowly stops fighting me, and I cradle her to me like a baby with her head on my shoulder.

I nod at them to leave, and they do. I hold her tight to my chest, "*Shh Principessa di papà, stai bene. Papà è qui adesso. Sei al sicuro o.*" (*Shh, Papa's princess you're okay. Papa's here now. You're safe.*) I keep whispering in her ear, and she snuggles closer to my chest. Her little arms are wrapped around my neck and her face is on my shoulder. I can hear her taking a deep breath of my cologne. I have come to find out she does this while she is upset. Her little legs are wrapped around my stomach as tight as she can. I keep gently rocking her. After a few minutes, she sobs and turns into sniffles, *"Va bene ora Principessa?"* (*You okay now, Princess?*) She nods her head, knowing she is now calm. I sit on the bed with her still clinging to me. I rub her back until I feel she is calmer. I have to figure out what she remembers and where her head is at.

"Baby, can you look at Papa for a minute, please?" I ask her. She shakes her head no at me. I sigh, "Alessia, I need to look at your eyes." She still refuses, so stubborn like her Mama. I get a bit sterner. "Alessia Rose De Luca," I say in a warning tone. She slowly looks up at me; I smile and give her forehead a kiss. "We have to talk about what happened, baby."

Her eyes have fresh tears in them. "It's my fault," she whispers. "What is your fault, princess?"

"Mama, getting hurt. If I didn't want mac n' cheese with hot dogs she wouldn't be hurt."

My heart shatters at her tears and her sad voice. "Oh, baby. This is not your fault at all." She is looking at the ground. I gently lift her head back up to look me in the eyes. "Alessia, you had no way of knowing someone was gonna have our house blown up. So, the only person who is to blame is the one who set up those bombs, and Papa will take care of them. Okay?" I ask her, and she slowly nods her head.

Over her head, I see Vincenzo pop his head in; he mouths if the family can come back into the room. I was shocked to see him since he wasn't supposed to be here until tomorrow. "Princess, can your crazy Zio Vincenzo, Zio Salvatore, Zia Julietta, Zio Adriano, Nonno, and Nonna come back in?"

She gives me a smile and nods her head. Vincenzo pretended to look offended that I called him crazy; I rolled my eyes at him and with the hand I have on her back I gave him the finger. I am glad he was able to get an earlier flight in, even though he usually gets on my nerves. His goofy personality is what Alessia needs right now.

While we are sitting there together, she says, "I hate when people get hurt to protect me."

Before I can respond, Adriano walks over to her and sits on the end of the bed. "Alessia, that is what you do for your family. You love them and protect them."

She turns her head to look at him. "But I never protect anyone."

I chuckle at her. "That is because you are our little princess; it is our job to protect you."

She is quiet for a moment and starts to look around. "Papa, where is Mama?"

I suck in a breath, knowing regardless of how I tell her, she isn't gonna be happy. But before I can Theo comes in wearing a crown, and his pen is a pink glittery wand. Ok, this man is definitely something else. Now I see why he and my wife are friends.

"I heard the Princess has awoken from her slumber," he says.

Alessia turns her head. "TEDDYYYYYY," and she jumps from my bed and tries to launch herself at him. I grab her by her waist and make her sit her butt back on the bed.

"Papa," she whines at me.

"Take it easy, baby girl; you are hurt." She looks at me, crosses her arms over her chest, and pouts her lip at me.

"You look cute when you're mad." She glares at me and pretends to give me the silent treatment. I chuckle at her, "You can hug Theo when he gets close to you." Theo is watching in amusement at our interaction; I clear my throat, which snaps him back to Alessia. When he gets next to the bed and picks her up, she gives him the biggest hug that she can with a cast.

"Teddy are you my doctor?" she asks him.

"That I am, Princess Alessia."

"Good, the other doctor was grumpy. You are a nice doctor." All the adults in the room chuckle.

"Princess, I need you to sit on the bed so I can check your injuries. Can you do that for me?"

"Any needles?" she asks.

"No needles," he tells her.

She smiles at him. "Okay, Teddy." He sits her down and tells her how she has to listen to his directions so she can feel better quickly. "Teddy, you know I listen better than Mama does."

He winks at her. "We know you do, but this time we have your Papa here to help us, when your Mama won't listen to doctor's orders. He can put her in time out if she doesn't listen." He winks at me. Of course, I get lots of ideas on how to punish my stubborn wife. I laugh and go along with Theo.

"Yep, I say we have Nonna beat her butt with a spoon."

Nonna pulls a wooden spoon out of her purse. Theo's mouth opens wide when Nonna starts waving the spoon in the air. But her four grandkids (including me), and Adriano gulp and shuffle away from her. Nonno laughs. "You all are grown adults and you all are moving away from her like she is the devil." Vincenzo cries out.

"Because with THAT in her hand, she is."

Nonna just glares at us. "I won't use it unless I need to. Do I need to?" We all either say no or shake our heads.

Theo chuckles, "This is gonna be the most fun I am going to have while treating a patient."

Alessia giggles at us. "Nonna, they are silly. You wouldn't hurt them with the spoon; spoons are for cooking."

Nonna tells Alessia, "I always had to smack them with the spoon. They were bad as children. But you are a good girl, so I won't have to use the spoon on my *pronipote (great-granddaughter)*. You will be a perfect angel, unlike them, who gave me a headache from all of their mischief." She just nods and smiles at Nonna, but her smile slowly fades from her face.

"Papa, you never told me about Mama," she says, looking at me.

"I will tell you, but first, I need you to tell me what you remember." She nods at me and starts playing with the buttons on my shirt, one of the signs that she is anxious. I just give her a bigger hug and wait for her to talk.

"All I remember is sitting in the kitchen with Mama. She was stirring the pasta, and I heard a loud sound. Then I heard Mama screaming as I was flying off my stool. I don't remember anything after that."

I take a deep breath. I am so glad she doesn't remember anything else, so she can be spared some trauma. "Baby, you know how we tell you to be careful around the stove because it can get really hot?" She nods at me. "Well, when the window shattered from the bomb exploding, hot water and glass hit your Mama. Even though she was in a lot of pain, she grabbed you to get you both to safety, and while doing that she got other injuries as well. So, Mama is asleep right now because she needs pain medicine to help her feel better, and the medicine makes her sleepy."

She has tears in her eyes and looks at me. "Will Mama die?"

I shake my head, "No, baby. Your Mama will not die, she is gonna be sore for a while, so we have to be very careful around her."

"Promise?" she asks me.

"Of course, Princess."

"Ok, Papa." She starts to yawn.

"Are you tired, Princess?" I ask her. As her head is on my shoulder, she shakes her head no. I just chuckle. "Go to sleep, Princess."

"No, it hurts too much."

My eyes pop out of my head. "What hurts?"

"My arm, leg, and chest."

I didn't realize Theo had left the room. I see Salvatore get up and say, "I will go get Dr. Walker."

Of course, even exhausted and in pain, Alessia has a comment, "Zio Salvatore, Teddy doesn't like family calling him Dr. Walker, and because we are his family, that makes you his family too."

He tells her okay and walks out.

"Little girl," I got her attention using a stern voice. "Why didn't you tell me you were hurting?"

She gives me a sheepish smile. "I felt bad everyone was already worrying about me. I didn't want to make anyone worry more."

I shake my head. "You are just like your mother, stubborn but always worrying about everyone before yourself. We need to know when you are in pain, okay?" That is when Theo walks in.

"Alessia. I thought you said you were gonna be a good patient? Good patients tell their doctor when they are in pain."

She gives him sleepy but innocent eyes. "Sorry, Teddy, I won't do it again."

"Good, I am going to give you some pain medicine. It will make you sleepy, but it's okay. You are still tired from everything that happened and need to get some sleep." Theo signals for me to have her focused on me. I lay down in the bed with her head facing away from her IV. I run my fingers through her hair; she has her head on my arm. I start humming the same tune Emilia would sing to her when she has a bad dream. Her eyes are getting heavier.

"I love you, Papa; you are my hero." I am the furthest from a hero, but I will always be a hero to my little girl.

"I love you too, Alessia. I will always protect you."

She gives me a sleepy smile as her eyes are shut. Everyone leaves, but I honestly pay no mind to them. I just lay here with my daughter in my arms. These past two days since I found out the mansion exploded, have been nothing but pure hell. As much as it sucks that both have a long and painful road ahead of them to recover, I am so relieved they are alive.

I get up slowly. Once I have her tucked in, I kiss her forehead and walk out of the room. I see Marcello's replacement is stationed outside Alessia's door. I tell them to keep guard, and they nod at me. I walk back to Emilia's door to suit up in the scrubs again. I walk in, and Theo is already in the room. Theo is doing another examination. I sit by her side, running my hands through her hair. Seeing her hooked up to all these machines and seeing her face scrunched up in pain even when she is asleep is killing me. Theo walks over to her IV, and he sees me look at him. "I am going to give her some more pain medicine. For the next couple of days, we are going to stay on a tight schedule with her pain medicine they will be the most helpful for her."

"Ok, I trust you, Theo. Since Alessia is up, how soon can you be ready to leave?"

"Give me a couple hours."

"Perfect, I will have the jet ready. I am going to take care of a couple things. I will be back in a few hours. If anything happens, call me." I lean down and kiss Emilia's forehead. *"Ti amo. Mia Regina."* I walk out of her room and tell Vittorio to keep watch and make sure both of my girls are safe and to call me if anything happens.

I walk out to where my family is, and when I walk up to them, I tell them I am going to the warehouse. As soon as I stepped out of the clinic, my facade dropped. I quickly walked to my car. I have so many emotions running through me. Anger being the strongest. Visiting our guest will be a good way to channel that anger. I get in and speed off to the warehouse. I turn off my emotions and go back to being the coldhearted bastard I am known to be. During the whole ride to the warehouse, I decide how I am going to torture the Russian.

Most Mafia Don's don't believe in being emotionally attached to their wives and children because it makes them weaker. I disagree, especially after seeing both of my girls injured from the bomb from the Russians. I have never been so angry; I was past seeing red. I had to reign in my anger. But then again, my anger escalated seeing both so upset and distraught over what happened. Alexei wants to play hard ball; he has no idea what he started and especially with my Queen next to me. Ready or not, Alexei, the devil is ready and his diabolical wife is coming out to play. No one messes with our family and gets away with it; we might not attack right away. We will plan, but when we attack, it will destroy you. We will watch your empire turn to dust.

TWENTY-SIX
MATEO

  I walked into my office at the warehouse, poured myself some whiskey, and sat behind my desk. I take a sip and sit my glass back down on the table. I lean back in my chair, reflecting again on how everything happened. Who could be the person Emilia saw before the bombs went off? Are they a rat? If they are part of my family and they broke Omerta, things will be very painful for them. I hear the door open, and I look to see the rest of my family walking into my office together.

  "I am going to make this simple, we can't all go to the safe house together. Vincenzo, Salvatore, and Zio Adriano, I need you three taking over for me over here. Julietta, you can choose who you are going to live with, one of them for the time being. Everyone gets at least two guards with them anytime they step out of the house. I don't care if you all go out together, each of you needs two guards," I tell them.

  Adriano orders, "You three come live at my house, you all will have your space, but it will put me at ease that you will be under my roof." The boys go to argue. "I wasn't asking. After all this I want you three close. Just deal with it."

  Nonno agrees with them. I turn to Nonno and Nonna. "You two can choose to come with me and the girls to the house in Milan, or you can stay with everyone else."

  Nonna gives me a gentle smile. "We already discussed it; we would like to come with you so we can help the girls recover."

  "Okay, we leave in three hours. Now that is done, I have a Russian downstairs who I need to chat with," I say with an evil smirk on my lips.

  I walk past my family members, not caring if they follow me or not.

  "What is your name?" I ask, standing in front of him with my arms crossed my chest and the whip still in my hand. *"Listen here, you Russian scum. Today would not be the day to test my patience. So talk, or I will make you... And trust me, I will make you talk."* He gives me a dirty glare and spits at me. *"Okay then,"* and I take the whip and smack him on his lower stomach.

  He grunts out in pain and shouts out. *"Fuck you, dirty Italian mother fucker."*

  I laugh. *"Uh oh, is the poor little Russian getting hurt?"* I mock him. *"I will ask again, what is your name?"*

  He still stays quiet, and I'm losing my patience. I take out my gun and shoot him in the knee. He screams out in pain but still doesn't answer. I'm fed up. I walk over to my table, lay the whip down on the table, put on industrial gloves, and grab the container of acid.

"Lower him till he is on his knees and put a chain to his waist so he can't move too much." Two soldiers do as I say. They wrap the thick chains that are bolted to the floor around his waist. Then they back up against the wall with the others. I walk over to him and say, *"Hope you enjoy pain because you are about to endure a lot of it."* I start pouring the acid slowly from his left shoulder over the back of his neck, to his right shoulder. He is thrashing around, cursing, and screaming. I stand back. *"Are you done being stubborn?"*

He nods his head. *"My name is Gabe."*

"Well, Gabe, why did Alexei bomb my mansion?" He looks like a deer in headlights.

"Who's Alexei?"

I roll my eyes at Gabe. *"I am not as stupid as you Russians. I clearly see the Russian Mafia tattoo on your shoulder. So again, tell me what Alexei plans on accomplishing by destroying my home."*

"I won't say anything. If I say anything, I will be killed."

I throw my head back and laugh. *"You are not gonna leave here alive, but it is your choice if you want your death to be fast or very slow and painful."*

I do have to admit Alexei has very loyal soldiers. But that doesn't matter; I am very angry and can unleash my anger here on Gabe until he decides to talk.

"Raise him back up." I walk over to the table and switch out the acid for the whip. A couple of lashes should open his mouth, especially since his back is nice and sensitive to the acid, a couple lashes should open his mouth. I don't even ask him the question again; I just pull my arm back and crack the whip down on his back as hard as I can. He screams out in pain; I don't bother stopping, I give him five more lashes on his back.

"He wanted to use the bombs as a distraction, and we were supposed to grab the whore and bastard child."

"Why?" I ask, taking a break from whipping him.

"The girl needs to start her training as a wife, and you all have messed up all of Seth's work. Then the whore was going to be put in one of the brothels to make money for Seth. Since she is now tainted from you. You dirty Italian cocksucker."

All I see is red at this point. I shoot his shoulder directly on a spot acid was poured on. I take the end of my gun and push on the bullet hole. In a deadly tone, I say, "No one, and I mean no one, gets to disrespect the Queen and Princess of the Italian Mafia and gets to live to tell about it."

"You will lose them, and we will watch your empire crumble."

"One problem with that little plan. You all know my wife as the quiet, obedient servant, who she was to protect our daughter. You don't know the vicious Queen. She is just as evil as I am, if not worse."

"Women are weak and are meant to do as we say."

I shake my head; Vincenzo walks up to me with a box I am very familiar with. It is one of Emilia's custom-made "torture toys." It is a dildo that is controlled by a remote. With a push of a button, blades pop out from the side, and another button controls the speed. What can I say? My wife is obsessed with blades and knives.

"Do you see this? This is something my wife custom-made just for when she gets her hands on anyone who abused her. But you can be the first to test it." I turn it on to the lowest speed, and you see small blades pop out of the dildo. You can see him squirm and sweat starts to build up on his forehead. I turn it off for the moment.

I look over and see my grandmother and sister standing with my cousins and uncle. "Nonna and Julietta, you may want to leave for this part. It is gonna get pretty bloody."

Nonna, without missing a beat, says, "Hell no, I want to see how Emilia's torture tools work."

I shake my head and turn back to Gabe. "Strip him, bend him over the table, and tie his arms and legs down."

I look over at Salvatore. "Salvatore, can you record this? I am sure Emilia would like to see it but since she can't, we can at least let her watch it later."

He smirks at me, "Sure thing, Boss."

I wait for Gabe to be in place and Salvatore to be ready. Once I see he is ready, I stand behind Gabe, and without warning, I shove it into his ass dry. He screams and tries to wiggle away from me. I push my hand on his lower back to keep him still. "*You already pissed yourself. This is gonna be fun.*" Once, it was fully inside of him, which needed some rough encouragement, I turn on the dildo and the blades pop out.

He is crying, "*Why are you crying? We are just getting started.*" I then turn it up, so the dildo starts to spin slowly at first. I hear a trickling sound in front of me. I look down and the fucker pissed himself again. I laugh and decide to speed it up. Not even a couple minutes later, the fucker passed out. I yank the toy out of his ass, and blood comes pouring out.

Vincenzo snickers. "Well, either it is very effective, or the fucker is a little bitch." We all chuckle at him. Vincenzo looks at me with a pleading look.

"Do you want a turn, Vincenzo?" I ask.

He nods his head, trying to act like he isn't eager as a kid in a candy store. He walks over and dumps a bucket of freezing cold water over his body. Gabe shoots awake; he realizes where he is and is begging for death. Vincenzo pays no mind to him; he grabs his favorite knife and starts to cut out the Russian Mafia tattoo. Once he has cut the tattoo from his body, he throws it on the floor. He pours salt over the exposed area. Gabe passes out again.

    I look at Salvatore and Adriano, saying, "Have fun with him and send his head back to Alexei to deliver a message."

    Adriano smiles at me. "You got it, boss."

    I leave the basement and head into the shower to wash off the blood from my body and put fresh clothes on. I shower quickly and go back to my office and gather what I will need. I plan on working from our safehouse for at least a month. My girls need me, and I am going to be there physically, not just pay Theo to do the things I can do. I walk out and my family is waiting for me. I see Adriano has a couple of big bags in his hand.

    "What do you have there, Zio?" I ask him.

    "Tablet with headphones for both girls, along with laptops and a new cell phone for Emilia. Julietta got them both soft and comfortable clothes and shoes. Nonna made some food for the plane ride. Nonno got Emilia new knives. The boys got the girls new boots and Alessia new stuffed animals."

    I hug him. "Thank you," I tell all of them. "Are you coming back to the clinic to say goodbye?"

    Vincenzo answers first, "Of course I am, plus I have to warn Theo not to try and take my spot as the favorite man in Alessia's life."

    I glare at him. "That spot has already been reserved for me as her father."

    He is about to open his mouth when Nonno says "Both of you hush. We all know I am her favorite."

    Nonna smacks him on the back of his head. "All of you are idiots, now get your asses in the cars, or I will pull out my spoon." We all scurry out to the cars quickly. Yes, I am a Mafia Boss, but that woman will still spank me like I am a little boy who broke an expensive vase. Hell, she did it after Emilia left; not saying I didn't deserve it. Of course, that crazy old woman is laughing at us.

    Once I get in the car and turn it on, I am about to leave when my passenger door opens. Julietta slides into the passenger seat. "Hope you don't mind but I wanted to talk before you leave, and I know once you get back, you will be finishing up orders for the flight."

    "Not at all, *sorella*. Everything okay?" I ask her as I pull out of the parking lot.

    "Yeah, I wanted to see how you are."

    I take a deep breath. "Honestly, I have never been as scared in my life as when I learned they were at the mansion when the bombs went off. Then when I finally saw their injuries and how they both reacted when they woke up, it tore my heart out."

Julietta puts her hand on my arm. "I know. I love them both too. I don't know how you have kept it together so well. When I saw both, I cried, but when I saw Emilia," she stops to take a breath. "If it wasn't for Nonno, I would have fallen to the floor. Haven't they suffered enough from those evil bastards? It pisses me off and breaks my heart that they are still suffering from them."

I give her a small smile. "I know, and once I have my hands on them, I plan on torturing every person who had a hand in the girls' abuse."

"I know you will, Mateo. Promise me something."

"What's that, Julietta?"

"Make sure the torture is long and painful for each one. Especially Seth and Boris."

I smirk at her. "Of course, but I will have to tell Emilia that. She already demanded to be in charge of their torture. Supposedly the dildo is just one of many toys she has created," I say, smirking.

Julietta chuckles. "If I were you, I would be afraid to piss her off."

I shake my head. "Oh, I am, but the makeup sex would be worth any torture she does on my body."

"Ugh, Mateo. TMI! I don't want to think about you having any kind of sex."

I throw my head back and laugh. "Well, we have to practice so you can have more nieces and nephews to spoil."

She rolls her eyes at me, "Still don't want to know details about the process. In my mind, they are conceived by miracle conception. Or I can always share about guys I have been with." She smirks at the look of disgust on my face.

"Ok, fine. I won't harass you anymore but tell Marcello to keep his hands off you or I get to cut them off. I am not ready to be an uncle until I see a wedding ring on your finger."

She rolls her eyes. "The most we have done is have secret kisses."

"Good, keep it that way. Is this what you really want? To be with him?" I ask her.

"Yeah, I am. He treats me like a princess. He is super overprotective, maybe worse than you, if that's possible, but pays attention when I talk to him. He is supportive of my business; he knows how I prefer the small things like just taking a walk or having a picnic outside instead of the fancy dinners. Yes, they are nice, but we have had that shoved down our throats by our father. Being around Emilia and Alessia made me realize how much more important the small things are."

We arrive at the clinic and I lean over and kiss her hair "As long as you are happy. But if he hurts you, I will put a hole in his body."

"Ok, overprotective brother."

I shrug my shoulders. "Not gonna deny it." I get out of the car and go to open the door, but I see Marcello already beat me to it and has her in a hug. I give him a blank stare.

He greets me, "Boss," and nods his head at me.

"I will say this only once. I will not give you a hard time because Julietta seems very happy but know this if I find out you make her cry, I will put bullets in your body. I don't care that we have been friends since we were kids."

He gives me a smile "Thank you, Boss."

"Good" I say and walk back in the clinic. I check my phone and see that the pilot is ready once we are. I walk to the girls' rooms and see both of their rooms have the three guards outside their doors like I assigned them.

I continue walking until I find Theo in his office. I knock on the partially open door. "Do you need anything before we load up?" I ask him.

He shakes his head. "No, just finishing packing these files, and then I have everything ready. Both girls have been asleep the whole time and they are ready to go as well. They will probably sleep for the ride." I nod at him and head back out to the guards. I am bringing all the guards who have been with the girls since they got to the clinic plus the safehouse we are going to already has guards there waiting for us to arrive.

I go to check on both girls. I first go into Alessia's room. She is sound asleep with her face snuggled into the pillow. I bend down and kiss her head. I walk into Emilia's room, and it still knocks the breath out of my chest seeing her in such a delicate state. I sit in the chair next to her and talk to her. "Alessia woke up earlier. You saved her, *Tesoro*. She barely has any injuries compared to you. We are soon going to leave for the safehouse. I will be here for both of you every step of the way, including any flashbacks. I love you so much."

She turns her head towards me and slowly blinks her eyes open. "Hey," she gives me a hoarse whisper.

"Hey beautiful. Did I wake you up?" I ask her.

She shakes her head no. "I have been awake for a while, listening to your voice is soothing."

I smile at her and kiss her cheek. "How are you feeling?"

"I am okay, pain meds are working."

"Good. We are going to be headed to our safehouse soon."

She nods at me. "Okay, good. How's Alessia?"

"She woke up scared even though our family was there because we weren't there. Once I held her, she calmed down after a couple minutes. We gave her some more pain medicine because she was hurting, and she is still asleep. Most likely she will stay asleep during the whole flight."

She nods, and I run my hand through her hair. She always relaxes when I do this, she leans into my hand. "What are you thinking about?"

She opens her eyes and looks at me with tears in her eyes. "I am scared. They bombed our home to get to me and Alessia. I am afraid of what else they are willing to do to get to us. Who all is going to be hurt or killed in the process? I hate feeling responsible for other people getting hurt, it already kills me that Alessia got hurt."

I kiss her lips to stop her rambling and grab the sides of her head and deepen the kiss for a moment. "Stop blaming yourself. You didn't ask for any of this. But what we can do is stop them and destroy the Russians, not only for what they did to the two of you, but also for how they hurt Zia Anna and Lilyana." I wipe the tears off her cheeks, she gives me a small smile. "I love you and there is nothing I wouldn't do for our family." I tell her.

She tells me, "I love you beyond my last breath."

I give her a gentle kiss, but before I can take it further, I hear the click of a camera. I pull away from her and see Theo smiling holding his phone. Emilia mumbles to me "Mateo will you shoot him in his ass for me?" I chuckle, especially at his fake hurt expression.

"Mateo don't hurt the goods. How do you think I get all of the dick I do?" Then he starts to twerk.

Emilia groans, leaning back into the pillow "This is gonna be a long recovery if I have to deal with him and I can't do shit to get him back when he is being a pain in my ass."

He smirks at us. "Emilia, that's Mateo's job to be a pain in your ass. As juicy as it is, you don't have the right parts for me."

I wiggle my eyebrows at her, and she shoots me a glare. I put my hands up in surrender, but I am biting the inside of my cheek from laughing at them. This is going to be fun to watch.

"Anyway, I came in here to say we are ready to head out, your uncle is carrying Alessia to the car, you want to carry Emilia?" I nod at him as he walks to the other side of her and unplugs her IV from the wall. I gently pick her up bridal style, being careful not to touch any of her injuries. And we slowly make our way out of the clinic. I feel terrible because every step she either winces or scrunches her face in pain.

"I am sorry my love. We are almost there." She doesn't say anything, just nods her head.

We get out to the van to transport the girls. It has two medical beds in it so they can both lie down. I step in with Emilia still in my arms. I lay her down with her head behind the passenger seat. I kiss her head as Theo sets up her IV's for the ride. Adriano has already laid Alessia down the same way. I take a seat on Alessia's bed. I look over and see the relief on Emilia's face, just from looking at Alessia.

"You saved her," I whisper to her.

Marcello and Theo climb into the front seats, with Marcello driving.

Salvatore opens the back of the van. "Ready, Boss?"

I nod at him, barely taking my eyes off the girls. Next thing I know Emilia's door is being opened and I see my family, except for Nonna and Nonno at her side. They all say their goodbyes.

"Let's go, Marcello."

"Yes, Boss."

Emilia looks at me with tears in her eyes. "Will they be safe?"

I nod at her and say, "Yes. Adriano demanded they all live with him, regardless how much they protested."

"Nonna and Nonno?" she asks.

I smile at her and tell her. "They will be with us. They want to be there to help you and Alessia's recover."

She closes her eyes and mumbles, "Okay."

I kiss her head and tell her to rest. We all left the clinic and headed to our private airport.

TWENTY-SEVEN
EMILIA
Waking Up In The Clinic

  I can't open my eyes, but I hear people talking around me. It was quiet for a moment, I tried to focus more on who was talking around me. I realize it is Mateo and another familiar male. "You have no idea how thankful I am that you saved our daughter today. I am sure you did more than what I was told but Emilia you truly are a goddess," he says as I feel someone rub my cheek softly. "I have said before and I will say it until the day I die. I am the luckiest bastard alive to be your husband and the father of our children. You are so beautiful Emilia on the inside and outside. I know when you wake up you are gonna be scared and hurt but know that I will be with you every step of the way."

  I try to move my fingers or open my eyes, but I can't. I am too exhausted so I give up and fall back asleep, hoping when I wake up again, I will be able to open my eyes. I have no idea how long it has been since I have been asleep but when I wake up, I have a headache. I slowly try to open my eyes. I am able to, but the lights in the room make me wince and close them again. I take a deep breath and open them again. The light hurts but not as bad as it did before. I slowly move my eyes around the room, I can see I am in a hospital room. I look down and see Mateo asleep with his face toward me, laying on his arms, by my hip. He must have left his meeting with the Irish Mafia early to come back here.

  I quietly start to cry, thinking to myself why would this man willingly stay with me. Look at all the trouble I have caused since we got together last year. I try to move my arms, but they are too sore, and I don't want to make any noise of discomfort to wake Mateo up since he looks like he hasn't slept well. You can see the dark circles under his eyes. I just keep staring at him with tears flowing down my cheeks.

  Mateo wakes up and looks so relieved. He is already asking me *"Il mio amore,* you are awake! Why are you crying? Are you in pain?" I shake my head no and open my arms regardless of how bad they hurt; I just need to feel my husband hold me. He gently holds me; I lay my head on his shoulder with my face in his shirt. I just let the tears flow; I can feel a wet formation on his shirt.

  He doesn't try to ask me what is wrong, he just whispers sweet things to me in my ear while he holds me. At this moment I feel safe, and I end up falling asleep again. When I wake up again, I feel better. Mateo is still by my side, and when our eyes meet, he gives me a smile. I immediately ask about Alessia. He tells me she is okay, and I can't leave the room because of my injuries. When she wakes up, I can see her even if it is through a phone. When Theo comes back in, he explains her injuries are not as bad as mine. I breathe out in relief; you could empty a clip into my body, and I would be okay as long as Alessia never got a single scratch on her. Theo gives me a look when he asks me if I will be a good patient and he knows damn well I am not a good patient. Even as a kid, it was difficult when I was sick. I hate to rest when I could or should be doing something else. I would drive Mama and Papa crazy. Theo knows this.

I was terrible last time after escaping from Seth, and I know my body is in worse condition than it was last time. I hate feeling worthless and having to rely on people to do anything. "Nope, got to keep you on your toes," I tell him with a smirk that hopefully hides my feelings, but he gives me a look I am too familiar with. He knows I am hiding my feelings, but in fairness to me a lot has happened, and it is a lot to process. He plays it off, though. He throws his head back and groans but then gets a mischievous glint in his eye.

"Misbehave, and I get to tell the De Luca's some stories of you. Maybe like ones of third grade?" I am glaring at him.

"You wouldn't dare."

"Oh, but I would."

"Fine. Asshole."

He does a small victory dance. "But that is only the tip of the iceberg of good stories I have of you Emilia…. How about when you snuck into your grandparents' barn?" I throw an empty cup at him. It hit him in the stomach.

"Rude." Mateo is trying to hide his laugh and shakes his head.

"Let me check over you and see how your injuries are looking." He checks over me. "You still have a concussion but everything else looks good."

I give him a small smile. "Thanks, Theo, for taking care of us, makes me feel safe knowing it's you."

"I will always be there for both of you." He gently pats my good shoulder and turns to walk away but before he walks out the door, he adds. "Keep your ass in the bed. There is no reason for you to get out of it."

I am too exhausted mentally and physically to be a smart ass. After Theo leaves the room, Mateo asks me to tell him what happened. I tell him everything from the suspicious man to waking up. I can tell he is pissed but he reigns it in for me, which I appreciate a lot. I have no energy to calm down a pissed off Mafia Boss. With the help of the pain medication, I fell back asleep. Which I seem to be doing a lot of.

I was awake but resting when I heard Mateo's voice again. I am not paying attention to what he is saying. All I know is that he is talking to me, and it is very soothing. I relax knowing he is here with me; I know I am safe with the guards posted outside my door but having him here with me helps my anxiety a lot. I wake up and Mateo tells me Alessia is asleep from the pain medication they gave her. I really want to get out of bed to see her, but I know I can't. And the thought of being so helpless doesn't help my anxiety and the thoughts swarming through my mind.

Mateo has been staring at me and he asks me what is wrong. Instead of keeping it to myself I decided to tell him. "I am scared. They bombed our home to get to me and Alessia. I am afraid of what else they are willing to do to get to us. Who all is going to be hurt or killed in the process? I hate feeling responsible for other people getting hurt, it already kills me that Alessia got hurt."

He kisses my lips to stop my rambling, then he deepens the kiss by holding my face with both of his hands. "Stop blaming yourself. You didn't ask for any of this. But what we can do is stop them and destroy the Russians, not only for what they did to the two of you, but especially for how they hurt *Zia* Anna and Lilyana." He wipes the tears off my cheeks, and I give him a small smile. "I love you and there is nothing I wouldn't do for our family," he tells me.

I tell him, "I love you beyond my last breath."

He gives me a gentle kiss, before it can go any further, I hear the click of a camera. I pull away from him and see Theo smiling holding his phone. I mumble to Mateo "Mateo will you shoot him in his ass for me?" He chuckled at me.

"Mateo don't hurt the goods. How do you think I get all of the dick I do?" Then Theo starts to twerk. Seriously, my friend needs some help.

I groan, leaning back into the pillow and say, "This is gonna be a long ass recovery if I have to deal with him and I can't do shit to get him back when he is being a pain in my ass."

Of course, Theo, the sarcastic dickhead he is, has to make a comment about my "juicy ass" and Mateo has his usual sexy smirk on his face. I glare at him because he knows damn well what it does to me when he looks at me like that. And obviously we can't be doing any kind of extracurricular activities so he is not about to get me riled up when I can't do shit about it.

Our playful banter stops as soon as Mateo picks me up in his arms. Even though he is gentle the whole time he carries me to the van, each step he takes hurts me. He apologized even though it is not his fault. Once he lays me down on the bed in the van, I look next to me and I see my sweet baby. I have to blink my tears away; I am glad I can see with my own eyes that she is okay, but then I have this rage brewing inside of me towards anyone associated with having our mansion blown up. They killed our people and injured others as well. I feel Mateo running his hands through my hair, but I don't acknowledge him. I am trying to control my anger until I can get my hands on those fuckers.

We arrive at the private airport and once we are all settled, we take off. Alessia is laying on the couch, with Marcello sitting in the chair beside her because I need room in the bed since my injuries are more severe. When Theo comes in to check on me, he shuts the door and he spins around with his hands on his hips. "Emilia Rose De Luca, you are keeping your emotions to yourself," he tells me. Fuck I am not gonna get away with shit between Theo and Mateo.

I glare at him and say, "I am processing everything."

He cuts me off, "Don't give me that bullshit. You're keeping your emotions to yourself in until you lose your shit and explode. Well, we aren't having that. I am sending your husband in here and you will talk to him about this."

I glare at him as he turns to leave. "As my doctor, you have a shitty bedside manners."

He looks over his shoulder and smirks at me. "Well, good thing right now, I am being your friend who refuses to let your demons get the best of you."

And then he walks out. Maybe I can hope Mateo will believe I fell asleep, so he doesn't talk to me.

I hear the door open; I regulate my breathing and keep the rest of my body still. I feel the bed dip, I feel him lean down next to my ear and he whispers, "Good try, my queen, but I know you're awake."

I squint my eyes at him and whisper, "Shh it's rude to wake the sleeping Queen."

He just chuckles at me, "Emilia," he says my name, and I shake my head trying to ignore him or at least delay the conversation. "Emilia" he says my name a little more firmly. "So stubborn. You better look at me." When I still refuse to look at him, he gently grabs my chin and turns my face to look at him.

"There she is my beautiful wife." I just look at him with a blank look. "Wipe that look off your face. You might have been able to get away with that a year ago, but not now."

I try to take a deep breath and stay calm, but he and Theo are starting to piss me off. I want to be able to bury my emotions for now, so I can deal with these fuckers. "Ah there we go. Now I am seeing how you feel."

And there goes my plan of staying calm. "Mateo. Let me be."

He shakes his head. "No can do. So, the sooner you open up, the sooner I will stop getting on your nerves about this."

I am trying to battle my emotions; I turn my head away from him. He knows me well enough, especially since he has been helping me with my PTSD therapy. He also knows how much I trust him. Without me realizing it, I have tears rolling down my face, and he wipes my tears away. He lays down and turns my head it's his chest, and he just runs his hand through my hair. I fucking hate how much I have been crying since I woke up.

"Talk to me, Emilia. Tell me what is going on inside that head of yours."

I try to talk to him, but it takes me a couple minutes to calm down enough so he can understand what I am saying.

Once I feel that I am calm enough, I take a deep breath and say, "I have so many emotions flowing through me. I am devastated we lost people when the mansion blew up. I am also beyond furious that those fuckers tried to hurt my baby. Like, hasn't she been through enough? Why can't they leave her alone?"

He gives me an encouraging smile when I take a breath, but I start again, "I want every motherfucker who had a hand in destroying our home to die in a long and painful death. They don't deserve any mercy."

He kisses my forehead. "And they will. Fabio is already working on accessing the surveillance from that day, but it is going to take some time. But we are going to tighten up security around the safe house for a while."

He pauses before he asks me, "I need to ask you if you want to be involved or not. I know you enjoy torturing people, but do you want in when we find out information?"

Without hesitation, I tell him, "I want to know everything. I am your wife, the Queen of the Italian Mafia. I need to know everything so we can take down these Russian fuckers once and for all. I was mad before, hearing about Anna and Lilyana but now they tried to kill my baby. I am a whole new level of angry." I give him an evil smirk thinking about how I can't wait to try some of my new toys I made out on these fuckers. "Just thinking how much fun it will be when I get to try out some of my new toys out on our guests."

He starts to rub the back of his head and gives me a sheepish smile; I glare at him "What did you do?"

"Well, the Russian was being difficult. So, I may have used the dildo with blades in it on him."

Oh, when I feel better, I am gonna whoop this idiot's ass. Better yet, I will have Nonna do it for me.

"What? I wanted to watch it." He pulls out his phone and starts to type on it. I am about to give this moron a piece of my mind when he turns the phone in my direction.

"You can watch it. I had it recorded for you."

I smile like a kid in a candy shop, with my hand open waiting for him to place his phone in my hand. As soon as he does, I hit play and lay my head back against his chest. I get excited seeing one of the sons of bitch squirm and scream in pain. But the happiness soon leaves my body when I hear what the pathetic man's plan is.

I can feel myself shake in anger. "I swear Mateo. When I get my hands on that Russian scum, he is going to learn what pain really is."

He puts his hand in my hair and angles my face towards him. He kisses me in a way that reaches into my soul. "No worries. We will have each and every last one of them suffer. Everyone will fear the name Emilia De Luca. You are my perfect Vicious Queen, and everyone who has wronged us will be begging at your feet."

I chuckle at him. "We are some very sick demented fuckers, huh?"

He laughs, "Yes, we are, but I wouldn't change anything about you."

I shake my head at him, "Corny fucker."

He smirks, "Only for you."

His phone beeps and he look at it and sucks in a breath.

"Get ready, we have to call your crazy godmother." I smile knowing we get to call my godmother, I miss her. Not even a minute later, we see her name pop up on the phone for FaceTime.

Esmeralda: Hello Mateo and Emil…. what the fuck happened to you? Oh, did that boy do something to you? Oi when I get my hands on him! Jose, get the plane ready, I need to go kill another Italian.

Emilia: Esmeralda, calm down. Mateo didn't do anything to me, he was in Ireland and rushed back here when he heard the mansion was blown up.

Esmeralda: I need my shotgun too.

Mateo: Esmeralda, it was Alexei who orchestrated the whole thing to kidnap Alessia and Emilia. Both girls are alive, and both have some injuries, Emilia's are, of course, worse than Alessia's because she thinks she is a wonder woman.

I glare at him; he knows that by him saying that to Esmeralda, I am gonna get yelled at.

Esmeralda: Emilia, do you want me to smack you?

Emilia: Ok, I was in the kitchen with Alessia when the bombs went off. I had to get her out of the house when I heard the Russians looking for us. So, I jumped out the window, but luckily, I caught up with some of Mateo's capos and we were able to get out of there.

Esmeralda: You are a danger to my health; you are absolutely crazy. You better rest and listen to the doctor, but speaking of the doctor that's the reason I called. Mateo, I hope you have a new doctor because yours will be unavailable.

Emilia: What did you do to Roman?

She smirks at us.

Esmeralda: Well… we had a little chat.

Emilia: Sure. Is that what you call your torture sessions now?

We both chuckle knowing damn well, it wasn't a friendly chat.

Mateo: What did you do to my doctor, Esmeralda?

Esmeralda: Well, I found out he was the one who provided the man who set up the bombs for an easy escape to Russia. He refuses to say who did it though. I would like to finish questioning him, but if you insist, I can have him sent to you. He also was giving the spoiled brat information about Emilia and Alessia. His sister is working with someone, but he refuses to say who.

Mateo: You can keep questioning him, but keep him alive, I want to end him. Since he broke Omerta, I will be the one to finish him. Honestly, you are saving me some time by questioning him, because I know a certain woman who is going to be a pain in the ass because she hates feeling useless while she recovers.

I try to give him an innocent look but that doesn't work when Esmeralda is cracking up on the phone.

Emilia: Esmeralda, you are supposed to be on my side!!

I pout at her. She rolls her eyes at me pouting at her.

Esmeralda: My dear goddaughter as much as I love you, I don't envy anyone who has to take care of you when you are sick. You would drive your parents loco, Mateo, you will probably have to tie her butt to the bed because she will try and get out of bed when she are not supposed to. Do you need me to send you one of my doctors since I took yours?

Mateo: Nope, we have Theo with us.

Esmeralda grins at us.

Esmeralda: Oh, I miss Mr. Sexy Australian. How is that boy?

Emilia: He is good. Already working my nerves, and he has Alessia on his side.

She laughs again.

Esmeralda: You two always acted like siblings and not friends. Well, I need to go and visit your doctor some more, but I will keep you updated. Adios.

She hangs up, without waiting for a response. I just chuckle at her quick goodbye. Before Mateo can respond there is a knock on the door. Mateo tells whoever to come in while he sits up and we see Marcello pop his head in the room. "Don, Donna, there is a little girl out here wanting to come see her Mama and Papa. Can I bring her in here?"

And I quickly respond, "Yes please, Marcello."

He nods and goes back to get Alessia. He gently sets her in the bed next to me. I have tears running down my face, which I didn't realize. Alessia wipes my tears when she sits on the bed next to me. I kiss her palm while she giggles at me but then she looks at me with a sad smile.

"Mama…. I am sorry you got hurt."

"Oh baby, I will be okay. Theo is going to help me feel better, plus I have you as my little helper to keep an eye on me."

Alessia giggles and nods her head. "Yeah, Mama, you are not a very good patient. Teddy says so."

I roll my eyes; he is already pinning my daughter against me. "I am a very good patient, little missy." I hear Mateo chuckle behind me. I glare at him, and he puts his hands up in surrender.

"Alright you two, both of you need to be laying down, even if you are not sleeping. So both of you lay your heads on your pillows." Alessia goes to open her mouth, "You can lay next to Mama, Princess." She smiles and snuggles next to me on my pillow. Mateo goes and collects extra pillows to support our injured limbs. Once we are propped up and blankets tucked around us, he kisses both of our heads and leaves us to talk alone. Knowing we both need to sort out our emotions from what happened at the mansion. Plus, I am sure he has calls to make.

It takes me a while to convince Alessia it is not her fault I got hurt. She feels guilty, which I understand. I feel the same, except my guilt is for the people who died in the mansion and all the trouble we have caused the De Luca's.

"Mama, will Papa take care of the mean men?"

"Yeah, baby he will."

"Good, I want you to be happy and they make you angry and sad. So, they need to go away," she tells me as she closes her eyes, while I run my hand through her hair.

I whisper to her. "My sweet little girl, you have such a big heart. I will always protect you." I kiss her cheek and close my eyes.

TWENTY-EIGHT
EMILIA

It's been two months since we settled into a villa that was his mothers, and the reason why he wanted to marry me in the first place. When we drove up the long driveway it gave you the horror movie vibes. The driveway had tons of trees on either side of it. Once we pulled up to the front of the house, I was blown away by its beauty. I can tell his mother was Greek. From the inside to the outside, it was a beautiful, wide-open house with an indoor and outdoor pool. This place is big but not as huge as Nonna's mansion. I honestly wouldn't mind staying here forever. It is a beautiful ten-bedroom villa. Alessia's room and our room are next to each other. Which calmed Alessia, even though she hasn't been sleeping in her room. My poor baby has been having nightmares more frequently. The only way she has been sleeping in her room is when Theo and she had a sleepover in her room. Even though he was in the room with her, she still woke up screaming and we heard her wake up. Mateo ran in there to help Theo calm her down, she has been extremely attached to Mateo.

She says she only feels safe because "Papa will keep us safe." To the point she lays on the couch in his office while he works. I am so grateful he has been here helping both of us recover.

I am worried about her when he has to leave the house for business. He says he will try and hold off until I am better so that I can help her since I still can barely move. Luckily, Alessia's therapist agreed to have her sessions with her through video calls, because we don't trust anyone besides the guards that Mateo handpicked and the family. I just hope, in time, she won't be as anxious, and her nightmares settle down.

FLASHBACK
A Month Earlier

"Theodore Fucking Walker! I swear to God if you don't bring me my walker so I can get out of this bed, I will kill you." He stands at the doorway with the walker which is the only way I can walk on my own but even then, it's only a few steps. I am still not that sturdy on my feet, having a shattered knee does that to your balance.

"No, if you want to go anywhere you will be carried. There are plenty of strong men who have nice muscles. Who can carry your ass where you need to go?" I glare at him and really want to throw something at him, but no, my jackass husband took everything besides my pillows away from the side of our bed so I could stop throwing shit at

Theo. I swear Theo is finding enjoyment that he is getting my anger to this point where all I want is to kill something.

Granted, my temper has been shorter than usual. I hate feeling useless barely allowed to leave the bed except to practice once a day to walk a few steps. Which makes me on edge. I feel like if we are attacked, I will be useless or dead weight. I hear a chuckle and I see Mateo walk out from the bathroom with only a pair of gray sweatpants hanging low on his waist. I slowly eye him down, taking in each and every divot of his muscles. I have to clench my legs together. Ever since me and Mateo started to sleep together, we couldn't keep our hands off each other. And this past month has sucked because I have been so horny, and it doesn't make it better when I can hear him moaning my name jerking off in the bathroom, making me want him more.

"Quit eye raping your husband when I am in the room, you will taint my virgin eyes."

I look away from Mateo. "You are not a damn virgin and don't think I haven't caught the way you have been eyeing a certain guard," I said to him with my eyebrow raised at him, and he blushed.

"Have no idea what you are talking about."

"Oh, so if I would tell a certain guard with shaggy blond hair with green eyes you aren't interested even though he is very interested in you?"

"Wait, he is interested in me?"

I roll my eyes at his stupidity. "For a doctor you are very blind to things that go on around you."

"Well maybe, I was just staying focused on treating my patients."

"You have always been blind to anyone who checked you out."

He scoffs and puts a hand on his heart. "You wound me bestie."

"Eh, you will be fine, you're a doctor I am sure you can treat yourself."

He is about to open his mouth, but Mateo turns him around and pushes him out the door while saying, "As amusing as you two bickering is I am spending time with my stubborn and hardheaded wife." Mateo shuts and locks the door. I hope he brings my walker back over to the bed, but he walks past it.

"Now, my *cara moglie*, why are you being difficult for Theo?" he asks me, crossing his arms across his chest, making his arm muscles bigger. I look away from him so he can't distract me like he has been when I want to kill something.

"Is me wanting to walk on my own being difficult?" I ask him, arching my eyebrow.

He shakes his head and walks over to me and picks me up to place me on his lap. "No, it's not, but pushing yourself past what your body can handle is being difficult." I lay my head on his chest and sigh. I know what he is saying is correct, but it doesn't help that I want to feel better.

He lifts my chin up so I meet his eyes. "Patience, my Queen. You will feel better soon, but once Theo gives us the clear, I am dragging your ass back to this bed and I am going to ravish and devour you. You will need that walker to walk after I am done with you," he says with a smoldering look in his eye. I have to squeeze my legs together again, and he smirked at me.

He gives me a passionate kiss as he opens my legs, putting his hand over my pussy but not moving his hand. I try to grind onto his hand to get some kind of friction. He chuckled into the kiss and with his other hand, he held my hip still. I groaned at him, and he pulled away from the kiss. He sits me back on the bed and stands up but leans into my ear. "That is your punishment for being difficult with Theo." He stands to his full height. I gape at him before I can respond. "Now you will lay your ass in this bed and rest." And then he walks out the door without looking back. That's it! When I can walk again, I am going to kill both of them.

EMILIA

Two Month Later

"Cazzo diavolo. Questo fa male come un figilo dick puttana" (Fucking hell. This hurts like a motherfucker) I say out loud as I am working with Theo on walking. I decided to wait and listen to Theo about my recovery. I became a little more bearable to be around since my burns are basically healed. I still have to put cream on my arms and wear long sleeve shirts for protection, but I can move around without being in pain.

"Take it nice and easy Emilia, just take two more steps and we can be done for the day." I nod and grip onto the walker, lifting my good foot, and pain shoots through my bad leg. I grit my teeth but push so I can get the pressure off the bad leg. I stop after one step and take a deep breath; my head falls down to my chest.

"Come on Emilia, one last step I know you can do it." I do the same thing as before and it still hurts but I push back, knowing I can lay down after this. As soon as I finish, I lean all my weight onto my good leg. Theo picks me up and sits me down on the bed, and he rubs my knee to help with the swelling, but it still hurts like hell.

"Do you remember what you did to Stefan McGregor in our freshman year?" he asks me, and I throw my head back laughing.

"Of course I remember what I did to the small dick prick. He deserved it for teasing you and calling you all of those homophobic slurs," I say. Even thinking about it pisses me off, but remembering what I did to him makes me smile.

"Yeah, he definitely did. Super gluing his ass to the desk, but then also coating the front bar of his desk with super glue so the top of his jeans would get stuck too, was pure genius."

I shrug my shoulders, that is when Mateo walks in and says, "You did what?"

We start laughing while Mateo is looking very confused. Once we catch our breath, I retell the story.

"Well, the quarterback of the football team was an asshole with a small dick attitude. He kept making fun of Theo about being gay and for being from Australia. So, I dealt with him by super gluing his ass to the seat and his jeans to the desk during Spanish class. We had the desks that were connected to the chair, and the best part is the dumb ass didn't realize he was stuck to the chair until the end of the class. I super glued his ass and the bar attached to his desk that was over his lap. I got suspended for a week, it was supposed to be for two weeks, but when you are a good student, and your Papa happens to be a cop and the friends with the principal, you tend to get lesser punishments."

Theo snickers, "Mama Angelica had the best reaction though."

I shake my head. "Yeah, Mama was a free spirit, she told me I should have recorded it." I smile a small smile; I really miss her and I have time to think about it during this recovery, and I also know if they were still alive, she would be fussing over me like a mother hen.

Theo gives my hand a squeeze not saying anything, but giving me a knowing smile. We have had talks about everything from my family passing away up until now. As much as I appreciate my new family being here to talk to me, it helps to have someone who knew my family and basically was like another son to my parents. Hell, Mama always said she had three sons and one daughter. Theo even left clothes at my house so he wouldn't have to worry about clothes or so he could stop stealing Franco's clothes. Franco hated when Theo borrowed his clothes.

Theo starts to randomly laugh; I look at him like he has lost his mind but, to be honest, I think he lost it a long time ago. "Your dad was a cop and here you are married to a Mafia Boss, ironic, huh? But again, doesn't surprise me. You always were the rebel child out of the three of you."

I shrug my shoulders, "I kept things entertaining. Franco was so serious, and a computer geek who always had his face in a book or on a computer screen. But he was fucking brilliant he did teach me a lot. Giovanni was a clown, boy did he love soccer. Scary how he should be graduating high school this year. I can only imagine what crazy party Mama would throw while Papa tried to control her craziness. Plus, I am sure they knew about Esmeralda and Jose being the Boss of the Spanish Mafia," I say, again giving a small smile.

Mateo kisses my forehead then squats down in front of my chair. "I didn't know them, but I know they would have been proud of you. Your Papa may not have been happy you married me, but they all would be proud of how you protected Alessia. You are an amazing person, never forget that." He then turns to Theo. "Is she done or is she just taking a break?"

"Nope, she is done. Hot bath, then make sure she elevates her leg with ice."

Mateo nods his head and picks me up in his arms bridal style. I lay my head against his chest with my arms around his neck. We walk into our bathroom. He sets me on the sink and starts the bath. Once he has the water at the perfect temperature, he strips naked. I keep my eyes on his face knowing damn well if I look below his neck, I will get horny, and since we still can't do anything, I have to try and control myself. He looks at me and smirks. "Is there a problem?"

I glare at him as he walks up to me, and I tell him, "You know damn well what the problem is."

He pretends to act all innocent but we both know damn well he isn't. He helps me get undressed but behaves like a gentleman the whole time and doesn't ogle my body.

He picks me up once I am undressed, and we both sit in this massive tub that could be a hot tub. I am sitting in his lap; I go to put my hair up in a messy bun on top of my hair, but he grabs my hair ties off my wrist and does it for me. I give him a kiss on his cheek, give him a small smile, and quietly thank him. It is when he does the little things that I fall deeper in love with him. I snuggle into his chest, and we don't talk for the first couple of minutes, which is honestly nice. I love how we have a balance of knowing when we have to talk and knowing when being quiet together is also good.

"So, I have a surprise for you," Mateo tells me.

I look at him and arch my eyebrow. "Okay, what is it?"

He chuckles at me. "I am not telling you what your birthday surprise is yet."

"Birthday surprise? But my birthday isn't until...shit today is my birthday."

He scoffs at me. "I can't believe you forgot your birthday."

I shrug my shoulders. "Last year with Esmeralda, was the first time I celebrated my birthday since my parents passed away. I never paid attention to my birthday when I was with Seth, I made sure I did something for Alessia but never myself."

"Well, that's gonna change. Even though my original plans were to have a huge celebration for both of my girls since your birthdays are a month apart, well we are gonna do something else instead."

"I am not going to be able to change your mind, am I?" I try giving him my puppy dog eyes, he puts his hand over my face.

"Nope and now, I can't see your puppy eyes." he tells me chuckling. I lick his hand that is on my face.

"Did you really... just lick my hand?"

"Maybe?"

He shakes his head. "You keep surprising me every day." And before I can respond with a sassy answer, he kisses me.

We finally get out of the bath, and he dries both of us off and we get dressed. He insisted on blow drying my hair for me, even though I was just gonna throw it into a wet bun. While he is drying my hair, Alessia comes barging into our room.

"Papa are you almost ready?" she asks him.

I arch my eyebrow at him. He looks down at her as she runs and hugs his leg.

"Almost done. I am just finishing your Mama's hair." She looks up at him, poking her lip out and giving him the puppy dog eyes.

"Can you braid my hair too, Papa? Please?" she says, dragging out the e. I try to hide my chuckle but miserably fail.

Mateo looks at me and attempts to glare at me while saying, "She learned that from you."

I roll my eyes at him and give him a knowing look because she has him wrapped around her finger.

And to prove my point he nods his head at her and says *"Sii paziente principessa." (Be patient princess)* Once I am done, he helps me get dressed because doing anything with my shattered knee after physical therapy is a bitch. Once I am done, I have my knee elevated on a pillow with ice on it while he untangles Alessia's messy hair and puts it into two braids. I look at Mateo in adoration. A year ago, I would never have imagined him braiding my daughter's hair, but today I don't think there's anything he wouldn't do for her.

Once he is done Alessia jumps down from the stool. I tell her to be careful and she comes over to kiss my cheek, saying. "Sorry Mama."

Mateo picks me up and he tells Alessia to open the door for us.

The three of us walk into the living room and before I sit down, I hear Vincenzo's voice. "Aww, look at them looking like a newlywed couple."

Then I hear a smack and him grumbling about being abused. I look around but I see Vincenzo, Salvatore, Adriano, and Julietta on the T.V. A huge smile comes across my face and Alessia is running closer to the T.V. Before I can say hello Alessia has started her rambling. I ignore her for a bit and lean my head against Mateo, enjoying spending time with our family. Theo walks in the room with an ice pack for me. I mumble a thank you. I hear Alessia say my name, so I decide to tune back into what I is being said.

"Mama always argues with Teddy. She isn't a very good patient but that's okay because she is beautiful and a great Mama."

Of course, the drama queen has to open his mouth "Alessia how could you say it is okay? Your Mama threw things at me!"

She rolls her eyes at him. "But you didn't get hurt plus Papa took away all her weapons so you couldn't get hurt."

Theo puts his hand on his head. "Oh no we are doomed she is turning into a mini-Emilia. The poor child."

Vincenzo is quick to be as dramatic as Theo. "Hey doc quit being dramatic, that is my role in the family."

I mumble in Mateo's ear, "I wonder if we lock the two of them in a room together, if they would annoy each other as much as they annoy us?"

He laughs, but of course it's not a quiet laugh so no one knows we are talking about them, he has a full belly laugh.

"Great idea."

Tweddle Dee and Tweddle Dum (Theo and Vincenzo) start bugging us about what we said, and I tell them and they both look offended. Theo tells us that we are rude. Vincenzo feels attacked by us saying he is annoying. Julietta tells Vincenzo, "Well you are, maybe if you had a girlfriend, you would be tolerable."

He shakes his head "I don't need a girlfriend." And before they can start Adriano stops them.

We all continue playful banter with each other. The boys tease Julietta about missing Marcello, she blushes and hides her face in her hands. Of course Alessia tells Julietta about what Marcello has been doing and Julietta has a small smile on her face hearing all the stuff Marcello has done with Alessia. After a while, the banter slows down, and we all update each other about everything that has been going on that Alessia can overhear. We have told her that Seth is looking for us and that is why we are at this house, so we can be safe.

After about thirty minutes of talking, Julietta told Alessia how she visits the horses, and the boys promised her once the new house is built, they will have a new playground built as well. Alessia is more than happy to talk to her extended family, which we have not talked to much because of safety reasons. After that, she gets bored and drags Theo out to go bake cookies together, which has Nonna and Nonno chasing after them because they don't trust the two of them together. Let's be honest, Theo has the mentality of a kid, yet he is a good doctor. I will never understand that. Julietta says goodbye and then the three men walk into another room.

After they are settled, I see they are in the basement, and the men smirk directly at me. "What did you do?" I ask them.

"Well, we got a very interesting visitor to come to the office yesterday," Adriano says. I nod at him to continue. "A delusional old man who says his wife was in danger. So, I brought him to the office, and he told me how her mother kidnapped her and fled the country. Then he proceeded to tell me that her mother got her involved with some bad people, and she needs to be saved."

"Are you talking about who I think you're talking about?" I ask him. He gives me possibly the biggest grin I have ever seen, and he nods at me. He turns the camera around, and I see Boris sitting in a chair. His head is hanging since he is still asleep. Salvatore tells me to hold on so he can set up the laptop so I can talk to Boris. I evilly grin and rub my hands together.

"Can you wake him up? I want to taunt him a bit," I ask, and Vincenzo is more than willing to comply. He grabs a metal bucket and fills it with water, and he grabs a hammer. Once he is next to Boris, he dumps the water over his head but leaves the bucket on his head. Vincenzo swings the hammer against the outside of the bucket. Boris groans and he jumps up but freaks out being tied to the chair and having a bucket on his head.

"Hello? Who is there?"

"Go ahead and take it off," I tell Vincenzo; he moves the bucket off his head. Boris's eyes frantically search around the room, and I keep a blank face on. Once he sees me, he goes from scared to pissed.

"Where is my wife?" he yells at me; I roll my eyes at him.

"She is not your wife."

"Yes, she is. Her father sold her to me."

"I would never do such a thing," Mateo replies to him.

"You are not her father."

"No, he is her father. The boy you are talking about is her sperm donor, and Mateo is her father. He is her father on her birth certificate. Seth had seven years to man up and be a father, but he never did. Oh, and he never got her a birth certificate, so the deal with Alessia is invalid," I say with a smirk at the end. Boris' eyes widen.

"What do you mean?"

"What my wife means, old fucker, is that Seth never got Alessia a birth certificate. My lawyers had to have one made for her because she didn't have one."

"But he promised me, I gave him money for her."

I can feel my temper rising, Mateo rubs his thumb across my knuckles to try and soothe my anger. "Don't worry about the money since you won't be leaving that warehouse alive," I smirk at him.

Boris yells back, "I will be saved, because I run Mr. Ivanov's brothels."

I look at Mateo and laugh. "We haven't done anything, and he is already spilling his secrets."

Mateo turns to the camera and says, "Don't rough him up too bad. Once Emilia is healed, he is hers to finish." Then he turns off the TV and he is carrying me in his arms back upstairs.

He lays me in the bed, and he walks over to my nightstand. He pulls out the dildo I have been using; since we can't have sex I was improvising. He snaps it in half. "What the fuck. Mateo?"

He is leaning over me "You don't need a dildo if you need to cum. I will do it for you, not some silicone toy."

"But we can't have sex."

"I have a tongue and fingers; trust me I have been wanting to taste you," he says while licking his lips.

He unties his tie and ties it around my mouth. He leans down and whispers in my ear, "We can't have the whole house hear you scream in pleasure; that is only for my ears."

He takes my shirt off and bra off. He leaves gentle kisses down my neck towards my chest. He is extra gentle on my burn scars. *"Bella assolutamente bella,"* he whispers against my skin. He plays with both of my nipples going back and forth between sucking both while his hand plays with the other one.

I feel the pressure build up, I grind on him to try and get some friction, but he holds my hips still. I whine at him through the tie. He chuckles, *"Qualcuno è impaziente." (Someone is impatient.)* I glare at him and reach for him, but he shakes his head when he reaches for his belt. He undoes his belt and grabs both of my wrists. He restrains both of my wrists together with his belt above my head. *"Non muovere le mani, o io ti punirò." (Don't move your hands, or I will punish you.)*

I do as he says because usually his punishments end up with my ass red or he denies me of an orgasm, and I really need an orgasm. *"Sembri così assolutamente sexy come questo alla mia mercé." (You look so absolutely sexy like this at my mercy.)*

He runs his fingers down my body from my neck down to my chest, over both nipples. He continues tracing down my body with his finger. Once he gets to the waistband of my pants, he takes off my pants and rips my underwear off. He brings me to the end of the bed. He props my legs on his shoulders and dives between my legs. He wastes no time diving his tongue deep inside of me. I moan out through the tie as he thrusts his tongue in and out of me. When he curls his tongue inside of me, I arch my back and I feel my orgasm rip through me so fast I have no time to warn him. My toes curl behind his back and my head is thrown back into the pillow. He continues as I ride out my orgasm and as soon as I am done, he laps all of my juices. "Let's see how many times I can make you cum."

This man is going to kill me. He switches his tongue with his fingers and moves his mouth to my clit. He brings my sensitive bundle of nerves in his mouth and starts to suck on it. I am withering under him, feeling that tightness in my stomach. He reaches up with his other hand and starts to play with my nipple. I am moaning but it is muffled by his tie. He curls his fingers, hitting my G-Spot over and over. I am grinding my hips up into his face.

Mateo is nibbling my clit but once he bites down on it, I fall apart and moan his name through the tie. I am completely spent after he devoured me. He unties my hands and takes the tie out of my mouth. He walks off and comes back with a washcloth to clean me up. I am almost asleep when I feel him slip a shirt over my head. I grumble to him about him being rude for disturbing my sleep.

He chuckles at me, and once he lays me down, he climbs in bed behind me. I turn around and snuggle into his chest, with his arms around my body, I wrap my arms around him, holding him closer afraid if I let go, he won't be here in the morning. Mateo kisses my forehead, and before I know it, I am asleep.

TWENTY-NINE
ALEXEI

I look at Seth sitting across from me, and I can see how this idiot is related to my wife. Both are complete morons. If my wife wasn't as sexy as she was and didn't obey my every command, I would have gotten rid of her a long time ago. She was a one-night stand that got pregnant and my father got wind of it and forced me to marry the bitch. She thought she got lucky, but she realized she entered hell.

"Are you fucking kidding me, Seth?" He shrugs his shoulders like his idea was a good one, which it was not.

"Are you telling me you sent Boris into De Luca Corp asking for his "wife" after we recently bombed the mansion they were living at? Oh, and the team we sent in tortured the only survivor. Boris is a bitch when it comes to pain, he would start spilling all of our secrets if they scratched him."

Seth just raises his eyebrows at me. "I wasn't going into the lion's den. And if he is so desperate to get his hands on Alessia then he can do some dirty work."

"I should shoot you right here for being so fucking stupid."

He gives me a cocky grin. "But you won't because it will upset Irina."

I laugh at him. "Like I give a fuck about that cunt. She is here to look pretty on my arm when needed and be a woman for me and my men to fuck." He looks shocked at what I told him; she must have been lying to him about how happy she is. "Now if you excuse me, I need to go check on my wife's punishment."

I walk out past a bewildered Seth and into the basement where my darling wife is serving out her punishment. She thought she could speak out against me about her training my niece how to be a proper wife, but it seems my wife needs more training herself. I walk downstairs to the basement and chuckle at the sight I see before me.

Irina is tied to the bars of her cell with her front flush to the bars. She can't move any part of her body besides her head. Her hands are tied inside of a bag so she can't attempt to escape. Her ankles are handcuffed together, and her body is tied to the bars of the cell by heavy rope. The man in front of her is savagely fucking her throat, and she is gagging. He grabs her hair and pulls her head so it smacks against the bar next to her head.

"Swallow every drop you whore," he tells her with a knife to her throat. I see she already has some cuts on her throat that are still bleeding. He holds her with his other hand at the back of her neck and slams her face to him, so her nose is flush against him. He pulls back, barely letting her catch her breath, and slams her face back against him and holds her in place.

He grunts out his release, and a couple drops leak out the side of her mouth. When he pulls away after she swallows what is in her mouth, he sees that she didn't swallow every drop. "Tsk, tsk, tsk, a greedy whore shouldn't waste what is given to her," he says while digging the knife into her shoulder. She screams out in pain as I walk forward and make my presence known.

"You may go now," I tell the man; he nods at me as he passes. I bend down in front of Irina. "Looks like my men are enjoying your punishment," I snicker at her.

I stand up and go to untie her from the front of the cell. I grab her by her forearm, dragging her to my playroom. I throw her to the ground, and she lands on her arm. She groans out in pain since she cannot break the fall with her arms and legs still bound. I lock the door and turn around to face her.

"Get on the bed now." She does as I tell her, and I uncuff her hands and legs. I tie her to the edge of the bed, so she is sprawled out on display for me. She doesn't make eye contact with me and is looking at the ceiling with no emotion. Well, I guess I will have to change that.

I grab one of my cigarettes to smoke, knowing she hates the smell of it. I watch her carefully as she scrunches her nose at the smell. I chuckle and burn the bottom of her foot. She starts to scream and thrash around trying to get away from me. I hold it there for a minute and takes it away. She takes a deep breath of relief, but it is short lived when I move to the other foot. She doesn't beg for me to stop, knowing I never will stop; I love her tears. When I pull the cigarette away from her foot, she is shaking, and her face is covered in tears.

I grab my knife and slowly cut her clothes off her body making sure to have the knife cut into her skin. She winches and has her eyes shut; her breath is labored. Once she is naked, I stand back to admire her naked with bruises and knife marks all over her body. I do admit, she has a hot body, which is the only reason I agreed to marry the bitch. "I heard you were telling lies to your brother. It seems your mouth is getting you in trouble recently." She doesn't acknowledge me, which pisses me off. I am the Boss and her husband, I will not be ignored or disrespected. I squeeze her foot and she scream out in pain. "You will respond when I ask you a question."

"I didn't want him to worry about me," she tells me.

I throw my head back and laugh. "Well, he now knows exactly what your place is around here as my wife, whore."

"What...what did you tell him?"

I stalk next to her by her face and pull my hand back and punch her across her jaw. Her head snaps to the other side and she just cries. "You don't get to question me. I own you, all you are good for is to please me and my men. Otherwise, you are useless."

"Speaking of pleasing. We are overdue for a night alone. Wouldn't you say.... wife?" And I say the word wife with the most hate in my voice.

I strip out of my clothes, settle myself between her legs, and thrust into her. She cries out in pain since she isn't wet. Oh well, it's not like I am going to stop either way. "What's wrong Irina? Being fucked by rich men doesn't turn you on anymore?" I taunt her.

She is crying, but again, she won't make any noise, and that's no fun. I bite down hard on her neck, over the bruise where I had grabbed her by the throat when I dragged her to the basement a few days ago. She cries out in pain.

"Such a good whore, the way you cry out. Let me hear you. Do you enjoy my cock destroying your loose cunt?" She continues to cry and wail as I continue to bite all over her neck harshly. I lean back up and look down at where we connect. Pull back to where only the head was in her and slam as hard as I can back into her. She is thrashing around.

"Stop, please, it hurts. I beg you please."

I smirk at her, grab her nipples and pull on them while twisting them at the same time. "Yes, beg me. I love when you beg me."

She stays quiet so I slap her across her face. "I said beg me."

She finally makes eye contact with me "Please, Mr. Ivanov, please have mercy on me and stop this torture."

I feel myself getting closer, so I take one of my hands and wrap it around her throat and the other pinches her clit as I continue to roughly slam into her harder than the thrust before. "Fuck," I grit out as I push as far as I can inside of her while I hit my release. She lays there, limp, and I know she will be very willing to do whatever I want to her. I uncuff her and drag her so only her top half is laying on the bed and her ass is in the air.

I smack her ass as hard as I can, and she whimpers and jumps. I push my erection in between her cheeks and grind hard on her, pushing until her chest falls flat onto the bed. I lean over her and whisper in her ear, "This punishment is for not agreeing with me. You still have your punishment for lying to Seth. Can't have my wife going around lying to people now, but that's okay. We will fix that." She whimpers about having more punishments, and I grow harder at the sound of her fearful whimper. I lean back up and smack her ass again. I watch as it jiggles. "Such a wonderful ass you have," I tell her as I pull her hips up higher to me.

I rub my cock from her clit to her ass a couple times. I then push my cock into her ass, going painfully slow so she can feel herself being stretched. She tries to move away from me, but I grab her by her hair and pull her up so her back is flush to my chest. That makes my cock fully settled in her tight ass. I groan in her ear, feeling her ass grip my cock so tight.

"Right, grip my cock with your ass, slut," I tell her as I start to fuck her. I have one hand wrapped around her throat, and the other is across her stomach. "Grind your ass on me.... like you mean it. NOW." I yell into her ear as I bite down hard on her ear lobe. She complies with me; I move my hand away from her stomach and up to her nipples, and I painfully twist and squeeze both nipples.

She is still whimpering and begging me to stop but I don't; instead, I push her back down on the bed. I lay my hand on her lower back so she can't move, and with my other hand, I reach into my bedside drawer and grab the vibrator. I turn it on full blast and shove it into her pussy. She squirms underneath me, and I hear her breath becoming labored. "My wife the whore is about to cum, hmm? Should I let the cum dumpster cum?" She nods her head. "Words slut," I demand of her.

"Please let me cum."

I think about it for a moment and get a wonderful idea in my head. I whisper in her ear, "If you want to cum, you will cum. You will cum all night."

I grind harder and deeper into her. Between me fucking her and the vibrator, she cums alright. She cums hard, which sends me into cumming in her ass. As soon as I am done cumming, I yank myself out of her. She cries out in pain, and I slap her hole hard. I go to the bathroom and clean myself up.

As I am in the bathroom, I smirk about her punishment. When I walk back into the bedroom, she is still in the same position I left her in. I pick her up and throw her in the middle of the bed. I cuff her arms and legs back to the sides of the bed. I walk into my closet and grab a couple toys of mine to use on her. She sees me walk back and looks to see what I have in my hands, and she gulps. I put everything on the bedside table, but I grab the blindfold and tie it around her eyes.

"You wanted to cum; well, you can cum. Every man and woman in the mansion will get a turn to do whatever they want to your body, as long as you cum at least once. And I will encourage them to be as painful and messy as possible."

I smirk as I see the blindfold getting wet from her tears, and her body shakes from the sobs wracking her. "But I am first," I tell her. I put on the nipple clamps, then I grab the dildo that has a clit sucker attached to it. I turn it on, and then I walk out of the room. I loudly slam the door and gather my high-rank soldiers. When I tell them to meet me in the playroom, they smirk and follow me.

Before we enter, I tell them, "Do not make any noise until I tell you to." I purposely open the door quietly and hold it for everyone to walk in quietly. We all stand there watching Irina as she squirms and moans. We all watch as she orgasms, but we still don't move. She really starts to move after she has come down from her high, as she is sensitive.

"Well, men, our whore decided to be a greedy slut and wanted to cum. So, I decided we should let her cum. She will cum all night long, and we all get to have a turn with her. You can do anything you want to her, but she has to cum. If she passes out, you may do anything you wish to wake her up."

They all grin as I walk over to Irina and remove her restraints because she isn't going to be able to overpower ten men, especially with how weak she is. I decide to sit this one out as I watch two of my men walk up and put her on her hands and knees. One stands in front of her face, he slams his cock down her throat while squeezing her throat, and the other slams into her ass. He grabs the dildo she had in her earlier but turns it on to full blast.

He smirks at me and says, "Let's get this party started," as he grabs the chain to her nipple clamps. She is crying, and he laughs. He slaps her pussy as he is roughly fucking her ass. They are in sync; they both enter her at the same time. They both take turns bruising her in some way. She cums and almost falls down. If it wasn't for her being held up by the men fucking her, she would have. The man who is fucking her ass finishes and walks away. The man who was getting his dick sucked off decided to be a sadistic fuck and cum on her cigarette burns from earlier. She screams, and you can see by looking around that her scream got all of us hard. And we all had some kind of fun; we all want at least two rounds each before we decide to let the lower rank soldiers have a turn.

The excitement on their faces when we told them how they could do anything to her as long as she orgasmed. Let me tell you, I have some evil men and women working for me, and I could not be prouder. My mistress was the worst, and it was such a turn-on to watch her whip Irina across her ass and pussy until she bled and then make multiple men fuck her relentlessly. My darling might be a bit hateful and petty towards Irina, and I know she abuses Irina on a daily basis, but I honestly could care less.

Knowing Irina would be in good hands, I walked back to my office to get a hold of my spy on the De Luca's to see where they were hiding now.

THIRTY
EMILIA

      I am lying on my back whistling while Theo takes another x-ray of my knee. We do this once a month so he can monitor my healing progress. He finishes taking the x-ray, and I sit up on the bed. He tells me, "Let me look over your x-rays then we will discuss what your plans for next month look like." He wiggles his eyebrows at me knowing I want to be able to fuck my husband. Even though his tongue and fingers are wonderful, I miss the anaconda that hangs between his legs. Stop, Emilia. Quit thinking about it or you will end up being a horny mess again. Plus, Mateo isn't here until later tonight.

      I rolled my eyes at him. "Well, I am going to go find Alessia," I tell him and hobble down the hallway. I hate wearing the full leg brace that doesn't let me bend my knee, but I know the more patient I am, the sooner I will heal. As I get closer to the kitchen, I hear Alessia and Nonno talking. I quietly peek into the kitchen. I see Alessia sitting next to Nonno, talking over some snacks Nonna must have made. Knowing Nonno, he is telling her stories about raising the grandchildren. I smile softly. Seeing Alessia this happy and having grandparents makes me happy, but it also makes me miss my parents, knowing how they would fuss all over her.

      Telling my parents not to spoil her would have been pointless. Mama would had said something like, "This is why we dealt with you even on your worst days. I wanted to hang you by your toes on the clothesline. She is my grandbaby. You won't deny me my right as a grandparent." I softly chuckle to myself and decide to go to Mateo's office to check for updates on the plan while Alessia has quality time with her Nonno.

      I walk into his office and get comfortable in his chair. I turn on his computer and lean back in my chair while I wait for everything to load. I hope the plan of revealing Mateo out in public works so we can catch some Russians to get more information. Granted, Boris has been a great help. I think it is hysterical that the sadistic bastard who did nothing but torture me for years can't handle a bit of pain. When I finally get my hands on him, oh, how sweet revenge will be. I hear a beep and see Mateo's GPS live on the map. It shows him going out to eat with a business partner. They are eating a couple blocks from a new brothel that just became open a couple weeks ago. Boris gave us a list of all the brothels he has been to, but I will say Alexei is smart and has other business partners besides Boris; otherwise, we would know all of his business.

      I can imagine Alexei isn't very happy with us since we have been destroying the businesses Boris told us about. Either by physically destroying them with bombs, sending the police in, or getting them to shut down financially. This brothel is the last one on our list that we have to destroy, which Mateo will do once he either sees any Russians near him, or after he finishes his lunch. He has a small remote so all he must do is flip the switch. I bounce my leg waiting for him to let me know he set off the bomb and he is safe.

Theo comes in and sits in front of Mateo's desk. "You can stop being so damn cranky, you can let Mateo fuck the attitude out of you," he says as he swings his hand like he is spanking someone's ass.

"Any restrictions?"

He nods at me. "Yes, you have to keep your leg straight, so you can't get on top of him and ride the man's dick to death."

I roll my eyes at him "I swear you are worse than Vincenzo and his stories about the different women he brings home. I honestly feel bad for Julietta having to live under the same roof as him."

Theo chuckles. "I can imagine he can be a bit much to handle."

I raise my eyebrow at him. "And you're not extra at all?"

He pretends to flip his hair. "Um, I need to be extra to keep up with you."

"Sure, that clearly is the reason you are extra." He looks at me with wide eyes and puts his hand on his chest.

"I am hurt you think that bestie." I roll my eyes at him; he snickers at me. "Better quit rolling your eyes before Mateo finds out and adds another punishment to your list," he says, laughing.

I glare at him. "You better not. I am so screwed, when he finds out he can start punishing me." I whine, and of course, my oh-so-loving best friend laughs at me.

"It's nice to see someone finally can keep your sassy, rebellious ass in line."

"I'd rather be called feisty, thank you very much."

"You are a pain in the ass, Mateo's pain in the ass, to be exact."

"Whatever, go bother someone else. I am waiting on a phone call, so shoo."

He dramatically says with sarcasm, "I can feel the love." I point to the door, and he flips me off as he walks out of the door.

After an hour of waiting, I am walking towards the door, about to start on our plan b if things don't go well, which it is looking that way, since I cannot get hold of Mateo or any of the damn soldiers that are supposed to be with him. Plan B is I get everyone out of this house in the cheaper-looking cars we have and drive towards the other safe house in Paris. I call Peter O'Sullivan, the head of the Irish Mafia, to fly us to his home in Ireland. Peter was the man Mateo was meeting when the mansion was bombed.

I felt a pit in my stomach about something happening to him, I love him so much and I don't want anything happening to him. But

Mateo made me promise I would do whatever was necessary to keep Alessia safe. I sent Jose a text letting him know Nonno, Nonna, Alessia, and Theo would be on a plane headed to their mansion in the next hour.

I walk out of the office and start looking for everyone else. I find Theo and Alessia watching the avengers. Theo sees the somber look on my face and says, "Plan B?"

I nod and say, "Plan B."

He comes over, hugs me, and whispers, "Everything will be okay. I am not leaving your side. Even with this mafia craziness."

"Thank you, Theo. I don't know what I would do without you. But I need you to stay with Alessia. I am sending everyone except Marcello and me to Esmeralda's home. I am gonna go to Ireland, an ally of Mateo's is there and see what I can find out. I'd rather have Alessia hidden away, even if it is away from me. All that matters to me is that she is safe, Theo. I trust you more than anyone else with my baby."

He goes to argue, but I stop him "Please, Theo, I am begging you. I don't know the Irish Mafia, but we know you all are safe with Esmeralda and Jose. Please think of Alessia's safety."

"Okay, but promise to take care of yourself."

I squeeze him tighter. "I will. Hurry and pack your stuff. The sooner we leave the better." He nods at me, gives me one last small smile, then heads to his room.

Alessia looks between Theo and me. "What's wrong, Mama?"

I sigh, walk to her and sit next to her on the couch. "You know how Papa has been working hard to make sure Seth and all of the mean men never bother us again?" She nods her head. "Well, your Papa always had a plan to keep us safe just in case something happens, because he loves us very much and wants to make sure we are safe."

Her lips start to wobble. "Is Papa dead?"

"I don't know, baby. No one has told me anything, but we have to leave this house just to be safe."

"But how will Papa find us if we are not here?" I wipe the tears that have fallen from her eyes. "Papa will know because he told us where we are going, but guess where you get to go?"

"Where?"

I smile at her. "You get to go see Esmeralda and Jose." She has a huge smile on her face.

"But I won't be with you."

"Please come with me, Mama. I promise I will be a good girl."

I brush the hair away from her face. "Oh, sweet girl. You are a good girl, but I am going to stay with a friend of Papa's who will be able to help me find Papa and get rid of these bad guys once and for all."

"Who will protect you if Papa isn't there?"

I smile at her, "I will have Marcello with me. And Nonna, Nonno, and Theo will be with you. Vittorio will be waiting for you at the airport, and you will have a lot of security around you. I need you to listen to the adults we trust. Okay, baby."

"I will miss you, Mama," she says as she hugs me tighter.

"I will miss you too. I promise we will talk every day, and if you can't get a hold of me, Jose has Peter's number. You can always ask him to call him, okay?"

"Okay, Mama. Please find Papa. I don't want to lose him."

"I promise I will do everything I can to find Papa. Now, let's go pack your stuff because the sooner we all leave, the sooner Mama can start looking for Papa."

I stand up and offer my hand to her. Alessia stands up and grabs it; together, we walk toward her room. On the way, I stop. I see Marcello, Nonno, and Nonna, I tell them that we are on Plan B. The men give me a stoic nod and go off to get ready, but Nonna comes over and gives me a big hug and I can feel her tears on my shoulder. "I know, Nonna. I will find him."

She leans back, "Take care of yourself too, okay. Please call us as much as you can. I need to know you are safe and healthy too. You are one of my grandbabies as well."

I kiss her cheek. "I promise, Nonna." She gently pats my cheek and gives me another hug.

"Well, let me go help Nonno pack our things." She heads to her room as well. When we get to Alessia's room, I grab a suitcase and open it up as she brings over her clothes and she puts them inside. I go and grab her stuff from the bathroom. Once that is full, we grab the second bag and fill it with her shoes and her toys. Alessia follows me to my room as I pack mine and Mateo's things from our bedroom.

Alessia is holding her wolf in her arms while she watches me. I run my finger down her cheek, "I know, baby, but before you know it, we will be together again."

"I know, Mama. I am gonna miss you and I am worried about Papa."

I bend down and kiss her head, "I know, baby. I am gonna miss you so much too and I promise you I will find Papa. Now come on, we have to pack up Papa's office."

She follows me to Mateo's office, and she packs her books and the art stuff she has left here. While she does, I pack up his laptop, paperwork, and I pocket the burner phone that I will use.

Marcello already has our bags in the car, and he grabs the ones we packed from the office. "Thanks, Marcello. Everyone else ready?"

"Yes, Donna. Just waiting on you two."

I nod at him. "Alright, let's go." Alessia grabs my hand tighter not wanting to let me go. And I feel the same way, but I know she is safer there than with me. I don't know the O'Sullivan's or if I can trust them, but she will have the Spanish and the Italian Mafia watching over her at all times. Knowing Esmeralda, she will be spoiling Alessia to the core, which I would complain about, but Alessia's world is getting flipped upside down right now.

We all drive to the airport where we say our painful goodbyes. I tell everyone to protect her and how much I love them. I hug Theo as tight as I can, "Promise me you will watch over her."

"Of course I will, she is my niece, and I will always protect and love her."

"Thank you, Theo., You have no idea how much I love you."

"I love you too Lia." He kisses my head and then lets me say goodbye to Alessia.

She wraps herself around me, "I love you, Mama."

"I love you too baby." I can feel her tears on my stomach. "Shh, baby girl. It's gonna be okay. I promise we will be home together soon."

"I know, Mama. It's not fair we have to go through this because of how evil Seth is."

I blink my tears away, "I know it's not, baby, but I promise we will get rid of them. But I am so proud of you for how strong you are, baby. Now go ahead with Theo."

She gives me one last tight hug around my waist. "Beyond my last breath," she tells me.

I smile and say to her, "Beyond my last breath." She slowly let's go while wiping her eyes. Theo picks her up, and she lays her head on his shoulder and her little body shakes with sobs. I feel like someone is tearing out my heart. I hold my tears in until Alessia is inside the plane. I can see her wiping her own tears through the window as she waves to me.

As soon as the plane takes off, that is when I let the tears roll down my eyes. I hope this is not the last time I see my daughter, husband, or anyone else in my family.

THIRTY-ONE
EMILIA

    I get into the passenger seat of the car with Marcello as fat tears roll down my cheeks. I can't wipe them fast enough. Marcello hands me a water bottle, and I mumble out thanks. I slowly sip the water and try to control my breathing. It takes me a few minutes I get myself in control. I lay my head on the window and mumble, "This fucking sucks."

    Marcello nods, "It is always hard separating from our loved ones."

    "Yeah, I know, but it killed me to see her so upset, and I couldn't be with her to comfort her. That was so upset was worse than any torture I went through with Seth," I say to him, still seeing in my head Alessia's body shaking in Theo's arms.

    "I know. Hopefully, soon Fabio gets us some surveillance from today's bombing, so we know where to start, and we can finally get rid of these Russians. You and Alessia deserve to live as normal as a Mafia boss's wife and daughter can live."

    I chuckled at him, "Yeah, it will be nice not to be looking over our shoulder waiting for the Russians to attack at any moment."

    "They have been an issue for way too long. Sadistic and evil bastards like them don't deserve to be walking this earth."

    I smile at him, "You will make one awesome brother-in-law."

    His whole face shines with happiness. "One day, I hope that is true. But I have some walls to knock down around Julietta's heart."

    I nod. "Yeah, I have noticed she has the fake smile plastered on her face, but if anyone can get her to open up, I feel like it would be you."

    "Thanks."

    "Of course, Alessia would be more than excited to have you as her uncle."

    "I would love to call her my niece. But that means she has another overprotective uncle." We both chuckle at how protective all the De Luca men are over Alessia.

    "Eh, regardless of if you being her uncle or not you still would be protective of her."

    He shrugs as we both chuckle.

    I pull my burner phone out of my pocket. I text Peter O'Sullivan, the Boss of the Irish Mafia the code word, "Plaid." I know he won't respond until our escort is at the safe house.

    We made small talk until I got a call from Fabio. My heart races when I see his name on my phone, I am worried he is about to tell me Mateo is dead.

    Emilia: Hello.

Fabio: Hello Donna. I got some CCTV. I am still working on getting more.

Emilia: Send it over and thank you so much, Fabio.

Fabio: Of course, Donna. It's in your email.

He hangs up the phone and I open my email from Fabio. I take a deep breath and hit play. I watch as Mateo is sitting there with a business partner, across the street from the camera. Then, all of a sudden, you see Mateo being tossed through the window of the restaurant and then he lays unconscious on the ground. Then you can see masked men try to grab Mateo, but they are killed by shots to their foreheads. All five men are shot down within seconds of each other.

"What the fuck?" I mumble to myself, but then I see a team of people put Mateo in the back of a van. They are giving him medical treatment and that is the end of the CCTV.

Was it the Russians who tried to kill Mateo? Who saved him? And where did they take him? And why were the bombs so close to Mateo? We didn't plan it to be that close to Alexei's hotel. And a lot of other questions buzz around in my head. I decide to call Salvatore so he can have people start searching for who tried to kill Mateo, because if it is someone else besides the Russians I need to know. I call Salvatore to give him an update.

Salvatore: Emilia what happened?

Emilia: Things didn't go as planned so we are on Plan B.

Salvatore: Fuck.

Emilia: Basically. I am going to send you the CCTV footage that Fabio sent me. After Mateo got tossed through a window, a team of five men tried to shoot Mateo. Luckily, someone else came to his aide, but send guys out to see who tried to kill my husband. We need to know if we have any other enemies.

Salvatore: Got it. Are you okay?

Emilia: Fuck no. Mateo is missing and it tore my heart out to watch Alessia cry as I left her with everyone else. Even though I know it is what is safer for her.

Salvatore: She will be happy and safe there. We will find Mateo, and soon we will be all back home. I will get people on this right away. Stay safe.

Emilia: I will. Stay safe as well.

This time I am the first to hang up. Marcello doesn't say anything, but it sounds like he is on the phone. I ignore him, being lost in my own head. I look at the time and see we have five more hours on our eight-hour car ride. I decided to take a nap, which is something I would normally do. I would have offered to drive but when my leg is in a straight leg brace, I can't exactly drive. I close my eyes and I hope this will soon be all over.

Hours later, I am shaken awake; I jolt up and quickly look around. I see Marcello in the driver seat, it takes me a moment to remember everything that happened before. "Fuck! That wasn't a dream."

He shakes his head. "No it wasn't."

I nod at him, "We are at the safe house, and it looks like we got company."

"Hold on," I tell him. I look at the burner phone and see Peter said he sent his two oldest sons to escort us the rest of the way to Ireland. It tells me that the car in the driveway is their car. I turn to Marcello. "That's our escort. Cillian & Oscar O'Sullivan, Peter's two eldest sons, will help escort us to Ireland."

"Okay, good. Are you ready to go inside?"

I nod my head. "Yeah." I open my door and slowly lower my legs to the ground and push myself out of the seat. My injured leg is really stiff. I stand there for a moment before I start to head towards the stone cottage. The house is so adorable and has a homey feeling, and we haven't even walked inside yet. The roof is an old tin roof and the house itself is made up of dark stones.

Marcello is next to me with both of our bags in his hands and is offering me my crutches. I give him a small smile. "Thank you, Marcello, for everything. I can imagine it isn't easy being away from Julietta this long."

He shakes his head. "I miss her like crazy but it's an honor to be protecting you and Alessia."

"Don't worry, after we deal with the Russians, I will make sure you have time off so you can spend time with Julietta uninterrupted, no matter how much the De Luca men protest." He chuckles knowing every last one of them will complain and protest about Marcello spending alone time with Julietta.

"I actually have been planning a trip for us when we have time."

"And where is that?"

"We would be traveling all over Europe and visit her favorite places for vacation, not for work."

"She would absolutely love that."

I hear the door slam open, and two men step out of the house. "Well, I'd be damned. She is prettier than father said." I have to admit the open flirt is cute, but I wouldn't be trading Mateo for this man who has shoulder length dark brown hair with bright blue eyes. My Italian husband is a work of art no man can come close to him.

We stop right in front of them, I stick my hand to introduce myself. "Emilia De Luca and this is Marcello Giordano. He is my personal bodyguard."

The other man, who is very stoic and has eyed me up and down, shakes my hand first.

"Nice to meet you, Mrs. De Luca. My name is Cillian O'Sullivan, and this is my younger brother Oscar. Sorry about him flirting with you, he will flirt with anything that has a set of boobs." Cillian has the same color hair as Oscar except his hair is much shorter and he has a goatee, and instead of blue eyes like his brother's, Cillian's eyes are green.

"I was not flirting; I was just paying the pretty lady a compliment." Cillian pushes him away from me.

"No, you were hoping to get your dick wet. We will not lose our alliance with the Italians because you can't keep it in your pants."

I chuckle at him, "I see you have one of those too friendly ones in your family too."

Cillian sighs, "Yes and I swear he's my biggest headache at times."

I chuckle, "Mateo has the same issue with his cousin."

Cillian holds the door open for us. Inside has a mini kitchen with a refrigerator, microwave, and a small table. In the living room there are two worn couches, a wooden coffee table, and a fireplace.

Oscar apologizes, "Sorry, usually we don't stay here more than a few hours before moving to the next stop."

I shake my head. "No it's actually quite quaint. I love it." He looks at me like I have lost my mind.

Marcello is laughing at him, "You need to understand, Emilia loves the simple things. She hates gaudy and overpriced stuff."

Oscar is still staring at me. "You seriously are not normal."

"Understand, Oscar, my past before I met Mateo was very ugly, and because of that, I rather enjoy the simple things of life."

"I guess that makes sense, but you're still weird."

"Eh, I can live with that," I say as I shrug my shoulders.

I didn't realize that Cillian was pulling out something from the refrigerator. "My mother made stew with fresh bread, she figured everyone would be hungry."

I nod my head. "Yeah it has been a few hours since we ate anything. Your Mama is so thoughtful." For the first time I see a glimpse of a smile on Cillian's face.

"Yeah, she is a sweet woman with a huge heart."

"She sounds like it." After Cillian heats up everyone's food, we all sit around the table and quietly eat.

While eating, Cillian's phone beeps and he looks at it. "Jet will be ready in an hour, so after we finish eating, we will clean up and then head out of here. I want to abandon your car before we get to the airport just in case, so we can lose any possible tail from the Russians."

"Sure, no problem."

It doesn't take more than ten minutes to finish eating and for all the dishes to be washed, dried, and put away. Marcello grabs our bags, and we all get into our vehicles. Marcello and me in the one we drove here and Oscar and Cillian in theirs. We follow them for about twenty minutes, and we are driving on a dirt road, you see a field filled with rows of old rusted cars. It is a glorified junk yard. We pull up next to their car, and I roll down the window.

"Do you want us to park there with the other cars?"

Cillian nods his head, "Yeah."

"Okay." I roll up my window and turn to Marcello, who has yet to start driving.

"Go ahead and get in the car with them, that way you don't have to walk as much."

"Okay, do you want me to take the bags?"

He shakes his head. "No, I will bring them with me." I nod at him and walk over to their car. When Cillian sees me walking over, he gets out and opens my door for me.

"Thank you," I say to him, and he nods at me while he shuts my door. He climbs in the driver's seat; I get a picture of Alessia in Esmeralda's arms with a smile on her face.

"Who is the lucky man who put that smile on your face?" Oscar asks.

"Not a man, my daughter," I respond.

"You have a daughter?"

I nod, "Yeah, Alessia, and she is the center of everyone's attention in the family." I text Theo back thank you and I love them both beyond my last breath.

Marcello slides into the seat next to me with both of our bags. He sees me smiling. "Alessia made it to Esmeralda's, okay?" I nod and show him the picture. "Look at that beautiful smile on her face. Much better than the tears she left us with."

"Yeah, seeing her so upset and knowing I couldn't stay and comfort her just about killed me."

Cillian starts the car and we make small talk. I text back and forth with Theo about how Alessia has given him the grand tour and demanded they have sleepovers. He also tells me he has seen quite a few pieces of eye candy he will be talking to later.

We pull up right beside the jet and we all walk. Okay they walk, I start to crutch my way up the stairs. Oscar picks me up, I shriek from him scaring the hell out of me. "Oscar next time give a girl a warning."

"Oh, so I will get to hold you in my arms again?"

I roll my eyes, "No, you buffoon."

He pouts at me, "Now that is rude."

"You will survive," I say as I stand on my feet. Once inside the jet, I quickly sit down and relax in the comfortable chair next to the window. The men also sit down, and we listen to the pilot make their announcements. Once we are in the air, we only have about an hour and a half until we land. So, I decided I was going to watch the clip Fabio sent me again.

I watched it a couple times, going very slow to see what we could have missed. I think of all the different questions I will have for Fabio and Salvatore when I call them both. I am so engrossed in dissecting the video I don't realize Oscar is sitting next to me.

"What are you watching?"

I basically jumped out of my skin.

"Fucking hell, Oscar. Are you trying to give me a heart attack?"

He chuckles, "Sorry, thought you heard me come over here."

"It's okay, I just was so engrossed in the video."

"I can see that."

"This is the video of the latest bomb we were doing on one of Alexei Ivanov's businesses, but something went wrong. I am trying to figure out what and other details."

He nods but whispers in my ear, "Why does your bodyguard look like he wants to shoot me?"

I look over and Marcello is glaring down at Oscar. "Maybe because you have been flirting with me, touching me, and getting very close to his best friend's wife."

"Oh, come on, you think Mateo will be that mad?"

Marcello laughs. "You better hope you can outrun a bullet."

Oscar shakes his head. "Yeah, right. Mateo wouldn't do that."

I smirk. "Yes, he would, he has already threatened to shoot any boy who looks at our daughter wrong. He is a protective asshole."

Cillian chuckles. "Maybe he can teach you to keep it in your pants."

"Brother, you are supposed to defend me."

"Not when you're an idiot."

They sound like Vincenzo, Salvatore and Mateo bickering with each other. The rest of the flight is spent with Cillian trying to ignore Oscar who is purposely trying to get on Cillian's nerves.

After that, I sit in silence, staring out the window. I hope and pray that Mateo is okay. I know he is hurt but I pray whoever took him isn't hurting him and isn't another enemy. Different scenarios of what has happened keep running through my head, and I blink away my tears. I keep my eyes locked on the clouds outside; right now I need my own space to think and not have anyone talk to me. I will have my moment of weakness, then I will turn into the cold-hearted Queen. I will find Mateo and bring him home and we will defeat the Russians and live our normal mafia life.

The jet jolts a bit when we land in the O'Sullivan's private airport, and we see two blacked out SUVs waiting by the end of the steps of the jet. Four men step out, the two with dark brown hair and blue eyes must be related to Cillian because they look like carbon copies of him except younger. As soon as we all have reached the bottom, the boys introduce themselves as Aiden, who is the third oldest boy, and Killian, who is the youngest boy. I think their mother must be a saint to raise four boys then I am told they have three sisters. I changed my mind. She isn't a saint; she is an angel.

The other man, Collin, has blond hair and blue eyes. He is friendly but doesn't cross the lines of flirting. But now, Brandon might be worse than Oscar. As soon as he could, he picked up my hand and left a lingering kiss while trying to give me seductive eyes. I forcefully took my hand out of his and told him to keep his mouth off me. Before he could reply Marcello was in his face and told him to remember he is a soldier, and I am the wife and Queen to Mateo De Luca.

I knew Marcello was protective, but I never saw him be like this against another man. It makes me happy that Julietta will have someone like this to love her. Before Brandon can respond, I get into one of the SUVs. I honestly don't have time for flirts or playboys. They might think I am fresh meat, but I will have them whimpering at my feet if they cross the line. No one gets to disrespect me or my marriage to Mateo and think I will tolerate it. We drive through the black gates towards their home, a huge colonial style white mansion. It's beautiful, granted I hate houses this huge, but that is my personal taste.

I take in the beautiful roses as we walk up the stairs, and the butler welcomes us and escorts us inside to the sitting room. Once inside, I see Peter and Grace. I remember meeting them at the ball Mateo threw to introduce me and Alessia. Peter's hair is slicked back, and he has a beard and green eyes. Grace is absolutely beautiful. She has bright red, wavy hair that stops at her shoulder and sparkling blue eyes. She is an angel who has raised seven kids, seven mafia kids. And somehow, she still has this gentle, sweet aura around her.

Peter man walks over to me. "Hello Mrs. De Luca, I am sorry we are meeting under these circumstances. My name is Peter O'Sullivan, this is my wife, Grace O'Sullivan. You met my boys and hopefully they behaved like gentlemen."

I chuckle, "They were fine, I have met worse men than your sons. This is my personal bodyguard while I am here, Marcello." Marcello nods at Peter, and Peter shakes his hand as they exchange quiet pleasantries.

"I am sure you have, but they better have been perfect gentleman. These three ladies behind me are my daughters. Ellie and Riley, they are twins." The twins have brown hair like their father and blue eyes like their mother. They have adorable freckles all over their faces, and they look like they are around fifteen years old. "My oldest daughter and my second oldest child, Kayleigh." She extends her hand to shake mine, while everyone else just waved and smiled. I shake her hand back and tell everyone it is a pleasure to meet them. Kayleigh is eyeing me up and down with her bright blue eyes, her red hair is pulled up in a high ponytail. Her eyes land on my leg brace.

"Oh my god. Is this part of your injuries from your mansion being bombed?"

I nod my head, "Yeah, it takes a while to heal a shattered knee cap."

Her hands go to her mouth. "You poor thing. Come, come and sit down, you shouldn't be on your feet. Let's have one of the maids get you some ice." She starts to fuss all over me.

I do follow her to the couch, I chuckle as I put my hand on top of hers. "Thank you, Kayleigh, but I promise I am okay. Thank you, sweetheart, for caring so much."

She gives me a small smile and her cheeks are covered in pink from her blushing. "Sorry, I hate when people are hurt around me, and I want to help them feel better or be comfortable."

I shake my head. "Sweetie don't apologize. You have a big heart and there is nothing wrong with that. Just protect that heart so no one takes away that sunshine inside of you." She hugs me, I am taken aback for a second but then I hug her back. I think I am going to enjoy her company while I am here.

Kayleigh reminds me of a ray of sunshine. Grace asks me, "Do you need anything for your knee Emilia?" I look at Grace as I pull away from the hug with Kayleigh.

"Besides a hot bath to soak my knee, no, I will be okay, but thank you."

"Emilia, this is Molly, she will be your personal maid while you are here. She will show you and your bodyguard to your rooms. I put him across from you so if anything would happen, he would be close, but you still some privacy."

"No, I am good. I trust my sister-in-law's boyfriend to respect my privacy."

He chuckles at me, "Yes, Emilia, I prefer not to have any bullet holes in my body because we know Mateo would do that in a heartbeat for his girls."

I shrug my shoulders, "He is just a wee bit overprotective."

Marcello chuckles while shaking his head. "Sure, we will go with that, but you need to go soak your knee. I don't need him or Theo to be all pissy with me if you're not taking care of your knee."

I groan but nod my head. "Okay, sounds good. Molly, can you show us the way please?"

She nods her head. "If you would follow me, Sir and Ma'am."

I shake my head. "Nope, none of that Ma'am nonsense. Just call me Emilia."

She smiles. "Okay, Emilia."

We walk up one set of stairs and Marcello takes me into my room to check it out for safety reasons. He checks the windows are firmly locked and that no one is hiding in the closet or bathroom. Once he feels the room is safe, he tells me he is gonna get himself settled in his room. I nod and tell him I'm going to take a nap after I take a bath since we have a few hours until dinner.

"Do you want me to unpack your stuff for you?"

I shake my head, "No thanks, Molly. I actually am gonna enjoy some quiet before dinner since I have barely had any time alone in over a day. If you could just come get us when it is time for dinner."

"Of course, Emilia. I will leave you to it. If you need anything, just hit the button by the bed and I will be alerted you need me."

"Thank you, Molly." She smiles at me once more before he closes the door behind her. I take a deep breath and grab my stuff out of my suitcase. I take off to the bathroom to try and unwind from the past twenty-four hours.

THIRTY-TW0
EMILIA

      I grab my stuff to take a hot bath to soak my aching knee. I wasn't about to tell anyone how much pain I was in. I can't seem weak in another mafia's house. Sure, they might be allies with Mateo and he trusts them, but until I trust them, I will go back to my cold-hearted bitch façade. I won't be mean or disrespectful to them since they are helping us, but I am not letting my guard down.

      I add bath oil and salt to the very hot water. I strip out of my clothes and stare at myself naked in the mirror. I run my finger over the bite marks around my panty line that Mateo gave me the other day when he ate me out and I returned the favor. I start to quietly cry, now that I am alone, I can let myself cry and temporarily drown in my sadness and fear. Through my tears, I step into the tub.

      I bring my good knee up to my chest and lay my face on my knee and just sob. The pain of thinking Mateo could be dead somewhere feels like someone is ripping my heart out. We didn't have enough time together, we wanted to expand our family. I wanted to be driven crazy by him being overprotective and overbearing with me while I was pregnant. To watch him dote on our other children just like he does Alessia. I wanted to grow old with him as we watched our children grow up, to try and scare every possible date that Alessia has because he believes no boy will be good enough for his princess. He won't be able to hold her and comfort her when a boy breaks her heart and watch him as he fights himself not to go hunt the bastard down to teach him a lesson. He won't walk her down the aisle to a man who we all approve of and who will protect and cherish our princess. He also won't be able to watch how his best friend and his sister have the most adorable relationship, get married, or have kids. He won't experience being an uncle to our adorable nieces and nephews. He won't witness his cousins fall in love, get married, and have kids. It's not fair. So many things we will miss out on doing together because of the fucking Russian Mafia.

      I see black dots in the corners of my eyes, and I know I am starting to hyperventilate. I take a deep breath and start to count backwards from twenty, and at each number, I take a big breath in and slowly let it out. At twelve, I feel myself breathing easier, but I continue to finish counting. I force myself to think positively, that I will no longer believe he is dead, hopefully a good Samaritan got him medical help. Soon he will be back at my side, and together we will show why we are the King and Queen of the underworld.

      Alexei, your days are numbered. I was angry before, but now I am a woman who has been scorned. I am coming for you, and you will regret coming after my family. First, killing Aunt Anna and Lilyana, then trying to kidnap me and Alessia, now injuring Mateo. I will be coming for you. I will be draining every ounce of your blood. You are going to beg me to let you die and go to hell. You will know what the hell is when I get through with you.

I am so pissed that I am digging my nails into my palms. I decide to finish up and get out so I can call my baby girl. Alessia always puts a big smile on my face. I put on leggings and one of Mateo's hoodies that smells like him. I lift the collar of his hoodie and take a deep breath so I can breathe in the scent of his cologne. It relaxes me for a moment. I grab my phone and sit in the chair by the window that looks over the rose garden.

I call Theo's phone; he picks up on the second ring.

Theo: *Hey, Lia.*

Emilia: *Hey, Theo. How is she?*

Theo: *Esmeralda is spoiling her rotten.*

Emilia: *I suspected nothing less, but she seems happy?*

Theo: *Yeah, she does. I got the grand tour and met all of Esmeralda's family and staff. Let me ask, why did you come back to Italy? There are some delicious pieces of eye candy to look at here.*

We both chuckle at that but he is not wrong, I swear there must be something in the water at the Garcia's mansion because everyone is very, and I mean very, good looking.

Theo: *Then she went to hip hop lessons and now she is on a trail ride with Jose. They have kept her so busy since she stepped foot in Spain, that she has barely had any time to think about anything that has happened back home.*

Emilia: *Good, and thank you, Theo.*

Theo: *You don't have to thank me. You are my sister from another mister and Alessia is my unofficial niece. I will always do whatever I can for both of you.*

Emilia: *I know, Theo. I love you. Have Alessia call me before she goes to bed.*

Theo: *I love you too and of course I will.* **Take care of yourself.**

Emilia: *You too.*

I ended the call because I needed to take a nap before I went downstairs. I set my alarm on my phone for two hours, so I had enough time to get ready before joining the O'Sullivan's for dinner. I am so exhausted from everything, it doesn't take me long to fall asleep. When I hear my alarm go off, I groan and roll over and turn it off. I slowly sat up and grabbed the clothes I sat on my end table before I fell asleep. I changed my shirt from Mateo's hoodie to a blue, lacy tunic dress top. I put on my ankle boots, then I put on my leg brace and pull the Velcro, to guarantee it is on firmly and it won't slide off. I am walking towards the door when I hear a knock on it.

"Hold on, I am coming." I get to the door and Molly is there with her sweet smile and I noticed her black hair is now in a bun. And her hazel eyes seem just as happy as she was earlier. "Hello, Emilia. I am here to escort you and Sir Marcello to dinner." I see Marcello smirking behind Molly's back at the fact she is calling him Sir Marcello.

"Of course, lead the way." We follow her and he is still snickering. I roll my eyes at him; I swear these mafia men and their huge egos. How more than two men can fit inside a room together with their huge egos, I will never understand.

The O'Sullivan family greets us when we enter the room. Marcello pulls my chair back and makes sure I am comfortable as I can be with my leg straight as a board while sitting down at the table. The maids serve us lasagna, it smells absolutely delicious. I smile, thinking of memories of Alessia in the kitchen with Nonno and Nonno making dinner together.

Grace calls my name, "Oh, sorry. I was lost in thought."

"That's okay. Is there something wrong with the lasagna? I can have one of the cooks make you something else instead."

I shake my head. "No, it just reminds me of home a bit. My daughter loved to cook with my husband's grandparents and one of their favorite things to make was lasagna."

She smiles. "How old is your daughter?'

"She just turned eight a few months ago."

"Aw, such a sweet age, but the attitude starts."

I chuckle. "Oh yeah, she has the sass down between her aunt and me. She isn't lacking women around her to learn how to be sassy, but even though she is full of sass, I love her new confidence."

"Aren't you worried that she might be too much when she becomes a teenager?" Grace asks me.

I shrug my shoulders, "Probably God knows I gave my Mama and Papa a hard time growing up, but I also know she is a strong and independent woman who can stand up for herself or anyone else."

Peter and Grace share a look together, I don't question it. Not my marriage, not my problem. We continue to make small talk, even Marcello talks to Cillian about guns and different fighting techniques. I am glad he isn't being the moody brute, but I know he is like that because so much of our world is uncertain right now.

"Emilia," Peter calls out to me.

"Yes?" I answer back.

"Would you like to join me in my office so we can start discussing how to track down Mateo or would you prefer to have a good night's rest instead?"

I shake my head, "The sooner the better."

"Good. Boys I want you in there as well. Well, that is if you don't mind them being there."

"Not at all. I have nothing to hide. But I am gonna have our consigliere and underboss on the speaker phone while we talk. Hopefully they will have information to add."

"Already have them working," he chuckles at me.

"Yep, our tech guy was able to pull part of a clip before everything happened and based on what we saw, we had sent people out looking for more information."

He nods. "Good."

It didn't take us long to finish eating dinner and I followed Peter to his office. He held the door open for me. I walked in and took a seat across from his desk. Marcello and Peter's sons follow inside the office. Marcello, Cillian, and Aiden all stand. I had texted Salvatore and Vincenzo earlier saying that I was gonna call them so we can discuss with the O'Sullivan's how to find Mateo. Once we are all settled in Peter's office, I call Salvatore's phone.

Salvatore: Hey, Emilia.

Emilia: Hey, Salvatore. How is everyone?

Salvatore: We are good, but we are worried about Mateo.

Emilia: Me too, but is doofus there with you?

Vincenzo: Hey!

Emilia: Well, that answers my question.

Vincenzo: I take offense at that.

Emilia: You will be fine, but we can discuss that later. I am going to put the phone on speaker with the O'Sullivan's so we all can discuss how to find Mateo.

I put my cell phone on speaker.

Salvatore: Okay, so we were able to look at the men before they were taken away since everyone was worried about the injured. It was easy to see they worked for Alexei Ivanov. They have the Russian Mafia Crest on their shoulder or upper chest.

Emilia: Those dirty mother fuckers are going to pay.

Salvatore: They will, but I have information about the woman who saved Mateo.

He says the word *saved* with heavy sarcasm.

Emilia: Why do I not like the tone of your voice?

Salvatore: That is because you are not going to like this. Her name is Rebecca Cavello, she has been fired from various jobs or been sued for being aggressive towards extremely rich men. She has gone under the radar; Fabio loses them when they head towards the country and not any surveillance cameras in the area because it is a very poor area. The vehicle used is her brother's, Tommaso. He is an ER doctor at our hospital. I have people watching him closely.

Emilia: One day, Salvatore. He is under tight surveillance then he is brought in for questioning by me. If you all don't want to do it, then fly him out here, and I will.

Salvatore: Are you sure? Watching him longer could give us answers.

Emilia: I am not letting him stay with that woman who is looking for a sugar daddy any longer than necessary. Her days are already numbered anyway, you all know no one fucks with my family and gets away with it. She fucked up when she kidnapped Mateo, and she will pay the price.

Peter: I agree with Emilia. If this woman is as driven by her illusions as you describe, we want information as soon as possible. A woman like that will get desperate if she doesn't get her way soon. And Emilia is more than welcome to use our basement and we will lend her a hand if she needs it.

Vincenzo: We will grab Dr. Cavello by tomorrow and we will Zoom call you, so you get to ask questions, but I get to do the physical hurting. Mr. O'Sullivan, you won't need to do any torturing for her, most likely you will have to be holding your stomach from her creative ways of torturing people. Her latest victim, a woman who assaulted her daughter and betrayed the family, has been in our basement for the past four months.

Emilia: Oh, Zaria. I forgot she was still at the warehouse. I can't wait to have another round with her. I thought of a new idea for her. Vincenzo if you touch any of my toys, you will be my next guinea pig.

Vincenzo: Oh, come on. I want to try your new knife.

Emilia: It's not finished yet and no; I get to try them first and maybe, if I feel like being nice, I will share with you.

Salvatore: Okay, psychos, you can fight over playing with Emilia's diabolical tools later.

Peter: I definitely want to see Emilia in action next time she decides to deal with someone, since it sounds like the rumors are true.

Emilia: They come short of what I can do to my victim's and certain Russians, I have a very detailed torture I have been planning for them.

Oscar: Sounds like we will be taking a family trip to Italy. He says with a smile as he rubs his hands together.

Cillian: Yeah, this sounds like a very educational trip.

Killian: I am definitely coming.

Aiden: I am not missing this.

Peter: Well, I hope you don't mind Emilia.

He says while chuckling at his son's enthusiasm.

Emilia: Not at all, but I will warn you I have made spectators empty their stomachs. Anything else anyone wants to discuss? I wait a moment for anyone to say anything, when I hear nothing, I continue. Good, I am going to go find your weapon room, Peter, and throw some knives or shoot a gun.

Peter: I will have someone escort you down to our weaponry room and you are free to use anything in there.

Salvatore: Marcello don't let her overdo it.

Marcello: Of course, Mr. De Luca.

Emilia: I would never do that, Salvatore. Do you really have such little faith in me?

Salvatore: Yes, I don't. You are a bit hardheaded.

Emilia: That's hurtful. But I will talk to you later. Tell everyone I love them.

I need to let this frustration and anger out soon before my demons consume me. I know Marcello won't let me do any kind of working out because Theo still has me restricted besides the workouts he left, but that won't work out my emotions. So I am left with no choice but to throw knives or shoot a gun, if not multiple guns.

I walk out of Peter's office, and I see Brandon is standing with his back against the wall. He looks up at me and pushes himself off the wall, "So the pretty lady wants to check out the weapon room. If you want, I can show you how to use them."

I smirk and take a step closer, but we still have some space between us. "That depends. Can I use you as target practice? And then when my husband gets here do you want to be at the end of his wrath for shamelessly flirting with his wife twice?"

Brandon smiles. "But I don't see your husband and who is gonna tell him? You? I know you won't, because you want the attention."

I laugh at him, "Oh, I certainly will because I find it rather hot when he gets possessive over my ass and gets physical with any man who tries to take me from him. So, I will definitely tell him, especially if I get to watch him torture someone shirtless and then watch as he washes the blood off his beautiful, sculpted body."

"You can always watch me do that if you want?"

I shake my head, "Yeah, I don't find you attractive at all. My body only wants my Italian Sex God with an anaconda between his legs. He is my King and the King of the Italian Mafia. No playboy soldier who doesn't respect women's wishes is someone I would ever be with. Now, show me to the weapon room." He glares at me.

Marcello firmly tells him, "Now would be great."

Brandon spins towards the stairs and basically stomps the whole way down to the basement. He opens a door, and the walls are literally lined with different weapons. They have knives of all different sizes with different blade sizes, so many different guns, bombs, and so much more. I am in heaven, slowly moving my eyes against the walls. Brandon says nothing else but slams the door behind me and Marcello after we walk in the room.

I roll my eyes and say to Marcello, "Sounds like someone doesn't like to hear the word no from the ladies."

"Yeah, but regardless, Mateo is gonna want his head." I chuckle.

"Oh yeah, he will, but let's get you out of their range so you can push your darkness away." I smile and give Marcello a friendly hug since he is my husband's friend and hopefully one day, he will be my brother-in-law.

I smirk at him. "Let's have some fun."

I hear him mumble "Why am I always stuck with her when she goes in psycho Queen mode?" I throw my head back laughing, as I grab a couple different knives and head toward the board so I can practice throwing knives. I let the motions and emotions swarm free, I pretend the board is Alexei, Seth, and Boris. As I said earlier, I have plans for when I get my hands on them and they will be begging for death.

THIRTY-THREE
EMILIA

After completely destroying one of Peter's dummies, I had worn myself out. I was hoping I would be able to get some sleep without waking up from a nightmare. I was right, I got maybe three hours of sleep after I talked to Alessia last night. As much as I missed her and wanted to be with her. I am going to be constantly working to track down every lead possible to Seth and the Russian Mafia. I am beyond pissed and fed up dealing with them, I want this war over once and for all. Plus, I trust Jose, Garcia and their family completely, unlike the O'Sullivan's who are strangers to me.

Since I didn't sleep much, I quietly went down to the kitchen to make myself some coffee so I can drink that while I work in the spare office Peter has generously let me use while I am here. I am in the office slowly sipping on my coffee. I start typing on the computer to find anything about where Alexei & Irina Ivanov or Elena Dubois could be hiding.

Honestly, how many people could be hiding these snakes? And how can Irina be okay with his mistress always around or is she being treated like shit? What about her son?

I keep looking. I start with Alexei, since he is the one with most money. I look at his businesses and look at who his partners are. See if any of them come off as doing anything illegal. At this moment, I am more than glad that Frankie would teach me some of his hacking skills while he was in college because, as amazing as Fabio is, Frankie was better, and right now I am still suspicious of everyone who isn't a De Luca. We still have a rat who assisted in blowing up the mansion and have yet to find out who it is.

I am hours into looking into Alexei and all of his partners, I have a list of people. I have not even started to look at Irina or Elena yet. I see that I have a Zoom video call coming through from Salvatore on my laptop.

Salvatore: Good morning, Emilia.
Emilia: Shit. It's already morning?
Salvatore: Did you even go to sleep last night?
Emilia: For a few hours.
Vincenzo: I am so telling Mateo. He is gonna deal with your ass.
Emilia: No, you're not, or I will come cock block you when you go to the clubs when I get home.
Vincenzo: Like you could sneak past the security in place.

Emilia: I smirk at him. *I did it before with Alessia. Do you think I couldn't sneak in and out of the mansion alone, undetected?*

Salvatore: *Ok, you two can fight later, we have a guest who needs to answer questions.*

Salvatore turns the screen to face a man with very broad shoulders and big chest muscles. Obviously, he works out. His hazel eyes are staring at me through the computer. You can see his lingering on my chest, granted I am in a push up sports bra under a tank top so you can see my cleavage.

Vincenzo smacks him on the back of the head.

Vincenzo: *Quit eyeing her chest. Your psychotic sister has her husband, our cousin, kidnapped somewhere and we want to know.*

Tommaso: *I don't know where she is. All I know is she took my van and said she needs it.*

Emilia: *Tommaso Cavello, is it?* Tommaso nods his head. *I am a woman who has very, and I mean very, little patience, especially when it comes to her family. And right now, you are not being honest with us, and do you know what that dishonesty is doing?* He shakes his head. *It is making a little girl who had a rough childhood and is very attached to her Papa, wonder if he will ever come home to her. As a doctor, how can you put a person, let alone a child, through pain? Aren't you supposed to help heal people, not give them pain?*

Tommaso: He hangs his head. *The only place I can think of that she would be is at our grandfather's house in Sicily, but I honestly don't know. We are not close, especially since I don't agree with how she tries to milk every rich guy she can before she moves onto the next one.*

Salvatore: *Why don't you or your family step in?*

Tommaso: *I have tried, but every time I try to get her help, my mother will have her bailed out. She honestly learned everything she knows from mother anyway. I don't think my mother has stayed married to the same man for more than five years. Rebecca is a loose cannon. She needs help or jail, but with mother having a lot of money at her disposable, her precious daughter will never be held responsible.*

Emilia: *If I find out you are lying to us, you will be brought back in, and this sweet visit will be nothing compared to what will happen to you. Next time, you will see me in person, and I will be able to torture you. I am not a woman to piss off, I am feared for a reason. With that being said, the men will give you ten minutes to think of anything to tell them.*

I don't mention that once I get my hands on his sister, I will be killing her. You kidnap my husband, you lose your life. It is as simple as that.

I say goodbye to Salvatore and Vincenzo, I turn my focus back on the blueprints I have of Alexei's casino in Paris. Since we have set off enough bombs to his businesses, I decide we will just go in gun blazing and take out more of his empire. Should I feel guilty that I'm organizing a lot of people to be killed? Maybe but did they care what they have done to my family. No. I am more than determined to bring Alexei's empire to dust that will be under my boots.

I hear a knock on the door, and I tell whoever to enter but I don't look up until I see a cup shoved in my face. I look up and see Kayleigh with a cup of coffee. "Thanks darling," I say to her.

"You're welcome. What are you working on?"

I look up away from the blueprints. "I am planning my next attack on my enemy." She nods, I refuse to go into detail about my plans because I don't want others over hearing. Call me paranoid, but right now I want to do whatever I can to have my family reunited as soon as possible. We have discussed this, so she understands my silence.

"Daddy says to let him know if you need anything, and Mommy said breakfast will be ready in an hour."

"Thank you, I will be down for breakfast," I tell her. She smiles at me and leaves the office, shutting the door quietly behind her. I go back to reviewing the blueprints; there are six exits, and we will need to disable the cameras and the elevator. I want a team at each exit. We are going to completely ambush them. Our spy on the inside told me that tomorrow night they are going to be holding a meeting. So, we can eliminate more of his empire.

The next day, we loaded up into Peter's jet to head to Paris. We landed at the airport in just under two hours. When we got there, we checked into the hotel, we are basically using the hotel to shower and take a nap. But once we take down the casino, we will get on the jet and head back to Ireland. Men from our mafia will be here soon. We will all meet up beforehand so I can tell everyone the plan. Vincenzo and Salvatore have flown in with the men from Italy. They said it was to protect me because they don't want to face Mateo's wrath if I get hurt. That maybe part of the reason, but we all know they both have personal reasons to kill the Russians, but I won't comment on that.

Six hours later, after everyone has cleaned up and rested, we check out of the hotel, and we meet up on a deserted road on the edge of town. Once all six Range Rovers have pulled over, I stand on the hood of one of them. I put my fingers in my mouth, whistling to get everyone's attention.

"Listen up I will only say this once, so shut up and pay attention. I have divided you all up into six teams. We are doing an ambush on the Russian's new casino. We are killing everyone on sight unless it is Alexei, his wife Irina, or his mistress Elena. Bonus if you catch one of his higherups. The goal is to kill as many Russians as possible. The high rank members have some questions to answer. When all the electricity is cut, each team will enter at different parts of the house. We are going to catch them off guard by hunting them at night. Use the night vision googles, as ridiculous as you might feel, they will help you take out the Russians. I want the least number of injuries and casualties on our side as possible. When we get there, we will park at the back of the parking lot until I get the signal that the electricity has been cut, and once I get the signal, we will quickly move in. Any questions?"

Everyone stays quiet. "Good. Make sure you wear your bulletproof jackets, night vision goggles, and arm yourself with weapons before we leave. Thank you all for what you are doing, this is going to make us one step closer to ending this drawn-out war between us and the Russians. Load up, we will see you on the other side." I hop off the hood of the Range Rover. We all load up and it takes us about thirty minutes to get to the casino, "Coins and Cards."

I read their sign out load. "Very original" I snicker.

Salvatore looks at me in the rearview mirror. "Don't be so harsh on the simple-minded." We both chuckled, it isn't a mystery to anyone in the mafia world that since Alexei took over after his father Maxim died, the Russian Mafia is not as powerful as it once was.

We see the lights in the parking lot and their sign goes off. "Let's go," I say to everyone in the car. I wait for everyone to exit their vehicles. We all split up into our teams and headed to each door. Once we are in position, I ask quietly to each of the leaders, "Everyone in position?" I get confirmed by all five teams.

"Marcello, you know what to do." His team enters in the back,

"Alright, boss, we are in."

"Good, everyone else move in." We all move in and at first no one is around, but when we make it into the lobby there is a woman, and she screams. I have no time for this shit, I shoot her in the head. Her scream must have alerted the security, because it sounds like a heard of elephants running towards us.

"Get ready," I tell my team. I have a gun in each hand, ready to go. About twenty men come running down the hallway. They all have flashlights, they outnumber us four to one, but we have the element of surprise on our side. I start shooting; unfortunately, with them having flashlights they were not as defenseless as we had hoped they would be.

When a flashlight shines on me, I try and duck behind the chair I am by, but it was too late, a bullet grazed my arm. "Motherfucker," I grunt out and drop down to my knees behind the chair. I peek my head around the corner, and he almost shoots me again. "Son of a fucking bitch," I yell as I get behind the chair again, but in the next moment, I feel the chair vibrate with bullets. I look around and decide to crawl over to the couch that is a few feet away. Hopefully, I can get to the other side of the couch and shoot this bastard.

As I am on my hands and knees crawling away, I hear Vincenzo yell, "Emilia, what the fuck are you doing? Take fucking cover."

I don't look up but yell out, "What the fuck do you think I am doing you *cazzo di idiota*." Once I get to the far end of the couch, I look around the corner and the bastard must have waited for me to poke my head out and shoots at me again. *"Ho intenzione di uccidere quel pollone di cazzo russo." (I am gonna kill that Russian cock sucker.)* I quickly peek around the side and shoot, I hit him in the knee. He goes down and I shoot him in his head.

"Finally," I say. I slowly get up and look around to see how we are doing. I see one down with a bullet to her shoulder, but otherwise, we look okay for now, but there are Russians still alive we need to finish eliminating. I quickly scan the room and one is about to shoot Salvatore behind his back; I quickly fire five shots. I am determined not to lose another member of my family. I may have gone a bit over kill because all five bullets went into his head; he is definitely dead.

I see Salvatore take out the last man by slitting his throat, blood pours all over his face. I chuckle, "I guess that is one way to kill someone." I look back at the woman who was shot in the shoulder. "Go back to the van and start getting that treated. Don't worry about us, I don't want anything else to happen to you."

She nods at me, "Thank you, Donna."

I nod at her and look at everyone else, saying. "Let's keep moving." I reload the clips in both of my guns as we keep walking down the hallway and you can hear a lot of yelling, mostly in Russian, along with gun shots. Vincenzo shoves me behind him as he opens the door.

He starts shooting as he enters the room, I see Marcello's team was in here and I look around and I see no higher ranked members. I do see a laptop though, so Alexei can actually have a smart idea. So, he had a meeting through his laptop so he would be safe from us. That is a major bummer, but he is just dragging out his death. It doesn't take us long to finish off everyone in the room.

Vincenzo sees the laptop and shuts it. "Bring it back to Fabio to work his magic. Maybe we will get lucky, and it will give us some information we can use." He picks it up and tucks it under his arms.

I speak into the Bluetooth. "Are we all clear?" I ask. I know only one team is not with us, I don't hear any gunshots, so I would assume we are all good.

"Yes, Donna," I hear.

"Good, let's quickly all get out of here. I am sure the cops are on the way. Remember everyone split up and we will meet at the airport in an hour." Each driver was assigned a route to take to the airport.

When we get to our Range Rover, I jump in the back seat and slump against the seat. My arm is now starting to hurt now we can relax and the adrenaline is wearing off. I take my knife and cut the bottom of my shirt so I can tie it around my bicep until we can get on the jet, and I can properly treat it.

"Emilia, what are you doing?" Salvatore asks.

I don't bother looking up, "I am temporarily wrapping my arm where I was grazed with a bullet."

"You were fucking what?" he yells.

I roll my eyes. "Salvatore, you know damn well a bullet graze is nothing for me."

"Yeah, I don't care. I am not listening to your husband when he finds out you were injured on this mission."

"He will get over it, it was a graze not a bullet hole. Anyway, what was the damage done on our side?"

He takes a deep breath, "We lost ten and four injured."

"Fuck." I say.

"Yeah, I know but unfortunately it happens when we are in a war. All we can do is make sure we win the war and make sure all of their deaths are not in vain."

I nod my head, "That will happen regardless. We will win this war and we all can live peacefully. Well as peacefully as you can live being in the mafia," I say, and we all chuckle because there is no such thing as peace and quiet when you are in the mafia.

THIRTY-FOUR
EMILIA

It has been a month since Rebecca has been taunting me with pictures of Mateo being unconscious and his face covered in bruises. He is tied to a chair; she must be keeping him drugged because there is no way she could overpower Mateo. Regardless that she is a woman he would have subdued her and got her back to the warehouse so I can deal with her.

This woman keeps toying with us, and every time I think we are getting close, we lose the trail. We did find out that she has no ties to Alexei, Irina, or Elena. Rebecca is just an obsessive woman looking for a sugar daddy; the little brat will be dealt with. I am extremely worried because it has been a week since I have received any pictures or any news about Mateo. Rebecca had found great joy in mentally tormenting me daily with pictures or a phone call about Mateo's condition.

If I let him go, he would no longer be suffering. "Let him go, he doesn't deserve to be tied down to someone like you when he could be married to me," is what she said to me. She will learn what happens when you mess with the Queen's King.

I decide after spending six hours behind my desk and staring at my laptop, it is time to step away and take a break. I walk, not hobble walk. Me sitting at my desk for hours a day has helped my knee heal, plus I do my stretches that Theo makes me do and I can walk on it with some pain, but it is bearable.

Kayleigh and I have been working out together because she doesn't want to be a meek woman and I told her I would teach her how to defend herself since all the Irish Mafia Men refuse to train her since she is Peter's oldest daughter. It is also nice to have company around here who isn't a man. Don't get me wrong, they have been extremely helpful but sometimes a girl just needs to talk to a girl.

I changed out of my jeans, shirt, and boots. I laughed thinking about how the O'Sullivan women, especially Grace, freaked out that I don't wear dresses or skirts everyday with heels. She even offered me some of her clothes. Supposedly, some of Peter's business partners believe women should be perfectly dressed every day and be the perfect wife. I am far from the perfect wife. Yes, I can keep my house clean, but I prefer to be in my house in jeans and my boots, and one of my favorite activities is torturing someone or building new torture tools. I don't think a typical housewife would enjoy that. I even told them if it bothers his business partners who see me at the house, tell them I am Mateo's wife.

I am twenty-seven years old, and I didn't let my parents tell me what to wear as a teenager. I am not about to let some entitled man think he can tell me what to wear because he is a businessman. If my husband had a problem with what I wore, he would have said something but if anything, Mateo loves it. Yes, when we go somewhere extremely fancy, I can dress the part, but Mateo says when I dress in my boots and jeans, I can kick ass better than I can in heels.

I think today I am going to take out some of my built-up anger on the punching bag after I work with Kayleigh. I have so much anger inside of be from Mateo being held hostage by some demented woman who fantasies about being married to a rich man, and that neither me nor Fabio can find those three snakes.

I quickly dress into my workout shorts and a tank top, and I head toward Kayleigh's room. My phone rings before I can leave my room and I see it's Nonna trying to FaceTime me. I sit on my bed and answer it.

Nonna: You aren't sleeping?
Emilia: Well, hello to you too, Nonna.
Nonna: Don't start with the sass, Emilia Rose De Luca.
Esmeralda: Oh, the full name. But why aren't you sleeping? Do I need to come knock you out?
Emilia: I am sleeping just fine.
Esmeralda: I smell bullshit coming from Ireland.
Emilia: I am fine, you both need to stop worrying about me.
Nonna: Yeah, you know that will never happen.
Esmeralda: Lia bug, you need to take care of yourself.
Emilia: I am okay. I am just under a lot of stress. Once I get Mateo home, I won't look like hell walking around okay.
Nonna: What can we do to help?
Emilia: Do what you are doing to keep Alessia and the family safe.
Esmeralda: What else can we do to help you?
Emilia: Nothing as of right now, but I am going to head to the gym to take some of my anger out on a punching bag. Have Alessia call me later.
Nonna: Of course, she is out at the barn again. I swear she would live in that barn if we let her.
Esmeralda: She is just like Emilia as a child, and don't worry Lia. I have shown your new family all of your old pictures.
Emilia: Please tell me you didn't.
Nonna: Oh, she did, and now we see why you are a perfect fit for Mateo. Both of you gave your elders migraines dealing with you as children.
Emilia: Thanks, Esmeralda.... On that note I am gonna go to the gym.

I end the call before they can lecture me again about not working out too hard or something else. I appreciate their concern, but right now it is the only way I can stay together. Between not sleeping, drinking way too much coffee, and then my stress level at trying to keep everything together for my family, it is too much at times. I will not tell anyone my nightmares are back and it's bad. They are not about my past; it is about Mateo choosing to abandon me and Alessia so he can stay with Rebecca. Or that we lose to Alexei and Alessia becomes Boris's wife. Me going into a brothel doesn't scare me as badly as Alessia having to be at Boris's hands every day.

I take a few minutes to get myself back in control of my emotions and I put on my fake smile, that no one can see through. Then I wash my face. I actually leave my room this time and I walk up the two flights of stairs towards the O'Sullivan's bedrooms. Kayleigh's room is the fourth door on the right. When I get closer, I can hear some muffled sounds that seems like crying.

I should knock, but if she is being hurt, I am not giving the attacker time to flee. When I open the door, the sight before me pisses me off beyond words. A man is on top of Kayleigh, and she is trying to get him to stop. I don't bother trying to find out who is on her, I shoot them in the back of both kneecaps. I grab the bastard and drag him off her.

Marcello and some of the Irish soldiers barged in the room when they heard my gunshots. "What happened?" Marcello asks me.

"This bastard was forcing himself on Kayleigh," I seethe out in pure anger. The bastard landed face down when I dragged him off her, I flipped him over and saw Conor Doyle, Robert's son. Robert is Peter's underboss. He tries to get up, but Marcello is quick to restrain him, and I turn to face the Irish Mafia members. "Go, get Peter and something to keep him tied up with." They are still staring at me. "NOW!" That finally snaps them into place, and they get their asses moving.

Marcello is holding Conor on his knees with his hands behind his back and he has his gun pointed at Conor's head. I ignore him crying and cursing at me. I go to Kayleigh and get her hands out of the belt that had her hands restrained above her head. I pull her up into a sitting position and wrap her blanket around her. Then I untie the gag from her mouth and untie her feet from the edge of her bed. I pull her into my arms as she cries.

"I know sweet girl, let it out. I got you now," I tell her softly as her body shakes with sobs in my arms.

The sound of Kayleigh's sobs are bouncing off the walls of her bedroom. There is nothing I can say to make her feel better.

"Shut up, this will not save you. You will marry me and be the mother of my child."

I quickly turned my head to face him. "The more you talk the worse your punishment will be."

He starts to laugh. "A woman can't punish a man. You are just weak."

I chuckle at him, and it isn't a sweet kind of chuckle. "No worries, I will show you and every other man in this mafia exactly what a woman can do to men who cross us."

Marcello says, "Nice knowing you, I almost feel sorry for you."

"No, you won't be able to do anything to me because of who my father is and his importance to Peter," Conor says cockily. Marcello shakes his head. He is probably thinking the same thing as I am. Conor is a sexist, entitled fuck boy.

"You think Peter is going to let the man who tried to rape his daughter live and go unpunished."

"He wouldn't do that to his future."

Conor is cut off as Peter slams the door open, Kayleigh jumps in my arms. "Shh it's your dad."

She looks up from my shoulder and over at Peter and says, "Daddy," through her tears. He was looking at Conor and Marcello but when he saw Kayleigh's tears, it took him two steps to be at her side. I walk over to Conor to give Peter and Kayleigh a moment together.

"Don't you dare lie to him you bitch." Okay my patience with this fucker has reached its limit. I pull my hand back and punch him in the face. Marcello let's go of him as he falls to the ground.

"I am gonna kill you, stupid Italian whore."

I look at him. "Is that the best you can come up with? I have been called worse than that and people have been threatening to kill me for years. Come on, be a bit more creative."

"Emilia, what the hell happened?" I keep my eyes on Conor and answer Peter's question.

"When I came here to see if Kayleigh wanted to go to the gym with me, I heard what sounded like someone struggling inside Kayleigh's room. I didn't bother to knock before I opened the door, and I saw a man on top of Kayleigh, trying to force himself on her. I didn't bother to ask who it was; I shot the man in the back of both of his kneecaps. After he fell off the bed and I rolled him over to see who it was, it was none other than Conor."

At this point, Peter is next to me, and he has his gun drawn. "Why were you trying to rape my daughter?"

"I deserve to be in the upper ranks of this mafia, not just some capo."

I kicked the bastard. "You don't deserve to lick the dirt off my shoe." I told him.

Peter calls over two guards and tells them. "Hang him in the basement by his wrists."

They drag out Conor as he is fighting them and yelling out, "I will kill you, bitch. I would have gotten what I wanted if it wasn't for you. You are a good for nothing whore. All women are useless whores."

I roll my eyes at him, I slam the door after he has left the room so we can't hear him anymore.

"I am gonna take Kayleigh to our medical wing to get her wounds treated. Would you mind waiting for me in my office?"

"Actually, I want to go talk with Conor, if you don't mind, and see what else he has to say. He might be willing to talk more because of his hatred toward women."

Peter nods his head, "Just be careful. I don't need Mateo killing me if you get hurt."

"Don't worry, I won't even touch him. Just taunt him verbally." I go over and kiss Kayleigh's forehead and tell her, "I am here if you need me at all."

She nods but doesn't remove herself from Peter. She is holding onto him like he is a lifeline right now. She needs to feel the safety and comfort of her father's arms.

Marcello is behind me; we don't say anything, but I know my body is radiating off my anger. The fact that Conor thought he had the right to do that to Kayleigh. The sweet girl is only twenty-two years old; she shouldn't have to be traumatized by someone trying to force themselves on her in her own room. Her room should be her sanctuary.

When we got to the basement, which wasn't hard to find, especially with how loud he was yelling, they were fighting him, trying to get his wrists wrapped in the chains. I stayed in the shadows of the room, against the wall. Their basement had one light above where Conor was now barely standing on his toes. Conor scrunches up his nose, "What the fuck is that smell?"

"You better answer me. I will be your boss one day. I will have you killed," He yells to the two men who chained him up but are now leaving the room.

The one turns to me and smirks. "Good luck with this one." I nod at him but don't say anything. Conor deserves to sweat a bit.

"Hello, who's there?" he asks, but I continue to stay quiet.

"I said, who is there?" he yells out.

"You better answer me."

"I will have you killed. You spineless coward."

He is quiet for a moment then he starts spilling his guts. "Kayleigh knows her place, and if she doesn't obey me, I will use one of the twins to get what I want."

Now that he is talking, I step out of the shadows. "YOU!" he yells at me with such venom.

"Yes, me. It was me hiding in the shadows that had you completely falling apart and starting to spill all of your secrets, but please, don't stop on my behalf. Please enlighten me."

"Peter will see the light. He will apologize to me for this misunderstanding and will let me impregnate one of his daughters. Then

I will marry her and become the Boss of this family, because Peter's grandfather made it so you couldn't become boss unless the boss is killed or your wife is pregnant. Since Cillian hasn't impregnated his bitch of a wife, I will impregnate an O'Sullivan girl. It is about time the old man retired; he is basically sixty."

I slowly circled him. "Honestly, I can see why Kayleigh is upset, besides the fact you were forcing yourself on her. There isn't one attractive feature about you. Your oily and unkempt black hair that is thrown into a ponytail is definitely a turn off, and your hazel eyes are probably the only tolerable thing to look at. You barely have any muscles, and your face is full of pimples and is pudgy. As the head of the family, you are expected to keep up your hygiene for appearances, which, obviously, you have a hard time doing."

"Says the woman who wears jeans and boots. That is man's clothing. You are not a proper woman," he sneers out at me.

"Are you sure you're in your twenties, not eighties? Because you are a real sexist pig."

"It seems like your husband doesn't know how to keep you in line. I should teach him some pointers that I will use on my wife."

Before he has a chance to say more, I am right in his face. "Keep me in line? Like, what, hit me, or better yet, rape me? Oh, darling, I have been there and done that already. That has no effect on me."

His face drops, and I smirk as I take a few steps away from him. "Oh, did I ruin your whittle plan? Oh, poor baby." I drop the baby tone out of my voice, and I use my ice queen voice. "News flash Conor, women are stronger than weak-minded fools like yourself. And no, Mateo never lays a harmful hand on me or has to rape me. Because we are a team. Sure, I can get mouthy, or he is an arrogant asshole, but we respect each other enough to hear each other. That doesn't mean I don't love when his beast comes out and he fucks me so hard that I am sure a whimpering mess of pain and pleasure that he has to carry me. I personally think it is hot as hell when he fucks me into a pile of mush. But that is something you will never understand how to do, because I doubt you are man enough to do that." I take a breath but continue to talk with a smirk on my face. "Oh and enjoy your last moments pain free. When I come back down, I will be enjoying hearing each and every moan and whimper of pain that escapes your lips."

"Untie me, and I will show you what I can do. You can't do anything to me," he screams out at me, but I can see the fear in his eyes. His eyes look like they are about to pop out of his head and his face is as red as a tomato.

"Oh, but I can, and I will. Sorry, I don't let little boys touch me, only my husband, who is very much a man. Peter will let me do whatever I want with you, especially after I share the information you shared with me. Well, I have better things to do since I am not draining your blood. So, toddles." I wave to him as I walk out of the basement. Marcello is already at the door, holding it open for me.

As soon as the door is closed behind us, he asks, "Did you really have to talk about your sex life with Mateo? That is something I could have lived without knowing." He adds with his face scrunched up in disgust.

"I can always give you more details like I love the way his fingers…" I am cut off when his hand covers my mouth. "No, don't you dare. Keep those details to yourself or if you have to share them, go share them with Theo. He is like a brother to me, and you are like a sister to me. Plus, I don't want to be shot by your husband if he knows I heard of anything like that. I prefer to get back to my flower without any new bullet holes."

I fake pout, "You are no fun."

"I am making Vittorio be your guard next time. Between you barely sleeping and constantly getting in trouble, I will stick with being Alessia's guard."

I put a hand on my heart.

"But I am just bonding with my future brother-in-law."

He rolls his eyes. "Well, let's not bond over sex stories."

"Fine, I will try to calm down my feisty side."

He laughs, "No, you won't."

"Yeah, you're right. I won't. But let's go check on Kayleigh." His mood changes to his usually hard-brooding self when I mentions Kayleigh.

"Yeah, if anyone knows how to help her, it's you."

My demeanor changes from playful to sad.

I give him a sad smile. "Yeah, but her safety has just been robbed from her. She is supposed to feel safe in her home. Conor took away that security from her."

I open the door to the medical wing, and when we get to Kayleigh's room, I see Peter standing at the foot of her bed, looking so distressed. Grace is holding Kayleigh's hand as Kayleigh sleeps in the bed. I quietly walk over and whisper, "How is she?"

Grace comes over to me and gives me a big hug. "Thank you so much. Regardless of what Peter says, if you need anything, we will do what we can to help you," she says to me, as she cries on my shoulder. There is not much I can say that will make them feel better.

As a parent, I am sure they feel powerless to help Kayleigh, I remember what it felt like when I was being abused, but as a parent, you want to protect your child at all costs. Before I pull out of the hug, I tell them, "If any of you need anything, don't hesitate to ask." We pull away from the hug, "We will always be grateful for what you did for our baby."

I smile at her, "I would do it again in a heartbeat. I wish I got there sooner."

"But you saved her from being raped. I can't believe the boy we welcomed into our home with open arms and loved like one of our own would do this."

I smile at her, "Sometimes a wolf will hide in sheep's fur."

"Yeah. I guess you're right. I just don't know how to help her." Grace says sadly, pushing some hair behind her ear.

"Just follow Kayleigh's lead. She will tell you what she needs."

"Emilia, would you mind coming to my office? I want to know what he said to you, but I don't want Kayleigh to overhear anything if she wakes up."

"Sure thing." I say goodbye to Grace and lightly squeeze Kayleigh's hand. I wonder if Peter will be okay with me torturing Conor for some answers, it would be fun. I smile evilly while rubbing my hands together.

"Okay, even as the Boss of the Irish Mafia, I find the look on your face pretty scary."

Marcello laughs and says, "You have no idea. Emilia is genuinely nice unless you abuse a woman or a child, then her diabolical side comes out."

I smile, "Mateo doesn't call me his diabolical wife for nothing."

THIRTY-FIVE
EMILIA

    Peter holds his office door open for me, I go to stand against the wall, but Aiden stands up and offers me his chair. "Aiden here, has the most manners out of all of my sons. At least one of you, has hope to have a wife and children."

    Aiden being the quiet but brooding one of the four brothers just nods his head. Of course, Oscar being the cocky comedian he is says, "Father, not all women want a gentleman." I bite my lip because Peter looks like his head could pop off, but I fail and laugh.

    "Peter don't worry about what he said in front of me. I have heard a lot worse, and Mateo's cousin is the same way. Some are hardheaded and take longer to learn."

    "I swear we did raise them with manners; it seemed like they just forgot them as they got older."

    I wave him off, "One day, they will mature. Well, we are still waiting on Vincenzo, so who knows if there is help for them? Anyway, Conor was very willing to tell me his plan."

    I heard someone take a deep breath, and I didn't realize Robert, Conor's father, was in the office with us until then. "Sorry, Robert, this might be hard for you to hear."

    "I know. I am beyond embarrassed about what he tried to do." he says, shaking his head and looking down with his fists clenched at his side. I do feel sorry for him. I can't imagine how he is feeling.

    "After he was restrained, the men left. One of the men told me good luck with him. Conor started to freak out that someone was there with him but he couldn't see who. I purposely hid in the shadows to make him sweat a bit. It didn't take him long to start spilling his plan. He threatened Kayleigh that if she didn't let him impregnate her, he would do it to either Ellie or Riley. He wants to impregnate one of your daughters, Peter, because of your grandfather's rule about becoming Boss of the Irish Mafia after you are married and she is pregnant. So, he figured he could force his way into the position."

    "I thought he got over his power trip and sense of entitlement," Robert says. "Peter, I am so sorry. He wanted to be in the upper ranks as a teenager, but I thought he had gotten over it. If I had any idea, I would have dealt with him. It makes me sick that I am his father."

    Peter gets up from his desk and clasps his hand on Robert's shoulder. "I know. We basically raised our children together after your wife ran away. You know, some people have demons in their heads that can't be changed no matter how hard we try to help them. I don't blame you, friend, but you also know what we have to do."

Robert nods his head, "I have to tell Quinn, but I don't want her there. She doesn't need to have that image of her big brother in her head. Even though I am beyond pissed at what he did, and he deserves his death, I don't want her seeing that at seven years old. I will let her believe he is a hero in her brain. I still can't believe he would do that, especially with how overprotective he is of Quinn."

I start to tell him that some people get so focused on greed and power they forget about logic and the consequences of their actions when the door is slammed against the wall. I spin towards the door and pull my gun out; I see Kayleigh's friend Hailey. I relax and start to put my gun away, but she yells "I am gonna kill you bitch," and charges at me. Before she can lay a finger on me, Marcello has her restrained.

I arch my eyebrow at her and ask, "Now, what is your problem with me?" Hailey has openly expressed on multiple occasions her dislike for me.

"You shot him; you shot my Conor."

I give her a blank stare. "So, you are telling me that you are more upset that I shot Conor than you are that Conor tried to rape Kayleigh," I ask her, if this is how she treats her friends. Kayleigh needs a better one.

"I faked being friends with that bitch. She gets everything she wants, and I have to work for everything I get. So, I faked being friends with her until he could man up and take action for our plan." She is yelling all this at me.

I have never liked Hailey, but now that I know she is the mastermind behind Kayleigh's suffering, I am gonna deal with her. I pull my hand back and punch her against her jaw. Marcello holds her so she doesn't fall over.

"Damn," Killian says.

I casually glance over at the men in the room, and all of them look shocked, amused, or intrigued.

"What? Have you never seen a woman punch another woman before?"

Cillian shakes his head, "Yes, but that was intense. Now I am starting to believe the rumors about you are true."

Marcello says, "The rumors look like kids play compared to what she has done."

"Seriously?" Cillian asks me, and I nod.

"Yep, my godmother, Esmeralda Garcia, taught me some basics, and then I put my own twist in my techniques."

Marcello scoffs, "Twists? Is that what you call your demented ideas?"

"Oh, hush. You know Zaria deserved that and so much more." I state, and he nods at me.

"Still, it had every man in the room cringing. Well, except for your husband, but he is just as fucked up as you."

I decided to explain what we are talking about since they all looked confused. I give them a quick run through of everything that led up to Zaira's imprisonment with us and a few details about the torture I've put her through while she has been our guest.

"Yep, not gonna get on your bad side," Aiden says.

I chuckle, "My morals go out the window when someone hurts my family, women, or children. Not saying I won't defend a man who needs it but after my past with Alessia's father, anyone who abuses women or children gets to see my diabolical side very quickly."

Hailey decides to open her mouth, "How could you hurt me? I am a woman."

I glare at her. "No, you are not a woman. You are an evil, coldhearted bitch. A woman would not plan for an innocent woman to get hurt, especially one who is supposedly her friend."

"Well, they should have given Conor what belonged to him. He is Robert's only son and he deserves to be the second in command."

I look at Peter. "Peter, do you have any problems if I deal with Hailey?" I ask him. I really hope he lets me have some fun.

He smirks. "Only if we can watch. It would be an honor to watch Mateo's Ruthless Queen in action."

"No problem at all," I say to Peter with a huge smile on my face.

Marcello sees my smile, "Oh boy, you already have plans."

I smirk at him, "Of course I do."

I turned back to Peter, "What is her biggest fear?"

Aiden speaks up, "Snakes."

Hailey shakes her head and says, "No it's spiders."

I snicker at her, "Oh Hailey your face said enough. You don't have to lie to me. I know you are afraid of snakes since all the color drained from your face and your brown eyes held nothing but fear in them as soon as Aiden told us." I look at Peter, "Can we put her in a room full of snakes?"

"Sure thing. Boys, take her to the basement. Keep the window on the door open so Conor can hear his precious Hailey screaming in fear," he says snickering.

"I am an innocent woman," she yells as she is fighting Oscar and Killian to free herself.

I roll my eyes. "Innocent as the devil," I mutter to myself. The men in the room laugh at me. They finally get her out of the office her whining and cries were getting annoying.

Peter says, "You must keep Mateo on his toes."

"Yep, he is never bored. I am gonna let her sit down there for a couple hours so she is on edge. I am gonna go clean my tools, once you are ready let me know." I don't wait for them to answer, I walk to my room in complete silence, lost to my own demons in my head. It never ceases to amaze me how evil this world is, but I am surprised about Hailey turning on Kayleigh. I know Kayleigh valued her friendship with Hailey and my heart once again breaks again for her.

I flop on my bed and bury my head in my pillow.

"Why don't you go take a nap until they are ready," Marcello says to me.

I barely lift my head and tell him, "I need to clean my tools." I flop my head back in my pillow.

"Emilia, we both know that is a bullshit excuse. You are neurotic about having your tools cleaned after you use them." I flip him off.

"Take a damn nap Emilia. You are not taking care of yourself. If you don't, I will tell Mateo and let him punish you."

I picked my head up again, "I thought you were supposed to be my bodyguard and keep me safe."

He smirks. "I am, even from yourself when you are doing too much. You forget you're not superwoman."

I sit up and glare at him, "I know I am not superwoman, Marcello, but I need to find and save my husband from a psychotic gold digger, find where Alexei, Irina and Elena are hiding, keep our family safe somehow, and get rid of the Russians. And now I am worried about Kayleigh. It is a lot on my shoulders, and I am doing the best I can."

Marcello comes and sits next to me on the bed. "I know you are Emilia, but you are not gonna do anyone any good if you are not taking care of yourself."

I nod but tell him. "I know, but the only way I can sleep is if I make myself completely exhausted. The nightmares are worse than they have ever been, and I am struggling."

He shakes his head, "And why didn't you say anything? We could have had the O'Sullivan's doctor give you something."

I shake my head, "I don't trust anyone but Theo and I don't want them to know how bad I am fucked up."

"Emilia, you are not fucked up. There is no hiding your past is ugly, extremely ugly, but you and Alessia survived because of what you did to protect her. You came to Italy with Roman on crutches and covered in bruises. Alessia had only two bruises, because you have kept the princess safe. You escaped from us after Zaria hit Alessia and you were beaten by Eleanor and the guards, even with your back raw and open wounds that were bleeding. Lastly, you jumped out of a second story window when the house was bombed, after you had just got nasty second-degree burns. Emilia, you are the definition of a strong person, but you need to know it is okay to ask for help. No one expects for you not to have some mental scars after everything you went through." He wipes away the tears that have fallen from my eyes.

I hug Marcello; he is more than my bodyguard. He is like another brother, I am glad he is here with me. Not that I will admit this, but I am extremely homesick. I have never been away from Alessia this long or not been able to talk to her, but I know we need to keep her safe.

"Thanks, Marcello."

He smiles at me as he stands up from my bed. "You don't need to thank me."

"One day, I hope I can call you, my brother-in-law," I tell him, and we both smile.

"I would love nothing more than to have my flower as my wife. Not sure Mateo will feel the same way."

I chuckle, "I don't think he would be okay with any man wanting to marry his sister. The De Luca men are a bit overprotective of the women in the family."

He nods "Yeah, they are but I am glad they are. It shows how much they love her, and I want everyone around Julietta to love her."

"You are such a good man, Marcello."

"Thanks, now go take a nap or I will tell Mateo."

I scoff at him, "Traitor."

He laughs as he shuts the door behind him. I lay back down in the bed on my back, staring at the ceiling and I keep thinking about Mateo. Is he safe? Is she still pumping him with drugs? Is he dead? Is that why she hasn't sent me any photos to harass me? Then I hope maybe he escaped, and she is freaking out. My mind is buzzing with questions and my worries about Mateo. At least I know the rest of the De Luca's are safe, even though Marcello is with me in Ireland, he has been on the security detail both in Italy and Spain. He has more men watching over our family and businesses. The De Luca men seem to be annoyed with the security, but I will not risk anyone else in the family being kidnapped or hurt.

I hear a knock on the door, and I look over. I see it has been two hours since Marcello left. I open the door and see Marcello on the other side of the door. From the look he gives me, he knows I didn't nap at all.

"Busted," he says.

"I did rest. I just couldn't fall asleep, so no need to tell Mateo."

He shakes his head.. "Nope I told you if you didn't nap, I was telling Mateo. So have fun," he says laughing.

"Fucker," I mumble under my breath. "I will be ready in a few minutes," I tell him as I go to change my clothes. Maybe Mateo will be too distracted after not seeing his family after a month and he won't punish me. I laugh to myself, knowing that is wishful thinking.

I dress in all black and pull my boots on and put my hair in a ponytail. Can't have my hair in my way when I am torturing Hailey. I open the door and Marcello is leaning against the wall next to my door with his arms crossed against his chest. He looks at me when he hears the door open.

"Ready?" he asked me.

I nod at him, "Yes. Let's go have some fun."

He shakes his head, "I think you will be the only one who will be having fun."

THIRTY-SIX
EMILIA

When Marcello opens the door to the basement, I can hear Hailey crying and screaming for Conor. He is yelling from the next room, "Stop. Let her go, I will take her punishment. Please just don't hurt her."

I smirk at Peter, "Let's bring her devoted puppet in here so he can watch the show."

Peter smiles at me, "I love your idea. Now I am seeing why Mateo calls you his Ruthless Queen. Oscar and Cillian, go get Conor."

"He has many nicknames for me: Vicious Queen, Feisty Tigress, and his Diabolical Vicious Wife, to name a few. But this is nothing compared to what I have planned for our mastermind here," I say, pointing to Hailey who is tied to a chair. Conor is dragged into the room with us, he is thrashing against Oscar and Cillian. Even with them dragging him. They both are holding his weight since he can't stand on his legs from me shooting him in the back of his knees. "Boys put him on his knees in front of Hailey, he can have a front row seat for what I am gonna do to his darling."

"Please don't hurt her, I will do anything please."

I look over at him and smirk. "Hmm. I guess I can hear your moans of pain and agony watching me torture Hailey. I was needing a way to release my anger and Hailey's plan just gave me a reason to." I bend down and pick up a snake, Hailey is shaking. "Aw, look at the Black Rat Snake. You are so pretty, aren't you?" I say to the snake, as I gently rub my fingers along its body. Obviously, she doesn't know that Black Rat Snakes are not poisonous, or she is generally that afraid of snakes. Oh well, either way I am gonna enjoy torturing her with her fear of snakes.

I walk up to Hailey. "Hailey, look how pretty it is."

"Get that thing away from me!" she screeches. I chuckle and move it closer.

"Who? This beauty? I think it wants to be your friend, Hailey."

She tries to move away from the snake but with her tied to the chair and the chair bolted to the floor, she can't move away from it except to move her head. There is no space between her back and the back of the chair, since she has scooted her body as far away from the snake as possible.

"Hailey, are you scared of the snake?" She nods her head. "Okay, I will move it away from your chest." Hailey takes a deep breath, but I don't put the snake down. I move behind her and gently put the snake on her shoulder, because I don't want to hurt the snake.

She screams loud enough to burst an eardrum; she is eyeing the snake as it slowly slithers all down her body. Hailey is taking short shallow breaths; I can tell she is about to hyperventilate. I stand off the side watching her being scared out of her mind. Conor has been yelling this whole time, begging me to stop torturing her. If he is this worked up with my mental torment on Hailey, I can't wait to see what happens when I start to physically hurt her.

I don't do anything else and wait until she has gotten herself worked up until the point she is about to pass out.

I will give her credit; it takes her longer than I expected to get to that point. About ten minutes later, I can see her struggling to breathe. I remove the snake that has settled itself in her lap, totally oblivious, its presence in Hailey's lap has caused her to soil herself and has given her a panic attack.

I set the snake back on the ground. I might see if I can bring it home with me. I think I will name it Draco, which means snake in Greek, but it sounds cool. "Marcello, look, I made a friend," I tell him as Draco is still by my foot.

He shakes his head, "I am not gonna be present when you tell Nonna you brought a snake home with you as a pet."

I put my finger to my lips, "She won't know about Draco."

He looks at Peter, "Hope you weren't attached to that snake. If she has named it, she will do whatever she can to bring it home."

Peter shakes his head laughing, "She can have the snake, plus it adds to the Vicious Queen look."

"See, Marcello. Peter understands. Thank you, Peter! And Draco would look perfect perched on my shoulder while I torture my victims. Don't you think so?" I ask while tapping my finger to my lips.

Oscar laughs, "Yep I am definitely not fucking with her ever. Not that I was planning on it, but I am definitely not now. Never trust a woman who treats a snake like a baby. And Emilia, you are treating that snake as if it is your baby."

I smile as I watch Draco slither around my feet and Hailey is still slowly catching her breath.

"You said you would move it away from me." Hailey says to me, now that she has calmed down.

I don't bother to answer her question. I stare at her and ask her, "Scary, isn't it? Being absolutely scared out of your mind but can't do anything to stop it? Now you know how Kayleigh felt when she was tied to the bed and gagged while Conor was trying to force himself on her."

"She was just a pawn we needed in our plan." She stops and takes a breath but looks at Peter.

"Peter, you need to wake up and realize you are making a mistake. You are getting older, and you need to retire soon. Since Cillian's wife isn't pregnant, let Kayleigh get pregnant and Conor will make a perfect Boss. Obviously, what he was going to do shows he is willing to do whatever that needs to be done for this family."

"No, I won't allow a rapist in my upper ranks, nor would I make my daughter be around her abuser. So no, Hailey, I won't regret killing Conor. Plus, how Emilia has become another daughter to me, a feisty pain in the ass daughter but a daughter, nonetheless. And I am not willing to risk a five point six billion euro contract with Mateo over a greedy bitch or a power-hungry fool."

"Conor is worth more than a 5.6 billion contract. He is willing to do whatever he needs to for this family. You would be a fool not to have him as the new boss of the mafia. He will raise it up to become the most powerful in the world. It shouldn't matter that he is a rapist, you all are monsters anyway. Obviously, you are not smart enough or ruthless enough Peter to have this mafia at the top. So, let Conor have a baby with one of your girls and let him do what he was destined to be."

Peter slowly claps, "That was a cute speech Miss McLoughlin but let me fill you in on a secret. I am a monster, but this monster will do everything it can to protect his family as long as I am still breathing. I am still alive and breathing, which means I am still the boss. As the boss you and Conor won't be leaving here alive. Now how long you both suffer. Well, that depends on both of you."

I have to ask. "If Conor would have impregnated one of Peter's daughters and married them, where would that leave you?"

She smirks, "Well I would technically be his mistress, but I would be his favorite, number one girl."

I roll my eyes at her. "You know if he is married, he can't take you shopping, or you can't be on his arm at events."

"So, I would be the one he treats like a Queen and in his bed."

"Wow, you are dumber than I thought," Cillian says. "Not only do we have to be married and have a child to be boss, but we have to remain loyal to our family. And if at any time, we are not loyal, the capos can take away our position. So, your little plan would have never worked."

She goes to open her mouth but I cut her off, "Honestly Hailey. I don't even want to hear the same bullshit you have been spewing. Conor deserves it, Kayleigh gets whatever she wants. No one, and I mean NO ONE, deserves to have someone try and rape them. You have no idea the power it takes from you, and the fact that you are so greedy that you were willing to put another female through it, well that pisses me off. Kayleigh is like a younger sister to me; she is a sweet and genuine person."

Cillian speaks up, "We all never liked you, but Kayleigh always said you just needed love because you were an orphan and you felt abandoned. She refused to abandon you, but obviously my sister was being too nice to you. We should have thrown you out with the trash when you first started coming around."

I don't say anything for a minute but shake my head.

She yells out, "She got whatever she wanted."

Peter finally loses it and raises his voice, "Because she is my daughter, and I chose to spoil and love my children. I am sorry your parents gave you up, but it is not Kayleigh's fault that she was raised in a family that spoiled her in materialistic things and in love." You can see him struggling with his anger wanting to physically hurt Hailey. The overprotective mafia daddy in him wants to deal with her, which I can understand. Look what I did to Zaria for slapping Alessia.

"Anything anyone else wants to know?" They shake their heads; I nod and without saying anything else I walk over to my bag of tools on the ground. I look until I find my "zapping knife" as Vincenzo calls it, since it is a knife that can electrocute you. Salvatore came across this during one of the weapon shipments. He got an extra one for me, knowing I would love to add it to my unique torture tool collection.

I stand back up in front of her. I know she can't hurt me since she is tied to the chair by her lower legs, upper arms and wrists. There is no way she can get any of her limbs loose and I can always have someone hold her head if she tries to head butt me. I don't waste any time and hold the button on the side of the knife, I can hear the electricity from the knife zapping in the air.

"What are you gonna do to me?" she asks, as she jumps every time, she hears the zap from the knife.

"Well, I am gonna do this." I quickly cut off her pinky finger.

"NOOO! Stop hurting her." Conor yells over Hailey's screams. I turn around and run the bloody knife over the side of his cheek.

"Conor, you have been so quiet, I forgot you were in here. Are you enjoying the show? Isn't it wonderful watching how people react to their fears?"

He shakes his head, "What do I have to do so you stop hurting her?"

I smirk at him, "Nothing, she will be tortured until she begs for death. If she can't handle any pain, then she shouldn't be a money chaser without being ready to deal with the consequences." I turn my focus back to Hailey and cut another two fingers off, she continues to cry. "Oh, quit being so dramatic or I am gonna shove your fingers in your mouth. Would you like that?" Hailey shakes her head. She is still crying but at least she stopped screaming.

"Bummer, I was hoping you would keep screaming. I haven't shoved someone's fingers in their mouth yet. Oh well, I can try it on my next victim," I say shrugging my shoulders. I walk over and grab the container of salt and without saying anything I scoop a bit of salt in my hand. I push the salt on the wounds where I just cut her fingers off. She is now thrashing around and keeps screaming. I put the salt back on the table and watch for a couple minutes as she thrashes around.

I have a huge smile on my face.

"You are a monster," Hailey says to me.

I give her a big smile. "You are right I am a monster, but I will show you what a monster I am." I start to carve the word monster on her forehead. I dig the knife in until I feel the bone of her head. And I drag my knife through her skin. I barely get through the first letter when she tries to stop me by shaking her head.

I look over at the men, "Can someone come hold her still." Killian walks up behind her, he grabs her hair with one hand and the other is wrapped around her throat. "Oh, a little suffocation play. What fun." I smirk at Killian; he just shakes his head. I continue to carve Hailey's forehead. I ignore her protests; I enjoy watching the blood drain from each cut and drip down her face.

"Now the mastermind is now a masterpiece, " I say standing back looking at her with my hands on her hips.

"How can your husband be married to a psychotic bitch like you? It's not like you're even that pretty." I roll my eyes and as I am about to respond I hear.

"You are wrong, she is the most beautiful goddess in my world. Not that someone like you would understand, but she is not only beautiful on the outside, but she is also an angel on the inside. Unlike most pure angels, she is my dark angel. She is loving, protective, and fierce, and will do whatever it takes to protect her family. She is also a true warrior; my wife has gone through hell and back, yet she stands here before us with her head held high. All of us should be on our knees kissing the ground she walks on and be appreciative that we are even in her presence. I am the luckiest bastard alive to be married to her and she is the mother of our daughter. I can only imagine what you have done if you are seeing her sadistic dark side. You must have done something pretty fucked up."

I hear that voice that is my solace I have been craving for over a month and can't believe my ears.

THIRTY-SEVEN
EMILIA

      I turn to see my husband with his usual cocky smirk. If he hadn't just been kidnapped at the hands of a gold-digging psychopath, I would make a comment to get rid of the smirk. But right now, I am more than elated to see that smirk on his face. He is here and alive in front of me and not just in my dreams.

      I dropped the knife I was holding and run into his arms. He wastes no time in catching me and lifting me into his arms, I wrap my arms and legs around him. I slam my lips on his, and I push myself as close as possible to him. I missed my irritating husband so much. He obviously missed me as much as I missed him. When he grabs my ass and pulls me closer to him, I can feel his cock has already sprung to life. His tongue brushes against my lips and as I am about to open my mouth to let him in, I hear someone wolf whistle at us.

      We pull away and Oscar is smirking at us, "Well that was a hot welcome Mateo got."

      I look over at Peter, "You're lucky he is your son otherwise I would throw a knife at him."

      Mateo chuckles, "We do not throw knives at people when they irritate you *la mia Regina diabolica*."

      I look at him and pout but say, "Fine." I unwind my legs from around his waist, and I slide myself down his body until my feet are on the ground. Mateo groans. I quickly step back and look him over.

      "What happened? Are you hurt? Oh, my fucking god. How could I be so stupid to jump in your arms like that? Of course you are hurt, that woman had you drugged up when she would beat you. I am such a careless wife."

      I am cut off when Mateo pulls me back to him and kisses me silently. After a few moments he pulls away. "Would you relax? I am not hurt unless you count my very hard cock that you rubbed your body against."

      I roll my eyes at him and, of course, he is smirking at me. "Can you not think with your cock for, oh, I don't know, five minutes a day?"

      "Well right now, no that's not happening. My sexy wife, who I have not held in my arms for over a month, was kissing me and slid her sexy body against me. And you also looked hot as hell torturing this woman here. Speaking of which, what did she do to be at your mercy?"

      "Mateo, Hailey here decided she was gonna convince Conor, who is Robert's son, to forcefully impregnate Kayleigh or one of the twins to become the boss. Unfortunately for them, I caught Conor trying to force himself on Kayleigh and stopped it before he could get too far.

She thought if Kayleigh was pregnant, she would marry Conor. Then he would become the Boss of the Irish Mafia, and keep Hailey as his mistress, with his relationship to Kayleigh only being for show when they are in public. Oh, and the icing on the cake is that she pretended to be Kayleigh's friend just to get closer to power and wealth."

Mateo went from playful and happy to murderous. "What kind of woman does that? No wonder Emilia decided to deal with you. Because I know the O'Sullivan's feel the same way I do about hurting women."

"I want and need the money. She doesn't."

I roll my eyes. "Blah, blah, blah. We have already heard it." I say to her, Mateo stands next to me with his hands on my hips.

Hailey looks at Mateo with a hungry and hopeful look in her eyes. "But he might save me from you."

Mateo laughs as he kisses my temple, "Oh no. You have it all wrong, I would hand her the weapon for her to torture you with. We both hate when people abuse women and children. Since you planned out what would happen to Kayleigh, I will help Emilia in any way to make the last moments of your life extremely painful."

"How can you allow that whore to treat my woman this way?" Conor yells at Mateo.

I look over and see Mateo's nostrils flare in anger. He steps in front of me, to protect me, even though Conor is on his knees being held by the O'Sullivan brothers. "What did you just call my wife?" he says with a deadly tone. I run my hand up and down his back to try and settle the beast in him down a bit.

Conor stupidly replies back with, "You heard me. I called her a whore. Only a whore would put on that kind of display when she was all over you. She must have no decency. Mateo, how faithful is your wife? Do you really think she has kept her legs closed while you were kidnapped?"

Okay now I am seeing red. Mateo marches over to him and picks him up the collar of his shirt. He gets about two inches from his face and tells him, "I know my wife. And I know she would never be unfaithful to me or our marriage. We both take our vows very seriously." He sends me an air kiss and I smile at him. He turns his attention back to Conor. "No one will get away with speaking about my Queen like that. As long as I am breathing no one will speak ill of her without consequences from me." Then Mateo punches Conor in the nose. Conor falls over and stays down. Mateo starts to taunt Conor.

"Come on, big man. You talk a big game and try to act all big and bad, assaulting women. Come on, get up and fight a real man." he says as he rolls up the sleeves on his black button up shirt.

Conor pulls himself up to a sitting position, "I can't stand because of your fucking wife."

Mateo wastes no time and kicks him in the ribs. Then he turns to me, "*Tesoro,* what did you do to him that he is claiming he can't stand on his own?"

Before I can respond, Hailey is crying, "Stop hurting him. You are all fucking monsters."

Okay that's it I have had enough of her voice. "Hey Mateo, come pry her mouth open for me." He grabs the bite block which is similar to what a dentist uses to keep your mouth open when they do a procedure. He hands it to me. "Hold her chin so I can stick this in her mouth."

He does and I roughly force it in her mouth, it cuts her lip and it bleeds a little. I go back to where I dropped the knife earlier on the floor. On my way back over, I grab some tongs so I can hold her tongue while I cut her tongue out of her mouth.

She sees what I have in my hand, and she must have figured out what I am gonna do. She is crying again and shaking her head back and forth. Mateo doesn't need me to ask him, he holds each side of her head still. He loves to taunt his victims, so he starts on Hailey. "Uh oh, not so evil as you thought you were. Oh well, that's okay because you won't be able to say anything soon anyway. Not after Emilia cuts your tongue out, besides your voice is really annoying. I wonder how Conor could actually tolerate listening to you?" I laugh as I grab her tongue with the tong and the next second, I am cutting her tongue off. I throw it so it lands in Conor's lap. He screams and moves away from it.

We both laugh as Mateo shoves Hailey's face forward so she doesn't choke on the blood; granted, she will be dead soon anyway.

"Now that we can't be interrupted, can you tell me why Conor can't stand on his own?" Mateo asks me.

I smirk down at Conor and watch as he glares back at me.

"Well, when I caught him trying to force himself on Kayleigh, I shot him in the back of both knees. I had to make sure he was immobilized so I wouldn't have to worry about him until Marcello could restrain him. Granted, I barely got the second shot off before Marcello was bursting in Kayleigh's room," I say with a smirk.

Mateo has a huge smile on his face. "Sexy, vicious, ruthless, protective, and intelligent. I am such a lucky bastard. Let me finish dealing with this idiot and then I will bring you to your room," he tells me with a smoldering look.

I nod my head and wait to see how he is gonna teach Conor to respect women the rest of his painful life because we all know the O'Sullivan's won't be letting him out of this basement alive. He yanks Conor up with his hair and pushes his gun in his mouth. Conor starts to cry. "Wow such a big man you are. I have only put the gun in your mouth, and you are already crying like a baby. My daughter is braver than you, but then look who her mother is, so it's no doubt she is brave.

Now if I find out you have been disrespectful to any woman in the remainder of time you have left on this earth, I will come back and bring you to my mansion. Where my tigers, who have not had any prey to hunt in a while, live, and I will let them hunt you. But I won't do this until after the O'Sullivans have tortured you. Even if all your limbs are missing, I will still throw you in the cage with them. Let me tell you, they love to play with their prey, so they will tear you apart and it will be painful before they finally kill you and eat you. Understand?" Mateo says with the gun still in his mouth and Conor nods his head with tears falling down his cheeks.

Mateo takes his gun out of Conor's mouth and wipes his saliva on Conor's shirt. After Mateo tucks his gun back into his pants, he punches Conor in the gut and watches as he falls to the ground.

"Do you want her alive or dead?" I ask Peter. It was his daughter who was assaulted and hurt by Hailey and Conor.

"Dead, you have given her a nice painful death. Conor's will be much longer and he will get a turn with each of my sons along with myself."

I nod at him. "That sounds like a wonderful idea." I walk over to Hailey and pick her head up by her hair.

"Hey Conor, look over here." He does, and I slit Hailey's throat. She is gurgling with more blood coming out of her mouth.

"NO! HAILEY!" Conor yells.

I walk over to him and wipe the bloody knife on his shirt. "And you think you could have gotten away with what you did. Conor, all you ever will be is a selfish boy in a man's body. You would never have made it in our world. It isn't a place for little boys like yourself." I pat his cheek with the knife and stand back up.

I am not sure if he heard me, as he was staring at Hailey dying in the chair. He looks helpless as he cries for her on the ground. I put the knife back on the table.

I walk next to Mateo and wrap my arms around him. I lean up and peck his lips.

He smiles at me, "You know you look extremely sexy covered in someone else's blood?"

"Good, well you can enjoy helping me wash it off in the shower."

A throat clears, interrupting us. "Emilia, I cannot thank you enough for saving Kayleigh from being raped and dealing with Hailey." I smile at Peter. At first, I was extremely skeptical of him and everyone else here besides Kayleigh, but now I consider them to be a great ally. "Of course, I would hope that god forbid Alessia was ever in the same situation someone would do what I did for Kayleigh. I see Kayleigh as a friend, and I always protect the people I care about."

"Sorry about me roughing Conor up a bit there, Peter. I won't tolerate anyone being disrespectful to Emilia or any women in my family," Mateo apologizes.

Peter sticks out his hand for me to shake, and then he shakes Mateo's hand. "I completely understand. I would have done the same thing if it was Grace or one of my daughters. You are one lucky bastard, Mateo, and now I see why you are married. You both are as crazy protective as the other one."

Mateo kisses the top of my hair, if he is being this touchy feeling right now but I am not complaining I have missed him. I have a feeling he is gonna wreck my body when he gets me alone and all to himself. "And I am especially glad we are allies because I think I am more afraid of her than I am of you." We all laugh at that.

"She is my perfect diabolical wife," Mateo says with a proud smile on his face.

"Well, go spend time together, it has been a month since you saw each other."

Mateo smirks, "Don't need to tell me twice." Then he swings me over his shoulder.

"Mateo," I say between a shriek and a laugh.

Before we get out the door, I hear Marcello call out to Mateo, "Hey, Boss, thought you should know that she wasn't taking care of herself while you weren't here."

Mateo stops in his tracks and puts me down so my back is flush with his chest. He has his arms tightly wrapped around my stomach. "Is that so?" he asks Marcello while I am glaring at him.

He is smirking at me with his arms crossed his chest. "Yep, she wasn't eating enough, barely sleeping, and drinking way too much coffee. For example, she would only step out of her temporary office to eat, shower, work out with Kayleigh, and maybe sleep for a few hours. And when I say few hours, I mean maybe three hours."

"Don't worry, I will add to her punishments that she accumulated while she was recovering from before," Mateo says, and I groan.

"You are gonna kill me." I tell Mateo, who just chuckles as he once again lifts me over his shoulder.

"Fucking brute. I can walk." He smacks my ass. Oh for fuck's sakes here we go with his damn obsession with him smacking my ass every time I cuss. Then I turn my attention to the men laughing at me, especially Marcello.

I yell out to him, "Marcello, you traitor! And here I was, planning to convince Mateo to let you and Julietta take a vacation together."

He continues to smirk at me. "Well, that is punishment for not taking care of yourself and you over sharing about what you and Mateo do behind closed doors."

I flip him off, "I think Salvatore is my favorite brother-in-law."

Mateo is quick to say, "Marcello isn't family."

I say, "Not yet at least."

Mateo grumbles, and I laugh at him for being all pissy and overprotective of Julietta being with his childhood friend.

"Keep laughing but we will see who is laughing tomorrow when I have to carry you around after I fuck you all night that you can't walk." He smacks my ass again.

"Don't you start, fucker." Of course, he smacks it again. I chose not to respond but I squeeze my legs together because, as much as I will cuss him tomorrow, the thought of being tangled with Mateo all night sounds really good right now. I have been a horny mess and the dildo Theo sent me isn't doing anything compared to the anaconda that hangs between my husband's legs

THIRTY-EIGHT
EMILIA

Once we are inside the room I have been staying in, he sets me down on my feet. "We have a very busy night, *mia Regina,*" he tells me as he quickly pulls his belt from his pants.

"And why is that *mio Rio*?" I ask him, not breaking eye contact with him.

"Because you have a very long list of punishments to make up for," he says slowly, dragging his finger down my neck. I go to open my mouth but before I can react, he is stripping me naked while he is kissing me. When I feel my nipples harden from the cool air against my skin, I break the kiss and decide to be brave.

"So, Mr. Big Bad Mafia Boss, what will my punishment be?" He cups my pussy.

"I will make you cum for every punishment you accumulated in the past three months since being injured. Maybe not all today, but you will receive each of them" He smirks at me as I gasp. "And I have been keeping count. Mrs. De Luca, you have been very naughty."

I whine out, "I am gonna die."

He takes the same hand that he cupped me with and now is circling his hand around my pussy not touching me, and says, "Maybe you should behave better."

He is in between my legs and looks at me and says "Let's see how many you can handle, *la mia tigre cattiva*. You have a lot of punishments to fulfill." My eyes bug out of my head and stutter on the word twelve as his tongue is already between my folds. I try to form some kind of sentence, but my mind draws a blank, and I throw my head back as the feeling of his tongue roams all over me except for entering my pussy. I whimper, wanting more and grab his hair to pull him closer and grind my hips closer to his face.

He pulls away "You better stay still, or I will tie you to this bed." I pout at him and release my hands from his hair and grip onto the sheets next to me. He is devouring me. I am wiggling and panting, when he gently bites down and then licks my clit. I grab the pillow and put it over my mouth as I moan out. I can feel him chuckle against me and plunge two fingers in me but pumps them slowly and deep until I fall apart.

I moan out under the pillow "Fuckkk, Mateo!"

But he doesn't stop once my orgasm is done; nope, he continues to suck me and has three fingers in me pumping fast this time.

I can barely catch my breath when I feel my second orgasm rolling in. I try to warn him that it is coming but all I can do is arch my hips up closer to his face and moan out. I hope he gives my sensitive pussy a moment to rest. I sigh a breath of relief thinking he is gonna give me a break when I feel his fingers being removed. My moment of relief is gone very quickly when I feel his tongue start lapping up all my juices. *"Fottutamente delizioso,"* *(Fucking delicious.)* he tells me as he licks his fingers, staring at me and then he starts to kiss back up my body. Once he has got to my lips, he puts a sweet and gentle kiss on my face. "How are you feeling?"

I look into his blue eyes and say, "Very good."

He smirks. "Good I barely quenched my hunger for you *la mia tigre sexy.*" I gulp at the hunger in his eyes as he stands up to finish undressing. He wastes no time kicking his pants and boxers off him. He is back between my legs, slowly grinding his hard cock against my sensitive pussy. I whimper from how sensitive I am right now, and how bad I want him inside of me.

He chuckles. "What is it my love?" And he grinds on me harder. I throw my head back, breathing hard. He grabs me by the back of my head so I can't move my head. "Keep your eyes on me, I want to see how much I affect you." I nod my head; he grinds a couple more times and I am a panting mess.

"Mateo please…. Need you inside me." I beg him.

"You want my cock inside of you?" he taunts me. Usually I would be pissed, but right now, I am a hot, horny damn mess and I don't give a damn.

"Yes, Mateo please. I need you."

"Whatever my Queen wants, she gets."

He grabs my legs and wraps them around his hips, he lines himself and slowly slides inside of me. I moan out in satisfaction; I roll my eyes in the back of my head.

He stops. "Eyes on me." He tells me again. I look at him as he continues to slide back inside of me. Once our hips are touching, he kisses next to my ear, "Are you okay?"

I nod my head and whisper out, "Perfect." I can feel him smile against my skin. He pulls back and starts pumping in and out of me as he kisses all over my neck. I hold onto his shoulders and grind back against him.

He grits out between his teeth, *"Cazzo diavolo. Sei così stretto."* *(Fucking hell. You are so damn tight.)* He kisses my head; he doesn't wait and plunges his tongue in my mouth and dominates my mouth. I don't fight it, I let him dominate all of me, because let's be honest, I absolutely love it. We continue kissing as he is thrusting in and out of me at a delicious pace. I squeeze my leg tighter around him when my orgasm is approaching. He reaches to the front of me and circles his finger on my clit. I moan into his mouth as I cum all over him.

I fall sluggish, once my third orgasm has run through my body. He grabs me so my butt is at the edge of the bed, he lifts one of my legs that was around his waist and puts the other over his shoulder. "Fuck, Mateo. You are so deep." I moan. He holds my waist tight, the mischievous on his face shows that he is about to destroy me. He fucks me, good, hard, and fast.

"*Gioca con le tette*"*(Play with your tits)* he demands from me. I obey him and I grab my nipples, pinching them between my fingers.

"*Cazzo. Cazzo, sei così dannatamente sexy. Ho così tanti piani per noi mia moglie cattiva.*"*(Fuck. Fucking hell, you are so damn sexy. I have so many plans for us my naughty wife.)*

I pant out, "What plans?"

He leans down next to my ear and huskily whispers into it. "*Mmm ti scopa in tutti I tipi di posizione, specialmente contro il muro della doccia dato so che ami il sesso con la doccia. Non sei mia piccola volpe?*" *(Hmm fucking you in all kinds of positions especiallu against the shower wall since I know you love shower sex. Don't you my little vixen.)*

Oh, shit imagining him fucking me against the shower wall with holding my hands above my head and relentlessly pounding into me. "*Ti piace? Penso che l'abbia fatto perché mi hai appena spremuto.*" *(You like that? I think you did because you just squeezed me.)* I nod at him; he sucks on my ear.

I moan out and push my hips harder at him to chase the next orgasm and he quickly pulls away from my neck so he can look at my eyes. "Hold it." I shake my head knowing I can barely hold it. "*Ho detto di tienilo,*" *(I said hold it)* he demands of me.

Fucking hell everything this man does is turning me on. A couple thrusts later he tells me to, "*Guardami quando sborri tutto il mio cazzo.*" *(Look at me when you cum all over my cock.)* And that triggers me to squeeze the hell out of his cock and I cum. I start to get loud when he quickly puts his hand over my mouth, and he is right behind me. He buries his face in my shoulder as he muffles himself as he cums. He moves his hand off my mouth and wraps his arms around my waist as he nuzzles himself deeper into my body. I just hold onto him as we both catch our breath.

I finally am able to form a sentence and say, "*Santo cazzo, è stato intenso.*" *(Holy fuck, that was intense.)*

He chuckles at me. "Yes it was. You are a goddess."

I am glad he can't see my face because it would be as red as a tomato. He kisses my forehead as he slowly slides out of me, and I whine. He kisses my forehead again and mumbles sorry. He climbs off the bed and I know he is headed to the bathroom; he comes back a minute later with a warm washcloth to clean up between my legs.

I give him a small smile and close my eyes as I snuggle into my pillow. I feel my upper body being lifted and something draped over me.

I barely open my eyes. "Shh, just close your eyes. I am just putting a shirt on you." I do as he says, and I close my eyes and fall back asleep. I feel Mateo climb in the bed and pull me, so I am laying on his chest. I feel him run his hand through my hair, and as I am about to fall asleep, I hear Mateo whisper, "I love you, my Queen. I have missed you so much."

Maybe I will get lucky, and he will reduce my sentence for my punishments because I only made it to four and I feel like I am going to die. That was my last thought before I let sleep consume me.

THIRTY-NINE
MATEO

The next morning, I woke up feeling a weight on my chest. I see my wife's beautiful brown hair sprawled across my chest and her arm thrown across my lower stomach along with her leg thrown across mine. She is holding me as tight as she can in her sleep. Before I got married, I would never fear death like I have now. With Emilia and Alessia in my life, I never want to leave them to fend for themselves in this world without me there with them. I know Emilia is more than able to take care of the both of them, but I don't want her to ever have to do that again.

I feel a feather-like kiss on my chest. I look down and see Emilia's green eyes looking back at mine. "You seem deep in thought," Emilia says to me, as she gently runs her finger over the wrinkles on my forehead. I grab her hand and kiss the inside of her wrist and give her a sweet smile that only my family sees.

"I was just thinking about how, for the first time ever being kidnapped, I was actually afraid of dying because that meant leaving you and Alessia."

She stops smiling and she quietly says, "I am sorry I couldn't find you and save you sooner." I shake my head.

"Don't apologize. Knowing my stubborn wife took all of my responsibilities plus hers on her shoulders made my kidnapping, and subsequent escape, less stressful for me. I could get back to you a little less loopy from the drugs she gave me."

She nods at me, "Yes, I did. Every time I would get close, she would move and then I would have to start all over again, looking for her next location. But Rebecca loved to taunt me with photos of you being drugged and beaten. She made sure to say that this was all my fault and asked if I would let her, have you. She said, if I did, you would be out of your pain and misery. But how did she know where you were?"

"She hacked my calendar, so she knew I was going to that meeting. And she contacted an ex-boyfriend of hers who had been arrested for possession of illegal explosions. They made a deal that he could use her body whenever he wanted if he would set up the bombs at the restaurant I was at so she could kidnap me. I did find out she has nothing to do with the Russian Mafia. That probably was the only time I was coherent before I escaped."

"Are you serious?" She asked. I nodded my head at her. "Okay, I thought she was crazy before now I know she definitely is. And what if her plan didn't work and you died in the bombing?"

Before I can respond, she adds, "But why did we find Russians there?"

"I think they were out looking for who set off the bombs at the hotel, and since the restaurant was a few miles away and it is one of my hotels, they were probably looking to see if they saw anyone from our mafia. And I assume when they saw me injured after the bombing, they figured I was weak and vulnerable, and they could take me out." I lean my head on hers and take a deep breath, "She tried to beat me into agreeing to divorce you. That would never happen. I love you so much. I am just glad I am back here with you in my arms, and soon, we will be with our princess too. Speaking of which, where is she?"

"She is with Jose and Esmeralda in Spain with Nonna, Nonno, Theo, Vittorio and other guards I sent with them."

I kissed her head, "Good, so why did I get a note while I was there saying. Quickly return to your wife, I prefer not to die. From a Doctor Tommaso?" Emilia laughs against my chest.

"He happens to be the brother of Rebecca. Supposedly he is a good and honest man. According to Tommaso, Rebecca has been unstable her whole life, chasing after men with money, but her mother was the same way and still is. But once we intel that the van that took you was his. I had Salvatore and Vincenzo bring him in and I questioned him. Even questioned him through the computer, I guess I scared him."

I shake my head, "Emilia, the devil is scared of you."

She shrugs her shoulders, "It's a talent."

I laugh at her but stand up and throw her over my shoulder. She laughs at me. I missed hearing her laughter. "Come on, let's go have a shower. I need to have you bent over with your hands on the wall," I say as I smack her ass.

"Mateo! Hands off."

I set her down on the bathroom sink. I kiss her lips and say, "Never!" I turn around and turn the water on and adjust it until it is the perfect temperature.

I face my beautiful wife who is sitting at the sink in nothing but my button-down dress shirt. She looks like the alluring temptress that she is. Her long brown hair has that adorable messy look, and her deep green eyes are watching my every move. I move in front of her and quickly unbutton every button of my shirt. I kiss her jaw very slowly to antagonize her because my wife, when horny, is the most impatient woman. Not that I am going to complain, I love that she craves my body and touch as much as I crave her. I take my boxers off and pick up Emilia and bring us to the shower.

Emilia's hair gets darker and longer when her head is submerged under the water in the shower. My cock is painfully hard. I sink down to my knees and lift one of her legs over my shoulder. I watch her as I latch my lips on her clit and start to lick in between her folds. My goddess throws her back against the wall and moans out. Her hands are in my hair, holding onto me as I pump two fingers inside of her while my mouth goes from sucking to kissing on her clit. She goes to start humping my face, but I hold her still. This time, I am in control.

"Mateo," she complains.

"No, this time, I am in control. And I will control when I let you cum." I smirk at her, "You didn't think I would let just last night be the end of your punishment, did you?"

"I was hoping it was."

I chuckle at her as I kiss up her stomach and continue to slowly kiss up her body until my lips are next to her ear. "Maybe, if you are a good girl, I will let your punishment be over by the end of the day." She opens her mouth to say something but decides not to say what she wants to say and just nods her head. I grab her leg and wrap it around my hip, and I grind into her. She holds onto my arms and digs her nails into my skin as she is panting. I am still holding onto her hip to control her from moving. I can feel how wet she is; she is dripping down my cock.

"Do you want it?" I ask her.

"Yes, Mateo," she says while nodding her head.

"Beg. Beg me to fuck you and sooth that ache in your pussy that only my cock can ease," I say as I grind harder on her.

Her eyes stare into mine, "Please, Mateo, only you can satisfy me. I need you. Please, fuck me."

I waste no time and thrust inside of her. I groan when she wraps herself around me. She is already squeezing my cock. I grab her other leg so now that both of her legs are wrapped around my waist.

I give her long and deep strokes; I can feel her body tighten every time I hit her sweet spot. "Yes, Mateo, right there, don't stop." I want to drag this out, and plus I decided that I will edge her a couple times as her last punishment. I start giving her slow strokes. "Mateo," she whines at me.

I don't respond but chuckle at her, almost pouting. I rub her clit while continuing my slow pace. "Hm, I wonder if I should let you cum or should I tease you some more."

Emilia shakes her head, "Please, Mateo. I need to cum." She is begging me with more than her words, her lip is stuck out, and her eyes are holding mine, begging me to let her get what she wants.

I decide I would bring her to the edge one more time. I keep circling her clit and quicken my pace. She throws her head back after the third thrust and lets out a loud moan that, if the room wasn't soundproofed, the whole mansion and everyone inside would have known. It doesn't take her long to start climbing to her release, but I pull out before she can finish. I have her spin around and face the wall.

"Bend over, spread those legs, and hands on the wall." She does what I ask. I watch as her ass bounces when she moves her feet apart. I smack it and watch it bounce again. I line myself up and sink back inside of her. I grab her wet hair with one hand and angle her head to the side so I can kiss the sweet spot behind her ear. And the other holds onto her hips because I am going to fuck her, so she won't be able to walk later.

I thrust into her fast. We both are so wound up from me teasing and edging Emilia it won't take long until we both cum. As I predicted, she is already squeezing me. "Let go," I demand to her in her ear. My hand that was on her hip moves to her clit and rubs it.

"MATEO!" she screams out as she wraps herself tightly around my cock.

It doesn't take me long to find myself overtaken with pleasure. "Fuck, Emilia." I keep thrusting in and out of her a few more times.

I lean my head in between her shoulders and try to catch my breath. I leave a gentle kiss on her back. "Are you okay?" I ask her as I remove my cock from her pussy. I slowly stand up and turn her to me; she stumbles a bit. I wrap my arms around her and bring her to my chest.

"Yes, except I can't stand on my legs," she grumbles, and I chuckle. I grab the shampoo and pour some into my hand to wash her hair. She closes her eyes as I massage her head while washing her hair.

"Feel good?" I ask, while I rinse her hair. She nods, and I kiss her forehead.

"I love you beyond my last breath," she tells me.

"And I love you beyond my last breath." I help her finish washing, and then I wash. I love doing this for her because she is such a stubborn, and independent woman that she usually refuses help. During this time, we aren't parents or the bosses of our mafia. We are husband and wife who are being vulnerable and are taking care of each other.

After we dry off, we get dressed and head downstairs to join everyone else to eat. While we are eating, I smile as I watch how sensitive and caring she is towards Kayleigh; Emilia has been where Kayleigh is and understands how she is feeling. I hear Emilia say softly to Kayleigh, "Remember I am here if you need anything." Kayleigh smiles and quietly whispers a thank you.

She truly amazes me; Peter is sitting next to me and is also watching Emilia, who is now being sassy with Oscar. "You are a lucky man, Mateo."

I nod at him and say, "Luck doesn't even come close to describing it."

"I have seen a lot in my old age but, never take for granted a woman who loves you and your family but also can juggle wearing multiple hats."

"Yeah, women are the ones who make our houses into homes."

"You are right but, honestly, she was definitely over working herself regardless of how much or who bugged her. I was getting extremely worried about her."

"When things start to fall apart around her, she will do anything to put everything back together. Regardless of what it does to her but if everyone around her is happy and healthy she will continue to sacrifice for them. I just can't wait to see Alessia, I miss her." I say smiling thinking about Emilia's mini me, my princess who has me wrapped around her pinky.

"Hopefully next time we see each other it will be under better circumstances, and I can meet your daughter and maybe some more on the way."

I just give him a knowing smile and say, "Once we have the Russian's dealt with, we want to try for a bigger family. Emilia is dead set on waiting until after the Russian Mafia are nothing but dust. She is afraid if she is kidnapped, another child will be in the same kind of situation Alessia was in. And as much as I want to see her stomach round with my child, I agree with her."

"That is completely understandable." After that, we continue to eat as everyone makes small talk.

After we eat, I decided Emilia and I would enjoy a day together going through everything she has been doing the past month to track down Alexei. When we get into the office, I have her sit on my lap. What Emilia has shown me is impressive, she has gone through all of Alexei's business partners and ruled out if they were helping him. She has a list of all the different companies, financial records, and other associates. She also has a list of people and companies she still must check out.

We each take a few names and work quietly in the office together. She looks absolutely adorable with her knees up to her chest, with her chin propped on her kneecaps sitting in her chair as she is working on her laptop. She hears me chuckling and looks up from her laptop, "What are you laughing at?"

"You just look absolutely adorable sitting there like that." She rolls her eyes.

"Focus, lover boy," she says and goes back to focusing on her laptop.

"By the way, we leave tonight to go get my baby because I can't wait another day to see my princess." That puts a huge smile on her face.

"I missed my baby too." After that we stayed focus because we both know once we get to the Garcia's mansion, we won't get anything done because we both are going to want to spend time with Alessia.

FORTY
EMILIA

After a few hours of working together, we had a few names that we went through. Only one was suspicious, and we sent that name to Fabio to look more into. We got all of our stuff packed up and had it sitting on the bed to be loaded up in the cars so we could leave. I wanted to have a proper goodbye and all of the O'Sullivan's came to the door.

I gave the twin sisters a quick goodbye, they were sweet girls, but we didn't spend much time together, since they were teenagers and were busy. The sons all hugged me goodbye, and they all showed how much they appreciated what I did for Kayleigh.

When I get to Kayleigh, she sobs in my arms when I hug her goodbye. "I don't know how to thank you."

I pull back from the hug and wipe her eyes and say to her, "Live and smile again. Don't let what he did and almost did to you steal you of your happiness."

"But what if I can't?" I smile at her.

"You will maybe not today, maybe not tomorrow, but one day you will. Remember, you have family who loves you, and you can always call me if you need me. Okay?" I give her one last hug and say my goodbyes to Grace and Peter.

"Thank you, Emilia, for everything you did. And next time we see each other hopefully it will be a joyous occasion," Peter says to me as he gives me a tight hug.

"Of course, Peter. Thank you for having me stay here this past month." Mateo, Marcello, and I all walk out to the cars and head off to the airport to go see my baby.

The plane ride was quiet and peaceful. I called Jose to tell him we were on our way to Spain but asked him not to tell Alessia we were coming. We wanted to surprise her. Santiago, Jose's second in command, picked us up at the airport. He filled us in on how she has been taking lots of dance classes, still improving in therapy, and using any free time she has to be out at the barn. I chuckle at my little barn brat, who is just like me, when I was her age.

Our bags are grabbed, and we go to find Alessia. She is in the kitchen with Esmeralda and Nonna baking, I was going to watch her and wait, but Mateo was too eager to wait.

"What is my little baker making?" he questions her. She turns and sees Mateo. She has the biggest smile on her face, and she runs to him. Mateo bends down and opens his arms and picks her up. She wraps herself around his body, and her face is in his neck, crying.

"Papa, you're not dead."

"Shh, my princess. I am here. I told you Papa would be here to watch you grow up. I am so sorry I was gone for so long," he tells her as he rubs his hand up and down her back. She hugs him tighter; I have to wipe my eyes from relief at being with her again and having our family back together. It was so painful not to know where Mateo was and being away from Alessia for so long.

"Mama," she says, and I look at Alessia who is wanting me to hold her.

I grab my baby from her Papa's arms. "I missed you, Mama."

I kiss her cheek. "I missed you too, baby girl. Where you a good girl?" I put her on her feet, and she nods her head.

"Yeah, Mama. I had dance class, I went to speech therapy, and I was at the barn a lot."

"Wow, it sounds like you were one busy little girl." She grabs my hand, and we walk over to where Nonna is peppering kisses all over Mateo's face. I chuckle at his face. I decide I will be a nice wife and save him.

"Hi, Nonna."

She looks over at me and she is glaring at me. "You were not taking care of yourself you are too skinny."

I hug her and say, "I missed you too, Nonna."

"Don't you try that sweetness on me! You need to be healthy, so I can have more grandbabies to spoil," she says, but hugs me even tighter. I pull away from Nonna when I feel something hit the back of my head. I turn around and Esmeralda has a flip-flop in her hand.

"Geez what a nice welcome I get from you as well, Esmeralda."

She glares at me and shakes her flip-flop at me. "You stupid girl. If you don't start taking care of yourself, I am going to smack some sense into you."

"I will do better. Happy?" I ask these two ladies; they both shake their heads.

"Don't worry, I will make sure she is eating better and gets back to the weight she was," Mateo tells them as he comes stands next to me and wraps an arm around my waist. They both smile at him being the doting husband. Geez, I didn't think I had lost that much weight.

Alessia has already grabbed onto Marcello and was talking to him, about everything she has been doing. As I have said before, Marcello is the perfect guard for her. He will be another amazing uncle.

"BITCH!" I hear, and I see Theo coming into the room. I laugh and hug him. "Girl there must be something in the water."

I throw my head back, laughing. "I know! I thought the same thing when I was down here. The asses on the men down here." I fan my hand in front of my face because they are some very hot-looking men around here.

"Emilia," I hear my name being said in a warning tone. I turn around and see my husband glaring at me.

I put on my innocent smile, "Yes, darling?"

He continues to glare at me, "That innocent look doesn't work after what I saw when I went to greet you at the O'Sullivan's in the basement and you better behave, or you won't be able to walk tomorrow."

He then turns to Esmeralda, "How did her Papa deal with her?"

Esmeralda pats his shoulder and laughs, "He barely did, and her Mama was just as bad as she was. But he also had her older brother follow her around like a hawk and scare all the guys off. You better hope Alessia will not be as wild as her mother or grandmother."

He groans, "So there is no help for my feisty wife?" She shakes her head no at him. "Well, Alessia will be home-schooled, so we can keep all the horny teenage boys away from her."

I smirk, "If she is anything like me, good luck with that idea. The apple doesn't fall from the tree. Plus, we will raise her to be smart but also an independent woman."

"Yes, we will, but I am hoping she won't give me as many migraines as you do, Emilia." he says, and I just shrug my shoulders.

"Oh, this is nothing compared to the hell I gave Papa. I fought him about clothes, going out with Theo, and partying with boys. But don't worry, we have years for that," I say, laughing. Mateo runs his hand through his hair and groans.

Nonno and Jose come into the kitchen and greet us all. While we are all talking, Alessia calls Mateo. "Papa, can you take the cake out of the oven, please?" He gets up and carefully takes it out of the oven and sits on the stove top to cool off.

"So, what kind of cake did you make Alessia?" Jose asks her.

"Banana chocolate chip cake."

"Sounds yummy, baby girl," I say, and kiss the top of her head as I get the plates down for everyone. We all enjoy the dessert Alessia made. That night Alessia insists that she can put herself to bed. We wish her sweet dreams and go to the room next to hers and fall asleep ourselves.

FORTY-ONE
IRINA

      I lay on the dirty floor of the cell in absolute agony after pleasuring all of the soldiers here at the mansion a week ago. I was treated and then thrown into this cold and dark cell. I get a slice of moldy bread and murky water once a day. I know I won't get any visitors until Alexei decides I "deserve" any visitors. I was already weak from serving out my punishment for telling Alexei I would not train Alessia to be a wife to Boris.

      I hate Boris; he is a sick asshole. He once tried to get handsy with Dimitri, but I put a stop to that. Granted, that earned me fifty slashes, but it saved Dimitri from that pedophile's hands, so it was worth it. I will do whatever it takes to prevent any child or woman from being at Boris' mercy. The fact that my brother sold his daughter to him is absolutely disgusting. I knew Seth was a monster, but to do that to his daughter is absolutely sickening, and if I ever get the chance, I will kill him myself. Seth is so greedy for money he loses what values he has left. Granted, he really never had values as a child anyway. My brother is a self-absorbed asshole. We didn't talk for over ten years because of his behavior, and he only came back into my life when he realized I was married to a rich man.

      I laugh to myself that Seth finally learned how low on the totem pole I am around here. I am pretty sure if I died, Alexei would leave my corpse to rot where I lay. Seth always thought he had some leverage on Alexei because of me. If anything, Alexei was using the favors from my brother against me, so in the end, I ended up paying the punishment.

      I honestly don't know why he married me. Yes, I was pregnant with Dimitri, but Dimitri isn't his. I am a spy for the Italian Mafia, and I am a soldier for them. Honestly, I have no idea if the mission is still going on, but I have no way to contact them since Alexei took my phone away from me. He has complete control of everything I do, from what I eat to what I wear. It is all in Alexei's control, and I absolutely hate it. If he lets me wear clothes, it is all very provocative, and I never wear stuff this low cut or tight. Sure, I would wear sexy clothes, but I never looked like I was desperate for dick. Dimitri is Damiano's son. We were constantly sleeping together, and we were exclusive with each other. I was pretending to be a party girl and got information from Alexei, who I was working for, but when Maxim found out I was pregnant, I was forced to marry Alexei by his father. Even though I kept saying I wasn't sure who the father was, he dismissed me and said I would marry Alexei and the child was Alexei's.

As soon as we got married, Alexei ignored me and put me in my own wing of the mansion with a maid. I was happy that he was leaving me alone, and the maid I had is Lilyana, but they called her Ana. We knew each other from our previous life, but we knew there were cameras. We couldn't risk being overheard, so we barely made conversation and gave each other small smiles, but she was someone who gave me comfort in this extremely fucked up situation. I really missed everyone back home and was extremely homesick, but even if I wanted to, I could never go back home. I had to think about keeping Dimitri safe. I knew if they found out the truth, they would kill him in the first place. When I gave birth to Dimitri, I was in the hospital wing, and Ana was by my side the whole time. I kept getting looks of pity and sympathy from all the staff that Alexei was not with me. I was honestly glad he was not in the room with me, especially after the beating he gave me after his father informed him he was marrying me because he got me pregnant. He tried to kill Dimitri and me that day, and if it wasn't for his underboss, I would have been killed. I was afraid of what he would do if he found out Dimitri wasn't his. Either Alexei is a complete idiot or knows Dimitri isn't his but doesn't care. I think he doesn't know because he has only laid eyes on him four times his whole life, and he is five years old. I try not to lose hope that one day we will make it out of here alive, but I don't think I will. Have they stopped looking for me? Do they think I have betrayed them?

    I close my eyes and think of how much Damiano would have loved Dimitri and how Dimitri wouldn't have been stuck in our small room all day and all night. He would interact with other kids his age. But most importantly, he would feel the love of a family even if Damiano and me never got into a relationship. I know we both would love him endlessly.

    I worry that I will be killed by Alexei or one of his men. Then Dimitri will be on his own with these sadistic men. I hope that never happens, because I don't want my baby to turn out like them. He is at such an impressionable age, that if Ana or I wasn't around, he could be molded into one of them. I am trying to raise him to be a gentleman like his real father, but our living situation makes that hard. When Dimitri was about two, Elena decided we didn't need a whole wing. So now we are both stuck in a room that is a cleaning closet that can lock from the outside. His mistress, Elena, has locked us in our room many times and then orders everyone away from us. Between me and Ana, we keep snacks hidden in our room so when that happens Dimitri won't go hungry.

    I think back to the day I met Damiano. He was having a big celebration for the new Gentleman's Club he had opened. I went with a group of my friends, and I will have to admit, the ladies who were dancing were sexy. When I went up to the bar, the bartender was relentlessly agonizing me for being gay because I was at a strip club. I was trying to be polite and tell him I am not, but he needed to mind his business. He finally pissed me off enough that I threw my drink all over him. He was about to hit me. That is when Damiano showed up. I thought I was going to get kicked out. I didn't know that he had already been watching the situation between the two of us. He fired the bartender and after that, we had drinks and talked for hours. By the time the club was closing, we were both drunk and we stumbled into a cab. We got to his penthouse; he spent no time stripping us down bare. I was beyond satisfied once he was done with my body. We went all night and even into the next morning. I was so deliciously sore from all the different positions he had me in. That man knew what he was doing when he played with my body. I have no idea if it was that night or one of the other times we met when Dimitri was conceived. We were not together long, but I felt like we had a true connection. I miss him, my friends, and my old life. One day I promise to get Dimitri out of here. And we both will be called by our real names Kelly Mae and Dante Mae (Morelli if his father wants him to). I gave him a Russian name to help protect him from Alexei's wrath. I was hoping that if he had a Russian name, it would be one less reason; he would question who Dimitri's father is.

MATEO

The next morning, I am dressed in my suit. I am sitting at the temporary office at the Garcia's mansion going through what Emilia found while I was kidnapped. I have to say I am really impressed; she really has been digging to find where they could be hiding. I keep reading through all her notes about all of his business partners and his other businesses.

I get a text on my phone from Chandler, who is one of my spies who is on the inside of the Russian Mafia. I have been trying for years to get Kelly Mae back. She was working as a dancer at one of his clubs, then not even a month later, she was married to Alexei. Kelly wouldn't jump into a marriage like that, but after she had her baby, she barely made any public appearances. Alexei has his mistress Elena out in the spotlight. They always say Elena is just a friend, but anyone with a friend can figure out that she is his mistress.

Chandler: Rumors going around that the men use Kelly for their sexual and physical pleasure. No word on the kid, but I still have not been to the main mansion.

Mateo: Ok, thanks for the update. Keep working on getting in on the inside.

Chandler: Will do, Boss.

I run my fingers through my hair. I hope the rumors aren't true, but with Alexei they are most likely true. He is just as sadistic as his father, Maxim. Maxim abused his wife terribly. The mission we sent her on was known as angel face, which was one of Lilyana's nicknames. We were looking for more information so we could destroy his empire. Kelly was great at getting us information; granted, it was all small details, but we knew it would take time to get more useful information. After all, he is the Boss of the Russian Mafia. He isn't going to blab details about it to some dancer he hooks up with. We wanted payback for killing Zia Anna, and Lilyana, but with no information from the inside, it was hard to move forward. Without Emilia realizing it, she helped us come closer to destroying their empire.

  Her connection with Alexei and his business with Boris helped us destroy about half of his brothels and kill many of his men. I wish I could be there to see his face when he heard they went up in flames or the police ambushed it. I darkly chuckle thinking about watching the torture that my cousins and uncle put the son of a bitch through. He was crying and begging for mercy at the first cut Vincenzo did to him, which was nothing. The man who physically and sexually abused my *mia Regina* for years can't handle being stabbed. They are keeping him alive because he is going to die at the hands of my Queen after I have my turn with him. He doesn't get to have an easy death after all the abuse he made Emilia go through and the fact that he has sexual fantasies about my daughter. He is going to be regretting that he breathed the same air as my girls. No one gets to hurt my girls in any way without being punished by me.

  I hear a throat being cleared, and I look to see my beautiful wife leaning her hip against the door. I go over to her, pick her up, and I sit her on my lap at the desk. She turns to me. "Are you okay? You look very deep in thought."

  I lightly kiss her lips, then tuck some hair behind her ear. "I am just worried *il mio amore*." I tell her.

"About?"

  I take a deep breath. "Well, about two years after Zia Anna, and Lilyana, were killed, we sent a girl undercover to get Alexei's attention. Well, she definitely gained his attention because within a month, she was married to him."

"Do you think she was forced?" she asks me.

  I nod my head, "Yes, because Alexei's father was alive during that time and his father is more sadistic than Alexei. His father multiple times reached out for a marriage between Alexei and Julietta, but I absolutely refused. I would not sell my sister to those bastards even if it was our last option. Julietta might be strong, but I know mentally she wouldn't be able to handle the abuse they would do to her."

  She is staring at the wall behind me, biting her lip, which I know means she is thinking. After about a minute, she turns to me. "Do you have any videos of them together in public?"

I nod and tell her. "I have the announcement they made about them being married and then announcing her pregnancy."

"PREGNANCY?" she yells at me and then smacks me on the back of my head.

"The hell, Emilia," I say, rubbing the back of my head, but she cuts me off.

"You dumbass, of course she was forced to marry that son of a bitch. Show me the announcement now." I pull the video up on my laptop and play it for her, we watch it one time all the way through. She scoots forward, almost sitting on my knees and pushes my hand off the mouse. Of course, I check out her plump ass as she is leaning forward to check out the video. Don't blame me, I am a man and my wife has a delicious ass.

"Would you quit perving at my ass?" she says without looking at me.

I grin at her and lean back "Nope, I will always look at how sexy my wife is. Plus, I have the perfect view of your ass, perched on my knee." And I continue to stare at her ass and start imagining having her bent over my knee and spanking that ass and watch it jiggle.

I get pulled out of my lusty thoughts when I hear Emilia cussing. "Holy mother… fucking shit."

I lean forward sitting my chin on her shoulder "What happened?" "

"Watch her hand that isn't next to Alexei." she tells me, and I watch as is signing letters.

"Wait, is she signing something?" I ask dumbfounded.

"Yep, I wrote it all out. Angel face forced Damiano baby."

"Fuck," I say into her shoulder.

"Oh yeah, definitely fuck." She says. "That means two of ours are being held hostage by that sadistic bastard."

"That's not all, one of my guys who is a spy says he has heard rumors of her being used sexually and physically by the men."

She shudders, having gone through that herself she knows the pain that Kelly must be going through. Since Kayleigh was assaulted and Emilia has talked to Kayleigh everyday if not multiple times a day, I know Emilia is struggling mentally. I let her have her moment to push through the memories.

I just rub her arm and kiss the side of her head. "We have to tell Damiano. He has a right to know." I nod at her; I decide this is a better conversation to have through video chat. So, I text him and tell him that I am calling him in a half hour.

"I told him I am calling him in a half an hour." She just turns around, so she is straddling me and snuggles into my neck. Her hands are gripping my shirt for life, I hold her tight against me. "What is it, Emilia?" I am not sure what is going through her mind.

She tries to keep her head in my neck, but I lean back and lift her head up with my fingers. "Talk to me baby. What is going on inside that head of yours?"

She looks at me with tears in her eyes. "I feel bad for what she must be going through. She was forced into a marriage with an evil bastard like Alexei. She is probably doing whatever she can to protect her child. And, no doubt, even though she doesn't regret doing what she has to do, the self-doubt and hating how dirty she feels after is happening. I know that pain so well, and I can't help but feel sorry for her."

I wipe away her tears, "You Mia Regina, are an angel. Even though you have gone through the pain and are still working on your own mental battles, you are more worried about everyone around you before yourself." I kiss her lips; she just gives me a small smile. We don't talk much, and she snuggles into my neck again. When she gets like this it is better for her to let it out, and not say anything. And that is exactly what I do, I rub her back and let her cry it out. Once she is better, she grabs a tissue off my desk attempting to clean her face off. Emilia mumbles a thanks to me. "Are you ready to tell Damiano?" I ask her and she nods.

I called him through Zoom, and he picked up on the second ring.

Damiano: Hello, Don and Donna. Donna, are you okay?

Emilia: Hello Damiano. I am okay, but I am afraid we have some bad news for you.

Before he can question her, I interrupt.

Mateo: Damiano do you remember Kelly Mae?

Damiano: Yes, Don. She went undercover with the Russians then married Alexei.

Mateo: Do you know her personally?

Damiano: I... Uh, we slept together a few times prior to her assignment. Why did something happen?

Mateo: Well, Emilia looked back to the announcement they made about them being married and her pregnancy announcement. Emilia noticed she was signing during it. And there's no easy way to say this, but Damiano, she was forced to marry Alexei and her child it's yours.

He gets up and punches the wall.

Damiano: *Cazzo sapevo che qualcosa non andava. Avrei dovuto dirle di non andare in quella missione, ma no, devevo esere orgoglioso stupido cazzo.*" (I fucking knew something wasn't right. I should have told her not to go on that mission but no I had to be a prideful stupid fucker.)

He was still pissed but I needed him to calm down.

Emilia: DAMIANO SIT YOUR ASS BACK DOWN.

Damiano: Sorry, Don and Donna.

Emilia: It's okay, Damiano. I know you are upset, and you have every right to be. But you need to know she isn't being treated right.

Damiano: Are you saying she is being r... raped?"

Emilia: Rumors that we have heard say yes, and also being beaten pretty bad.

Damiano: I am going to fucking kill him. Do you know anything about my child?

Mateo: Only thing we know is that he is a five-year-old boy named Dimitri.

Damiano: Will you please give me any updates about them regardless of how bad they are? Please?

Emilia: Of course, we will. Do you need anything?

Damiano: No thank you Donna. I just need to absorb that the woman who bewitched me is being raped and beaten probably daily and I have a little boy out there in Alexei's hands. I mostly need time to absorb all of this.

Mateo: Take your time. If you need time off from the club and to have Salvatore look after it, I will tell him you might be needing his help.

Damiano: Thank you.

Then he hangs up, I take a deep breath. I truly feel bad for Damiano, I don't want to imagine how I would feel if Emilia was in his hands, especially with Alessia there. I call Salvatore and tell him about what happened and tell him to inform Vincenzo and Adriano but not of the other capos. Damiano needs this time to absorb all of this information, his whole world just got flipped upside down. But if anyone can help Damiano, it's Salvatore. Damiano helped Salvatore when he was grieving Lilyana.

FORTY-TWO
DAMIANO

   I lean back in my chair and run my hands through my hair. I can't believe we missed the signs that *la mia stella splendente" (my shining star)* was forced to marry that worthless fucker and our son is there with him. Does he refer to Alexei as his Papa? Does he know I am his Papa? Is he being treated right? Is he being fed enough? All the questions run through my head, and I don't have any answers to them.

   I can feel my anger building up inside of me and I decide to leave my paperwork for tomorrow. I am not going to get anything done today. I jump on my motorcycle, a Ducati Superleggera V4 and decide to head to the gym to see if I can work out some of my anger. As soon as I turn the key, I am revving my bike and speeding off I try to relax. Usually, I am not reckless on my bike but today I am letting my emotions drive me. I don't care that I am cutting people off or that they are honking and cursing me as I weave in and out cars. I quickly park my bike and storm past the receptionist who has been attempting to seduce me. Usually, I would entertain her games but fuck I can't stomach the thought of being friendly with any female now.

   I don't bother wrapping my hands and start to take everything out on the punching bag. I remember after I slept with Kelly that first night and how, after she slept, I stole her number out of her phone because I was so mesmerized by her. It wasn't just the sex, granted, that was mind blowing. It was the way she carried herself and her disposition. She was strong and never let anyone take advantage of her, she showed the bartender to respect her. She also knew how to be respectful because when Mateo and his cousins came around, she was so polite and never threw herself at them and called them by their correct title. I had no idea she was one of the new assassins until Mateo mentioned it. And God don't even get me started on how smart she was, as she talked business with other men.

   By the end of the night, we were drunk but we were having a great time. Cracking jokes and listening to her laugh. I acted like a lovesick puppy, but Kelly had me under her spell. After that, we kept meeting up so we could hang out but always lead to us fucking, which I never complained about. Kelly had the body of a goddess and a face of an angel with her hazel eyes and dirty blond hair.

   I had no idea someone was talking to me until I saw someone grab the punching bag. "Fuck off and let me be. I grunt out and go to grab the bag, but I see Salvatore De Luca is the one holding the bag. Mother fucker. I didn't want to deal with anyone right now.

"Yeah, you know that isn't gonna happen." I ignore him, turn my back on him and go get my water, I flinch when I go to wrap my hand around the bottle. I gulp half of the water down and place it back down. Of course, the relentless fucker is following me, if he wasn't my friend I would turn around and punch him in his face. "That is why you are supposed to wrap your hands before you decide to brutally attack the punching bag."

I spin around and glare at him. "I am not in the mood for your shit, Salvatore."

"Too bad. You are stuck with me until you simmer some of this anger down, so you don't do anything stupid." I chuckle at the memory of him being stuck in an underground fight after Lilyana passed away. Salvatore was going down a slippery slope fast. He was either illegally racing his bike or fighting in the underground fights, hell sometimes he did both the same night. Some days I could talk him out of it but other times I would just follow him around to stop him from getting into too much trouble. Especially since Abramo was still Don then, and I can only imagine the punishment Salvatore would have gotten if he got caught. Abramo would not have cared that it was his nephew, hell he would have made an example out of him; god knows he did it to Mateo.

He throws a set of wraps at me; I chuckle but still wrap my hands. Once that is done, I walk back over to the punching bag. Salvatore stands a bit to the side, so I won't hit him with the bag. He asks me. "What is eating you the most?"

"Guilt. I should have done something, both of them are at his mercy. And if he has figured out my son isn't his, what will he do to him? How bad is she being treated? I can't help but all of these questions are buzzing through my head."

"Why do you feel guilty? Were you the one who forced Kelly to marry Alexei? Or did you force all those men to hurt her? And we have no idea about the treatment of your son, but we will do everything to get them back."

I shake my head "Fuck no. I would never do that to Kelly or my son. I wish I knew sooner so they would be safe."

"Then why do you feel guilty?"

I stop punching the bag, letting it swing, and look at Salvatore. "I should've never let her leave. She was so damn persistent at proving herself worthy to Mateo, but fuck I wanted to keep her locked up so she couldn't get hurt. I know I sound like a bitch, but she bewitched me for any other woman. And I worry about my son. Is he calling that son of a bitch his father? Is Alexei abusing him?" He raised his eyebrow at me "Yes, I know I am just as bad as your brother about sleeping with woman but that was to attempt to move on. But fuck it didn't work."

He shakes his head "Once you love a woman, truly love a woman, you will never be the same. It has been years since my Lilyana died, but I can never look at another woman the same as she was and is still my whole world."

He walks over to me and slaps my back. "Now, you are gonna go home. Take a shower, have the rest of the day off but tomorrow we will start figuring out how to get Kelly and your son out of there safely and back where they belong," he tells me with a smirk, he turns to walk out but stops to look over his shoulder. "Oh, and don't be driving recklessly anymore, you're a father now. You won't be doing him any good six feet under."

I nod at him as he leaves the gym, grab my stuff, and head home. I get on my bike and whisper into the air. "I promise you Kelly, I will get you both home safe where you both belong. Just hold on a bit longer."

EMILIA

Two Months Later

I hate having to hide in this safe house. Yes, I understand why we are doing it, but we need to draw these fuckers out and us being hidden isn't gonna do that. I am ready to lure them out, kill the fuckers, and move on with our life. I decided to go convince my overprotective, pain-in-my-ass husband to agree with me. I knock on his office door; I hear him talking so I open the door enough so I can peek my head through, and I mouth to him, asking if this is a good time. He nods at me and points to the chair in front of his desk. Hmm, this actually might work better for me to do a bit of teasing before I can ask him.

I walk over to the chair, and I see him eye my outfit up and down. I am wearing yoga pants with a sports bra and a jacket zipped over it. I sit down and unzip my jacket, so my cleavage is showing, I look up at my husband. His eyes show his hunger and lust for me. I smirk when his hand is clenched in a fist on his desk. I keep teasing him by leaning forward a bit in my chair and biting my lip. Not even a minute later, I hear him tell whoever he was on the phone with that he would have to call them back. He hangs up and sets his cell phone down on the table. He looks at me with a mischievous smirk. He unties his tie and undo the cuffs of his sleeves, rolls up the sleeves of his white button up shirt. I gulp and remember I came with a goal and not to be distracted by my sexy husband.

"*La mia vixen* is there something you need?"

I bat my eyelashes at him innocently. "I have an idea I would like to share with you?"

He leans back in his chair and scoots his chair back. "Come over here and tell me about this idea you have *Mio caro*" he tells me as he motions me over with his index finger. I slowly walk over to him and sway my hips a bit knowing he is watching my every move. I go to try and sit at the edge of his desk but that sly man grabs me by my wrist and pulls me to him until I am in his lap. I glare at him; he chuckles at me. He kisses the inside of my wrist looking up into my eyes "Now, what is your idea you want to tell me?" I shudder at the look of his eyes, he looks like he wants to devour me again, not like we didn't have sex this morning in the shower.

"I say we use me as bait to lure the Russians out." His face quickly goes from wanting to devour me to anger. I try to look away, but he doesn't let that happen.

"Are you out of your fucking mind?" he seethes at me.

"No, I am not. It makes sense Mateo; they will see me and try to grab me."

His nostrils flare, "I am not willing to have them kidnap you. They know you are my weakness, and I can't handle knowing you are in their sadistic hands."

I almost roll my eyes, but I can understand why he is pissed. "I know that *il mio re* but if anyone has to be kidnapped I would rather it be me." He goes to open his mouth, but I put my finger to his lips "I know but I went through years of their abuse, and I can handle it. I do not want them getting their hands on anyone, especially not Alessia or Julietta."

I move my fingers off his lips, and he grumbles "I hate when you make sense."

I chuckle at him and try to give him a sweet kiss, but I should've known better with Mateo. He grabs my hips and pulls me so there isn't any space between us and deepens the kiss. He pushes his tongue in my mouth while he squeezes my ass, I moan into his mouth. I feel him smirk against me, he puts both of my hands behind my back and holds them there. I don't pay attention to what he is doing until I feel something being tied around my wrists, and I pull away from Mateo. I look over my shoulder and see the tie that was around his neck is now tied around my wrists.

"And why are my hands tied behind my back?" I ask him, arching my eyebrow. He smirks at me but not answering my question. "Mateo?" I call his name trying to get his attention. He continues to ignore me as he is kissing down my neck, but I attempt to stay in control.

"Mateo, I asked you why my hands are tied behind my back?" He chuckles, as he can hear the frustration in my tone but continues to kiss my neck.

I try to grind on him, and he smacks my ass hard "Quit being an impatient brat." I go to respond but he grazes his teeth against the shell of my ear. He chuckles as I shudder and lean into him, he whispers against my ear, "You need some kind of punishment for teasing me while I was on my phone call with a business partner."

He leans back and sits me on his desk, he reaches into the drawer in his desk and grabs a knife. "Hope you don't love this bra too much," he tells me as he cut the straps off my sports bra and then another cuts down the middle. I gasp at him; I want to be mad at him, but him going all dominate on me turns me on.

He stands up and sits me in his chair, he walks over to the door and locks it. Mateo walks back over to me while he undoes his belt. I cross my legs to try and temporarily soothe the ache between my legs. He is standing in front of me and smirks. "Does it excite you, *mia piccola vixen* that I am going to dominat this sexy little body?" I nod my head not trusting myself to talk. He lifts my head with his fingers under my chin. "You love using that mouth, use your words."

"Yes" I barely breathe out. He has his button undone and zipper down and is taking them off. He stands before me only in his black boxers which shows how excited he is.

He runs his hand slowly down my cheek to my throat and gently squeezes it, "Hmm now what should I do to you, maybe I should fuck that smart-ass mouth of yours?"

That makes me even wetter than I already was, if that was even possible, and I squeeze my thighs together. He has a mischievous smirk on his face, He uses his other and takes off his boxers. His very hard, erect cock is eye level with my face. I lick my lips. He puts his thumb on my bottom lip, opening my mouth a but until he can fit his thumb in my mouth. I waste no time sucking on his thumb. His eyes become more hooded with lust.

"*Questo e tutto, succhia il mio pollice come una brava ragazza.*" *(That's it, suck on my thumb like a good girl.)*

I decided to suck harder on his thumb which earns a groan from him. He releases my throat and slowly trails that hand down to one of my nipples and tweaks it between his fingers, I am squirming under his touch. He removes him thumb from my mouth with a pop, and he grabs his cock, runs it over my lips. I open my mouth wider for him and he inserts his cock in my mouth. He adds more of himself inside of my mouth until all of him is fully in my mouth.

"*Cazzo, Emilia. Avvolgi quelle labbra intorno al mio cazzo.*"*(Fuck Emilia. Wrap those lips around my cock.)* I do as he says, I wrap my lips around his cock and start to bob my head up and down on his cock, but he has other plans. He wraps a hand in my hair to control my head as he starts to thrust in and out of my throat. We keep eye contact the whole time as he fucks my throat. I love that he dominates my body but also will stop at any sign of distress. But I trust Mateo he would never hurt me. If anything he is too overprotective of me. I continue to suck his cock as he fucks my mouth, he starts to play with my boobs. He squeezes them and also plays with my nipples, making me moan around his cock.

"*Cazzo diavolo. Continua a farlo e non durerò a lungo.*" *(Fucking hell. Keep doing that and I am not gonna last long.)* He starts to thrust himself in and out of my mouth faster and I feel him twitch inside of my mouth. I know he is getting closer; I suck him harder. He shouts my name as he cums. I try to swallow all of it, but when some dribbles down from the side of my mouth, I use my tongue and lick it off.

"*Sei troppo sexy per il tuo bene.*" *(You are way too sexy for your own good.)* I smile at him. "*Ora è il mio turno di avere il mio dessert.*" *(Now it's my turn to have my dessert)* He lifts me up, so I am standing with my ass in front of his desk. He pulls my thong and leggings off my legs in one quick motion. Before I can respond, he is kneeling between my legs and his mouth is on my clit. I moan out and have my head tossed back. It doesn't matter how many times he has gone down on me; his tongue is fucking magical.

He isn't teasing me. I feel like he is going to pull as many orgasms out of me again as my punishment. Fuck, those are torture after a while. He distracts me from my thoughts when he bites down and then licks my clit. "*Fanculo, Matteo.*" I moan out. He chuckles against me, and the sound sends shivers all the way down my spine. He pumps two fingers in and out of me, and my legs start to shake. He holds me steady with his other hand so I don't fall into a puddle on the floor. "*Proprio lì Mateo. Non fermarti.*" *(Right there, Mateo. Don't stop.)* He doesn't respond except to finger me faster. Oh, fuck, when he inserts that magical tongue inside of me, I lose all of my control. I feel myself tighten around his tongue.

He stops, spins me around, and pushes my chest against his desk. He wastes no time and fucks me from behind. He grabs my hair with one hand, the other hand is holding onto my hip. I push myself back onto him matching his thrusts.

"*Una ragazza così avida che sei. Vuoi che ti fotta forte?*" *(Such a greedy girl you are. You want me to fuck you hard? Is that it?)*

I nod while whimpering out. "*Sì, Mateo. Vaffanculo, non trattenermi.*" *(Yes Mateo. Fuck me, don't hold back.)*

"*Tu vuoi duro, ti darò duro.*" *(You want hard, I will give you hard.)*

He pushes me further onto the desk and holy fuck, he fucks me. He gives me long and deep strokes, and his desk keeps inching forward with every thrust. I don't even bother to contain my moans of pleasure. He smacks my ass; he groans as my walls tighten around his cock.

"*Ti piace quando ti fotto la figa forte?*" *(You like when I fuck your pussy hard?)* I whimper out yes. He keeps at it with the deep and hard thrusts in me, I feel myself getting closer to orgasming.

"*Mateo, sto per sborrare.*" *(Mateo, I am gonna cum.)* He reaches around and puts his thumb on my clit. Within a minute I am screaming out his name as I cum all over his cock.

"*È giusto tesoro. Spremere il mio cazzo.*" *(That's right baby. Squeeze my cock.)* I fall limp the rest of the way on his desk, a few hard thrusts later he cums inside of me. Once he has come down from his high, he leans his head on my back and gives me gentle kisses from the middle of my back to my shoulders.

"Are you okay?" he gently asks me.

"Yeah, just been thoroughly fucked."

He chuckles at me, "Even having been fucked you still have a witty comment."

I shrug, "It's a gift."

"No worries one day I will fuck you so good that you won't have any smart-ass comment afterwards."

I laugh at him "Promises, promises." He stands up and smacks my ass. I turn my head and look over my shoulder and glare at him. "My ass is gonna have a permanent handprint on it from how many times you smack my ass." He chuckles as he grabs a tissue to clean us up. Once he does that, he unties my hands. He massages my wrists even though there aren't any marks and continues to kiss and massage up my arms all the way to my shoulders. When he gets up to my face, he gives me a sweet and gentle kiss which I respond to. He pulls away and helps me redress, I have to zip my jacket up since he decided to cut my bra off me. I sit on his desk while he redresses, once he is done, he pulls me into his lap as he sits in his chair.

"I will think about your plan, I just don't want anything to happen to you." I snuggle into his neck as he rubs his hand up and down my back.

"I know you don't. And that is one of the reasons I love you so much. You always make sure you keep us safe but we might have to take this risk so we can get rid of the damn Russians once and for all. One day Alessia is going to have to go to school." He shakes his head.

"Nope, she can have private tutors. No private school because she will be around boys, and I am not sending my princess away to an all-girl boarding school. I need my baby close." I roll my eyes and smack him on the chest.

"Mateo, you cannot keep her locked up away from boys her whole life." He smirks at me.

"I can try, or I get to shoot any boy who looks at her the wrong way."

"You are not going to be shooting boys."

"Yes, I can. No one will make my baby cry. Plus, I have a warehouse full of guns and bullets, so I can afford to waste a few hundred bullets on anyone who makes her upset."

I shake my head at him. "We can discuss this after the Russians are dealt with, Mr. Overprotective Father."

He smiles at me "Sure we can discuss it, but I am not changing my answer, my daughter will be protected." Geez, I hate to see what happens when she gets a boyfriend, I have a feeling me and Julietta are gonna have to help sneak her out so she can go on a date.

"Whatever you say Mateo."

FORTY-THREE
MATEO

    I came back to the office after I carried a very satisfied but exhausted Emilia back to our bedroom. Good thing it was after dinner, otherwise she would have heard comments from Theo. Not sure which one is more immature Vincenzo or Theo. Theo loves to rile my feisty tigress up.

    I chuckle to myself thinking about how many times I have had to save him from Emilia or Alessia coming to get me to deal with Emilia when the two go at it. You would think they are siblings not friends the way the fight. And my wife plays dirty and Theo doesn't stand a chance.

    I love seeing her so happy and carefree, she deserves to be able to act a bit immature at times. But she also can act like the Queen she is when she needs to, especially when she tortures people who have wronged our family. She is so sexy when she taunts them and how precise she is when she uses a knife. Emilia definitely loves her knives, especially the ones she makes. I can tell who her mentor was, Esmeralda is very eccentric about her torture techniques. As much as I cringe about how they torture especially the men, her teachings made Emilia stronger.

    I lean on my elbows on my desk and put in my hands. I know what Emilia said was right about luring out the Russians but doesn't mean I want to put my wife in direct danger. I can feel the headache coming on from thinking of another solution that can keep my family hidden behind a locked door. I really want to avoid putting my wife in Alexei's hands. I was so engrossed in my thoughts that I didn't hear Nonno enter my office.

    "Burning the midnight oil, son?" I look up at my grandfather as he sits in the chair in front of my desk and give him a knowing but exhausted smile.

    "Always, Nonno." He chuckles and shakes his head.

    "Don't miss that part of the job. Looks like something is eating at you. Want to share?" That is the thing about Nonno that I respect. He will point out when you need help but won't force you to accept his help.

    "Yeah, Emilia wants to use herself as bait to make the Russians come out of hiding. In her words she can handle what they might do to her instead of the other women in the family. Which I am not doubting but the thought of her being in their hands makes me see red. It also makes me absolutely petrified because if something happens to her, I will be absolutely heartbroken, and I don't know if I am able to raise Alessia on my own. Emilia is raising her to be an amazing girl. I don't know if I could do it."

"You are right Emilia has done a phenomenal job raising Alessia despite all the obstacles thrown at her. But one thing is clear how much you love those girls. If you, didn't you wouldn't be up so late worrying about what could happen to them if Emilia is kidnapped." He pauses for a second "You are stronger than you realize. You push your past away or ignore it. Don't forget how your father tried to break you but you ended up becoming stronger." I grimace thinking about the shit my father put me through.

Flashback to 17-year-old Mateo

I was hanging by my wrists from the ceiling only down to my boxers. My body was scattered with burns and whip marks all because I killed one of my dad's precious guards who had gotten handsy with Julietta. When father saw that I shot the bastard., he was furious that I killed one of his men and not the fact that someone had tried to rape his daughter. I knew he was a bastard, but he took it to a whole new level.

I was dragged back into my thoughts when I felt the cow prodder was pushed against my arm. I bite the inside of my mouth; I refuse to give the son of a bitch any gratification that he is hurting me.

"Dai ragazzo, cedi e tutto questo si fermerà." (Come on boy, just give in and all this will stop.)

I looked back up at him and just gave him a blank look "Non ti darò mai la posizione di Julietta." (I will never give Julietta's location to you.) That's right after I shot the bastard, I sent Julietta to my grandparents and had them take her to one of the safe houses, but it is one I bought that no one knew about until now. Perché difendere quella puttana? Le donne sono usa e getta. Hanno lo scopo di compiacerci e darci eredi. Non hanno altro uso." (Why defend that whore? Women are disposable. They are meant to please us and give us heirs. They have no other use.)

I shake my head "Sei davvero un patetico figlio di puttana, vero?" (You really are a pathetic son of a bitch, aren't you?) You see the anger rolling off him in waves.

"Bene, vuoi farlo nel modo più duro, quindi sia." (Fine you want to do it the hard way so be it.) He then goes and grabs a knife and starts carving the word useless in my shoulder. I grunt out in pain every time he would dig the knife a little deeper, he would laugh enjoying my pain. After he finished, he decided to rub salt in the wound, I bite my lip hard enough for it to start bleeding. He came up and patted my cheek with his bloody hand. "Sei ancora un figlio giovane e ingenuo. Un giorno imparerai come gli uomini governano il mondo e le donne sono destinate a seguire i nostri ordinal." (You are still a young and naive son. One day you will learn how men rule the world and women are meant to follow our orders.)

Back to Present

He was pissed he never knew where she was for a year until Julietta was ready to be around our father again. When she finally saw him, our stepmother slapped her across her face but by this time, I had already become Don and I had my soldiers drag her worthless ass down to the basement. When the soldiers had grabbed Eleanor, they were not exactly gentle with her. I had changed the way of loyalty to the way it was when Nonno was Don, and that is that you protect family. Eleanor might be my father's wife, but she was never our mother, she never tried to be. All she cared about was the money attached to my father's name. A whore like that will never change and that is one of the many reasons why I never took Zaria as my wife. I knew she was a money hungry slut, and I wanted no part of that.

I looked back up at Nonno and said, "I know I just remember your anger and Nonna devastation when you found me in the basement."

He grits his teeth "I was so close to killing him that day, but I am glad we forced his hand when you were eighteen to have him hand you over the title." He shakes his head laughing at the memory "Who knew your father would easily step down for two billion dollars. He is an idiot. If he would have stayed as Don, he could have had more money for that gold digger. He has been complaining of her spending too much money, she was going to bankrupt him."

I smirk. "Well, it would have been fun to watch him go from king of the underworld of Italy to homeless. Cause I know neither of us would have helped him out and you know Adriano wouldn't help him especially the way Adriano beat his ass after he recovered from your beating and the best part was, he did it in front of all of his men."

Nonno was laughing so hard he was wiping away tears off his face. After a minute he had calmed down and got a serious look on his face. "I know you want to keep all the women locked up behind a key but that won't work for Emilia. She is a very strong woman; most women would be afraid to be around any man after all the abuse she went through but look at her. Within under a year and a half she has conquered most of her fears. She can order the men around when she needs to, she is respected because she respects them, she is an amazing mother, daughter, granddaughter, sister, friend, and wife.

"You don't have me fooled about what you two are doing, disappearing for hours at a time to "nap" I was young once."

I shrug with a smirk, "I never said you were a fool old man, but we can't exactly tell my daughter I was fucking her mom."

He rolls his eyes. "One day, she will figure it out and she will react the same way all of you do when I mention that your grandmother and I do anything together."

I gag, "Come on, Nonno, I don't want that image in my head. You won't taint the image I have of her being a pure angel unless she has that wooden spoon in her hand."

"Oh, your grandmother is anything but an angel."

"No, nope, not hearing any of this," I say cutting him off.

I rolled my eyes at him knowing the old man did it on purpose, since he is holding his stomach laughing at my reaction. "But I hope you realize when this war is over, Nonna is gonna start bugging you both for more grandbabies to spoil."

"I have no problem with that, but I will wait until Emilia is ready." I want to say more about how she is petrified that her body won't be able to get pregnant again after all of the abuse she went through and is afraid of disappointing everyone. My heart breaks thinking of her breaking down in tears about it a couple of weeks ago. She hasn't told anyone but me and Theo, but her PTSD has been bothering her and she constantly is soft doubting herself and her worth.

He nods his head at me in understanding but doesn't comment about it. "Do you want my opinion?" He asks me and I nod at him. "I say we all move back to the other mansion; they will hear that it is busy again and that we have moved back. You don't have to put her out in public, so it will help drag the Russians out and keep her safe. And after some time, if that doesn't work, we can consider her idea. We both know you have increased security around the family, plus you have the dogs trained in identifying bombs, and they can live at the mansion with us."

I take a sip of my whiskey as I think about it. "That is actually not a bad idea. We'll leave in a week. That way, it gives me time to have everything ready. I want this move to go flawlessly, and I also need to explain this to Alessia since she is still very scared which is why it is time to end these Russians once and for all."

He nods, "I won't say anything so you can break it to everyone." He smiles as he walks out of my office, and as he reaches the door, he stops. "Oh, and Mateo," he says.

"Yes, Nonno"

"Get to bed, you look like shit."

"Geez, thanks, old man," I say, laughing as he flips me off, walking out of my office.

I chuckle at him flipping me off. I owe that man so much. He helped raise me and Julietta. And for the first year I was Boss he helped me turn it back the way it was before my father took over. We had to "clean house" because too many refused to be loyal to me but stayed loyal to my sadistic father.

I decide to listen to him and go to bed since it is two in the morning and tomorrow, we are having a family day just the three of us. I walk out of my office and nod as I pass all of my guards on the way to my room. I first stop at Alessia's room and quietly open the door and see her hugging her wolf stuffed animal. I had Vincenzo search to find a replacement for her after the mansion was destroyed. Let me say it had been worth listening to him bitch about doing it. Not that he minded doing it for Alessia, but he said, him walking in and out of different kid shops made him lose his manly vibe but he melted when he saw how happy she was getting her wolf back. Her smile on her face and the big hug made me want to do anything and everything to keep her happy. I smile as I walk over to her and tuck the blankets back around her, she is just a wiggle worm in her sleep but holds onto "Wolfie" the whole time. "*Sogni d'oro ti amo principessa.*" (*Sweet dreams I love you Princess.*) I say to her as I kiss her forehead, she smiles in her sleep as she snuggles into her pillow.

I quietly walk out of her room and into our room. I chuckle at how adorable my wife is asleep with her head on my pillow, she always seeks me out in her sleep and if I am not there my pillow becomes my replacement. Especially after I was kidnapped, I feel guilty I have been coming to bed so late since we have been back here, but Emilia never complains. I have a feeling part of the reason she thought of her plan is also to make me get some sleep because she has noticed how exhausted I have been recently to the point she locked me in our room without my phone or laptop so I would take a nap last week. Stubborn vixen didn't realize her actions would get her a punishment from me, not that I mind.

I chuckle at the memory of spanking her ass, then bending her over the bed and sinking my cock into her wet and needy pussy. I walk into our closet, changing from my suit to gray sweatpants. My sexy wife is wearing one of my shirts, and I can see the sexy ass blue thong she is wearing, since the shirt has rolled up a bit. When I get into the bed next to her. I slide in next to her, wrap my arms around her and bring her to my chest. "Hmm, Mateo," she says sleepily.

"Shh, go back to sleep; sorry to wake you, *Tesoro.*" She doesn't say anything else as she snuggles into my chest. I close my eyes as I kiss her head, and before I know it, I fall asleep with her.

The next morning, I am woken up by little hands on my face and someone whispering "Papa?" I open my eyes and see my princess smiling at me.

"Good morning, baby," I say to her as she snuggles into my chest.

"Good morning, Papa. Do you have to work today?" She asks me to look up from my chest that she is snuggled up against.

"No, I figured we could have a family day today. You, me, and Mama." She has a huge smile across her face and jumps off the bed, pulling on my hand and trying to drag me out of bed. I shake my head laughing at how excited she is.

"Hold on Alessia, Papa needs to put a shirt on." I pick her up and sit her on my bed, then I quickly walk into my closet, grab a white shirt, and put it on. I quickly walk into the bathroom, do my business, and walk out to see Alessia waiting for me. As soon as she sees me, she grabs my hand and trying again to pull me out of the room, I get a better idea, I grab her and give her a piggyback ride to the kitchen.

She giggles as soon as she is on my back, she wraps her arms around my neck, and I hold onto her legs. As we head down to the kitchen we spin, jump, and run to the kitchen. You can hear our laughs through the whole house. Do I care if I woke anyone up? Nope not at all because I know soon enough, she will not want to do these silly things with me, so I am soaking them up.

"Look at my two troublemakers," Emilia says to me as I place Alessia on the ground. I put my hand on my heart and mock a look of hurt across my face. I look at Alessia, who is pretending to look hurt as well.

"Us troublemakers. Never Mama, maybe you are just old." Alessia says.

Emilia has a glint in her eyes. "Old, you say? Well, little girl, you better run because this old lady is about to get you." Alessia shrieks and takes off down the hallway almost running into Theo.

He walks the rest of the way into the kitchen and asks, "What was that about?"

"Alessia teased Emilia about being old." I say, laughing, and he laughs along with me. I walk over and pour my coffee while I wait for the girls to come back. I hear Alessia giggle; Emilia must have caught her. Emilia and Alessia walk, and I shake my head as I grab Emilia's wrist.

I spin her around and give her a light kiss on her lips. "Good morning, beautiful," I say to her and she gives me a small smile as we hold hands walking into the dining room for breakfast. She is trying to hide her blush from me. I think it is funny that the same vixen who has the same libido as me always blushes from any sweet gesture I give her. I pull back both of my girls' chairs before I settle into my chair. The maids begin to serve our food as I greet my grandparents. It is just my grandparents, Theo, Emilia, Alessia, and myself since the Garcia's are all busy today.

I decided to break the news to everyone while we were all eating together. "So, I have an announcement to make." Emilia looks over at me with a questioning look; I give her hand a squeeze as I continue. "In a week we will be headed back to our mansion," I look over at Alessia and see her looking down playing with the hem of her shirt. I lift her head and have her look me in the eyes. "Alessia, I know you are scared, but I promise you. You will be safe. I will never let anyone hurt my princess, okay." She nods even though I can see the wheels turning behind those big doe eyes. "Plus, I know some people who miss you and can't wait to see you." She looks confused. "Zia Julietta, Zio Salvatore,

Zio Vincenzo, and Zio Zio." That earns me a big smile. "Eat, Princess. The sooner you eat the sooner we can have a family day," I tell her.

Emilia pipes in, "Family day?"

I nod at her. "Yes, it has been a while since we had a family day, just the three of us. Plus, I know as soon as we get to the mansion, I will be busier. So, I am taking today to enjoy being together." She leans over and gives me a kiss on my cheek and starts eating her breakfast.

I look over at my grandparents and ask in French so Alessia doesn't know what we are saying. She is just like her Mama and very quick to pick up a new language fast. She has been learning Italian and loves to talk to me in Italian. *"Qualcuno di voi ha domande?"* (Do either of you have any questions?)

Nonno shakes his head, but Nonna says, *"No, mi fido di te, ragazzo mio."* (Nope I trust you, my boy.) I hear someone huff out in annoyance and I see Alessia pouting.

"I need to learn more languages, so I know what you are saying."

I chuckled at her. "That is why I said it in French so you, Miss Nosy, didn't know what we were saying."

She pouts at me. "One day, Papa I will know every language in the world, and you can't hide your secrets from me," she tells me while attempting to glare at me.

I point my fork to her plate. "Then you will be a very smart young lady but now eat your food so we can start on family day." She does without complaining. I look over at Emilia, she and Theo are biting their lips to contain their laughter. I roll my eyes knowing exactly what they are thinking about the sass from Alessia. Once we finish, I tell Alessia to go get changed into something comfortable. I decided to look up some easy and fun activities to do besides watching movies, not that it isn't fun, but I want to do something else. I find something fun, I run up to our room and grab Emilia's new camera. We will be needing this and while we are busy, I will have the maids set up pillows and blankets inside the canopy gazebo so we can watch a movie or two while we enjoy lunch.

When I walk back inside, I have the camera strap over my shoulder, and I grab both of my girls hands and lead them outside to start our family day.

FORTY-FOUR
EMILIA

Alessia runs out of the kitchen and up the stairs to her bedroom. I yelled to her, "Stop running in the house."

You can hear her yell back, "Sorry, Mama." Mateo follows me over to the sink to put our dirty dishes in the sink until the maid can wash them. I usually try to wash them, but no one lets me. Before I can pick up the sponge, I feel two arms wrap around my stomach and pull me away from the sink.

"Don't even think about it. You need to change into something comfortable."

I look over at him and smile. "Any hints about what we are going to do?" I ask with a pout hoping he will give in.

He kisses my lips and says, "Nope, now go get changed." He moves my arms away from him and smacks my ass when I start to walk away.

I glare at him, and he chuckles at me. I grumble as I walk away, "Fucker can't ever leave my ass alone." When I get up to my room, I decide to change into black yoga pants and a George Strait t-shirt. I laugh when Alessia comes in, matching Mateo with gray sweatpants and a white shirt.

"Mama match with us please." I pretend to think about it, knowing Alessia is obsessed with matching outfits. Thank you, Julietta… not the heavy sarcasm.

"Okay I will change."

"Wait, let me pick it out," she says and runs into my closet. I follow behind her to see her grab a gray pair of leggings and a white very low tank top.

"Alessia, let's pick another shirt."

"Why, Mama?" Shit. How the hell do I explain her father is very overprotective and will go all caveman on my ass if he sees me wearing a very low-cut top?

"Well, that is one of my fancy shirts, let's find something else just in case we get dirty." She nods at me and keeps looking through my clothes and finally decides on a plain white shirt. "Ok, go sit on the bed and I will quickly change." She smiles and skips out of the closet. I quickly changed into the outfit she picked.

When I walk out, she is waiting by the door instead of the bed, I chuckle to myself knowing she isn't very patient. She opens her hand out to me so I can hold her hand, I firmly grab it. We start heading back downstairs to find Mateo, I swing our hands as we are walking. Hearing Alessia giggle makes me laugh with her. We see Mateo sitting at the kitchen island with a piece of paper in his hand and my camera bag on the island. Ok I am totally confused about what he has planned.

"Well look at us matching. We will have to have our picture taken later but we are going to be doing a scavenger hunt."

"Really?" Alessia asks, jumping up and down, Mateo nods his head.

"Yep, and when we find the item on the list, we will take a picture of it." He helps Alessia up on a stool so she can see the list and I walk to the other side of her.

Photo Scavenger Hunt
-A relaxing place
-The biggest tree
-Something shiny
-Something that starts with the letter W
-Something orange
-Light
-Someone's eye
-Something round
-A shadow
-Movement
-Letter L
-Something silly
-A group photo

I finish reading the list. "Okay let's start with a relaxing place. Where is somewhere here that is relaxing to you Alessia?" She sits tapping her fingers on her chin, like Mateo does.

We both wait for about a minute and she is jumping off her stool. "Come on," she tells us, and I grab the camera. We follow her to Mateo's office but in her chair with her bookshelf next to it.

"Good idea. Why don't you sit in your chair, and I will take your picture." She runs over to her chair and sits down. She has her knees up to her chest and her arms resting on top of her knees with her chin on her hands with a beautiful smile on her face. I mentally gush at how adorable she looks before I take the picture.

Mateo looks over at the camera "I want a copy of that for my desk."

I nod at him. "I think many of the family members are going to want a copy." He kisses my cheek and Alessia walks over and sees the picture.

"Mama, look, you made me look beautiful." My breath catches in my throat, did I just hear that right? Does my baby think she is not beautiful? And who the hell made her feel that way?

Mateo bends down to her and I follow behind him. "Princess, do you think you're beautiful?" She looks to the ground wiggling her feet, she shakes her head no. I grab Mateo's hand because I feel like someone just punched me in the gut. I feel terrible that my daughter feels this way.

Mateo raises her chin to look up at him. "Now, why don't you feel you are beautiful?"

She stays quiet, so I decide to pick her up in my arms and move over to the couch. I have her sit in my lap. "Baby girl, you need to talk to us."

She tries to stay quiet, but Mateo isn't having any of that. "Alessia," he says in a bit more of a sterner tone.

"That is what Seth had told me. That I am not beautiful enough to be his daughter and some of the ladies who were friends with the mean lady said I was ugly and" she takes a pause and whispers, "a bastard child." I pull her into me and hug her tight, I fight the tears in my eyes. After a moment, I pull back to look at her in her eyes.

"Alessia, I want you to understand something. Whatever Seth or anyone in that house ever told you do not believe them. They are very mean and nasty people. Okay?" She nods at me.

Mateo tells her, "Alessia what he said was a lie. You are a beautiful girl, you are not just beautiful, you are smart, silly, kind, generous, sweet, you give the best hugs, you have an amazing laugh which I love to hear every day, you are an amazing baker, you are really good at drawing pictures. You are an amazing little girl, and we are so lucky we are your parents. You have so many people who love you and they love you just as much as we do." She reaches over for him; he grabs her and holds her in his arms as she cries. I rub her back and with my other hand I am wiping away my tears.

I look over at Mateo and he has tears in his eyes as well, I mouth to him, "Seth is gonna pay." He nods at me. Seth just earned a longer death than I already had planned.

After a couple minutes, she has calmed down and she pulls away. Mateo uses his thumbs and wipes away her tears. While he is doing that I go into her room and grab her small hand mirror. When I come back, I hand her the mirror and sit down next to her. "Look at yourself in the mirror, what do you see?" I ask her.

"I see me."

I nod at her, "That's right, I see Alessia Rose De Luca. Now I want you to repeat after me." She nods at me. "I am beautiful and strong."

"I am beautiful and strong."
"I am smart, kind, and helpful."
"I am smart, kind, and helpful."
"I am loved by my family."
"I am loved by my family."
"I can do anything I put my mind to."
"I can do anything I put my mind to."

I take away the mirror "Now I want you to remember that, okay?"

"Yes Mama."

Mateo tells her, "Now I don't want to hear you put yourself down ever again. If you're upset, that is okay, but remember we are always here to talk with you. Nothing is more important than you." He kisses her head. "Okay let's continue our scavenger hunt."

When we continue our scavenger hunt, Alessia is happy and loving every moment looking for the stuff on the list. I have been helping her take pictures of the items. We get to something silly, and she runs to the hallway down to her room where Nonna has a bunch of portrait pictures on the wall. She stops at Vincenzo's picture. "Papa, can you take Zio Vincenzo's picture down so I can take a picture of it since he is not here?"

Mateo chuckles. "Sure, Princess." He sets it on the ground, but Alessia props it up against the wall and sits on the floor in front of it and is gonna take the picture but is getting frustrated. I sit next to her and see what's wrong.

I look at the screen and see the flash is still on. "Need help?" She nods at me, and I show her the button for the flash and how it takes it on or off. She turns it off and takes the picture again and smiles when it turns out the way she wanted.

"Thanks, Mama."

"No problem baby girl." Mateo puts the picture back and we look at the list to see that our group photo is last. Mateo tells us to follow him because he knows the perfect spot, we follow him out to the canopy tent he has set up for us. I asked one of the soldiers to take a couple pictures of us because it has been a while. First, I am sitting between Mateo's legs and Alessia is sitting between mine. We are all smiling. Next Alessia is sitting between us, and we both kiss her cheeks while laughing. The last one Alessia decided that Mateo should kiss my cheek and give me a happy smile. After the soldier took the last one Alessia was jumping up and down smiling. I thank him, we all lay in the tent and lay down. Somehow Mateo got a projector inside the tent so we could lay on our backs and watch the movie. I wondered how he would make it work since it is around noon but then I realized he has black out curtains inside the tent, so he does have his smart moments. We lay back on the pillows with Alessia between us and the new Spirit movie is playing. I love these moments with the two of them, I love all the De Luca's but sometimes it is nice to have it be just the three of us. I kiss Alessia's head. She is so into watching the movie she doesn't realize. I look over at Mateo and he is smiling at us, he mouths to me, "I love you."

I mouth back to him, "I love you beyond my last breath."

He mouths back, "Beyond my last breath," which I finally told him where that came from. My Mama and Papa would say this to us and to each other every day and especially before Papa went to work since we didn't know if he would come home. After the movie ended, we ended up having a picnic lunch together. The maids provided us with sandwiches, fruits, chips, and juice. After we finished eating. Alessia said, "Papa?"

"Yes Princess."

"Thank you for doing this. I am having so much fun today." She smiles at him.

"I am glad you are having fun, but guess what we get to do next?"

"What?"

"We get to bake dessert for dinner. But first we need to clean up our lunch." We all help put everything back in the basket. Mateo grabs the basket and I grab the blanket.

Once we have everything put away, Alessia is already looking through Nonna's cookbook. "I don't know what to cook. I want to cook something new."

I go and sit next to her. "Well what kind of dessert do you want to make ? Cake, cookies, pie, or something else?"

"Cake."

I nod at her. "Okay. I know, what about the cake my Mama would make for me on my birthday?"

She smiles at me. "Yeah! What kind of cake would Nonna Angelica make for you Mama?"

"She would make my favorite Strawberry Angel Cake."

As we are mixing the ingredients together Alessia looks up at me. "Mama what was your family like?" I take a deep breath; Mateo stops breaking up the pretzels and gives my hand a reassuring squeeze.

"Well, my Papa was a cop. He loved playing sports and never missed a single sports game that me or your uncles played."

"I have more uncles?"

I give her a small smile. "Did, Alessia. My Mama, Papa, and my brothers Franco and Giovanni, all passed away in a house fire before you were born." She hugs my waist really tight.

"You have us, Mama."

"I know, baby. Let's see Papa was a quiet man but he loved and protected his family. He also scared all the boys away who wanted to date me because he claimed no boy was good enough for me," I say smiling.

"Papa, says the same thing."

I chuckle, then Mateo tells us, "That is because no boy is good enough for my princess."

I roll my eyes but continue "Mama, well she was crazy. A free spirit and she was a nurse. She loved being outside in the country, in the open air. That is why we lived in a cottage and in between two farms. I act more like her than Papa, but she wouldn't hesitate to put anyone in their spot who needed it. She also had a big heart. Esmeralda was best friends with Mama, they would get in all kinds of trouble when they were younger."

"Really? Nonna was crazy like Esme?"

I nod at her. "Yeah, she was. You also had two uncles. Giovanni was my younger brother. He was eleven years older than you. He loved soccer and video games. He also was extremely silly and loved to play pranks on people. Lastly Franco, or Frankie as I used to call him, hated when I used to call him that. Franco graduated college being an I.T. Tech and actually taught me some stuff while he was learning. Franco was five years older than me; we were attached at the hip most days. He loved running. We actually would run together every morning before he had to go to work. He was super protective of me to the point he would pick me up from work every day after he got off work, and I always had to inform him where I was. We used to laugh that we weren't sure who was more overprotective of me Papa or Franco." I chuckle while wiping a few tears away.

"Do you miss them, Mama?"

"Everyday baby girl, but I am also glad I have the memories I do have with them."

"Do you think they would have loved me?"

"Alessia, you would have been so spoiled by them. Mama would have told me that I cannot tell her no about her giving you anything because it is her right as a grandmother. And the boys would have spoiled you as well and made sure you had no boys around you without being approved by them. Just like your Papa and uncles."

She gives me another hug. "I love you, Mama."

"And I love you, Alessia, beyond my last breath."

We make small talk while we finish the dessert and we set it in the refrigerator until after dinner. After we clean up, the maids start coming in to make dinner, so we leave to give them space to work. I tell them we made dessert for tonight. They smile and thank me, using Mrs. De Luca. It is still weird being referred to anything instead of Emilia. I sometimes forget how much power comes with being married to Mateo. At dinner, Alessia tells Theo, Nonno and Nonna about our day; she is so animated with everything she is telling them. We all enjoyed dinner and dessert.

At the end of the day, I expected Mateo to head to his office to catch up on all of the work he didn't do today. No, he surprised me by following me into our room after Alessia fell asleep. I had decided during dessert I was gonna enjoy taking a relaxing bath with a glass of whiskey. I went and poured myself a glass, turned to Mateo, and asked him if he wanted a drink, he asked me to pour him a glass of whiskey as well. I walk over to him, hand him his glass. I kiss his cheek and begin to walk away. "Where are you going tigress?"

I look over my shoulder. "To take a relaxing bath with a glass of whiskey." I continue walking in the bathroom ignoring him but knowing Mateo will join me. I turn on the water for the bathtub and find the perfect temperature. The water fills the tub up while I start to undress, I barely get my shirt off when I feel lips kissing my shoulder.

Mateo whispers in my ear, "Did you think I would turn down the offer to be naked with my sexy wife in the bathtub together?" I shrugged my shoulders, looking over at him, seeing he was already down to just his black boxers, and I could tell someone was excited.

"I see it took you no time at all to strip down."

He moves to stand in front of me as he reaches behind my back to and unhook my bra. I let it fall to the floor, even though he has seen me naked plenty of times, but each time he sees me naked his eyes devour me. "I am not going to waste any time when my wife is naked. I would be a complete idiot and if I ever do, I will give you permission to shoot me."

"Ok, Mr. Dramatic." He yanks my leggings and thong down my legs and helps me out of them. He stands to his full height and kicks off his boxers. He grabs my hand and holds my hand as I get into the tub. He gets in right behind me, and I am seated comfortably between his legs. "I thought this was supposed to be a relaxing bath," I said, and he kissed the column of my throat.

"Oh, don't worry, it will be very relaxing." He turns my head and locks our lips together; he licks my lips, asking for entrance, but I decide to deny him. He plays with my nipple which makes me moan out, and he thrusts his tongue into my mouth. He dominates the kiss, not leaving any surface inside of my mouth untouched by his tongue.

I am putty in his hands as he is holding my head with one hand and the other is playing with my boobs. He slowly leaves my lips and kisses from the corner of my mouth all along my jawline but keeps traveling his lips until he gets to my sweet spot behind my ear. I lean my head to the side to give him more access to my neck. I grind my ass on him and start to moan out. *"Hai il lamento più sexy,"* *(You have the sexiest moan)*, he huskily whispers in my ear, which causes me to shiver down my spine. I bring one of my hands down to reach for my clit, but Mateo grabs it. *"Hmm vuoi che ti tocchi la figa?"* *(Hmm, do you want me to touch your pussy?)* He asks me. I nod at him. He has his hand on my hip, squeezing it but not moving his hand any closer. I whine out in protest; he gently bites my ear then licks it to soothe the pain. *"Parole, tigre"* *(Words, tigress)*

I moan out. *"Sì... sì Mateo toccami per favore"* *(Yes...yes Mateo touch me please.)*

He chuckles at me, and I whine at him, *"Mi piace quando mendica."* (I love it when you beg.) He reaches down and inserts two inside of me while his thumb circles my clit. I throw my head back and moan when his other hand starts tweaking my nipple.

"Oh... proprio lì Mateo. Non fermarti. Oh, per favore non fermarti." (Oh...right there Mateo. Don't stop. Oh, please don't stop.) He doesn't. If anything, he speeds up. *"Sto per cum"* (I am about to cum) and as I am about to cum, he stops. Before I can protest, he grabs me by the hips and pushes me so I am leaning forward with my hands on the edge of the tub. I feel his cock at my entrance, and he slides it inside of me. Since I was already so close, I am already gripping onto his cock as he begins to thrust in and out of me. He isn't as rough as he usually is, but he is still bringing me to my climax. He grabs my hair with one hand pulling my head back and has the other one hand is on my lower back. *"Oh cazzo. Sto sborrando."* (Oh fuck. I am cuming) He reaches down and vigorously rubs my clit. "MATEO!" I yell out, as I begin to slump, but he has other ideas. He pulls me so my back is flushed with his chest. I look in front of me into our mirror that is over the sink. And holy hell, watching him as he fucks me in the mirror is so hot.

"Ti piace guardarti scopare?" (Do you like watching yourself being fucked?)

I nod and say, *"Sì, Don."* He growls at me as he starts pounding harder and deeper into me. Mateo keeps hitting that spot with his cock over and over again; I can feel myself tightening around him. I start to pant out another moan. My orgasm is rolling in faster than I can warn him, but he notices and takes his one hand and firmly wraps it around my throat as I cum again; he follows a few pumps later. He emptied himself inside of me, continuing to thrust until we both caught our breath. He moves his hand off my throat and moves my hair away from one side of my neck and gives me sweet butterfly kisses along my neck. He pulls out of me, and I try to hold my balance but fail. Luckily Mateo hasn't removed his hands from my body. He pulls us back down into the tub, and I sit back down between his legs. He is rubbing his hands across my body in a sweet way; I lean my head back on his chest. I look up at him and say, "This was supposed to be a relaxing bath."

He chuckles. "Are you not relaxed?"

I shake my head. "Oh, I am relaxed, but I also feel royally fucked."

Mateo tilts my head up. "Good, and I will make sure you always feel like that." We wash each other and snuggle together until the water gets cold, and we both get out of the bathtub. We both change into night wear and climb into bed.

I lay in Mateo's arms, thinking that we have a week until we go back to the mansion. I am excited but nervous, I can't wait to see the rest of the family, but I am also anxious about the Russians. I want them finished; we need to live our lives. I know being married to a mafia boss we will always have a target on our back, but this war needs to be stopped. Obviously, Alexei is a nutcase and can't be reasoned with, so that leaves our only choice eliminate the Russians once and for all.

FORTY-FIVE
EMILIA

    It is the night that we move back to the mansion. We loaded up in the van in the middle of the night for safety. It also makes the long car trip a little bit more bearable not having Alessia awake. I love my daughter, and I love that she is no longer mute, but my god the child loves to ask a thousand questions when we go anywhere. The flight back to Italy was quiet, especially since Alessia slept through all of it and was still asleep in the car. Marcello is driving with a soldier in the passenger seat. They are quietly talking. Once this war is over, I am telling Mateo that Marcello and Julietta deserve to have a vacation, even though the asshole snitched on me when we were in Ireland. I know he has been missing her, he hasn't seen her since we left for the safe house and that was over three months ago. Alessia is asleep in her own seat, and Mateo is next to me busy checking email on his phone. I decided to try and fall asleep too. I grab my blanket, cover myself up and lay my head in Mateo's lap. He looks down at me and quietly asks, "Tired?"

    I nod and say, "I am going to try and get some sleep." He gives me that sweet smile that always melts my heart. He puts his phone away and runs his hand through my hair. I close my eyes and relax into his touch.

    "Go to sleep, my Queen." I gently kiss his leg that my head is resting on, and he brings the blanket under my chin. I close my eyes and it takes me no time at all to fall asleep.

    When I wake up, I can hear Alessia talking and Mateo attempting to keep her quiet. "Alessia, shh. Your Mama is sleeping."

    I hear her whisper, "Oops, sorry."

    I open my eyes, and Alessia sees me. "Mama, you're up."

    I chuckle at her enthusiasm "Yes, baby girl. I am awake." I slowly sit up and look around. We are still in the car.

    I turned to Mateo to ask how much longer, but he said, "We are pulling in the mansion." I look out the window, and I see a beautiful mansion; the outside is absolutely beautiful. I can only imagine how beautiful the inside will be. Mateo told me this is the mansion he had bought as a teenager that only his favorite family (everyone except Abramo and Eleanor) knows about.

    Alessia goes to open the door and is ready to run inside, but Mateo's voice stops her. "Alessia Rose, freeze." She stops in her tracks; I laugh at how she does whatever Mateo asks her. She idolizes her father, whereas she is now starting to fight me on things. He opens his door and holds his hand out for me. I put my hand in his hand as he helped me out of the car. We walked over to the side of the car. Mateo opens the door.

Before she can get out, he squats down so he is at eye level with her. "Alessia, do you know why you shouldn't open your door as fast as you did?" She shakes her head. "You are a lady, and as long as you have a gentleman around, they should open the door for you." She looks confused "You are a special lady and should always be treated with respect. And a gentleman should open the door for you."

"Like you do for Mama?"

"Yes, like the way I do for Mama. But the other and most important reason is, we need to make sure it is safe for you to get out. Okay?"

She nods, "Okay Papa. I will wait for someone to open my door." Mateo kisses her forehead and stands back to his full height and holds his hand out to her the same way he did for me. She grabs it and gets out of the car. He is holding her hand but has his hand wrapped around my waist.

Guards nod or acknowledge us by saying "Welcome back, Don, Donna, and Princess" Alessia just smiles and waves at each one. They all give her a small smile back.

After the door is opened for us Alessia lets go and dashes right for Adriano and yells, "Zio Zio!" He squats down, opening his arms to give her a hug. She runs right into his arms and gives him a big hug. To see Adriano hold her so tight and give a gentle smile to her is sweet. Because usually he is very serious and stoic. Mateo told me he wasn't as serious until after Lilyana and Anna passed away.

I am broken out of my thoughts when Vincenzo says to Alessia, "Um, hello, your favorite Uncle is here."

She lifts her head from Adriano's shoulder, "Uncle Uncle gets the first hug because he checked on the horses and called me every day Zio Vincenzo."

He goes to open his mouth to give her a response back.

Adriano stops him, "Hush, boy. Don't be jealous."

Nonna comes up and hugs him. "Don't worry baby, I love you."

He smirks and says, "See, Nonna loves me."

I roll my eyes. "Nonna loves all of you even when you are being little punks," I would say assholes, but I don't feel like getting the wooden spoon from her. She believes Alessia shouldn't hear any cuss words, even though her mother cusses like a trucker.

Alessia moves to each of the De Luca's, Mateo whispers in my ear. "She is our family's sunshine." I nod at him.

I hear Mateo gag; I look over at him questioning why he is doing that. I see what he is looking at, but of course, Vincenzo and Salvatore are gagging as well. I roll my eyes at them being immature idiots. They are seriously gagging over Julietta reuniting with Marcello. All it was a sweet innocent kiss on the lips and then hugging. "If you all don't knock it off, you will be the next test subject on the newest weapons I created…" I drag out, and they all stop gagging and teasing Julietta and Marcello, knowing how diabolical my weapons can be, they don't like Julietta being affectionate with any man. Julietta looks over at me with red cheeks.

"Thanks, Emilia."

I go over and take her out of Marcello's arms and give her a hug. I whisper in her ear. "Of course, we need to stick together. Plus, we will have to start planning how to sneak Alessia past all these De Luca men so she can go on dates." We pull away from the hug and we both laugh. The men look at us confused, but I wink at Nonna; I am sure she knows exactly what I am talking about.

Salvatore asks, "Are you gonna fill us in on the secret?"

I shake my head. "Nope."

He shakes his head. "Mateo, she is your problem."

I give him my mischievous smile. "Can't have you all getting bored with us, now can we?"

I start heading for the kitchen but before we get too far. "Hold on, we have to discuss a couple things first," Mateo says.

We follow him into the room and take a seat. We all find a seat on the couches in the living room. He sends a quick text and then looks at all of us but mostly has his eyes on Alessia, which causes me to worry a bit. "As we all know, we have yet to catch Seth and Alexei. And because of that, we have increased security, and you will see them more than we have in the past. I am not willing to take any chances with anyone in this room. I would prefer it if you wouldn't leave the mansion, but if you need to, you must have a minimum of five guards per family member. I will also be following this rule. Even if you go out to the garden, have guards with you. I will not take a chance with any of your safety. With that being said, Vittorio has been training four dogs to be guard dogs." Mateo gets up and introduces the big but beautiful dogs. "This is Wolf, Brutus, Spike, and Tank. They will be walking the property with one of the guards. They are not pets; they are trained guard dogs. They have been trained to protect us, against other attacks."

Wolf is a white and light brown Akita, Brutus is a brown and white Boxer, Spike is a brown and black German Shepard, and last, but not least is Tank, who is a brown and black Doberman Pinscher. I look over at Alessia, and she has the biggest pout on her lips. Knowing my daughter, she is gonna see who she can sucker into getting her a puppy.

"Alessia put that pouty lip away. We will talk about a puppy if you can keep your grades up, and we feel like you are responsible enough for one." I smirk at Mateo, seeing in his eyes it is killing him not to give in to her. She has all of De Luca's wrap around her pinky. He dismisses everyone to come and do their own things.

Mateo walks over to where I am sitting on the couch, sits next to me. He wraps his arm around my waist and pulls me against his side. "I am gonna meet with the capos and get caught up on everything we missed while we were at the safe house."

I nod at him. "I am gonna spend time with Julietta since Marcello is with you."

"Sounds good. Please stay in sight of your guards."

I smiled at him. "Of course, *il mio re*." He cups my cheek and gives me a sweet kiss.

"Eww, and you give me shit about kissing my boyfriend," Julietta interrupts us.

Mateo looks over at her.

"She is my wife, and you are my little sister; I do not want to think about your extracurricular activities in between the sheets," he says shaking his head as if he can shake the image out of his head.

Julietta being a De Luca of course has a response. "They are not always in between the sheets. Sometimes it is against a wall, door, window, bent over something. That is actually my favorite, especially when their hand is wrapped around my hair." She shrieks when Mateo throws a pillow at her.

"Julietta, that motherfucker better have not touched you."

She rolls her eyes, "No, Mateo he respected the family and wouldn't touch me like that without us being official. And we have not been alone to do anything since the old mansion blew up."

Mateo is quiet, then says, "Then who the hell deflowered my sister."

Julietta smirks. "Nope, not telling you. Now shoo you have a meeting to go to and I have a sister-in-law and niece to bake cookies with." He rolls his eyes and kisses me again before kissing Julietta on the cheek. He heads to his office in the mansion for his meeting.

I follow Julietta to the kitchen where I see Nonna and Alessia in their aprons, baking. Alessia looks up and says, "Zia go talk to Mama; I am making you a surprise."

Julietta puts her hands up in surrender. "Okay. Let me get drinks for me and your Mama and we will stay out." She goes and gets a bottle of wine with two wine glasses. I smirk at her, loving her idea. Nonna looks at us with a raised eyebrow and I shrug my shoulders. I grab the bottle from Julietta and go to the sunroom which looks out to the beautiful garden. She puts the wine glasses down on the table and I pour wine into both glasses. I hand her one and I take the other, while we get comfortable on the couch.

"So how are you?" she asks me.

"A lot better. I have moments when my leg will hurt but I have complete mobility. To be honest my biggest obstacle has been dealing with the nasty scars left behind from the burns."

She gives me a knowing smile. "I can understand that. Have you talked to Mateo about it?"

"Yeah, I have. He has been nothing but amazing with everything. Between running the mafia, his legal businesses and helping both Alessia and me recover, plus trying to find Rebecca and trying to finish off the Russian Mafia, I can never thank him enough."

Julietta shakes her head. "You don't have to thank him. He would do it again in a heartbeat. One time when I called, he said he was exactly right where he was meant to be nursing his girls back to health."

I smile at that.

"For a Mafia King, he is really a sweet and lovable man. I am lucky that I am one of the few people he shows that side too."

"He has a demonic side to him."

I smirk. "And I can't wait to see it."

Julietta throws her head back and laughs, "You both are made for each other. Who the hell gets excited watching her husband kill and torture someone in the cruelest way possible?"

I shrug my shoulders as I lean further onto the couch while taking a sip of my wine. "Well, my husband is Mateo De Luca who is known to be a devil and plus my godmother is who taught me my love for torture."

Julietta shakes her head but goes quiet for a moment and is staring at the wall blankly. "Julietta, are you okay?"

She blinks and looks at me for a second and plasters a fake smile on her face. "Yeah I am good." I grab her glass out of her hand and put both wine glasses down on the coffee table.

"No, you're not. Don't even try and lie to me. You are talking to a woman who faked happy smiles on her face for years. So, what is going on?" I grab her hand and give it a gentle squeeze letting her know I am here for her.

"I was thinking of asking Mateo to send me to Mexico after this is over so she can teach me to protect myself without all of the damn overprotective De Luca men and Marcello. They all flip if I get as much as a paper cut. I want to feel like I can protect myself. But I don't want to intrude on them."

I roll my eyes "First of all Esme is my godmother, and you are family to me which makes you family to them. Not to mention you are Mateo's younger sister. And Esmeralda loves teaching people her ways...a little too much. I will warn you she will push you way past your limits. I hated her during our sessions but the whole Mexican Mafia will teach you something. They will rotate teaching you something, but I don't regret it at all. It made me feel more confident in myself and safer. If you want, I will ask her and even help you break it to the overprotective idiots."

"Yeah, I am tired of feeling like I can't defend myself and have to rely on the guards."

I take my phone out and text Esmeralda, but she calls me instead.

Emilia: Hello, Esme.

Esmeralda: Hello, my godbaby. Are you okay? How was your flight home? How is my other baby? Did Mateo do something? Do I need to castrate him?

I chuckle at her.

Emilia: No. Everyone is okay. I am actually calling to ask you a favor, if you are interested.

Esmeralda: Sounds interested. What is the favor?

Emilia: Do you remember Julietta? Mateo's little sister?

Esmeralda: Ah yes, the adorable flower. I do remember her. Why is she hurt?

Emilia: No, but she wants to learn to be a crazy badass like us.

Esmeralda laughs on the other end of the phone.

Esmeralda: Does she now? Is she near you?

Emilia: Yes, she is sitting right next to me. I will put her on speaker.

I put the phone on speaker.

Emilia: Ok, you are on speaker.

Esmeralda: Hello, Julietta. How are you darling?

Julietta: Hello, Mrs. Garcia. I am well. How about yourself?

Esmeralda: You are a sweet and polite girl, but you are my goddaughter's sister-in-law which makes you family, so don't be so proper. Call me Esmeralda or Esme. I am sure you will have other names for me once we start training.

Julietta: Of course, Esmeralda.

Esmeralda: So, you want me to train you?

Julietta: Yes, if you don't mind.

Esmeralda: I don't mind at all. I love teaching men and women to be scary badasses! I am warning you; I am tough, I will push you past your limits, at times you will feel like giving up but I won't let you and I can guarantee you will hate me. It will be worth it in the end if you push yourself.

Emilia:(mumbles) That is an understatement.

Esmeralda: Emilia Rose De Luca, you are not too old to be smacked with *Chancla (flip flop)*

Emilia: Well, you're in Spain and I am not.

Esmeralda: Do you really think I am not friends with Nonna Francesca? After spending time together. I am sure she will have no problem smacking that ass of yours, or I can always ask your husband.

Julietta gags while Esmeralda laughs.

Emilia: You are mean. You are supposed to love me, not threaten someone else to beat me and don't call Nonna. I don't need her to smack my ass with the wooden spoon again.

Esmeralda: Wooden spoon? Hmm, I like her thinking. It seems like Francesca, and I need to get together again soon. But you never said no about your husband spanking your ass. Is my goddaughter a little freaky in the sheets?

Emilia: Yeah, I am not discussing my sex life with you, and I doubt Julietta wants to hear about what I do with her brother behind closed doors.

Julietta: Yeah, I will pass on that.

Esmeralda: Fine, at least tell me if he is as good as I imagined.

Emilia: Oh, he is much better than you could even imagined. He knows how to work what he was blessed with; I can never feel my legs afterwards.

Esmeralda: Well shit, that's the best kind of sex.

Julietta: Ok changing the subject before I throw up the wine we were drinking.

Esmeralda: Ok fine. I will corrupt you sexually too. Julietta, do you have a man? If not, I know plenty of men down here who could rock your world.

Emilia: Oh yes, she does. It is none other than Alessia's main bodyguard.

Esmeralda: Well, I be damned. Vittorio?

Julietta: No Vittorio runs the rest of the security. Marcello is personally in charge of Emilia and Alessia's security. Even though someone…. Emilia (fake coughs) gives him a run for his money.

Before I can reply a guard comes in and says "Excuse Donna. You have a visitor." I nod and tell them I will be there in a moment.

Emilia: Esme, we have to go, but we will be in touch. I love you. Tell everyone we say hello.

Esmeralda: Ok, my godbaby, I will. Be safe, I love you.

I hang up the phone and Julietta follows me to the entryway. When I got there my blood boiled at the sight of a man who was my last resort to save me and my daughter and turned his back on us for money.

"You have some fucking nerve showing up here, you low life piece of fucking shit."

I hear Julietta say, "Oh shit," but I tune everyone else out except my Uncle Andrea who is standing in front of me.

"Oh, Emily, my sweet niece, I have been looking all over for you."

I just stand there and say "Emily?" I say not at all shocked that he doesn't know my name, after all he has always been self-absorbed. "Shows how much you know and care about me if you call me Emily."

"That's your name."

I chuckle at the audacity of this man. "No it is fucking not. My name is Emilia Rose De Luca and don't pretend you give two shits about me. Let me guess the only reason you looked me up is because you are out of money and heard my husband is rich. And you low life piece of shit wanted a handout, once again. No wonder Alonzo and Mama were the favorite out of the triplets. At least they made something out of themselves where all you do is mooch off everyone around you."

He gets pissed off at what I said to him, he swings his arm back to hit me. Before he can he is shoved against the wall with my personal devil's hand around his throat. "Well, the rat finally comes out of his hole." He grips Andrea's throat a bit tighter, Andrea is trying to pull Mateo's hand off his throat. "Here is the thing, you abandoned my girls when they needed you the most. You collected the money and ran away from your family. They are my family, and, in my family, you don't turn your back on family." He let's go of his throat and roughly tosses him to the floor Andrea is trying to catch his breath. Mateo puts his boot on his throat and says, "And no one disrespects my Queen without any kind of punishment from my hands." Well shit I just got turned on again, fuck Julietta is right I am as fucked up as him. Mateo looks at me and gives me a knowing look with his smirk. *"Mia Regina*, do you want me to let him live? He is, after all, family."

I shake my head. "Nope, he is not family. Family doesn't turn their back on each other."

He tells Vittorio to put him in the basement. He moves his foot off his throat and walks over to me.

Andrea is yelling insults at me, calling me a whore and all kinds of names. I can tell it is pissing Mateo off. I walk around in front of him and give him a hug. He wraps his arms around me and kisses the top of my head. "Are you okay?" he mumbles into my hair; I look up at him.

"Yes, if anything, I am pissed. He dared to try and come back into my life when he abandoned us."

"I know, but I will deal with him later. He will regret turning his back on my Queen."

I kiss him. "Can I watch please?"

"I could never deny letting you watch someone being tortured," I smirk at him; he knows how excited I get when I get to watch him kill someone. Yes, it is my uncle, but he deserves it. I can guarantee if Mama was alive, she would be beating his ass, and so would my Uncle Alonzo. I do miss Alonzo. He died from lung cancer. He smoked a lot. We all knew it would kill him but as he would say "If I am gonna go out, might as well go out happy." I shake my head from my sad thoughts, but of course, the sadness in my eyes doesn't get past Mateo.

"Later," I tell him. He nods and grabs my hand, dragging me with him to his office.

I thought I was brought in here so they could finish their meeting but no one else followed us to his office. "Where is everyone?" I ask Mateo, as he sits me down in his lap.

"We had already finished up and were casually drinking when the guard burst through the door saying some man was here and my wife was looking very lethal, and you were about to tear him a new asshole." I shrug my shoulders and snuggle into his chest.

"Sorry. I just have a lot of anger towards him."

"It's understandable. Come, let's go see if our baker is done in the kitchen and after she goes to bed tonight, we will deal with your uncle." I kiss him and jump off his lap. I start walking towards the door when Mateo smacks my ass. I stop, turn around and glare at him with my arms crossed over my chest. He shrugs his shoulders. "What? Your juicy ass was tempting me to smack it."

FORTY-SIX
EMILIA

    Our little baker decided on a triple layer chocolate cake to make with Nonna. It was absolutely delicious and Alessia was very proud of herself since she cooked all by herself besides putting in and out of the oven. I am still very pissed at my uncle showing up trying to weasel money out of me. I think what pisses me off more is that he lied to my face saying he looked for me, but I pushed that aside while I am currently putting Alessia to bed.

    Alessia is reading another chapter of *Heartland* to me and Mateo before bed. This is our routine; it is nice to have some normal in our absolute crazy mafia life. Mateo helps her sound out some of the words that she struggles with her stutter. She has gotten a lot better, but she gets nervous when she comes across a word that she doesn't know how to pronounce. After a couple tries, she is able to say it without stuttering over it, Mateo kisses her temple, and she soaks in everything Mateo does with her. She worships the ground he walks on; they have only been a part of each other's life for two years. They have such a great relationship. He has given her the one thing I had always wanted for her, a father who loves and cherishes her. I am sure I will be saying something different when she is a teenager and especially if she is anything like me. She finishes reading the chapter after about fifteen minutes, I kiss her goodnight then Mateo takes his turn to tell her goodnight.

    Before we walk out of the door Alessia calls Mateo, "Papa?"

He turns around. "Yes?"

"Will you always love me?" I see Mateo take a harsh breath and go to sit on the bed right next to her. She is looking down, but he lifts her head with his finger and makes her look him in the eyes.

"Now would you ask a question like that?"

"Because Seth was supposed to love me and never did. And I wonder if I am unlovable."

I look up at the ceiling to try and stop the tears from escaping my eyes. I hear Mateo say "Alessia, since the moment I laid my eyes on you. You became my daughter, and you will always be my daughter beyond my last breath." I walk over to the other side of the bed next to Alessia, Mateo is giving her a hug. She sobs in his arms. I rub her back while Mateo is whispering, "Shh, Princess take a deep breath." She keeps trying to catch her breath but is struggling.

"Alessia, you need to try and calm down, but remember we all love you." She keeps crying and Mateo goes to try to stop her but I mouth to him just to let her cry it out. Listening to her breaks my heart and I surrender to the tears. I silently let them fall but wipe them away before Alessia or Mateo can see.

Mateo, being the very observant husband, saw my tears and used his one hand to wipe the tears off my cheek. "I know, baby," I am not sure if he is talking to Alessia or to me honestly, he is probably talking to both of us.

It takes her a while to calm down, Seth better hopes he dies before I can get my hands on him because he is going to have a long and painful death. "Alessia, I want you to remember that there are evil people in the world who will look for ways to hurt people. But there are also good people in the world who will love you and want nothing but the best for you. Seth and all the men who were at that house were evil, very evil. While all of our family here they are good, and they want to see you happy. Seth should have loved you but obviously he wasn't meant to be a father, but we are lucky enough that Mateo loves both of us. Especially you, he loves you so much," I tell her.

Mateo responds to Alessia with, "Alessia you are my daughter and there is nothing in this world that would make me not love you. I hate how much Seth has hurt you and has made you sad, but I promise to remind you how much you are loved." She nods at us and snuggles back into his arms. I give him a small smile seeing them together.

"Baby girl, what brought on this question?" I ask her.

"I just wonder why he never could love me, and I remember you both telling me I should talk to you if I am upset. I am sorry if I made you sad, Mama."

"Alessia, I am happy that you came to talk to us. Even if what you say makes us sad, that is okay because we are your parents and will be there for you whenever you need us."

She gives me a sad smile. "Can you lay with me until I fall asleep?" she asks.

"Of course," Mateo responds. Mateo wraps his arms around her, and she lays her head on Mateo's shoulder while I run my hand through her hair and hum songs to her like I used to do as a baby. My poor baby basically passed out once we all got comfortable, but I don't think either of us wanted to leave her.

We finally leave both of us giving her a kiss on her head. We leave for the warehouse; I want to deal with my uncle as soon as possible. I will not keep anyone alive who is a threat to myself or my family. Andrea is so money hungry that he would sell us out to anyone who will give him money. We walk into the basement of the warehouse, I see my uncle tied to a chair, I stand next to Mateo smirking.

Mateo wastes no time in punching him across the face, "Now tell me why you came to our home?"

Andrea spits out the blood in his mouth. "I am not telling you shit unless you pay me."

I roll my eyes, "You will never change. But you think you actually have a choice. You are not leaving here alive, so if you want to spend the rest of your life down here then be my guest and keep your mouth shut. But if you want to leave here, I suggest you open your mouth."

"How can you be married to this monster and have your daughter around him? What kind of mother does that make you?" Andrea says to me.

Mateo stabs Andrea in the stomach with a knife I didn't realize he had in his hand. He makes the cut from one side of his stomach to the other side. "You are right I am a monster, but you have made this monster very angry, so you can deal with the consequences." Mateo turns to me and asks me, *"La mia regina* do you mind if I deal with this?"

I walk up to him. "Only if you finish him off by our pets," I tell him as I kiss his lips.

He pulls away and smirks, "It has been awhile since they hunted their prey. But first, I will deal with him."

I kiss his cheek and say "Do whatever you want *Il mio re*." I go back and stand against the wall, watching Mateo.

"You have pissed me off. You want to call me a monster, I actually perfered beast but monster is fine to. But being disrespectful to Emilia and claiming she isn't a good mother. You have no right to question anything she has done or does for our daughter. You had a chance to save them but money was more important than family. No one gets to disrespect my Queen without having to suffer the consequences. That is why you earned yourself a very painful death."

Andrea says, "I am sorry. Please forgive me."

Mateo chuckles as he runs the bloody knife down the side of his cheek. "Begging for forgiveness won't help you. If you want to help yourself start talking."

He stupidly stays quiet, he must like pain, Mateo gets the bolt cutters hanging off the wall. He whistles as he is walking over to Andrea who is fighting to get out of the chair. "W-what are you going to do with those?"

Mateo smiles innocently, "These? Oh, I am going to use these to cut off your fingers until you start talking."

Andrea shakes his head, "Okay then," Mateo says as he brings the bolt cutter around his right pinky finger and quickly cuts it off.

"Fine. Fine. I will talk." Mateo moves the bolt cutters away from his ring finger, Andrea looks at me begging me to help him.

"Don't look at me. You deserve everything and more than what he has done to you." I say to him.

Mateo smacks the side of his leg with the bolt cutters, "I am waiting. Starting talking, or you lose your ring finger next."

"Okay I was given this address and told to ask for money and once I did that I was to call a number to let them know if you were living there."

"Who gave you the address?" I asked.

Andrea says, "He didn't give me a name. All that he said was he is going to bring you down and start training your daughter and placing you where he wants."

"Fucking Alexei. Do you know what that means if you would have called them?" Andrea shakes his head. Mateo tells him, "It means Alessia would be training at the age of eight to be a wife to a man who is forty years older than her and Emilia would be sent to a brothel."

Andrea's eyes go wide, "I...I didn't know."

"Of course you didn't. We didn't publicize what his plans were to the world. But it's not like you actually cared because they were in their hands before when you sold them out for money before. So why should know be any different?"

Mateo puts the bolt cutters down and then he grabs his knife and cuts the rope off of Andrea's arms and legs. Andrea smiles thinking he's free, but I laugh, "Don't be so excited. You aren't gonna be leaving here alive."

"But I told you what I know."

I raise my eyebrow at him, "And that is supposed to make the fact that you are a danger to my family any different?"

Andrea tries again to save his skin by saying, "We are family. Your Mama and Papa would be disappointed in what you are doing."

I shake my head. "No, Andrea, you have it wrong. They would be disappointed in you for not only selling Alessia and me out to sexual predators once but almost doing it a second time. Papa would have to hold Mama back from beating your ass, but then he probably wouldn't. Then Papa would beat your ass himself too. I was his *principessa selvaggia*, and he was fiercely protective over me. But you would know that if you spent any time with me as a child."

"Emilia, can you open the door for me?," Mateo asks. As he hands Andrea off to Vittorio, who I never realized was in here with us, I open it, and it is a jungle habitat.

"Wow," I say. It is absolutely beautiful.

"Beautiful, isn't it?" Mateo asks me. I nod. "This is Lucifer and Lilith's home. Here they have everything they could need; they have a pond so they can cool off. When they want, they can walk outside inside the fence." He whistles three times and you hear heavy paws hitting the ground. A minute later, you see two tigers come out between the trees; I am in complete shock. They are so beautiful and majestic, and they seem so excited to see Mateo. Mateo walks further into their habitat. They come and sit in front of him; they act like they trained big dogs.

"*Ciao Lucifero e Lilith. Ti sono mancato i miei bambini?*" (*Hello Lucifer and Lilith. Did you miss me, my babies?*) Mateo cooes to the tigers as he rubs the top of both of their heads, and they make a strange sound in approval. "*Mi sei mancato anche tu, i miei bambini. Ma ho portato qualcuno che ti incontrasse. La nostra regina.*"(*I missed you too my babies. But I brought someone to meet you. Our Queen.*) He looks over at me and waves me closer. I slowly walk over to him, not wanting to frighten the tigers. "Stick your hand out and let them smell you." I do, and they both take a turn smelling my hand. When one of them licks it, I laugh because their tongues are rough like a cat's.

The tigers make that sound again, I smile at them and with my hands I pet them both on the head like Mateo did. "Wow, you take Mafia King to a whole new level."

Mateo laughs at me, "Well I am glad you think so."

"I am excited to see them hunt our guest." I say smirking at him. He kisses my cheek.

"This is why you are the perfect wife for me." He looks back and calls Vittorio. "Vittorio, bring him in."

Andrea is fighting him and begging for us not to kill him. The tigers stand on their feet and their tails are swinging in excitement. "*aspettare*"*(Wait)* Mateo tells them, and they do. Vittoro pushes Andrea inside the habitat, he falls to the ground. Mateo walks over to him, towering over him. "Run. You have one minute before I release them."

"Please," Andrea begs but he is cut off when Mateo starts counting down. "60..59..58" Andrea gets up and is slowly moving past the tigers and into the thickness of the trees. "You better move faster than that or they will catch you in no time," Mateo yells out. Andrea is trying to move faster but I can imagine trying to walk when your stomach is cut open can be difficult. After a minute is up Mateo looks down at the tigers, says, "*Caccia,*"*(Hunt)* and they take off.

It doesn't take long before we hear Andrea yelling out to me to save him, "Emilia please. I am sorry. I am your uncle. Please save me." I chose not to answer him so he can understand how it feels to be alone and abandoned by your blood family. We hear him screaming and the sounds of bones breaking. That goes on for a few minutes and then we don't hear Andrea anymore.

Mateo grabs my hand and we walk out, I look back and he says "They will be busy for a while." I nod and follow Mateo out with Vittoro behind us. Do I feel guilty that I had my uncle killed by my husband's tigers? Not at all. I know if we would have let him go he would off sold us off to Alexei for money and as long as Andrea was alive we were not safe.

Mateo tells me he is going to go change and I just look out of his office window, it is a beautiful view it over looks a beautiful garden. I feel hands wrap around me and I smell Mateo's cologne, "You okay."

I nod, "Yeah I am fine. I honestly I barely saw him growing up because Mama and Papa knew what kind of man he was and they didn't want us around him. I am glad he is gone because as long as he was alive any enemy of ours could use him to sell us out and we would never be safe. Plus he isn't what a true uncle should be, Adriano is a true uncle who loves all of us selflessly and is always there for us when we need him. Not when he can get a payment from us."

Mateo kisses my temple, "You are right about that. You ready to go home?"

I turn around and kiss his cheek. "Yeah let's go home, I am exhausted." He grabs my hand and walks us out to our car.

FORTY-SEVEN
EMILIA

Mateo holds my hand the entire ride back to the mansion which doesn't take long. The whole mansion is asleep besides the guards who are on duty. They all nod and greet us saying "Don, Donna." We nod back at them. Mateo opens our door for me and I walk in headed towards the shower, to clean off before bed. I know Mateo needs to take one as well, to wash all the blood off of him.

I pull all my clothes and put them in the laundry basket. I start to walk naked to the bathroom but I feel a smack on my ass. I look and see Mateo looking me up and down slowly. "You are so sexy." He says to me. I roll my eyes and keep walking to the bathroom, I hear him take off his clothes and I know he is gonna join me in the shower.

I turn the water on and stand under the water as it pours down on me. I hear the door open and I feel a very excited Mateo stand behind me. He doesn't say anything. Instead just massages my shoulders, and I melt into his hands. Then he massages my neck softly and moves his way up to my temples. I moan when he rubs my head, I am leaning into his body. "You okay?" he asks me.

"Yes and no. Yes, I am okay that Andrea is dealt with but I keep thinking about what Alessia said to us before she went to bed."

"I know but remember we will deal with him too. She will no longer wonder if she is loved. Even when she will make us mad, we will always love her. And I plan on making sure she knows how much I love her as my daughter every single day."

I turn around and hug him, "I know and I couldn't be more grateful that you are her father and my husband. For a beast you are our guardian angel."

He chuckles, "I wouldn't go that far." I roll my eyes at him, I feel his cock against my stomach.

I reach down and start to stroke him, he groans out in pleasure. He puts his hand over my hand, "If you don't want me to fuck you up against the wall of this shower. I would advice you to stop touching me."

I lean up and whisper against his ear, "Who says that isn't what I want?" He turns us so my back is flushed with the wall and he reaches down and runs his finger in between my folds.

"So wet for me and I haven't even started." He says as he rubs in perfect circular motions on my clit.

I throw my head back against the wall and moan. Mateo starts to kiss down my neck, he lifts me up in his arms and I wrap my arms and legs around him. He pushes me back against the wall and starts to grind on me, "Yes, Mateo. I need more."

He gently bites on my ear lobe, "More. Hmm. Do you want my fingers, tongue or cock?" He asks and pushes his cock further in between my pussy lips.

"Cock." I pant out, "Please I need you inside of me." I beg him. He wastes no time and thrust all of him inside of me at once. I scream out in complete pleasure. He pushes me further into the wall but he grasp on my ass is tight as he uses it to grind me into him. This man knows how to move my body in ways I never knew could bring me so much pleasure. I swear each time gets better and better. "Yes, harder. Fuck me harder." He does as I ask and fucks me harder and faster. I am digging my nails into his shoulders and holding on. He keeps fucking me hard and fast while he grinds himself harder into me with each stroke.

"Fuck. Mateo. I am so close." I moan out.

"I know you are squeezing the hell out of my cock." He grits between his teeth.

It doesn't take much longer for me to get pushed over the edge and I moan out his name. "MATEO!" He doesn't slow down his thrusts after I have calmed down but I am sensitive from just having an orgasm. I am already feel myself being built up for a second one, he moves one of his hands that was holding my ass and starts to rub my clit again.

"Cum one more time for me." I nod because I can't seem to get any words out between my pants. He does this for a minute but switches from rubbing my clit soft to rubbing it harder. It is building me up faster than I expected him to.

He kisses all over my neck but once he gets to the spot behind my ear, I am a thread away from falling into the bliss of pleasure.

"Cum, like a good girl."

Fucking hell. I scream out his name "MATEO!" at the same time Mateo grunts. Both of his hands are grabbing my ass tight, I am sure I will have bruises on them tomorrow. But it was definitely worth it. He keeps thrusting in and out of me a lot slower until we both have calmed down from our orgasmic highs.

He slowly unwraps my legs and pulls his cock out from inside of me. He looks down at me with a smile, he holds both sides of my face and gives me a passionate kiss. I hold onto him because my legs are shaky. He pulls away from the kiss, "So damn beautiful and perfect. Let me wash you up. It's really late and we both need to get some sleep." He spends the next ten minutes washing both of us up. Once we are all clean from the shower he wraps the towel around me and dries me off including wrapping my hair up in a towel.

He quickly dries himself off and has me sits at my vanity with a towel wrapped around my hair and another wrapped around my body. He comes back in changed into gray sweatpants that hang dangerously low on his hips but he has a baggy shirt and a pair of cotton shorts for me in his hand. Mateo pulls the towel away from my body, he bends down and slides my panties and shorts up my legs. "Lift up your hips", he tells me and I do as he asked then he slides the baggy shirt over my head. I figured he would be done but I should have known my husband loves to take care of me.

He grabs my hair dryer and stands behind me. He takes my hair out of the towel and starts to blow my hair dry with a hair dryer. He blows it into soft waves. We don't say anything but we talk with our eyes and smiles. I am more than appreciative for these little things he spoils me with. He finishes and he turns it off and holds his hand out for me. I put my hand in his hand, we walk over to the bed. He pulls back the covers and has me slide in and he covers me up before he goes to the otherside of the bed and climbs in on the otherside of the bed. He pulls me so I am laying on his chest, he runs his hand up and down my back.

I get lost in my own thoughts while we lay together in complete silence. I am hating how much everything we went through and Alessia suffered silently. I wish she was never around them; I can handle anything they do to me but to know she is suffering is killing me. And the fact she could still possibly suffer again from something they do is torture. Mateo gets in bed and turns me over facing him, "Talk to me."

I sigh. "I hate that she has suffered because of the choices I made. I don't regret having her, but I am worried she might still suffer at whatever they are planning." I look at him.

"*La mia moglie perfetta.* Because of what you did they were only able to lay a hand on her after they threw you into a wall. Even though you were in absolute pain you pushed through to knock them out and you both were able to escape. So, stop blaming yourself," he tells me, and I'm about to argue with him when he shoots me a look. I shut my mouth, he continues, "And I will do everything I can to protect you both from them."

I stroke his cheek with my thumb. "I know, you have been working so hard keeping us safe. And I know you will continue too. Once this is over you can also get some well-deserved rest."

He leans over and gives my lips a gentle kiss and pulls me closer. "Go to sleep, baby." I snuggle closer to him if that is possible.

"You go to bed too." I feel his chest vibrate against me as he chuckles.

FORTY-EIGHT
EMILIA

I am woken up when I hear my bedroom door slam open. I jump up and grab my gun point it to my annoying best friend who is standing there with a smile on his face. I put the gun down and lay back down muttering, "Oh, it's just you."

"Excuse me? What the hell do you mean it's just you?" Theo exclaims.

"Theo, you are a pain in the ass. And you have that smile on your face that means you are up to no good. So, I am going back to sleep until I have the energy to go along with whatever crazy idea you have." I mumble into my pillow.

He jumps into the bed next to me, "No can-do bestie. We have a shopping date," he says. I crack my eye open and look at him while he is waving a black card around.

"No! Now you can exit the same way you entered but preferably quieter," I say, as my face falls back into the pillow.

Does Theo listen? No, of course not. "Come on… Please your hubby was generous enough to let us use his black card. So that means we are going on a shopping spree."

I close my eyes hoping if I pretend to be asleep, he will leave me alone and let me sleep. Can a woman not sleep in after she watched her uncle being tortured and then had hot sex with her husband last night. Plus, I haven't slept much. Let a woman sleep.

"Faking sleeping isn't going to work," he says as he gets closer to me.

I roll my eyes even though my eyes are closed. "Will shooting you get you away for a couple hours so I can get some more sleep?"

He shakes his head no. "Get up or I get to pick your outfit, and I already saw a pretty dress and heels that you can wear."

My head pops off the pillow. "There is no way in hell I am wearing a dress or heels if we are going shopping. Shopping with you is like running a marathon. Why don't you go ask Julietta she has the same enthusiasm as you do when it comes to shopping."

"But she isn't my bestie and plus she won't sit and judge other men's asses and other muscles with me," he says giving me the puppy dog eyes and pouts his lips.

I groan and say "Fine. Let me go get up and get dress." As I take my first step, I groan a bit because I am sore from how Mateo wrecked my body.

Theo laughs at my misery. "Looks like you were royally fucked last night."

I glare at him over my shoulder, "And what gave you that idea, jackass?"

"Oh, just a guess from the way you are walking like you have a stick up your ass," he snickers, I flip him off as I walk into my closet and change into jeans, a tunic shirt, and boots.

I come out and he sighs, "I guess that will do. I swear one day you will be my doll and I will dress you however I want. I can guarantee Mateo won't be able to keep his hands off you."

"He can't keep his hands off me now. If you doll me up like you want, I will never leave my bedroom," I say to him as I grab my purse so we can leave. The sooner I get through this shopping torture with Theo, the better.

We walk down the steps and see Vittorio, Marcello, and a couple other guards. I skip over to Marcello. "Marcello are you excited to be going shopping with us?" I say laughing at the look of horror on his face.

"Oh no, I had enough of guarding you for a while. I am going to be with Alessia, Vittorio gets to deal with you shopping. I almost feel sorry for him, but that happens when I can lift more than him."

I put a hand on my chest. "Marcello you wound me."

He rolls his eyes. "You will be fine. Vittorio have fun." He says laughing as he walks into the house in the direction of the kitchen.

Vittorio looks at me. "You can't be as bad as he is describing, right?"

I smirk at him. "Only one way to find out. Let's go boys." I say and head for the door but before I do, I hear my darling husband call out to me.

"Are you forgetting something?" he asks me. I turn around knowing he wants a kiss, but I decide to give him a hard time since he gave Theo approval to go shopping when I wanted to be lazy today. I put my finger on my lips and tap it a couple times, pretending to think. "No, I don't think so."

He raises an eyebrow at me, "Are you sure about that?"

"Yep. I am. So, see ya later, I have to go get tortured shopping with Theo. That, someone approved of." He snickers at me as he comes down the stairs, he wraps his hand around my waist and gives me a sweet kiss.

"Boo." I hear and pull away and see Theo smirking at us.

"That's not a kiss." Mateo smirks at me, I pull myself out of his reach.

"Nope, you are not getting anything more than that since you gave him," I stop and point to Theo, "permission to torture me by shopping."

Theo whines "Oh come on Lia. We will have fun."

"I am not responsible for whatever we do while we are gone," I laugh as I run out of the house and into the Range Rover and Theo jumps in behind me. We are both laughing, I smirk at him. "If I am being tortured by you, we are going to a thrift store."

Theo complains, "NOOO! Come on Emilia we are going to all the high-end stores."

"Ok I will get out then," I say as I go to grab my door.

He grabs my hand away from the door. "Fine."

I pump my hands in the air. "Let's see what ridiculous outfits we can put together." We both laugh as Vittorio and one of the guards get in the front of the car. They have no idea about the entertainment they are about to endure.

I tolerate going to all of the stores Theo wants to drag me into, Theo got me to buy some clothes there or he would tell some embarrassing stories of me. I did not need my husband to know about my NSYNC love I had as a teenager, or how I embarrassed myself at the concert. So, I got a few designer jeans and some cute knee length dresses I can wear to cocktail parties. Since I do have to go to parties being the wife of Mateo. Plus, they make it easier for a quickie. Maybe I should start wearing dresses more often.

After that I went to Victoria Secret because Mateo keeps ripping my thongs and bras when he is too impatient. "That man is hungry for you." he said to me laughing after I told him, I needed to buy more. I get an idea in my head and I smirk at Theo. When he sees the smirk on my face, "Now what are you planning in your evil mind?" He asks me.

"Oh, just a bit of payback on my husband for not letting me sleep in." I chuckle, "And that would be what exactly?" I tell Theo, "Just sending him some photos of what I am going to buy from here while he happens to be in a meeting at the moment."

"All that is gonna get you is your ass red and fucked until you can't walk," he says laughing.

I shrug my shoulders. "Who says I don't rile up my husband so he does exactly that."

"Your a little freak," he says laughing.

"Damn right I am. Have you seen my husband?" I snicker.

Vittorio mumbles behind me, "No wonder Marcello won, now I see why he didn't want to guard you. I am not sure who is worse Emilia or Vincenzo." Theo looks at me and we bust of laughing.

"Oh, Vittorio this nothing compared to what Marcello had to go through when I was in Ireland."

His mouth falls open. "Great," he says sarcastically.

I finally decided on the lingerie set I took a picture with; it was a black strappy bra and thong that leaves little to the imagination with garters. After I had bought about twenty sets of thongs and bras, we finally headed to the thrift store.

I turn to Vittorio, "You are about to have the time of your life."

He shakes his head, "I seriously doubt that." I start skipping down the isles looking at stuff, I start grabbing the most ridiculous and bright color things I can find. I grab a neon green feather boa, neon pink tutu, rainbow stripped leggings, a shirt with a neon yellow sun on it, huge sunglasses, and an obnoxiously big sunhat. I go and try everything on, and Theo sees me and busts out laughing.

"You are ridiculous," he says, and I chuckle with him. We basically got kicked out. If Mateo didn't own the shopping center, I am sure we would have been kicked out. The manager didn't appreciate Theo's comments about what Mateo would do seeing me in the different lingerie sets. I modeled each one and Theo would say things like Mateo's cock is going to combust seeing you in that or he will shred that off you so he can bend you over and fuck you until you can't walk.

Theo goes and finds a neon green speedo and holds it out in front of himself. I chuckle, "Get it and strut your stuff." He puts it on over his jeans and is walking around the thrift store like it is his own personal runway. After he takes the speedo off, he switches to a beer hat. We keep pulling out the most obnoxious outfits one after another. We goofed off trying other ridiculous outfits including me wearing extremely high stiletto heels and falling on my ass. We both decided that I was not made to walk in stripper heels.

Even though I complained about coming out to shop I needed this alone time with Theo. Life has been so stressful recently and it was nice to pretend I am not a mafia boss's wife and not a mother for a few hours.

When they pull in, I don't see Mateo when I get out of the car. I am literally getting out of the car like I am a ninja or something. I tell the maids to put my bags in my room, I keep being careful as I am making my way through the mansion. I know my little stunt from earlier is going to have my ass in trouble. I walk in my room and the room is dark, the curtains are shut, and the lights are off. I shut the door and quickly turn the lights on. I don't see him, the coast is clear. I walk over to my bed so I can take my shoes off since my feet are killing me. I hear the lock on the door click. I spin around and I see Mateo. I pretend to be innocent maybe that will save me from being put over his knee.

"Hi honey, how was your day?" I say sweetly when he stalks toward me not saying anything. I start backing up. With every step he takes toward me, I take one back. Until the back of my legs hit the bed. "Shit," I say quietly.

He finishes walking up to me and says, "Turn around, hands on the bed. And watch yourself in the mirror." I quickly spin around facing the bed and bend over with my hands on the bed. I stare at the mirror that is hanging above my vanity across the room. Mateo quickly pulls down everything from the waist down to my ankles. He has me spread my legs as far as possible. He has a box in his hand and he opens it, but I can't see what it is.

"Take your punishment like a good girl," he says huskily as he agonizingly slowly runs finger up and down from my clit to my hole. I moan out, he spanks my ass and I feel my thighs getting wetter. He removes his finger and I feel something metal run through my folds and I look down where his hand is and I see he is rubbing a vibrator between my lips. I look back at him through the mirror and smirks, he slowly inserts the vibrator inside of me but this one also has a part that sits on my clit.

Mateo moves it to where he likes it, then he bends down and grabs my pants and pulls them up. He spins me around when my pants are on my hips, he zips and button my jeans. "What the hell Mateo?" I ask.

He pulls out his phone and I feel the vibrator come to life inside of me. I grab on to his arm for support, it keeps vibrating inside of me for a minute before he turns it off. I am panting. He smirks at me and says, "Behave or I will have no problem turning it on while we are in front of our family." My mouth opens wide, he wouldn't, right?

"Maybe if you are a good girl, I will fuck you tonight if not you will go all night without have any kind of pleasure." Without waiting another moment, he walks right out of the room. I follow him down the stairs to go eat with everyone else. During dinner he would constantly turn the vibrator on and off. I was biting the inside of my cheek hard enough I was tasting blood so I could avoid moaning and embarrassing myself. At one point while we were eating, he reached over and pushed the vibrator harder against my clit. I was panting squeezing his wrist, he whispered in my ear, "You're doing so good, being a good girl." I looked down at Mateo's lap and you could see he was enjoying this.

I was lucky he gave me a break from the torture when we were putting Alessia to bed. But he kissed her goodnight first and let me read her the story but before he left the room he whispered in my ear, to come straight to our room when I was done. Two stories later I am opening our bedroom door to Mateo laying on our bed with only his black boxers on.

He sits up. "Take everything off." I do as he says, and I strip everything off and he motions for me to come closer. When I get next to the bed, he puts the leather handcuffs around my wrists. "Kneel on the bed by the headboard." As I passed him he smacks my ass, I squeal and jump. I quickly scramble to the headboard and kneel in front of it. He gets behind me and grabs my hands and attaches them to the hook that hangs from the ceiling.

I start to pant in excitement of what he has planned for me. He kisses my jaw. "You okay?"

I nod my head and say, "Yes."

He puts his hand at the back of my head and turn my head so he can kiss me. It was a brief but passionate kiss. "Good, tell me if it's too much."

I whisper my agreement. He lays down but scoots himself so that his mouth is below me. Holy shit. Does he want me to do what I think he does?

"Sit on my face."

I lower myself a little. "I don't want to suffocate you."

He smacks my ass. "I said sit, not hover. If I die by suffocation of my wife's pussy at least I will know what heaven tasted like before I died." Then he grabs me by my hips and brings my lips to his. His tongue goes in and out of me, his one thumb is pressing on my clit. It doesn't take long for me to start feeling the coil of pleasure tightening. I start grinding on his face, with my head thrown back and I let the moans fly from my mouth. He uses the other hand that isn't constantly rubbing my clit to smack my ass. I start to fall apart and arch my backwards, shoving myself closer to his mouth. After I have finished, I thought I would be done but no. I feel him shift under me and he has sat up. Somehow, he took off his boxers.

"Mateo. I can't." He grabs my hips and rubs his cock through my slick folds. "Mhm, Mateo," I whine out because I am so sensitive.

"You have one more in you, then you can rest and be done." I raise myself a bit and start to sink down on him, Mateo grunts and squeezes my hips. I keep sliding myself further down on him, once he is all the way inside of me. I start rocking back and forth on him.

Mateo leans forward and kisses me; I can taste myself on his tongue. He plunges his tongue inside of my mouth and grabs my ass with his hands, pushing me to grind harder and faster on him. I gently scrape my teeth across his tongue. He squeezes my hip but doesn't pull away from the kiss at the moment, but I pull away when I am almost out of breath. He sucks on my nipple with his mouth and his hand is playing with the other one, my back is arched, and my head is tossed back.

I can feel myself getting closer and I can tell he is too because his grip on my hips is getting tight. I am sure they will leave bruises. But fuck it is so worth it. This man is blessed with an amazing cock, and he knows how to work it. It is not long after he switches that I fall apart, he keeps me rocking against him until he finishes. I lay my head on his shoulder and his is in my boobs. He stands up with him still inside me and pulls the handcuffs off the hook. My arms fall down around his neck, and I snuggle into his chest.

"You okay?" I nod but I am exhausted, all I want to do is sleep. "Put your arms in front of us, darling." I move my arms and he unlocks the handcuffs off my wrists. He takes each arm and kisses the inside of my wrists even though there isn't any bruises.

He finally pulls himself out of me when we get in the bath together, but he keeps me snuggled into his chest sitting on his lap. He kisses all over me and makes sure I am completely okay. I start dozing off while we are still in the bath. I get out, only half-awake with Mateo's help dry off and put one of his shirts on before I climb into the bed. I barely notice Mateo climbing in behind me before I have completely fallen asleep.

EMILIA
A Week Later

I am going to strangle my stupid husband! I tell myself does his dumb ass wouldn't think I wouldn't pick up on his change of behavior. What the hell is he hiding? I swear to god if his ass isn't being faithful, I will be damaging his cock. I am going to ask him one last time what is wrong with him, if he doesn't tell me I will be figuring out myself and he doesn't want that. I walk to his office and knock on his door, he says, *"Entrare."* I walk in and he is busy typing on his laptop and doesn't look up. I take a seat and wait for him to finish what he is doing on the computer. *"¿Dirai quello che... oh ehi Emilia."* *(Are you gonna say what you...oh hey Emilia.)*

I glare at him. "Do you talk to everyone else like that?"

He shrugs his shoulders as leans further back in his chair. "I am the boss; I can speak to anyone how I want."

I shoot my eyebrow up at him. "Really, you want to try and talk to me like that?"

He shakes his head "No I don't have a death wish. I would rather be at the end of one of Nonna's beatings than deal with the consequences of talking to you like that."

I smirk. "Smart man."

He sticks his chest out like he is a caveman who is gonna beat on his chest. "I am a smart man."

"Don't let your ego get any bigger otherwise you won't fit through the door. But anyway, I came to talk to you."

He has his arms propped up on his elbows and his chin resting on his interlocked fingers. "What do you want to talk about?"

I lean further back in the chair while crossing my legs. "Mateo what are you hiding from me?"

He sighs and says "Not this again. I told you I am not hiding anything."

I sigh, he wants to keep lying to me. "Do I look stupid to you?" I ask him, getting mad he is lying to my face again.

"When have I ever said you were stupid?" he asks me. I stand up from my chair and stand at the front of his desk.

"Well you must be thinking I am either stupid or a fool which I am neither. I can tell you are hiding something Mateo. We have yet to keep secrets from each other, but you decide to start now."

"When I tell you, don't worry about it. It means don't stick your nosey ass in my business."

"Oh, so now me worrying about what is bothering you and you being secretive is being nosey. Sorry, how dare I worry about my husband," I say, getting louder.

"Did I ask for your concern? No I didn't. I am the boss around here, not you. It would be wise for you to remember that. You only have this much power because me." He leans forward on his desk, yells at me.

"So now, when you want to hide shit from me you are the boss. But when you don't want to hide things from me, we both are the boss?" I say to him. I can feel my patience with him about to snap.

"I am trying to protect you," he yells at me.

"I don't need your protection Mateo. Wasn't it you who has called me your diabolical wife? That sounds I can hold my own," I yell back at him.

"Wasn't that why we got married? Because you couldn't protect Alessia?" His words feel like a slap to my face. I see the moment those words left his lips he regrets it. He knows damn well that Alessia's safety and protection is a sensitive subject for me because I feel like I have failed her in the past, so for him to bring it up and throw it in my face is a low blow.

"Emilia."

I stop him by putting my hand up. "At least I now know how you truly feel about me." I turn and head for the door. I can no longer stand to be in his presence.

"Emilia. Please I am sorry, I shouldn't have said that. I just want to protect you from seeing your past that haunts you."

He goes to grab my wrist, but I pull it away from him and snap at him. "Are you telling me they are in the same house I was forced to live in with Alessia?"

"Emilia. Please don't do this. I am sorry, I just didn't want you to go back to that house." He basically begs me to see why he said it.

"Yes or no Mateo?" I am demanding an answer, I don't care if he wants to tell me or not.

He hesitantly nods his head and says "Yeah, they are at Boris's house in Virginia. I didn't tell you because I was worried you would try to go there and save them."

"Of course I would, because I know that house like the back of my hand but don't worry, I will stay out of your way."

Mateo goes to open his mouth; I hold my hand up again to him "Don't! You have said enough." How dare he say that to me, he preaches for me to realize I am not a helpless woman and when I question him. He throws my past in my face. I wipe my tears; he wants to act like that. It hurts that he still thinks I am weak. Well, that's fine. I turn and leave his office. I walk into our room and grab my laptop. I decide I am gonna go to the library and see what he else he is hiding from me. I lock the door, sit in the far corner of the library, and start going through his emails, I see nothing in his legal business emails. So, I assume it is in his illegal businesses, I go through some and see his numbers for guns have increased. Obviously, that isn't the issue, I know he is still looking for a new doctor to replace Roman and Theo said he would help Mateo find a good doctor, but he didn't want that position. I think Tommaso would be a good fit but what do I know I am just a woman. And you see the emails back and forth with Theo, but I see an email from Fabio. In the email is a video of Kelly being hung from the ceiling by her hands being whipped, and I just cry. All my emotions are coming out from her and Damiano's child being in that situation to being hurt by what Mateo said. Then rage courses through my body at the Russians and Mateo.

After I finish crying and am able to watch the video, I see the address below. I suck in a breath knowing that it is Boris's old house where me and Alessia were held there for years. I know the inside of the house like the back of my hand. I sit there and contemplate if I should go rescue them. Fuck it, it would take less time to just go save them myself instead of telling him about the inside of the house and him arguing with me about helping. I hear the front door slam and I peek out the window, Mateo is speeding off in his car. Alessia is out shopping with Julietta, might as well sneak out now when some of security is gone. I quickly wrote a note for Mateo.

Mateo,
I am going to save Kelly and her child. I saw the email from Fabio with the video. I have no idea why you thought about keeping something this important from me. That was your choice, this is mine, I will do everything I can to save them. Don't worry about me, even if I get caught my wellbeing is no longer your concern.
I wouldn't want you to be worried about a weak and pathetic woman. All I ask from you since I am still your wife is to keep Alessia safe, if you can't give her to Esmeralda and Jose. I will be back for Alessia after. I want nothing from you except to have Boris and Seth killed.
Thanks for everything you did for us. Tell Alessia I love her and will always love her beyond my last breath.
Emilia

I wipe my eyes as I finish writing the note and place it on his end stand. I should wait and talk to him before I plan like this but if anything from my past has taught me is to know my worth. I will not stay with someone who thinks I am pathetic; I rather be single then tolerate being treated like that. I grab cash out of my wallet and see I don't have enough. I will stop and get cash before getting rid of the card. I only take the clothes on my back. My phone, wallet and rings are next to the note. I walk down to the garage and climb into one of the Range Rover's, the men see it is me and open the gate. They probably assume I have guards with me, and they are sitting in the back since I love to drive. I go to the closest bank and withdraw a couple thousand dollars, so I have enough to get there and back for everyone. I leave the keys and card locked inside the car. Knowing he has GPS on the car, and he will also trace my card, I am sure it will take no time at all for him to find it. I walk towards the airport and get a flight back to the states, headed back to my personal hell in Richmond, Virginia.

  I keep my head down while I am purchasing the tickets, I am lucky that the flight leaves in an hour. I sit down in the chair waiting for my flight, I play with the end of my shirt. I just hope I am making the right decision about leaving Italy. I won't regret going to save them, even if I don't make it out alive. They will and hopefully one day they can live a life of peace. I will regret it if I don't make it out alive or if Mateo decides not to give me Alessia back but if he does that he will be at the receiving end of my wrath. "Calling for flight to Virginia, USA" I hear them call. I get up, show the attendant my ticket and sit down in my seat. As we take off, I lean my head back in the seat and just pray everything works out in our favor.

FORTY-NINE
EMILIA

Twelve hours later, I am landing back in Richmond, Virginia. I hoped I would never set a foot back on this continent let alone this state. A place that used to have so many wonderful memories from me growing up. Now holds nothing but my worst nightmares. With only myself and my money, I decide on my first plan and go back to where I used to work before all hell lets loose. I hail a taxi and head to Mimi's diner, as soon as I open the door. I take a deep breath and smell the greasy food and coffee, it brings me back to my high school days, when Theo would be harassing me while I worked.

I was interrupted by the hostess, "Welcome to Mimi's. Would you like to sit at the bar or a table?"

"Table, please."

"Sure thing. Follow me." I follow her and sit down and order a burger with a coke. I think about Kelly and her son, I am worried how traumatized they both are being at the hands of Alexei and his goons. "Here is your coke."

"Thank you. Does Mimi own the diner?" I ask.

"Yes, she does. Why?"

"Oh, I am an old friend and would like to say hello."

"Oh, sure thing. I will tell her that she has a visitor."

"Thank you." She leaves and I am back to my own thoughts.

Before my burger comes out, I hear a sweet southern voice that never have seemed to lose her southern accent. "Oh my gosh. I must have died and went to heaven because I see my angel has returned to me." I stood up and embraced Mama Mimi, she demanded that I call her that since she was great friends with my Papa.

"Hi, Mama Mimi."

She leans back and cups my face "Look at my sweet angel is all grown up, and so beautiful. Tell me, to what do I owe this visit." She gives me a knowing look, not to lie to her.

"Can't get anything past you, can I Mama Mimi?"

"No, you can't, little missy. Now let's sit and you can talk to me." I nod at her and sit down; I start playing with the end of my shirt. "Emilia Rose Lombardi. Look at me and talk to me." I grimace when she calls me by my maiden name. I want to correct her, but I might have to get used to it again.

"It's actually Emilia Rose De Luca, well at least for now. But it is a long story." I look at her and she raises her eyebrow.

"Well I am no psychic, so open that big mouth of yours and fill me in." I chuckle at her attitude; she was always able to match my attitude and could put my ass in line when I needed it. So, while I eat my burger, I tell her everything from what happened after the murder of my family to the abuse of Seth. I had to stop during that so we both could work through our tears. After we have caught our breath, I tell them about my time with the De Luca's. And I finished telling her about what Mateo said and I told her why I left.

"I doubt I will still be married to him after everything is over but honestly, why would he want a pathetic, used woman like me when he could have any beautiful model or celebrity with a lot less scars mentally and physically."

She looks at me for a second then slaps the back of my hand. "Ouch, Mama Mimi! What was that for?" I say rubbing my hand.

"Because you're dumber than you look."

"Well, geez. Thanks."

"You dumb girl. That man was being stupid trying to protect you. And if he loves you like he claims to be, I am sure he was regretting what he said the moment those words came out of his mouth. But you said you needed help, what do you need help with?" I take a deep breath knowing she isn't gonna be happy I am putting myself back at risk. "I am going back to that house to rescue that woman and her child." She goes to stop me "I know Mama Mimi, but I know that house is like the back of my hand, and I can sneak in and out of there and save them then I will. But God forbid I can't escape with them. I want to leave you a number and money for them to be able to get back to Italy. And there is no one I trust more than you to do that."

"I absolutely hate this, but I see that fire in your eyes. Your Mama had that, and I know I can't talk you out of this."

I shake my head. "No Mama Mimi, my mind is made up."

"Okay, I will do it."

I give her a smile. "Here is the money, if I am not with them save a thousand for me just in case. And only give them money and phone number if they say angel face to you. It is a code so no one tries to trick you."

"Ok I will. What if your husband shows up looking for you?"

I sigh knowing he probably will be a couple hours if not a day behind me. "I am sure he will but anyone in the De Luca family will know the answer to this question. Who did I deal with after they slapped Alessia when we met the family? And the answer is Zaria."

She shakes her head. "I would have loved to see that."

"Oh, I am sure you would, but you would have asked us to stop so you could get popcorn knowing your crazy self."

She shrugs her shoulders, "Popcorn always goes well with entertainment." I laugh with her. I sat there with Mama Mimi for about another hour talking and reminiscing about Alessia. I purposely don't talk about Mateo. I am still very pissed at him. When it was time to go, we hung onto each other knowing we might not see each other again. She handed me a pocketknife, so I had some way to defend myself if I needed to. She did make me promise once I escaped that even if Mateo rescued me that I would let her know. She would prefer to see me, but she would settle with a phone call.

  I grabbed another taxi and had it stop at the end of the road. Luckily it was starting to get dark, so I was able to sneak onto the property. This is almost too easy; I know they are dumb, but I honestly didn't think they were this dumb. I don't ponder this at all and keep going the sooner I get them the sooner we get out the better. I walk around to the back of the house; the laundry room is right next to the closet that me and Alessia were kept in. I am going to start looking for them there and if not, I will work my way through the house until I find them. I put my hand on the door handle and slowly twist it and no surprise it is unlocked. I crack it open to listen for anyone in the room, I hear nothing but silence, so I slowly open the door the rest of the way and walk in. I quickly but quietly shut the door behind me. I walk to the other door for the closet inside the laundry room door and listen for movements inside the room. I hear a small child and one woman talking in hush voices. I smile knowing I have found them. I open the door, but I don't see a boy and a woman, but I see a little boy who has Damiano's face and two women who are guarding him from me. I see Kelly but the other woman has me completely shocked that I take a step back. I pinch myself and when she is still in front of me. I realize that she was still alive standing in front of me.

  "What...how...but he saw you die? How...shit," I stammer out. I take a breath to compose myself.

  "Lilyana is that you?" Her eyes look like they could pop out of her face.

  "How do you know my name? Everyone who cared about me died." I shake my head.

  "No, Anna De Luca died a week after they killed you. But Salvatore hasn't forgotten about you."

  She smiles. "Salvatore is still alive?" I nod my head.

  "Yes, he is along with my hardheaded husband Mateo and Dumbo Vincenzo." She giggles quietly.

  I look over and see Kelly is tense, so I tell her, "Kelly Mae, it's okay. Angel face."

  Kelly relaxes but asks, "Who are you?"

  "Emilia De Luca, Mateo's wife. But we don't have time to talk. We need to get the three of you out of here. Do not wait around for me; if you get out, run to Mimi's Diner. Go in and ask for Mama Mimi and tell her Angel face. She will give you money and Mateo's phone number so you can get back to Italy. I will find a way out; hopefully, we can leave together. Now let's go." I walk over to the door and put my ear against the door to listen, and I hear voices. I turn and put my finger to my lips, continuing to listen as they get closer. I pull out my pocketknife.

The door is snatched open, and I see my daughter's sperm donor. "Well, look here, boys. Looks like the kitten came back because she knows where she belongs. Serving us."

I roll my eyes. "No, Seth, I would never come back to you. I have a man who knows how to use his impressive cock, unlike that pathetic toothpick you call a cock." He slaps me, hard enough for my face to turn to the side.

"You have gotten mouthy since you left. That is okay. We will have no problem reminding you where you belong."

I again laughed at him. "Oh, Seth, you may have had me obey you when my daughter was under the same roof as me for her safety, but she isn't here. You have no idea who I am, so you want to try and break me. Be my guest, and I will make sure to make it difficult for you. But I have been planning my revenge for you after everything you did to me and MY daughter. I promise I will be brutal and vicious. You will be begging for mercy, but I will never give in to you." Seth's patience snaps, he had always had a short temper and hated when I disrespected him.

He punches me in the nose, and it starts to bleed. I wipe under my nose; I see the blood on my finger. I look at him and say, "Well that's cute."

He goes to swing at me again, but I kick him in the knee, hard. He falls down, and I slam my fist into his collarbone. He is hollering and cussing me. "You stupid whore. I will make you pay."

I raise an eyebrow at him on the floor shouting in pain. "Sure, you will, Seth."

"You think because you married a rich man, you are something special. You are nothing but a whore, which is all you ever will be."

I pick at my nails, waiting for him to finish his rant. "Are you done bitching?"

He stands up. "Oh, you are so gonna get it."

I open my arms out wide, "I am right here Seth. Do something." He goes to punch me, grabbing his wrist and pulling his arm behind his back. I kicked the back, all while. Kicking the back of his knee; I had already kicked. Now that he is down on his knees, I grab his other hand. He is thrashing around in my hold. He tries to stand up, but I stand on his calves. I lean down and whisper in his ear, "Now you will know how it feels to be the bitch. Get ready, kitten; you are about to be at my mercy. And I will make it long and painful."

I punch him in the side of his head and knock him out cold. I turned to Kelly. "Sorry but your brother is a sadistic bastard, and he has dues to pay."

She shakes her head. "None taken. He stopped being my brother a long time ago."

I must have alerted the other goons, I mean security. I look at them and realize they are too close for them to sneak out. "Get back in the closet." Kelly pushed her son in and locked it from the outside. I tell them to not be in direct sight. We all stand ready; I flick the pocketknife open. I turn to the girls, "The only ones to be left alive are Alexei and Seth. They will be dealt with by the De Luca men and Damiano," I say with a wicked grin.

Before anyone can react, Alec and two other men come down the steps. I know each one as they had raped me in the past. I step out of where I am hidden. "Hello boys. It's been a while," I say as I twirl the knife between my fingers. Alec looks at Seth unconscious while I have my foot on his back.

"What the fuck happened to him?"

I shrugged my shoulders. "He pissed me off. Plus, he is gonna be dragged back to Italy. He has some very eager people who are waiting to teach him thing or two before he is greeted by his maker."

Alec smirks at me while eyeing me up and down. "Why? Is your husband upset that we have used your body?"

I shake my head as I toss my knife into his shoulder. "No, he has an issue with rapists and abusers. Oh, Alec, he has plans for you too. That's if I don't kill you myself."

He yanks the knife out of his shoulder and puts a hand over his wound. "You were always a bitch." He says as he goes to try and punch me, but he is too slow. I hold his hand and kick him in the balls. He groans and bends over, grabbing his balls. I walk over and smash my knee into his nose. "Fucking cunt."

I snicker. "If I remember correctly, you enjoyed this cunt," I say to him as I slam my elbow on his back as he is slowly regaining his balance and is attempting to stand up. He falls to the ground; I kick him in the rib.

"Who the hell are you?" he asks. I push him so he is on his back.

"Emilia De Luca, the Queen of the Italian Mafia, and my husband's diabolical vicious wife, but you are about to find out how ruthless I can be," I tell as I slam his head on the concrete floor. His hands drop to the ground, I check for a pulse, and he is dead. "Fucking pussy, didn't give me a challenge." I grab his two guns out of his pants and pick up my knife. I look, and Kelly has snapped the man's neck.

But the sweet angel Salvatore talked about has her face covered in blood. Lilyana has slit his throat and is standing back with her arms crossed as she watches the man bleed out. I evilly smirk at her "You are gonna give Salvatore a heart attack. He still thinks of you as his sweet and innocent angel."

She gives me a small smile. "I won't interfere in his life just because I am back."

I shake my head. "Good luck with that. He is gonna cuff you to him. He has not moved on from his tiger lily." She scrunches her face when I say the nickname, she hated that Salvatore used to call her. "But we will talk about that after we kill the rest of these fuckers."

I start to whistle different songs as I make my way through the house. Luckily Alec had a silencer on his gun. I keep shooting every Russian scum I come across. I empty one gun and toss that one and switch to the other one. Between Lilyana and me, it takes us no time to kill the twenty or so men here. Kelly stayed to protect her son. I learned his Italian name is Dante, but the Russians, they call him Dimitri, so they don't suspect anything.

Alexei, unfortunately, isn't here; he took his mistress Elena out to go shopping. So, we have time to kill. I grab one of the dead men's phones to call Mateo. He picks up on the first ring.

Mateo: Hello. Who is this?

Emilia: Wow, don't you sound like a bucket full of sunshine.

Mateo: Emilia! My love. I am so sorry. I am an asshole. Are you okay? Are you hurt? Where are you?

Emilia: I am fine, but you need not worry about me. But I am at Boris's house. I have Seth here unconscious, ready to be transported to Italy, or should I just torture him here and kill him?

Mateo: Don't worry about you? You are my wife, I will always worry about you. Especially when you are in our enemies' hands. You could have been hurt?

Emilia: Whatever. You know I have been through hell. A couple bruises won't kill me.

Mateo: That isn't the point. I was trying to protect you.

Emilia: I don't need you protecting me from everything, Mateo. And there was no way in hell I was letting them stay here any longer. Plus, you would have fought me about coming here. I know this house just as well as the dead dumb fucks.

Mateo: What do you mean dead?

Emilia: We killed about twenty Russians including Ivan and Alec. But I've got to go, Mateo. It looks like we have company. Toodles.

That's the last thing I tell him as I hear cars pulling up in the driveway.

FIFTY
EMILIA

I am sure I pissed him off. Oh well, he can get over it.

We are back in the basement, so we can catch them off guard since it has the most coverage. We also can see how many get out of the vehicles from the small window over the washing machine which I am currently perched on, peeking out. I see Alexei, Elena and ten more guards, including his second and third in command, getting out of their vehicles. I am glad Mateo had me learn about all the different mafias and their high-rank members. They are making this too easy.

They open the door, and I hear Elena scream. Kelly quietly snickers, "Weak bitch."

I have to bite my tongue from laughing at her. We hear Alexei yell for his men to check the house. I mouth to both women, "Ready?" They nod. I am glad we swiped the weapons from the men we killed. We can hear them closing and opening doors upstairs.

We don't have to wait much longer until the first set of footprints start coming down the stairs. Once the man's feet hit the final step. So, I shot him in the back of his head. Lilyana and Kelly drag his body out of view. We do this with four other men, we start fighting them off.

I hear Kelly yell, "Leave him alone." I see a man drag Dante out of the closet we had him hiding in. Lilyana shoots the man who is holding Dante. He scrambles over to his Mama, but I look over in Kelly's direction and my mouth falls open. I see a red dot on Dante's chest.

"Kelly!" she turns and looks at Dante. She quickly shoves Dante out of the way, and he falls to the ground. Kelly is shot in the chest instead of Dante.

Lilyana runs over to put pressure on her wound. I see red and start shooting every man that comes down the steps. I have no idea how many men I have killed. I barely hear Lilyana and Dante screaming and crying for Kelly to not leave them. I scream when shot in my arm. I scream not from the pain but for the pain of Dante seeing his Mama shot. And all of the abuse from these monsters I went through and Alessia had to witness.

I turn around and see his second-in command Ivan snuck in through the back door. "You are so much of a pussy that you have to shoot me behind my back?" I taunt him.

"No. I just wanted the kitten's attention."

"Most people call someone's name when they want their attention. Not shoot them, Ivan. But why would I expect anyone who works for Alexei to have any brains." He tries to shoot me again; I move but not fast enough. The bullet hit me in the lower abdomen by my hip bone. I stare at him, gritting my teeth through the pain.

I realize he is drunk the way he is extremely uncoordinated on his feet and is using the wall for support. It also would explain his terrible aim. "Uh oh I think someone is drunk or is your aim that bad?" He gets angry and before he can I shoot his hand; he drops the gun.

"Fucking slut. I am gonna kill you."

"I have heard that all day. Yet here I am still standing." And I shoot both of his knees and he falls down. "You can't say the same, can you?" He tries to move but I shoot him in the neck. "Bye bitch." I hear two sets of footsteps come down the steps. One is someone with heavy shoes like boots and the other is a pair of heels.

The woman, who I could be called her pretty if you are into artificial women, has bleached blonde hair and bright green eyes. I can tell she got plastic surgery on her lips which are huge and disproportioned to her face. And her boobs are huge, yeah, she got a boob job too. Why the hell would Alexei willingly sleep with that? Kelly is so much more beautiful.

Elena shrieks in happiness. "Finally, the slut is dead. Now we can get married."

I come out of my hiding spot. "Well, whore, that means you both have to leave here alive."

They turn in my direction. Alexei smiles when he recognizes me. "Well, if it isn't the famous Emilia De Luca."

I point my gun at him and say, "The one and only."

"It is a pleasure to finally meet you." he tells me. I sneer back in response.

"Wish I could say the same thing."

His face goes from amused to angry and points his gun at me. "Tsk, tsk, tsk, such bad manners in a lady. No worry, we can fix that."

"And how will you teach me any manners when you will be locked up in our basement. While I torture you?"

He chuckles. "What makes you think that will happen?"

"Oh, I don't know most of your men are dead," I say, as I tilt my head to where most of his men are lying dead.

Elena screams at Alexei. "Fucking kill her."

He takes the gun and smacks her across the mouth. "I am the boss, not you, slut. Now get out of my face."

She quickly scurries away, but before she is out of the basement, I yell to her, "Make sure you hide really well, Elena, because you have a target on your back." She lands on her hands and knees. She stumbles a few times to get on her feet but gets up and quickly runs away from us. One day I will deal with her, I promise myself.

"You have a real winner there," I say laughing. He gets more pissed and goes to charge at me, but the basement door slams open. I see Mateo and Damiano come down the steps.

Damiano sees Kelly and yells, "No," and runs to her side. I see him cup her face; she puts her hand on his cheek. He turns his head and kisses her palm. They are quietly talking, but both of them have tears running down their cheeks. They both know she isn't gonna leave here alive. She has lost too much blood. They won't get a chance at a future outside of this hell.

I hear Mateo yelling at Alexei. "I am going to enjoy killing you very slowly." I roll my eyes. He doesn't really have to be so dramatic. The yelling is not necessary.

My vision starts to blur, so I lean against the wall for support but that doesn't seem to help. I fall to my knees; I hear someone yell my name. I don't respond and fall over onto my side. I hear my name being yelled; I try to see who is yelling my name, but I can't see who it is. I am moved to my back, and someone is hovering over me. Then it all goes silent and everything around me is slowly turns black.

FIFTY-ONE
MATEO
Back To The Night Of The Fight With Emilia

  "Don't. You have said enough," she said, as she basically ran out of my office.

  "*FANCULO!*" I yell in my office and throw my cup of coffee at the door. Why the fuck would I say something so stupid and hurtful to my Queen? I sit back down in my chair and run my hands through my hair. My big mouth just added to my stress. I worry about Emilia more than the Russians right now. I want to go after her, but I think we both need a few minutes to calm down. I should have been honest with her. What the fuck would it have hurt? Obviously, I suck at keeping shit from her since she picked up on something that wasn't right within hours. I decided to go see and see if she is ready to talk to me and prepare for whatever punishment she released on my ass that I very well deserve.

  I first walked into our bedroom; she isn't on our bed. Maybe she is taking a bath, and she isn't in there either. Okay instead of trying to try and hunt her down I sit on the bed and watched the CCTV from when she left my office. I watch as she leaves my office, passing the guards who all give her a concerned look, but she plays it off. Shit as if I don't feel guilty enough, she walks into our room. She walks out a minute later with her laptop in her arms, I follow her on the CCTV to the library. I should have known my little bookworm would have gone to the library. The far corner that overlooks the front garden is her reading area. I personally went out and picked out a comfortable chair with pillows and blankets once I saw how much she loves reading. I turn off my phone and start walking to the library. I barely get out of my bedroom door when my phone rings when I see Salvatore is calling.

  Mateo: What.
  Salvatore: Damn, who pissed you off.
  Mateo: Myself. What do you need?
  Salvatore: What did you do this time?
  Mateo: I said some fucked up shit to Emilia and I am about to grovel at her feet. So, what do you need?
  Salvatore: We had a shipment of guns stolen.
  Mateo: Fuck! I am on my way. No one leaves until I get there.
  Salvatore: Got it, Boss. And it was nice knowing you.

  I don't bother responding to him, I hang up and continue to walk to the library. I get another four texts from Salvatore by the time I walk to the library, which only adds to my foul mood. I go to open the door and I hear her sobs. I stop and rest my head against the door, I get another text from Salvatore. He is asking for a bullet; fucker knows I am in the doghouse and keeps blowing up my phone. I rest my forehead and hand against the door and whisper *"Mi dispiace mia regina. Sono uno stronzo stupido completo. Devo sistemare qualcosa, ma non appena torno a casa, mi brancherò ai tuoi piedi o farò qualsiasi cosa tu voglia aggiustare il mio cazzo."* (I am sorry my Queen. I am a complete stupid asshole. I have to fix something but as soon as I get home, I will grovel at your feet or do anything you want to fix my fuck up.) I grudgingly walk away from Emilia and head to the warehouse.

I get into my car, and I can honestly say this is one of the first times I actually hate being the boss. I rather be staying home with Emilia instead of heading to a warehouse and I swear if it is a stupid mistake, I will be emptying my clip into someone. I speed out of the driveway and it takes me half as long as it should to get to the warehouse. I want to get done as soon as possible so I can get back to my wife. I get into the warehouse and my anger is radiating off me, honestly, I really could care less. Salvatore sees me and hands me the invoice we were getting from the French Mafia, which is twenty dozen of the FR F2. It is the French version of the sniper rifle.

"Quindi, quale di voi figli di puttana incompetenti ha trascurato di fare il vostro lavoro?" (So, which one of you incompetent motherfuckers neglected to do your job?) Silence is all I hear. *Quindi, nessuno vuole ammettere chi era troppo occupato o stupido per rendersi conto di controllare l'inventario prima di finire la transazione con i francesi. Quindi, chi è l'idiota?"* (So, no one wants to admit who was either too busy or stupid to realize to check the inventory before finishing the transaction with the French. So, who is the moron?) I see one man start to squirm around from my hard gaze. *"Non iniziare a parlare, inizierò a sparare finché non farò del male all'uomo giusto. Quindi, scegli, fai un passo avanti o fai morire il tuo prossimo per te che sei un codardo."* (Don't start talking, I will start shooting until I hurt the right man. So, pick, you step forward or have your fellow man die from you being a coward.) I pulled my gun out of the waistband of my pants and walked to the first man and shot him in the chest. *"Ancora non sto parlando. Ok, continuerò a sparare."* (Still not talking. Okay I will keep shooting.) I am about to pull the trigger when I hear *"Aspettare. Ero io."* (Wait. It was me.) I stop and turn to face the man who cost me millions of dollars. I call him over to stand in front of me.

He stands in front of me. I put my gun to his head, and I asked him *""Come ti chiami, ragazzo?"* (What is your name, boy?)

"Wyatt, capo," (Wyatt Boss) he stutters out.

"Wyatt, dimmi perché hai pensato che sarebbe stata una buona idea tradirmi?" (Wyatt, do tell me why you thought it would be a good idea to betray me?)

"Mi sono appena distratto Boss. Mi dispiace." (I just got distracted Boss. I am sorry.)

"*Scusa? Oh, ti dispiacerà.*" (Sorry? Oh, you will be sorry.) I smacked him on his temple with my gun, hard but not hard enough to knock him out. He stumbles a step back; I send a quick punch to his jaw that sends him to the ground. "*Perché eri distratto, Wyatt?*" (Why were you distracted Wyatt?) He doesn't answer and I am in no mood to play around with him, so I shoot him in the shoulder. He groans and reaches up and puts pressure on it. I shoot his hand holding the bullet hole, he screams out in pain. He must think I am stupid, knowing he was paid to fuck up the shipment. *Non sono dell'umore giusto per giocare. Dimmi chi cazzo ti ha detto di non controllare la fottuta spedizione di armi.*" (I am not in the mood to play games. Tell me who the fuck told you not to check the fucking shipment of guns.)

He attempts to stop screaming but when he hears my gun click "*Ok te lo dirò.*" (Ok I will tell you.)

I arch my eyebrow at him "*Inizia a parlare o continuerò a mettere proiettili nel tuo corpo.*" (Start talking or I will keep putting bullets in your body.)

He nods his head "*Erano i francesi. Non vogliono fare affari con qualcuno che sta inseguendo i russi.*" (It was the French. They don't want to do business with someone who is going after the Russians.)

"*Erano i francesi. Non vogliono fare affari con qualcuno che sta inseguendo i russi?*" (And why would the French care if I am at war with the Russians?)

You see him swallow so obviously he is about to lie to me. Stupid boy.

"*Non so*" (I don't know)

I shoot him in his kneecap and step on his knee. "*Smettila di mentirmi. Dimmi quello che sai, ADESSO!*" (Quit lying to me. Tell me what you know, NOW!)

He nods his head while he shakes. "*Tutto quello che so, i francesi non vogliono più fare affari con te perché sua nipote è importante per Alexei. E non vogliono che si faccia male.*" (All I know the French don't want to do business with you anymore because his niece is important to Alexei. And they don't want her to get hurt.)

I nod at him and shoot him in between the eyes. I look to the rest of my men and say "*Questo è ciò che accadrà a chiunque ci tradisca. Hai preso Omerta. Mi aspetto che tu obbedisca a quella promessa fino a quando non fai il tuo ultimo respiro. Altrimenti, implorerai la morte. Pulisci questo pasticcio.*" (This is what will happen to anyone who betrays us. You took Omerta. I expect you to obey that promise until you take your last breath. Otherwise, you will be begging for death. Clean this mess up.)

I walk out of the warehouse; I hear Salvatore behind me. "Tell Vincenzo to get ahold of the fucking French to set up a meeting."

"Got it. Do you need anything else?"

I shake my head. "No but unless it is an emergency don't disturb me." I get into my car and speed off back to the mansion. I replay what I said to Emilia in my head. I grip the steering wheel in anger. "Did I ask for your concern, no I didn't. I am the boss around here, not you. It would be wise for you to remember that. You only have this much power because me." Why the fuck would I even say anything like that to her, she is so much more than that. I slam my fist on my steering wheel multiple times, it starts to bleed but I could care less. I park my car in front of the mansion and toss my keys to Sergio, my driver, to park my car in the garage. I run up to our wing and head straight to the library. I see she isn't there, but her laptop is sitting on her chair. I decided to check our bedroom. It is empty as well; I get an uneasy feeling something is wrong. I call her phone and I can hear it ring inside the bedroom, I see it on my end table. I drop my phone. I see a note, her phone, wallet, and her rings sitting on my end table. "Fuck! No, no. This isn't happening." I pick up the note and read what it says.

I grab the lamp on my end table and throw it across the room, it shatters into pieces as it hits the wall. After that I see red and destroy the room, I destroy the bed, furniture, I am about to grab the big family portrait from our last day at the safe house. My eyes land on Alessia and I run my finger down my daughter's face. "No one will take you away from me, baby." Emilia you can be mad, and you have every right to be, but you married the mafia dear. We are married until death to do us apart. I dare you try and leave. No way in hell are you taking my princess from me. I will find you if you leave and drag your ass back here where you belong.

I walk back into the library and see what she was doing on her laptop before she got this stupid idea to try and save Kelly on her own. I swear if she has one scratch on her, I am gonna kill the fucker slowly. And her ass is gonna get punished, well more punished. I open her laptop; fucking hell I forgot her older brother was a hacker and taught her. According to Fabio he was legendary he basically fangirled over the fact my wife is related to him. She has my email open, specifically the one Fabio sent me with the address and the video of Kelly being whipped. Shit! I didn't want her to see that knowing it could trigger her.

I know why she decided to go save her but on her own. Fabio was working on getting blueprints so we can be successful in killing the Russians except for Alexei and hopefully if Seth is there. I send Fabio a text "I need those blueprints asap" he doesn't respond which isn't unusual when he is in his "zone" hacking he hates being disturbed. I decide to go to my office and see what else I can find out. I walk in and look at the chair Vincenzo is sitting in knowing that was the last time I saw her. Even though I am mad at her for being reckless, I am more pissed at myself. I ignore my cousins as they greet me, and I walk over to the bar and pour myself a big drink of whiskey. I drink it all in one shot, I feel the burn in my throat, but I don't care. I go to pour myself another drink, but Salvatore grabs the bottle out of my hand.

"Don't fuck with me right now Salvatore." Salvatore holds the bottle out of my reach, so I decide to grab something else instead when Vincenzo pulls me by my shoulder and turns me away from the bar. I am about to swing at Vincenzo, but he grabs my fist.

"What the fuck did you do Mateo?"

"Remember who you are talking to."

He snorts at me. "Oh, I know who I am talking to. I am talking to my dumb ass cousin who did something stupid, and who is pissed and going to try and drink his problems away. Knowing that drinking will add to his problems, not solve them."

I pull out of his grip and reply with a, "Fuck off." Vincenzo might be a goofball at times, but he is the biggest asshole out of us and will call you out on your shit. And not give a damn if he hurts your feelings or how much he pisses you off.

I sink into my desk, run my hands through my hair. "You're right but I fucked up bad," I say.

Salvatore asks, "How bad is bad?"

"Bad. I was trying to keep that email from Fabio away from Emilia, she called me out on hiding stuff from her. I threw her past in her face when she cornered me about hiding shit. I gave her some space and dealt with the warehouse bullshit; I came back to a note from her saying she left to go save Kelly. That she is no longer my concern and when she returns, she is coming to take Alessia. She hacked into my email and saw the email from Fabio."

Vincenzo whistles. "Fuck, Mateo. When you fuck up you fuck up."

I glare at him. "You think I don't know how bad I fucked up? I know what I did. I am fucking regret it; I was just trying to protect her from getting triggered seeing the video."

"You will be at her mercy when she gets back. So good luck with that. But the better question is how does she know about the house? Does she know it, or did she just go in blind hoping for the best?"

"I am pretty sure that is where they lived since, they were with Seth..."

"Fabio needs to hurry up with those blueprints." I say exasperated, and Vincenzo nods.

"Yeah, we need a plan before we go there guns blazing. As much as I would love to eliminate the Russians, I don't want to risk Emilia, Kelly, or her son's life." Salvatore nods with him, he is about to say something when I hear a small knock on my door.

I smile, knowing it is my princess. "Come in baby girl." She slowly opens the door and peeks her head in. She has a smile on her face when she looks at me. She comes in the rest of the way; she sees her uncles go and kisses each of them with a kiss on the cheek before coming over to me. I open my arms out to her and give her a hug and a kiss on her hair. She climbs on my lap and lays her head on my chest, "How was shopping with Zia Julietta?" I ask her and she looks up at me.

"Exhausting, but I found some pretty boots."

I chuckle at her boot obsession. "Am I going to have a bigger closet built for you?"

She rolls her eyes. "I am not as bad as Zia Julietta, Papa." I kiss her forehead, but she wrinkles her face when she looks at my laptop. "Papa, why do you have a picture of our old house?"

"What do you mean Alessia?" I play dumb to see what she knows.

She points to the laptop. "That was the house we stayed in with Seth and Boris until Mama got us away from them." I look at Vincenzo and Salvatore giving them a knowing look. I pick Alessia up in my arms and bring her to sit on the couch, Vincenzo and Salvatore sit on either side of her. She looks at the three of us "Am I in trouble?"

I shake my head. "No, *Principessa*, but can you help us with something?"

She nods her head. "Sure, Papa."

"Can you tell me anything about the inside of the house?"

"Our room was in a small closet in the laundry room. And you could go outside through a door in the laundry room." I squeeze my fists hearing about my girls living in a closet for years, but they will never live in rough conditions like that ever again.

"What about upstairs? Can you tell me about anything upstairs?"

She shakes her head no. "I only went upstairs the day we left because I heard Mama yelling and Mama never yelled at them. I was afraid she was hurting, and I was right, Seth hurt her really badly." She starts to cry; I wipe her eyes.

"Shh, Alessia, it is okay. Thank you for telling me this, we found out someone else is being held in that house like how you and your Mama were. And your Mama is busy helping an old friend, but we want to go save the person at that house."

Her eyes open wide. "Yes, Papa. You need to save them; they are mean people. I don't like them."

Vincenzo grabs her hand. "We will, Alessia, and you are right they are very mean, but we will make sure they go away for hurting people like they did." I glare daggers at him, why would he say that to her. He shrugs his shoulders,

"Okay. When will Mama be home?"

I take a deep breath. "Not sure baby girl, but I will know later. It might be a couple days, but you know what that means?" She shakes her head no. "That means we can eat ice cream before bed."

She squeals in excitement "With chocolate syrup and rainbow sprinkles?"

I wink at her. "Of course but it is our secret."

She puts her hand on her head and salutes me like a sailor "Aye, aye captain." The three of us laugh at her silliness.

I stand up and hold my hand out for her. "Let's go see what boots you bought with your aunt." She grabs my hand, and we walk into her room; she is talking to me about the different kinds of boots. Let's be honest I have no ideas about the different kinds of boots but if buying them makes her this happy I would buy her every pair of boots in the world. Good thing Emilia balances everything out because if I was to raise Alessia on my own she would be a spoiled brat.

We get into her room, and I see her big pile of bags in her closet that Julietta is putting away. I smirk at my sister. "Did you buy out the whole mall?"

She turns around with her hands on her hips. "No, but I can always go back and buy it out if you want." I want to roll my eyes at her, but I don't. I get a notification from the bank letting me know someone has withdrawn a large amount of money out of Emilia's account earlier today. Julietta must see the look on my face and distracts Alessia by putting stuff away then helping her with designing her own shirt. Alessia is more than excited to help Julietta. I say to her thank you, I kiss Alessia on her head and tell her I have to go finish my work so we can have our ice cream date tonight. She barely acknowledges me being so excited to help her aunt.

I text Fabio to get the security cameras from my bank and see who is withdrawing the money from Emilia's account. Vincenzo and Salvatore are still in my office when I walk back in. Salvatore says, "Well now we know why Emilia decided to go and rescue them on their own."

I nod at them. "And I got a notification from the bank that someone withdrew five thousand dollars out of Emilia's account. I have Fabio pulling up security cameras from inside and outside of the bank." Salvatore looks at me like I am stupid, before he can answer "I know it is probably her, but I want to confirm it."

About twenty minutes later, Fabio sends me the footage and you can see Emilia in one of our jeeps parking in the parking lot. She walks into the bank and withdraws the money; I expect her to leave in the jeep, but she doesn't. She opens the door, puts the key and bank card in the jeep, locks the jeep. Then she walks down the road. What the hell is wrong with her? Why the fuck is she being so careless? Is she trying to get kidnapped? She shouldn't be so damn careless, knowing the fucking Russians are after us. Walking in town in broad daylight with no protection. They could easily kidnap her; she has no protection. I swear she must want to be punished when she keeps doing stupid shit like this. At the rate she is going I am going to tie her ass to our bed until her hardheaded ass stops making stupid decisions. Fabio knows me well enough that he got other security cameras to follow my rebellious wife.

She walks to the airport and books a ticket to the states. And once she gets on the plane, we don't have anything since she should still be on the plane since it is a twelve-hour flight. She got on the plane five hours ago.

Vincenzo and Salvatore are smirking at me. "What?" I say to them.

Vincenzo shakes his head. "When Emilia wants to leave, there is no stopping her." Salvatore joins him in laughing at my misery.

"Laugh it up now but when we return, she is screaming down the walls after I tie her ass to the bed. I will make sure you are in the same house as us."

Salvatore shakes his head "I love you but no way in hell do I want to be in a ten-mile radius when she unleashes her wrath on you. I actually will take Alessia and take her on a vacation."

I roll my eyes. "It won't be that bad," I say confidently.

They both chuckle at me "Whatever you say."

I sit back in my chair and think if we should go ahead and fly over there to try and stop her or at least drag her ass out of there. "I think we should leave tonight to the states. I don't feel comfortable being twelve hours away from her if shit hits the fan." Salvatore nods his head, Vincenzo tells me he will call the pilot, I tell them we will do it after Alessia goes to bed in two hours. Before my date with Alessia I call Peter and Jose to have them meet us in Virginia to take down these fucking Russian's once and for all. We will be going to Boris's mansion and Peter and Jose's groups will be taking down their warehouse. I am going to enjoy this night with her especially with her Mama gone and I am going to leave the same day. She needs this but I also know she will be in good hands. I tell my family after dinner when Alessia is changing into her pajamas for our ice cream date. Nonna gave me good smacks with her broom instead of the spoon and everyone else is pissed at me as well. I honestly don't care, the only thing I care for is bringing everyone home where they belong. Luckily Julietta and Marcello will be with Alessia the whole time along with Nonna and Nonno, but I have put our family on lockdown until we return home.

I pray we all make it out alive and home in one piece.

FIFTY-TWO
MATEO

After my daddy daughter ice cream date with Alessia, I explained to her that I had to go help Mama.

She was extremely happy to be having a sleepover with Julietta until we got back. As much as I don't like the idea of Marcello sharing a room with my sister, I told him to sleep in the room with them. I am not taking any chances of either one of them getting hurt when I am across the country. I know Marcello and his team will keep my family safe while Vittorio has organized a team that will come with me to rescue Kelly and her son.

Hours later, I am sitting on my laptop on the plane finishing some work for De Luca Corp because I know when I bring Emilia home it isn't going to be a peaceful ride. I am lost in my thoughts when I get a call from an unknown number.

Mateo: Hello. Who is this?

Emilia: Wow, don't you sound like a bucket full of sunshine?

Mateo: Emilia! My love. I am so sorry. I am an asshole. Are you okay? Are you hurt? Where are you?

Emilia: I am fine, but you need not to worry about me. But I am at Boris's house, the one Fabio emailed you about. I have Seth here unconscious ready to be transported to Italy or should I just torture him here and kill him?

Mateo: Don't worry about you? You are my wife. I will always about you especially when you are in our enemies hands. You could have been hurt.

Emilia: Whatever. You know I have been through hell. A couple bruises won't kill me.

Mateo: That isn't the point. I was trying to protect you.

Emilia: I don't need you protecting me from everything, Mateo. And there was no way in hell I was letting them stay here any longer. Plus, you would have fought me about coming here. I know this house just as well as the dead dumb fucks.

Mateo: What do you mean dead?

Emilia: We killed about twenty Russians including Ivan and Alec. I've got to go, Mateo. It looks like we have company. Toodles.

Mateo: Emilia don't hang up. Hello, Emilia?

The call ended. I push down my anger that she hung up on me but worry about who her company is.

I lean back in the chair; I take out my phone and look at the photo of me and Emilia on our family day. I rub my thumb on her face. She is sitting in between my legs in the opening of the canopy tent, just looking up at me with the biggest smile on her face. I remember I was gonna go give her a sweet kiss, but my feisty wife decided to lick my cheek and run off laughing. I chased her around the garden and eventually caught her and threw her over my shoulder. We both were genuinely laughing. I wipe a tear from the corner of my eye.

  I never understood what my father said about love makes you weak, but he was also wrong because my love for Emilia can have me on my knees, but she also makes me stronger. My Tigress, oh how I miss you. As soon as I save you, I am going to be punishing you and you will never be leaving my sight again my sneaky wife. I close my eyes thinking about Emilia, Alessia and our future children in our own farmhouse. She would love that; we would have farm animals and land for her to do whatever she wanted. I tried to get some rest, but none was available, so I decided to go back to finishing more work. Fabio calls me to give me updates about Emilia.

  Fabio: Boss, I have more updates about Donna after she left.
  Mateo: Go ahead, Fabio.
  Fabio: She took a taxi to a diner called Mimi's Diner; they do not have cameras on the inside but what I could tell from the camera from the store across the street. Emilia met up with an older lady and talked, they seemed friendly like they had a past. After that she left in another taxi to go to the street of Boris's house. I sent you a picture of the lady in your email.
  Mateo: Thanks, Fabio

  I look at the woman Mimi Gallagher. She owns Mimi's café. I am shaken awake by Vincenzo telling me we have landed. I grab my stuff and walk to the SUV's; we decide to follow in Emilia's footsteps to see what my Tigress has planned plus it gives Fabio more time to gather everything together. As much as I want to swarm into Boris's house, we could do more harm than good if we go in unprepared.

  I walk into Mimi's Diner with Salvatore and Vincenzo, the waitress sits us at a table and attempts to flirt with me. I ignore her, that might have worked before Emilia, but I definitely am not interested, nor do I need her to find another reason to be mad at me. I know I already am digging myself out of the hole my mouth got me in.

  She realizes that I am not giving her any attention then tries it on Salvatore. And we all know he hasn't been interested since he laid his eyes on Lilyana. I figured she would stop trying to get our attention but no, she then tries to be sexy with Vincenzo.

  Well, Vincenzo being the asshole he is tells her, "Darling you are wasting your time. If my brother and cousin turned you down for being desperate, what makes you think I will be interested? Desperation is a big turn off."

She puts her hands on her hips "You don't know what you are missing. I don't mind sharing." I gag at the concept, one thing we will never do is share a girl.

She glares at me, and I cut her off "Sorry, but we don't share girls. We need to speak to your boss."

"You really think you are all that because you are rich?"

I take a sigh and stand up so I am towering over her and say, "No, I could care less about you being poor. You are throwing yourself at us, your customers. You are lucky I don't own this diner, if I did you would be fired. Now run along and get your boss."

"Jennifer, you're fired. I told you if you flirted or acted like a hussy again you would be fired. Pack your stuff and get out." Jennifer goes to open her mouth when the same old lady says. "NOW." Jennifer stomps her way to the back of the cafe. The old lady comes to our table. "I am sorry about that. I heard you want to speak to me."

I am still standing when I introduce myself, "Yes you must be Mimi. I am Mateo De Luca, and these are my cousins Vincenzo and Salvatore De Luca. My wife was here earlier, and I wanted to know what you talked about. It is really important."

She squints her eyes at me to see if I am lying. "Who did Emilia deal with after they slapped her daughter after she met your family?"

I smirk as Vincenzo laughs and Salvatore has a slight smile to his face. "I see my wife was being smart and calculated as always but your answer is Zaria."

"So, you are my angel's husband." Then she reaches up and smacks my cheek. I rub it; damn, for an old lady, she can hit hard. "Now that is for being stupid and not realizing when to shut your mouth. Also don't keep secrets from her she has always been able to tell when someone is lying to her. She is your wife; trust her she is stronger than you realize. But let's sit down and we can talk." I agree with Mimi. What is it with my wife being friends with women just as scary as her?

"Emilia came to tell me she was going to save a friend and her child from the same hell she was in with her daughter."

I interrupted her, "Our daughter. She isn't just Emilia's daughter. She is mine as well."

"Hush boy. Anyway, she said she knows the place like the back of her hand and was determined to get them out of there. She said she was willing to risk her life if they would be able to have a better life. I saw the same fire in her eyes as her Mama and knew there was no talking her out of it."

I run my hand through my hair at times. I love having a fierce wife but right now I wish she wasn't because she put herself right in my enemy's hands. They will continue to hurt her until I get her safe in my arms, then I am not letting her out of my sight. I mumble "Of course she would. I swear I am gonna lock her up in our mansion when I get her away from him."

Mimi just laughs. "She has the fire like her Mama but the big heart like her Papa," she says with a smile.

Salvatore asks Mimi, "You knew Emilia's parents well?"

Mimi chuckles. "Yes, I did. I was Alessandro's neighbor and Angelica's best friend. I was a second mom to Franco, Emilia, and Giovanni," she says with a small smile. "I never liked that man she was with after her family died. I wish I could have stopped her, but she was grieving and acted recklessly. I tried so hard not to have her tell him she was pregnant; I could just tell there was something not right about him."

I nod at her. "Yeah he is a real evil bastard. What he put my girls through." I stop and take a deep breath and finish "I can't wait until he is six feet under."

Mimi nods at me. "I agree with you. But good luck. She is convinced you are going to divorce her after your fight."

I take a harsh breath, "Over my dead body will we be getting a divorce."

Mimi laughs at me; she pats my clenched fist. "I can see you are a good man Mateo. You just need to know when to put your foot in your mouth. But my angel needs a man who is strong enough to deal with her when she is being bullheaded." I look down to see a text from Fabio telling me Peter & Jose has landed with their trams and everyone is ready.

"I hate to leave Mimi, but we need to leave so we can go save my stubborn wife. But here is my number, if you ever need anything, I mean anything do not hesitate to reach out. And I will make sure Emilia stays in contact with you."

She takes my business card; she looks at me. "By the way she thinks you want a divorce."

My nostrils flare. "Over my dead body am I getting a divorce from her."

She laughs. "Good luck with her hardheaded self."

I chuckle knowing she is right, "Thank you, Mimi."

She hugs and kisses each of our cheeks. "Go save my angel. And you're family now. Come back anytime."

Once we leave Mimi's Diner, Vincenzo chuckles, "I think her and Nonna would be best friends."

I laugh. "I agree but that could be dangerous for everyone else around them. Especially since by the picture on the wall Mimi knows Esmeralda. And I don't want to imagine them all together." Salvatore chuckles at my statement. But I cringe knowing I will most likely be at Esmeralda's wrath if she finds out about our fight.

Once we get back to the SUV's, I pull out my laptop and we start looking through the blueprints. It is a mansion off of a suburb development so if the neighbors hear gunshots, they will call the cops, so we need to use silencers and knives. But I change my mind when I see the front entrance is heavily guarded, but I am in no forgiving mood. I look over at my cousins. "How does driving through their gate sound to you?"

Vincenzo smirks. "We might stir attention."

"So? And I might just happen to know the chief of police neglected my in-laws' homicide case and it could easily be brought to light if they try anything with us. And Fabio has other blackmail on this chief of police that we can use if we need to. Like his hand in distributing drugs to the local teens." I smirk along with my cousins; we have no problem getting our hands dirty when it comes to family. "Plus, the chief of police is a crook. After we drive through their gates, they will be opening fire on us. Everyone else can be killed except Seth and Alexei. If we get our hands on his mistress, well that is just icing on the cake." I say with a malicious smile on my face, it is time for the Russians to see the beast within me. She is my diabolical wife, and no one gets to hurt what is mine.

We pull off the side of the road about two miles away from Boris's mansion. I gather my main men around and tell them the plan. While Peter and Jose go over there plan. Alexei's warehouse is about thirty minutes from here. They have about fifty men with them, so it shouldn't be hard to kill off the Russians, take whatever merchandise then blow the place up. "I want every Russian killed besides Seth, Alexei, and his mistress. They are to be brought back to Italy alive. The main goal is to get Kelly, her son and Emilia out alive. If you see them and can get them to the SUV's safely, do it and get them to the airport, but let me know. I want silencers on your guns. Let's bring the women and Damiano's son home safely."

They all respond with *"Si, Don."*

We all go to our SUV's and gear up. Everyone is armed with all kinds of weaponry from bulletproof vests, guns, knives, brass knuckles, bombs. We are not playing anymore with these Russian scum, it is time to take them down once and for all.

Jose sees me. "Where is Lia?"

I look around and don't see Esmeralda I don't need to be injured before attacking the Russians. "We got in a fight. She got pissed and decided to sneak off and get here before us."

He chuckles at me and slaps my back. "Good luck." He tells me as he walks away. I am not sure if he means good luck with Esmeralda or Emilia. I decide to focus on rescuing our people then I will deal with the consequences of my big mouth.

I am in the passenger seat of the first vehicle with Vittorio driving. We approach the suburb development and I tell Vittorio "Floor it". He nods at me and does as I ask. Might as well make an appearance known. We are speeding towards the gate; his men are already shooting at us, but we are in bulletproof vehicles. They realize Vittorio isn't gonna stop and try to run out of the way. But they were already shot at by my men, the front of our SUV slammed into the gate, sending the gates and any men left standing in front of the gate flying backwards. Vittorio skids the van to stop at the front of the entrance of the mansion.

I get out and start shooting at the Russians who are rushing out the mansion, it doesn't take long for us to kill them all. Disappointed I haven't seen any of my targets yet. I walk into the mansion and more men shoot at us.

Vincenzo is having a blast playing with them *"Vincenzo ha smesso di giocare a cazzo. Uccidi questi stronzi, puoi divertirti con quelli che portiamo a casa. Non farmi ripetere me stesso o ti sparerò io stesso."* (Vincenzo quit fucking playing around. Just kill these fuckers, you can have fun with the ones we bring home. Don't make me repeat myself or I will shoot you myself.)

"Bene. Rovini tutto il divertimento, cugino." (Fine. You ruin all the fun, cousin.)

If I wasn't in the middle of shooting fucking Russians, I might put a bullet in him. I might do it afterwards anyway. It takes us not much longer to minimize the Russians to where my soldiers and Vittorio can handle it. I make my way downstairs to where the basement would be, Damiano calls out to me, I look down the hall and see him pointing to a door. You can hear people struggling on the other side. I can hear Emilia's voice muffled and I slam the door open and run down the stairs with Damiano on my heels. I open the door and see Emilia in Alexei's face. Damiano yells "no" and runs to Kelly's side, she has been shot in her chest. A woman and her son are both crying at her side.

When I take a closer look at the condition of Emilia, I let the beast inside of me emerge. Alexei smirks at me and goes to shoot me but I easily dodge it. He goes to take another shot at me, this time it grazes my arm. "Wow you shoot just as well as you run your family's empire." He goes to shoot me again, but he comes up empty. He tries three more times to shoot me. After finally realizing he ran out of bullets he throws the gun at me. He charges at me; I can see Emilia is white as a ghost. I decide to knock him out fast so I can get her help fast.

I shoot him in his thigh, he falls down like a stack of bricks. He is on the ground holding his leg, I walk up to him and tell him "It is time for you to enjoy De Luca's hospitality to those who hurt my family. I am going to enjoy killing you very slowly. Night, Alexei," I say, then I kick him in the head, which knocks him unconscious. As much as I would want to cause him to be in pain, Emilia needs me more.

I see Emilia leaning her body against the wall. I run over to her but before I could she falls down to her knees. I yell her name, but she falls to her side, I watch as her head bounces off the concrete floor. "Emilia," I yell louder and fall to my knees in front of her. I turn her to her back and tap her cheeks, her eyes keep fluttering. I tap her cheeks. "Keep your eyes open Emilia." She shuts them, so I tap her cheeks harder, and she opens them. She looks directly with those deep green eyes that makes my heart skip a beat. But a moment later she closes her eyes and won't open them. I pick her up and run out to the first SUV. Vittorio sees me running with Emilia in my arms and he runs ahead and opens the door so we both can get in quickly. The SUV fills up, but I pay no mind who is with me. I keep all of my focus on Emilia.

FIFTY-THREE
MATEO

Vittorio and I don't talk the rest of the way to the jet. I am too focused on keeping pressure on her stomach and shoulder. The blood is pooling around my hands, "Stay with me Emilia, you have to stay alive. Please baby. We still have more kids to grow and raise with Alessia. And the farmhouse I have finished working on for us so we can have our own private house for just our small family and our own space. We have to create our own memories in our new home. Please Emilia, wake up I beg you." I am crying over my unconscious wife who it seems has blood all over her body.

I feel the SUV jerk to a stop and Vittorio barely has the van parked when the door is snatched open. I look up and see Theo. "I swear she is going in a fucking bubble."

"Fuck off, Theo. Quit bitching and start helping her, she is fucking unconscious."

"Get her inside the jet." I don't respond to him; I pick her up again in my arms and carry her onto the jet. I waste no time and bring Emilia into the room already set up for Theo. The first jet is basically a flying hospital, we had rearranged so Theo could treat everyone. And the second jet is for the soldiers who traveled with us or the minor injured ones. Plus, our guests will have special arrangements for them. As soon as I lay Emilia down, Theo pushes me away from Emilia.

I go to fight back but Vittorio and Vincenzo each have one of my arms pulling me back. "Get the fuck off me. I need to be with her."

Theo turns around. "If you want me to save her, you will go sit your fucking ass down. You know I am more than capable of taking care of her. Now quit being a hotheaded asshole and let me do my fucking job, I have other patients who need my help. I don't need to deal with your ass. Sit down before I knock your ass out." I don't have time to respond or react because I am dragged out of the room by Vittorio and Vincenzo.

They sit me down in a chair, I run my hands down my face. Vittorio walks away and Vincenzo is next to me. I look over at him. "I can't lose her; I love her so fucking much."

He puts a hand on my shoulder. "I know you do Mateo but fighting everyone on the plane isn't going to help her. As soon as you can, you can go sit with her."

I nod, he looks over at me "Go clean up, you have blood all over you. I doubt she will appreciate it if you are covered in blood when she wakes up." I laugh knowing my wife will fuss at me if I am covered in blood and I would cave in right away since she has me wrapped around her finger.

I walk into the bathroom with a fresh suit, Vincenzo is right. My white dress shirt is mostly stained with blood, my face has blood on it and my hair has blood in it. I decided that taking a shower would be the easiest and fastest way to clean myself up. I look down and watch as the water by my feet is red. I am washing her blood down the drain. I am so petrified about losing her, I break down and cry again in the shower. I put my hand on the wall and lean forward as I let my silent tears fall down my face. Call me weak or whatever you want but I will not be embarrassed for loving my family and I am on the edge of losing it knowing my wife, my best friend, may never wake up again. I don't waste too much time in the shower because I need to be by her side, and I won't waste another moment crying in here. I quickly get dressed and get out.

I walk back where everyone else is, Theo is walking out of Emilia's room, he calls me over. "Mateo, let's talk in private." I nod and follow him into the room, I walk next to Emilia. I can hear the heart monitor beeping which a huge comfort to me is knowing she is alive. I hoped never to see her in this condition again, but I am grateful she is still alive. "She lost a lot of blood, but she will recover." He takes a breath. "What worries me the most is the baby."

My eyes shoot up to his. "Baby?" I ask.

"You don't know she is pregnant?"

I shake my head no. "And I doubt she did either."

He nods at me. "Yeah, she is too fiercely protective of Alessia, and she wouldn't put another child in a dangerous situation but with the gunshot wound in her abdomen, when we get back to Italy, she needs to have an ultrasound done right away. But regardless, she is on bedrest. I don't want her walking to the bathroom by herself."

I nod at him. "I will have one at the mansion when we land. What else are you not telling me?"

"The heartbeat sounds good, but without me seeing the baby, I have no idea the condition of the baby. I am not going to promise you the baby will survive, and this gunshot wound might kill the baby or Emilia most likely will be in for a rough pregnancy." I lay my hand gently on her stomach and rub it with my thumb. I close my eyes to swallow the pit that is in my stomach. I feel nauseous at the idea of losing our baby. We have wanted to continue our family but that was away from us. Then a wave of anger washes through me that they hurt my wife and might have killed my unborn child. "Her nose is broken. Shot in her shoulder went through so I didn't have to dig it out. Unlike the shot in her abdomen. But when she wakes up, she needs to take it easy."

"Okay, thank you, Theo. Sorry about earlier, I just lost it thinking I could lose her."

He gives me an awkward hug and pulls away. "I understand Mateo. She is too stubborn to let something like this kill her. I am going to go check on the other patients." I nod my head at him, I bend down and kiss her forehead.

"You are gonna give me a heart attack before I hit forty *la mia bellissima moglie*. You have to stop playing hero and let me take care of our family, I can't stand seeing you like this. You are my world, the light to my world would be filled with darkness again if you didn't come back to me. Emilia I am so scared, you are pregnant. I am beyond excited you are pregnant, but I am scared shitless that the baby won't make it because of the gunshot wound. But we have Seth and Alexei, in our custody but not his mistress but we will find her. They will all pay for everything they have done to you, Alessia, Lilyana, Kelly, her son, and Zia Anna."

She doesn't wake up and as much as I want her to, I know she won't wake up for a couple hours. I need to go check on everyone else, but I really don't want to. I text Julietta to have Alessia stay with her at her penthouse, she doesn't need to see Emilia like this, and I have no idea about the baby or Emilia's mental state when she wakes up. And I need to focus on Emilia and the baby. I have no idea what everyone else's condition is, I tell her I will fill her in on more details later.

After about an hour I walk out and see that Theo is walking back toward me. "How is she?"

"The same, no change."

He nods at me. "It probably will be like that for a couple hours. I am gonna do another check up on her and the baby." Theo says they both are doing okay and right now I will take that. I thank him and go check on Damiano's son, I see he is asleep on Damiano's chest and Damiano looks like he could fall asleep himself. I grab a blanket for them, I whisper to him that we will talk later, he nods at me and says thank you.

I walk over to the other woman Salvatore hasn't let out of his grip. I wonder why he is so protective of her; I look over at her and my mouth falls open. I am in complete shock; I walk over to her and pull her into a hug. Salvatore is already protesting. "Mateo, boss or not, if you don't get your hands off my woman…"

I look over her shoulder. "Fuck off, Salvatore. Lilyana is a sister to me, and my wife is in the other room. I have no interest in her like that. You are more possessive and protective of her than before." I put my hands on the side of her face in disbelief that she is here and alive. I kiss her forehead "I am so glad you are alive *la farfalla (butterfly)*. We all missed you, especially the grumpy fucker behind you."

She smiles at me and gives me a hug. "I missed you too, Matty." I grumble at the terrible nickname she gave me back in high school.

Vincenzo walks over. "Hey, how come he gets to hug her, and I got a punch to my jaw?"

Salvatore grumbles, "Because, dickhead, you were trying to hit on her. She is back and I will be damned if anyone takes away *la mia angelo (my angel)* from me. Especially the manwhore brother of mine."

Lilyana laughs at our bickering. "Somethings never change," she says.

I shrug "Well do you see who I have to deal with." She gives me a hard look then smacks my head "Ouch Lilyana. What the hell?"

"You are not innocent and don't think me and Emilia didn't talk while we were there together." Shit, I gulped knowing I am about to get my ass chewed out by Lilyana.

"I am an asshole and an idiot."

"Oh, you definitely are. Seriously, where in your small pea sized brain did you think saying something like that to her would be okay?"

"I was freaking out because she was calling my bluff about hiding things from her and I was afraid she would try and do something stupid like she did. She has been through enough. I just wanted to protect her."

"And that got you where?"

I shake my head. "With my wife fighting for her life and me on my knees in the doghouse begging for her forgiveness."

She mutters to herself, "And he runs the Italian Mafia, that's scary."

"Hey. I do a good job running the Mafia. Thank you very much."

I give her a playful glare; she rolls her eyes at me "So are you a shitty husband or are you just an idiot."

Salvatore comments, "No she has him wrapped around her finger."

I raise an eyebrow at "You are one to talk, your hands have barely left her since you laid eyes on her again."

He shrugs his shoulders, "I am not denying it, she was taken from me for years. You would be the same way if this was Emilia."

I nod in agreement, next thing I hear is a scream. A scream I know too well. "Emilia," I say and take off running to her room.

I open the door into her room, and she is tossing and turning in her bed. I shake her gently calling her name. "Shh Emilia, you are okay. I am here with you." She isn't responding to me; I am worried she is going to fall out of the bed the way she is moving. I pick her up bridal style and settle her into my arms while I sit on the bed.

She is still yelling. "No, don't hurt him. Hurt me instead he is just a child." I just hold her and keep talking to her quietly, after a few minutes she stops thrashing but is still shaking. I get a quick glance at

Lilyana, Salvatore and Vincenzo who are hovering by the door. Lilyana asks if we need anything. I tell her, "Water for her when she wakes up." She nods at Vincenzo to go get it. He does and brings back two water bottles for her. I thank them, Lilyana has tears in her eyes looking at Emilia.

"She is so strong, Mateo. I barely know her but the way she put herself in the way so she could take the blunt of the hits… she is strong mentally and physically."

I shake my head. "I am not surprised. She always puts everyone else before herself." Lilyana pushes the two men out the door to give us privacy. I run my hand through her hair. "You awake, *Mia Regina?*"

She nods. I move my hand from her hair to cup her cheek. I raise her head to look at me. "Shh. You are okay." Tears keep leaking from those beautiful green eyes.

"They were gonna shoot Dante, he is a child, Mateo! A fucking child."

I cut her off, "I know and right now he is asleep on his father's chest. We have Seth and Alexei tied and gagged on the other jet. They will get what is coming to them. You need to relax."

She nods "Did everyone make it out alive?"

I take a deep breath "Unfortunately, no. When we got to you, Kelly was barely hanging on, and she didn't make it on the plane alive, and we also lost a couple of soldiers."

She covers her hand with her mouth. "No. That poor boy had to go through what he went through from Alexei's abuse but now he has to grieve his mother's death that he witnessed."

"I know but we will be here for both of them in every way we can. I have a feeling they will be good friends with my girls since they went through something similar."

She tries to get up and I hold her back. "Where do you think you are going?"

She gives a duh look. "To go see everyone and how they all are doing."

"You are on bedrest. Salvatore's hands have barely left Lilyana, he already punched Vincenzo when he tried to make a joke about Lilyana being with him instead of Salvatore. He got pissy when I gave her a hug."

She chuckles but then gives me a hard glare. "I am not on bed rest because you think so."

I shake my head. "It was Theo's call. Emilia, you are pregnant," I tell her, and place my hand gently on her stomach.

"Pregnant…. Is the baby, okay? Oh my god. I was shot, the baby?" Her breathing starts becoming labored.

"Shh, calm down. You have to stay calm for the baby. Theo said the heartbeat was strong but as soon as we landed at the mansion you are getting an ultrasound so we can know. He said this pregnancy could be high risk because of the gunshot wound, so we are going to follow every order from the doctor okay." She nods while more tears are falling from her eyes.

"I know. We will do everything we can."

"I didn't know, Mateo. I swear I didn't."

I hugged her to my chest, "I know you didn't, let's lay down so you can relax okay."

She nods at me; I lower us to the bed and keep her lying on my chest.

"I am still mad at you," she mutters to me.

"And that is okay, as long as you both are here and alive. I will deal with whatever punishment you give me for being such an asshole to you. I am sorry I said that I didn't mean it. I love you and there will be no other woman besides you as my wife." I kiss her forehead. She doesn't respond but let's me hold her as I run my hand through her hair. She eventually falls asleep.

Theo walks in. "I heard you told her, how is she?"

"Emotional but I expected that. She didn't seem like she was in any pain but that is probably the adrenaline in her system."

"Yeah, plus the pain reliver in her IV helped with the pain for now."

I nod at him. "The ultrasound machine is in the medical wing of the mansion, do you need anything else?"

"No, Emilia got the worst of the injuries. Dante and Lilyana just have old cuts and bruises." I nod "Call me when she wakes up so I can check on her again and be careful of the gunshot wound on her stomach."

"I will."

It doesn't take me long at all to fall asleep with her in my arms. The past two days have been long, and I have barely slept. There is also peace knowing that we finally have her tormentors in our custody, and I can finally rain hell down on them. I will not indulge in my anger at them right now, right now I am where I need to be with my Queen in my arms. I close my eyes and the last thought before I fall asleep is my girls are safe and we can start living again.

Next thing I know is I am being gently shaken awake, I slowly open my eyes and I see Lilyana next to me. "We are about to land."

"Thanks, *la farfalla*." She nods at me and walks back towards the door where Salvatore is waiting for her. I gently rub my hand on her arm and start to stir Emilia. "Emilia, we are about to land, you need to wake up."

She looks up at me and glares. "No, go away."

I shake my head, and she wonders where Alessia gets it from. "Okay, my sleeping beauty. I will carry you out but if you are still asleep, I guess you will miss our baby's first sonogram," I say in a teasing tone. She opens her eyes and glares at me. "Asshole." I chuckle at her and kiss her lips quickly. She rolls her eyes at me but doesn't get up, I pick her up in my arms and carry her out of the room and head toward the door so we can get off the damn jet. Theo is carrying her IV bags.

Theo is in front of us as we get off the jet. Nonno, Nonna, and Zio Adriano are all waiting for us also. Nonna cries at the sight of Emilia, and they all run to her. She smiles at them. "I will be okay. Where's Alessia?"

Nonno tells her, "Mateo had her go stay at Julietta's with Marcello. We didn't know what you all would be like coming home and rather her not see something so traumatizing." He looks behind us and Nonno continues to talk, "Like Vincenzo tossing a man down the steps of the jet." He says with a chuckle. We turn around and see Vincenzo toss Seth down the steps of the jet.

"What I think Alessia's sperm donor is getting is a special treatment. Don't you?" I chuckle, and then I hear Adriano gasp, and he sees Lilyana.

"*Mia figlia è viva. Oh, quanto mi sei mancato*". (*My daughter is alive. Oh, how much I missed you.*) He is in tears and is holding her tight, I smile as I see Nonno, and Nonna joins in on hugging her. We all love Lilyana and were so devastated when we thought she had died. I continue my trek into the house. Emilia complained that she wanted to watch the rest of the reunion.

"Nope, we can catch up with everyone later. We have an ultrasound appointment to get to." She nods but still pouts.

I walk into the medical wing and set her down on the table, "Ok Emilia, the gel is going to be cold." She nods and squeezes my hand; I give her a gentle squeeze back. "Let's see here." He doesn't say anything but has a small smile on his face, so I am guessing it is good news. "Well damn Emilia, when you do something, you do it big." He smirks at us; I look at him confused. "Well congratulations. Emilia, you are ten weeks pregnant with triplets." Did he just say triplets? I feel nauseous, and the room starts spinning. The next thing I know is everything is dark.

EMILIA

I hear Theo tell me I am pregnant with triplets and I hear a thud. I look over and Mateo is passed out on the ground. "Really I go through hell with killing off the Russians and don't pass out until I lose too much blood, but you pass out when you hear we are gonna have triplets?" I say to Mateo and shake my head. Theo chuckles and waves some smelling salt over his nose; Mateo opens his eyes.

"Was I dreaming, or did he really say you are pregnant with triplets."

"You are not dreaming; I swear if you pass out again, I will knock you out myself."

He gives me a sheepish smile. "Sorry, I got a bit of a shock."

I shake my head. "No shit sherlock. Anyway, Theo, are they okay?"

He smiles at me, "Yes, the gunshot wound barely missed your uterus, so the babies were not harmed. But because of the stress on your body from your rescue mission and you having triplets you are at a high-risk pregnancy. You will be having weekly checkups and for now I want you on a modified bedrest. Limited walking, eat healthy, take your vitamins and rest when you need to. Right now, you need to take care of your body so the babies can be healthy as well. I am going to take some blood so I can check your levels so we can make sure you don't need anything else. I should have the results in a day or two but take it easy."

I nod and hug Theo. "Thank you," I tell him.

He kisses my cheek. "Of course. Now stop getting hurt or I swear I am buying you a personal bubble." I laugh at him; I wave bye to him as me and Mateo walk out of the medical wing together.

I am still shocked. Holy hell, I am carrying triplets, but I guess triplets run in the family since Ma was a triplet herself. I keep smiling while I rub my belly. We walk into our room in silence as soon as we get in the room. Mateo shuts and locks the door. I turn around and see him walk over to his end table and grab something, and I see he is playing with my rings between his fingers. He has a dark look in his eyes as he looks at me. He slowly walks toward me; I glare back at him and stand my ground. He doesn't get to say what he said and get away with it.

"The next time you think about leaving me, I will have you bent over the closest piece of furniture, and I will fuck that stupid idea right out of your head." I go to open my mouth, but he puts his finger over my lips. "No, you will keep that mouth shut until I am done, or I will help you find something to fill it until I am done talking." Fuck that shouldn't make me horny, but it does. His eyes darken when he sees me push my legs together. "I will help you with that problem later, if you behave." I glare at him, if he doesn't want to help, I will take care of it myself. That is, if I let him touch me. "I am an asshole, and you can be mad at me, but you are my wife and the only way you are getting out of this marriage is through death. Trust me people have been trying to kill me for years and have been unsuccessful, so you... Emilia Rose De Luca are stuck with me until we are buried side by side six feet under and even then, we will be together in hell." He wraps his arm around my waist and brings me closer to him, I try to push him away, but he just holds me tighter. "No, you're not pushing me away. I didn't mean what I said. You are not pathetic you are stronger than you realize. You willingly went back into a house that was your personal hell to rescue people who were going through the same thing you did. You did that knowing you could possibly not make it out alive. If you did you would have new scars physically or mentally or even both. I only said that I was hoping to distract you by being mad at me so you would forget about what I was hiding. I didn't want you to see that video, I was afraid it would cause you flashbacks. You have been doing so well, with hardly any nightmares and I wanted to continue to let you have that peace. Me being the idiot that I am I thought of something that would get you distracted. Obviously, my whole plan backfired on me, and I know I should have been honest with you. I regret saying it the moment the words came out of my mouth."

I looked up at his eyes. "When you said that to me it hurt but also pissed me off. You made me feel less than my worth. I won't stay where someone doesn't value my worth."

He nods. "I am sorry. I should never have said that to you."

"You're right. You shouldn't."

He cuts me off. "But you are not leaving. If you even think of it, I will tie you to the bed."

I glared at him. "Don't you dare."

He raises his eyebrows at me. I roll my eyes at him and try to push him away, but he won't loosen his grip on me. He smacks my ass; I glare at him again. He grabs my hand and puts my rings back on my finger. "These belong on your finger." He kisses right below my ear and whispers, "I love you." I fucking shiver; the asshole knows how to get my body to react to him.

"Go ahead and try, but you will find yourself tied to my bed. You know I have no problem tying you to shit."

I try to ignore him; I love him, but I am pissed at him. Mateo isn't having any part of that; he grabs my chin and has me look him in the eyes. "Be mad all you want but you are my beautiful, feisty tigress and I love you beyond my last breath."

"I love you, but you're not getting anything from me. Have fun with blue balls." He looks at me, shocked; I guess he figured I couldn't torture him. I will be torturing him, but I will punish him sexually by not letting him have me. Knowing my husband is gonna be extra touchy and possessive with me being pregnant, well, sucks to be him. He better get acquainted with his hand. I chuckle at him. "Enjoy your punishment, honey." I say with a sickly-sweet smile and I walk out, swaying my hips.

I hear him groan. "Fuck, this is worse than physical pain. She is gonna kill me from blue balls."

I smirk to myself. Let the games begin. And I am going to be ruthless with his punishment

FIFTY-FOUR
EMILIA

  It literally has been one day since I put Mateo on his punishment, and you would think he would appreciate it. I chose this punishment instead of letting him be at the hands of Esmeralda but no he is whining. She even offered to deal with him for me. She had flown here after Jose told her I was hurt; I did break down in her arms about being mad at Mateo, but I was mostly worried about my babies and wishing my family could be here. She held me and let me cry it out. I wasn't able to feel like this when I was pregnant with Alessia since I was trying to survive. Unfortunately, Mateo walked into our room after a meeting he had with Jose and Peter about the warehouse being taken down.

  Mateo went into an over-protective husband mode. He rushed to my side and started bombarding me with questions. "Baby? What's wrong? Are you in pain?" I shook my head and continued to choke on my sobs. Mateo pulled me out of Esmeralda's embrace and pulled me into his lap. My chest was flushed with his chest, and he rubbed my back up and down. With Mateo's help, I was finally able to calm down. I gripped his shirt and greedily took deep breaths of his cologne. After I had finally calmed down, he pulled away and wipes my tears.

  "What happened, baby?"

  I sniffle and say, "I am scared our babies won't make it."

  He kisses my head and cradles my head into his chest. "Of course, they will. They have the strongest Mama in the world; they will be okay." I nod in his chest; he rubs my back, and I feel myself getting tired. I feel someone kiss the back of my head, and I open my eyes and see Esmeralda. She has a smile on her face looking at us. She told me to take a nap and that we will talk later. I fall asleep on Mateo's chest with his fingers running through my hair.

  I wake up to me snuggling with Mateo's pillow. I sit up and wince at how tender my eyes are from crying. I can imagine I look like a mess. I see Mateo on his laptop on the chair in our room. He must have heard me shuffling because he put his laptop down on the table and walks over to the bed and sits beside me. He holds my face with his hand and strokes my cheek with his thumb.

  "Did you have a good nap, my Queen?" I lean into his hand and nod my head, closing my eyes for a moment.

  "Good." I feel him kiss my forehead. "Esmeralda and Jose had to leave. The French Mafia is stirring up problems back in Spain." I open my eyes.

  "What happened?" I asked Mateo.

"Supposedly, they are demanding a meeting and are being complete assholes. I have a feeling it has something to do with us destroying the Russian Mafia. I told them if they need anything, just to ask."

I pull away from Mateo and nod. "Good. Do we still have that meeting with the capos?"

"Yes, in thirty minutes, but if you need to rest, you can."

I shake my head, "Let me get dressed, and I will be ready."

I get up and put on a red blazer with black dress pants and black heels. I throw my hair in a ponytail and do a natural look make-up with red lip stick. I walk out. Mateo is waiting for me by the door. I grab my phone and try to get past him to leave, but he refuses until I give him a peck on his lips.

He has a maid get me warm apple cider; he knows it is my comfort drink. I try to sit in another chair, but he is having no part of that. He makes me sit on his lap. Mateo hands me my drink. How sweet of him.

I started my torture by very slowly grinding my ass on his cock. He held my hips in place with his hands, so I very slowly and teasingly ran my finger up and down his leg. I could feel him take a deep breath to try and stay calm.

Lilyana is sitting on Salvatore's lap and looks just as annoyed as I am. If he is this bad now, I can only imagine her pregnant. Salvatore starts telling us about everything that happened, and I learned about what Alexei did with their daughter Serenity. You can see the guilt all over her face. I took her into my office and let her talk. She did the best she could to protect her daughter and we will find her.

We walk back in. Mateo has me sit back on his lap; I feel his friend has deflated since I left. I decided to make his friend make another appearance. He grips my hips as a warning to stop, but I just grind on him harder. I can hear him taking a deep breath, but after ten minutes, he gives up and surrenders, dismissing the meeting. But getting back to Mateo's torture, everyone but Salvatore, Lilyana, and Vincenzo left the office. Mateo is extremely uncomfortable with having a hard-on with his family members on the other side of the desk. "Emilia, I swear if you don't quit moving when the punishment is over, you will not be able to walk for a damn week." He mutters to me.

I laugh at his misery and say, "Promises, promises."

He arches an eyebrow at me. "You're enjoying this, aren't you?"

I look over my shoulder at him. "Every second." He groans and throws his head back.

Vincenzo looks between us. He must realize what I am doing to Mateo. He is laughing, holding his stomach; it takes him a minute to compose himself before talking to Mateo in a baby voice. "Aww, poor Mateo has a stiffy from his wife sitting on his lap."

Mateo glares at him, "No fucker. My cock is fucking hard as steel fucking steel because she." He stops talking and glares at me, which I return with an innocent look "has been grinding her ass on my cock or teasing me during the damn meeting." Lilyana hides her laugh in Salvatore's shoulder, but the men don't hide their laughing at Mateo's dispense. Mateo is still glaring at all of us, I feel a bit of sympathy for him, so I stop teasing him for now.

Salvatore snickers. "You have one hell of a punishment *cugino*."

Mateo responds, "The sexual teasing is torture. I will keep my mouth shut. This is fucking hell especially since she is."

I elbow him in the gut before he can spill our pregnancy secret. "Ouch, fuck!" He says, I look at him and glare at him. He gives me a sheepish smile. "Oops sorry."

Vincenzo leans forward. "Since what?"

I shake my head. "Nope, Alessia will be the first to know and then she will be the one to tell our secret."

Vincenzo pokes his lip out. "But that's not till later. Tell us we will act surprised."

I shake my head "Nope. Not happening and no you are not gonna get it out of us."

Vincenzo looks at Mateo. "Mateo, I think we need to talk."

I roll my eyes. "Vincenzo, try to be a little more discreet, dumb ass. Thank God Lilyana is here. We need more women around here to help keep these idiots in line."

Lilyana turns to me with an evil glint in her eyes. "Emilia I think we need to find Vincenzo a woman, not a plaything. Then maybe he actually might use his upper brain. Those women he fucks must be sucking the small amount of intelligence out of him when they suck him off." I choke on my drinking but after a moment, I laugh with them. I already love this girl; she is my long-lost soul sister. Vincenzo was first shocked with his mouth wide open but then he composed himself and now is glaring at Lilyana. Oh, I am going to enjoy having Lilyana around. "Oh, my god. That was perfect, and his face was priceless."

Vincenzo grumbles "You definitely haven't lost your sass since you were gone."

Lilyana smirks. "Oh no worries, Enzy. I saved it all just for you."

He rolls his eyes. "How lucky of me. Don't you have something better to do then harass me."

She sits there with her pointer finger tapping her chin, pretending to think. "Nope, I actually don't."

"Why don't you go fuck my brother and stop harassing me."

She laughs. "The King of Cockblocking is now encouraging us to go fuck?"

"If I get you to stop harassing me then yes. Plus, maybe he can fuck the sass out of you, and you can suck the grumpiness out of him." I see the dark look in Salvatore's eyes, so I decide to jump in before Vincenzo has a broken jaw. I swear Vincenzo never thinks before he speaks.

"Seriously, we need to find you a woman. So, what are you looking for?"

He smirks. "Someone who looks good on their knees in front of me."

"Eww"

"You pig," both me and Lilyana say simultaneously.

He laughs while he stands up. "As much fun as this has been, I have stuff to do. *Dopo.*" *(Later)*

All of a sudden, I start feeling a bit nauseous and dizzy and lay my head on Mateo's chest, he looks down at me. "You, okay?"

I shake my head no. "I need to eat something." Without saying another word, he picks me up and brings me to the kitchen. He sits me down on the counter. He pours me a glass of orange juice with some fresh fruit and crackers. While I slowly eat my fruit, I admire his ass and back as he moves around the kitchen. It is a sight I usually don't see that often so when I do see him being domestic, I take full advantage and ogle my husband's body, very slowly. He must feel my eyes on him, he peeks over his shoulder and winks at me while blowing me a kiss. I chuckle at him; he comes over to me and kisses my temple. We don't talk while I eat, he is busy going through emails but honestly, I don't mind. I am just enjoying the food and the fact is I am not dizzy anymore.

After I eat, he carries me up to our room and makes me take a nap. As much as I want to fight it, I know I need to. I know this pregnancy will be completely different than my pregnancy with Alessia. Obviously, I will have Mateo doing everything he can to make it easier for me, but I am pregnant with triplets, so it will be more draining for my body. I still am shocked about that, but I am still grateful for all of my children. My brain stops buzzing with thoughts and I finally let myself fall asleep.

I was trying to fall back asleep after I woke up to pee. I hear the click of our door handle as someone is opening the door. I turn over and see my baby girl running into our room. "Mama," she yells I open my arms and she runs into them. I gave her a big hug, god I missed my baby so much. I had not seen her for five days. I pull back and kiss all over her face, she starts to laugh "Mama" she tries to act mad, but she is laughing.

Mateo walks into the room and sees us laughing and being silly. "Alessia, I told you not to wake your Mama up, she needed to sleep." He tells her gently.

I tell him "I was already up." He comes over and sits next to us and kisses Alessia's head. He picks her up from my lap and places her in his lap, I give him a pout. He just pecks my lips, asshole. I wanted to snuggle with my baby, but he always hogs her.

"Alessia, me and your Mama have something to tell you."

She looks between us. "Okay?" she says questioningly, and I jump in.

"Alessia, do you remember what you asked for on your birthday and I told you we would have to wait?"

Her eyes pop open. "Are you talking about a baby brother or sister?"

I nod my head. "Yes but not one baby. Three babies."

She jumps up from Mateo's lap. "Three babies?" She screams, I am so glad our room is soundproof, since she is jumping up and down screaming.

Mateo chuckles at her enthusiasm "Yes, baby. Your Mama has three babies in her belly."

She stomps jumping around and tilts her head to the side, like tilting her head will help her understand better. "Why are they in your tummy Mama? Did you eat them?"

We both laugh at her. "No silly girl. That is where they will stay until they get big and strong enough to come and play with us. Just like you did," I tell her.

"I was in your tummy when I was little?"

Mateo smiles at her. "Yes, you were."

I hope she will stop but no my curious daughter will keep asking questions until she is blue in the face. "Well how do the babies come out when they are ready?"

Mateo looks at me with a worried look, probably wondering how to handle this. "Well, when it is time, I will go to a special doctor who will help me take the babies out."

She shrugs her shoulders. "Okay," but I see the wheels turning. "We have to tell everyone."

She basically sprints for the door, Mateo catches her. "Park the breaks speedy. We will tell everyone at dinner, which will be soon. So, go wash your hands, then we will head down for dinner."

She kisses both me and Mateo on the cheek and skips to the bathroom, while singing to herself, "I am a big sister, I am a big sister." I shake my head at her silliness.

I stand up, Mateo being right next to me helping me. Even though I don't need it, I appreciate his offer. "You ready?" he asks.

"Yeah, I am. We all could use some good news."

He nods, "Oh Julietta doesn't know about Lilyana so expect tears and dramatics. They were best friends growing up and honestly Julietta's only true friend until you." I smile, that is another reason I am glad she is home.

Alessia comes back out of the bathroom and reaches for both of our hands, she loves holding our hands as a family. I bend down and whisper in Alessia's ear, "We will tell everyone after dinner, okay." She looks up at me and smiles nodding at me.

We all take our seats with Mateo at the head of the table, me next to him, and Alessia next to me. I look around and am happy to see our family has expanded and will continue to expand in the next year. Julietta and Lilyana are next to each other, obviously we missed their reunion but by the smiles and dry tear stains on their faces they are nothing but thrilled to be with each other again. Alessia gently tugs on my shirt and whispers "Mama who is that?" pointing to Lilyana, Lilyana must have heard and is looking at us.

"That, Alessia, is your Zia Lilyana."

Lilyana says quietly, "I am not her Zia. I want to but I am not related to her."

I shake my head "If tweedle dee and tweedle dum are her *Zii* then you are her Zia." Pointing to Salvatore and Vincenzo who both say "Hey" to me while scowling.

"You are Salvatore's woman right?"

She goes to protest but Salvatore says, "I dare you to try and deny that, Lilyana Marie O'Milloy. You know what happens when you say you are not mine." Well shit, Salvatore has a secret dominant side I was not aware of.

Alessia has no idea about the sexual tension that is floating between the two of them, but she asks. "What happened to Zia Lilyana wasn't she the same woman that Zio Salvatore would tell me about that he missed her?"

Nonna jumps in, "You're right, *fiore*. Remember how you and Mama were in a place that wasn't safe, but you couldn't leave because they would hurt you and your Mama?" Alessia nods "Well those same people tricked us into thinking Lilyana was dead when she was alive the whole time but when your Mama went to help those people, she found Lilyana. We will finish that conversation later, okay?"

"Okay, Nonna. Zia Lilyana I am glad you are back home. Maybe we can go shopping with Zia Julietta. I like shopping for boots." and then Alessia, Julietta and Lilyana got into a conversation about shopping and fashion. I let them have their niece and aunt bonding time.

While they are talking about that, I turn to Mateo. "After Alessia goes to bed, I am going to chat with Seth."

Vincenzo joins in "Oh. I want to see this." And the other men agree.

Mateo turns to me. "Are you sure? I don't want to stress you out."

I shake my head. "I want it done so we can live our lives stress free knowing he is dead."

They all agree, finally desert comes around. It is blueberry cheesecake, Alessia is bouncing in her seat to tell everyone, I am biting my lip from trying to hold my laugh in. I look at Mateo and he is doing the same thing as me you can see the laughter in his eyes. "Mama, can I tell them? Pleaseeeee?"

I chuckle, "Go ahead, since you are bursting at the seams." She gets up from her chair, goes to the kitchen and grabs her cooking stool.

"I have an announcement to make," she announces, and, of course, all the adults give her their full attention. "I am a big sister! To THREE babies!"

Nonna rushes to my side, stands me up into her arms. "Oh, three babies. What a blessing." I get hugs and congratulations from everyone. Everyone is happy for us. We passed around the sonogram picture that Theo printed off for us. We answer all the questions they have for us saying we are ten weeks and even with the gunshot wound that barely missed my uterus they are healthy. I just have to be careful with my stress levels and make sure I eat enough since I am anemic. Of course, Nonna is already making plans for my diet and what snacks I should be eating, I chuckle but also am extremely appreciative of having more people around us to be there and love our children as much as we do. Mateo leans over and kisses my cheek while he has his hand on my belly and his thumb is stroking my belly.

Alessia was so excited even after dinner that it took her longer than usual to settle down for bed. Mateo came up with the idea to have her read to the babies, which does the trick. We both kissed her goodnight. I walked to our room to change my clothes, so I don't ruin the ones I am wearing now and why not tease my husband more. I closed the door and stripped out of my clothes, I heard the door open, and Mateo walked in, shutting the door behind him. He looks at me standing in my lacy red bra and thong, which leaves little to the imagination. "Are you trying to torture me?" He asked me, I just give him a smile. He keeps going back and forth between lusting after my body and glaring at me for torturing him with my punishment. I chuckle and walk into the closet and I change into my tight black jeans, black tight long sleeve shirt and my leather jacket with my boots. Mateo changes into basically the same thing as me but he definitely looks more delicious to me.

I sit down at the edge of the bed. I bend down to tie my boots up, but Mateo stops me and bends down on his knee and puts my foot on his leg and ties my boot. "You didn't have to do that," I tell him.

He finishes tying my boot, looks at me, and says, *"Un re si inchinerà sempre davanti alla sua regina"* (A King will always bow down before his Queen.) He puts that foot on the ground and grabs my other one and ties it. After both of my feet are planted on the ground he rises up to his full height, he pulls me up, so I am standing in front of him. He leans down and kisses me. When I say kiss, I mean kiss. One hand on my neck and the one wrapped around my waist pulling me closer. I give in to him and let him dominate the kiss, we don't kiss long but long enough to get the message across to each other. We pull apart from each other, but he steals another quick peck on my lips. Then hugs me close to him, we both know this is going to be emotionally draining on me.

"Cheater," I say to him.

He chuckles. "I never play fair."

I pull back and look at him with another glare but say, "I am ready."

"I know you are, but if it gets too much you let me know. I will have you out of there. I have the nanny watching over Alessia while we are gone just in case." I nod, he grabs my hand, and we walk down to the front door where the rest of the De Luca's and Lilyana are there waiting for us. We all get into our vehicles; I settle into the passenger seat while Mateo is driving. He has hand on my thigh giving me gentle squeezes. I am running my fingers through his hair while he is driving, I know he wants me back at the mansion. But he also knows I need to do this as much as he hates it.

When we pull into the warehouse parking lot, Mateo walks around the car and opens my door for me. I give him a smile and thank him; he just kisses my cheek in response. I see all the other cars are already here, I give him a questioning look. "How did everyone get here before us?"

He shrugs his shoulders. "I may have taken the long way here. I just wanted a few moments of peace for us before we face your nightmare."

I shake my head laughing at him "After we finish them, we can enjoy our new peace. With our growing families, we have Lilyana back and the triplets on the way. So, let's go give them worse than payback."

He smirks at me. "Well, let's go my Queen, it is time to show them why you are my Diabolical Queen."

We get into the basement of the warehouse, and I see the viewing room empty. I am kind of shocked that the women are not in there. Mateo opens the door, and I see the pitiful men hanging from their wrists by chains. I get an excited smile on my face and become giddy at seeing they are using my special chains. "Oh, I see my new chains are being used."

"Well, our Queen is a genius when it comes to torture," Vincenzo tells me when he comes over and kisses my cheek.

I give him a small smile, but my breath catches in my throat when I glance behind him and I see who all is in the room with us is. Not only are all of the De Luca's and Lilyana in here but all of the Capo's are here too. I mumble under my breath, "Holy fuck." Zio Adriano comes over to me and guides me by my hand to a beautiful chair. The chair is a beautiful black velvet chair and has a medieval look to it. The chair is a fucking throne chair. I am flabbergasted. I turned and asked him, "What? Why?"

He chuckles. "Well you're pregnant with the Don's babies and you can't overstrain yourself. Plus, these worthless bastards need to realize that a true Queen that is in their presence." I smile at him.

"Thank you, Zio Adriano. I know this was you're doing." He smiles at me and winks. He walks back to the rest of the family, and I see the other ladies are sitting on chairs with their men standing behind them. I feel a hand on my shoulder, and I see Mateo standing next to me. He leans down and kisses me. My king is at my side supporting me.

Seth yells out. "Get off her you filthy bastard, she is mine."

I look at Seth and see he has some additional injuries that must have happened after I knocked him out. I look at Vincenzo and ask, "Was this you're doing?"

He smirks at me. "I was just making sure he felt welcomed."

We all chuckle at Seth's body which is covered with more cuts and bruises. I slowly stand up, pick up a knife, and throw it at Seth in his leg. "Oops. Did that hurt, kitten?" I say kitten with the most hate in my voice.

"I am not a kitten, whore. That is you," he says through his grunts of pain.

Before I could respond, Mateo has punched him across his cheek. "You better watch what you say to my wife."

Seth goes to open his mouth. "Seth, for once shut your mouth because Mateo will have no problem in making you beg for death. But your wish won't be granted because you are mine to torture and kill."

Seth just scoffs, and says, "Wow, you must be desperate if you took this whore as a wife. Tell me how that bastard child of mine is." I stand up from my chair and very slowly slice up the side of Seth's ribs very slowly. He is grunting in pain and moving around which causes the chains with spikes along his wrists to dig into his skin. "Oh, Seth don't worry this pain is going to feel like a papercut compared what I have planned for you."

I put the knife back on the table, I motioned to the guys to have him be put in the chair. Vincenzo jumps up at the opportunity to help.

When he grabs his chains, he pushes on the chain, so they dig a little more in his wrists. I chuckle at Vincenzo's enthusiasm to physically hurt him. Seth grunts out in pain; he is strapped in the chair with metal restraints around his arms and legs and waist. I walk over and get a towel and a huge bucket of water. Time to do some waterboarding for some answers.

"Mateo come hold his head back." Mateo grabs his head, so he is looking at the ceiling. "Now, Seth, I am going to ask you questions, you have one chance to answer them. If not, you will regret not answering me."

"Fuck you bitch," he tells me.

I punch his rib but continue. "Why did you even want me to live with you if all you were gonna do is abuse me?" He just laughs. "Ok, you think this funny, let's see how funny you think this is then." I throw the towel over his face, and I lift the bucket and pour the water over his face. He is drowning, he is trying to get out of Mateo's grip since the rest of his body is restrained. After a minute I stop and remove the towel. "You want to try that again." He is still coughing from drowning, I punch his chest, he groans but starts talking.

"Because you were mine and you will always be mine."

"You decide to fuck me a few times when I was completely drunk out of my mind, and, because of that, I became yours."

He shakes his head. "No I watched you for a month before I killed your family."

I take a step back. "W-what?"

He grins at me. "Yep, I knocked out all the men in the house out and tied them to a chair and we waited for your Mama to come home. Once she did, we put on a nice display after everyone woke up. I will say you definitely got your good looks and stunning body from your mother, but I enjoyed your body better since you were younger and tighter." I see red thinking about how he raped my mother, but I stop myself from reacting. I need to know what else he did.

"What else did you do?" I say emotionless.

He still has a big grin on his face, hoping that this will break me. "While I was enjoying your mother, your brothers and father were crying and begging me to stop through their gags, but I just laughed and continued to rape her until I was finished. After that, I slit her throat and tossed her at their feet. That is when I decided to pour gasoline all over the house. When I came back to the room and your mom was trying to move, I decided to hog tie her so she wouldn't try and help the others escape. But the best part was when I was raping her, I told her how I was gonna make you my new sex toy and she begged me not to hurt you. That she would do anything but not to hurt her children. But you see that did no good, your family died, and you still became my sex toy."

I tell Mateo to waterboard him a few more times, I turn my back to him, so I can compose myself.

I am sitting in my chair; I can hear in the distance Seth choking on water, but I am not focused on that. I can only focus on the tears coming down my face and falling into my lap, I don't bother to wipe them. I feel two hands on my face wiping my tears, I look up and I see Nonno is knelt in front of me. "Don't let that crown fall, it is okay to cry. But we all know you are stronger than this. Take those emotions and fuel it into letting him suffer from everything he did to your family and plus you might want to stop Mateo before he kills him." He says with a chuckle, I look up and Mateo is punching the shit out of Seth with a set of brass knuckles.

Is it bad I am so turned-on by Mateo going into beast mode on Seth in my family's honor? Oh well. I really don't care; I am fucked up in the head. My husband is sexy, and I love enjoying his body. Plus, pregnancy hormones don't help when your husband looks that good. "Mateo, stop," I say to him, but he doesn't hear me. I get up from the chair, go behind him and give him a hug. He tenses, but I whisper in his ear, "Stop. He deserves a slow and painful death but thank you for roughing him up for me." I kiss his back and step next to him.

"Didn't I tell you to be careful what you say?"

Seth gives me a death glare as if that bothers me. His face is all bloody.

I am gonna listen to Nonno's advice and make him pay for everything he did to my family. I remember what they did to me after I gave birth to Alessia and decided to let him fuel that agonizing pain he put me through. I grabbed a knife and cut him across his stomach similar to a c section cut but not as deep. Seth is screaming and writhing in pain "What's wrong Seth, can't handle a bit of pain? Well, sucks to be you because your last moments will be filled with nothing but agonizing pain for all that you have put my family through." I keep making small nicks all over his body, just not enough to kill him.

"Stop, you're hurting me."

I laughed at him. "As I said, Seth, this is nothing compared to what I am going to do to you." I step back after the front of him is covered in small nicks. I grab the lemon juice and pour it over his head. "Here is some lemon juice so you don't smell as bad," I say, chuckling knowing damn well the lemon juice will burn every cut I just made.

"You are fucking psychotic bitch."

I pat okay more like slap his cheek. "Oh, darling, I am more than that. I am aware I am a psychotic bitch, but here is the thing, Seth. I behaved when we lived with you for Alessia's safety but see she isn't here but safe at our home. You get to see why they call me the Diabolical Queen and why my name is feared in the mafia world." I turn to the men. "Strip him of his boxers and hang him back up." I walk over to my chair and get the drink of water that is waiting there for me. Once I feel hydrated enough, I walk back over to the whips and grab my favorite that has small blades wrapped in the end of the whip. I start circling Seth and have the whip graze his legs, he tries to shift away from the whip. I crack the whip down on his feet, hard.

He pisses himself. "Would you look at that, someone peed themselves." And the whole room burst out with laughter. Not only am I gonna hurt him physically I am going to embarrass him like he did to me. "Aww poor little Seth can dish out abuse but can't take any. Poor baby, the fun is just beginning." I turn behind him and start whipping his back. And I ask the question I want to ask but am not sure if I can handle the answer "Why did you sell Alessia to Boris?" He doesn't respond, still being stubborn. I whip his back harder and see his back starting to bleed.

"I said WHY DID YOU SELL MY DAUGHTER TO THAT PEDOPHILE," I yell at him; I walk around and whip him across his stomach wound five times.

He finally gives in, "Because then she would be out of my way, and I can have all of your attention on me."

"ARE YOU FUCKING KIDDING ME? SHE IS JUST A CHILD; YOU SHOULD HAVE BEEN HER HERO AS HER FATHER NOT HER MONSTER." I continue to whip any part of his body; I am beyond pissed at this point. I have no idea how long or where I have been whipping him. I feel the whip being taken out of my hand and my body turned around and I am being hugged. I take a breath and smell Mateo's cologne; he just caresses my back. He places his hand on my stomach and I know I need to calm down.

After I have taken a deep breath, I walk over and grab my newest toy. The one I have made especially for him. I walk over to him with the toy and a knife in my hand. I cut his piss covered boxers off him. Funny how the man who used to get hard when I was being beaten shows no interest in being hard when he is the one being beaten.

"Seth, this doesn't excite you? Wait, I forgot. You like your woman drunk or you get off on beating them half to death before raping her. Do you remember all of those times you would beat me than rape me?" I ask as I trail my finger down his chest. Seth nods and his little friend starts to grow. I keep going because he needs to be fully erected for the penis cage. He will be the first to have it used on him, but all the other rapists will have their turn in wearing it as well.

"Or how about all the times you watched me being taken over and over without a break?" Bingo! That brought his friend back to life. Before he can lose his erection or Mateo stops me. I secure the metal penis cage around his cock. Seth looks down and is trying to move his body away from the cage, but it is too late for that. I snap the buckle on the outside of the cage.

"What is that?" He asks while he is shaking like a leaf from head to toe.

"Oh, this? This is my newest toy I made especially for you. It is a penis cage. Right now, you might be a bit uncomfortable but whenever I want when I hit this little button. The cage will get tighter around your cock, and you will feel lots of small blades pierce your cock. There are over two hundred small blades in the cage." I look over at Vincenzo who has been itching to get his hands on Seth.

As Mateo is walking up to Seth, I hit the button to tighten the penis cage. Seth grunts and says, "Fucking shit." I chuckle this is only the first level it can go up to four levels before it is at its maximum, for now until I tweak it. Seth here is my guinea pig to see how it works.

"Vincenzo, do you want a turn?"

He bobs his head up and down "With pleasure, Emilia." I head back to my seat, but Mateo has me sit on his lap. I slowly sip my water as I watch Vincenzo having fun cutting Seth's ear off and making him eat it. Ok, Vincenzo is a different kind of fucked up, but I love his idea.

"Are you okay?"

"Yeah, I am better."

"Good sit here and keep drinking your water, I have some questions I need to ask him myself." I nod at him.

"Go ahead but make it painful." He stands up and places me back in his seat.

"Anything for my Queen.

FIFTY-FIVE
MATEO

Hearing what Seth said about my girls and Emilia's family added to the fury raging through my body. I will not act on it if she wants to be the one to kill him, but I have some questions I have for this worthless son of a bitch. She decides that I can finish him off and am more than willing to do so. I don't even care what knife I grab, all I care if it can cut off parts of his body because he got pain from Emilia and as beautiful as it was to torture someone, she has yet to master her technique like I have. He winces every time he moves, which entertains the rest of us, and we laugh at him in pain. But this is only nothing compared to what he did to Emilia so he should be grateful.

    I circle him, he is shifting in his chains that are still holding him up by his wrists. I stab the outside of his thigh deep, so the four inches of the blade are inside his leg, and I drag it down until we get to his knee. He is crying which is pissing me off, "Quit your crying bitch. If you can't take a bit of pain, you should have thought about that before you hurt my Queen and Princess. It is finally time for you to suffer from my hands." I stick two of my fingers in the cut and I say, "Welcome to my hell." He stops when he sees the look on my face, I am not playing around, he is going to be in agonizing pain.

    "Why did you keep Emilia and Alessia for all those years?"

    He takes one look at the deadly expression on my face. "I wanted Emilia, and I was going to force her to give up the baby. But when Boris found out it was a girl, he told me when she got older, he would buy her and make her his wife. I would get money for all my troubles dealing with that brat. He found Emilia hot and decided he would use her until Alessia got of age." Absolutely disgusting, he won't be living another day.

    I decide that I will start to skin him starting with his back, I dig my hunting knife which is made for skinning animals. I dig it into his collarbone and drag out towards his shoulder. "She is a child. You should protect her, not feed her to the monsters of this world." I go to his other collarbone and repeat what I just did except I connect them together so I can work on peeling his skin from his body.

    "Monsters! You all are monsters!" he exclaimed.

    I look at him. "You are right. I am a monster, but I could never do what you did to her, and I will protect her from anyone who wants to harm a hair on her head," I say with so much hatred in my voice, and another wave of anger trembles through me thinking about anyone harming or upsetting Alessia. I hear a buzz and Emilia is smiling at me, waving the remote around in her hand. I have to admit the penis cage she created is very frightening. I am pretty sure every man had shifted or grabbed their cocks like that would protect it, every time Seth's cock was being pierced by those blades.

He pisses himself again. "I thought you already pissed yourself, boy." I chuckle darkly at him and continue to cut down his back. "So, what was your plan? Sell Alessia and keep Emilia as a sex slave until you got tired of her? Then what, dispose of her?" He quickly nods.

"Yes, she waited on me while she was working at the diner, and she bent over to pick something up. I immediately got a hard on and decided she would be mine until I got bored with her." He says the last bit drowsily, I punch him across the cheek. He jumps at the contact of my fist hitting his cheek.

"Can't be falling asleep on me now. We are not finished."

He starts crying again. "Please, just kill me. I am sorry."

I grin, he finally knows what it feels like to be the victim. "Hmm let me think about it... Did you stop when Emilia begged you to stop when she was beaten or raped? No, you didn't. So, no I will not kill you that easily, you will suffer." I go back to skinning his back while I ask questions, "How did you meet Boris?"

"I have a gambling problem and came into debt with the Russian Mafia. He willingly bailed me out of debt if I helped him lure girls into his prostitution business. It wasn't hard to get a girl drunk or high; they would agree to anything. So, getting them to sign a business contract with Boris was a piece of cake. It also helped that I got part of the profit he made off them." He is a crying blubbering mess as he finishes talking, I keep separating his skin from his back at one point I had to tug a bit hard to pull it off his muscle. He puked all down the front of himself.

"I am so glad he didn't puke on me," I say out loud.

Of course my lovely wife says "Then you wouldn't be joining me in the shower when you finished killing him. I love you, but I don't think I can tolerate the smell of puke right now."

I chuckle at her. "Good thing he didn't then. Cause I quite enjoy our showers together." I have Marcello bring me over the hose that is attached to well water, which is ice cold. I soak Seth with the cold water.

"What the fuck," he sputters.

"Sorry I need to cut your dick off, and I am not touching puke."

"W-what? Why do you need to cut my dick off?"

I laugh. "Oh, I don't know, maybe because you raped my wife countless times." My men better be able to handle this, since this is nothing compared to the training they have gone through, especially to become one of my capos. They don't call me the beast of the underworld for nothing.

Nonna smirks. "You see one dick, you seen them all. Some are just nastier to look at then others."

Julietta smirks but Marcello is trying to have her leave. "I am staying here Marcello; I will stay here with Emilia until he stops breathing. She is family. Plus, I have no interest in his dick, you know that."

He covers her mouth. "*Fiore*, as much as I love you, please shut your mouth so I don't get shot for something I have not done yet." She is laughing behind his hand, but I am more than appreciative that he got my big, mouthed sister to shut up. Lilyana is glaring at Salvatore to say something about her leaving, but he is wrapped around her finger. He just nods and stands behind her chair, but I have a feeling he will cover her eyes once I start cutting. I look at Emilia in her eyes and she walks next to me and gives me a kiss, which is all I need to know she is ok with being in here while I finish this asshole off.

I turn my attention back to Seth. I take the cage of his cock which is all bloody, but he is definitely below average. When I see what he is, or I should say what is not packing. I smirk, "No wonder you had to have girls drunk to sleep with you. No sober girl would be willing to fuck that small prick."

We are all laughing at him, he is getting pissed. He decides to try and save himself by trying to embarrass Emilia. "Laugh it up, but remember, I fucked your wife in all of her holes."

Emilia rolls her eyes. "Seth they all know you raped me for years, I think they can figure out you used me in any way you could. It is nothing to brag about." She then turns to me and says, "No wonder it hurt the first time we had sex, you are huge compared to him." Well shit, woman, you just inflated my ego and crushed him at the same time. I am definitely not complaining.

I just smirk at her and smack her ass. She pretends to scowl at me, but I chuckle at her cute fake glare she is giving me. I quickly slice his dick off, and it falls to the ground and blood pours from where I cut it off. I pick it up and shove it into his mouth and put duct tape over his mouth. I can see he is getting close to dying, so let's finish this so we can all go home. I put on the apron and gloves that come up to my elbows. I see Emilia is curious, but I move her behind me and tell her to keep back. I don't want any of this splashing and getting on her. I grab the acid and slowly pour it down Seth's open back. He screams extremely loud, to the point that mostly everyone either shifts further away from us or covers their ears. I pour from shoulder to shoulder until all of the five-gallon container of acid is empty.

I put everything back and look over at Seth, and he is hanging on by a thread. I look at Emilia "Do you want to finish him, or do you want me to?" I ask, holding my gun in front of her, she looks at me and then the gun. She picks the gun up from my hand and struts over to Seth, his head is hanging towards the ground as he is taking shallow breaths.

She lifts his head by putting the gun under his chin. "Seth, as much as I hate you, I do have to thank you. You gave me the best gift in the world, my daughter. And you ran us to the man we both love, my husband, and her father. But for everything else you did, I hope you suffer in hell ten times over what you did to us." And after that she moved the gun to his forehead and shot him point blank in his head.

"Vincenzo, make sure he is disposed of," I tell him.

"Sure thing, Boss."

Emilia is staring at Seth in a trance, I walk over to her. I take the gun, turn the safety back on and stick it in the back of my pants and wipe her face off with a hand towel. *"La mia bella moglie diabolica,"* I tell her, and kiss her sweetly.

She smiles at me. "Is it really over?"

I nod at her. "Yes, and soon Alexei will get his as well but for now let's get cleaned up and go home." I hold out my hand to her; we go past Alexei, but I stop him and say, "This is child's play compared to what I have in store for you."

He smirks and looks directly at my sister. "Did you keep our secret *piccola colomba (little dove)?*"

Julietta keeps a neutral face and doesn't react, but I am not fooled. I won't push the issue now. Emilia walks back to Seth, rips off the tape, pulls his dick out of his mouth. She grabs the tape and Seth's dick and shoves it in Alexei's mouth and seals it with the tape. She tells the men they can take it out in three days."

I tell him, "Enjoy your brother-in-law's cock. Your last days breathing are numbered." And we walk out of the basement with everyone. We separate from them, and we head to my office which has a bathroom off it. "Go ahead and get in the shower, I will grab our extra clothes." She walks into the bathroom; I lock my office door because no one gets to see my wife naked besides me. I grab the duffel bag I packed earlier with extra clothes.

I slowly eye Emilia's perfect body, and you can see her stomach has a slight bulge to it. That brings a smile to my face that our family will be expanding in a couple months, and I can experience it all with her. Emilia will be able to focus on enjoying her pregnancy. She is perfect for me; she has her Mafia Queen side, but she also is so loving and caring to our family. I am truly a lucky bastard to be married to her and her to be the mother of our children. I strip out of my clothes and join her in the shower. I am definitely taking advantage of this before she continues my punishment. I slide the door open, and she peers at me over her shoulder. "Behave or I will find other ways to punish you."

I put my hands up in surrender. "I am in here to wash the blood off of you, I have the purest intentions."

She lowers her eyes to my cock which is already hard. "Clearly you do."

"What? I am a man, and my sexy naked wife is in the shower. I can't help to get turned on, but I will behave myself especially since my office is not soundproof. You moans and screams are only for my ears only."

She rolls her eyes at me. "Caveman," she mumbles under her breath.

I chuckle but we both quickly wash off all the blood from our bodies. After we get dressed, we walk back out together to the car. I turn the car on and turn to her. "Do you want to go anywhere before we go home?" I ask, she shakes her head no. "Good I have a surprise I have been planning that I want to show you."

"Okay?" she says questioningly.

"I promise you will love it." I drove past the mansion. About twenty minutes past the mansion, I pull the car into our new home's driveway.

Emilia's eyes look at the farmhouse in adoration. "Whose house is this?" I don't answer her and come around to her side of the car. I helped her out of the car "Mateo, who's house is this?" I stand behind her, wrap my arms around her but have my hands on her belly which is slightly swollen.

"Ours, this is our new home."

She turns around "Are you serious?"

I nod at her. "I know your dream home is a small quaint little farmhouse. Now you have it, it is fully furnished but you can change anything you want." She is still looking around as the sun is about to rise so I grab her hand and unlock the door. "I will show you around, but first, let's watch the sunrise from the best spot."

We walk into our master room straight onto our patio, yes, we have a patio off our bedroom that has a hot tub along with patio furniture. This is our little sanctuary, I wanted somewhere we could unwind. "Oh my god, Mateo. This is absolutely beautiful, it's perfect."

"I am glad you like it; this is our personal sanctuary. No kids, no mafia, no work, no family drama. This is just for us to be a normal married couple." She wraps her arms around me and kisses me with so much hunger and passion.

I soak it all in, I wrap my hands around her waist and pull her closer to me. "*Ti amo.*"

I peck her lips and she whispers against them, "*E ti amo.*" We get in bed and snuggle together, and I just hold her and relax knowing all the years of this war between us and the Russians is finally over.

Yes, I am sure we will have more issues, but I have such a strong woman at my side. Seth is dead Alexei will be dead soon, but after his comment he made I have a feeling we might need him around longer than I want. He was going to get a longer and more painful death anyway. I will see if someone can get Julietta to open up because she clammed up after Alexei spoke to her. Maybe she will open up to Marcello. If not, maybe her going to Spain and having Esmeralda train her isn't such a bad idea, it did wonders for Emilia.

I can only hope that this family can start moving forward from the scars of our past. I look down at my fierce wife and place my hand on her stomach knowing this amazing woman hasn't already given me my princess but is also going to bring three of our children into this world. But god help me, she is already crazy without the pregnancy hormones. I have a feeling her pregnancy is going to test my patience.

And I have a feeling my punishment is far from over. This woman is ruthless and loves to torture people but that is my wife the Diabolical Queen is feared in the underworld but loves her family fiercely and will do anything to protect them.

FIFTY-SIX
MATEO

      The next morning, Emilia woke up to a surprise when she found herself chained to the bed by her ankle. I was downstairs drinking my coffee while I was reading my emails when I heard her yell, "MATEO MOTHERFUCKING DE LUCA. YOU BETTER GET YOUR ASS UP HERE." I chuckled that she thought she wasn't going to get punished for her little stunt of running off and being so careless putting herself in danger. She was very wrong, and I wanted my stubborn and hardheaded wife to learn her lesson. I decided her punishment would be that she would be chained to the bed; the chain was long enough where she could walk all around the room, but she couldn't make it out the door. I purposely didn't come up the stairs for a few minutes to let that anger boil. She looks hot as hell when she is pissed.

      I walk up the stairs and open the door and she is searching through the drawers in the end tables. I lean my shoulder against the door frame with my arms crossed over my chest. "You looking for something, my Queen?"

      She stops looking in the drawer and stands up. Emilia marches her way over to me and stands in front of me with her hand out. "Give me the key Mateo!"

      I pull the key out of my pocket and lift it above my head, knowing she won't be able to reach it. "Yes, that fucking key Mateo. Hand it over fucking now!"

      I chuckle. "Nope, you think you can do what you did without any punishment?" I say to her, I put the key on top of the door frame knowing my wife she will get it out of my pocket if I put it there. I let my anger show how much she pissed me off being so careless and reckless.

      "You think you can leave this house without any form of protection? Were you trying to get kidnapped?" She goes to respond but I shake my head. "No, Emilia, we have more than one enemy. The whole world knows you are my weakness and would use you against me to bring me to my knees."

      She looks down and I see her wipe her eyes. Which kills me, and I want nothing more than to bring her into my arms and hold her but she needs to realize how much power she has. When I said that I gave her this power, I was partially right but in the sense that she has the power to completely destroy me in every way. I would be completely lost if something happened to her.

      "I am sorry, Mateo," she says quietly and she raises her head. Her eyes meet mine and I cave and walk up to her. I hold her in my arms, I kiss her head as her head rests on my shoulder.

"You have the power to destroy me, you are my world my Queen. I wouldn't be able to survive if anything happened to you. I can't and won't let anything happen to you." She nods in my chest. I pull back to wipe the tears off her cheeks. "No more doing stupid and reckless shit. Okay?"

"I promise."

I kiss her cheek, "Good girl. By the way, I have increased your security." I tell her smirking as I walk away, knowing my tigress is about to get mad.

"Mateo! You better be kidding; I already have a team."

I shrug my shoulders. "Obviously you need more, if you can sneak past your team."

"Oh my fucking god. I snuck away to save Kelly and Dante from Alexei since I knew that house like the back of my hand," she yells at me with her hands thrown in the air.

I walk back over to her. "And I almost lost you. So if I have to have someone glued to your side every minute of every damn day, I will. I have seen you too many times laying in a hospital bed fighting for your life and I prefer never to see that again," I tell her. I will not budge on this.

"Enjoy your punishment being in this room until we leave later to go get Alessia." She doesn't respond all she does is get back in the bed staring out the window. I decide to give her some space.

A few hours later, I bring her something to eat she eats in complete silence. I unchain her ankle so she can get ready. I try and talk to her; she doesn't acknowledge my presence. She stays quiet the whole time by the time we get in the car, before she can open the door I have her caged between me and the car. "You better change this attitude, or you will have another punishment when we get home." She rolls her eyes at me; oh, she is asking to be put over my knee. We get in the car, and she slides to the other side of the car. I don't push her but if she doesn't stop her ass is going to be nice and red when we sit down at Nonna's.

We get to Nonna's, she tries to walk past me; I grab her wrist and pull her back to me. "Enough."

She shakes her head. "No, Mateo. You want to punish me, fine. But never chain me like I am some dog. I am your wife."

"Yes, you are my wife, but my wife likes to run off and I have to keep chasing her."

"TWICE! I have run away twice when I felt like we needed to. Don't give me a reason and I won't have to run." She stomps past me; I pick her up and throw her over my shoulder. I head straight to the basement; we are dealing with this once and for all. When she realizes, we are headed to the basement she starts thrashing in my arms, we get in the weapon room. I grab a few guns and set her at the gun range. I know this anger isn't just at me and she needs to get it out.

I place her down and hand her a gun. "Shoot," I tell her. I watch as she fires round after round off. By the time she has emptied her second clip her hands are wobbling, and her body is shaking. I take the gun out of her hands and lay it on the table. I turn her in my arms and hold her. Her knees give out, but I just pick her up in my arms. After a few minutes she goes from sobbing to sniffling. "Better?" I ask.

She nods. "Sorry I was being a raging bitch." I chuckle and kiss her head.

"It's okay, but what else had you pissed?"

"A lot. Knowing how my family died, especially my Mama, how unfair everything me and Alessia went through because Seth had some weird obsession with me, missing my family more than ever now that I am pregnant again. I also feel terrible about Dante and Damiano grieving Kelly," she says, still sniffling. I hold her face in my hands and wipe her tears with my thumbs.

"I know what Seth did was absolutely terrible, but he can never hurt you or Alessia ever again. Alexei soon will pay for what he did, and we will help both Damiano and Dante while they grieve Kelly. You ready to go upstairs?"

She nods. "Yeah, I am hungry." I kiss her lips and grab her hand as we walk upstairs. We enjoy the rest of the day with the family and when we brought Alessia home she absolutely loved the new house.

A few weeks later, after Theo gave Emilia the okay to have sex again. Alessia was having a sleepover at Nonna and Nonno's house and I was going to spend the whole night in between my wife's legs.

After Alessia leaves, Emilia smirks at me. "So, we have the whole house to ourselves?" she asks as she straddles my lap. I nod and she leans in next to my ear. "Then why don't we christen our bedroom?" And she stands up heading towards into our room, she barely gets two steps before I have swooped down. I pick her up in my arms bridal style and run into our bedroom and toss her onto our bed.

"Sorry, it has been weeks since I have been able to touch your body and I am going to soak in every moment." I waste no time climbing over her, I whisper in her ear.

I start to slowly kiss the spot behind her ear, her weak spot. She is starting to turn into a moaning mess. "No more punishment for you."

I smirk "Okay, my love." I keep kissing down her body until I get to the collar of her shirt, I move my hands behind her to support her to sit up. I peel her shirt off her and unhook her bra, I lean her back against the bed. She grips my hair bringing me back to her mouth. I oblige and kiss her; I lick her lip and she eagerly opens her mouth. My tongue caresses every part of her mouth, and I slowly grind on her. She grips my hair tighter as she moans into my mouth. I move one hand to the back of her hair, and I angle her head so I can have better access to her mouth. My other hand is resting above the waistband of her pants, and I just caress the skin. I am going to take my time with her right now. No more threats hanging above our heads, our family is growing, life is as perfect as a mafia power couple can get.

She breaks away from the kiss to catch her breath, I smile at her and whisper. "I love you," but move down to her breasts.

I start sucking on her nipples she winces; I pull away and look at her. "They are tender," she tells me.

I nod and say I will be gentle; I gently kiss and lick her nipple while playing with the other one. It doesn't take long for them to perk up, I switch and start kissing and licking the other one. I softly blow on both of her nipples. Emilia is moaning out my name as she grinds up into me. I smirk against her nipple and grind back onto her. Once I feel both nipples are hard enough, I make my way further down until I get to her pants. I pull her pants and the thong of her long perfect legs. I pull her to the end of the bed, so her ass is at the end of the bed. I smack her ass; she jumps but I also see she is wet for me. I run a finger down her slit, she shivers and moans at my touch. I get down to the floor on my knees in front of her pussy, I lick my lips looking at my desert that I am about to devour.

I throw both of her legs over my shoulder, and I start sucking on her clit and insert one finger inside of her. Almost instantaneously she is moaning my name and listening to her moan and whimper in need makes me so much harder than I already was. I reach down with one of my hands and squeeze my cock. I stay focused and go back and forth between licking and sucking her clit, while I add another finger to finger fuck her. "Oh, shit. Fuck, Mateo. Fuck, fuck." I can feel her tightening around my fingers, so add my third finger. I curl my fingers to hit her g-spot while I suck harder on her clit, within a couple strokes she is almost there. "Yes, oh please don't stop." She grabs my hair in her hands and grinds herself onto my face, which is one of the hottest things I have seen her do. I mentally roll my eyes in the back of my head, but, physically, I don't because I am not looking away for a second to witness the goddess that is my wife in the throes of her orgasm. "Oh, fuck. Mateo!" and she drags the O out in my name as she cums. I continue until she rides out her orgasm high. I lick everything up; I stand up and quickly strip out of my clothes.

"Give me a second and I will return the favor."

I shake my head. "No, you will not. You are going to be a good girl and lay your sexy ass in this bed while I see how many orgasms, I can pull out of you while we make love." She doesn't get a chance to respond when I settle myself between her legs and insert all of myself inside of her. I groan into her ear, "Fucking best place to be." I start thrusting in and out of her, I kiss all over her neck and chest as I continue to thrust in and out of her at a steady pace. Between barely recovering from the first orgasm and being extra sensitive being pregnant she is already starting to tighten around my cock. I pull her one leg over my shoulder and give her deeper strokes.

"Oh fuck, I feel so fucking full." I bite the inside of my cheek to stop myself from smirking, she is definitely stroking my ego today, not that I am complaining. I rub her clit and keep giving her deep and long strokes inside of her and within no time she is cuming again. I move her legs so they are bent toward her chest but out to the side. She is so sensitive and responsive to my touch that I pull three more orgasms out of her before we finally both cum together.

After we both have caught our breath, I go into the bathroom for a washcloth to clean us both up. Within minutes she is asleep, with her head on my shoulder. I look out our window and see nothing but wide-open spaces, I rub my thumb across her belly. I kiss her stomach, *"Papà non vedo l'ora di incontrarvi, bambini miei." (Papa can't wait to meet you, my babies.)* I am so excited for our future together.

FIFTY-SEVEN
EMILIA

  It has been a year since returning from the states and a lot has changed. One thing is that our family has grown by three. Alessandro, Antonio, and Arianna came eight weeks early and were a force to be reckoned with. I was thirty-two weeks pregnant, bigger than a damn whale. While I was enjoying some mint chocolate chip ice cream while I was in the middle of an Avengers marathon, my water broke.

  Mateo was at the office and in the middle of an important meeting. He thought I was calling for my latest craving. "Hello, *mio caro*. What would you like me to bring you home?"

  As I was about to answer a contraction hit so I grunted out in pain and Mateo, being the overprotective husband he is started to freak out. "Emilia. What is wrong?" I was barely able to get out of that, my water broke. Adriano was home and he drove me to the hospital. Adriano is a saint for rushing to my side when he heard me yell out in pain, helping me to the car and holding my hand through the car ride. Mateo had beat us to the hospital and was waiting out front with the wheelchair for me.

  Mateo had stayed on the phone with me and tried to keep me calm but I was in pain. I know I should have been okay because I went through labor already with Alessia and it wasn't an ideal delivery but with how many close calls I had during this pregnancy I was beyond scared and the fact that they were eight weeks early. I was very anemic and had preeclampsia during my pregnancy. I was rushed up to the maternity ward of the hospital and quickly was prepped to have a cesarean delivery. Luckily Mateo was allowed in the operating room with me, but we all know he would have threatened his way in the room with me, regardless. Alessandro was the first to be born he scared us because he was quiet for the first few moments, but he finally made a small cry. Then came Antonio who cried louder than Alessandro but wasn't that loud. Finally came Arianna and I think people could hear her cry outside of the hospital. Mateo was ready to fight the doctor thinking he did something wrong and had hurt her. I reassured him she was fine and that she was just being loud. Let me say she has her Papa wrapped around her finger. He loves all the babies, but Arianna makes a whimper, and he is already picking her up and fussing over her.

  But now back to the current issue: pulling Mateo off Alessia so we can take her to her first day of school. Yes, I am having to pry Mateo off Alessia. He has fought me since I brought up her going to school, but she needs to interact with other kids her age. His response was "Private school has boys, and no boys deserve to look at my princess." Alessia gave Mateo the puppy eye pout telling him she wants to make friends. He tried saying no but that didn't last with the threat of him sleeping in the guest room until he changed his mind. He didn't last the night before he came storming back into our bedroom saying she can go but he had security around her, and she could not friend any boys. I laughed and reminded him that she is friends with Dante who is a boy. He muttered, "Unfortunately. That boy stares at my princess too much." I had to remind him that they are blood cousins.

We are walking out the door to drive Alessia to school and Mateo is trying to convince Alessia she doesn't need to go. "Princess, are you sure you want to go?"

She smiles up at him and nods. "Yes, Papa. I really want to go and make friends. Please don't make me stay home."

He sighs. "Fine but if you want to come home all you have to do is call and I will come pick you up."

She hugs him. "I know, Papa. I love you."

He kisses the top of her hair. "I love you too Princess."

While we are driving to school and Alessia singing along to the music, I see Mateo keep glancing in the rear-view mirror, watching her, sing and dance around in her seat. I squeezed his hand. As much as I pushed for her to go to school doesn't mean I am not sad that she won't be home with us, but I know she needs this. This is the first time she will be going to any kind of school that isn't private tutors inside of our home. He looks over at me and gives me a small smile and kisses the top of my hand. Alessia talks about all the things she can't wait to do once she starts school like field trips and making friends.

We pull into the school parking lot and Mateo parks the car; he turns around facing Alessia. She leans forward and kisses his cheek. "It's okay, Papa. I will miss you too, but I will see you when I get home from school."

He strokes her cheek. "When did you get so smart?"

"It kind of rubs off on you when your parents are pretty smart."

I chuckle at her. "Ok, cheeky girl. Let's get you inside." Mateo opens both of our doors and helps us out of the Range Rover. Mateo holds onto my hand and keeps squeezing it the whole way into the office. When we get in Alessia has a big smile on her face and you can see she is basically bouncing on her feet in excitement.

We meet Principal Ricci; we talk about how Mateo will have a man keeping an eye over Alessia for her safety. Mr. Ricci doesn't object; I doubt he will object to anything Mateo says with the huge donation we made to the school. This beautiful little angel with brown hair and bright blue eyes comes in.

She's around the same height as Alessia and says, "Hello Mr. Ricci. You called for me."

He smiles over at the girl "Ah yes Aurora. I would like you to show our new student around. Alessia De Luca, these are her parents Mateo and Emilia De Luca. Alessia, Aurora is in your first period with you and has a couple of other classes with you. Aurora will show you around today and help you so you can find all of your classes and other important rooms like the cafeteria and library." Alessia waves her hand at Aurora and the girls say hello to each other, then she turns to us and sticks her hand out to introduce herself to me and Mateo.

"Hello, Mr. and Mrs. De Luca, my name is Aurora Romano. It is nice to meet you."

I smile at her and shake her hand. "Hello Aurora. It is a pleasure to meet you. Thank you for showing Alessia around today."

"Of course, Mrs. De Luca, I hope Alessia enjoys coming to school here."

She shyly reaches for Mateo's hand because he is showing his Mafia Boss side. I glare at him, and he gently reaches for her hand. "Hello, Aurora. Thank you for helping Alessia today."

She smiles and says, "It's no problem at all."

"Alessia, why don't you say goodbye to your parents so Aurora can see where your locker is before the first period," Principal Ricci says.

Alessia walks over to Mateo first, and he bends down so he is on his knees in front of her. "Remember what I told you." She nods as he continues talking. "I am so proud of you. You have come so far from that scared little six-year-old hiding behind your Mama's leg. I know you will have a wonderful first day today and we can't wait to hear about it when you get home. I love you, *Principessa*. Now go give your Mama a hug and have a great day. We will pick you up after school."

She hugs Mateo tight around his neck. "I love you too Papa. And don't worry when I get home, we can have a snack together since I won't be there for lunch."

He kisses her cheek. "It's a date."

She then walks over to me, and I copy Mateo and crouch down in front of my baby. I hold her cheeks in my hand. "Oh my precious strong girl. Remember who you are, a princess and you keep that head up high. Don't let the crown fall, you are a De Luca and so brave and strong. I love you baby girl."

She smiles at me and hugs me while she whispers. "I love you too, Mama. Thank you."

I smile at her. "Anything for you." I stand up and tell her. "Go on, have fun, baby. We will see you after school."

She nods, blows us both a kiss and says, "I love you, Mama and Papa beyond my last breath."

And we tell her, "We love you beyond our last breath."

I wipe my eyes after the girls leave the office. Mr. Ricci offers me a tissue and I thank him. He gives me a smile and says, "It is usually harder on the parents than it is on the kids."

"I know. Thank you, Mr. Ricci."

He walks us out to the front door and says, "Of course, Mrs. De Luca. Call at any time if you want." We all wish each other a good day.

I hold my tears in until we get inside the Range Rover and then the water works fall. Mateo is wiping them as fast as they are falling. "It's okay darling. She will be okay."

I nod and start to sniffle. "I know, I just can't believe my baby is finally going to school. I know she needs it especially since she is nine years old, but I will miss seeing her at the house during the day."

"I know," he tells me and kisses my lips softly.

He pulls away and starts the engine and we head back to our farmhouse. I sometimes can't believe Mateo built me our very own farmhouse, don't get me wrong, I love it. In the basement, the "mafia floor" as Mateo calls it, it has a gym, and a weapon room. Alessia and Mateo spend time alone down there and no one disturbs them. Vincenzo made the mistake of walking down there while Mateo was teaching her how to take down someone. Let's just say, Vincenzo became the dummy and was sore afterwards.

Mateo and Alessia walked out with proud smiles on their faces while Vincenzo was limping out of the basement behind them. Salvatore and Lilyana were quick to laugh in Vincenzo's misery. Mateo says he will train all of our children to take down anyone, and when they get old enough, they will be a master of all weapons. As a mother, of course, I don't want them playing with weapons, but the reality is their parents are the head of the Italian Mafia and unfortunately, they will have a target on their backs. And I would rather have them be prepared than be unprepared.

We walk into the house and we both pause; Mateo looks at me with a mischievous look in his eye. "Do you hear that?" he asks me/

"Hear what?" I asked him, confused. He turned to me, so I am in his arms.

"Exactly. It is completely silent. We are alone. The terrible trio are with Nonna and Nonno. Alessia is at school. So that means Mrs. De Luca you have one minute to be up in our room naked on our bed before I start ripping your clothes off you." I laugh and he gives me a smoldering look. "Unless you want me to throw you over my shoulder?"

I shake my head and run off to our room. As I am finishing stripping off my last piece of clothes, I am bent over, taking off my thong. I feel Mateo smack my ass, but before I can say anything, he has me sitting on the bed. I stare at him as he unties his tie and throws it on the bed next to me.

And he slowly starts to unbutton his shirt. "I am going to enjoy taking my time with you mia Regina" he says as he licks his lips.

I run my hand down my body. "And what do you want to do to me, *il mio re?*"

"I am going to devour your body and have you making those sweet noises I love hearing, especially when I make you cum over and over again." I squeeze my thighs together. "Seems like someone likes that idea." I am unable to make any words without moaning so I just nod my head. Mateo starts rubbing my clit, I bite my lip to hold in my moans. He pulls my lip away from my teeth with his thumb. "Don't you dare hold in those moans, I want to hear them. Understand?"

I nod my head, and he gently grabs my throat "Words, Emilia."

"Yes."

He leans down and says, "Good girl," against my lips before he slams his lips on mine. I immediately respond back to the kiss; I push his shirt off his shoulders, and it falls to the floor. I then unbuckle his belt, unzip his pants, and push them down. He kicks them off his feet, we break away from the kiss. He stares at me, eyeing me up and down. "You truly are perfect. So damn sexy."

He kisses all over the column of my neck while he continues to rub my clit, I am squirming under him, I feel him smirk against my neck. He loves to tease me and pull back multiple times until I can't take it anymore. "Please, Mateo, don't tease me," I moan out.

"What do you want?" he asked me.

"YOU! I want you inside me right NOW!"

He flips me over, so I am on my hands and knees. Mateo doesn't waste any time and plunging himself into me and says, "Whatever my Queen wants she shall get." We both moan out when his cock is fully inside of me. He leans forward so his chest is flushed with back. He whispers in my ear "Is this what you want? For me to ravish you?" as he pulls on my ponytail. I arch my back and push my ass into his groin.

"Yes" I moan out when he uses his other hand on my ass to stabilize himself and to squeeze it. I moan out again when he squeezes my ass.

"Touch yourself," he orders me. I wait and don't obey him, but Mateo isn't having any part of it. He gives my hair a firm yank. "I said touch yourself or do you want to be punished by not cuming?" I quickly shake my head and I start to play with myself. He smacks my ass; I squeal out his name and tighten myself around him.

He lets out a deep groan from his chest and pounds into me harder and faster, "Fuck. Yes, Mateo right there." I say as he keeps hitting my G-Spot over and over again, it won't be long until I cum. He pushes himself deeper inside of me and that is when I fall apart. "Mateo!" I shout as my walls squeeze the life out of his cock. His grip on my hips tightens as he continues to pound into me as I continue to ride out the high from my orgasm, I slump myself against the bed. He is getting faster and sloppier in his thrust; I know he is close.

"FUCK!" he grunts out as he cums inside of me. I am so glad I got an IUD.

He slumps against my back and we both are breathing hard. After about a minute we both climbed into bed and just lay together in the bed in silence. Mateo says, "You, okay?"

I nod my head. "Yeah, I am more than good." He chuckles and kisses my head. I look over and see we have less than an hour until we have to go get the triplets. "As much as I would love to stay like this, we need to go get ready to go get the babies."

He whines. "Do we have to?"

I shake my head and laugh. "Yes, we do. Now get up, let's go shower and maybe if you're lucky, you might get a round two?" He quickly jumps out of bed and is running to the bathroom; I laugh shaking my head following him into the bathroom.

After a long and heated shower, we went to pick up the babies. Nonna and Nonno love spending time with their grandbabies, even the adult ones. We decided to have a family dinner tonight to celebrate Alessia's first day of school. Mateo goes to get some paperwork done while I play with Alessandro, Antonio, and Arianna. It seems like the day goes slower without Alessia popping in randomly throughout the day to come say hello.

When four o'clock hits we are in the pickup line to get Alessia from school. Mateo and I quietly talk since "the demon spawns" as Mateo was calling the babies earlier are finally asleep. "Do you think she had a good day?" he asks.

"Yeah, I think she did plus Marco would have said something if she didn't."

He nods. "Yeah, I guess so. I just hate that she is growing up."

I smile at him. "It's only gonna get worse. One day she will be dating, driving, then graduating, going off to college, getting married and one day, having her own babies."

He cuts me off by putting his hand over my mouth. "Are you trying to give me a heart attack? I barely got through today and you want to talk about her moving away to go to college." I chuckle at him.

"Look," I say and point to Alessia who has a huge smile on her face. She is hugging Aurora. We both step out of the car; Aurora says something to her and Alessia turns around and sees us. I wave to her; she waves and runs over to us.

"Mama, Papa," she says as she runs to us. "Thank you. I had so much fun today and I made a lot of friends."

I smile and push her hair behind her ear. "I am so happy for you, baby girl. But guess what?"

She looks up at me and says, "What?"

"Everyone is coming over for dinner tonight to celebrate your first day of school."

"Really?" she asks.

"Yep."

"YAY!"

Mateo clears his throat. "Hello, Princess. Where is my hug?" She gives him a sheepish smile and hugs him.

"Sorry, Papa. Can we still have our snack date?"

"Of course we can. That is a silly question. Get in but be quiet; terror trio are finally asleep." Alessia giggles as she scolds Mateo for calling them the terror trio.

As soon as we get home, Mateo and Alessia rush up to his office for their date, and Mimi helps me put the triplets in their cribs. That is another thing Mateo surprised me with. He paid Mimi to be our live-in nanny because we both didn't trust a stranger. I love having her here, and she is amazing with them. Hopefully, they stay asleep long enough so I can get dinner cooked. I hum and dance around the kitchen as I cook chicken breast with mashed sweet potatoes and asparagus. Alessia's new favorite. I could never get her to eat macaroni and cheese with hot dogs in it after the old mansion was blown up. But thankfully, she rarely has nightmares of that day anymore, it took years and a lot of therapy for both of us to be able to move past that traumatizing day.

Mateo and Alessia came back down from his office and Mateo was pouting at Alessia. She was laughing at him. "Papa, I will tell everyone all the details of my day at dinner. It's not fair to everyone else."

He shrugs his shoulders. "But I am your Papa. I deserve to know first."

I laugh at him. "You De Luca men have no patience. They will be here in ten minutes, so both of you go wash up for dinner. And Mateo, go check on the babies."

"But they will smell me and wake up," he whines at me.

I roll my eyes, point the spoon at him and say, "Go."

He loves the babies, but he isn't wrong in saying they are a lot to handle. I wink at Alessia for keeping her nosey father away from her for a couple minutes. When the doorbell rings, Nonno and Nonna are the first to arrive with a blueberry cheesecake in hand, no surprise there. I knew they would bring some kind of dessert, especially since most of the De Luca's have a sweet tooth. I kiss them both on the cheek and take the cake from Nonna to put in the refrigerator.

Alessia comes downstairs as the doorbell rings again; Marcello and Julietta come in. Julietta decided to stay longer in Italy before heading over to Spain to train with Esmeralda. I know everyone is happy about that, especially Marcello, but I know she needs it, and when she is ready, I will help her deal with these overbearing men in our lives. "Celly, Zia Julietta!" Alessia says excitedly and hugs them both. No surprise, Marcello has a sweet treat in his pocket that he tries to sneak her, she winks at him and sticks it in her pocket. Julietta looks at me, and we both smile. I don't say anything because Marcello is so good to her, and those two are so close; he is more than just her bodyguard. He was just as picky as Mateo about who would be her guard at school. He was one of the first men she trusted, and he never stepped over the lines. Also, he will be her Zio one day, and three Zio's already spoil her. Having Marcello spoil her too won't hurt.

Speaking of Zii they barge into the house with Lilyana. She looks beautiful as always.

She has put weight back on, so she is no longer skin and bones. She is scowling at Vincenzo. "There is a thing called knocking."

He rolls his eyes "Yeah, what is that?"

Before the two of them can start, I pull Lilyana in a hug, and whisper, "Is he being a pain in the ass again?"

She nods her head. "I swear, he is the king of cockblocking." We both laugh; the men have realized we won't share what we talk about no matter how much they annoy us.

After Damiano and Dante arrive, yes, they are now included in our family since Alessia and Dante are cousins by blood. Also, we owe Damiano a lot for keeping Salvatore out of getting into major trouble after Lilyana was supposedly killed. I also have been trying to have the capos and us be like one big happy family, but certain wives are not as willing. As annoying and irritating their catty behavior is towards Lilyana and me, we don't let it bother us. Maybe one day my wish for all of us to be like one big family, but if not, oh well, it's not like I didn't try.

We all sit down for dinner; everyone is eating but now is hanging onto every word that Alessia says about her first day of school. "Aurora showed me my classes; we have literature, math, and music together. I also made friends with Emily and Emma. They are twins, and I have music with them. Emma can sing really well, and Emily plays the flute. I didn't hear her play since today we focused on singing today in class. Tomorrow, we get to use instruments. I hope I can play the violin since it is my favorite and Brian told me at lunch that I have pretty eyes."

Oh shit. "Brian?"

"A boy?" the men all say.

I roll my eyes. "Alessia, is Brian, a boy?"

"Yes, Papa. He is nice. He has a nice smile."

I look over at Mateo, and I swear he looks like his head could explode. I laugh at him but then look at all the other men in the family. "Seriously, it is a simple crush. She isn't about to run off to elope with the boy. Chill out."

Salvatore shakes his head. "Nope, we need to do a background check on this boy Brian." Okay, now I am completely shocked.

Damiano smirks; oh no, it isn't a good smirk. "Alessia, what do you say if your Papa, Zii, Zio, Nonno, Marcello, and I all bring you to school tomorrow? We want to see where you go to school."

Julietta speaks up, "Oh no, you don't. Leave the poor girl alone. You overgrown cavemen are not going to scare every boy that looks at her like you all did to me." And that is how the rest of the dinner goes, with all the men, even sweet Nonno deciding how to scare this nine-year-old boy away from Princess Alessia.

I shake my head. Three years ago, when we finally escaped Seth and his goons, we find a family who welcomed us with open arms. They have been there for us through every high and low. We are so lucky. I have a husband, who is a wonderful father to my children, a sweet sister-in-law, and hopefully, an additional cousin who will help me keep the two De Luca cousins in line, two crazy cousins, a supportive uncle, and wise grandparents. But most importantly we have people we love and love us, who we call family. A crazy, very dysfunctional, mafia family but still family. And every day, I will be grateful for having each and every one of them.

Want more Emilia and Mateo?

Let's be honest you are not ready to let them go. You are not alone; I wasn't ready to say goodbye either.

Yes, we will see them in the upcoming books, but we will miss their shenanigans.
Are you ready for Emilia to complete her vengeance for her family?

This is your warning the content contains violence, graphic bloody torture. Sexual content.

ONE
EMILIA

I sit in my office like I have for months since I had the triplets. Searching all over the web for him. I was not going to let what he did go unpunished.

Ryan Funkhouse or what I knew him as Sergeant Henry Dwight, the man who gave the order for no one to enter my family's home while my family was being burned alive.

As much as I don't regret having Alessia, maybe we could have never been held captive by Seth for all those years. Maybe things would have been different, maybe they would have been the same. I just wish my family was still alive and that they didn't have a painful death.

I'm just glad that the outcome was a happy ending and a new beginning for Alessia and me. We have Mateo, who is an amazing husband and father to our children. I wouldn't trade any of them for the world. That doesn't mean I will forget about Sergeant Henry. He deserves to die the same way my family did, but his death will be much more painful.

I found that after my family's death his hush money was deposited in his account and he left with a new identity. He moved to California and has tried to stay under the radar, but you can only stay under the radar for so long. I booked myself a ticket on a flight to California that leaves in a few hours. Hopefully I will be able to get on the plane before any of these pain in the ass guards that my husband has on me get wise to my leaving and alerts him.

He is in Canada handling business, he is hoping to set up trade with them, he is supposed to be there for a week so fingers crossed he will be too busy to deal with me. My goal is to get to California interrogate and torture Henry for a few hours. Watch as his house burns with him inside, then hop back on the plane back to Italy without my husband knowing I was gone until I am home, so I won't be punished but I seriously doubt that. A woman can only dream. Right?

I get to my room and pack a light bag for my short trip to California. The house is empty since the kids are all at Pa's. I asked if he would take them for a night so I could have a bit of me time with Mateo away. He was more than happy to have them stay with him, not sure if he was more excited to take the kids or that Mimi would be staying with them. It's no secret that Pop is pinning after Mimi but they both lost a spouse and I can only imagine how painful that is.

As much as Mateo plucks my last nerve on a daily basis, I would be completely heartbroken if he wasn't here with me. He understands me better than anyone ever has. He embraces me after I am done torturing and covered in blood, he holds me tight when the memories from the past resurface and protects me from my own mind. Loves every part of me like I love every part of him, especially the naughty side.

"What are you doing this time?" I hear from the sweet voice, who I love. I slowly turn around, Mimi has her hands on her hips with her eyebrow arched at me.

"Going to see Mateo. Spontaneous trip."

"You might be able to fool the De Luca's with your white lies, but I basically raised you. So try again."

"Pain in my ass." I mumble under my breath, I look up to see how likely I am able to get out of this without her giving me shit. And by the look on her face that is a big fat not happening. I sigh, "I am going to California."

"And what is in California?"

"The son of a bitch who thought he could hide after ordering his men not to save my family from the fire." Anger pours from every word that comes from my mouth. Mimi knows I have been looking for Henry.

Mimi walks over to me and embraces me in a hug and just holds me to her. I wrap my arms around her. Closing my eyes I feel myself back there being restrained watching as my family is burned alive and there was nothing I could do to stop it.

"I wish you wouldn't put yourself in danger but I know I can't stop you. All that I ask is that you be careful and check in with me regularly."

I nod against her chest, "I promise I will."

"Good. Now what do you need?" She asks as I move away from her and finish packing my bag.

"I have to leave in an hour for my flight. I need to sneak past the goons." She chuckles with me.

"How about you get in the back of my car, I will drive you out of here?"

"Perfect, I just need to make it ten minutes away, that's where my ride will be waiting for me."

"I will be ready in an hour." She smiles at me as she walks out the door.

"Passengers please buckle your seatbelts. And please turn all phones off." The pilot calls over the intercom. I am situated and have my bag that has a few books I will read while on the flight. I curl my nails into my palm as the plane takes off. No matter how many times I fly with Mateo I still hate the take-off and landing.

It only takes a few minutes for us to be coasting in the air, instead of taking out a book from my bag I lean my head on the window letting the chill of the glass cool my hot skin.

I go back to that day. I had closed the diner with Mimi and had driven back to our house. Mama had insisted that me and Franco continued to live at home until we had enough money to buy our own home. She was never ready to let us go, no matter how badly we wanted to spread our wings. We both loved Mama too much to hurt her feelings.

Papa used to joke about kicking us out, but he wanted us at home just as bad as she did. He claimed he needed Franco home so he could help Papa keep an eye on me. No shocker that I have always been a wild child but what do you expect when you are your mother's daughter and she is a wildflower. You tend to take after her.

It breaks my heart all the suffering they went through because Seth became obsessed with me. I have fought the darkness inside of my head for so long after what Seth told me. How he raped Mama in front of my father and brothers and tied them so they had no way of escaping as they burned alive.

They had so much more life to live. Mama and Papa should be retired, traveling back and forth between Virginia and Italy to visit and spoil their grandbabies.

Franco would be a kickass computer genius, maybe I would convince him to be a part of the mafia. If not, I know I would be turning to him when I had doubts about Fabio's abilities.

Giovanni, sweet Gio. He would have been graduating high school this year. He hadn't even started living his life. Maybe he would go to college on a soccer scholarship. Or who knows what he would have decided to do with his life but I know he was so vibrant that you couldn't help but be happy around him.

I wipe my eyes as the tears pour down my cheek. The old lady next to me hands me a tissue, I quietly thank her. And all she tells me, "One day at a time, my dear. One day at a time."

TWO

MATEO

  I am sitting in my hotel room sorting through the contract I am negotiating with Canada for their diamonds in exchange for some of my family's wine to be sold in Canada. Supposedly the wife of one of the diamond jewelers had recently traveled to Italy and had our wine. She had been complimenting it and demanding her husband get some.

  I look away when I get a text message on my phone, hopefully it is from Emilia, something has been bothering her for the past few weeks. I almost canceled this trip but she assured me she was okay. I still wasn't so convinced, but when I see a message from Mimi saying Emilia took a flight to California. I am now confused about what is in California and why didn't she take one of our planes. I would know because they are to notify me anytime they take any member of my family anywhere.

  I pick up the phone and call Mimi, knowing she pried answers out of Emilia before she left.

  Mimi: You waste no time, do you?

  Mateo: When it comes to Emilia or my family. No. Absolutely not.

  Mimi: I know and that's why you are a good man.

  Mateo: Thanks Mimi. Did she say why? Is she okay? She said she was okay.

  Mimi: Easy Mateo, she is okay. She found the man, Henry Dwight, who ordered his men not to go and save her family in the house fire.

  Mateo: Shit.

  Mimi: Yeah. You could tell she was reliving the day when I was holding her. I did have her promise me to check in.

  Mateo: Okay, good did she tell you when her flight was?

  Mimi: No but I figured it would be soon.

  Mateo: Okay thanks Mimi. Don't worry about Emilia.

  Mimi: I know you will take care of her. Just make sure the two of you make it home.

  Mateo: We will. How are the kids?

  Mimi: Well they are left alone with Adriano so who knows what kind of trouble they have landed themselves in.

  Mateo: Not sure who is worse, the toddler triplet tornado or Zio Adriano.

  Mimi: No idea but I am on my way over there.

  Mateo: Okay go save my princess from them. Call me if you need anything.

  Mimi: I will.

I text Fabio.

Mateo: I want the address for Henry Dwight in California ASAP.

Fabio: Done.

Hopefully it isn't too hard to find, I look up when the next flight to California is. The plane leaves in forty minutes, I could have men sent after her but knowing Emilia she mind is in a whirlwind. I will give her time on the plane to settle her mind, but I will meet her in California and help her get the last of her vengeance for her family.

I change my time in Canada to be shortened by a day, I'm sure they'll try to give me grief about it. One thing that will never change is that business will never come before my family.

The following day I am stepping off my jet into the California heat. Fabio had sent me the address a few hours later, he had narrowed down the list he had. I get into the rental I ordered and drive over to what I think is supposed to be a house. It looks like a trailer that is literally being held up by plywood and tarps. I look around and it isn't the nicest neighborhood, thankfully I have one of my men with me who will be sitting in the car around the corner until we are ready to go home.

I walk up to the door and knock. I see movement in the window and I see his beady eyes staring at me, "I can see you Henry. You can open the door willingly or I can open it on my own. Choice is yours."

"Go away or I will call the cops." I chuckle, "Sure. Go ahead and do that. While you are at it, let them know you took money to make the call to let a family burn alive in their house." I purposely say the last part loudly. He quickly opens the door.

"Who are you?" I push past him and move my body in a circle to take a look around his home. I turned back to him, "My name is Mateo De Luca. Not that will do you any good because you won't be leaving here alive."

He goes to take a step back, but I grab him by the collar of his shirt.

"Now we won't be doing any of that now Henry or should I call you Ryan since that is your new name right?" I taunt him. He tries to fight against me but his beer belly and out of shape body is no match for me.

I pull him into the kitchen and force him in the chair, I quickly get to work restraining him to the chair.

"Why? Why are you doing this to me."

I sinisterly chuckle at him, you can feel the fear rolling off him in waves.

"Why? You ask. It's because of a choice you made years ago that has made my wife suffer for years. So it's time for her to get her revenge on you for that."

He starts to cry and beg me not to kill him. Usually I love to hear my guests cry and beg me but this fucker is grinding my last nerve and as much as I want to put my hands on him for what he did. I know this is Emilia's kill, so I will wait. She needs this.

I look around and see a dirty dish rag. I shove it in his mouth and use the duct tape I brought and tape his mouth shut. Finally peace and quiet, I look at my watch and see I still have time until Emilia will arrive. Let's see if this fucker has any half decent alcohol to kill the time.

I see he has beer, well better than nothing. I sit in the chair opposite him and take a sip of beer and grimace.

"Fuck how the hell do you drink this shit. It's like drinking piss." He just glares at me, "That's right I gagged your mouth because you wouldn't stop crying. Such a shame that you have to die such a painful death today because you were stupid and greedy."

He starts crying again, "Don't waste your tears. I can promise you that when my wife gets here, you will be crying and begging for death. My wife loves to be covered in blood while she tortures her victims. She has a thing for knives. Lucky you or maybe unlucky you, that she has held a hatred for you since the night you let her family die and it's now time for you to pay for your sins."

THREE
MATEO

  I smile when I hear the unmistakable sound of a car door opening, knowing it's my diabolical wife arriving. I moved my chair a while ago, that way I can see her shocked face when she sees me.

  I watch her face looks shocked to see Henry gagged and tied up. Then her eyes go to me, I stand as my eyes meet hers and they are red and have dry tear marks down her face. She walks into my arms, "How? Why?" She mumbles into my chest.

  I rub my hand up and down her back, "Mimi called me. There was no way I was letting you do this on your own." I pull away from the hug and wipe the tears off her cheek.

  "Do you want me to do this for you?" She shakes her head, "No. I need to do this and doing this is the final part of my revenge for them. I have to say goodbye to them but I'm not ready to do that yet. It's like as long as I have been holding onto my vengeance for them, I've been able to keep a part of the alive in me.

  "But now you can finally properly grieve for them." I say to her.

  "Yeah." She says quietly.

  "What do you need?" I ask her, "Just a knife. I couldn't bring my bags of tools on the plane so I will just use one of the knives he has and then let him burn to death like he did to my family." She starts going through his kitchen and grabs a few knives.

  Emilia violently rips the tape off his mouth, and he screams out but not for long as she back hands him hard across the mouth.

  "Shut up, you will not make a sound unless I say so." His eyes are wide, but he nods his head. Hell she didn't even hit me, and I am afraid to say something. She pulls the dish rag out of his mouth, she looks at me. I shrug, "He kept crying and begging. It got annoying after a while."

  "Why did you accept the money?" He stares at her, her whole-body tenses. She takes a step closer to him and puts the knife to his throat. She pushes hard enough that the knife knicks his throat.

  "I asked. Why did you accept the money?"

  He swallows, "Because it was ten grand."

  Emilia chuckles, "Wow. What a great sergeant you are. You can let a woman be raped in front of her husband and sons, then have all four of them burned alive. Leaving their daughter to stand outside and watch as the house collapses on them. Killing them." She pants out in anger.

  He doesn't respond, Emilia continues.

"How can you even look at me in the eyes Henry. My mother was the nurse who treated you when you broke your leg in a work accident and even brought you food when you were at home those first few weeks. How could you betray us like that." I walk over and hold her. "You knew my family; you would tease my father how firefighters were better than cops. You watch me and my brothers grow up."

I watch as Henry looks ashamed and regrets what he did. Emilia drops the knife and buries her face in my chest. "I can't," she whispers.

"Do you want me to take over?" I whisper in her ear, she nods.

"I am not strong enough."

"You are but you hit your max. That's why I am here." I say kissing the top of her hair. I hold her in my arms and look over at Henry.

"Unfortunately for Emilia it didn't stop there. The man who paid you was so obsessed with her he raped her for years. She got pregnant with our daughter and he held them hostage for years. Emilia was beaten and raped every day for six years until she was able to escape."

"I…I didn't know."

I scoff, "Of course you didn't. You took the money and disappeared. Your selfish actions not only cause Emilia extreme trauma but also my sweet princess was mute when I met them and she was petrified of men. Imagine being born into this world and watching your mother be physically hurt everyday by every man that stepped foot into the house they were being held in."

He goes to speak, but I hold my hand up. "There is absolutely nothing you can say that will fix what you did." He nods his head as the tears fall down his cheeks. I want to wrap my hands around him or at least have my hands covered in his blood. He doesn't get to cry.

"Let him burn to death, I can't be around him anymore."

"Whatever you want, My Queen." I kiss her head, I grab the gas cans I found earlier when I was snooping around his property. I start pouring gasoline all around the trailer, on the furniture, curtains, anything, and everything. Then dump the remaining gas over Henry's head, tossing the can at his feet.

Emilia opens the book of matches and lights one tosses it in his bedroom, lights another and sets the kitchen curtains on fire. The last one she lights and watches it for a second but looks at Henry.

"I hope your death is more painful than my family's. Remember their names: Alessandro Lombardi, my father. Angelica Lombardi, my mother. Franco Lombardi, my older brother. Giovanni Lombardi, my baby brother. See their faces in your mind as you take your final breath." She says in a deadly calm voice, and she tosses the match at his feet and tosses the rest of the matchbook in his lap.

I hold my hand out for her, and we walk out of his trailer hand in hand.

I wait to see if she wants to stop and watch as it burns to the ground but she doesn't; she just keeps walking.

Emilia remains quiet as we step inside of the car, as soon as the driver takes off for the airport. I pull Emilia over me, so her legs straddle mine and just hold her tight to my chest. No words are needed, I can feel her pain. I hope what I have planned for her won't backfire but I also feel like she needs this final closure.

FOUR
EMILIA

Mateo kept me in his arms throughout the ride to the airport, and even carried me onto the jet. Usually I would fight him that I can walk but right now I need him to hold me. Be my anchor because I am tethering from falling over the edge, the demons in my mind are whispering in my ear.

My whole-body tenses when I close my eyes tighter hoping to push the demons out of my head.

Mateo sets me down; I jerk open my eyes. We are in the bedroom of the jet.

"Come on, let's get you out of those clothes." I nod, he helps me change into some clothes. After we both are changed, we lay in the bed as he holds me.

There is so much I want to say, where do I start? Right now I can barely breathe let alone attempt to dissect how I am feeling.

"Don't force it. Right now just feel. Feel your head laying on my shoulder, feel my arms wrapped around you pulling you against me, feel me breathing under your hand."

I nod and push myself closer to him.

"It's okay. Let it out, let yourself fall apart. It's only me here. You don't need to pretend to be strong in front of me. I already know how strong you are." Damn him. Damn him for knowing I was trying to be strong.

I bury my face in his neck and just let the tears flow. Mateo runs his hands up and down my back, I eventually end up crying myself to sleep.

"Emilia, love." I smack at whoever is calling me. Don't they know not to wake a sleeping Queen? I hear a deep husky laugh, and my core knows exactly who is trying to wake me up. I peek and see Mateo next to me looking at me smiling.

"Why the hell do you look so happy for?" I grumble as I close my eyes and snuggle further into his chest.

"Come on, wake up. I have a surprise for you."

"Only surprise I want is to sleep without interruptions."

I hear him laugh again but he sweeps me into his arms. My eyes pop open, "Mateo! I'm Fucking serious!"

"That's three."

My eyes widened in shock, "How do I already have three punishments?"

He glares down at me but sets me on my feet. He has me stuck between him and the wall.

"One, sneaking past the guards. AGAIN. Two, riding in a plane full of people without any protection. Any one of them could have easily hurt you. Three, for cursing."

I go to open my mouth, but he stops me. "Do you want four?" I shake my head because with this man my punishments can range anywhere from spanking, hours with a vibrator inside me while he holds the remote, his sexual punishments are endless. Usually I would test him but not today.

"Good." He says taking a step back, I grab his hand he has out for me. I follow him off the jet and into one of his cars. He drives us to a funeral home; I look at him confused.

Mateo parks the car and looks at me, "It's time to give your family the proper burial they deserve. Let's go buy them urns they deserve and then we can give them a proper De Luca send off."

I am floored again. I shouldn't be surprised that he set this up for me but still. I am barely able to get a thank you. He just gives me a sweet kiss on my lips. Gets out of the car, comes around, opens my door, and holds me as we walk inside.

Mimi is inside the office and on the desk I see the four boxes holding what is left of my family members. I have never seen the boxes, I was never ready to see them but I look at them and each name that is on the box.

I first ran my hand over Papa's box. Alessandro Lombardi. "Papa" I say quietly as the tears gather in my eyes again. I move onto Mama's box and do the same thing. I run my finger over her name, I wipe the tears that fall down my face.

Franco Lombardi and Giovanni Lombardi, the size difference in these two boxes makes me sick to my stomach. I know it is time to let myself fully grieve without any hate for what happened.

Mama would say everything happens for a reason, and if I follow her logic. The reason would be Alessia and Mateo. If it wasn't for Seth raping me, I would never got pregnant with Alessia. Then I would have never pushed so hard to escape and I would never have met Mateo or the De Luca's and be married into such a wonderful family that opened their arms to us without a question.

Mimi helps me pick out proper urns that fit their personalities the best. When we got to the Nonna's mansion I see all the De Luca's, Esmeralda, Josie and even the O'Sullivan's are here. They all greet me and tell me they are proud of me. Never thought I would hear the day where someone would tell me they were proud of me for killing someone but I didn't exactly marry into a normal family.

Later on Nonna walks me over to the family wall, and I see Papa, Mama, Franco, and Giovanni's picture as well as some of mine from when I was a child and teenager.

"What? How?"

"Mimi gave them to me a while ago. I figured you wouldn't be ready until you finally got your vengeance."

I nod my head, "Yeah." I pause for a moment, "It's bittersweet ending this."

"How so?"

"As glad I am for finally killing everyone who had a hand in what happened. Ending it means I have to let them go. And to be honest, I am not sure if I am ready." She gently pats my back, "You never are but you have a huge family here. Who love you and will support you at every step." She gives me a kiss on my cheek and Esmeralda comes next to me as I stand staring at these pictures.

"You know they would be so proud of you and the woman you have become." She says to me, I look over at her with a watery smile.

"Don't question yourself. You are loyal and very protective like your Papa. You have your Mama's spunk and wild streak." We both chuckle knowing Mama was a hell raiser.

"Franco would be proud of how you fought against all odds to keep Alessia safe. Giovanni, well he would be happy if we have chocolate cake." That has me laughing, he would have lived off chocolate cake if he had his way.

"It's time to let go. You can move on but still remember them and one day it won't be painful when you think of them."

FIVE
EMILIA

Later that night, I know the moment I walk in my bedroom after getting all the kids to and I see Mateo staring out through the window looking at the night sky. I knew something was up.

He is standing there shirtless, shoulders squared, hands crossed behind his back but waiting. What is that in his hand? I take a small step closer but freeze when I see the leather handcuffs hanging from his fingers.

Maybe he doesn't know I am in here; I can walk out and hide.

"*Regina*, come here." Mateo says without turning around. I look back at the door, debating if I can get out of here.

"Emilia" he growls at me, as he faces me. "Don't even think about it." I wait to see what he is going to do next. He ushers me over to him. I walk and stand in front of him. He pulls me closer to him by the belt loops of my jeans until there is no room between us.

He curls his other hand around the back of my head and pulls so he can hold my eyes. "Did you really think I would let your punishment not be fulfilled?"

Shit. I was hoping he forgot about that.

"I was hoping you forgot." I say staring at him, he nods.

"But I didn't, and you have three punishments." He pauses, "Now what to do to my wife who seems to have no concern for her own safety."

"The choices are endless." Mateo chuckles and it vibrates through my body, he whispers in my ear.

"I want you naked bent over the foot of the bed."

"And if I don't?"

"Then I will punish you without any reward tonight." I glare at him but strip off my clothes and toss them at his face. Mateo chuckles, "Feisty tonight, I see."

Once I am bare I bend over, I purposely rotate my hips when he stands directly behind me. I jump when his palm connects with my cheek.

"Behave." I bite my lip, wanting so badly to mouth off. He slides the blindfold down over my forehead and over my eyes before he ties it behind my head.

"Hands above your head." I do as he says. I shiver when he moves himself away from me. I listen carefully to see if I can hear what he is doing but it is dead silent.

Is he still here? Did he leave the room? Or is he watching me teasing me?

I jump when I feel a leather wrap around my wrist, Mateo kisses behind my ear as he tightens it, then does the same with the other one.

I pull on them, and feel the resistance of the chains, but I know these are the safety ones that have a release latch on them. Not that Mateo would keep me bound if I started panicking but the reassurance that I can get out on my own, helps my anxiety.

Mateo runs his finger through my folds pressing on my clit and moves his finger past my entrance and then back to the top of my clit.

I wiggle my hips each time he gets to my entrance, hoping he will slip his finger inside of me. He pinches my clit, not hard but enough for me to feel a sting of pain.

"Stay still or next I will cuff your ankles to the bed." I whimper, he already has my body worked up and he has barely started. He goes back to make leisure strokes through my folds. My fingers dig into the blankets, wanting more but damn well know that isn't an option.

He continues the torture for another few minutes, "You can be such a good girl."

I whine when I feel his finger move from my body only to feel his tongue thrust inside of me.

"Yes, fuck, Mateo." I groan into the sheets. The vibration of him chuckling against my mound heightens the pleasure. This man knows how to work my body, with his tongue deep inside of me and his thumb circling my clit.

"Mateo, please." I beg him to do a little more. He doesn't slow down or speed up. I groan in frustration because he has me immobilized.

"Mateo, please. I need more." I am on the verge of tears; I need him to make me cum.

I whine in desperation when he pulls away from me, "That's one."

I hear him move around, I wonder what he is going to do to me this time. Mateo lifts my hips a bit higher, "Stay just like that."

He uses his fingers to separate my folds and with his other hand I feel something pushing inside of me. He pushes it all the way inside of me and another part is laying across my clit.

FUCK. He is using the remote vibrator on me, dammit he really is going to punish me.

The heat from his body moves away from me, I jolt when the vibrator comes to life. He turns it up high right off the bat taking my breath away, I push my hips into the edge of the mattress. And as fast as he speeds it up he slows it down to where I can barely feel it. He does this for what seems hours, he works me up to the point I am about to break but then brings it all the way down.

My body is covered in sweat, I am squeezing the blanket in my hands, and my legs are trembling. I honestly have no idea how much more I can take of this.

"Mateo" I say with my voice is hoarse from crying and begging.

The vibrator is turned off, and I groan when he removes it from me but he doesn't give me much time to think about it. I feel his cock at my entrance, he enters me hard and fast.

He leans over me and takes off the blindfold and undoes my handcuffs but he intertwines our fingers as he leans over me, thrusting in and out of me without any mercy bringing me exactly where I want to be. Mateo grinds himself harder into me, all glorious eight inches of him goes deeper inside of me.

"Fuck, yes. Mateo, yes." I keep chanting over and over.

"Are you going to stop putting yourself in danger?" He harshly whispers in my ear; I am so lost in pleasure that I can't seem to respond.

Mateo leans back, bringing me with him so we are both standing. He stabilizes me with one hand around my waist and his other wraps around my throat. He gives it a squeeze.

"Do you want to answer my question?"

"I-Uh-uh." I mumble out, my head still lost in the cloud of pleasure.

"Do you want to cum, Emilia?" I nod my head.

"Then answer the question. Are you going to stop putting yourself in danger?"

I can't promise that because if I can save someone in our family then I would in a heartbeat.

"Emilia." He growls at me, I shake my head.

"I can't."

"Do you not want to cum?"

"I can't promise not to put myself in danger if it protects our family."

He quickly pulls out and flips me over onto my back. He slides back inside of me, this time instead of it being fast and punishing it is slow and sensual.

"Don't you realize that you are my world. I would give away everything I have for your safety."

I smile, place my hand on his cheek. "I know and I would do the same for you, but after everything that happened. If I can stop someone else being hurt, I will."

Mateo puts his forehead to mine while lifting my hips higher, pushing himself deeper. I clench around him, feeling myself come closer.

We stare at each other not exchanging a word but letting our eyes communicate to the other's heart.

I shattered around him, anchoring myself onto him. He grips my hips as he shatters along with me as he continues to thrust in and out of me riding out our orgasmic bliss.

He pulls me into his arms as he rolls us into the bed on our sides. My head rests above his heart, I trace his tattoos on his chest listening to his heartbeat. He gently yanks on my hair, having me look up into his eyes, "I love you, my Queen." He says against my lips.

"I love you too, my King."

Afterword

Want more of the De Luca's?

Salvatore and Lilyana's Story Is Next

Lilyana has been held hostage for years. She misses the life she had before with her boyfriend, family, and friends. Her life was just beginning, she has now accepted that she will never have the happy life she once had.

Salvatore has not been the same since Lilyana, his angel has been killed but he keeps himself busy with being the consigliere of Italian Mafia Boss. When Salvatore finds the woman who owns his heart, things have changed in the years she was gone.

She is not the same woman she once was, but he is also not the same man either. Salvatore finds out what she went through while she was kidnapped.

They don't call him the Angel of Darkness for nothing. He will get retribution for his family once and for all.

💚 Long Lost Love
♥ Italian Mafia Consigliere
💚 Dark Mafia Romance
♥ Missing daughter
💚 Sweet but Sassy Heroine
♥ Touch her and 💀
💚 HEA
♥ Angel of Darkness

https://books2read.com/u/mZqYgy

Acknowledgements

To all my supporters thank you, I am beyond grateful for your support. To my PA, Jessie. Thank you so much for all the work you put in behind the scenes to help me get these books out.
Seriously thank you.
To Chrisandra's Corrections, thank you so much for all the hours you put in editing to polish Reign of Vengeance to perfection.
Lastly, thank you Crazy Knight Book Creations for the cover and teasers.

About
Annalynn Nicole

    Annalynn Nicole is a mother of two autistic boys, and she is married to her high school sweetheart. Every day she is determined to be the best mother and wife she can be.

    At the end of the day she emerges herself in writing her books of her strong heroine characters who have to overcome many obstacles.

    When Annalynn Nicole isn't writing she loves to get lost in a good book with unexpected twists and turns that keeps you on the edge of your seat.

Follow Me

Did you enjoy Reign of Vengeance? Come follow me for sneak peaks and more.

Tik-Toc: annalynn.nicole.author.

Bookbub:authorannalynnnicole

Instagram: author.annalynn.nicole

Facebook: Author Annalynn Nicole

Join my Facebook group

Mafia Mistresses and Madness

Goodreads: Annalynn Nicole

Pinterest: Annalynn_Nicole

Reviews

Thank you so much for reading Reign of Vengeance and I hope you loved it as much as I do.

Please help me out by leaving a review on Amazon and Goodreads.

Bonus if you share the book on your social media.

Made in the USA
Coppell, TX
10 July 2024

34495130R00252